THE COLORS OF DRAGONS—

Sioned threaded a few strands of sunlight together, cautiously extending the silken gold weave toward the young female dragon.

The female turned her head questioningly. Sioned displayed her own colors—emerald, sapphire, onyx, amber. Then she sought a closer contact and the dragon whined through her long nose, shivering a little.

Suddenly the sunlight exploded into a rainbow of color. Sioned cried out at the same time the little dragon threw back her head with a howl of terror. All the other dragons sprang up in the sky, keening a chorus of fear and warning as they fled.

"Mother!"

Pol tried to hold her up as she crumpled, Walvis right beside him. Trembling with the shock, Sioned whispered, "I'm fine."

"The dragons aren't," Walvis said grimly. "Listen to them."

The wild music echoed down from the cluster of dark shapes in the sky. "I was too clumsy. I frightened her."

"What are you talking about?" Walvis asked. "My lady, what did you do?"

Pol answered for her. "She used the sunlight to touch a dragon. . . ."

Melanie Rawn's magnificent saga of love and war, of sun-weaving magic and princes' honor—and of the dragons, deadly dangerous yet holding the secret of power beyond imagining. . . .

DRAGON PRINCE
(Book One)

THE STAR SCROLL
(Book Two)

SUNRUNNER'S FIRE
(Book Three)

available February 1990

DRAGON PRINCE: BOOK II

THE STAR SCROLL

MELANIE RAWN

DAW BOOKS, INC.

DONALD A. WOLLHEIM, PUBLISHER

1633 Broadway, New York, NY 10019

First Printing, May 1989

3 4 5 6 7 8 9

PRINTED IN THE U.S.A.

for MaryAnne Ford

PART ONE

The Scroll

Chapter One

Graypearl, Prince Lleyn's elegant jewel box of a palace, nestled atop its hill in a sculpted setting of lush spring grass and flowering trees. Built of stone that gleamed at dawn and sunset with the subtle iridescence from which it drew its name, it was one of the few princely residences that had never been a fortress. No defensive architecture had ever been needed on the island of Dorval, at peace with itself and the nearby continent for longer than anyone's great-grandfather could remember. Graypearl's towers had been fashioned for beauty, not war.

Gardens spread in curved terraces overlooking a tiny harbor where boats sailed out in season to harvest the pearl beds. A small army of groundskeepers kept the luxuriant spring growth of flowers, herbs, and trees from running riot—but no one could impose similar order on the boy who ran an intricate pattern between the rose trees, kicking a deerhide ball before him. He was a slight youth, rather small for his fourteen winters. But there was the promise of height in his long bones and he moved with an agility that older squires had reason to bemoan in games of skill with blunted knives and wooden swords. Dark blond hair crowned a clever oval face whose most vivid feature was a pair of large, fine eyes that changed from blue to green depending on his mood and the color of his clothes. It was a quick face, intelligent and sensitive, with its share of inherent pride in bones which were becoming more visible as his features lost their childish roundness. But there was nothing about him to suggest that he was anything more than a squire fostered to Prince Lleyn's court for training, released from afternoon duties and playing happily by himself in the gardens. Certainly there was no indication that he was the only son of the High Prince, destined to inherit not only his father's Desert lands but those of Princemarch as well.

9

Princess Audrite, wife of Lleyn's heir Chadric, watched the boy with an indulgent smile. Her own sons had gone to other courts just as this youth had, and returned as young knights skilled in all the graces—not her little boys anymore. She spared a sigh for having missed their growing years, but other youngsters had filled up her time and, some of them, portions of her heart. Maarken, Lord Chaynal of Radzyn's eldest son and cousin to the boy playing in the gardens, had been one of her favorites, with his swift mind and sunny smiles. But this golden princeling she watched now was special. Made of air and light he was, with a temper like flashfire through summer-dry timber and a streak of mischief that had more than once landed him in trouble. In fact, he ought not to have been excused his duties like the other squires this afternoon, for he still owed her the copying of a hundred lines of verses after a misdemeanor yesterday in the kitchens—something involving a large quantity of pepper and an exploding fish bladder. She was not sure she wanted to know the particulars. An inventive mind, had young Pol, and Audrite chuckled in spite of herself. She had chosen a most appropriate punishment by selecting poetry for him to copy; had she specified a hundred mathematical problems, he would have completed them in a wink and considered it no punishment at all.

The princess shook out her thin silk gown and settled on a bench, not wishing to interrupt Pol's game until she had found the right phrases for what she had to tell him. But all at once the deerhide ball shot past her, propelled by an enthusiastic kick, and the boy skidded to a stop before her. Surprised by her presence, he nevertheless gave her a bow worthy of the most elegant young lord.

"Your pardon, my lady. I didn't mean to disturb you."

"It's all right, Pol. Actually, I came here looking for you and thought I'd sit in the shade for a little while. It's quite hot this spring, isn't it?"

He was not yet skilled enough in the art of polite conversation to take her lead on to further chat about the weather. "Do you have news for me, my lady?"

Audrite chose to be as direct as he. "Your father has asked permission to take you away from us for a time.

He wants you to go home to Stronghold by way of Radzyn, then to the *Rialla* with him and your mother.''

Excitement shone in the young face. "Home? Really?'' Then, realizing that his reaction might be taken amiss, he hurried on, "I mean, I like it here and I'll miss you and my lord Chadric and my friends—''

"And we'll miss you, Pol.'' Audrite smiled her understanding. "But we'll bring you back to Graypearl with us after the *Rialla* so you may continue your training. It's unusual, you know, for a squire to be allowed a holiday from the work he must do in order to become a knight and a gentleman. Do you think what you've learned thus far is enough to uphold Prince Lleyn's reputation?''

Pol gave her a cheerful grin. "If it isn't, then Father will know it's *my* fault, not anyone else's!''

Audrite grinned back. "Yes, we had a long letter about you when you first came to us.''

"But I was just a child then,'' he assured her, blithely forgetting the transgression of the previous day. "I won't do anything to embarrass anyone. I've outgrown all that.'' He paused, glancing at the sea far below. "Except—I'll have to cross water, won't I? I'll try to behave better than I did the first time.''

The princess ruffled his blond hair. "It's nothing to be ashamed of, Pol. Indeed, you ought to be proud. All Sunrunners lose their dignity along with their breakfast when they cross water.''

"But I'm a prince, and I should be in better control of myself.'' He sighed. "Oh, well. Once to Radzyn and once coming back—I suppose it won't be too bad.''

"There's a silk-ship leaving in two days for Radzyn port, and Prince Lleyn has bespoken a place for you on it. He's sending Meath with you for company.''

Pol made a face halfway between a grin and a grimace. "Then we can be sick together!''

"I'm convinced it's the Goddess' way of keeping you *faradh'im* humble! Why don't you go upstairs now and start packing?''

"I will, my lady. And tomorrow—'' He hesitated, then went on, "Could I go down to the harbor and find presents for my mother and Aunt Tobin? I've saved almost everything Father's sent me since I got here, so I've money enough.''

He had the right instincts; he was already generous and thoughtful about pleasing ladies. That face and those eyes would be breaking hearts before he was too much older, Audrite reflected, and relished the notion that she would be around to watch. "You and Meath may be excused tomorrow for the day. But I seem to recall you have a certain project to complete for me first. How many lines was it?''

"Fifty?'' he asked hopefully, then sighed. "One hundred. I'll have them done by tonight, my lady.''

"If they're not in my hands until tomorrow evening, I'll understand,'' she suggested, winning another of his wide smiles and a bow of thanks. Then he ran back up the terraces to the palace.

Audrite spent a few more moments enjoying the shade before she, too, left the gardens. Her steps were lithe and energetic as she climbed; a passion for riding had kept her slim and supple for all her forty-nine winters. She unlatched the gate that led into the private enclave and paused to admire the oratory that rose like a shining gem from the formal gardens. It was said that the one at Castle Crag, a crystal dome built into the side of the cliffs there, was the most splendid in all the thirteen princedoms, but she could imagine nothing more beautiful than this oratory at Graypearl—and not only because she had had a great deal to do with its construction.

Carved stone columns had been taken from an abandoned keep on the other side of the island to support walls of pale wood and brilliant stained glass. The painted wooden ceiling rose far above, punctuated with small, clear windows in an uneven pattern that looked random but was not. It could be said that the oratory was in reality a temple: lit by the Fire of sun and moons, open to the Air, built of the things of the Earth, and circled by a stream of Water that irrigated the gardens below. Audrite crossed the little footbridge and stepped between the columns, catching her breath as always at the beauty of the place. It was like walking into a rainbow. And if standing here embraced by all the colors in the world was a moving experience for her, it must be near ecstacy for *faradh'im*.

The ceiling had been the hardest to reconstruct. Some of its supports had been demolished, and it had taken years of study for Audrite to discern the proper placement of windows. The tiled floor had been painstakingly lifted from the soil and overgrown grasses on the far side of Dorval, and was marked with various symbols for the seasons and indicated the position and phases of the three moons on any given night of the year. Audrite had spent years checking its accuracy, and several new tiles had been fashioned at her direction to replace ones worn or broken long ago at the other keep. Her calculations on the exact relationship of ceiling to tiles, and the observations of Lleyn's Sunrunners, Meath and Eolie, had awed everyone. For the original design of this oratory had been correct down to the slightest nuance.

Twenty-one years ago, Prince Lleyn had learned from Lady Andrade—she who ruled Goddess Keep and all Sunrunners—that the abandoned castle had once belonged to the *faradh'im*. Stone had been taken from it for hundreds of years to construct other places, including Graypearl, but on Lleyn's return from the *Rialla* that autumn an excavation had begun in earnest. This masterwork had been their most important find, save one. Audrite walked softly over the summer tiles, a smile on her face for the sheer beauty of the oratory and the sheer joy of understanding it. The structure had become again what it had been meant to be: the most remarkable calendar in all the princedoms.

She heard steps on the footbridge and turned. Meath entered the oratory and bowed a greeting. "Full moons tonight," he said, smiling as he shared her delight at their knowledge.

"You can use them to contact Princess Sioned," Audrite told him.

"You've talked to Pol, then?"

"Yes. I'll have to give you my notes on the scrolls." She frowned slightly. "Meath, do you think it's wise to give them to Andrade now? She's very old. It may be that she won't have time to discover their meaning—and it may also be that the next Lady or Lord of Goddess Keep won't use the knowledge wisely.''

The *faradhi* shrugged and spread his hands wide, rings glinting in the colored sunlight. ''I'm convinced she'll outlive us all, if only through pure cussedness.'' He smiled, then shook his head. ''As for the other thing—I agree that it's a risk. But I'd rather have Andrade examine the scrolls now and decide what to do with them than wait and see who next rules Goddess Keep.''

''You were the one who found them,'' she said slowly. ''I've helped with as many of the words as I could—and, Goddess knows, there wasn't much I fully understood,'' she added regretfully. ''But the responsibility for them is yours.''

''Well, it's true that I dug them out of the rubble, but I'd prefer not to have the choice of what's done with them. If they're as important as we suspect, then it's knowledge I'm not qualified to deal with. I'd rather see the scrolls in Andrade's hands, not mine. She'll either understand them and use them, or destroy them if they're too dangerous.''

Audrite nodded. ''Come by my library later tonight and I'll give you my notes.''

''Thank you, my lady. Andrade will appreciate it, I know.'' He smiled again. ''I wish you could be there to see her face!''

''So do I. I just hope the shock isn't too much for her.''

* * *

The hundred lines of verse duly copied and presented to Princess Audrite, Pol was free by late morning to ride to the harbor with Meath. Shops snuggled along the village's narrow main street, not as varied in their wares as the stores in Dorval's main shipping center down the coast or in Radzyn's port. But there were interesting things to be had here—crafts native to the island and not much traded elsewhere, small items made of silk remnants, jewelry cunningly fashioned to hide defects in pearls not suitable for the general market. Pol and Meath tied their horses in front of a dockside inn where they planned to have lunch later, and walked up and down the street, window-shopping.

The merchants all knew Pol, of course, and were of two attitudes when it came to selling him things. Some, aware of his father's great wealth, quoted outrageous prices in hopes of siphoning off a little of that wealth for themselves. Others cared more about royal favor, and underpriced their wares in a shameless bid for Pol's further patronage. The young prince usually did his looking through the windows, then consulted with companions on the fair price of goods that caught his eye before making his purchases. Patient for the first and second tours up and down the street, Meath finally asked Pol if he intended to spend all day at this. A third perusal was all the Sunrunner would stand for; he ordered the boy back to the inn for sustenance.

Prince Lleyn did not tolerate seafaring roughnecks in this port. He discouraged them elsewhere, naturally, but here in the precincts of his palace they were forbidden. Thus everything catering to such men—taverns where strong drink was served and brawls were common, disreputable lodgings where they bedded down between voyages, and the girls they bedded down with—were missing from Graypearl's little harbor. The law assured domestic peace and the safety of the residents as well as of the highborn youths who came to Dorval as squires, and the old prince himself often ventured down to the port for a meal or a day's ramble in the fresh air. The inn Meath chose was one Lleyn had introduced him to years ago, a clean and merry establishment perfectly safe for the heir to the High Prince. But even if it had not been, Meath's great height, broad shoulders, and *faradhi* rings would have ensured Pol's safety.

"Goddess greeting to you, Sunrunner! And to the young master, as well!" The innkeeper, Giamo by name, came out from behind his counter and bowed his respects before escorting them to a table. "Honored to be of service to you both! Now, we've some fine cold roast today, and bread right out of the oven, and the first berries of the season, so sweet that they don't need any honey dolloped on them—although my good wife having a tooth for it, she slathers it on anyway! Will that suit?"

"Perfectly," Meath said with a happy sigh. "You can

add a tankard for me and something appropriate for my friend, here.''

Pol cast him a deeply reproachful look, and when the innkeeper had gone to fetch the meal said, ''What's 'appropriate' for me, anyway? A glass of milk? I'm not a baby, Meath!''

''No, but not tall or hefty enough for a bout with the ale Giamo brews, either. Not at just over fourteen winters! Put on a few fingers' height and some flesh on those bones, and then we'll see.'' Meath grinned. ''Besides, all I lack is your mother raving at me for letting you get drunk.''

Pol made a face, then turned his attention to the other noontime patrons of the inn. There were a few pearl-fishers, easily identifiable by their lean, lithe bodies, well-developed chest muscles, and the scars on their hands from digging shells out of rock crevices. Skin weathered by sea and salt had paled a little during the winter months, but soon they would be out in their small boats again, browned from head to heels by summer sun during the annual harvest. Lleyn's squires often enjoyed the treat of a day's sail in the pearl coves—but not Pol. The first time he'd taken a look at those tiny, flat-bottomed boats bobbing gently at their moorings, he'd been most humiliatingly sick.

In one corner of the room a pair of merchants haggled pleasantly over their meal, swatches of silk on the table between them. A young man wooed a pretty girl nearby, their lunch forgotten as he whispered in her ear and sent her into gales of laughter. Near the door sat five soldiers, four men and a middle-aged woman, all dressed in light harness but without swords, according to the law here. They wore the solid red tunics and the white candle badge of Prince Velden of Grib.

''Meath?'' Pol asked softly. ''What are they doing at Graypearl?''

''Who?'' he glanced around. ''Oh, them. The Gribain ambassador got in this morning. Something about arranging silk trade.''

''But there's been a treaty forever that says all silk goes through Radzyn.''

''Well, they can try to convince Lleyn, can't they? But

I don't think they'll get anywhere. I wouldn't be too worried for your uncle's revenues—or your own," he finished teasingly.

Pol bristled. "Dorval can do as it likes with its silks—"

"As long as the Desert sees the profits?" Meath laughed, then held up a placating hand as blue-green eyes began to flash. "Sorry. Couldn't resist."

"I was talking about treaties and the law, not profits," Pol said sternly.

"I think you'll find such things are flexible when it comes to making money."

"Not since my father's been High Prince," he stated. "The law is the law, and he sees to it that laws are obeyed."

"Well, it's all beyond a simple Sunrunner like me, your grace," Meath said, barely controlling another smile.

Giamo arrived with a tray, and set before them two huge plates of food, a tankard of ale for Meath, and a Fironese crystal goblet filled with a clear, pale pink liquid that frothed gently with golden bubbles. Pol took a sip under his host's watchful eye, and smiled in delight. "Wonderful! What is it?"

"My own brewing," Giamo answered, pleased. "The most delicate and refined of ciders, barely blushing."

"It tastes just like spring itself," Pol said. "And I'm honored by the goblet it's served in."

"The honor is my wife's," Giamo replied with a bow. "It's not every woman can say that so important a lord has eaten at her table and sipped from her most treasured possession."

"If she's not too busy, then perhaps I can visit her in the kitchen and thank her."

"After you've finished your meal in peace," Giamo grinned. "My good wife Willa could talk the tail off a dragon."

Sunrunner and prince dug into the food. The healthy appetites of a growing boy and a large, active man required seconds; Meath requested a third piling of meat and flaky bread, and Pol was sincerely sorry that he was too full to do likewise. He lingered over a dish of berries in honey glaze and sipped at his cider, wondering if he might persuade Giamo to part with a bottle as a gift for his mother, who adored fine wines.

The pearl-fishers had gone, replaced by a trio of ship-wrights come to enjoy a few tankards of ale. The young man and the girl were now being teased by the two silk merchants; Pol grinned to himself as the couple blushed. In a few years that would be him over there, enjoying the company of a charming lady. But he was in no hurry.

Replete at last, Meath leaned back with tankard in hand, ready for conversation again. "You didn't say if there was anything in the shops you liked well enough to buy."

"Well . . . the green silk slippers were pretty, and that comb of pearl shell. But Prince Chadric told me that a man should never buy a gift for a lady unless he takes one look at it and can see her wearing it or using it."

The Sunrunner laughed. "An excellent policy—and doubtless the reason Audrite always looks so lovely."

"You might try his advice out on that new maid in the west wing," Pol said, his eyes at their widest and most innocent. "I hear you haven't had much luck so far."

Meath spluttered on a swallow of ale. "How did you know about—"

Pol only laughed.

Willa, Giamo's wife, emerged from her kitchen then, wiping her hands on her apron and obviously intending to gather compliments from her exalted guest. The merchants had risen to leave, still arguing amiably over their silk. The young girl squealed, "Oh, Rialt, you're terrible!" in response to some sally of her companion's; the shipwrights laughed in response and raised their cups to him. All was warm good cheer—until one of the soldiers suddenly shoved his chair back and sprang to his feet, growling a difference of opinion that turned every head in the room. Meath saw the glint of steel and rose, his substantial frame instinctively placed between the soldiers and Pol. The merchants, caught between their table and the angry Gribains by the door, sent a look of frantic appeal to the Sunrunner, and he nodded reassurance.

"Here, now," Meath said casually. "You can settle this outside, can't you?"

Usually his height, his breadth of shoulder, and his rings made his point. But these were seasoned troopers, angry and resentful of any interference, even that of a *faradhi*. The bearded one who seemed to have started the quarrel snarled, ''It's no concern of yours, Sunrunner.''

''Put the knife away,'' Meath replied, his voice less pleasant now. The merchants were trying to slip past, silk swatches rustling in their clenched hands, and the girl had shrunk back in her chair.

Willa marched forward, hands on hips. ''How dare you threaten the peace of this inn?'' she demanded. ''And in the presence of—''

Meath interrupted before she could identify Pol. ''Get out of here before you make a very serious mistake, my friends.''

The woman—their captain judging by the braid at her throat—drew her own knife. ''You have a loud and offensive mouth, *faradhi*. And *you* are mistaken in using that tone to members of Prince Velden's own guard.''

The bearded man brought up his knife in obvious threat, sunlight through the windows striking silver off the blade, and the innkeeper's wife shrieked a protest. The merchants tried to vanish behind a couple of chairs. And the knife sped through an abrupt silence toward Meath's chest.

''No!'' a young voice cried. Meath rocked easily out of the knife's path as a fountain of Sunrunner's Fire rose from the middle of the soldiers' table. They yelled and leaped back, and in that precious moment of their startlement Meath surged toward them. He slammed two into the wall and shoved the woman at the terrified merchants. Rialt shook off his girlfriend's clutching hand, jumped to his feet, and launched himself at the bearded soldier. The three shipwrights, bulky muscles barely covered by thin shirts, hastily downed the last of their ale before leaping up to join the fight.

By brawl's end, Meath had a sore jaw and a shallow slit in his arm. Neither deterred him from overturning a table on top of the Gribain who was foolish enough not to stay where Rialt had kicked him. Two of the shipwrights were holding a second soldier so Rialt could take whatever punches he liked; Willa was engaged in tying up the unconscious woman with knotted napkins. The fourth soldier had gone headfirst into the brick hearth; the fifth sprawled on the floor, and the shipwright seated casually on the Gribain's spine looked up with a grin at Meath.

"Many thanks for the entertainment, my lord Sunrunner! I haven't had so much fun since I worked over to the other port!"

"My pleasure," Meath answered, and looked around for Pol. The boy was administering ale to the white-faced girl. He was unhurt, and Meath felt relief shake his knees just a little. He didn't want to consider what he would have told Sioned if her son had been injured.

Giamo puffed up the cellar stairs and gave a shocked cry. Meath patted his shoulder.

"All taken care of. But I'm afraid we've made a shambles of your room." He glanced down as capable hands went to work on his wounded arm. "It's nothing," he told Willa.

"Nothing?" She snorted and tied off the bandage she had made with strips torn from her apron. "Nothing that could have been deaths in my house, that's what nothing! Now, you find out who these ruffians are and what they're about while I find some good strong wine to restore the blood you've lost."

Meath was about to protest that it was only a scratch—then remembered the glorious wine Prince Lleyn had treated him to at this very inn last autumn. He nodded enthusiastic approval and Willa snorted once more.

There were more casualties among the furniture and plates than among the people involved. Rialt would have a sore shoulder for a few days, and the merchants' dignity had been more bruised than their backsides. Meath righted an overturned chair, tested it for soundness, and pointed to the Gribain commander, who sat on the floor with her hands bound behind her. "Have a seat," he invited.

Sullenly and awkwardly, she obeyed. Her red tunic was a little darker along one shoulder, but Meath judged the wound to be superficial. Of her companions, three would have very bad headaches and the other would not be walking entirely upright for a while. After assuring himself of their relative good health, Meath stood before their captain with arms folded, unimpressed by her arrogant demand to be released on the instant.

"Captain," he told her, "I don't care if you stand guard outside Prince Velden's own bedchamber while he favors his wife with his attentions. You know the law here."

"It was a private matter between me and my men," she snapped. "You have no right—"

"I have the right of any man or woman to make sure the law is obeyed. I want several things, and I want them now: your name, those of your men, and the reason for this outrage against Prince Lleyn's peace. And then you may make your apologies as well as restitution to those you've offended here today."

"Apologies!" She sucked in a breath and glared at him.

Meath glanced down as Pol plucked at his sleeve. "What is it?"

"I've sent Giamo to fetch the patrol. They should be here soon."

"Good thinking. Thanks." The boy looked a little pale, but seemed in perfect control of himself. "Are you all right?"

"Fine. But I don't think this was any simple disagreement," he added thoughtfully. "In fact, I'm sure the one with the beard started it on purpose."

Meath was almost afraid to find out why. Neither was he looking forward to an explanation about Pol's conjuring of Fire. Meath and Eolie had never shown him how. Perhaps Sioned had before Pol left Stronghold, but somehow Meath doubted it. Pol would have told him.

The *faradhi* looked down into clear eyes. "Why would he start a fight?" he asked quietly.

"Because he wanted to kill me." Pol shrugged. "Rialt kept him from throwing his second knife. You were busy with the others and didn't see. But he wasn't aiming at you the first time, either. He was after *me.*"

It wasn't natural for a fourteen-year-old to speak so calmly about such things. Meath started to put an arm around his shoulders, but Pol slid away and went to the cellar door, where Willa had just appeared with clay mugs

of wine. Pol appropriated one and took a long swallow,
then helped her serve the rest. Meath downed the contents of his mug in two gulps and then approached the
man who lay trapped and unconscious beneath the overturned table.

He was unremarkable in every way—height, weight,
coloring, features—and that very plainness signaled danger. Who would notice this man, but for the uniform and
the beard? Yet both were too easy to identify, and Meath
could not help but wonder about them. Even if Velden of
Grib had had a compelling reason to kill Pol, Meath
couldn't believe anyone was stupid enough to send an
assassin dressed in the colors of his own princedom—
unless he *counted* on everyone's assuming that no one
would be that stupid. Intricate schemes made Meath's
head ache. And he could just hear himself accusing a
ruling prince of attempted murder. It was much easier to
absolve Velden of complicity and decide that the uniform
was borrowed protection, gaining the assassin access to
Graypearl as part of the Gribain suite, with chance placing the soldiers here at the inn at the same time as Pol.

Besides, there was the beard—a disguise that could be
discarded almost as easily as the uniform. Meath
crouched down to peer at the man's face.

"What are you looking for?" Pol asked over his shoulder.

"I'm not sure," Meath admitted. "I don't think he's
had his beard very long. It's uneven and hasn't grown
long enough to trim neatly. And that place on his chin is
practically bald."

The boy knelt and fingered the beard. When he met
the Sunrunner's eyes, his own were haunted. "Merida,"
he whispered.

"Impossible. They were all but wiped out the year you
were born. Walvis got them at the Battle of Tiglath."

"Merida," Pol repeated stubbornly. "The scar's on
his chin in just the right place. They're trained assassins.
And who else would want to kill me?"

Meath heard reaction beginning at last as Pol's voice
rose slightly, and he pulled the boy to his feet. He
snagged another cup of wine from the tray on the table
and gave it to Pol after seating him firmly in a chair.

Rohan had sent his son to Dorval for its safety, with the understanding that Meath, Sioned's friend since their student days at Goddess Keep, would act as bodyguard whenever the boy was not in the immediate confines of Graypearl. Meath's hands shook as he thought about what might have happened here today.

Pol's color and poise had come back. He complimented the merchants and shipwrights on their fighting skills, speaking as easily as if this had been a simple tavern brawl, not an attempt to kill him. But Lleyn's carefree squire had vanished, replaced by a young man who now knew how much his death was worth. Rohan and Sioned would find that their son had taken a very long step toward manhood in the space of a few moments. Pol's identity known by now, as he thanked Rialt for his quickness the low bow he received seemed to embarrass him. This reassured Meath for reasons he did not immediately understand.

The patrol arrived and Meath was glad to hand over the prisoners to their keeping. They would be brought before Prince Lleyn; he looked grimly forward to hearing the Merida explain himself.

"I'm sorry about the damage," Pol was saying to Giamo. "And your goblet was broken. I'll find a replacement for it at the *Rialla*, I promise."

"My goblet?" Willa exclaimed. "Great Goddess watch over us, what's a foolish goblet? If your Sunrunner hadn't called Fire and startled them so much, more than my goblet and a few sticks of furniture would have been broken!"

Pol did not correct her impression that the Fire had been of Meath's making. "Well, just the same, you'll get another Fironese crystal when I return this autumn."

One of the merchants cleared his throat. "Well-spoken, your grace. But I differ with good Willa here. It was your shout that distracted them and probably saved me a bloodletting—if not my life. It may be the duty of a prince to be brave, but courage always deserves a reward."

"We know you'd not accept anything for yourself," said his companion. "But come to our warehouses when you've time and choose whatever you fancy would suit your lady mother's famous beauty."

Pol began a protest, but Meath interrupted smoothly, "You're very generous, and on High Princess Sioned's behalf, we accept." Refusal would have offended, and Pol did not yet know enough about being a prince to understand that. It was in the nature of most people to believe that highborns were special, braver and better than ordinary folk. They must be trusted to govern the princedoms and holdings, and if they were not better, then what hope was there? A tribute of fine silk would symbolize the belief as surely as Willa would find justi-fication of it in her new goblet. Pol's instincts had guided him correctly there, even if he did not yet understand that he did something far more important than provide restitution for something broken.

But he did know enough to take Meath's lead. "Thank you. My mother will be very grateful. Will you be at Waes this year to see her wearing your silk?"

"Dragons couldn't keep us away, your grace." The pair swept him elegant bows, and Pol smiled. Only Meath saw the brief flash of amusement in the blue-green eyes.

Later, on the ride back to Graypearl, Meath held his tongue and wondered how to explain this to Prince Lleyn. The events themselves were straightforward enough, but he worried about the Merida and the calling of Fire. Halfway up the hill he glanced over at Pol and said, "You know, there were probably easier ways of saving yourself the expense of buying a present for your mother."

"Is that the tale you're going to tell her?"

"I just might. But what I'm really thinking about is your little display of Fire. Oh, I'm not complaining, mind. They were startled and thus didn't fight well. And you didn't even leave a burn scar on the table," he ap-proved.

"Maybe Lady Andrade will give me my first ring," Pol replied lightly.

"And maybe you'd better tell me who taught you how to do that," Meath said, unsmiling.

"No one. I just—I needed to distract them, and it seemed the best way."

Meath stared between his horse's ears at the road ahead. "You've the heritage on both sides, so I guess it's not surprising that you gave in to your instincts." He reined in beneath a shade tree, and Pol did the same. Meath looked the boy full in the face, holding his gaze with deliberate intent. "Do I have to tell you how dangerous your instincts can be, my prince?"

The use of title rather than name made Pol gulp. But he could not look away from Meath's eyes. The Sunrunner speculated on how long he would be able to influence Pol this way. It was something all *faradh'im* learned from Lady Andrade during training, this absolute concentration that captured another as surely as a dragon could spear a sheep or a deer with a single look. Holding Pol's gaze, it occurred to him that despite their coloring the boy's eyes had nothing of the sea. There was sunlit Desert sky in them, limitless blue like his father's eyes; there were emeralds, too, bright as the one his mother wore on her finger, the color of moonlight through a leaf. But not the sea, not for this son of the Desert.

Meath lifted his hands so his rings caught the light drifting down through the shade above them. "My father was a metalsmith in Gilad, and my mother was a fisherman's daughter who hated the sight of the sea. It was from her that I received the gifts that made me a *faradhi*. The first of these rings is for calling Fire. It took me three years of training before I earned it. I was past twenty before I was worthy of my fourth ring, and two years older than that before I received my fifth and sixth. It may be you have more of the gift than I—but you also have more to lose by it than I ever did."

"More to *lose?*" Pol frowned, bewildered. "Don't you mean more to gain?"

"No," Meath said in harsh tones. "You were born to two kinds of power. You're a prince and one day you'll be a Sunrunner."

"And I could lose all of it, is that what you mean?" the boy whispered, his fingers white-knuckled around the reins. "Meath—"

"Yes?" He lowered his hands to the horse's neck.

"You're right to scare me with it. Did you do the same for Maarken?"

"I did." He consciously relinquished control of the blue-green eyes, and the blond head bent. Meath knew this lesson ought to have come from Sioned—who herself knew both kinds of power. But the right time was now, and he had to make sure the right lesson was learned. "It scared me, too," he admitted. "Every day of my life, until I learned to know myself. That's what the training at Goddess Keep is for, Pol. It teaches you how to use your instincts and your powers, but it also teaches you when not to use them. It's the same way with your training as a squire and a knight. You're learning your powers as a warrior and a prince."

"But there's one thing a prince sometimes has to do that Sunrunners are forbidden."

Meath nodded. *"Faradh'im* must never use the gift to kill. When you know and trust yourself, Pol, you won't be afraid." He brushed the boy's shoulder with his fingertips, rings glinting. "Come, let's ride on. It's getting late."

They were nearly to the gates when Pol spoke again. "Meath? Did I do the right thing today?"

"Is that for me to say, or you?"

"I think—I think I did. No, I'm sure of it." As they rode below the stone archway he added, "But you know, it's the stupidest thing. I can't stop thinking about Willa's broken goblet."

They separated at the stables, Pol to report to the Master of Squires and Meath to inform Chadric and Audrite of the day's events. Word and the prisoners had gone ahead, and Lleyn was even now interviewing the Gribain captain. Chadric's eldest son, Ludhil, brought the ominous news that the bearded soldier had somehow managed to hang himself in his cell.

Lleyn came into Audrite's solar a short time later. Past eighty, frail as parchment stretched over brittle glass, he leaned on a wooden cane and refused the assistance of his son and grandson in taking a seat. Narrowing his fine, faded eyes at Meath, he folded his hands over the cane's carved dragon's head handle and said, "Well?"

"From your expression, my lord, the Gribain captain knows nothing of the Merida's origins and has nothing to say about the cause of the argument." Meath shrugged. "I imagine she is telling the truth."

"I'm not interested in imagination," Lleyn snapped. "I want to know what happened."

"Pol believes the Merida provoked the fight on purpose. And since he killed himself, I'd say he had something to hide."

"But why attempt Pol's life now?" Chadric asked. "Surely they had plenty of chances while he still lived at Stronghold."

"You should pay more attention to rumors," his father told him. As Audrite caught her breath, Lleyn nodded. "I see you've taken my meaning, my dear."

Chadric's plain, pleasant face tightened to grimness. "If you're talking about that possible son of Roelstra's—"

"He'll be nearing twenty-one. Pol's barely fourteen," Lleyn remarked.

"But it's ludicrous!" Audrite protested. "Even if the boy *is* Roelstra's, he'd have to rally all Princemarch behind him. And that won't happen. Rohan has done well by them in making Pandsala regent—no one but a fool would trade certain prosperity for an unknown pretender."

"Nicely put," Lleyn grunted, fingering the dragon's head. "But it so happens that Rohan is an honorable fool. He'll feel compelled to meet this young man and hear him out."

"No proof one way or the other," Chadric said. "It's all supposition."

Meath said, "Lack of proof makes Roelstra's supposed son dangerous."

"There's Lady Andrade," Audrite reminded them. "She was there the night of the births."

"She might know what happened, and she might not," Lleyn replied. "And for all her authority as Lady of Goddess Keep, she's also Rohan's aunt and not exactly an impartial witness."

Chadric shook his head, rising to pace the solar. "The issue isn't the pretender's identity, Father. It comes down to this: Does the claim of someone with Roelstra's blood weigh more heavily than the years of good governance established by Rohan in lands he won by right of war?"

Lleyn's eyes sparkled. "I'm gratified to see that my training hasn't been wasted—and that you inherited your mother's wits as well as her eyes. You have the right of it, Chadric. Who do we support when and if it comes to it? If this youth is indeed Roelstra's son, do we take his side and support the blood-claim that keeps all princes in power? Or do we back Rohan and the things he's done in Princemarch?'' He smiled without humor. ''It's not the kind of choice a prince finds comfortable.''

Meath sat forward, elbows propped on his knees. ''Your grace, it's yet to be proved that the person is who some say he is. But even if he isn't, there will be those who choose to believe—''

''Or *act* as if they believe,'' Lleyn agreed. ''Just for the sake of making mischief. Real proof to the contrary will be needed.''

''I see why Pol is suddenly a Merida target,'' Audrite said unhappily. ''Miyon of Cunaxa still shelters them, though he says he doesn't. He's probably behind what happened today. There'll never be proof, of course. But without Pol to inherit Princemarch, this pretender might be welcomed outright—and Miyon would rather deal with anyone else than Rohan or his son. And I see, too, why Rohan wants the boy with him this summer and at Waes.''

''There's a progress planned for them to Castle Crag,'' Lleyn affirmed.

Chadric gestured the pretender away with one hand. ''Once they see Pol and he wins them the way he does everyone—''

''There's still the matter of proving this claimant a liar,'' Lleyn said. ''Do you think people like Miyon will support Pol on the strength of his admittedly charming smile?''

''It's the people of Princemarch he'll win,'' Chadric said.

''The people of Princemarch do not attend the *Rialla* and vote on who and what is the truth. Andrade is the only reliable witness and the evidence will have to come from her in a manner the princes will accept as absolute truth.''

''There's Pandsala,'' Meath reminded them.

''Oh, yes, Pandsala.'' Lleyn snorted. ''May I remind you that if this boy is acclaimed, the regent would be out of a job?'' He shook his head. ''I don't like this. Not at all. Meath, before you leave Radzyn for Goddess Keep, make sure you have a long talk with Chay and Tobin.''

Much later, in his own chambers, Meath pulled out the case made for the scrolls dug up at the ancient Sunrunner keep. They were written in the old language; though script had not changed much from modern writing, the words meant nothing to him. Yet certain words survived to the present day nearly unchanged—personal names, for instance, were usually chosen with their ancient meanings in mind—and as he unrolled one of the parchments he bit his lip. The usual sun-and-moons motif was missing from this first page. The sources of light for *faradhi* weavings were not depicted here as they were on all the other scrolls. This one had a different pattern, a design of night sky strewn with stars. He stared for a long time at the title that had so shocked him on first seeing it, words he had had no difficulty translating.

On Sorceries.

Chapter Two

Pandsala, Regent of Princemarch and daughter of the late High Prince Roelstra, scowled at the letter on her desk and told herself that life would have been much simpler without sisters. Her father had provided her with seventeen of them. Though ten were dead now—some in the Plague of 701, others since—and good riddance, she was still left with far too many for her peace of mind.

The survivors were a plague in themselves. Letters such as the one now before her arrived constantly here at Castle Crag; petitions for money or favors or a word in High Prince Rohan's ear, and especially requests to be allowed a visit to their childhood home. Pandsala had spent the first five years of her regency removing her sisters from Castle Crag by various methods; she was not about to let any of them come back, not for so much as a day.

But it was the youngest of them, the one who had never even been here, who was the focus of Pandsala's present irritation. Chiana's letter could not have irked her more had the girl written every word with a calculated eye to insulting her powerful half sister. She presumed an intimacy repugnant to Pandsala; she even styled herself "princess" as if her mother, Lady Palila, had been Roelstra's wife instead of his whore. Born in Waes and raised in various places, including Goddess Keep for the first six winters of her life, Chiana evidently chose to forget that Pandsala had shared those six winters and knew every detail of her character in excruciating detail. Their rare encounters since and the letters Chiana wrote were ample evidence that maturing had not changed her. At nearly twenty-one, her haughty selfishness had grown worse. In this letter Chiana implied that if Pandsala extended an invitation to Castle Crag for the summer, Chiana might be persuaded to grace it with her presence. But Pandsala had long ago vowed that Chiana would never set foot here so long as she was the keep's mistress.

A few of the other sisters had shared Chiana's rearing after Lady Andrade had flatly refused to have her back at Goddess Keep. Lady Kiele of Waes, wedded to that city's lord, had taken the girl in at first. But she had eventually wearied of Chiana's pretensions and packed her off to Port Adni when Princess Naydra had married Lord Narat. The island of Kierst-Isel had been an excellent place for Chiana, distance being a thing to be cherished insofar as Pandsala was concerned. Yet after a few winters even Naydra's patience had given way. By that time Lady Rabia, Chiana's full sister, had married Lord Patwin of Catha Heights, and the pair had invited the homeless girl to live with them. Rabia's death in childbed had ended Chiana's time in Catha Heights, and she had lived in Waes again for a time before Kiele had caught her trying to seduce Lord Lyell. It had been back to Naydra, from whose seaside residence she now wrote.

Pandsala looked sourly at the royal title and thick flourish of ink Chiana used as her signature. She knew very well why the girl wanted to come to Castle Crag—so that at summer's end, she would naturally become part of Padsala's suite at the *Rialla,* with access to all the princes and their unmarried heirs. Landless though she was, she would yet have a considerable dowry from Rohan, as had all the sisters who had chosen to marry, and her beauty alone would make her a desirable match. But Pandsala was damned if she'd lend her own countenance to her loathsome little sister.

She penned a brief, firm denial, then scrawled her own titles and signature. Leaning back in her chair, she contemplated the words that meant her power and thought of her other surviving sisters. She and Naydra were the only ones left of the four daughters born to Roelstra and his only wife. Lenala had died of Plague and Ianthe was dead at Feruche Castle these fourteen years. Foolish, harmless Lenala and beautiful, brilliant, ruthless Ianthe; they represented the extremes found in Roelstra's offspring. The other surviving daughters all fell someplace in between. Kiele was a fool, but not harmless—nor, fortunately, ruthless enough to be any real danger. Naydra was intelligent enough to have schooled herself to acceptance of her lot. Pandsala suspected she was even happy as Narat's wife. Chiana, on the other hand, was beautiful, brilliant, and a constant irritant. As for the others— Pandsala could barely remember what they looked like. Moria lived placidly on a manor in the Veresch foothills; Moswen divided her time between a townhouse in Einar and visiting Kiele in Waes and Danladi, Roelstra's daughter by Lady Aladra, at High Kirat. Fourteen years ago at Stronghold, when Rohan had been acclaimed High Prince, Danladi had become friendly with Princess Gemma, last of her branch of the Syrene royal house since her brother Jastri's death. Prince Davvi had taken his young cousin under his protection and Danladi had become part of Gemma's suite. But whatever the rest of Roelstra's daughters were doing, thinking, or thinking of doing, Pandsala knew she could safely ignore them. They each had a share of beauty and a modicum of intelligence, but none of them was a threat.

And Pandsala herself? She smiled slightly and shrugged. Neither as beautiful nor as clever as Ianthe, she was nevertheless far from stupid and had learned many things in her years as regent. She wondered if her dead sister, in whatever hell she surely inhabited now, could see Pandsala's current position and influence. Pandsala hoped so. The knowledge would torment Ianthe more than anything else that could be devised for her punishment.

Pandsala's dark eyes squeezed shut, her fingers curving into claws at the thought of Ianthe, for all that her ruin at her sister's hands was over twenty years past and she had long since tasted her revenge. Their father's last mistress, Palila, had been pregnant and due to deliver sometime after the *Rialla* of 698. But just in case she was early, three other child-heavy women had been brought along—for Ianthe planned that if Palila delivered the precious male heir, then a girl born to one of the others would be substituted. At least, that had been the plot outlined to Pandsala.

Rising from her desk, she went to the windows and stared across the narrow canyon gouged out of the mountains by the Faolain River. She could hear the rush of water far below, but no sound of the keep's daily life reached her in this aerie. Gradually she calmed down enough to recall the past without succumbing to blind fury, and even with something resembling dispassion.

Most people would have said she deserved what she had received that night long ago. She had promised Palila that if yet another girl was born, she would find a way to substitute a boy birthed by one of the servant women, who would be drugged into early labor. Roelstra would have his long-desired heir, Palila would be the all-powerful mother of that heir, and Pandsala would have first place in the pursuit of young Prince Rohan. Both plots had been insane gambles based solely on the sexes of unborn children. So insane, in fact, that Ianthe had had no trouble denouncing Pandsala to their father the night of Chiana's birth. Clever, ruthless Ianthe—Pandsala could still see her smile as Roelstra condemned his newborn daughter and Pandsala to the exile of Goddess Keep. Ianthe had been rewarded with the important border castle of Feruche.

But the real irony was not Pandsala's discovery of her *faradhi* talents under Andrade's tutelage, nor even her present position of power. The laughable part was that only moments after Ianthe had betrayed her, a boy had indeed been born to one of the servant women. Had the timing been just a little better, Pandsala would have been the victor, not Ianthe.

Her gaze went to her hands and the five rings of her earned Sunrunner rank. Another ring set with topaz and amethyst symbolized her regency. The golden stone of the Desert shone brighter and more compelling in the sunlight than did Princemarch's dark purple gem. And that was how it should be, she told herself.

Her lack of filial devotion to her dead father's aims troubled her as little as her lack of sisterly affection. Years ago she had accepted a charge from the man who might have been her husband, on behalf of the boy who might have been her son. Her life had found focus when Rohan made her Pol's regent. For them she governed sternly and well; for them she had made this land a model of law and prosperity; for them she had learned how to be a prince. For them, anything.

She returned to her desk and sealed the letter to Chiana, watching her rings gleam. She alone of all Roelstra's daughters had inherited the gift; it ran not through his line but that of her mother, Princess Lallante, his only wife. Had Ianthe been similarly gifted—Pandsala shuddered, even at this late date. Ianthe with Sunrunner powers would have been well-nigh invincible.

But Ianthe was dead, and Pandsala was here, alive, and second among women only to the High Princess herself. She remembered then that she had a report to write to Sioned, and forgot Chiana, her other half sisters, and the past.

* * *

Lady Kiele of Waes was also at her desk that evening, and also considering the gift Pandsala possessed and she did not. Kiele did the best with what she had—but how much more she could have done had she the ability to weave the sunlight and see what others might not wish seen.

Smoothing the folds of a gown made of green-gold tissue, she consoled herself with what she *did* possess. But in a short while she would preside over a dinner for Prince Clutha, in Waes to discuss arrangements for this year's *Rialla,* arrangements that would nearly bankrupt her and Lyell. Again. Clutha had never forgiven Lyell for siding with Roelstra during the war with the Desert, and all these years of being watched and suspected had not been amusing. Clutha had hit on the idea that making Waes pay the entire expense of the triennial gathering would keep its lord and lady too short of funds to work mischief elsewhere. Treading the extremely narrow path their overlord had decreed kept Kiele in a near-constant state of nerves. Lyell, however, never seemed to mind. He hadn't enough wits to mind; he was too busy being grateful that he still possessed his life, let alone his city.

Kiele's fingers trailed along the gold headpiece on her desk. It was not quite a coronet, for not even she would dare that in the presence of her prince. Her pretty mouth twisted as she calculated yet again the chances of wearing the real thing one day. None, unless a great many people died. Though elderly, Clutha was in the best of health, as was his son Halian. The blood connection between them and Waes was in the female line and so remote that Kiele had no hope of its ever becoming applicable to the inheritance of Meadowlord.

The best she could do was set up one of her half sisters as Halian's wife. She had been well on the way to it some years ago when her choice, Cipris, had died of a slow, mysterious fever. Halian had been sincerely attached to Cipris, but that had not prevented him from taking a mistress to console himself. He had sired several children on the woman—all girls, for which grace Kiele thanked the Goddess. Had there been a son, he might have become the next heir to Meadowlord, with no blood ties to Kiele at all.

Halian had been quite happy in his illicit domestic life and reluctant to exchange it for legal marriage. But now his mistress was dead. Kiele smiled as she put her signature to a letter inviting her half sister Moswen to Waes for the summer. Moswen would make Halian an excellent wife—although Kiele wondered why she took the trouble to elevate one of the hateful Lady Palila's daughters. Then she shrugged. She worked with what she had. Moswen was the right age, reasonably pretty, and grateful to Kiele for past favors. She was also hungry for the trappings of power. She saw the jewels, the lovely clothes, the deference, and it was these things she desired. Of the realities of power she saw and understood nothing. Kiele considered her the perfect choice, for she would be easy to instruct and influence. Once Clutha died and both Halian and Lyell were out from under the old man's eye, Meadowlord would be Kiele's to play with as she wished. Halian had proved himself the type of man who could be led by what was between his legs—just like Lyell. With Moswen leading Halian, and Kiele leading *her*. . . .

A shift of light in the mirror caught her attention, and the door behind her swung open to admit her husband. Lyell was an angular, pallid man whose blue eyes and nearly colorless blond hair were more faded than ever by the Waesian colors of red and yellow that made up his formal clothes. Kiele frowned slightly as he approached her, for she had ordered his squires to dress him in a shade of green to complement her own gown. They would have been a matched set, and Clutha would have been honored by their wearing his color. But Lyell was stubborn about his family dignity and wore his own colors on all formal occasions. In some ways his stubbornness had served Kiele well, for she might have made some tactical errors in the past if not for Lyell's insistence on the rigidities of tradition. Faint gratitude stirred at the memory, and her frown became a smile by the time he crossed the chamber and stood behind her.

"You're so beautiful," he murmured, stroking her bared shoulder.

"Thank you, my lord," she said demurely. "I had thought to save this gown for the *Rialla,* but—"

"Wear it then, too. Not even High Princess Sioned can have anything so magnificent."

Mention of Rohan's Sunrunner wife, who with her fire-gold hair and forest-deep eyes wore green even better than Kiele did, decided her against making the dress part of her *Rialla* wardrobe. "Did you have something to tell me?"

"A letter arrived for you from somebody in Einar. You said you didn't wish to be disturbed while dressing, so I opened it for you." He produced a piece of folded parchment from his pocket.

A curse nearly left her lips when she recognized the handwriting and the remains of a dark blue wax seal.

Forcing herself to stay calm and casual as she placed the letter aside, she said, "It's from my childhood nurse, Afina, who married a merchant in Einar." It was the truth, but she did not add that Afina had been the only servant at Castle Crag to care for her after her sister died of Plague. Afina had wanted to come to Waes, but had been persuaded that she could be much more useful in the vital port of Einar, the first link in Kiele's chain of informants. Merchants heard everything, and usually passed it on to their wives.

"A boring letter, really—just family news. I don't know why you bother with a former servant, Kiele."

"She was very kind to me when I was a little girl." To distract him from the subject, sure to touch soon on the unsuitability of the Lady of Waes corresponding with a mere merchant's wife, she brought her arms closer together to deepen the valley between her breasts. Lyell's fingers strayed downward from her shoulders, as she had intended.

"Let's go down late for dinner," he suggested.

"Lyell! It took me all afternoon to put this on!"

"It'll take only a few moments to get it off you."

"We don't dare insult Clutha," she scolded, winking at him. "On any other night—"

"But it would be perfect *now*. I've talked with your women. This is the right time to make another heir."

Kiele vowed to dismiss whichever of her maids had been blabbing. She had learned long ago that men strayed when their women were child-heavy; her father had never been able to bear the sight of his mistresses during pregnancy. Kiele had fulfilled her duty by giving Lyell a son and a daughter. Conception tonight would mean she would be bulky and uncomfortable by the late summer, when she would need all her wit and charm—and when other women would be at their loveliest in pursuit of the richest and most powerful men. Lyell had been the key to the locked walls of Castle Crag for her; she did not love him and never had. But he was useful, and he was hers, and she did not intend for him to seek other beds. Once she ruled Meadowlord through Moswen and Halian, then Lyell could mount as many mistresses as he pleased. But not now.

She smiled at him. "Anticipation always enhances enjoyment, Lyell. Now, be a darling and find my green slippers, please? After all, you're the one who kicked them under the bed the other night."

He kissed her shoulder and obeyed. Kiele locked Afina's letter in her jewel box and replaced the key in a pocket of her underskirt. Lyell returned from the bedchamber just in time to see her smoothing her green stockings. He knelt beside her to slide on the velvet slippers.

"If you don't put your skirts down, I'll forget Clutha even exists," he said playfully.

She deliberately hiked the gown a little higher. "Does he?"

"Kiele!"

But she glided smoothly from her chair and out of his reach, laughing as she placed the golden headpiece on her piled dark braids.

Dinner in the banqueting hall was endless. Prince Clutha was full of plans for making this year's *Rialla* more splendid than ever, and, Goddess knew, the cost of the last one had been such that Kiele had gone for half a year without a new gown. She was forced to listen in angry silence with a smile on her face as Lyell's pride made him agree to schemes that would beggar him. Most entertainments were put on by the princes, with the burden falling on Rohan as usual, but the prizes for horse races and the spectacle of the last evening's banquet were Lyell's responsibility, with only nominal assistance from Clutha. Kiele promised herself that once Halian was Prince of Meadowlord with Moswen as his wife, this triennial penury would cease.

Clutha had brought his Sunrunner with him, a frail and withered old man with very dark eyes that saw too much as far as Kiele was concerned. She knew that whenever he accompanied Clutha to Waes, Lady Andrade received detailed reports. When dinner was over, the old *faradhi* wheezed his way into the dining room, Clutha's squire at his side. The young man gave Kiele a slight, elegant bow, his fine dark eyes flickering with disapproval of her almost-crown. She favored him with a lifted brow, wondering if his place on the social scale of nobility was low enough to allow her a calculated insult in return.

Clutha glanced up from the written list of expenditures. "You've the look of the last sunlight about you, Tiel."

"Indeed, your grace, Riyan and I have just received word that Prince Ajit of Firon is dead. A seizure of the heart, it was."

Kiele made appropriate noises of shock and grief, but her mind raced. Ajit had no direct heir. She tried to recall the collateral branches of the Fironese royal house, and if she was allied with or related to any of them.

Clutha gave a heavy sigh, shaking his bald head. "Unhappy news. Many times I've told him he should live life more easily, as befits men of our age."

Kiele coughed to hide a giggle, remembering that Ajit had planned to take yet another wife—his seventh—this year at the *Rialla*. Halian caught her eye and his lips twitched.

"There'll be one less wedding at Lastday this year," he remarked.

His father thundered, "You will mourn our royal cousin with respect, you insolent fool!"

"I mean no disrespect," Halian said contritely, but there was that in his eyes that told Kiele he wished the old man dead, burned, and out of his life. She lowered her gaze to her lap after casting a careful look of sympathy at him. Yes, he was ripe for the plucking, if Moswen was clever and played on his impatience with his father. Clutha behaved as if his son was still a lad of barely twenty winters, not a man nearly forty. Kiele would have to remember to tell Moswen the best approach to use. She would be a princess before autumn.

News of Ajit's death dampened Lyell's ardor, for which Kiele was profoundly grateful. While he slept in the huge state bed, she returned to the dressing chamber and lit the candle on her desk. Its reflection in the mirror gave her enough reading light as she scanned the letter from Afina.

You may recall my sister Ailech, who was in service at Castle Crag during your childhood, though not in the honored place I had at your side, but in the kitchens. We

were never very close, for she envied me my place. But I
have had news of her family after these many years. As
you may know, she went to Waes with Lady Palila, both
of them big with child, and it happens she bore a son, a
fine young man with dark hair and green eyes. Ailech
died shortly after his birth, and her husband also having
died, Masul was raised by my parents where they are
pensioners at the manor of Dasan in Princemarch. Masul
is something of a hawk in a sparrow's nest, for with his
black hair and green eyes he is unlike the rest of our
blond, brown-eyed family. Ailech's husband also had dark
eyes, and was small of stature like us, but they say Masul
is the height of your late father. But I chatter on about
matters that could not interest you.

Afina never wrote about anything that did not interest
Kiele and they both knew it. Kiele had asked her to use
her contacts in Princemarch to get definite news about a
boy said to be Roelstra's son. She had been toying with
a particular scheme all winter, working out ideas—purely
speculative until now, when it seemed that her arrow shot
in darkness had hit an unexpected target. Delight brought
a soft burst of laughter from her throat. She glanced at
the open door to the bedchamber, but there was no sound
from Lyell.

That night at the *Rialla* had always intrigued Kiele.
Four newborns in one night; a princess exiled and a princess rewarded; a mistress burned in her bed. Of the four
babies, one had been Chiana—insufferable girl. If Kiele
shared anything with Pandsala it was an aversion to their
half sister.

But was Chiana Roelstra's daughter? Kiele chuckled
silently as she set fire to the letter and watched it burn to
ash on a polished brass plate. Afina had not had to repeat
that part about the green eyes. Roelstra's eyes had been
that color. And Masul was nearly Roelstra's height, was
he? Kiele bit her lips to keep from laughing aloud.

She pulled out parchment and pen, and wrote a swift
letter to Afina thanking her for her letter and asking for
more interesting family news to distract her from the
strain of organizing the *Rialla*. She ended by expressing
a desire for a gift, one of those trinkets Afina often provided to cheer and amuse her—something in shades of

black and green. This would be correctly interpreted to
mean that the gift was to be Masul himself. As she signed
and sealed the letter, another idea struck her. She wrote
a second letter, this one a prettily worded invitation for
her dear younger sister Chiana to do her the favor of coming to Waes to help her plan this year's entertainments.
That Chiana herself would be providing Kiele's entertainment caused another chuckle as she folded and sealed
the parchment.

Kiele weighed her letter to Moswen in her hand for
some moments before burning it, too. With Chiana here,
Moswen could not be. And with the thought of her other
half sister she nearly laughed aloud—for what could be
more hilarious than setting Chiana's hopes on Halian,
only to have him reject her utterly when her lowly birth
was made public? Kiele hugged herself as the letter
burned, rocking back and forth with suppressed mirth.

After a time she sobered. She knew she would have to
be cautious. The physical characteristics Afina had mentioned would be a help, no matter what the boy's true
ancestry. Once Kiele had Masul to hand she could judge
whether the green eyes and height were matched by reasonable facial resemblance. Lady Palila had had auburn
hair; if Masul's was very black, Kiele could heighten the
illusion of his parentage by application of a subtle reddish
dye. Proper clothes were essential as well. And jewels.
She rummaged in her cases and came up with an amethyst brooch that could be redone as a ring to hint at
connection with Princemarch. She could slip it in with
jewels due to be reset in time for the *Rialla*. At worst, if
the boy was impossible, she would have a new ring.

But if Masul was believable as Roelstra's son, then even
if he was truly baseborn there were endless ways to use
him. Chiana's public mortification when her birth was
doubted was worth anything. The burden of proof would
be on those who suspected his ancestry to be common—
for the only thing certain about that night had been its
chaos.

And if the rumors were true, and Masul really was her
half brother. . . . Kiele grinned into the mirror, contemplating the delightful prospect of Pandsala ousted from
Castle Crag, Pol disinherited, and Rohan humiliated. She

pictured Lyell as Masul's champion and herself as his
mentor, teaching him how to be a prince—and through
him ruling Princemarch.

She gazed at the two letters. One would go to Einar
and bring Masul, the other to Port Adni and bring Chiana.
She would keep Masul in hiding until the *Rialla*, school
him, attach him to her as his only hope of winning his
cause. It would not do to have him meet with Chiana
before the princes assembled.

But it all depended on his ability to pass himself off as
Roelstra's son. Kiele regarded her own reflection by candlelight, asking herself if it might be true—and if she
wanted it to be true. She decided not. A fake, with reality to hide, would be much easier to control than the
real son of the late High Prince. She knew the characteristics of her father's breeding only too well.

Chapter Three

Pol had dreadful memories of his first trip across the
straits between Radzyn and Dorval. His mother had
warned him that *faradh'im* and water were in no way
compatible. But, wise in the way all eleven year old boys
think themselves wise, and very conscious of his dignity
as the son of the High Prince, Pol had not believed her.

His first step on board ship had taught him otherwise.
He remembered turning to look at his parents, who stood
on the dock with Aunt Tobin and Uncle Chay, all of them
waiting for the inevitable. The ship moved fractionally
on the tide. Pol felt himself turn green. He staggered to
the rails, was grabbed by a sailor before he could fall
overboard and, after being dreadfully sick, fainted. A
long day's misery in a private cabin had been crowned
by the indignity of being carried off the ship that night
and put immediately to bed.

The next morning his eyes had ceased their imitation
of hot coals and his stomach seemed inclined to stay
where it belonged. Pol pushed himself upright, every

muscle in his body bruised with the violence of his reaction to crossing water, and groaned. A very old man
was dozing by the empty hearth. The noise made him
start awake from his nap, and a kind smile further wrinkled his face.

"I thought you'd appreciate a good night's sleep on
solid ground before riding up to Graypearl. Feeling better? Yes, I see you are. You've freckles on your nose now,
not green splotches."

Thus had he made the acquaintance of Prince Lleyn of
Dorval. Pol had felt unequal to the breakfast the old
prince proposed, and they had ridden to the great palace
where the entire household had assembled to greet the
future High Prince. The night's rest enabled Pol to behave with suitable dignity, and his gratitude had been of
such proportions that it had been only a short step to
outright worship of the wry old man to whom his parents
had entrusted him.

Similar arrangements were made in Radzyn so that Pol
and Meath could sleep off the crossing in private before
their official arrival at Radzyn Keep. Assisted from the
ship to a small house Lord Chaynal kept in the port, they
were tucked up between cool sheets and in the morning
were greeted by Pol's cousin Maarken.

"I won't ask about the crossing," he said, smiling in
sympathy as the pair woke up bleary-eyed. "I remember
it all too well myself. But you both look as if you'll live."

Meath glanced at him balefully. "I had my doubts last
night." Turning to Pol, he asked, "Are you recovered,
my prince?"

"More or less. It never gets any easier, does it?" Pol
sighed.

"Never," Maarken affirmed. "Do you want something
to eat?" Their winces made him grin. "All right, stupid
question, I know! There are horses outside if you feel
capable of sitting a saddle without falling off."

They did. There was no special welcome from the people of the port, though they paused in their daily routines
to greet both Pol and their own young lord. Maarken was
the image of his handsome father: tall, athletic, with dark
hair and gray eyes like sunlight through a morning mist.
He was more lightly built than Chaynal, however; the

slender bones of his grandmother's people had lengthened in him, not thickened. At twenty-six he had fulfilled the promise of height and strength that for now was only hinted at in his young cousin. He also wore six Sunrunner's rings where Pol had none. As they left the precincts of the town and started down the road between newly sown fields, he caught the boy's envious look and smiled.

"You'll have your own one day. I had to wait until after I'd been knighted before Father would let me go to Goddess Keep and Lady Andrade."

"What's she like?" Pol asked. "I remember her from when I was little, but not very clearly. And the only thing Meath and Eolie ever say when I ask is that I'll find out sooner than I want to."

Meath grinned and shrugged. "It's only the truth, isn't it, Maarken?"

The pair were old friends from Maarken's days as a squire at Lleyn's court, and they shared a chuckle. The young lord told his cousin, "You'll have the chance to see for yourself in Waes. It'll be a real family reunion this year, in fact. Andrade's bringing Andry with her, and Sorin's to be knighted by Prince Volog."

Andry and Sorin were Maarken's brothers, twenty-year-old twins whose lives had taken divergent paths. Andry had *faradhi* gifts, just as Maarken did, but had seen no reason why he should go through the usual pattern of squire's training and knighting when all he had ever wanted to be was a Sunrunner. When Sorin was fostered to Volog on Kierst, Andry went to Sioned's brother, Prince Davvi of Syr. But after only a few years he had successfully pleaded his case to his parents. His progress in earning his rings had confirmed his choice.

Maarken glanced over Pol's head at Meath. "When do you ride for Goddess Keep?"

"Tomorrow morning, after I've paid my respects to your parents."

"You'll need an escort, if I'm not mistaken." He gestured to the saddlebags slung across Meath's horse. When the older man's shoulders stiffened, Maarken went on, "Don't worry, I won't ask. But even in your misery last night you didn't let go of them when the rest of the baggage was taken off the ship. That means they're important, and you'll need an escort to protect them—and you.''

Meath smiled uneasily. ''I didn't know I'd been so obvious. I don't want more than a couple of guards, Maarken. More might arouse suspicion.''

Pol eyed his friend. ''Then they must be *very* important. Why didn't you tell me you were going to Goddess Keep? You told Maarken on the sunlight, didn't you? How am I ever going to be a prince and make the right decisions if nobody ever tells me what's going on?'' Then he shrugged. ''You don't have to say it. I'll learn what I need to know when I need to know it.''

''Enjoy ignorance, Pol,'' Maarken said. ''When you're older, you'll know more than you want to, sometimes—and they'll usually be the wrong things, anyway.''

The road curved through pastureland where tall spring grass waited for horses to crop it. Ahead of them rose the magnificent towers of Radzyn Keep, seat of Maarken's paternal forebears for hundreds of years. To the left was the sea below ragged cliffs; on the right, far beyond the grasslands, Pol glimpsed the beginning of the Long Sand, shimmering golden in the sunshine.

Again Maarken understood his glance. ''It's always out there, isn't it?'' he murmured. ''Waiting. We work so hard to make this little green ribbon along the coast, but the sand would take it back in a single winter if we ever got careless.'' Changing his tone, he asked, ''How is the old prince these days?''

''Hale and hearty for his age, and asks to be remembered to you. As if anyone could ever forget him!''

''He does tend to make an impression—especially on your backside when he's caught you doing something you shouldn't.''

Pol started. ''How did you—?''

Maarken grinned. ''Oh, you're not alone, believe me. But it's a relief to know he applies the same remedy to princes as well as lowly lords. How long was it before you could sit down?''

''A whole day,'' Pol admitted sourly.

''He must like you, then. It was two days before I recovered.'' Maarken stood in his stirrups and peered at the bulk of Radzyn Keep, then smiled in delight. ''There's

Mother and Father with the new foals! They were going to come meet you today, but the Master of Horse insisted the inspection had to be this morning, and he's a real tyrant. Come on, let's go watch.''

A wild ride and several jumped fences later, they drew rein. Princess Tobin, neat and trim in riding leathers, gave a glad cry and jumped down from her horse. Pol dismounted and went to be hugged and kissed. He was then held at arm's length while his aunt's black eyes regarded him in astonishment.

"Chay!" she called to her husband. "Come over here and see what Lleyn sent us in place of the hatchling we gave him three years ago!"

Pol found that he was no longer at eye-level with his aunt. He hadn't realized he'd grown so much taller. She was grayer around the temples and white threads wove through her black braids now, but otherwise was just as he remembered: beautiful as a starry night. Pol looked up as Chay came over to them, and was startled again to find he didn't have to tilt his head as far back to look into those piercing gray eyes.

"Don't be silly, Tobin," Chay admonished, giving Pol a quick hug. "It has to be Pol—either that or Rohan all over again at that age. My own gray hairs tell me that time hasn't gone backward, so it must be Pol. You don't look any the worse for the crossing," he added, ruffling the boy's hair.

"Not now, I don't. But you should've seen me last night. And I have a feeling I did something awful all over the deck!"

"Never you mind," Tobin soothed. "It's just proof that you've the *faradhi* gift." She turned and smiled at Meath. "Welcome to Radzyn. And thank you for taking care of Pol on the way."

"I can't make any claims to having done so, my lady," The Sunrunner said as he swung off his horse. "Goddess greeting to you both, my lord," he went on, bowing to Chay. "I bring you fond words from Prince Lleyn and all his family."

"Glad to have you here at Radzyn," Chay replied. "And it's good to know the old boy's well. If you're not too tired, why don't the three of you come look at our new crop of foals?'' He slung a companionable arm across Pol's shoulders. ''I'm disgustingly proud of them—like all my brood,'' he added with a smile for his eldest son.

As they walked to the paddock fence Meath remarked, ''The Desert breeds sons and Sunrunners as fine as its horses, my lord. I've reason to know.''

Tobin nodded proudly. ''I think you'll find that this year, they're all something very special. Pol, do you see those six little beauties over there? Three grays, a sorrel, and a pair almost golden?''

Pol caught his breath at the sight of them. Long legs carried them in playful leaps that were more graceful than awkward despite mere days of life. The golden duo in particular caught Pol's eye, so alike in color and size, and the darkness of mane and tail, that they could have been dragons hatched from the same shell. ''They're wonderful!'' he exclaimed.

''They ought to be.'' Chay folded his arms on the top fence rail and gazed dreamily at the foals. ''Bloodlines from here to the start of the world and back again, by my best mares and your father's old warhorse Pashta. If there's royalty among horses, you're looking at it. Pashta's last are even finer than his first.''

''His last?'' Pol glanced up at his uncle.

Chay nodded. ''He died over the winter, very easily and full of his years—and his self-importance, too! Almost as if he knew how these six would turn out. By next *Rialla* they'll be ready for you.''

''Me?'' Pol was unable to believe his luck.

''Who else?'' Chay squeezed his shoulder. ''It's Radzyn's duty to keep its princes decently mounted, you know. All six are yours.''

The boy stared in awe at the foals, imagining them full-grown. He could see old Pashta's siring in their depth of chest and the cant of their ears—his father's beloved Pashta, ridden in a *Rialla* race to win his mother's wedding emeralds. ''Thank you, my lord,'' Pol breathed. ''Are they really to be mine?''

''Of course.''

''But I don't need six horses just for myself. Would it—would you be angry if I gave the others as presents?''

"Who'd you have in mind?" Chay asked curiously.

"My father would like like one of Pashta's colts, wouldn't he? And Mother would look wonderful riding one of the golden ones—she and Father could have those two, like a matched set." He paused. "Would it be all right, my lord?"

"Perfectly all right. And no more of this 'my lord' business, unless you want me to start calling you 'your grace'! Well, now that that's settled, would you like to see the mare you'll be riding to Waes for me? I need steady hands and an understanding rider for her. And if you'll do me the favor, you can exercise her out in the Desert this summer. Will you?"

Pol's eyes shone. *"Will* I!"

They spent the rest of the morning looking over various mares and geldings that would be taken to Waes for sale, including the horse that would be Pol's for the summer. A pretty bay mare, she inspected Pol with large dark eyes for several moments before nudging him with her dainty nose in token of friendship. He was enchanted, as the horse had obviously intended him to be, and only his growing weariness kept him from trying her paces there and then.

After a casual midday meal in private at the keep, Tobin sent Pol off for a rest. Not even healthy young boys could weather a water crossing with aplomb when they were *faradhi*-born. Maarken disappeared soon after on his own pursuits, but Meath lingered behind.

"My lord, I have a favor to ask for reasons I cannot reveal to you. It has to do with Lady Andrade."

Chay shrugged. "Reason enough—and favor granted."

"Thank you, my lord. Will you lend me two guards for the journey to Goddess Keep?"

Tobin cocked her head to one side. "Maarken mentioned something about that. You need more than the protection of your rings? What are you carrying, Meath—information in your head or on your person?"

He shifted uncomfortably and apologized, "I'm sorry, my lady, but I can't tell you."

"Sunrunners!" Chay complained in a teasing voice. "And Sunrunner secrets! Certainly you may have your guards, Meath. I'll order it this evening."

"Many thanks, my lord. And now I have something I must tell you that is also a secret, and must be discussed in private."

The princess' eyebrows shot up, but she rose smoothly and suggested, "Perhaps a turn in the back gardens, by the cliff path?"

Meath said nothing until they were strolling the gravel pathway between plantings of herbs, the surf pounding far below. No one else was in this section of the gardens, and they would be able to see any intruders long before they were within earshot. He told them about the incident in the tavern, Pol's conclusions about it, and especially Lleyn's conversation with him, Chadric, and Audrite afterward. Chay's fists clenched and Tobin's black eyes narrowed dangerously, but neither said a word until Meath had finished.

"Does Sioned know?" Tobin asked.

"I told her yesterday on the sunlight, my lady. She wasn't pleased," he added with gentle understatement.

"I can imagine," Chay muttered. "Well, Pol will be watched by even more eyes than usual, though none of us will breathe easy until he's safe back at Graypearl. But the *Rialla* worries me. Do you think Rohan might be persuaded to change his mind and not take the boy?"

"Sioned didn't tell me otherwise, so they must feel they can protect him," Meath answered.

"And Rohan's had this progress planned since last year. Damn!" Tobin kicked at a rock, her fists jammed into the pockets of her trousers. "I thought we'd rid ourselves of those damned Merida years ago!"

"I don't like to leave Pol," Meath said slowly. "Not even to the care of his own parents. He's that important to me, and not just as the future High Prince and the son of my old friend. I love that boy more than if he was my own son. But I must go to Goddess Keep at once."

"What you carry is that important?" Chay asked, then held up a hand. "Forgive me—I won't question you any further about it, whatever it is. My best horses and two of my best people will be waiting for you tomorrow at dawn. They know the fastest and safest route." He smiled slightly. "And they'll look after you when you cross the rivers."

Meath winced. "Please, my lord—don't remind me!"

The *faradhi* left them. Chay and Tobin continued walking along the cliff path, mulling over the news. At last they sat down on a stone bench, their backs to the sea. Their castle rose before them: coveted, never breached, holding a young boy safe as he slept.

"There's not a hint of her in him," Chay said suddenly. "His hair's a little darker than Rohan's, and his jaw's going to be longer, but otherwise it's as if he had no mother at all."

"More to the point, it's as if Sioned very well *could* be his mother."

"When are they going to tell him?"

"I don't know. It's not something anybody ever talks about. He must be told one day, I suppose—but when he's older and can understand."

"You mean when circumstances force it. You know as well as I that left to herself, Sioned would never let him know she's not his real mother."

"She *is* his real mother! In all but birthing him, Pol is Sioned's son, not Ianthe's!"

Chay pressed her hand in his own. "I don't need convincing. But what would it do to him if he found out from somebody other than her or Rohan? Every year the chance grows."

"Diminishes," Tobin replied stubbornly. "There's never been the slightest whisper. If anyone knew, they would have spoken up before now."

"There's knowledge and then there's proof," Chay reminded her. "It's the latter I worry about."

"Find me proof," she scoffed. "The few who were at Skybowl and Stronghold love us and him and will say what Sioned and I tell them to say. As for those at Feruche—bah!" She dismissed them with an arrogant shrug. "The word of a few servants against that of two princesses!"

Chay knew that the surge of royal arrogance meant she felt threatened. "Let's make a case," he suggested despite the flash of warning in her eyes. "Let's say there are women still alive who helped Ianthe that night, washed the baby, rocked the cradle—"

"They'd never be believed."

"Then count how many hundreds knew Rohan was held at Feruche. And how many of *them* can count the appropriate number of days without using their fingers."

Tobin was unperturbed. "She delivered early. They'll think she was pregnant before she captured Rohan."

"So who was the father?"

"Who knows? And who cares? They believe the baby died in the fire with her, so it doesn't matter whose child he was."

Chay shook his head. "There are three elder half brothers still alive who were brought in to see their mother's latest son. *They're* not servants, Tobin. They're the sons of a princess and three highborn lords. And what if Sioned were asked to prove that she'd borne a child? There can't be a mark on her that would indicate it."

She gave him a triumphant smile. "Yes, there is! Myrdal knows of herbs that bring a woman's milk, even when she hasn't given birth. Nursing changes a woman's breasts."

"I hadn't thought of that," he conceded. "But it still doesn't negate the fact that there must be someone who recognized you and Sioned and Ostvel at Feruche the night the castle burned."

"You're shadow-fearing like a one-ring Sunrunner, Chay."

He eyed her beneath frowning brows. "You don't think Pol *should* be told, do you? You'd keep it a secret. Don't you understand that he *must* be told? And not find out through rumors that would hurt him and make him doubt who he is! And what might be worse, rumors like that could unsettle everything Rohan's built so far! Look at this nonsense about Roelstra's supposed son!"

"Chay, it's just that: nonsense. If he dares show up at the *Rialla,* he'll be laughed out of Waes. And the same thing will happen if there are ever rumors about Pol," she finished.

"You're as stubborn and blind as Sioned!"

"Stubborn, certainly. But not blind. I understand what you're saying. But I don't see why Pol should ever be told. The whole foundation of his life is the royal heritage from his father and the *faradhi* gifts he believes he gets from Sioned. How do you tell a child that he's the grandson of someone like Roelstra—or that his father killed his grandfather?''

''You don't tell a child such things, no. But once he's grown, and has his knighthood and a few Sunrunner's rings to his credit—''

''No. There's no need for it.''

Chay knew his wife's mind well enough to know there was no further arguing with her. He rose, drew her up beside him, and they started back to the keep.

''At least you'll agree,'' he said, ''there's a need for his physical protection right now. I'm going to set a special watch over him. Maarken's perfect for it. He's good with sword and knife, he's a man grown, and a *faradhi* as well. Pol won't be suspicious or resentful if it's his cousin guarding him.''

Tobin smiled up at him. ''The way you've guarded Rohan.''

''It's another duty that Radzyn never cedes to any other Desert lord.''

* * *

The future Lord of Radzyn was at that moment some distance physically from his inheritance and even farther removed from it in his thoughts. Maarken had left the stables mounted on Isulkian, which in the old language meant ''swift wind.''

Chay had named him for the nomadic Desert tribes that appeared and vanished as they pleased—usually to steal one of his studs. The Isulk'im never kept the stallions they spirited away, sometimes in broad daylight, and returned them in excellent condition after their mares had been serviced. He would have gladly given them a prize stallion, just to save the wear on his nerves from wondering when his horses would disappear, but the Isulk'im scorned all such offers. Borrowing a stud from under Chay's nose was much more fun.

The stallion lived up to his name as Maarken guided him along the road leading south from the castle. At length the young man drew rein and smiled as the horse tossed his head, still eager to be racing the spring breeze.

''Just hold that thought, my friend. We'll be racing in earnest at Waes, and for more than the fun of it. I have need of a few sapphires to grace a certain blue-eyed lady's neck.''

Continuing at an easy walk, Maarken was not too surprised to find he'd instinctively chosen the way to Whitecliff. Some measures down the coast from Radzyn, it was where the lord's heir lived after he took a bride. Chay had never inhabited it, for he had been Radzyn's lord by the time he married Tobin, and for years Whitecliff had been run by stewards. But if Maarken had his way, it would be in use by autumn, and for the purpose for which it had been built.

He knew he should have said something to his parents long ere this. But somehow he did not feel equal to telling them that picking through the various maidens at Waes this year was not his intention, for he had already found the woman he wished to wed. Or perhaps she had found him. He was not entirely sure which, and did not much care. He was only glad it had happened. Just thinking about Hollis brought a smile to his lips—and that this attitude was slightly adolescent bothered him not at all. He had had plenty of examples of foolish lovers all around him since childhood, his parents being the prime culprits in unwittingly nurturing his ideas of romance in marriage. His father had passed his fifty-first winter and his mother was only a few years younger, yet the looks they exchanged when they thought no one was looking were unmistakable. Rohan and Sioned were just the same, as were the Lord and Lady of Remagev, Walvis and Feylin. Even serious Prince Chadric and Princess Audrite had provided an example. Maarken had always wanted the same things for himself: the smiles, the secret glances, even the flashfire of temper. He wanted a woman he could work beside as well as sleep beside, someone he trusted with his thoughts as well as his heart. Without that kind of partnership, wedded life would be little more than waking up each morning to a stranger.

His cheeks flushed as he recalled the many times he'd done just that—and the first morning he'd awakened to Hollis. He should not have, and Andrade had been livid when she found out. But he cared nothing for his greataunt's displeasure.

He had been nineteen, and by no means inexperienced.

Indeed, his father had once shown him a letter from Prince Lleyn in which the old man wryly complained about Maarken's propensity for attracting women of all ages at Graypearl. *Practically everything in my palace that wears a skirt has chased him quite devotedly since he turned fourteen, and of late I do not believe he has been running as fast as he might. In fact, I believe he enjoys being caught.* Chay had waited to show him that letter until Maarken had been knighted and was on his way to Goddess Keep for *faradhi* training. They had laughed over it, Maarken with crimson cheeks, Chay with smug pride.

But those encounters had been experiments only, quick desire and curiosity easily satisfied. Hollis had ignited in him a fire that had burned steadily for six winters now.

He had been at Goddess Keep only a little while when Andrade had decided that his unorthodox first ring was indeed valid. Rohan had given him the circle of silver set with a garnet during the campaign against Roelstra, when Maarken had called down Fire. He had proved to Andrade that he deserved the ring, and she had given him a plain silver band to wear with the garnet on his right middle finger. Looking into her pale blue eyes, he had heard her tell him that the next day he would go alone into the forest and consult the Goddess regarding his future as a man—but that before then, at midnight, a *faradhi* woman would come to him and make him a man.

In theory, one never knew who that first sexual encounter was with. It was considered very bad form to try to find out, and it never really mattered anyway. The Goddess herself shrouded the Sunrunner in mystery, concealing identity from the girl or boy who by morning would no longer be virgin. It was only *faradhi* men and women of seven or more rings who possessed this skill, only they who had the responsibility of making girls into women and boys into men.

Hollis had worn but four rings that winter night. He wondered sometimes if he would have guessed anyway. Even in total darkness, her hair had *felt* golden in his fingers. Maarken drew in a long breath as if to scent again the tender fragrance of her body.

It was forbidden to speak. They both knew that. Lips

were only for kisses and caresses, voices for calling out
in delight. Yet when it was over and he rested by her
side, his heart still thudding in his chest, he whispered
her name.

She gasped and went rigid. Maarken tightened his arms
around her, holding fast when she would have escaped
him. "No," she whispered, "don't, please—"

"You want to be here as much as I want you here."
But then, because he was only nineteen, he added hesitantly, "Don't you?"

She trembled for a moment, then nodded against his
chest. "Andrade's going to murder me."

Maarken felt slightly delirious. "She'll have to get past
me to do it," he answered lightly, "and she won't risk a
hair on my head. Kinsman, future Sunrunner Lord of
Radzyn—I'm much too important! She may rant and rave
a little, but we've both heard her do that before!"

The tension went out of her. "There's still a problem,
though. This was supposed to be your man-making night.
I have only four rings, so I can't have instructed you
properly. I'm afraid I haven't done my duty by you, my
lord."

Maarken gasped in astonishment before he recognized
the teasing note in her voice. In his silkiest tones he said,
"You'll have to lesson me again, my lady. I'm a very
slow learner. In fact, it's quite possible you'll have to go
on teaching me all night."

They forgot that at midnight another woman would
come to Maarken's chamber. They forgot everything but
the sweet joy of each other's flesh. Her hair was a river
of gold that seemed to glow with a light of its own in the
darkness; almost blind, he brushed the delicate strands
from her face, tracing the contours of nose and cheeks
and brow with his fingers, learning her face with touch
as he had long since learned it with his eyes. His hands
learned everything about her, all the colors of her body
as clear as the colors of her mind. He lost himself in the
sapphire and pearl and garnet of her, deep shining colors
that were flung around him like velvet, a perfect pattern
of a luminous and beautiful soul.

They were lying together, trading idle kisses, when the
door squeaked softly open, Maarken sat straight up in

bed and Hollis gave a little cry of fright. A voice Maarken did not recognize came from a woman wrapped in silk shadows.

"Well, well, well." Suddenly the woman laughed indulgently. "You might as well finish your night so well-begun. Peace, children."

The door closed, and she was gone.

Maarken gulped. "Who—who do you think it was?"

"I don't know. I don't want to know. But whatever she said just now, we're in trouble, Maarken."

"I love you, Hollis. This was right."

"For you and me, yes—but not so far as Andrade is concerned."

"The hell with Andrade," he said impatiently. "I told you, she won't punish us. You heard what whoever that was just told us. The rest of the night is ours. I'm not going to give it up. And I'm certainly not going to waste it!"

"But—"

"Hush." He silenced her with a kiss. Desire glided through his veins, turning his blood to slow molten sunlight. She resisted for a moment, then sighed and clasped him in her arms.

The next morning he went alone to the tree-circle where *faradh'im* sought their futures. Kneeling naked before the motionless pool below a rock cairn, he faced not the Child-tree or the Youth-tree but the Man-tree. One day he would turn toward the huge pines symbolizing his fatherhood and old age, but not yet. Today, in Sunrunner ritual, he was a man. He conjured Fire across the still Water, plucked a hair from his head to represent the Earth from which he was made, and blew the Air of his own breath to fan the flames. In them he saw a face: his own, matured and proud, with his father's strong bones and his mother's long-lidded eyes. The Fire flared then, and another face appeared beside his own. It was an older version of Hollis that he saw, her tawny hair sleekly braided around her head and bound with a thin silver circlet set with a single ruby, marking her as Lady of Radzyn Keep.

On his return, after more or less recovering from stunned happiness, he found a summons from Lady An-

drade waiting. He was impervious to her wrath as she
raged at him for disregarding the traditions of Goddess
Keep. When she finally snapped out an angry question
about his penitence, he smiled at her with perfect serenity.

"I saw Hollis in the Fire and Water."

Andrade sucked in a breath and gave a terrible frown.
But nothing more was said and neither Maarken nor Hollis had been punished. Still, he was heir to an important
holding, a grandson of Prince Zehava, and cousin to the
next High Prince. He could neither marry nor make a
formal Choice without the consent of his parents and his
prince. But he was only nineteen, Hollis was two years
older, and there was time.

On receipt of her fifth ring that next summer, Hollis
had been sent to Kadar Water in Ossetia. The holding
was close enough to allow occasional visits and easy
communication on sunlight between a trained *faradhi* and
a mere apprentice, and the facilitation of such contact
motivated Maarken to excel at his studies. The days were
endurable, with the touch of her colors available to him
on the sunlight; the nights were very long.

Hollis herself had been the one to plead patience. She
was adamant that he not approach his parents or the High
Prince until they each had a sixth ring, signifying they
were capable of using moonlight as well as sunlight.
"They have to know I can be of use to you and to them,"
she told him quite frankly. "And you have to prove you've
gained all the skills your gifts demand. I'm learning what
I need to know about courts and manners, and how to
run a holding—things I can only learn here at Kadar Water. I have to be able to function as your lady as well as
a Sunrunner. Besides, if I'm to be at Radzyn one day,
I'll have to learn about horses—and where better to do
that than at Kadar Water, the competition?" And though
they had both laughed at this, she had quickly become
serious again. "It's important to me, Maarken—as important as your knighthood was to you."

He had reluctantly agreed. Now, looking down at the
six rings glinting on his fingers as he held Isulkian's reins,
he wondered why he still hesitated. He could tell his parents, or wait for the *Rialla* until they met her and saw

her worth for themselves. Andrade had recalled Hollis to the keep with the understanding that the young woman would be part of her suite at Waes. Maarken was grateful but suspicious; he knew his aunt, and she never did anything without a specific goal in mind. If she wished him to marry Hollis, it was not for reasons of their love, although she would have no objections to their being happy. No, Andrade must have something else in mind, and it worried him.

He could not count on his parents as allies yet, no matter how often they said they wanted his happiness above all else. He was, after all, their eldest son and heir, a powerful position even without his blood bond with Pol. He would rule the only safe port on the Desert coast, through which all important trade passed: horses, gold, salt, and glass ingots going out; foodstuffs, manufactured goods, and especially precious silk coming in. Radzyn bred horses of a quality that brought higher prices every *Rialla,* but its real wealth was in the trade it administered. Maarken's grandsire had been rich, his father was richer still, and he did not yet adequately appreciate just how rich *he* was going to be. By all the rules, he ought to marry a woman of birth if not fortune to match his own.

Hollis was an uncommon woman, but she was common-born of two *faradh'im* at Goddess Keep, who had themselves been of no recognized family connections. Her children with Maarken would certainly inherit the gifts, reinforced through both parents. Maarken had already had experience with the suspicion and envy attached to being both Sunrunner and son of a powerful family.

He walked his horse along the road to Whitecliff, stopping at the stand of trees his mother had ordered planted before his birth. The cool shade spread out around him, and he ignored Isulkian's impatient prancing. He could see the manor through the trees, the solid stone walls gentled by flowering vines. Stables, pasture, gardens, a sandy beach below the cliffs, a comfortable and cozy home—all of it would be his, and he would bring Hollis here before the stormy season began. They would spend winter listening to the rain and wind, snug beside their hearth. He had always envisioned it so, ever since childhood when he and his twin brother Jahni had ridden here to play young lords of their own manor. They had been much too young to include anything so alien as the idea of wives in their games, but sometimes in the years since his brother's death Maarken had wondered how it might have been, the pair of them and their wives sharing this fine old house, children overflowing its many rooms and playing at dragons in the courtyard. A small, sad smile crossed his face, and he rode nearer.

Whatever Andrade wanted, she would get her way. She always did. She had married off her sister to Prince Zehava in the hope of a male heir with *faradhi* gifts. Instead, Maarken's mother had been the one with potential. Andrade had then put forth Sioned as Rohan's bride, and this time the union had borne fruit in a son who would be both *faradhi* and High Prince. She had bred them all to each other like prize studs and mares. Maarken wondered whether she already had a girl in mind for Pol, despite his youth. She would not object to his own mating with a Sunrunner, guaranteeing the next generation's gifts. But he also knew that his great-aunt's fine, elegant fingers would close around his life if he was not careful. There were intimations that this was the source of the coolness between her and Sioned. Andrade had used her and Rohan to get her Sunrunner prince, and they resented it. Moreover, since Pol's birth Sioned had worn only her husband's emerald ring, not the seven others she had earned as a *faradhi*—visible reminder that she was no longer ruled by Andrade and Goddess Keep. And that was precisely what made other princes nervous.

Not that they would have been comforted by the idea that Andrade ruled through Rohan and Sioned. It was the notion of the two kinds of power merging in *any* combination that bothered them. And there were others besides Pol: Maarken himself, his younger brother Andry, Riyan of Skybowl. The other highborns feared the power of a lord who could summon Fire on command, watch any court on a weave of light, use eyes and ears not his own to observe wherever he chose. There were ethics involved in being a Sunrunner: the strict prohibition against using the gifts to kill, the equally strict injunction that the good of one land should not be sought at the expense of another. Yet what had Andrade expected when she created rulers who possessed both kinds of power?

It was a thin and difficult line to walk. Maarken had not yet been faced with a crisis of choice, but he knew that one day he would be. From the sometimes haunted look in Sioned's eyes, she had already done so—and whatever the outcome, it had scarred her. He could not talk to his parents about this kind of thing; despite her three rings, his mother would not understand. Though influential in her own right and as Lady of Radzyn, Tobin did not *think* the way Sunrunners did. She had never been formally trained at Goddess Keep. But there was Sioned, and Maarken relaxed a little at the prospect of talking all this out with her. She had been the first to wield both kinds of power. She would have the same fears for her son as Maarken felt stirring for himself and his unborn children.

He turned his stallion before he reached the gates of Whitecliff, not yet ready to enter it as its future master. A word to his father about the possibility of refurbishing its interior in anticipation of his marriage would clue his parents that he was at last thinking seriously about taking a wife. But he would wait, talk with Sioned, and at Waes allow everyone to see Hollis' merits for themselves before he said anything.

He would ride through the gates of Whitecliff with her at his side, or no one.

Chapter Four

The High Prince lazed late abed, finishing off a breakfast of fresh fruit and flaky rolls washed down by watered wine. A pile of parchments was at his elbow, the top one sporting a smear of apple butter. Usually Rohan even worked through his meals, but this morning he ignored duty in favor of the fun of watching his wife give in to nerves.

Her turquoise silk bedgown billowed around her as she paced. Three times she had braided and unbraided her long firegold hair, dissatisfied by every effort. With each sharp movement of her fingers, her emerald flashed in the sunlight. A selection of gowns was heaped on her lounge chair, but she had not even begun trying them on, occupied for the moment with doing something about her hair. Her muttered curses and the occasional hiss of sheer annoyance amused her husband greatly.

At last he said, "You never took so much trouble dressing for *me*."

Sioned scowled at him. "Sons are more observant than husbands—especially when the son has been gone for three years!"

"May a mere husband make a suggestion? Why don't you just look the way you always look? Pol will be expecting to see his mother, not the High Princess in all her silks and jewels."

"Do you think so?" she asked forlornly, and blushed when he laughed at her. "Oh, stop it! I know it's stupid, but I can't help thinking how much he must have changed."

"Taller, with better manners and an increased sense of his own position," Rohan enumerated. "I was the same way as a squire. But he'll be the same in all the ways that count—and he'll find you every bit as lovely as he remembers." He grinned and brushed off his hands. "Trust me."

"You've gotten crumbs all over the bed again."

"I'm persuaded that Stronghold boasts a sufficiency of sheets, and servants to change them. Now, come over here and let me fix your hair, you madwoman."

She sat on the bed with her back to him, and he deftly wove her hair into a single braid. "You've hardly got any gray at all," he said as he worked.

"When I find any, I pluck them out."

"If I did the same, I'd be going bald. Give me the pins and hold still." He wrapped the braid into a smooth roll and kissed the nape of her neck before securing the knot with plain silver hairpins. "There. Go take a look."

She went to the dressing table mirror and nodded. "If you ever get tired of being a prince, I'll hire you on as my maid. This isn't half bad. And as for going gray—all you're doing is turning silvery instead of golden. I didn't know you were so vain.''

He grinned. ''I only say things like that so you can be a good, dutiful wife and compliment me.'' Throwing the sheet over the parchments, he got to his feet and stretched. Running his fingers back through his hair, he yawned widely and stretched again—not *quite* preening under her gaze.

''Your good, dutiful wife begs to remind you we have work to do this morning,'' Sioned told him.

''We do?'' He looked over his shoulder at the bed. ''I remember some reports, but they seem to have vanished.''

She chuckled. ''Has anyone ever told you you're impossible?''

''Yes. You. Constantly.'' He approached and untied the belt of her robe. ''Get dressed. The hatchling will be here before we know it.''

But the party from Radzyn was late. Rohan and Sioned waited in the Great Hall and Sioned resumed her pacing, boot heels clicking on the blue and green tiled floor. Rohan sprawled in a window embrasure near the squires' table and watched her, vastly entertained by her impatience. He, too, was anxious to see his son, but some perversity of his temperament decreed that the more she fidgeted, the more he relaxed.

A servant finally arrived with the news that the young master's party had been spotted from the Flametower, and Sioned flung a guilty look at Rohan. Her expression saved him the trouble of asking who had posted a lookout way up there. She smoothed her hair and straightened her clothes, taking in a deep breath before walking through the huge carved doors held open for the High Prince and High Princess. Rohan surveyed his wife with a smile, thinking that lovely as she could be in full dress and his emeralds, nothing suited her so well as riding clothes cut to emphasize her slim, long-legged figure. Well, he amended, either riding clothes or nothing at all except the masses of her unbound hair.

They stood together on the top step of the porch, Sioned rigid with nerves. Rohan noted the growing excitement among their people gathered in the courtyard below. The grooms were still arguing over who would have the honor of holding Pol's reins as he dismounted; the cooks muttered about which of them had remembered his favorite foods, a conflict Rohan had thought settled days ago. Stronghold's guard lined up in strict formation, their commander, Maeta, brushing imaginary dirt from spotless blue tunics and gleaming half-harness. All this for one boy, Rohan marveled, conveniently forgetting that he had received just the same welcome home from his training at Remagev. He heard the shouted query from the gatehouse that demanded to know who wished entry into Stronghold. He could not hear the answer, but knew what Chay's reply would be: "His Royal Highness the Prince Pol, heir to the Desert and Princemarch!" Pride welled up in Rohan; he would give his son half the continent, from the Sunrise Water to the Great Veresch. He would also give him laws to rule those lands in peace, the power to enforce the laws, and *faradhi* gifts to keep it all safe. He glanced at Sioned, who had kept *him* safe for twenty-one winters—half his life. She had used her skills and wisdom on his behalf, and to hell with Andrade's disapproval. Together they were the perfect team. Pol would have Rohan's power and knowledge combined with Sioned's Sunrunner gifts. Never mind that she had not physically borne him.

Instinct told him that he had hit on the cause of her uneasiness. Had there been more time, he would have found a way to laugh her out of it. Pol was her son as much as his, and certainly more than he had ever been Ianthe's. Thought of the dead princess tightened Rohan's shoulders; he consciously relaxed and took Sioned's hand. Whatever her outward demeanor he could always tell what she was truly feeling when he touched her. The long fingers quivered just a little, chilled despite the spring warmth, and responded to his gentle squeeze not at all. Was she afraid that in growing up, Pol had grown away from her? Did she not yet understand that her claim on him through love was infinitely stronger than any claim of blood?

The gates of the inner court opened and the riders came through, Pol first as was proper for a young lord returning home. Chay, Tobin, and Maarken followed with ten soldiers. But Rohan had eyes for no one but his son. Pol rode forward to the steps amid the cheers of his people, and gave his parents a formal bow from the saddle.

Rohan and Sioned answered the salute with regal nods and suppressed smiles at Pol's youthful solemnity. From a corner of his eye Rohan saw Chay grin and Tobin's eyes roll skyward. He sternly refrained from winking at them. As Pol dismounted, Rohan descended the steps with his wife at his side.

"Welcome home, my son," he said, and Pol gave him another ceremonious bow. Lleyn and Chadric had certainly taught him pretty manners—but, judging from the smile that suddenly transformed his whole face, they had not done so at the expense of his spirit. It remained only to see if he could abandon formality in the presence of the castlefolk, who had known him all his life and were just as proud and amused as his parents.

Pol passed the test. Royal manners disposed of, he bounded up the steps into his mother's open arms. Sioned hugged him close, then released him so he could embrace his father. Mussing his son's dark blond hair, Rohan grinned down at him.

"I thought we'd never get here!" Pol exclaimed. "I'm sorry we're so late, Mother, but Maarken wanted to chase down a sandbuck—we lost him in Rivenrock, though."

"Too bad," Sioned sympathized. "Perhaps we can go after him tomorrow. You look thirsty enough to have been out hunting all day. Shall we go in and have something cool to drink?"

"May I have some time to greet everyone first? And I should take care of my horse, too. Uncle Chay gave her to me for the summer, and I get to ride her to the *Rialla!*"

Rohan nodded permission and Pol ran off. His pride in the boy knew no limits now. Stronghold had seen the changes in Pol's appearance and behavior, every bit the proper young prince. Now his instincts told him to re-establish the friendships of his childhood. Rohan wondered if Pol knew what made him do it and what the outcome would be, then decided he did not. The actions were all the more engaging for their genuineness and spontaneity.

Chay had dismounted and was approaching the steps, wearing a devilish grin as he made Rohan a low, elaborate bow of homage. Rohan snorted.

"Don't *you* start!"

"I thought only to follow your son's excellent example, my prince," Chay responded. "And if you'll forgive my humble self and my insignificant son, we'll follow the rest of Pol's example and tend our horses. With your gracious leave, my prince?"

"Get out of here, you great idiot," Tobin scolded, swatting him on the seat as she passed him on the steps.

Rohan looked around for Pol. The boy was in the center of a knot of chattering, teasing soldiers, archers, grooms, maidservants—even Rohan's chief steward, who evidently felt he should be attending the young master rather than the older one. Rohan shook his head ruefully as he hugged his sister, slightly bemused by the hitherto unrealized power of his son's charm. But as Tobin kissed Sioned and they went inside, she set him right about things.

"He's exactly like you at that age," his sister informed him. "I swear to you, he had everyone at Radzyn ready to battle dragons for him, and I can't imagine he left Graypearl behind him much different."

"At a little less than his age," Rohan reminded her, "I was acting as go-between for a certain princess and her intended lord. Midnight meetings, secret afternoons—is Pol accomplished at that, too?"

Tobin had the grace to blush, even at her age. "I don't know, but if he is I'll wager he's not half as clumsy about it as you were! I lost ten years off my life that time Father caught me with Chay!"

"That wasn't my fault," Rohan protested. "And you were only found the once, of all the hundreds of times—"

"Hundreds! Listen to him!" She stepped back on the coolness of the foyer and inspected them both. "Rohan, you've been eating. I don't believe it."

Sioned chuckled. "One of the privileges of encroaching middle age is getting fat."

"I am not," Rohan said. He pinched Tobin's waist that was still as firm as a young girl's. "*You* don't seem to have taken advantage of it."

"If she did," Chay said from the open doorway, "I'd throw her in my dungeon and starve her. Sioned, you're more beautiful than ever—as always." He kissed her, then paused a moment and kissed her again for good measure. "What's all this about middle age? And as for you—" He clasped Rohan's shoulders in both strong hands and grinned. "You could still hide behind your swordblade. Why am I the only one getting older?"

Sioned's brows arched. "The mere sight of you sends every woman at Stronghold into a flutter, and you ask that?"

"I adore this woman," he sighed happily. "But it's not me, it's Maarken. Do you know he's asked for Whitecliff to be redone this summer?"

"Oho!" Sioned laughed. "Do I detect grandchildren soon?" Catching sight of Maarken in the doorway, crimson to his earlobes, she beckoned him over for an embrace. "Not another word about it, I promise."

"*Thank* you," he said feelingly. "Pol wants us to go upstairs without him. He'll be along in a little while. Myrdal's got hold of him."

Tobin nodded and started up the main staircase. "And she won't be giving him up for the time it takes us to discuss the danger he's in."

The warmth of the family reunion turned to chill silence. Several steps above them now, Tobin sighed, turned, and shrugged an apology.

"It has to be talked about. Come on, all of you."

Rohan, in an attempt to recapture a little of the former mood as they followed her, whispered loudly to Chay, "Why is it she can make me feel like a guest in my own castle?"

"Better a guest than a servant," Chay responded philosophically. "You should see what she does to lords and princes foolish enough to invite us for a hunting party or a harvest festival."

"I've seen, thanks—every three years at the *Rialla*. She and I had the same parents and the same upbringing, Chay—why can she do it when I can't?"

Tobin had reached the landing by now and glanced over her shoulder. "Oh, poor, awkward, tongue-tied High Prince," she scoffed. "You do it, too—only you realize it as little as Pol does."

When Rohan had assumed the title of High Prince, the number of people coming and going at Stronghold multiplied fourfold. Ambassadors from other princedoms arrived with increasing frequency and stayed longer, although Rohan refused to keep the kind of permanent court Roelstra had established at Castle Crag. Sioned's skills as a Sunrunner made resident representatives unnecessary; she could communicate more swiftly and effectively to *faradh'im* at other courts than messages could go back and forth via couriers. Moreover, the interplay between Sunrunners was brief and to the point, unlike the endless civilities and obfuscations by which officials justified their existence. The lack of a formal court was a relief to both Rohan and Sioned. During Pol's childhood especially they had wanted to preserve some semblance of family life despite their exalted position.

Nevertheless, emissaries still came and went, and it had been necessary to modify Stronghold to accommodate the increased traffic. Sometimes every chamber, anteroom, and even the hallways were jammed full of people who had had the misfortune to arrive all at the same time. If there were complaints, Sioned never heard them. She never apologized, either, for the inconvenience. She looked on anyone but her family and close friends as interlopers in her home: tolerated, fed, and conversed with, but encouraged to leave as soon as they had finished their business. Rohan's mother, Princess Milar, had changed Stronghold from warrior's fortress into family dwelling; Sioned had no intention of its becoming a court that functioned only for the comfort and ease of outsiders.

Rohan had insisted on one thing, however. There was a large, formal audience chamber directly off the main foyer, but it was much too grand for confidential talks in a relaxed atmosphere. He had therefore claimed a smaller and less formal room within the precincts of their own suite. In the downstairs chamber the floor was bare, the few chairs were uncushioned, and one wall was covered with a huge tapestry of Stronghold itself in an unsubtle reminder of the keep's strength and its rulers' powers. But upstairs a gorgeous Cunaxan rug covered the stone floor in restful colors of green, blue, and white; the seating was casual and plentiful; smaller tapestries depicted the Vere Hills in spring bloom. The windows overlooked the courtyard where castlefolk went about their business and provided a pleasant background noise. In this beautiful room many profitable discussions had taken place between Rohan and his *athr'im* or the officials sent by one prince or another to talk over problems.

As her family arranged themselves on sofas and chairs, Sioned signaled the servants to provide everyone with cool wine and then withdraw. A cup was left for Pol on the side table. Sioned hoped he would take his time; there could be no discussion of danger with him in the room. Not that concern for his safety would frighten him; quite the opposite. He would instead try to find ways of giving everyone the slip to escape the oppressive sense of being watched—thereby increasing the danger.

"With your permission," Chay said to Rohan, although his expression implied that the request was a mere formality and he would do as he planned with or without permission, "I'll set Maarken as Pol's guardian on this Princemarch trip. He ought to get some experience of the place, anyway. Not only for his own education but with an eye to its military layout—if you plan to make him Pol's field commander eventually, that it."

"It's become one of Radzyn's duties by now," Rohan replied. "Maarken merits the position by training and wits as well as birth."

"Thank you, my lord," the young man responded.

"It'll be a long while before your father gives up his post, though—despite his advancing old age. I assume there's more, Tobin."

"Of course." She tucked one booted foot beneath her, careless of the velvet upholstery. "I'm worried about what Meath told us regarding this supposed son of Roelstra's. It didn't bother me before—the claim is absurd, after all— but the boy might become an annoyance through those who are foolish enough to support him for whatever reasons of their own. It'll be difficult to tell if they truly believe in his claim or if they're only pretending to believe for the trouble it'll cause. What do you plan to do about him. Rohan?''

''Nothing, Not directly anyway. If I even admit that the problem exists, I lend credence to the rumors, you see. Our visit to Princemarch will do more to squelch the hopes of this pretender than anything else. I'm taking enough swords with me to show strength, but only as many as are proper for a royal party. Besides, we've been planning the trip for a long while, before these rumors really got started. So it won't seem as if this is a deliberate bid for the area's support.''

Tobin nodded her approval. ''A hasty journey, previously unannounced, would be taken as a sign of worry and weakness.'' She sipped at her wine, then nodded again. ''With Maarken along to keep close watch on Pol without his knowing it, he'll be in a position to learn all he can about Princemarch just in case it comes to a fight.''

''There will be no war.''

Rohan said it softly, but the words were all the more potent for the quiet of his voice.

His sister's black brows slanted down. ''If it's necessary, you'll fight. Whatever pretty notions you have about honor and law, there are times when steel is the only answer. You know that as well as I. And Pol's training will make sure he knows it, too.''

''He will not live by the sword as our father did.''

If Tobin heard the warning in his voice, she ignored it. ''Don't be a fool. I'm not saying Pol ought to enjoy war the way Father did. I'm saying that at times a prince has to fight or he's no longer a prince.''

Rohan met her gaze calmly. ''You're correct, Tobin. No longer a prince, but a barbarian. And *that* is what I intend my son to learn, much less painfully than I did.''

Into the awkward silence that followed came Pol, all fair hair and bright eye and limitless energy. His excited smile died away as he slammed up against the room's tension. After a swift inspection of each face, he said, ''I can always tell when you've been talking about me—you all *stop* talking.''

The peevish tone hit Rohan all wrong. ''Perhaps if you

knocked at a door and waited for permission to enter, we'd be able to change the subject gracefully.''

Pol blinked and turned crimson. Sioned cast a disgusted glance at her husband and rose. "Come have something to drink" she said to her son.

He followed her to the side table readily enough, but once there he asked, "Is he angry at me?"

"No, hatchling.''

"I'm not a baby, Mother. When is everybody going to stop treating me like a child?"

"You *were* a child when you left us. We're just not used to you yet.''

"Well, I've grown up," he stated flatly. "I don't need to be protected. What could be so awful that you have to stop talking about it when I come into a room?"

Sioned bit her lip. In trying to mend the damage of Rohan's flash of temper, she had only made things worse. Her hand moved toward Pol's shoulder, fell back. He was so different, this youth who had returned in place of her little boy, adult lines of cheek and jaw showing in his face now, adult perceptions in his eyes. An ache tightened her throat. She wanted her child back. But Pol was right; he was no longer a child. Yet there *were* things he must not know—and one truth from which he must be protected as long as possible. If she could not hold onto his love and trust now, when he finally found it out she might lose him forever.

"Mother? What were you talking about?"

In her heightened state of nerves she could not face his direct challenge. *Treat me like an adult,* his eyes said.

Maarken saved the moment by asking Pol to explain aspects of squire's training that they both had in common under Chadric's direction, and gradually the mood in the room eased. Under the interested questioning of his elders, Pol began to chatter like any other boy who had been away from home and learned a great many things. But Sioned mourned the easy manner of his first greeting, lost when she had disappointed him.

When the wine was gone, Chay took Tobin off to their chambers to rest. Rohan still had his parchments to attend to, as Sioned reminded him sweetly, earning herself a disgusted look. She asked Pol if he'd like to help her

supervise the spring planting in the gardens, and tried
not to be too hurt when he mentioned a previous promise
to spend more time with Myrdal at the guardhouse. The
retired commander of the stronghold guard, Maeta's
mother was a particular friend of Pol's, and Sioned could
not deny the old woman the pleasure of his company.

Maarken asked if she would mind if he accompanied
her instead, and she accepted his offer with a degree of
curiosity. He had no interest at all in herbs and flowers.
Strictly speaking, neither did she, particularly; it was her
duty as Stronghold's mistress to make sure it bloomed.
They walked the gravel paths and crossed the little bridge
arching over the garden stream whose dual purpose was
irrigation and beauty. The trickle had swollen with spring
runoff from the high Vere Hills and culminated in Princess Milar's fountain. Sioned spoke with the groundskeepers along the way, attending to her duties with one
part of her mind while the rest of her chased an elusive
memory. When she and Maarken were alone beside the
tall, fluted blossom of water, she caught the memory and
smiled.

They had walked this path the morning after he had
convinced his parents that he should go to Goddess Keep
for more than just rudimentary training as a Sunrunner.
Tobin had three rings betokening skills taught her by
Sioned with Andrade's approval, but she had never lived
the whole cycle of training. Chay had been frankly opposed to the idea of his son's education in such things;
he had never been entirely comfortable with Tobin's
skills, though he valued the advantage they often gave
him. But he was concerned that the powers of a *faradhi*
added to those of an important lord would create enmity
and suspicion. Sioned had helped Maarken convince
Chay that his talents deserved nurturing to their fullest,
and the following morning they had strolled the gardens
while he tried to find words to express his relief and gratitude.

She sensed that he again needed her support, but waited
for him to broach the subject himself. They stood watching his grandmother's sparkling creation of playful water
in the Desert, and at last he spoke.

"About Whitecliff," he began, then sighed. "It's not

in hopes of finding a wife that I want it made ready. I've already found her.''

Sioned nodded slowly, following the dance of tiny crystal drops that plunged into the greater pond and sent out conflicting circles on impact, replaced every instant by another drop and then another. ''She's a Sunrunner.''

''How did you know?''

''If she were not, you would've told your parents you had someone specific in mind—perhaps even brought her to Radzyn, or asked that she be invited here for the summer. But because you have not done any of those things, you're apprehensive about their approval—which points to her rings.''

He kicked at the white gravel around the fountain. ''Then you know why I'm telling you this, and not them.''

''You think you need my help.'' She faced him, put a hand on his arm. Her emerald caught possessively at the light, glinting its ownership of the sun. ''You've done everything a young lord is supposed to, Maarken. Lleyn taught you your role as knight and *athri*, and you've been to other princedoms and holdings to see right and wrong ways of governing. But Andrade taught you how to be a *faradhi*, and that makes you different. I think you believe your choice of a Sunrunner as your wife will set you firmly on one side and not the other.''

Maarken bit his lip. ''She and I decided that we'd both have to be fully trained before we could marry. Well, I'm wearing my sixth ring, and I'm still worrying like a dragon at a stag's bone.''

They sat on the edge of the fountain, and Sioned kept her hand on his arm in comforting encouragement. He extended long legs, boot heels digging into the gravel, and stared at his knees.

''I thought I wanted to wait because at the *Rialla* they could meet her without prejudice, see what she's like for themselves. But you're right, Sioned. I don't know which is going to be more powerful in my life, being Lord of Radzyn or being a Sunrunner. I don't know how much they'll influence each other or how to reconcile them. I always thought I'd serve my lands and my prince and myself better if I was both—but choosing a Sunrunner makes it seem like I'm more one thing than the other. And that brings Andrade into things where she doesn't belong. Sioned, I *can't* let her in, not to the part of me that will be Lord of Radzyn.''

"Maarken.'' She waited until he met her gaze, then touched her own cheek where a small crescent scar curved near her eye. "I was burned by my own Fire because I put the needs of my prince and my princedom above all else, including my *faradhi* oaths. I believed more strongly in my own wisdom and my choices—destiny, if you will— than I did in being guided by Andrade. Don't ask me what happened or how, because I can't tell you that. But I used what I am to get what I believed was right.'' The authority of a princess had gained her the loyal lies of her people about Pol's true parentage, but Sunrunner's Fire had destroyed Feruche and Ianthe's corpse after Sioned had taken Rohan's son. It was only through the grace of a friend that she had not actually murdered Pol's mother with Fire, a thing utterly forbidden Sunrunners. But it would not have been the first time she had killed using her gifts. The *faradhi* in her writhed in shame, but the princess knew quite coldly that such things were necessary.

She held Maarken's gray eyes with her own. "It's a difficult choice to make, and a lonely one. But it teaches you something very important. Fear.''

"How to fear Andrade?''

"No. Your own powers. Maarken, you're a strong man and you know your strength could kill. You've learned to be careful in practice combat for fear of hurting others. Being a Sunrunner is like that—even more so for one who is also a great lord. What you do will set the standard for Pol and Andry and Riyan. There'll be more in the future. But you're the first.''

"What about you? You're Sunrunner and princess both.''

"I'm a half-breed of sorts. I wasn't born royal, no matter what my family's connections with Syr and Kierst. I was a *faradhi* before I was a princess, and that's always influenced my choices. I sometime react one way as a Sunrunner and quite another as a ruler, and the two aren't always compatible to my aims.''

"I think I understand," he said slowly. "I know the kind of power I have as a warrior—and one day I'll be Pol's field commander with an army behind me. I also know my influence as my father's son, and how careful I'll have to be with that power." He held out his hands so the rings caught the sunlight. "These are another kind of power. And it might conflict with the other. But you made your choice, Sioned. The only ring you wear is Rohan's."

"The others are still there, like scars," she murmured. Then, more calmly, she went on, "I'm willing to bet your Chosen appeals to everything you are, Maarken. She matches you in gifts, but she'll also make a fine Lady of Radzyn. Doesn't that show you've already woven the two kinds of power together, whether you realize it or not? What you did at the Faolain years ago proved it."

She saw the memory in his eyes. At barely twelve winters old, he had recognized the military necessity of destroying bridges across the Faolain River, and used his Sunrunner gifts to do it. Fire-bearing arrows would have been risky, for Roelstra's troops might have swarmed onto the bridges to put them out and might have died. But Maarken's Fire had frightened them into doing nothing. No one had died. Rohan had told Sioned about it, marveling at the boy's mature decision that had combined duty to his prince and *faradhi* ethics: it was for this act that Rohan had given Maarken his first ring.

"I'm glad you're to be the first," Sioned told him. "Rohan knows the ways of princes, and I know those of Sunrunners. But you're both. Pol could have no finer example than you." Pausing for a moment, she waited until he again looked at her, and smiled. "Because of that, you don't really need any help when it comes to this lady. You have it, of course. But you won't need it."

"Maybe not—but I'll be glad to know you're there, just the same."

"You mustn't tell me her name yet, you know," she continued in a lighter tone. "I want to see if I can pick her out from among Andrade's suite. And I'll wager you whatever jewels she fancies for your wedding necklet that I *can* pick her out!"

Maarken smiled at last. "Sioned! You don't need to provide a dowry!"

"Who said anything about her dowry? Haven't I the right to see my nephew in something magnificent at his marriage? If I lose, then you can have that tapestry you've always liked. I always thought it would be most properly displayed in a bedchamber."

He blushed, then gave up and laughed with her. "All right, done! I win either way—and don't think I don't know you planned it like that!"

"There's something about a *Rialla* that makes me want to wager. Did I ever tell you that I bet one of Roelstra's daughters she'd never catch Rohan? This emerald against all the silver she had on—and she was clanking like a wind chime."

"I know you—you only bet when you're sure of winning. You'd never have risked that ring otherwise."

"How very perceptive of you, my lord." A smug grin on her face, she rose and brushed the dark, sun-warmed hair from his forehead. "It's getting too hot out here. Can you imagine what summers are like at Remagev? Walvis and Feylin will be here in a few days with the children to escape the heat."

"Remagev always reminds me of a dragon sleeping in the sand. Do you think I could ride out to see it and come back with them? I hear Walvis has worked miracles with the old place the last few years."

"You'd hardly recognize it. I—" she broke off as the air around them shimmered with color, patterns of light she could touch with her thoughts. She gripped Maarken's arm with both hands, seeing that he was as caught as she by the woven rays of sunlight that thickened urgently as a *faradhi* voice spun down the threads with a brief, frightening message, crying out for help.

* * *

It had not taken Meath long to find out that pleasure rides through the hills on Dorval were no proper training for the long journey to Goddess Keep. Each time he began to think that perhaps the misery of a sea voyage would have been preferable to the mutiny of every muscle in his body, he forced himself to think of yesterday's crossing of the Pyrme River in a tiny, leaky raft. He had been given scant time for recovery; when Lord Chaynal told his people to be somewhere quickly, they obeyed. Meath reminded himself that at least there had been a bridge over the Faolain River and fresh horses at one of Prince Davvi's holdings, but he was too exhausted to appreciate the fine animal under him. They were out of Syr now, riding the open pastureland between the Pyrme and Kadar Rivers, and as the afternoon wore on Meath began to wonder with a hint of desperation if his escort would ever call a rest stop. A broad-shouldered man of about thirty winters and a slightly older woman, they seemed tireless. Meath had to admit they'd made excellent time, though he suspected that by tomorrow they would have to strap him to his saddle to keep him in it.

Revia rode ahead of him, her companion Jal just behind him. Their swords and bows were augmented by his Sunrunner status that completed their armament. His rings had commandeered the raft ahead of several other passengers, and at manors and villages along the way a glimpse of them had brought swift service. Lady Andrade was known, respected, and generally feared throughout the princedoms, and assisting one of her *faradh'im* was good politics as well as good manners.

When the first two riders appeared over the low northern hills, Meath felt only vague curiosity. The addition of a third, fourth, and fifth did not concern him. But when they chose an intercepting path and he saw the glint of unsheathed steel, he tensed in every aching muscle. The sluggishness of his body's responses warned him he would be slow until battle warmed him, for nothing other than battle was indicated by those drawn swords.

The bow came off Revia's shoulder. She looped her reins around the saddle horn, guiding her mount with knees and heels while she drew her first arrow. The five riders increased their pace and Meath tried to guess when they would be within range of that long, deadly bow. Hitting moving targets from a moving horse would be difficult for even the best archer. But Lord Chaynal had promised him the best—and Meath gasped aloud as Revia's second arrow was nocked and drawn before the first had even found its target. The red-and-white fletching sprang up like an exotic flower against the green grass just ahead of the galloping horses; a warning only. If they did not turn aside, the next shot would be in earnest.

Jal came up beside him, bow at the ready, saying, "Go on, my lord, ride ahead to those trees. We'll take them down if necessary, then join you."

When the lead horse neatly sidestepped the first arrow and the riders kept coming, Revia let fly. Jal kept perfect time with her, shooting as she withdrew another arrow, taking another one himself as she shot.

Meath's primary urge was to stay and fight alongside his escort. But the scrolls he carried were too important. He was about to follow Jal's suggestion when another ten riders crested the hill, sun shining on naked swords.

"Quickly, my lord! The trees!" Jal shouted.

"Or Lord Chaynal will have us scrubbing the middens for life," Revia added calmly, never losing rhythm with her bow.

Rather than obey, Meath reined in so hard that his horse reared back on its haunches. He tied his reins as Revia and Jal had done, freeing his hands. But he did not take up his sword. Instead he lifted both palms so his rings caught the sunlight. He did not do it to warn the attackers that they violated the law by approaching a Sunrunner with swords drawn, for they were clearly intent on assault, laws or no. He instead gathered in skeins of sunlight and sent an urgent message flashing toward Goddess Keep.

The Radzyn soldiers placed their horses ahead of his, protecting him. Meath was dimly aware that one man had fallen and two more had wounds, and the fourth man's horse shrieked with the pain of an arrow in its neck. But distance had softened the impact of the arrows, and the others kept riding.

Meath raced down the weave of sunlight to the western coast. A chill gray fog stopped him. He cursed the spring weather that shrouded the keep in impenetrable mist. Instantly he returned and cast the skeins in the other direction, east and north toward Stronghold. Sioned's emerald and sapphire and onyx and amber were long familiar to him; he wove light around the pattern of her colors and touched them. Briefly he communicated his location, the danger, and that what he carried must not fall into the wrong hands.

Without waiting for any answer, he pulled away from her and kicked his horse forward until he was beside Revia. Then he lifted his hands again. He could call down Fire if he had to, but Fire might kill—or blaze through the grasses if his control was not fine enough. He had no desire to leave behind a conflagration as token of a Sunrunner's passage.

So he summoned Air. The dust of the fields rose up behind the first group of enemy riders, gathered loose grass and tiny pebbles, swirled into a whirlwind the size of a small dragon. Through its thickness he saw horses rearing in terror and men trying to regain control.

Jal gave a startled curse. Revia kept shooting arrows, but with a grin on her face now that her targets were nearer and she need not worry about the second wave. One man went down screaming, an arrow through his cheek. But another, infuriated, dug his heels into his stallion and hurtled forward, ignoring the shaft Jal placed in his thigh. He raised and let fly a knife.

Meath grunted with the impact in his shoulder. He lost control of his whirlwind, the shock of the wound devastating. But that should not have been, he told himself fuzzily; it was only a throwing knife stuck in his shoulder, not through his lung or heart. He fumbled for the haft, drew the steel knife from his flesh with agonizing effort. It seemed to him that he toppled very slowly, his bones water. Countless colors shattered all around him; the hues of trees, flowers, meadow, and sky becoming as stained Fironese crystal, losing depth, paintings on glass that splintered with a terrible sound and crashed into jagged shards. He fell onto them, soft blades of spring grass now blades of colored crystal. And then all the colors were gone.

* * *

Sioned gasped with the force of Meath's weaving, and again when he abruptly vanished. ''Maarken! Help me find him! Quickly!''

He followed her down the paths of plaited sunlight, seeking the familiar pattern that was Meath. But he had not Sioned's skills, and so found only the colors, not sight of Meath himself. Sioned saw; Meath conjuring Air, Meath felled by the slick, glittering knife. She saw her friend go down and a sound left her throat that was half sob, half snarl.

The enemy riders regrouped as the whirlwind spluttered to nothingness. They thundered down on the two Radzyn guards and the Sunrunner lying prone in the grass. Sioned knew they would be slaughtered. She did not make the choice consciously; she did what was necessary. With the ruthlessness of need she grasped every mind with *faradhi* potential she could find nearby. Twirling all the colors together, light bright threads of silk in the hands of a master weaver, she spun the sunlight as she had once spun the glow of the stars, and directed its brilliance to the road immediately in front of the assassins.

Sunrunner's Fire sprang up, a thick wall of roaring flames. They rode directly into it, too late to stop their horses' momentum. Sioned could not hear the screams or the thuds as they fell. But she could see her Fire licking at their clothes as they rolled about in the dirt, trying to douse the flames.

The woman wearing Radzyn's colors leaped down from her saddle, lugging Meath's long, brawny frame up as best she could. Her companion was soon helping her, casting fearful glances over his shoulder at the Fire. Meath was thrown over his saddle and within moments the trio were heading for the sheltering trees. When they were out of sight, Sioned let the Fire die away. It left a scar across the field, blackened dirt like a line drawn daring the enemy to cross.

They did not. Dust rose nearly as high as Meath's whirlwind as they scrambled for what horses they could catch and rode away at speed, leaving their wounded behind to fend for themselves.

Sioned waited until they were gone, then turned her energies to untangling the taut weave of colors. Elsewhere at Stronghold, Tobin shuddered in the sunlight coming through her bedchamber window and Chay shook her by the shoulders, calling her name frantically until sense returned to her eyes. In the sunlit outer courtyard hear the guardhouse, old Myrdal hung onto Pol's slight form, feeling the boy tremble in a storm of power. She had seen the High Princess conjure Fire and the like, but now something else was happening to Pol. At length he gave a convulsive tremor, awareness back in his face, and even smiled at her a little before fainting in her arms.

Maarken, the strong central thread of her weaving, was the last to be released from it. Sioned separated herself from him and together they moved back along the strands of light to Stronghold. She spared no glimpse for the rich Syrene meadows below them, nor the proud rise of the Vere, intent on seeking the safety of the garden.

But all at once there were other colors—a blinding, amazing whirl of rainbow hues as startled by them as they were by it. Sioned shied away and the other did the same. Opening her eyes, she found herself staring at Maarken—and could not rid herself of an impression of wings.

The young man was drenched in sweat, shaking. He hung onto Sioned's hands so hard that the emerald ring bit into her flesh. His own knuckles were white. She could not recall when they had linked fingers as well as gifts.

"Sioned," Maarken whispered, his voice not quite steady. "Wh–what *was* that?"

She met his gaze and said carefully, "I think . . . I think we bumped into a dragon."

Chapter Five

The woman had been beautiful in her youth. Yet even with the marks of sixty winters on her face and her black hair gone iron-gray, there was about her an eagerness that the years normally stole when youth was irretrievably gone. Ambition shone in her gray-green eyes, and malicious amusement for its certain culmination. This absolute faith in her eventual success gave her the look of a woman half her age. Her body was still lean-fleshed and supple, though the quick grace of her youth had been replaced by a deliberate elegance. She was stately now, impressive with consciousness of her worth, the kind of woman who should have been ruling a principality rather than a tiny settlement in a remote mountain valley. But in her eyes was sureness that she would not be here forever—and would indeed rule one day, and not just a single princedom but all of them.

Dusk in the Veresch brought a chill. The woman waited, facing the cairn that marked the eastern arch of a circle of stones. The rocks were tipped by the last fiery rays of the setting sun, and soon the first stars would appear directly above them. It had pleased her to assemble everyone while there was still sunlight; the swift descent of darkness and the sudden appearance of the stars was powerful, primal drama, especially here. Let the *faradh'im* have their sunshine, their trees, their three pale moons. She and her kind had known for uncounted generations the potency of stones and stars, and a different kind of fire.

A full circle of ninety and nine ringed the glen outside the flat granite markers, hands clasped and breathing nearly stilled in the silence. In times past it had been difficult to gather so many, but rumors this spring were as plentiful as newborn lambs, and had brought people to her. Waiting for the last sunlight to vanish, she mused on the magic of this multiple of three, a special number since the beginning of the world. Three moons in the sky, three winters between dragon matings, three great divisions of land in Mountain, Desert, and River Meadow. The princes met once every three years. The ancients had honored three deities: The Goddess, the Father of Storms, and the Nameless One who dwelled in the fastness of these mountains. The *faradh'im* had long ago denied the power she would call on tonight—the more fools they. For there were three kinds of light as well: sun, moons, and stars. With ninety-and-nine here, she became the one hundredth, representative of the Nameless One who ruled all.

Three was also the number Princess Ianthe's sons, each poised a third of the way around the circle at the hip-high standing stones. She could sense their raw, half-trained powers, inherited from a grandmother who had been among the last purebred *diarmadh'im*. Lallante, a simpering coward who had rejected her true heritage, had nevertheless used it to ensnare High Prince Roelstra. The marriage had produced Ianthe, who had in turn produced three boys both ambitious and malleable. They were the cornerstones of the power she would call on tonight, and they were the reason she was certain of eventual triumph.

Fourteen winters past, victory was a word for other people. There had been only survival for her, as there had been for all her people through hundreds of winters, ever since the return of Sunrunners to the continent from their island exile on Dorval had destroyed the *diarmadh'im*, their power and their language and their way of life. Driven to the remote mountains, they had been hunted down and slaughtered by ruthless Sunrunners led by three—that number again, she thought bitterly—whose names were even now forbidden lest their wind-borne spirits find these last hiding places.

But now she had three of her own, she told herself, sensing Ianthe's strong sons all around her. They would do her work and her will, and she would triumph. Youth had begun anew for her the day they were brought to her in the shelter of the mountains.

The sunlight was gone and darkness brought the first star. The woman spread her hands wide so that the single pinprick of light was centered between her splayed fingers. The starshine stretched between her uplifted arms and she clenched her fists, half-closing her eyes as she wove the cool fire, centering the weave before she wrapped the fabric of light around and through the stones.

Her anchors, Ianthe's sons, began to tremble. Their shivering raced through the ring of hands and bodies around them, and the woman's strength increased as she drew in the energy of ninety-nine lives joined by starfire. This power she directed into the circle of stones. And an instant later the source of her kind's name was revealed: *diarmadh'im*, Stoneburners.

She became as the unmoving rock of the cairn, watching a scene form in the cool glow of tiny white flames. Long, fine fingers were what she saw first, held out to a hearth. Ten rings studded with gems circled the fingers; thin chains of gold or silver led from each ring to bracelets on bony wrists. Sight of a sharp-featured, proud face came next. The hair had once been blonde. The eyes were still fiercely blue, narrowing slightly as fire found fresh wood and burned more brightly. But the thin hands moved closer still to the blaze, rubbing together for warmth. Lady Andrade of Goddess Keep was feeling the cold.

A man only a little younger than she placed a heavy fur-lined cloak around her shoulders. The man was Lord Urival, Master of Sunrunners and Lady Andrade's steward. Beautiful eyes of a curious golden-brown were set into a craggy face of no beauty at all. He pulled a table over between their chairs and sat down, chafing his nine rings before pulling the folds of his brown woolen robes around him.

They exchanged a few words, inaudible from the stone circle, and then their heads turned as one. Into the vision came the tall, wide-shouldered, dark-haired Sunrunner who had narrowly escaped death only two days ago on the road to Goddess Keep. His face was pinched with exhaustion and pain. He held one arm awkwardly to his side, instinctively protecting the bandages that bulked at his shoulder. He bowed, spoke, and placed his saddle-bags on the low table.

The watching woman hissed in frustration. Her minions had failed to stop this man; by the Nameless One, it was hard to see the precious scrolls bulge within the leather bags. She fixed her gaze on them hungrily. When she turned her attention to the larger scene, the wounded Sunrunner was gone.

Lord Urival opened the saddlebags and extracted four long, round cases. A moment later he had the first of the scrolls spread out on the table before him, turned so Lady Andrade could see. The woman in the stone circle caught her breath as she saw the exquisite script. Much of the old language had been lost, and she was one of the few who knew more than a smattering of its words. But given enough time, the scrolls would be translated, and that must not happen.

Lady Andrade peered at the writing, shaking her head. She said something to Urival and he bowed, leaving the frame of vision. Soon he returned with a youth of no more than twenty winters who wore four rings, each set with a tiny ruby. He directed his attention to the scrolls, bending over them with a look of dawning fascination on his face. After a moment he straightened and rubbed his eyes with a comical grimace that brought a small answering smile from Andrade.

But all at once Lord Urival whirled, his fingers rubbing spasmodically at his rings, and stared into the flames—straight at the woman in the starlit circle, it seemed. The youth turned as well, blue eyes wide with astonishment beneath a shock of light brown hair.

She broke off the conjure with desperate haste, unthreading the weave of stars between her hands. The fire along the circle fled back to the cairn, which flared bright and fierce for an instant. Then it darkened, an uneven stack of granite rocks in the night, nothing more.

Some of those in the circle swayed and moaned at the abrupt termination of the vision. The woman scowled, reminding herself that next time she would have to test them all for strength and not just the willingness brought by fear.

"Bring to me the young man named Masul, who lives at Dasan Manor in Princemarch. Bring him however you must, but make sure he is alive, well, and in possession of his wits. I don't want him damaged."

All but three of the ninety-nine bowed to her and melted away into the woods, many of them leaning on their fellows for support. The woman flexed her hands, rubbing her palms where they felt slightly burned. This had been a potent working; she would need time to recover.

"Why do you need him?" the eldest of Ianthe's sons asked resentfully. "You have me."

"Us," his next youngest brother corrected smoothly.

"It is not your time yet," she said firmly.

The youngest of them smiled slightly. "Yes, my Lady Mireva. Of course."

She looked them over, remembering the three dirty, barbaric little boys she had turned into young princes. Ruval, at nineteen the eldest, had reached his full height but had yet to acquire the muscle and firm flesh of manhood. Dark-haired and blue-eyed, he favored the late High Prince his grandfather in features, but the shape of his eyes was Ianthe's. Marron, a year younger, was still awkward and bony with late adolescence. Of the three, he looked the least like his mother, having inherited his father's heavy-lidded eyes and fiery red hair. The youngest, Segev, was barely sixteen and still a child in most ways. His eyes were gray-green like Mireva's own and shaped like Ianthe's, but his hair was as black as Roelstra's had been. He was the most intelligent—and, paradoxically, the most biddable. Mireva understood that, and valued it; he trusted her wisdom and would do exactly as she bade him, for there was a hunger in him that her promises and power fed most adequately.

"Why him?" she asked suddenly, echoing Ruval's earlier question. "Because none of you is old enough yet. You have much to learn about the powers your grandmother gave you. For now, this Masul is an amusing feint who will cause interesting trouble for Rohan."

"Especially once you get your hands on him," Marron remarked with a smile.

Mireva chose to ignore the mockery beneath the admiration. "More important right now are the scrolls. You saw them, of course, though no one else did. When our people ruled here, the *faradh'im* stayed on their island and did nothing. Then, without warning, they were here, opposing us. They spent years watching us in secret, learning our ways for their own ends, using them against us. They drove us from power and chased us into these mountains. And then they erased all memory of us from the minds of the people, causing us to be forgotten along with our ways. But what they knew of us was written down. And now someone has found the scrolls and put them into Lady Andrade's hands."

"It didn't seem as if she understood a word of them," Ruval commented.

"But she will. She's clever—and ruthless. She will want the *faradh'im* to know the power *we* once had."

"So the scrolls must be destroyed," Marron surmised. "That's easy enough to do, even at this distance. A little starfire, nicely directed—"

"No! I must know what's in them! I must know how much has been lost!"

"They they must be stolen," Segev said. "As the knowledge was stolen from us. What if. . . ?"

Mireva narrowed her gaze at him in the starlight. "What if?" she prompted.

"Someone with the gifts could go to Goddess Keep to be trained, gain their confidence, and steal the scrolls."

"Who did you have in mind?" Marron asked silkily.

"Not you," his youngest brother shot back. "You have all the subtlety of a rutting dragon."

"And you think *you* could do it?" Ruval scoffed.

"I can. And I will." A smile stole across his sharp features. "And maybe I can even things up with dear Aunt Pandsala as well for betraying Grandfather during the war with Prince Rohan."

"Your primary concern must be the scrolls," Mireva said. "Leave the Princess-Regent to me—and to Masul, who may or may not be her brother." She laughed softly with excitement. "Excellent, Segev! A scheme worthy of a prince and a son of *diarmadh'im*. But there are things I must teach you before you leave. Come tomorrow night to my dwelling."

They understood this as dismissal, and left her. She heard the clink of bridles as they mounted the horses left deeper in the forest, and Marron's voice as he taunted his brother about becoming a weakling *faradhi*. When their arguing had faded, she began the long walk back to her house, relishing the touch of cool starlight through the trees.

She lived in a low stone dwelling much larger than it looked, seemingly built out from the side of the hill but in reality dug deeply into it by generations of her forebears. There were two outer rooms that appeared to be the whole of the place, but the wooden planks that formed the back wall hid a door leading into the important part of the house. Mireva paused to build up the fire against the night chill, then went to the rough paneling and pressed a catch concealed in a seam. Grunting a little with effort, she pushed on the door and it swung open with a protesting creak. The hallway beyond was black as the night outside. Mireva struck iron to flint—she could call Fire if she wished but never used Sunrunner ways if she could avoid it—and a flame burned obediently atop a slim column of wax. She plucked the candle from its niche and walked down the packed earthen floor, not even glancing at the low-ceilinged corridors that branched off from the main one. At last she reached the door she wanted, and set the candle into a holder within.

There was the glint of golden things and silver, and gems that stained the room with rainbow colors. A massive mirror stood in a corner, shrouded in midnight-blue velvet sewn with silver thread in a pattern of stars. Most of the space was taken up by huge chests and boxes resting on tables. Mireva took a small coffer and opened it, removing a piece of parchment folded around something minced and brittle. There were only five similar packets left, she noted; she would have to go harvesting soon, high in the mountains where the herb grew strong and potent.

She returned to the outer rooms then, sliding the heavy door back into place. There was no indication that it even existed. Gathering a bottle and winecup, she settled into a soft chair before the fire and stirred the contents of the packet into the bottle. She waited for the herb to mix, then poured a measure of the wine and drained it in three long swallows. Earlier today she had consumed a similar cup, but the effects had worn off and she needed more. A smile touched her face as the drug began its work in her blood. How stupid the *faradh'im* were to be so afraid of this. But perhaps their powers of sun and moons were too fragile for *dranath*. The ancients had found it a source of sure and sustained strength, addiction to it an assurance of potency.

Mireva drew in a deep breath to prolong the light-headed glow and closed her eyes. No, the Sunrunners were weaklings who could not tolerate use of *dranath*. The one enslaved to it by Roelstra had burned out after only a few years. She remembered very well the day she had presented the herb and knowledge of its addictive properties to Lady Palila, Roelstra's last mistress. Mireva had been young then, and only playing the part of old wisewoman from the hills. Her bedchamber mirror told her that far less effort would be required to sustain the image these days, and the opposite deception would be needed tomorrow night. She sighed, then shrugged. She had the ability. And she would win. The Sunrunner corrupted and used by Roelstra had been an amusement. But now she would play the game in earnest. The gambit with Masul would test her opponents, Segev would gain her the scrolls, and in only a few years Ruval would bring her final victory.

The rush of *dranath* peaked, centered in her belly. She shifted slightly, enjoying the tingle of sensual pleasure. Andrade might have her ten rings and her position as ruler of all *faradh'im*, but Mireva knew she had never know the sheer glut of power brought by *dranath*. To ensure that she never would, Mireva took out pen and parchment, closing her eyes the better to remember the words of the scroll. After a few moments her hand began to move, copying what she saw in her mind.

* * *

Urival accepted the glass of wine Andry gave him, nodded his thanks, and drank deeply. Setting the cup down, he sagged back in his chair and exhaled. He rubbed the ring on his left thumb absently. "I'm too old," he muttered. "I haven't the strength anymore."

"At least you felt it," Andrade said. "I didn't even catch a flicker." She looked up at her grand-nephew and namesake. "You either?"

"No, my Lady." Andry stared down at his four rings, each set with a small ruby token of his status as son of a powerful *athri*. Chay's colors were in his clothing, too, his tunic decorated around the throat with interlocking red and white knots. "I thought I saw the fire jump, but. . . ."

Urival said, "That had nothing to do with what I sensed. Someone was watching us. It was subtle, but it was there. And it had no basis in the fire—not Sunrunner's Fire. It's night, the moons aren't up—there's only the stars."

"You've said what it wasn't," Andrade snapped. "Tell me what it *was*."

Andry crouched down with his back to the hearth, sitting on his heels. With his lithe body curled up thus, and his too-long hair drifting untidily around a nearly beardless face, he seemed much younger than his twenty winters—except for the sharply intelligent eyes, a deeper blue than Andrade's. "We conjure with Fire to show us things, but we can't actually watch events except on woven light of sun or moons. Yet Urival says we were being watched. If not in the usual ways, then how?"

Andrade tapped the scroll with one long finger. "Not us, Andry. This." She traced the title page with its two ominous words and its strange border design. "Look at this and tell me how it was done," she added grimly.

Urival stared. "Impossible!"

"Sioned did it," she reminded him. "She used starlight." She met his gaze and they shared the memory of the night Rohan had killed Roelstra in single combat. The two had been protected from interference by a dome woven by Sioned of shining silvery starfire. She and Urival had both been caught up in the powerful conjuring. Pandsala, present at the scene, had been trapped into it, and Tobin, who had been with Sioned far away at Skybowl. And, though barely a day old, Pol too had been woven into that dangerous, forbidden fabric of light.

"Aunt Sioned has done it?" Andry looked up, frowning. "But it's not possible, and even if it were—"

"If it were not possible, why bother to forbid it to us?" Urival asked. "It's not something we do, but we know it can be done because Sioned did it."

"Whoever it is must have powers beyond ours."

"Not necessarily."

"Look at this page." Andrade traced the pattern of night sky with stars again. *"On Sorceries."*

"No wonder Meath was frightened by it. And no wonder somebody tried to kill him in order to get it. Knowledge left behind on Dorval by our ancestors—things they didn't want remembered?"

"And somebody doesn't want us to discover, that's certain," Andry said.

"The temptations must be very great." The Lady of Goddess Keep folded her beringed hands tightly together. *"I* am tempted. I choose to give in to that temptation. I must know what the scrolls teach. Others know it. So must I."

"They had reasons for leaving this behind," Urival warned. "Reasons for the prohibition against using starlight. Andrade, the danger—"

"—would be in not knowing," Andry interrupted, rude in his excitement. "The Lady is right. We must know what's here and how to use it. If only to know what to guard against.''

His attention was on the scroll, and thus he did not see the glance that passed between his elders. Through no special power but long years of familiarity with each other's thoughts, Andrade and Urival shared reaction at Andry's use of the plural. He had counted himself among those who must know. Andrade had summoned him here tonight because he was her kinsman and extremely gifted, but he did not yet know what she and Urival had decided this winter: that when she was dead, Andry would be Lord of Goddess Keep. Young as he was, he was the only possible choice. His relationship to the High Prince had only sealed what his talents would have earned him had he been born in a cottage instead of a castle.

"Use their own weapons against them, whoever they may be?'' Andrade asked him now. "Ways our ancestors thought best forgotten? Ways dangerous and forbidden to us?''

Andry rose fluidly to his feet, and there was nothing boyish about him as he looked down at her. There was the look of his father about him now, strength of will, clear-sightedness, and firmness of purpose adding maturity to his face. But more than his sire, Andrade suddenly saw his grandsire in him, saw Zehava's single-minded acquisitiveness, his drive to possess. Zehava had wanted land and unquestioned authority over it; Andry wanted knowledge. Both ambitions were perilous.

Andry's eyes shone with ambition as he said, "How do you think our ancestors won in the first place?''

Urival gave a muffled exclamation. Andrade did not react outwardly at all.

"Go on,'' she said quietly.

"You said that long ago they left Dorval and came here to involve themselves in the world. Why? It can't have been for the sake of power, for they didn't take over as princes, and our history hasn't been one of meddling in the affairs of the princedoms.'' *Until recently,* his eyes said, *until you, Aunt Andrade.* "Thus it must have been not for their own gain, but for the people. Because they were needed. And yet they left certain knowledge behind on Dorval. Why didn't they want us to know these things?

More importantly, why didn't they want us to know how to use starlight, the 'sorceries' this scroll implies? Tonight we learned that others know what these Sunrunners wanted forgotten. Is it so great a leap of logic to think these were the people our ancestors came here to oppose?

"And why learn the ways of the enemy in the first place? Knowledge is to be used—else why learn it? They must've carried it with them inside their heads and once the others were defeated, never taught it again, so of course it's been forgotten."

Urival roused himself from appalled reaction to Andry's words and said, "That's a long way from saying they used what might be in this scroll to battle these unknown enemies—existence of which hasn't even been proved!"

"Hasn't it?" Andry faced his great-aunt. "You saw, when you first became Lady here, that High Prince Roelstra was too powerful."

The jewels of her rings quivered in the firelight, betraying the sudden tremor in her hands. "I knew long before that what he would become. He came to my father's keep as a youth, looking for a bride."

Andry's eyes widened, for he had never heard that part of the story before. "But you must already have been a Sunrunner."

"Yes. Home to visit my father and my twin sister—your grandmother Milar. I know what you're about to say, Andry. I saw the power of the *faradh'im* dwindling, our influence threatened as Roelstra's power grew. So I married off my sister to Prince Zehava, hoping one of their children would be a son with the gifts, someone I could train up to be the first Sunrunner prince."

"Only it didn't turn out that way," Urival murmured.

"No. Your mother showed the gifts instead, Andry. And so I arranged for Rohan to marry Sioned, whom I knew to be powerful." A twinge of bitterness crossed her face.

"And now Pol will be the prince you wanted," Andry went on. "But it's happened even before him, my Lady. Sioned is High Princess, with no hesitation in using her gifts as she sees necessary to governance. Pandsala does the same as Regent of Princemarch. My brother Maarken, and Riyan of Skybowl—and maybe others we haven't identified yet—they'll all be Sunrunner lords, just like Pol will one day. *Faradhi* ways are merging with those of princes, because you decided they must.''

''And must our ways now merge with those of our enemies, because *you* decide they must?'' she snapped.

''Not merge. But why shouldn't we do what our ancestors probably did?''

''Because they had good reason for leaving that knowledge behind and forbidding us the starlight.'' She leaned back in her chair, looking very old. ''Talk with Rohan sometime about using methods you despise to gain something you know is right. Why do you think his sword has hung idle in the Great Hall of Stronghold since he defeated Roelstra?''

''Yet he did battle, and he won! And because of it, he's had the chance to make this a world of laws instead of blood brought by the sword.''

''Would you make us into users of dark stars rather than the clean light of sun and moons?''

''By your own admission, Sioned used starlight—and even though she wears no *faradhi* rings now, there can be no doubting her heart.''

Urival pushed himself to his feet. Andry was too clever by half and had learned logical argument all too well. ''Leave us now. You've made your case. And I don't need to tell you not to speak of this.''

''No, my lord. You needn't tell me.'' The words were spoken without rancor, but the blue eyes were shaded with defiance. He bowed to them both, and left.

Andrade was silent for a time, then said, ''If I don't live long enough to instill some caution in that boy, we're lost.'' She tilted her face up to Urival's. ''Do you think I'll last?'' she asked almost playfully, but her eyes were bleak.

''You'll drink to the sight of my ashes floating away on the breeze,'' he told her. ''But not if you don't get some rest.''

''I won't argue. Put the scrolls away somewhere safe.''

''I will. And then come back to make sure you're sleeping.'' He smiled. ''Stubborn old witch.''

''Foolish old bastard.''

After the scrolls had been put in a place only Urival knew about, he returned to her chambers. She was seated on her bed, long silver-gilt braids undone and forming a pale, rippling cloak around her. She had changed into a nightrobe, but seemed too listless to finish the job by sliding between the sheets. Urival had seen her like this more and more often in the last two years, and fear for her health was a stab of anguish in his breast. He drew back the covers and helped her into bed, feeling how light and frail she had become. Extinguishing the candles, he moved silently to the door.

"No. Stay."

From any other woman it would have been a command to offend even the most loving heart. From her, it was as close to a plea as her pride would ever allow. Urival was frightened.

"As you wish, my Lady." He stripped down to his long undertunic and lay down atop the covers, dragging the quilt up from the foot of the bed to drape around him. He did not touch her, only waited, the hearthlight playing soft shadows across the room.

"If it were Maarken instead of Andry, I wouldn't be worried," she said at last. "He was born with a sense of honor as strong as Chay's or Rohan's. But Andry is cursed with the wrong kind of cleverness. Why do all my relations have to be so intelligent?" She sighed. "There's something different about him from his father or his uncle or his brothers. Perhaps he gets it from Zehava."

"Or maybe even from you."

"Yes, I've always been terribly clever, haven't I?" She gave a harsh laugh. "Andry's going to be even more dangerous than I. And I beg the Goddess I'm not doing wrong in making him Lord of this place once I'm dead."

"He's young. He'll learn."

"And he'll have you to guide him."

"Always assuming I outlive you," he bantered as lightly as he could manage, not wanting to think about a world that did not have her in it. "Besides, there's Rohan, his parents—and don't underestimate Maarken's influence or Sorin's. Andry adores his brothers."

She shifted beneath the blankets and her fingers closed

around his. "Not the first time we've shared a bed," she remarked. "Do you remember?"

"Of course. I always knew it was you who made a man of me that night."

"I do good work," she replied, real laughter in her voice now. "Had to fight Kassia for you, too. It was to be one or the other of us. I don't think she's ever forgiven me."

"*I* would never have forgiven you if it had been her."

"But how did you know? None of my others ever did."

He did not tell her that because it had been him, she had not woven the Goddess' illusions as carefully as she should have. Forty-five years later, she still did not realize that she had wanted him to know. "Gift of the Goddess," he replied, meaning it.

"And all the nights since. That must be how you recognized me. Repetition of the experience. Did Sioned ever know it was you?"

"She may have guessed. I don't know. I must say, I've been tempted to collect my full share of gratitude from Rohan, though. I do good work, too."

"Conceited old lecher." She moved closer and he put his arm around her. "They've been good for each other. Will Maarken and Hollis be the same, do you think?"

"As good as you and I have been through the years." He pressed a light kiss to her forehead. "And neither of us is so old that come morning, when we're rested, there won't be a way to prove it."

"Shameless."

"You were the one who taught me," he answered, smiling. "Go to sleep."

Chapter Six

Sioned was not in the habit of deceiving her husband on any matter, nor had she ever avoided his presence for any reason. How deceive or avoid one's second self? But she found it necessary to do both during the days

after her rescue of Meath and the shocking encounter
with the dragon.

Worry about Pol and Tobin, who had reacted badly to
the drain on their energies, took up the afternoon and
evening. By the time she was certain that both would
sleep it off with no real damage done, Sioned was so
exhausted she fell into bed, oblivious until the next noon.
The arrival of the Lord and Lady of Remagev with their
children occupied the rest of that day; their welcome and
settling in gave Sioned further opportunity to deceive Rohan about her troubled thoughts and to avoid being alone
with him.

He waited her out, but every time she looked at him
the concern in his eyes was deeper. By the third morning
he had had enough of waiting, and rather than go downstairs to share breakfast with everyone in the Great Hall,
he ordered the meal sent to them in their study. It was
understood that they were not to be disturbed—and
Sioned knew there would be no fortuitous interruptions,
for the command would remain in force until Rohan was
satisfied in his own mind about what had occurred on the
sunlight.

She sat opposite him at the large fruitwood table that
served as their desk, reminded of times at Goddess Keep
when she had been called on to explain some misdeed or
other. Certainly there was a family resemblance between
Rohan and Andrade, emphasized now by the stern set of
his features.

Neat piles of letters, blank parchments, writing materials, and the other accoutrements of a voluminous cor-
respondence had been shoved aside to make room for a
meal neither of them touched. Near Rohan's right elbow
was the huge book of law and precedent, bound in slightly
iridescent green-bronze dragonhide and resting on a
carved wooden stand given them by Prince Davvi of Syr,
Sioned's brother. On her side of the table was a matching
wooden box that held their various seals: one each for
their personal letters, another pair for more formal documents, and the great dragon seal, wide as Sioned's palm,
that was pressed into pendants of blue wax hung from
green ribbons on all decrees of the High Prince. Two
walls were lined to the ceiling with books, volumes neatly

arranged in subject order; a stepladder stood abandoned by the section on geology and metallurgy. The door cramped into a corner, more books above it, and a tapestry map took up most of the third wall. Heavy silk and wool stirred sluggishly in a warm breeze through open windows on the wall to her left.

Sioned loved this room. In it Urival had taught her probably more than he should have of *faradhi* secrets her first summer at Stronghold, before she had become Rohan's princess. Here she had learned Desert law and the principles of justice her husband valued so dearly. And for the past twenty-one years she had worked with him in this chamber, governing their lands and planning the future they would give their son. But now she wished guiltily that she was anyplace rather than sitting across from Rohan, his cool blue eyes fixed on her so grimly that she wanted to squirm like a child caught breaking a rule. She held herself still, aware that at this moment he was not her husband but the High Prince. Neither was she his wife; she was his Sunrunner.

"A dragon," was all he said.

She nodded, deciding to get it over with so she could have *her* Rohan back. She explained what had happened from the time Meath contacted her on the sunlight, and finished with, "We've always suspected dragons are highly intelligent. If I'm right, and they have thought-colors *faradh'im* can perceive, then it may be that they're even more intelligent that we originally thought."

"Why has this never happened before? With all the *faradh'im* weaving sunlight and all the dragons flying Goddess knows where over the years, why didn't anybody ever 'bump into' one before now?"

"Perhaps they did, but didn't understand it. Or perhaps I'm completely mistaken. But I swear by what I felt, my lord. I touched colors and I felt wings, and so did Maarken. Pol and Tobin were safely back here before it happened, so they can't verify. But Maarken can."

Rohan placed his hands flat on the table. Like her, he wore only a single ring, a topaz that had been his father's. The gem had been reset some years ago into a circle of tiny emeralds, tribute to the color of his wife's eyes. His hands were lean, powerful, the long fingers bearing faint battle scars; they were hands that could control the most mettlesome horse with ease, or caress her skin as lightly as the merest breath of wind, or wield sword and knife with killing strength. They were the hands of a knight and a prince, but also those of a poet. Sioned could not recall a time when she had not coveted the touch of those hands.

It was a long while before he spoke again, and with his words his fingers drew in to fists, bones standing out pale against sunbrowned skin. "Could you do it again? Touch a dragon?"

Startled, she said the first thing that came into her mind. "Why?"

"I don't know. Could you?"

She thought for a long moment, then shook her head. "How would I know what to look for? Nobody's ever thought to memorize the colors of a dragon. And it's the owner of those colors who discerns their shape and tone, communicates them to others."

"I remember Andrade explaining it to me when I was little," he mused. "People are like windows of stained glass, each one unique, colors to be touched and woven with the light the way sun shining through a window throws colors into the air. Sioned, if dragons have those colors, too, and could be taught to understand them, what if we could—I don't know, speak with them somehow, or see through their eyes? They'll return to the Desert soon to mate."

"I don't think it would be dangerous, my lord—just startling." She smiled slightly. "You've always loved them so much. I'll try to touch one of your dragons for you."

He shrugged. "Others don't see dragons as I do."

Sioned thought a moment, beginning to frown. "You'd never use them wrongly, but others might. Dragons in battle—if there's a way to do it, someone will. Goddess, why does everything have to come down to killing?"

A smile played around his lips as he held her gaze, the prince becoming her Rohan again. "My father wanted me to have a wife, the way other princes have wives. He didn't know Andrade would bring me a princess."

"If I am, then it's you who taught me how, beloved.

I'll try to touch a dragon for you. But don't expect too much.''

"I expect everything of you—and I've never been disappointed." He glanced at the windows, judging the time. "Feylin wants to talk dragons this morning, too. Did you see that sheaf of parchments she came armed with? More facts and figures than anybody but she understands."

"Have something to eat first," Sioned suggested, gesturing to their untouched breakfast. "You know that when the two of you get to discussing dragons, you forget everything else—including your stomachs."

"I thought you agreed with Tobin that I'm getting middle-aged and fat."

She laughed and tossed a marsh apple at him. "Every man should have a middle age like yours, my lord, with a waist no wider than Maarken's. Hush up and eat."

Pol and Feylin were waiting for them in the upstairs reception chamber, her daughter Sionell with them. The Lady of Remagev smiled a greeting and said, "The others are out playing—including Walvis and Chay, who call it 'inspecting the horses.' "

"I would've thought you'd be out there, too," Rohan said to the children, ruffling Sionell's mop of russet curls.

Pol answered, "Lady Feylin says you're going to talk dragons, Father. May I stay and listen?"

"Of course you may. What about you, Sionell?"

Sioned's eleven-year-old namesake was a round and rosy copy of her mother, with the same dark red hair and the same triangular face. Her eyes alone had been inherited from Walvis, a startling blue fringed by thick black lashes over which equally dark brows arched. Her smile was his, too, a marvel of carefree good humor. "I like dragons, my lord. And I like this room—it's my favorite at Stronghold. It's the summer room."

"Then we'll name it that," Sioned told her. "I'll mention it to the steward this afternoon, that the Lady Sionell has named this the Summer Room in honor of the tapestry. And so it shall be called from now on." She met Rohan's amused gaze briefly, and winked. They both knew that Sionell had set her heart on Pol, confirmed by the look of triumph the child directed at the young prince. Pol pretended not to notice, and Sioned hid a grin.

They settled on the rug and Feylin spread out a formidable array of charts, maps, and lists. The lecture began with the yearly census of dragons.

"The most reliable reports place the total number at one hundred and sixty, of which thirteen are sires and fifty-five are females of mating age. The rest are three-year-olds who won't be involved in the mating this year. The population has taken on a fairly constant cycle, as you can see from this chart, my lord. Attrition due to old age, disease, and accident brings their numbers down to about one hundred fifty, and then after the hatching the total increases to three hundred or so."

"But we should have close to four hundred after hatching," Rohan said. "With fifty-five females—"

"But there are only forty-three usable caves," Feylin told him. "You see the problem."

Pol frowned. "What happens to them if they can't lay their eggs?"

"They die," Sionell replied succinctly. Pol looked slightly miffed that she knew more about dragons than he did, but she ignored his expression and went on, "Eight females died last time. We lost not only that year's hatchlings, but all the others they would have produced in their lifetimes."

"But if the population remains constant, what's the trouble?" he asked.

"What if there's another Plague?"

"Let's get back to the caves," Feylin chided gently. "Unless we find enough to hold them all, the extra females will die. Pol's correct that the population has stayed fairly constant within its cycle, but it can't grow beyond three hundred because of the lack of proper caves. I won't feel easy until there are at least five hundred dragons at the top of the cycle, preferably more."

"Are there any caves we might lure them to, Feylin?" Sioned asked.

"It's too cold up in the Veresch—the eggs wouldn't bake enough to hatch. And further south than Rivenrock there aren't any suitable caves at all."

"Rivenrock," Rohan echoed. "There are plenty of

caves there, excellent ones. Do you have any suggestions for coaxing the dragons back there, Feylin?''

"I'm sorry, my lord.'' She shook her head. ''The bittersweet they feed from in mating years is thicker there than anywhere else. The caves are perfect, as you've said. They've hatched a thousand generations there, for all I know. But they won't even fly over it anymore.''

"I don't understand, Mama,'' Sionell complained. ''I know they died of Plague there, but the ones old enough to remember that are all dead now, aren't they? How do the younger ones know to avoid Rivenrock?''

"I think they're much smarter than we've ever imagined,'' Sioned replied thoughtfully, remembering those brilliant colors touched for only an instant. ''If they can communicate with each other beyond the usual ways of animals, then the older dragons may well have warned the younger to stay away from the place where so many died. Then again, perhaps the young ones were never even shown the place by their elders, so they don't know it's there.''

Rohan met her gaze with intense interest. He said nothing, but she knew his thoughts as if he'd spoken them. If she could communicate somehow with the dragons on sunlight, then it might be possible to lure them back to Rivenrock, where the availability of caves would ensure their increase in numbers.

Pol, sensitive to the glance his parents exchanged, asked, ''Do you have an idea how to bring them back, Father?''

"Nothing I'd care to commit myself to right now,'' he smiled. ''Feylin, how many hatchlings are we likely to see this year?''

"About a hundred and fifty, if we're lucky. And by the way, Sioned, you're mistaken about dragons having to be shown their caves. Some collapsed up in Skybowl a few years ago, and the dragons went out looking for others nearby. So I'd say they know Rivenrock's here. They just won't go near it.''

"I wish the sires didn't kill each other off,'' Sionell said unhappily. ''It's awful, watching a dragon die.''

"It's the way the strongest survive,'' Pol informed her.

"If there were enough caves for all the females, then the weakest of them would survive, too."

"That's true," Rohan said. "But Lady Feylin has the right of it. First there has to be a large enough population base so the dragons aren't in danger. When they build up their numbers to that point, then the rule of the strongest surviving to mate will hold sway without risk."

"It's like princes," Pol said. "All trying to kill each other off, fighting over the best pieces of land. Until *you* showed them that you're the strongest," he added with pride, and Rohan frowned. "Because it's the laws that make the greatest strength, isn't it, Father? The power of an army is uncertain, but the law stays the law." He sneaked a glance at Sionell to see how she was responding to this princely wisdom, and Sioned hid another smile as the little girl nodded solemnly.

Feylin noted the byplay as well, and didn't bother hiding her grin as she met Sioned's gaze. "Dragons are my specialty, not princely politics," she announced, tidying up her parchments. "I'll leave these for you to study, my lord. Sionell, aren't we supposed to join your father and brother and that new pony you wanted to show Lord Chaynal?"

"Yes, Mama. Pol, come see my pony, please?"

For a moment Sioned thought he'd agree. But then he shook his head. "I have to stay here with my mother and father, and discuss what Lady Feylin has told us. Perhaps later."

Sionell's black brows rushed together as she sprang to her feet. "Perhaps later we'll be out riding and you won't get the chance!" She remembered to bow to Sioned and Rohan before running out the door.

The adults heroically kept mirth in check as Pol glared at the empty doorway. Feylin managed to restrain herself until after she had closed the door behind her, but Sioned thought she heard a gasp of uncontrollable giggles a moment later—and wished she could indulge in the same.

Pol muttered something under his breath, and Rohan turned a bland gaze on his son. "What was that you said?"

"Nothing. What are we going to do about the dragons, Father?"

"For starters, we're all going up to Skybowl to watch them this year."

"Everybody?"

"Why, yes," Rohan replied, all innocence, and Sioned nearly lost her battle with laughter. "Walvis will stay here and take care of Stronghold while we're gone, of course. But everyone else will come along."

Sioned took pity on the boy. "Feylin will be with us, naturally, but I think Sionell and Jahnavi will want to stay here with their father. It's a very long ride, even when one has a new pony."

Pol nodded, trying not to show his relief and failing utterly. "It's too bad they'll have to miss seeing the dragons," he said, able to be generous now that he knew his pest would not be joining them.

Rohan wore a thoughtful expression. "I think it's about time I expanded your education, Pol. I've taught you to ride, how to win a knife-fight, and the basics of swordsmanship, and Lleyn has said he's pleased with your progress in all three. But now I'm going to teach you something else that will come in very useful." All at once he grinned. "I'm going to show you how to beat a woman at chess."

"Brave words, my lord dragon prince," Sioned scoffed. "Bring the board and set, Pol, and watch me trounce him for the twentieth time this year!"

"And it's only twenty days into spring," Pol said impishly, running to get the chessboard and pieces.

Rohan set the game up on the carpet, Pol sitting at his side. Sunlight burnished the two fair heads, shone on identical smiles. Even the gesture of brushing the hair off their necks was the same. Pol's coloring was a little stronger than Rohan's, his hair and lashes a shade or two darker, his eyes glinting green as well as blue. But there was nothing of Ianthe in him, nothing to remind Sioned of the princess who had birthed him.

Opening gambits completed, she surveyed the board and confided to Pol, "He'll try to trick me into a mistake now. Just watch."

"Would I do that to you?" Rohan asked, eyes wide with injured innocence.

"Every chance you can get."

"You're using Grandmother Milar's defense, aren't you, Mother? Maarken taught it to Meath, and he taught it to me."

"She loved chess and played very well," Sioned replied. "Andrade was the only one who could win against her very often. And stop trying to distract me, hatchling," she added, making a face at him. He laughed and she knew she had been forgiven the contretemps of his arrival.

"Mind you," Rohan said, "she's a terrible loser."

"They way I've heard it, she hasn't had much practice at losing," Pol answered with a grin. "And it doesn't look as if you'll be teaching her how this time, Father!"

"Oh, so now it's compliments to lull me into complacency!" Sioned reached over and tweaked Pol's ear.

Rohan moved a piece on the board. "Remember, my boy, the main thing about playing chess with a woman is always let her win—even after you've married her."

"Let me win—?" She launched a playful fist at his jaw. He caught her wrist, tugged, and succeeded in toppling her to one side of the chessboard. Sioned went for his ribs, knowing every vulnerable spot in his body. The chess pieces went flying and Pol yelled, "Forfeit!" as the three of them tumbled around on the carpet, laughing and tickling. Sioned's hair came loose from its pins and Rohan grabbed the thick braid, pulling her down for a kiss. Then they both went after their son. Captured, Pol squirmed helplessly with laughter.

"Well, now," said an amused voice from the doorway. "Is it a castle revolution, I wonder? Bets on the winner, Maarken?"

"Pol," the young man said at once. "Chadric teaches dirty tricks in unarmed combat, Mother."

The royal trio sorted themselves out and sat up, still laughing. Rohan grinned up at Maarken and Tobin. "Always bet on the younger man—especially when he's your future prince!"

"It's only good politics," Maarken agreed, chuckling, and helped Sioned to her feet.

She thanked him and tried to make some order out of her hair. "Are you just going to sit there?" she inquired of her husband. "Pick yourself up and at least pretend to a little princely dignity."

"Make it a good show," Tobin advised. "I've come to announce the Fironese ambassador."

Rohan groaned and shook his head. "She wasn't due for another day, according to their Sunrunner."

"Lady Eneida is right behind me, brother dear."

Maarken and Pol searched for the scattered chess pieces while Tobin replaced the board and righted an overturned chair. Rohan and Sioned tidied each other up, then grabbed their son on his way by and performed the same service for him. They slid into seats, Maarken standing behind his mother's chair as was proper for a young lord in the presence of his princes, just as a knock sounded on the door.

"Come," Rohan said, raking his hand one last time through his hair.

The Fironese ambassador was a thin dark woman aged somewhere between forty and seventy. She was as cool and brittle as the crystal for which her land was famous, but there the resemblance ended; the airy grace of Fironese fantasies in glass was utterly lacking in her. Fragile as she seemed, there was something stolid about her, and though Rohan's casual court saved her from being further weighted down by stiff formal robes, her woolen gown had been made for the colder climate of Firon and her brow was slightly damp as she made her bows before the High Prince, the High Princess, and the heir.

"It is generous of you to receive me in private, your grace," she said to Rohan.

"Exceeded by your generosity in making the long journey from Firon in such haste," he responded. "Please, my lady, sit and be comfortable."

As Maarken placed a chair for her, she murmured her thanks and folded her narrow hands in her lap. "Our governing council has sent me to consult with your grace about the unhappy state of our princedom," she began. "As you know Prince Ajit died without heirs this New Year Holiday."

"We had news of his death on the sunlight, and were grieved," Rohan said. He remembered very well the prince who, at Rohan's first tumultuous *Rialla,* had openly doubted his ability to understand even the basics of government. He had never held it against Ajit; indeed, he had been grateful for the expressions of misgivings, for it had been a tribute to his acting skills. Borderline idiocy had been precisely the impression he'd wished to create, the better to cozen Roelstra into concessions. Everyone knew better by now, of course.

Lady Eneida continued, "The days since his grace's death have not been easy. We have been in constant receipt of . . . suggestions . . . from other princes."

"I am aware of them. How does your council view them?"

She condescended to give him a frosty smile. "With suspicion, as you may well imagine, my lord."

"Indeed," Tobin murmured.

"Most of these suggestions concern bloodlines, both real and imaginary. And thus they concern your graces." She included Sioned and Pol in her glance now.

"I'm afraid I don't understand," Sioned commented. "I'm not sufficiently informed about princely genealogy, Lady Eneida."

"That is not surprising, your grace, as the point is a rather obscure one. The High Prince's grandmother was a daughter of our Prince Gavran, who also had two sisters—who married the ruling princes of Dorval and Kierst."

Tobin leaned a little forward in her chair. "Thus there are four possible heirs to Firon—the sons of Volog of Kierst, the sons of Davvi of Syr, the grandsons of Lleyn of Dorval, and my nephew, Prince Pol."

The ambassador inclined her head in tribute to Tobin's succinct summation. "The Desert claim is stronger, coming through the High Prince and also through High Princess Sioned's connection with the Kierstian royal line."

Rohan was frowning, irritated by his sister's eagerness. "My lady, you realize that by making my son the heir to Firon, it might mean the disappearance of that land as an independent princedom."

She answered with a shrug. "The prospect does not please us overmuch—with all due respect, your grace," she directed at Pol, who nodded his understanding. "But it is infinitely to be preferred over being swallowed by Cunaxa."

"I appreciate your position," Rohan said, and Lady Eneida's fragment of a smile told him she appreciated his geographical pun; Firon was right next to ever-hungry Cunaxa. "Such an event would not please us much either. Still, there is much to be said for putting, say, Prince Lleyn's younger grandson forth as the heir. Firon would retain its independence."

Tobin shifted slightly in her chair and slanted a look of disgust at her brother. Maarken, standing beside her, put an unobtrusive hand on her shoulder. He understood his mother's acquisitive instincts as fully as Rohan did.

"Dorval is far away," Lady Eneida said bluntly. "Ten days' sail in good weather, should we require assistance against the Cunaxans. But we also share a border with Princemarch."

"A difficult one," Sioned pointed out. "Solid mountains with only one decent pass through them."

"There is also the proximity of the Desert to Cunaxa," Lady Eneida said expressionlessly, her eyes sharp as splinters of dark glass.

Rohan let the ensuing silence draw out, knowing what she implied. A treaty establishing Lleyn's grandson Laric in Firon would intimidate the Cunaxans much less than if Rohan actually owned the place. An attack on Firon would become a direct threat to him, unfiltered through any agreement of defense with an independent princedom. Kierst was closer to Firon, but only the Desert could attack across the shared border with Cunaxa in response to a march on Firon. Prince Miyon would never be so foolish as to invade in the west when he could be certain of a counterattack from the south that would necessarily split his forces and their effectiveness in half.

Lady Eneida finally broke the quiet by saying. "The stronger claim comes from the Desert. Prince Pol is a full generation closer to Firon through you, my lord. Combine this with her grace's Kierstian blood. . . ." She finished with a shrug that indicated the inevitability of Firon's end as an independent princedom.

"Your council is agreed or you would not be here, I take it," Tobin said.

"Yes, your grace—agreed reluctantly. Again, no insult implied. It is not that we worry about the suitability of our choice."

"Only that you regret that it had to be made at all," Rohan supplied. "I, too, regret the necessity, my lady."

"May I consider then that the suggestion of the council is acceptable to the High Prince?"

"Our answer cannot be forthcoming until the *Rialla,* when we have consulted with the other princes as law demands."

Tobin drew in a swift breath and Maarken's fingers tightened on her shoulder in silent warning. Lady Eneida's backbone became a shaft of ice.

"Please believe me," Rohan said, "when I tell you that all will be done to ensure the safety and integrity of Fironese lands. But the law is the law and must be observed. I can put forth no claim and I certainly cannot agree to anything until all the facts have been presented at Waes."

"My lord, perhaps I have understated the danger from Cunaxa. It will be a long spring and summer before the *Rialla.*"

"Nevertheless I will abide by laws I myself wrote," he said quietly. "Your *faradhi* at Balarat is only a ray of light away from Princess Sioned. Should you require assistance, it will be forthcoming—according to the law."

And with that she had to be content. She took her leave with frigid dignity and closed the door behind her with a sound like cracking ice.

Sioned spoke before Tobin could let loose her outrage. "Maarken, will you go find your father, please?"

A flicker of disappointment went over his face at being denied the witnessing of one of his mother's famous tempers, but he bowed and obeyed. Rohan nodded his gratitude to his wife and turned to Pol.

"You've had the benefit of lectures from Lleyn and Chadric. What do you think about this?"

The boy recovered quickly from his surprise at being consulted. "We have to take Firon. We supply their glass ingots, and I can't believe the Cunaxans would let that trade continue even if it cost them much of their revenues. Especially not with the Merida at their court speaking against us. And they're right across the border from Firon, with two good mountain passes to use.''

"Three," Tobin snapped, black eyes blazing. "Rohan, what ails you? They're handing you a princedom wrapped in silk ribbons! And you're going to wait until the end of summer to take it?''

"Yes. Can you tell me why, Pol?"

"Because it's the law, just as you said." The boy hesitated, then shrugged. "Besides, the princes can't do anything other than agree, can they? Our blood claim is the best, and you're the High Prince, after all.''

"Then why doesn't he act like it?" Tobin demanded. "It's very pretty and noble of you to observe the forms, Rohan, but in the meantime the Cunaxans might cross the border and then we'd have to *fight* for what the Fironese want to give us without a single sword unsheathed!''

Rohan paid no attention to her, instead gazing thoughtfully at his son. "Because I'm the High Prince," he echoed. "Does that make my wishes law?"

"No, but—"

He was interrupted by the entrance of Chay and Maarken. Tobin sprang to her feet and ordered her husband to talk some sense into her brother. Chay's brows arched at her vehemence, but he said nothing until he had turned Lady Eneida's chair, sat with both arms folded across its back, and spraddled his long, booted legs.

"I'm told the Fironese want to give you a present," he remarked mildly. Then he grinned, a wicked gleam in his gray eyes. "What a perfect summer this is for military maneuvers up around Tuath Castle. And how fortunate that it's only fifty measures from the Cunaxan border."

Tobin's breath hissed through her teeth and she glared at her lord. Pol's eyes went wide with astonishment; Sioned contemplated her hands to hide her amusement. But Rohan was openly grinning at his sister.

"You should know better than to doubt my sanity, Tobin," he admonished. "Miyon and his council will be so nervous watching us across the border that they won't have time or nerve to think about Firon."

"So you say," she retorted. "But why not agree to the

Fironese proposal now? It would save a lot of time. Pol's right—they can't do otherwise than agree with the High Prince."

"And if *I* don't conform to the law, who else will?" he countered. "Do you understand, Pol?"

The boy looked at Maarken, who smiled encouragement, and then said, "It's kind of like being a Sunrunner, isn't it? You're the High Prince and you have a greater responsibility to the law than anyone else, even when the law is awkward. And being a *faradhi* is the same. More duties and obligations come with more power, don't they?"

"Indeed they do." He could barely keep the glow of his pride from outshining the sunlight, and reminded himself to thank Lleyn and Chadric and Audrite. "Tobin, you've the best head for maps. Would you work on a proposal whereby Firon is divided between Princemarch and Fessenden?"

"Fessenden!"

Pol's jaw dropped; Sioned winked at him. Chay rested his forehead to his folded arms and shook with silent laughter. After a moment he raised his head and murmured, "Tobin, Tobin, haven't you learned yet not to outguess him?"

Her shock had given way to disgust. "Oh, so we don't want to appear the greedy prince, do we? Just so long as all the best crystallers come under Princemarch's jurisdiction!"

"It will leave Fessenden with a nice chunk of land and a nice degree of gratitude for our generous expansion of their territory. Maarken, perhaps you can contact Eolie at Graypearl and ask if Lleyn knows of any strong ties or stronger aversions between people along the borderlands. I want to make this as easy and painless for everyone as possible."

Maarken grinned his appreciation of the plan. "It will be a pleasure, my lord. Lleyn is a font of information on everybody's holdings after the border arguments three *Ri-all'im* ago. He knows who's been fighting over what down to the last blade of grass—even though it bores him silly."

"I'm sure you'll all find this little bit of geographical

rearrangement interesting," Rohan said. "Be sure to mention to him that there will be compensation for removing his grandsons from the consideration of other princes for the Fironese throne—if he's so inclined."

"I think he will be. The elder son, Ludhil, swears he'll never set foot off Dorval except to attend the *Rialla,* so I doubt very much he'd want Firon. And Laric is more scholar than prince."

Rohan thought for a moment. "I'll have a little talk with Davvi at Waes about Tilal. Now, *he'd* make an excellent prince."

"It's what we trained him to be," Sioned agreed. "But what about Volog's younger boy? His claim is just as good."

"I'll sit down with him, too. The Goddess must be smiling on me, that I can speak to them as kinsmen as well as princes."

Tobin gave a delicate snort. "Oh, yes, keep it all in the family, shall we? You remember, of course, that you arranged it so Volog's grandson will rule both Kierst and Isel one day. Are you going to add a third princedom to his list?"

"I would hardly say I arranged it, Tobin! Could I have foreseen that Saumer's only son would die without an heir?"

"No, but things have a way of working out to your advantage," she retorted. "Very well, I'll rearrange your map for you. But I still say you should take it all, and right now."

"You're just angry that you didn't think of the Fessenden angle first," Chay said. "Rohan, I assume you want Walvis to lead the maneuvers at Tuath?"

"Unless Maarken would like to." He looked a question at the young man, who lost his smile. "If you don't—"

"I will if you ask, my lord."

"But I'm sure Andrade will want to see him at the *Rialla,*" Sioned insisted. "Send Walvis. They know him well in the north after what he did at Tiglath. I'm positive Maarken could impress the Cunaxans and our own people, but the idea is to avoid battle, not to demonstrate how able Maarken is by provoking one."

It was all perfectly logical—but Rohan knew that her stated reasons for wanting Maarken in Waes and Walvis at Tuath were different from her real reasons. The relief in Maarken's eyes confirmed that the *Rialla* was his wish as well. Rohan eyed his wife suspiciously, then nodded agreement. He'd get the truth out of her later.

Pol gave a dismal sigh. "I guess that means—"

"Chay," Sioned interrupted smoothly, "why don't you and Maarken talk to Walvis this afternoon?"

Tobin was still nursing her irritation with her brother, but Chay had picked up on the undercurrents. He said nothing to the point, however, merely nodded and ushered his wife and son from the room—but not before giving Sioned a long, laughing glance that she returned with perfect composure. Rohan saw him grin and shake his head.

When the three of them were alone, Sioned turned a sly look on Pol. "Yes, it does mean that Sionell and Jahnavi will be coming with us to Skybowl. You'll live."

Rohan chuckled as the boy's cheeks reddened. "I give it another five winters or so, Pol, and then you won't have to worry about her. There'll be plenty of young men more than willing to take her attention away from *you.*"

Pol stared, utterly amazed that Sionell might possibly attract young men to her plump, pestilential little person, or that he might care if she did. Rohan, knowing he really shouldn't laugh, laughed anyway.

"Well, anyway," Pol said, "it's kind of appropriate that my claim to Firon comes from both of you, just like my Sunrunner gifts. I'm glad it's that way—reinforced. I don't think I'd feel quite right about it otherwise."

Sioned nodded easily, but her eyes had gone blank. Rohan knew why. There was no claim to Firon through her, nor were the talents of her giving. She was much too sensitive. "Does the prospect worry you, son?"

"No—not much, anyway," he amended honestly. "It's just that now I'll have to worry about yet another princedom." He gave a whimsical smile. "Just make sure this is the last I'll have to add to the list, Father. I don't think there's room enough in my head to keep any more princedoms straight!"

"As High Prince you'll have to worry about *all* of them."

"Then I'm going to keep everybody very busy answering about a million questions!"

"We'll do our best to answer. And that reminds me, how is Chadric these days? I haven't really had time to talk to you abut your training and your life at Graypearl."

"But shouldn't we start planning things?"

Rohan laughed. "Consider it the first lesson in being High Prince. I've sent everyone off to do work they know very well how to do without me. Chay and Maarken and Walvis will present me with excellent plans for Tuath, Tobin will bury herself in books and maps for the next ten or twelve days, and when they're ready, my experts will tell me what they've come up with. But until then my time is my own. Never do yourself what someone else can do for you better and faster, Pol. Now, tell me what you think of Chadric. He was a squire here, you know—he arrived the year I was born and left when I was only six, so I don't really remember him all that well."

Pol launched into a description of Chadric's many virtues, and during his recital Sioned recovered her poise—as Rohan had intended. They went on talking for a time, and then he suggested that it might be polite for Pol to go compliment Sionell on her new pony. Pol grimaced, then sighed.

"I guess she can't help it," he observed philosophically. "She's only a little girl, after all."

Neither Rohan nor Sioned missed the authority lent by a whole three years' advantage in age, but neither gave in to further amusement. Pol left them, and Rohan took his wife's hand in his own.

"It hurts me to see you upset, love."

"I just wasn't expecting him to say what he did, that's all." She shrugged. "I hate to have him grow up believing a lie—I know, I know, it's a necessary lie until he's old enough to understand what really happened, and why we never told him. But it's lucky that the Fironese claim doesn't come *only* through me. In honor, we would've had to refuse."

"And think up a very good reason why. But not much will change in Firon, you know. Pimantal of Fessenden isn't likely to close his fist tight around his new possessions—especially after I've had a little talk with him.''

"The same tactic you use with Princemarch. It's been fourteen winters since Pandsala became regent, and the people have learned where their advantage lies. By the time Pol is old enough to rule there, they'll find our methods completely natural.''

"I wonder if the other princes will.'' He rose and went to the windows, looking down at the courtyard. "Firon is too good an opportunity to pass up—and the fact that they came to me instead of the other way around soothes my conscience a bit. But I'll have to be careful, especially with this Roelstra's son business to deal with, now of all times.'' He snorted with sudden laughter. "Can you believe it—old Ajit had six wives and was thinking of taking a seventh, and he still couldn't get sons any more than Roelstra could!''

"Sometimes it depends on the woman, you know,'' she murmured, and when he turned with a stricken look on his face, smiled at him. "Oh, stop it. I'm not sensitive about *that* anymore, Rohan. I did give you a son, after all. And besides, Ajit did have an heir who died many years ago.''

"That's right, I'd forgotten.'' He heard shouts and laughter outside in the courtyard, and beckoned Sioned over to the windows. "Come look at this!''

She joined him and together they watched as Walvis, playing dragon for his son and daughter, fluttered an immense green cloak like wings as they tried to ride him down on their ponies. Shrieking with laughter, the children were barely able to stay in their saddles. The outraged ponies were forced to trot up and down, up and down, while wooden swords were waved at the dragon. Pol stood nearby, his face eloquent: he longed to join in the fun, but his sense of dignity as Rohan's heir and Lleyn's squire forbade it. Sionell solved his problem for him by kicking her pony over to where he stood and tossing him her sword. Pol swept her a low bow, then sallied forth to oblige her by slaying the dragon.

"Oh, she's marvelous!'' Rohan laughed. "Just what he needs!''

"Well, we'll have wait until he's older to see if he inherited his father's taste for redheads," she teased.

"It'd be nice if it happened. But he can choose his wife from scores of girls."

"They way you did? I can still see you that year in Waes, hip-deep in princesses!"

"And drowning in one pair of green eyes," he responded gallantly, kissing her.

"Very romantic," she approved. "Teach Pol some of that, and they won't let him alone."

"I don't recall that it was a very agreeable experience, personally. And speaking of Waes, what was all that about Maarken?"

"I'm not telling. You can torture me, starve me, pull out my fingernails, throw me in the dungeon, or even tickle me—and I won't say a word."

"I don't *have* a dungeon. And I'm all tickled out for today, thanks. Torture is messy, my own faithful guard would use me for target practice if I tried to starve you, and as for fingernails. . . ." He picked up one of her hands and nibbled her fingertips. "It's an idea," he admitted. "At least I wouldn't get scratched in bed. You can be so emphatic, Sioned."

Sionell was congratulating Pol on his conquest and Walvis had disappeared into the keep, presumably to consult with Chay and Maarken. Rohan saw Jahnavi, eight years old and already an accomplished horseman, execute a series of showy maneuvers around the horse trough. But his main attention was focused on Pol, who shrugged away Sionell's attentions and went off to the gardens. The little girl stamped her foot and ran after him.

"You know," Rohan mused, "I think I'd like to build him a castle."

"You already have several."

"Well, not a castle, really, but a palace. Something along the lines of what Lleyn has at Graypearl. Not a keep ready for war, but a peaceful place, with lots of gardens and fountains and all those things."

"And where would you site this marvel?"

"Halfway between Stronghold and Castle Crag. In fact, I'm going to inspect a few places on the progress.

Think of it, Sioned—a new palace for a new prince, uniting two lands. I'd like to start building next spring, so it'll be ready by the time Pol takes a wife.''

"I'll bet it's Sionell. And as stakes—"

"Extortionist. What do you want if you win?" He smiled at her.

"Feruche."

The shock went through his whole body and he drew back from her. "No."

"The pass through the Veresch is important, Rohan. Feruche always guarded it—but now there's nothing, not even a garrison. Feruche should be rebuilt."

"I don't want to have anything to do with that place ever again," he rasped, looking out the windows with blind eyes. Feruche—the beautiful rose-pink castle rising from the cliffs; the deadly woman who had ruled it; the night he had raped her and she had conceived his son.

"You promised a long time ago to give me Feruche," Sioned reminded him. "There are dragons near it who need watching and protecting. I want Feruche, Rohan."

"No. Never."

"It's the only way either of us will ever forget what happened to us there. I destroyed it with Sunrunner's Fire—for me, it lies in ashes. But for you it still stands, because you never went back to see it razed to the ground. I want it rebuilt, Rohan, so that it's not Ianthe's anymore but *ours.*''

"No!" he shouted, turning on his heel for the door. "I won't rebuild it, I won't set foot within ten measures of it! And I won't have you speak of it again!"

"When we tell Pol the truth, shall we also present him with the charred ruin where he was conceived and born—and where his mother died? Or will we make a new place that has nothing in it of the old, nothing to bear witness to what happened there?"

He stopped, his hand on the doorlatch. "If you love me, you will never say the name of that place in my hearing as long as we live."

"It's because I love you that I have to say it. I want Feruche, Rohan. And if you won't rebuild it, then *I will.*''

Chapter Seven

Lady Andrade stood at the closed gray library windows with her back to Urival and Andry, unwilling for them to see her chafing her hands together. Pride forbade her to huddle by the hearth as her chilled flesh begged her to do, and especially did she reject the plea put forth by her aged bones for the warm softness of her bed. She glared resentfully at the rain-wrapped tower across the inner court of Goddess Keep. Had the winter cold and spring rains been worse this year, or was she only feeling her age? This last New Year Holiday had been the seventieth of her life; compared to Prince Lleyn, she was a mere child.

"Whatever possessed them to leave Dorval for this dismal place?" she muttered.

Urival came to stand by her shoulder, soundless as an expert huntsman seeking skittish prey. "This will be the last storm of the season. But you're right—clouds are a Sunrunner's natural enemy. Why *did* they choose to build here?"

She put her hands in the pockets of her gown to hide their trembling, then turned to her young kinsman. "Well? You've had a while to puzzle out the scrolls."

"Not very long, my Lady," Andry reminded her. "But I think I may have a few clues. It's maddening, though—some words are very like the ones we use now, but they've changed over the years in context. I've had to be more careful with them than the ones that made no sense at all in the beginning. But I think I've found something interesting." He ran a finger over the section of scroll they had been examining all morning. "A little mark like a bent twig appears over and over. The first few times I thought they were just blots on the page, mistakes—but now I think they're quite deliberate."

"And they mean?" she asked impatiently.

Andry hesitated, then shrugged and plunged in. "I think they mean that the word above them is to be taken as its exact opposite. You know how strange it's been, reading one thing and then later finding it contradicted.

But the mark appears with suspicious regularity on the places that seem to be the opposite of what went before or after.''

''What a delightful confusion!'' Andrade snorted. ''Are you saying they deliberately wrote untruths, trusting their little twigs to signal the lies?''

''I think so.'' Andry began to speak with more enthusiasm for his theory, even in the face of her obvious mockery. ''For instance, there's one place that says Lady Merisel stayed on Dorval for the whole of a certain year, but later on it says she stayed with a powerful lord in what's now Syr that same summer. Later still there's mention of an alliance between the Sunrunners and this man that was formed that summer—and in that very first passage I told you about, that little twig sign appears.''

''You need a better case than one instance that's probably a mistake,'' Urival frowned.

''But it's the only thing that makes sense! Otherwise it all comes out as a series of statements that constantly negate each other until we don't know what's right or what's wrong—which is probably what Lady Merisel intended when she had this written, as a matter of fact.'' He unrolled the parchment to another section. ''In all the parts I've studied, where one place says one thing and somewhere else it says the opposite, the mark always appears at the key word. Listen to this.'' He found the place he wanted and read aloud, '' 'The twin sons who were Lady Merisel's by Lord Gerik were treated by Lord Rosseyn as his own.' And the mark shows up below Lord Gerik's name.''

''And what does this mean?'' Andrade put acid into her voice to disguise her growing excitement.

''I think it means that—that the boys weren't really Lord Gerik's sons at all! They might even have been Lord Rosseyn's! Please, just listen to me. If I read it as the mark indicates—'The twin sons who were Lady Merisel's but *not* by Lord Gerik were treated by Lord Rosseyn as his own.' Couldn't that mean that *he* was the father?''

''Evidence,'' Urival demanded. ''Give us proof, not conjecture.''

''Here it says they fought over a few measures of land near Radzyn—but I know that area. Why would they contend over a worthless plot of Desert? The mark confirms it, for it indicates that the land was *not* the reason why they fought the battle. And in this section later on it says Lord Gerik was pleased that Lord Rosseyn used his powers in battle. But only a page before it states that he and Lady Merisel had *outlawed* the use of the gifts to kill—and there's the sign, right below the word for 'pleasure' in reference to what Rosseyn did.'' He raked the hair out of his eyes and looked at Andrade. ''It's the only possible way to explain all this, my Lady.''

Urival peered down at the scrolls. ''They gave us two versions of their history, then? Good Goddess, it will take years to sort through it all!''

''What we have to remember is that they weren't giving anybody anything,'' Andry said. ''They couldn't know who'd find the scrolls, or even if they'd be found at all. This must've been their way of confusing anybody who shouldn't be reading this—the contradictions would drive you crazy. It nearly did me, until I figured out what their twig sign must mean.''

''But why confuse the issue so?'' Andrade asked. ''Who'd care at this late date whether this Rosseyn, whoever he was, sired Merisel's twin sons?''

Andry pulled in a deep breath and stared at his four rings. ''I think it's far more subtle than that, my Lady. Why were these scrolls buried along with the one on sorceries? To provide the clue that would help us interpret correctly that one essential, dangerous scroll—and to keep people who weren't as persevering from discovering what that scroll meant.''

Andrade returned to her chair and sat, hands clenched into fists inside her pockets. ''Show me the Star Scroll,'' she ordered.

Andry took it reverently from its case and unrolled it atop the other. ''The marks are all over it,'' he explained. ''This formula, for instance. It says it can cause loss of memory. All these roots and herbs and directions—but instead of leaving *out* an essential ingredient that would cancel its effectiveness, they put *in* something that would ruin the recipe just as surely. Here. This flower nobody around here has ever heard of, with the little mark beneath it. And look at this one—directions on how to boil a certain ointment that can make a wound fester instead of heal. But the sign indicates that it shouldn't be boiled at all! And here—this recipe for a powerful poison. It's just the same, my Lady—the list of ingredients with the little sign beneath several of them that I'd swear combine to produce the antidote within the poison itself, so it wouldn't be dangerous if anybody happened upon the scroll! In all the ones that could be dangerous, the little twig appears somewhere—telling us *not* to do something that the uninformed reader *would* do in following the directions.''

''The false step added to make the formula worthless in case it got into the wrong hands.'' Andrade gave in to wonder and admiration, convinced now. ''From what you've told me of Lady Merisel, she was devious enough to have thought this up. Can you imagine her in her old age, writing all this down as the first scroll says she did, laughing herself silly while she made sure no one would make use of this knowledge even if they found it?''

''And the clue is in the histories,'' Andry agreed. ''It really is the only thing that makes any sense.''

''Hmm,'' Urival said, still skeptical. ''The only way to prove it would be to pick a recipe and follow it both ways. With your permission, Andrade, I'll do just that—choosing something we know we can cure, of course.''

She nodded permission, then turned to Andry again. ''Read me a section that doesn't have to do with potions. I want to find out if this holds true.''

Andry immediately chose a few lines of cramped script, giving Andrade the correct impression that he had planned the whole conversation to lead up to this point. '' 'The herb *dranath* cannot augment powers,' '' he read aloud, then met her startled gaze. ''The mark is below the word for 'cannot.' ''

She knew for certain that he had deliberately maneuvered her to this. She resented his skill and admired it, but stronger still was her fear. ''If it cannot augment, then it must increase. Was that their secret? 'The herb *dranath* can increase powers'? The damnable herb that corrupted my Sunrunner to Roelstra's use?''

Andry flinched slightly. ''My Lady—I'm sorry—''

She stared into the fire. ''It enslaves, addicts, kills—

but it also healed the Plague. And now you tell me it enhances power.''

"It would seem so," he said cautiously.

"I don't believe it!" she stated. "Prove the rest of it as you wish, but this I will not believe." Rising, she turned her back on him, needing the fire's warmth to soothe more than the chill of a spring storm. It was a gesture of dismissal, and she listened as the scrolls were gathered up, slid whispering into their leather tubes, replaced in the saddlebags. There was a breath of air around her ankles as the door opened on silent hinges and then closed.

Urival knelt to put new logs on the fire. "You lied to him. You believe."

"He led me by the nose where he wanted me to go!" She backed off a step as the flames rose hotter. "Urival— I didn't even sense it. He deceived me completely with his fine little show."

"He'll make a properly devious Lord of Goddess Keep."

"Yes, he is as we've all made him. Especially me. He's good, is young Lord Andry. Very good. When he's ruling here, from my chambers and my chair—" Sinking into her chair again, she closed her eyes. "Goddess be thanked that I won't be around to watch."

* * *

For all the privileges due to his kinship with Lady Andrade, Andry wore only four rings and took no special precedence at Goddess Keep. Officially he was an apprentice, though he hoped that by summer's end he would earn the fifth *faradhi* ring, marking him as a fully trained Sunrunner. The sixth would signify his ability to weave moonlight with equal skill; the seventh, that he could conjure without Fire.

He closed the door of his chamber behind him and sat on the bed, staring at his hands, seeing them empty of the honors he knew one day would be his. But in all honesty he knew he would have to learn much before he was worthy of the rings, including the eighth and ninth he intended to earn. He had botched his ploy for convincing Andrade and Urival about the scrolls. Their belief had been within his grasp, but he had made a mistake.

If he ever hoped to wield real influence among *far-adh'im,* he would have to learn subtlety.

For the first time he dared to imagine the tenth ring, the gold one on his marriage finger and the thin chains that would lead from it and all the others to bracelets clasping his wrists. Lord of Goddess Keep. Master of this place and all Sunrunners—and of the princes and *athr'im* who possessed the gifts. The number was very small now, but would grow. He intended that it should grow, for he believed wholeheartedly in Andrade's long-term scheme.

Andry bit his lip and tried not to see all ten rings on his hands. Yet part of him argued that there was nothing wrong with aspiration to high position. Certainly his siblings were not shy about their abilities. Maarken with his six rings would one day be Lord of Radzyn and military commander of the Desert and Princemarch. Andry's twin brother Sorin was to be knighted this year at the *Rialla,* and had made no secret of the fact that he wanted an important keep of his own, which their uncle the High Prince would undoubtedly give him. But Goddess Keep was the only place Andry wanted, the only honor he coveted, the only life he had ever believed would suit him. He had the gifts in stronger measure than Maarken, and no desires toward Sorin's knightly accomplishments. He wanted ten rings and this castle, the right to govern all *faradh'im,* and the privilege of guiding the princedoms as Andrade had done for so long.

He heard footsteps outside in the hallway. It was time to go down for the evening meal, yet he made no move from his seat by the small brazier that barely lit and rarely warmed his chamber. He never felt the cold; the joke at the keep was that he had soaked up so much Desert sun and heat in his childhood that nothing short of a winter at Snowcoves would ever chill him. But he did regret the feebleness of the brazier's light that did not allow him to read until all hours, and looked forward to the fifth ring that would bring with it a larger chamber, one floor below, complete with its own hearth.

"Andry! I know you're in there, I can hear you thinking," a familiar voice called from outside his door. "Hurry or you'll be late."

"I'm not hungry, thank you, Hollis," he replied.

The door swung open and his elder brother's unofficial Chosen stood there, hands on slim hips, braids like twin rivers of dark sunlight falling down past her waist. She gave him a grimace of good-natured exasperation, and he smiled. He liked Hollis and approved of his brother's choice—the two of them were certain to produce not just handsome, intelligent children but *faradhi*-gifted ones as well. But he wondered how his parents were going to take to the idea of Maarken's marrying a woman without family, possessions, wealth, or anything else to recommend her besides her beauty and her Sunrunner's rings. Of course, they were concerned with their sons' happiness above all things—Andry would never have been allowed to choose this path otherwise—but Maarken was their heir. Andry wished Sorin had already met Hollis so they could compare notes and work out some sort of strategy for supporting their elder brother in his aims.

Hollis had not gone out of her way to make Andry's acquaintance or to make him her ally. Indeed, she had avoided him quite devotedly for some time after her return from Kadar Water this winter. Andry had been insulted until it had suddenly dawned on him that she had been sick with nerves, afraid he wouldn't like her and that he would disapprove of her less-than-highborn blood, and hadn't dared approach him for fear he would think her currying his favor. Andry had spared a shake of the head for the incomprehensible ways of women and sought her out. Within a day they had reached a good understanding, helped along by her shock and then her laughter when he had opened with, "So you're the Sunrunner my brother's going to marry." His bluntness had been matched by her honesty in confessing her trepidations, and they had become friends quite apart from their love for his brother.

So it was that she scolded him like an elder sister. "Not hungry? And what do you expect to live on, then? The sheer brilliance of your intellect as you sit here thinking great thoughts? Comb your hair and let's go eat."

He stood up, made her a humble low bow marred by a grin. "Goddess help my brother once you're wed."

"Goddess help the poor girl who weds *you*," Hollis

replied tartly, smoothing his hair into place. "Come, you don't want to miss the presentations, do you?"

"Oh! Of course not. I'd forgotten it was tonight. Thanks for coming to get me, Hollis. I love watching them make their first bows to Andrade." As they left his chamber and descended the staircase, he went on, "Even though I'd known Andrade all my life, I was *terrified* that night! I always try to smile at them so they see at least one friendly face. But I don't know how much good one smile does."

"Not much," she admitted. "It was different for me, being born and raised here—although when I made my first bow my knees knocked so hard I had bruises!"

"How many are there tonight?"

"Six. Urival says he's expecting another six or so before summer's over. We hope to get twenty per year, but we're lucky if we get ten."

They turned the landing and took the next flight of stairs. These were carpeted, unlike the bare stone higher up, indicating they had reached the more public areas of the keep. Andry shook his head at Hollis' last remark. "I can't imagine why anyone who even suspects they've got the gifts wouldn't want to get here as soon as possible."

"Your father didn't need you to work the land or inherit his trade," she pointed out. "You've a brother to rule Radzyn, and another to carry on the knightly tradition—and marry some rich, landed girl," she added a bit wistfully.

"Which leaves Maarken free to marry where his heart is," Andry told her firmly. "But I see what you mean. It works the same way for women, doesn't it? They're needed at their keeps or their trades—or to form marriage alliances. It's too bad. All of them should come, no matter what."

"Others have different duties and points of view. Besides, I think Andrade sits there being scary just so the timid ones who *aren't* sure can be weeded out."

"If they don't want to be here, they shouldn't be. But I still can't imagine anybody who *could* be a Sunrunner not fighting for the chance."

They were at the bottom of the stairs now, emerging into a long, wide corridor that led in one direction to the refectory and in the other to the archives, library, and schoolrooms. Andry and Hollis were among the last to walk down the high-ceilinged passage, and as they went by a window embrasure they saw four boys and two girls huddled together, listening wide-eyed as a Sunrunner instructed them in making their obeisances to Lady Andrade. The girls and one of the boys were no older than thirteen winters; the other three boys were older, fifteen or sixteen. The tallest of these was a handsome, self-possessed youth with glossy night-black hair and deep gray-green eyes. He met Andry's smile with perfect calm, and did not return it. His gaze shifted to Hollis with the appraising, approving expression of a male who knows his own attractions and how to use them. But there was something more about him, a consciousness of rank and worth that surprised Andry. The slight flush on Hollis' cheeks surprised him, too.

They separated inside the huge refectory, she to join the other ranking Sunrunners, he to sit with his fellow apprentices. The meal progressed through the usual three courses of soup, meat and salad, biscuits and fruit. Andrade set a plentiful though plain table, and Andry was looking forward to the elaborate meals served at the *Rialla*. He had a sweet-tooth that fresh berries and spice-dusted biscuits did little to satisfy. Steaming pitchers of taze were passed around last of all, and as he poured himself a full mug he inhaled deeply of the sharp scent, faintly tinged with citrus. He missed nothing about his life at Radzyn so much as expeditions with his family to collect various leaves, bark, and herbs to be ground up for his mother's own special blend. Taze was her favorite domestic ritual. She would spend several evenings a year in the kitchen creating just the right mix, while her husband chased the servants out and donned an apron to bake fruit tarts that were his contribution to the family ceremony. Andry had wonderful memories of hours filled with laughter and companionship—and flour fights with his brothers—as his father placidly negated his warrior's image by baking and his mother filled huge sacks with another season's grinding of taze.

Memories slipped away as the six new arrivals were brought into the hall. He tried to see them as Andrade might, as a Lord of Goddess Keep might evaluate new-comers. His attention soon fixed on the black-haired youth. A glance at Hollis told him that she, too, looked only at the boy, who moved with an easy assurance worthy of a lord's son. There was a look of highborn blood in his fine, handsome features, and his hands were well-tended, though his clothes were simple and rather worn. Andry was too far down the hall to catch his name, but he could easily read Andrade's reaction. It took long familiarity with the nuances of her lips and brows and the muscles around her eyes, but Andry knew immediately that she was impressed. As the six returned down between the tables from making their bows, heading for the lowest seats, Andry saw the boy catch and hold Hollis' gaze as long as he could, a smile in his eyes.

As soon as Andrade had dismissed them all and withdrawn to her own chambers for the night, Andry sought out his brother's Chosen and asked, "Who was that, anyway? Did you hear his name?"

"Whose name?"

"You know very well who. The one with the black hair and the strange eyes."

"Did you think they were strange? His name is Seldges or something like that. I didn't hear clearly."

"I wonder where he comes from," Andry mused. "Did you see the way he never once looked down, but stared right into Andrade's face?"

"Any boy who looks the way he does is used to being stared at, himself. I imagine staring right back is a defensive reaction. But one thing's for certain—that one was made a man quite some time ago. The night of his first ring won't be anything new to him at all!"

Andry smiled to hide the embarrassment that could still come to him years after the fact. He himself had been very much the virgin on that night. He had no idea which of the women here had come to him, and he trusted to the Goddess' mercy that he never *would* know, for he suspected he had been nothing to marvel at. Maarken, who had still been resident here at the time, had guessed—not that he'd said anything directly, of course. But within a few days he had found the opportunity to make the casual observation that it was damned inconvenient sometimes, being unable to find attractions in any woman but his absent lady, and that it seemed to be a family failing. Andry had correctly interpreted this as a comforting reassurance that he would enjoy things much more with a woman he truly loved. That night was, after all, supposed to demonstrate the difference between physical desire and genuine love, and how infinitely preferable the latter was. Andry trusted that one day he would be as lucky as Maarken and their father and Rohan. Yet even the prettiest girls at Goddess Keep roused no more than passing admiration in him.

Recently he had come to the somewhat bemused realization while working on the scrolls that he had fallen a little in love with the remarkable Lady Merisel. Her anonymous scribe had not been immune to her either, though she must have been nearly ninety when she'd dictated the scrolls to him. Otherwise impersonal accounts of her were salted with such phrases as *luminous eyes, gracious smile,* and *peerless beauty,* as if the man could not help himself. Even without these hints of her personal charms, her wisdom and the scope of her powers and interests were evident in each line. She had much to say on almost every topic imaginable, and those of her opinions not etched in acid were often very funny—and sometimes were both. His favorite so far in his translation mentioned ancient superstitions about the symbology of numbers, then remarked:

There are four Elements: Fire, Air, Water, and Earth. Each of these has three aspects, making twelve total. Twelve is the digits one and two together; add them and get three, which is the number of moons. Add the twelve to the Four and you get sixteen, which is one plus six, or seven, which is indivisible. I am told that if one added together all the stars, then added the result to the number of moons plus the sun, then added those digits, a similarly mystic number would result. Which only shows how silly the whole thing is.

Andry imagined her as combining the qualities of his own fiery, fascinating mother, the quietly fierce Sioned, and Lady Andrade in all her pride and power—with enough cunning and intellect to make all three women seem simpletons by comparison. He had always known, with a kind of rueful resignation, that the woman he himself Chose would have far to go to measure up to the major feminine influences in his life. His admiration for Lady Merisel wasn't helping much.

He wanted his lady to appear before him simply and irrevocably, the way Sioned had arrived in Rohan's life. He wanted to be as absolutely certain as his parents had been when they first set eyes on each other. He was as uninterested in the process of finding a wife as he was impatient with the steps that must be taken to earn his rings. He knew himself worthy of the woman and the honors; false modesty was absurd when one was personable in one's own right, royally born, and as gifted in the Sunrunner arts as he.

Knowing he would have to wait for all of it didn't help much, either.

* * *

The black-haired boy returned to his bed in the dormitory well-pleased with himself and the evening. The name he had given was not Seldges but Sejast, and his ears had been trained to respond to that name rather than his own. He had passed every test he had set himself: facing Lady Andrade, identifying Lord Andry of Radzyn without difficulty, even making tentative choice of the woman who would be his on a man-making night Mireva had rendered totally unnecessary.

Segev smiled in the darkness as he remembered his brothers' astonishment the morning after his night in her house. He turned over to stifle a chuckle in his pillow, but the shifting of sheets against his body reminded his flesh of that night.

Riding up to the house huddled against the hill, he'd told himself that Ruval and Marron had no right to treat him as if he were still a child. He was just as much High Prince Roelstra's grandson as they, and Mireva had agreed that he should be the one to undertake this essential task at Goddess Keep. He entered the dwelling, anticipating lessons in how to fool Lady Andrade. But Mireva had not been waiting for him.

The girl was a few winters his senior, and at close to

sixteen Segev was more than old enough to appreciate
her beauty. Slender through the waist, richly curved above
and below, she wore a silk shift three shades lighter than
her pale blue eyes. Black hair cascaded in thick, loose
waves from beneath a wispy golden veil weighted at its
three corners with silver coins. Her face was round of
brow, pointed of chin, with lips the color of summer
roses and eyelashes that swept demurely down as she
murmured, ''You're much handsomer than your brothers,
my lord.''

The next thing he knew for certain was her voice again.
They lay on the familiar carpet before the hearth, both
of them bathed in the sweat of their labors, and she had
said, ''More of a man than your brothers, as well.'' And
then she had laughed.

Head spinning, Segev spasmed away from her. It was
not the young girl who lay next to him but Mireva, a
woman old enough to be his grandmother.

Yet she did not look like a grandmother. Though the
guise had been shed, he recognized the knowing touch
of her fingers and suddenly craved the taste of her mouth.
By dawn they were in her bed, and Mireva was still
laughing.

''Your brothers managed thrice each. But you've satisfied me four times!''

''Five,'' he said, reaching for her again.

''Ah, you may be young and there's new fire in your
blood, but I don't relish another scorching so soon. You
must not be so eager when the night comes for you at
Goddess Keep, nor let the woman find out how much you
know.''

She had explained then that the *faradhi* ritual was a
perversion of the old ways, when only the most powerful
had initiated virgins—as was their right. Sunrunners were
so feeble in their spells that they performed the act in
total darkness and total silence, lest their weavings un-
ravel around them.

''Any fool of six or more rings may bed the virgin—
probably because those who think themselves the most
powerful are too old.''

''Then it won't be Andrade,'' he replied with a relieved sigh.

Mireva had pretended insult. "She's only ten winters my senior!"

"Say thirty, and I might believe you."

The answer pleased her so much that it was a fifth time before they resumed their conversation.

Segev turned once more in his dormitory bed, cursing himself for remembering so vividly, and forced himself to think about the tasks ahead of him. The first was to maintain the illusion that he was simply another student of the *faradhi* arts. The prospect of classes and discipline bored him, but he would see them through to reach his next objective: the beautiful golden-haired Sunrunner he intended for his man-making night. He would have to make sure she won the right to go to his bed, when he would give her wine laced with *dranath* as Mireva had instructed. Thereafter he would find other chances to drug her, gently and slowly so that she would not realize her growing addiction. She would be tired sometimes, her bones would ache—and then Segev would be there, all tender solicitude, offering wine or taze as a restorative. If he was clever, she would come to think that it was he and not the drug that caused her improved health and mood. When time and opportunity came to steal the scrolls, she would be his willing accomplice—not that he would ask anything unusual or impossible. Only a horse made ready at the gate, a few lies to cover the time needed for the theft—and, once he was gone, he would have a passionate defender who would sicken and slowly die for lack of *dranath*.

There had been another Sunrunner years ago who had died of it. Mireva had told him the details as he'd dressed that morning, and explained the complexities of the night Masul was born. Segev had been unable to share her regret that Ianthe had not won Prince Rohan for her own, pointing out that he could hardly be expected to mourn circumstances that had led to his own birth.

He remembered very little about his mother. Lustrous dark eyes, a rare and costly fragrance, a rustle of skirts, a soft lap—those were his only memories. His brothers had told him that in the last year of her life she had grown big with child, but he recalled nothing of it. The brother or sister had died with her on that fiery night that was Segev's first clear memory.

Torn from a sound sleep to the smells of smoke and fear, the sounds of screaming death and fire, the sight of a hideous greedy glow outside his chamber. Carried roughly down the blazing staircase in bruisingly strong arms. Unable to breathe through the thickness of smoke and flames. Screaming for his mother, pounding on the guard's chest, half-smothered in the folds of a smelly cloak. More pain as he was slung across a saddle. Looking back at the false eastern dawnlight created by the burning of Feruche.

Marron delighted in tormenting Segev with his fear of fire. But Segev had eventually learned that his brother was even more afraid of it than he, and one very satisfying midnight had shocked Marron into a shriek of terror with a candle held near his sleeping face. That had been the end of Marron's teasing.

Segev sighed again, rolling himself tighter in his blanket. The cold here was different from that of the mountains: wet with the sea, leaking ice along his bones as crisp snowy chill did not. His gaze flickered to the hearth, far from him beyond the other beds, but though he could appreciate the fire's warmth he could never regard it as a friend. Fire belonged to Sunrunners.

He lay very still, hearing the murmur of voices at the doorway as the new arrivals were checked for the night. The name he had given himself plucked at his ears, and he grinned into the pillow. He knew some of the old language, and Mireva had been vastly amused when told the word he'd decided to be known by: Sejast, meaning "dark son."

The voices went away, and the door closed again, leaving the hearth as the only source of light. He would have to conjure Fire before receiving his first ring and spending the night with the blonde woman. He must remember not to call it too powerfully in case he aroused suspicion. He did not look forward to the test, but he knew he could do it—must do it, and soon.

And then, when the first ring glinted from his right middle finger and the lovely *faradhi* was his through *dranath*, he would show Lady Mireva that he and not Ruval should be the one to challenge Prince Pol.

Chapter Eight

Just before spring gave way to summer, the dragons returned to the Desert.

Within Stronghold, Rohan and Tobin both looked up at the same time from the desk where she had been explaining a map. Brother and sister rose as one to gaze north from the windows, tense with anticipation. Sioned shared a wry smile with Chay, and they began tidying the spread of parchments on the desk. There would be no more work done that day.

Pol was out walking with Myrdal in the sandy plain below Stronghold, detailing his experiences as Prince Lleyn's squire. The old woman nodded approval of his training; in her day she had been in command of the castle guard and schooled more than one boy in the knightly arts—including Prince Chadric, which in a way made it seem as if Myrdal had trained Pol, too. He was smiling at the realization when she suddenly stopped walking and planted her cane made of a dragon's bone in the sand. Her face lifted to the sky.

"Listen," she murmured. "Can you hear them? Listen to the wings, Pol!"

It had been said of his grandfather Zehava that he could glance at the formation of clouds and predict to the day when the dragons would return. Myrdal was rumored to be Zehava's cousin; she certainly seemed to have the same talent. Pol closed his eyes and concentrated, hoping with all his heart that he had inherited the ability, too. Very faintly, on the edges of his mind, he sensed the wings, not hearing them so much as feeling them all along his nerves, a delicious tingling, a flash of excitement through his blood.

Maarken was in the courtyard with Sionell and Jahnavi, telling them a story while he whittled a flute for the

little boy. He gave a sudden start and got to his feet,
catching his breath. Jahnavi, named for Maarken's long-
dead twin brother, tugged at his sleeve in bewilderment,
face creased with worry. Sionell started to speak, but
then the cry came down from the Flametower: "Dragons!"

All of Stronghold abandoned tasks and duties, scur-
rying for vantage points at windows, atop the gatehouse,
along the walls. By the time the dragons had become a
faint smudge against the northern horizon, people were
jostling for the best places to see them—all in a strange,
awed silence. Rohan, Sioned, Tobin, and Chay met Feylin on the way up to the Flametower, their running footsteps the only sound. The lookout had already opened the
stone door of a huge circular room at the tower's pinna-
cle, where a fire burned year-round as a beacon light in
the Desert and to symbolize Rohan's rule. Not even the
open windows all the way around the room could cool
the heat given off by the fire blazing in the chamber's
center. Sweat immediately beaded foreheads and trickled
between shoulder blades as the five clustered around the
windows.

In the silence could be heard the rush of wings. The
hazy blot grew larger, separated into individual dragons.
Sunlight gleamed off dull hides: brown, russet, ash gray,
green-bronze, dark gold, blue-black. And suddenly there
came the music of dragon voices. A tremor ran through
all who heard the arrogant bellows of ownership, of triumph, of warning. Wings stroked powerfully, fore- and
hind-legs tucked in with shining talons barely visible. As
they reached the hot thermals they soared higher, gliding
easily with wings outspread, veering east to trumpet their
mastery over the Long Sand before turning once more
for the hills.

A huge sire, gold-speckled brown with black undersides to his wings, snapped at a smaller male of silvery
hide and aggressive tendencies who flew too close. They
roared out their rivalry loudly enough to shake the stones
of Stronghold and swept insolently close to the keep,
thundering their contempt of the puny beings below who
watched them in wondering silence.

"Father of Storms!" Feylin blurted. "I'm forgetting to count them! Quick, somebody—pen and parchment!"

"In your hands," Chay told her. She looked down with a start of surprise, then thrust the implements at him along with a bottle of ink from her tunic pocket.

"Take notes for me!" She leaned precariously out a window and Rohan grabbed her by the waist to steady her as she recited, "Group of eight youngsters, all brown—five females, varying gray—fourteen, no *sixteen* more females, bronze and black—" She paused for breath, counting frantically. "Thirty-six immatures, brown sire, black sire, two grays, three golds—Goddess, look at that flight of reds! Forty of them!"

"Forty-two," Tobin corrected from the next window as the dragons flew past.

Chay could hardly write fast enough. He sprawled on the floor and scribbled with all his might as the two women called out numbers and colors. Rohan hung onto Feylin as she climbed up on the sill.

"And bringing up the rear—twenty-eight immature dragons, gray and greenish and bronze!" Her balance chose that moment to desert her. Rohan yanked her back into the room and they toppled onto the floor near Chay, spilling the ink in a black splash.

Sioned stood over them, laughing. "Feylin, my dear, you know how deeply I value your friendship, but if you don't unhand my husband this instant—!"

Rohan helped Feylin up and winked at her. "She wouldn't mind so much if I didn't have a preference for redheads. I thought you were going to take off out the window and go flying with them!"

"I came near to it," she admitted, rubbing one hip. "Did you get it all down, my lord?" she asked Chay.

He looked up from the floor. "If any of you can make sense of the scrawl, we're all right, But I wrote it and *I* can't even read it!"

"I was listening," Sioned informed him.

"You and your *faradhi* memory tricks—why didn't you tell me earlier?"

"You mean you didn't see her over there, still as a stone?" Tobin asked. "Although I'm sure the blank stare is something Andrade teaches along with the tricks themselves, just for show. Feylin, you and Sioned go downstairs with Chay and make a clean copy while she still remembers everything.''

When they were gone, she helped Rohan mop up the spilled ink. ''Look at this. It's soaked right into the stone!''

''Next time let's do the count from the battlements.'' He wiped sweat from his forehead, leaving a streak of black behind.

Tobin scrubbed it away. ''I agree. It's a furnace in here. That was probably the most chaos I've seen since my sons grew up. But the dragons *are* beautiful, aren't they?''

''Don't tell me you've finally come round to my way of thinking about them!''

''I don't appreciate losing our stock to them, no. But they're wonderful creatures. Besides, you always pay for what they gobble down.''

''I pay inflated prices,'' he accused, following her out of the room. The heavy door swung shut behind them with a hollow thud that echoed down the empty stairwell.

''That wounds me deeply, little brother.''

''I don't hear you denying it.''

''Well, if you're foolish enough to pay for what the dragons steal. . . .'' She grinned at him. ''Besides, thanks to the dragons themselves, you can afford it. How much gold did you get out of their caves last year?''

They turned a corner and nearly bumped into Pol. His face seemed unable to decide whether excitement, shock, or bewilderment was the expression it wished to convey; his eyes said one thing, his brows another, and his slack jaw a third.

Rohan threw his sister a disgusted glance, and she had the grace to blush as he told Pol, ''I hope you won't follow her example by chattering that piece of information all over the keep.''

Pol shook his head, wide-eyed.

''And remember to make more noise when climbing stairs,'' Rohan advised. ''Unless you enjoy embarrassing people who get caught saying things they shouldn't. Now, what have you run up here to tell me?''

''What? Oh—Myrdal and Maeta want to know if we'll set out for Skybowl tonight or wait for tomorrow.''

"Hmm. Let's go tonight. The moons will be up, and I fancy a ride while it's cool. When we get to Skybowl, I'll answer all the questions you're having such trouble swallowing."

"Yes, Father. I'm sorry, Aunt Tobin."

"It was my fault, Pol." As he ran back down the stairs a good deal more noisily than he'd come up them, she turned to Rohan. "I didn't mean to—"

"I know you didn't. But I'd hoped to wait before telling him."

"I really am sorry, Rohan. It was careless of me."

"The day we have to watch everything we say at Stronghold is the day I trade this pile of rock for a tent with the Isulk'im and let somebody else play High Prince for a while." He put an arm around her waist. "Come. They'll have finished the tally by now. I only hope Feylin is pleased with the total—she has this way of looking at me as if it's my fault there are fewer dragons than she'd planned on!"

Sionell waylaid Pol on his errand, trying to capture his attention by running beside him and calling his name. He ignored her. Frustrated, she grabbed at his sleeve. "Slow down! Where are you going so fast?"

"I'm on my father's business. Let go." He tugged his arm from her grasp.

"Can I come with you?"

"No."

She followed anyway, listening from the doorway as Pol informed Myrdal and her daughter Maeta that they would depart for Skybowl tonight.

"Good," Maeta said. "It's a long ride—but with Ostvel's kitchen and wine cellar at the end of it!"

"If there was a horse in the stables that wouldn't shake my old bones loose, I'd come with you," Myrdal sighed. "Chaynal, bless the boy, never bred a slow animal in his life."

"You could ride my pony," Sionell offered shyly. "We could use lots of saddle blankets."

"Thank you, child, but a horse made of feathers wouldn't do for me at my age." Myrdal smiled.

"I'll give the necessary orders, my lord," Maeta said to Pol. "If you'd be so kind as to tell your father—"

"Of course." He started back across the courtyard, annoyed when Sionell skipped along beside him.

"I'm going, too," she announced. "On my new pony."

"That's nice," he muttered.

"Is Myrdal really your kinswoman? I heard somebody say she's your grandfather's cousin. Is she?"

"You shouldn't listen to other people's conversations. It's rude." He conveniently forgot that he had done the same thing himself that day, though unintentionally.

"I can't help it if people talk and maybe say things they shouldn't. Mama says the Goddess gave us eyes to see with and ears to hear with—"

"And a mouth to repeat everything you hear?"

"You're the one who's rude!" Sionell darted ahead of him and made an absurd attempt to block his way, small feet planted on the cobbles. "Apologize."

"What for?"

"Your manners! Say you're sorry!"

"No!" He knew he was being childish, but something about this little brat irked him beyond all patience. The thought of her tagging along after him all over Skybowl was intolerable.

"Say it!"

"Don't use that tone of voice to me," he warned.

"Why not? Because you're a prince? Well, I'm not just anybody—I'm Lady Sionell of Remagev, and you're nothing but a rude boy!"

He drew himself up, goaded beyond control. "You're ruder than I am, if I was rude, which I wasn't! And *I* happen to be the heir of the High Prince!"

Another voice spoke behind him, sharp with disapproval. "You are an insolent child who ought to be spanked for that statement. Apologize at once," Sioned snapped.

Pol's mouth set in mutinous lines and he shook his head.

His mother's green eyes narrowed for a moment, and then she looked at Sionell. "What's this all about?"

"Nothing, your grace," the girl whispered. "I'm sorry, my lord prince."

Pol blinked, more astounded by this sudden reversal

than by her use of his title. But if she could be generous enough not to tell his mother how badly he'd behaved, and apologize into the bargain, he could do no less.

"I'm sorry, too—my lady," he managed in a low voice.

Sionell's blue eyes rounded with wonder as he gave her the honorific—the first time someone of highborn rank had seriously addressed her by her title.

Sioned eyed them both. "I suppose I'm not going to be told exactly why we're in need of all the apologies. Sionell, would you do me a favor, please? Tell Maeta that if Selca's hoof is healed, I'd like to ride her tonight."

"Yes, my lady." She ran off.

Pol looked up at his mother and tensed for a scold. When it came, it was both less than he deserved and worse than he expected.

"A prince who reminds people of his rank isn't much of a prince," she said. And that was all.

He gulped, nodded, and followed her silently back into the keep.

* * *

By late afternoon of the next day they were at Skybowl. The keep itself was invisible from the dunes below, and the only signs of habitation were the small terraced fields of waxy-leaved plants that grew best when exposed to the incredible heat. Scrub and tufts of goat-tail cactus dotted the slopes of the ancient crater, but the greater part of the mountainside was bare and gray.

As the trail crested before winding down into the cone, however, visitors discovered the reason for Skybowl's name. A perfectly round, intensely blue lake nestled in the hollow of the volcano. No one knew how deep it was. On the far shore was the keep, which could have fit into Stronghold's courtyard. Built of stone taken from nearby cliffs, chips of shining black glass caught sparks off the sun where they were embedded in pale gray rock. A pennant bearing a brown stripe on a blue field stirred lazily atop the castle's single tower, and those who looked closely enough saw the gleam of gold atop the standard, a golden dragon in flight.

The party from Stronghold rode over the lip of the crater and a horn sounded from within the keep. A few moments later the pennant came down, to rise again with the blue-and-gold Desert banner preceding it, signifying that the prince was now in residence. Rohan slowed pace to give Ostvel time to come out and greet them, using the moments to breathe deeply of the fresh, cool air. The lake beckoned invitingly; he gestured to it and asked his wife, "Join me?"

"Not a chance! Ostvel always claims Sunrunners are frightened of drowning in a bathtub."

"Do you think it'll take a royal command to get him to Waes this year?"

Sioned waved as their old friend and former steward emerged on horseback from the gates. "I'll work on persuading him," she promised. "Riyan would be heartbroken if his father's not there to see him knighted. Besides, Ostvel hasn't left the Desert in years. When we made him Lord of Skybowl, it wasn't to see him immure himself in the keep."

Rohan lifted one hand in salute as Ostvel cantered toward them. "He still grieves, Sioned. After so many years, he still misses her."

"As if he'd lost her only yesterday." Camigwen, Ostvel's wife, mother of his only child, had been a Sunrunner and Sioned's dearest friend. Her death of Plague was still an open wound; Ostvel never made any show of his grief, and lived quite contentedly here at Skybowl, but he left his lonely keep only with reluctance. Sioned glanced up as she felt Rohan's fingers brush her arm.

"Smile for me, love," he murmured. She did so, seeing her sorrow reflected in his eyes—and her terror that someday one of them might have to bear the same kind of loss.

Ostvel reined in his horse and bowed deeply from his saddle. "Goddess blessing to you, my prince, my dearest lady," he greeted them. "And welcome to Skybowl. But I'm afraid I don't recognize several of your escort."

Sioned chuckled as his gaze went first to Pol, then to Sionell. "Surely you know Lady Feylin and Lord Maarken," she said, aiding and abetting.

"Of course," he responded with a bow in their direction. "But I see two strangers here. Oh, certain things about them are familiar, perhaps, but—"

"Oh, Lord Ostvel!" Sionell scolded. "You know it's me!"

The *athri* of Skybowl clapped a hand to his forehead, playing the scene for all it was worth. "The eyes, the voice, the hair—" He guided his horse around to make a full inspection and gave her an elegant bow. "My eyes do not deceive me! It is indeed the fair Lady Sionell!"

The little girl laughed merrily. Ostvel then straightened up, squinting at Pol. "Can it be—? Do I behold—'"

Sioned moved her mount over so she could bat playfully at his head. "Oh, do stop being so silly."

"Gently spoken as ever, " he observed, "and just as accurate in your aim." He rubbed ruefully at his ear. "It's nice to know some things never change!" He bowed to Pol. "My prince, welcome to Skybowl."

"Thank you, my lord," Pol said with proper dignity.

"Food and drink is ready for you—and baths for the *faradh'im*. I assume you'll perform your usual ablutions in the lake, Rohan?"

The High Prince returned from his swim to find his wife still soaking in a cool tub. He had never considered it strength of character to resist such temptation as the sight of Sioned wearing only water and her own long, unbound hair. So he climbed in with her, giving the innocent excuse that he would help her wash. The tub was not conducive to dalliance without some interesting gymnastics and a great deal of laughter, but they managed.

Afterward he lazed back in her arms, fingers idly chasing floating strands of red-gold hair. She chuckled softly and he asked, "Mmm?"

"I was just thinking that it *is* possible to drown in a tub, even if you're not a Sunrunner."

"Don't be absurd. We splashed most of the water onto the floor."

"Ostvel knows us too well. We got the suite with the best bathroom drain." She pointed to the little grill set into the floor tiles.

They found further evidence of their host's thoughtfulness in the main chamber which connected to the bathroom through a dressing area. Silk robes had been laid out on the bed, and two comfortable chairs faced each other across a table laden with dinner.

"Ostvel keeps the best cook in either of my prince-doms, damn him," Rohan said after finishing off a miraculous concoction of hot pastry wrapped around chilled fruit. He stretched, rubbed his silk-clad shoulders, and sighed. "You don't suppose I could connive him into a trade, do you?"

Sioned poured out the last of the wine and shook her head. "We might send our cooks up here for a while though, to learn a few things."

"I doubt it. His resident magician trained in Waes, and they don't give up their secrets. Not even to High Princes. And speaking of secrets, Tobin let it slip yesterday about the dragon gold where Pol heard her."

"He had to know sometime," she said philosophically. "I assume you're going to make the revelation properly dramatic?"

"Sneak him into a darkened cave and suddenly light a torch, you mean?" He laughed. "It's an idea. Sort of like the way we found out, remember? I'll never forget the shine of the sand and digging through it with your Fire over my shoulder."

"Actually, you might ask Pol to conjure the Fire for you. I've tested him, Rohan. He's an instinctive talent. It's uncanny."

"If Andrade thinks she had her hands full with Andry, she's going to get a shock when it comes Pol's turn at Goddess Keep. I've been thinking about that, by the way. If he's knighted at eighteen, it will be a *Rialla* year and we can give him a send-off to Andrade from Waes itself— making it very obvious that he's going to be a fully trained *faradhi* as well as a prince."

"Not exactly subtle," she remarked.

"And if we tried to do it less than publicly, the other princes would grow even more suspicious than they are right now."

"It was always comes back to that, doesn't it?" she mused, propping her elbows on the table. "Pol makes them *very* nervous, with the potential for all that power. But he'll have Maarken to show him how it's done, and there couldn't be a better example—not for him or for the other princes."

"Tobin and Chay are so proud of him they're ready to

burst," Rohan agreed. "What a family my sister produced! Two *faradh'im* and another son who bids fair to becoming an even finer knight than his father. Volog's last letter almost glowed. He's going to knight Sorin this year, did I tell you? Goddess, they're all growing up so fast."

"I wish we didn't have to send Pol back to Dorval. Laugh at me if you like, but I hate missing any part of his life."

"I'm not laughing, Sioned. But it's best for him to be at Graypearl. He's learning so much from Lleyn and Chadric. And it's safer there."

"The Merida—"

"—threatened once in the years he's been there. And it happened outside the palace. We can't keep him wrapped in silk, and he'd never stand for it if he tried. You wouldn't want a son who did."

She sighed. "I know, I know. But I can't help worrying."

Rohan got to his feet and stretched again. "We should be up early tomorrow," he reminded her. "We'll go out and have a look at the dragons, then I'll take Pol on a tour of the caves."

"Do you want me to try and touch a dragon tomorrow?" She joined him in bed after draping her robe over a chair.

Rohan gathered her close beneath the light sheet, stroking her damp hair. "It might be interesting. They're all thinking about nothing other than mating, and who knows what you might sense—and want to act on?"

"Don't you just wish!" she retorted, biting his shoulder.

"Stop that. Or at least do it as if you mean it."

She raised her head and looked into bright blue eyes that danced with humor and desire. "If this is middle age, then it's a wonder we both survived our youth!"

* * *

Chay leaned back in bed, a thoughtful frown furrowing his brow. "Tobin. . . ."

She stopped brushing her long black hair. "You honor my ears with speech, O light of my eyes?"

"Don't be impudent, woman, or I'll beat you senseless."

"You and what army?"

"Well. . . ." He cleared his throat. "Tobin, that boy is too damned perfect."

"What boy? Pol? What's wrong with him?"

"Just that. Nothing's wrong with him except that there's nothing wrong with him. He adores his mother, worships his father, is reasonably obedient, doesn't pick his nose in public, washes behind his ears, and is entirely too smart for his age."

"And this is cause for complaint?"

"It's unnatural. No, it *is,*" he insisted when she laughed. "He doesn't get in trouble. Our boys were never so well-behaved."

"Or so clean," she added, grinning.

"I want to know what's wrong with him."

"Nothing, according to you."

"That's the whole point. Consider Rohan at his age."

"My darling brother was perfect, too. Just ask him."

"He was the slyest, wickedest, most impossible brat I ever met. He just never got caught at it."

"Well, perhaps Pol's like him—too clever to get caught."

"I don't think so. Not that he's not clever. I mean. But I don't think he has to use it to keep himself out of mischief. I wish he deserved a few swats now and then. It's good for the character."

"Are you aware that this is one of the most ridiculous conversations we've ever had?" She slid into bed beside him.

"No, it's not. The prize for that goes to anything we said to each other before the first time I kissed you. Thousands of words, all of them a complete waste of time."

"So is this discussion." She made several unsubtle movements designed to distract him.

"Stop that."

"Two more ridiculous words." She gave him a look of vast patience. "Chay, Pol is a polite, respectful, mannerly, conscientious fourteen-year-old boy." Snuggling back into his embrace, she added, "But don't worry. I'm sure he'll grow out of it soon."

* * *

Maarken had been bred to the Desert through at least fourteen generations on both sides of his family. He loved the wildness of the land, knew its moods, respected its dangers. He asked nothing more of a day than to spend it watching the delicate sunrise colors flare into dazzling noon, then slowly mellow to the rose and purple shadows of dusk that gave way to sparkling black skies and silvered dunes. He relished the heat that seeped into his bones, the soft whispers of sand beneath his feet, the shimmer-visions that danced enticingly just out of reach. In this place where others could not even survive, his people had thrived; he had his share of pride in the accomplishment, his share of love for the harsh land that, testing them, had not found them wanting.

But though he intended to spend his life in the Desert, at present it was the last place he wanted to be. A ride of thirty measures, a long walk, and hours of waiting had not sweetened his mood. He crouched in a sandy hollow watching dragons, and chafed at the slow passage of the sun across the sky.

Hollis had promised to contact him sometime today. Her duties at Goddess Keep varied, and it was uncertain when she could be alone. His mind understood; but his heart, like that of any other ardent lover, resented anything that diverted her from thoughts of him and him alone. His sense of humor provided a balance between the two extremes, for he knew she could scarcely go through her day languishing over him, nor would he want her to. He also knew she would have laughed herself breathless at the very thought. Still, he told himself, she was supposed to be in love with him. Surely she could make time to reach across the sunlight to him, if only for a little while.

Boredom did not help his temper, either. He had chosen to join the observation party for something to do that would keep him out in the sun and reasonably occupied, but thus far absolutely nothing had happened. The she-dragons, back from an early morning foray to feed, lolled in the sand, baking their egg-swollen hides. The immature dragons had been chased off for the duration, though Maarken knew they had probably found some vantage point, just as the humans had. Of the sires there was no sign at all, although the occasional distant roar from the canyons made everyone start in surprise. But the females paid not the slightest attention to the bellowings of their mates; they only yawned.

Maarken glanced at Pol, who sat beside him in the sand. The boy's dusky yellow-brown cloak was pulled around him, the hood up to protect his blond head from the heat. He looked like a miniature tent. Maarken grinned, seeing the rest of the group spread out along the dunes like a little village of Isulki tents, all in lightweight cloaks that blended with Desert colors. Dragons were keenly sensitive to color, as Feylin had discovered some years ago.

She had conducted an experiment involving some humiliated sheep dyed garish shades of blue, orange, scarlet, and purple, which the dragons scrupulously avoided in favor of their unaltered tan and white brethren. Maarken remembered the trouble Feylin had taken to make sure no scent of dye clung to the wool, and especially he recalled the chaos they'd watched from a hilltop as the poor undyed, unsuspecting sheep had tried to escape thirty-five gleeful young dragons presented with a free meal.

He had to chuckle under his breath as memory stirred of the subsequent experiment. Feylin had used more subtle shades this time, browns and grays that were nearly the usual colors of sheep. The dragons had not been so choosy that time, and it had been concluded that protective coloration would only work if the most lurid hues were used. They had all had a good long laugh at the idea of convincing shepherds to watch over flocks of purple sheep.

Still, the tests had shown that dragons were sensitive to color. Maarken adjusted the hood of his own tazebrown cloak and recalled the shock of bumping into a dragon on the sunlight. He had talked it over with Sioned at great length, agreeing with her that it might just be possible to pattern and understand dragon colors. But the problems presented were serious ones.

Those not *faradhi* never understood the limitations of the gifts. A steady source of light was essential. A cloud over the sun or moons, a venture timed too close to sunset or moonset—and shadows drowned all color. Shadowlost was the most hideous death a Sunrunner could face. Spark of mind gone with the lost color-pattern of thought and personality, the body lived for only a little while longer in consciousless, empty void.

Maarken fixed his gaze on the great lolling dragons half a measure from where he sat. What if a *faradhi* in contact with a dragon was pulled into a cave or the shadow of a mountain? What if the dragon flew into fog, or from day into night? No one but Sunrunners comprehended the vulnerability of their kind to darkness. He wondered if Rohan had any idea of the real dangers—or if Sioned would tell him.

The pair were seated together a little beyond Pol, two matching triangular tents of dull gold silk. They would have been anonymous but for the small dragon cypher stitched at the right shoulder of each garment, the same symbol that appeared on Pol's cloak. Other princes had adopted Rohan's innovation of a device in addition to colors, and some were quite beautiful—Ossetia's golden wheat-sheaf on dark green, Fessenden's silver fleece on sea-green. The *athr'im* were clamoring for similar privileges now, and the *Rialla* this year would decide if such were to be granted. Thus far only one of the lords had been given the right to use a cypher with his colors. Maarken smiled and glanced to his left, where his parents sat side-by-side, their tan cloaks distinguished by the symbol Rohan had given them: on a red field bound in blue, a sword was stitched in silver thread, signifying the role of Radzyn's lord in defending the Desert. On Chay's pennant and battle standard the whole was bordered in white, and looked magnificent. Maarken dreamed a little of the time when he would give Hollis a cloak carrying that symbol. . . .

His mother looked around at him then, and Maarken tensed slightly as if suspecting she had read his thought. But she only smiled and rolled her eyes expressively, and he grinned back. She had the least patience for sitting still of anyone he had ever known. She hated lack of physical activity, and even when discussing a problem she tended to pace, drum her fingers, tap her feet, shift position constantly. Her activist approach to everything was occasionally her husband's despair; she believed that there was nothing in her world that could not be helped, solved, or conquered if only one got up and did something about it. Rohan was her opposite in that way, as in most others; he believed in allowing things to develop, in not forcing events. In the very personal matter of Hollis, Maarken knew he could count on his uncle's quiet support, and that was a help. But if Tobin decided she approved of Hollis, she would do everything in her considerable powers to facilitate the match. Maarken did not like to think what she was capable of if she did not approve of his Choice.

It amused him that his quiet, serene Hollis was so different from his mother. She would never fly into a tearing rage, give imperious commands, or escalate a difference of opinion into a shouting match. Tobin did all these things with as much relish as she lived the rest of her life. Maarken adored his mother—but he did not want to marry a copy of her.

Without warning a dragonsire trumpeted a challenge across the dunes. Maarken nearly jumped out of his skin. The deep, hoarse cry echoed all the way out to the Long Sand. Feylin stirred from her perch on the highest dune and slid down to where Sioned and Rohan sat. Maarken strained to hear their whispers, and saw his uncle and aunt straighten expectantly. A ripple of alertness went through the she-dragons as a shadow appeared across the sand, then another, then another. The sires were ready at last.

The females shifted, moved from the low hills that bordered the plain and grouped together in bunches of five to ten. Feylin moved over to Pol and began a low-voiced explanation of the hierarchy.

"The youngest are to either side of the senior females. You can't really tell them apart except for their wings. See the scars on the older ones? Mating gets pretty rough. But there's another way to tell the younger from the elder. The ones who've been through this before are pretending to be bored." She chuckled softly as Pol blinked at her.

"The sires will have to impress them. The youngsters will be the first to choose their mates, but the others will wait a while. They've seen it all before, and, like most ladies, they want to be wooed."

Maarken whispered playfully, "Bear that in mind, Pol."

"I'll be marrying a *girl* someday, not a dragon," he scoffed.

"My husband says there's no discernible difference!" Feylin laughed softly. "Watch the sires now. They're just about ready."

The three dragons made a delicate landing in the sand and were joined by a fourth and a fifth. Two were golden with black underwings. The third was russet-colored, the other two black and brown. Maarken had seen their dances before, but never so many dragons at once. He glanced up and saw the remaining eight sires hovering watchfully on thermals high above, waiting for the first dragons to exhaust themselves; when one tired, a fresher male circling overhead would land and take his place.

The five took up position before their audience, rearing back as one with wings spread wide and heads thrown up to the sky as they howled their opening music. The chord slid up and down the scale, wailing like five separate wind-storms. Maarken fought the urge to put his hands over his ears and knew the others were just as disturbed by the wild music. Feylin huddled in her cloak. Pol froze in place, eyes huge as he listened to the terrible dragonsong. But the females reacted with the dragon equivalent of shrugged shoulders, and the older ones opened their jaws in wide, insulting yawns.

The reddish-brown sire was the first to move. His head dropped down and his wings swept sand before him in great glistening waves. His song became a low, keening moan as he reached up, claws extended as if to tear down slices of sky. Neck writhing, wings sweeping back and forth to spew sand in all directions, his voice rose to a screech once more. And then he began to dance.

Poetry in flight, dragons ought to have been lumbering lumps on the ground. But their grace in the air was nothing compared to the elegance of the sand-dance. Swaying from side to side as smoothly as a slim willow in the breeze, the russet dragon folded his wings, spread them, swept them out once more as he paced with nimble ease across the sand. He was soon joined by the black dragon with rose-brown underwings, then a gold, then the brown and the second gold. The sequence of movements was as orderly and patterned as a Sunrunner's colors, repeating from dragon to dragon as each followed the other in ritual steps and wingsweeps.

Sand flew high and wide as the dragons repeated the steps over and over, each marking out his territory, each rising to full height with wings spread before dipping down again to pace the dunes, swaying gracefully until the end of the sequence when it was his turn to repeat the song. The younger females were shifting in rhythm with their tentative choices, sometimes changing in mid-beat as their attention was captured by another male moving in a different place in the dance. The older she-dragons had abandoned their pretense of indifference, but still sat back on their haunches, waiting to be impressed.

The black dragon tired first. He missed a step, one wing folding down to keep his balance. An ash-gray sire instantly saw the opening and swooped down, calling out derisively to his faltering rival. The black snarled, but the pattern had been broken and he could not recapture it. He took a few reluctant steps back, then beat his wings to lift away from his landing challenger. The gray sire then began his dance, fresh and energetic. The young females immediately focused on him, and the first rear-rangement of their ranks came as they were attracted by his vigor.

But when he accidentally caught the first joint of a wing on one foreclaw, the females hissed their disapproval and abadoned him to watch the other sires. A gold had dropped out, replaced by another brown with gorgeous red-gold underwings. Another dragon, very young and without a battle scar on his hide, was bold enough to join in without taking the place of a faltering sire, spreading his wings in defiance of the older females' snorts at his insolence. It was as if he knew very well that his green-bronze hide, accented by startling silver underwings, made him easily the most beautiful of all the sires—and he intended to take advantage of it.

They were moving apart now, slowly, subtly, and the females were moving with them. The dance continued. The russet sire who had begun it all drifted farther and farther from the territory he'd marked out; he had lasted the course and would now see how many mates he had won. Seven followed him, young ones who waddled egg-heavy after him. It was his turn to pretend to ignore them, sweet revenge after their seeming indifference earlier. One of them cried out plaintively, and another hurried forward to nip gently at his tail, but he showed no sign of noticing them at all. This impressed one of the older females, who started after him. A few moments later, another followed.

The group was well away from the others when the sire suddenly sprang up with a single powerful stroke of his wings and landed neatly behind the two older females. His attempts to herd them after the other seven brought howls of protest and a few angry snarls. One eluded him and returned to the watching group. The sire bellowed at her on her way past him, but evidently felt she was not worth going after; he gave a yowl obviously meant as an insult, to which she responded by baring her teeth. The russet sire then gathered his eight females and they took off at his side for the caves above Skybowl.

This process was repeated seven more times. Eight sires captured anywhere from five to nine females each. But there were still five males unmated at the end of the dance, and their furious screams of rejection made the sands tremble and the watching humans shrink into their cloaks.

Maarken, enchanted during the dragons' performance, abruptly felt the delicate brush of familiar, beloved colors. Startled, he turned his head instinctively to the west, where the sun was still above the Vere Hills.

Is that how you'd behave if I refused you? came a teasing voice in his mind.

Worse! he replied, gathering Hollis' brilliant colors to him and steadying the weave of sunshine. *How long have you been watching?*

Only a little while, and with much less devotion than you were. It took me four tries to get your attention! But they're magnificent, aren't they?

Next time you'll be here with me to watch them. Where've you been all day?

Working since dawn with your fiend of a brother, helping him translate those scrolls Meath brought. I'm surprised I'm able to communicate in words less than four hundred years old!

There are a few words I'd like to hear right now, he suggested, and smiled as her colors laughed around him. *But I'll say them first because I'm a knight, a gentleman, and a lord. I love you! And Sioned knows it—not that it's you specifically, but we have her help if we need it.*

The legendary Sunrunner Princess. Is she really as beautiful as they say?

If you like redheads. I like blondes. Hollis, I've spoken to my parents about opening Whitecliff, so they know I'm ready to marry. Why don't I tell them now instead of waiting?

Maarken, I love you, but—don't we owe them a look at me first? What if they don't like me?

Don't be ridiculous. And whatever you say, I'm going to marry you.

Could you go against your parents' wishes?

Just see if I don't, if it comes to that, which it won't! I'll wait for the Rialla if that's what you want, but the Lastday marriages are going to be led by us, my love.

Ah, Maarken—damn, I can hear Andry yelling for me. I have to go. Take care, beloved. Goddess keep you.

He became aware of Pol beside him, tugging his sleeve, and sighed. The threads unraveled and he was back in the Desert, and Pol was whispering, "You were Sunrunning, weren't you?"

"Maarken nodded. "Yes."

"Where to? How far? Who did you talk to?"

"Taking your questions in order—a long way, very far, and none of your business." He softened the words with a smile. Getting to his feet, he stretched the stiffness out of his muscles and saw that everyone else was doing the same. Pol, with all the supple resilience of early youth, jumped up and ran to his parents to share his excitement at witnessing the sand-dance. Maarken joined his own parents, grinning as Chay heaved himself to his feet and rubbed his backside.

"How can I be numb and still ache?" he complained. "I'm too damned old for this nonsense."

"The walk back to the horses will take the kinks out," Tobin said. "Pol and Rohan are going to the caves, Maarken. Do you want to go with them?"

"I promised Sionell and Jahnavi a full account before dinner tonight, so I'll ride back with you to Skybowl."

"And to enough bottles of Ostvel's best cactus brew to soothe my old bones," Chay added. To Rohan he called out, "If you're back late, don't expect me to save any for you!"

"Not even for your prince?"

"Not a thimbleful. It's your fault I'm out here roasting like a prize sheep in the first place."

"Not just any old sheep, darling," his wife said sweetly. "Definitely a ram."

"Tobin!" He took one long braid in each hand and tugged her to him for a kiss. "You're shocking the children."

Maarken grinned as he pictured himself and Hollis similarly "shocking" their own children. One day people would say their names in the same breath, the way they said "Chay and Tobin" or "Rohan and Sioned." One day very soon.

Chapter Nine

The people of Skybowl were close-mouthed, even with their prince and his heir, when it came to gold. Men and women who had given warm welcome the day before had only polite nods as Rohan and Pol tethered their horses in Threadsilver Canyon. They had ridden up into the hills from the dragon plain, then cut north through a narrow gulley to join the trail leading to Skybowl and the gold caves.

Wind and sand had worn down the rocks into odd shapes; huge cacti grew here and there along the canyon, broad green platters bristling with needles the size of spikes. There was water deep underground still, but nothing remained of the river that had long ago gouged out the softer stone.

The lower caves of Threadsilver were used for refining gold mined from the upper ones, something Pol deduced from the faint glow of firepits within. His father confirmed his guess as they dismounted for the climb on foot to the higher caverns, but volunteered no other information.

The boy squinted up at narrow shelves connected by a path just wide enough for a single pack horse. Work had nearly finished for the day and most of the men and women were on their way down. They favored the two princes with those slight nods of recognition and respect; one or two smiled, but there were no verbal greetings at all. Pol wondered about that, and the fact that his father seemed undisturbed by the silence. Curiosity was near to killing him.

As they waited for the last horses to come down, Pol could contain his questions no longer. "We're supposed to be mining silver here, aren't we? I mean, that's what everybody thinks—including me."

"That's the story, yes. And there really is a vein of it running through these hills. Hence the name Threadsilver."

"And we pretend this is an extension of it, to make everybody think our wealth comes from silver."

"Of course. Occasionally we do hit silver around here. It's useful."

Rohan started up the trail and Pol hurried to keep pace. "But why keep everything secret?" he asked.

"It's a complex arrangement," his father replied cryptically.

Pol paused, allowing a young woman carrying waterskins to get by him, and caught up to his father. "How do we hide the fact that we take gold and not silver from the caves?"

"We have ways to disguise the yield. Lleyn helps. So does Volog."

Pol wanted desperately to hear the full details of this ongoing fiscal fraud, but his father had signaled to a bandy-legged man up on the first shelf of rock. The boy held his peace during the climb, and was introduced to one Rasoun, who managed the whole operation for Ostvel. The miner bowed his respects and gave quiet welcome.

"Thank you," Pol replied politely. "Are you going to show us the caves?"

"I think I'll let his grace have that honor." Rasoun smiled. "I was about your age when my own father gave me my first sight of the gold caverns. He was overseer for Lord Farid, who held Skybowl for your father's father Prince Zehava."

Pol did some fast calculations in his head. Farid had died the summer before Pol was born; Zehava had died six winters before that; tack on another few years of work under his grandfather's rule and factor in Rasoun's probable age—and the caves must have been in production for at least thirty years. How had they managed to keep so much gold so secret for so long?

"Can you suggest a cave for us to explore, Rasoun?" Rohan asked.

"The far middle one should do, my lord. We plan to start up there next spring, so there should be a lot to see. You'll want a torch."

"Thank you, no. My son has another type of Fire at his disposal."

Pol's jaw dropped slightly. Rasoun looked a little startled, then murmured, "Ah, yes. Of course, my lord."

As they climbed the switchback trail to the indicated cave, Pol asked, "Father, do you really want me to call Fire for you?"

"Your mother says you're quite competent. Why? Does it make you nervous?"

"Well . . . yes. Some."

"We won't need a conflagration, you know," Rohan told him, amused. "Just something to see by. But wait until I tell you, and be careful." He lowered his voice to a conspirator's whisper. "And *don't* tell Lady Andrade!"

Pol shook his head emphatically, and Rohan grinned.

The path was steep, not yet graded to allow easier access for workers and pack horses. Pausing halfway up to catch his breath, Pol looked out over the emptying canyon. Neither as long nor as wide as Rivenrock to the south, and with only a quarter of the number of caves there, it was still an impressive sight in the late afternoon glow. The walls were gilded with the rosy light that came to the Desert in late spring and autumn, deepening to purplish shadows where the canyon curved and narrowed to the north.

"Father? Don't we set guards at night? And why aren't all the caves being worked instead of just a few? And nobody I've seen so far looks big and strong enough to dig gold out of rock."

"You'll have to let me tell this my own way, Pol," his father said moodily.

"But *when?*"

"Patience."

At last they reached a narrow ledge, having to scramble on all fours the last few paces. After taking a moment to brush off his hands and clothes, Rohan said, "Did Maarken ever tell you about the day a hatchling dragon nearly fried him and his brother for dinner?"

Pol nodded. "He and Jahni went to look in a cave without permission."

"That they did. And they got the fright of their lives when that dragon popped out of his cave. It was the last Hatching Hunt ever held," he went on softly. "A hideous custom—not sport but wholesale murder."

"Why didn't Grandfather ever outlaw it?"

"Because he thought there would always be enough dragons. No more questions now, not until I've told you the whole thing."

Pol nodded, holding his breath, staring into the dark hole of the cave.

"That day Maarken and Jahni went exploring—that was the same day your mother and I first went into a dragon cave. It was the summer she spent at Stronghold before we were married. We found out that day what my father had known for years and never told me."

They went into the cave. Impenetrable shadows swallowed up all light in a chamber at least three times the height and breadth of Pol's room at Stronghold. The ceiling and walls formed a ragged arch above a sandy floor that extended back into a darkness that might have ended there or reached a whole measure into the hillside. Rohan gestured Pol forward until they stood just inside the shadow curtain.

"Now you may call up a little Fire, please."

He did so, centering the finger-flame on the sand a few paces ahead of them. As it steadied, the cave began to shimmer. Pol tried to plant his feet more firmly into the sand, confused by the sensation of movement—but it was only the light that moved, striking a glisten of gold all around him.

Rohan went to the nearest wall, stooped down, and returned with a hand-sized shard of what looked like pale pottery. It, too, shone.

"It's part of a dragon shell," he explained. "And this is where we get our gold."

The little Fire flared as Pol reacted, and he hastily got control of himself.

"They breathe fire to dry their wings after hatching. When the shells are seared, some of the gold is freed. Over the years it's all ground down into the sand. There aren't many shells left here, but at Rivenrock I could show you big chunks left by dragons not much older than you are." He handed Pol the shard. "It's not rock we dig out of the caves at all, you see. No one uses a pick-axe, and no one has to be all that muscular to sift the sand that goes into the pack horses' bags. That was a very astute observation of yours, by the way—I'll have to talk to Rasoun about it, and get some heftier men up here to create the right impression. The gold is taken down to the smelting caves below, and everything important is done where not even Sunrunners can get a look at it."

"Father. . . ?"

"Let me guess. What happens to the gold, right?"

Pol nodded, turning the glistening fragment over and over in his hands.

"Most of it is made into ingots, much like the glass we trade with Firon and elsewhere. It goes into the treasury—not the one at Stronghold, but the secret one here."

"And the rest?"

"We send some to Lord Eltanin at Tiglath, where crafters make various items—plate and jewelry that are sold in the usual way. But we can't get rid of much using that ploy. An influx of gold would make people suspicious about its source, and ruin the market value of the work. So some of it goes on Lleyn's ships to Kierst, where Volog has a gold mine—a real one.'' He smiled and shrugged. ''It's nearly played out, though. We have a few people there who . . . shall we say it took us years to figure a way to make the gold seem like it comes directly from that mine.''

''But how many people really know? About the dragons, I mean.''

Rohan crouched down and dug up a handful of sand. Grains slid between his fingers like dried sunlight. ''Lleyn only knows that he's paid handsomely for Radzyn's exclusive right to the silk trade. Volog doesn't know that the gold isn't really his. And don't think it's sentiment for an old friend or your mother's family that makes me do it, either.'' He glanced up with a smile.

Pol thought furiously, trying to recall everything he knew about Kierst and any changes made there in recent years. But the shock of the gold, the shard of dragonshell in his hand, and the sand sifting slowly through Rohan's fingers slowed his thought processes. All he could come up with was, ''Volog's an important ally.''

''Indeed he is. But there are greater reasons than that, Pol. In the four years we've been supplying his mine, he's had the wealth to support some valuable work— woodcrafting, improving his herds, parchment-making, planting new orchards. He never had the money to spare before, you see, and while a good bit of it goes to what some people might call frivolity—well, that keeps other crafters fed and happy, too. But if it was anyone other than Volog, I wouldn't be doing it. He's not a greedy man, or one who sees wealth as a means to making mischief. He wants to improve his princedom, and our gold lets him do it.''

Another palmful of sand was gathered and Pol watched it trickle down, enthralled by the golden stuff that had financed his father's dreams.

''It's the parchment I'm especially interested in, and the herds he's raising. This year I'm going to suggest that he establish a scriptorium. Can you imagine it, Pol? Books at a price affordable not only to princes, but to all the *athr'im*—and eventually to almost everyone. If I'm lucky, the scriptorium will evolve into a school. We'll have people trained in the arts and sciences just the way *faradh'im* are trained at Goddess Keep, who can take their knowledge to every princedom and teach others. People who'd never get the chance to learn to read can be educated as far as their minds can take them.''

The little Fire leaped gently again as Pol caught his father's excitement. ''All the stories and history and music and *everything* can be written down and shared—''

Rohan was laughing again. ''Father of Storms, you're my son, all right! Any other boy your age would moan at the thought of still more schooling!''

Though Pol blushed a little, he laughed, too. ''As long as it's other people doing the hard parts, I'm all for it!''

''The hardest part is really our responsibility as princes. Soaking up words out of books is fairly easy, you know. Applying them to the world around you. . . .'' He shrugged and gave a self-mocking grimace. ''I learned that at my first *Rialla*. Come and sit down, Pol. There's more.''

''There is?'' he asked, amazed.

''Oh, yes. Much more.''

He settled near his father in the sand, still holding the shell. ''Wouldn't Prince Volog understand about the scriptorium and the gold and everything?''

''He's a good man, basically. But like all the others, he'd see only the gold. Besides, even a High Prince can't simply order a thing done when it's so closely involved in another princedom. I can only suggest things, try to make it seem as if the idea was Volog's, not mine.''

''And then praise him for his cleverness—while reaping the rewards.'' Pol nodded sagely.

''I just hope none of them are clever enough to puzzle it out about the gold. If they ever do. . . .'' He shook his head, light from the Fire playing off his fair hair and turning it almost the same red-gold as Sioned's. Pol watched his father's face, as familiar to him as his own. In time he hoped it *would* be his own, for it was a proud face, strong, unafraid of the hard work demanded by dreams.

''It really started the year of the Plague. Your mother and I had discovered the gold in Rivenrock earlier, but I

was still trying to find a way of extracting it in secret.
Then the Plague came. So many died, Pol—your grandmother, Jahni, Ostvel's wife Camigwen. . . ." He stared
down at his now empty hands. "There was an herb called
dranath that could cure the Plague. It grew only in the
Veresch, which meant that High Prince Roelstra controlled the supply. The dragons were dying, too—scores
of them. I was here at Skybowl and Lord Farid and I
came up with the notion of putting *dranath* beside the
bittersweet plants on the cliffs. That way, when the dragons ate, they couldn't help but get a dose of the herb as
well."

The muscles of Rohan's face drew tighter, deepening
the thin lines framing his mouth. "But first we needed
dranath—a huge supply of it. Roelstra was selling it
through his merchants at an incredible price. There
wasn't that much money in the world. In some places he
held back the supply until an enemy was dead. I could
never prove it, but I knew it was true."

"You should've killed him *then*," Pol whispered. "Not
waited for later."

Rohan glanced up, startled, as if he'd suddenly remembered he had an audience. After a long moment's hesitation, he finally said. "I wanted to, Pol. Perhaps I should
have. But then Farid showed me the caves here, and the
gold my father had taken from them but never told me
about." He shook his head at that, still bemused after so
many years. "He didn't want things to be too easy for
me, my first years as prince. If I'd known about this
wealth, I might have tried to buy my will with the other
princes. They would've found out about the gold if I'd
used it foolishly, and landed on us like a hawk on a sand
rat.

"But we had to have the *dranath*. So we emptied the
treasury here and paid what Roelstra asked. Over the next
years we had to make it seem we'd beggared ourselves to
do so. The gold had to remain secret. But after Roelstra
died and we took all of Princemarch, people expected us
to be rich and we could start building again. Tiglath and
Tuath Castle were improved. Baisal of Faolain Lowland
got his new keep. And a great deal of the money went to
reclaim Remagev from the Long Sand."

"And you paid back a lot of what Roelstra had demanded of the others for *dranath*," Pol deduced, based on sure knowledge of his father's character.

Rohan smiled slightly. "A portion of it, yes. Tobin convinced me that to pay any more would be foolish—after all, it was my gold that had bought enough *dranath* to distribute through the princedoms, so she said they owed me for their lives. In any case, Ostvel and I started the operation you see here today, as large as we dared, and put out word that a new vein of silver had been found.

"So, Pol, as rich as you've always known we are, we're very much richer even than that. But the real source of the gold must remain a secret."

Pol heard himself say slowly, "It's bad enough that I'm going to inherit two princedoms. It's worse that I'm going to be a *faradhi* as well as a prince. But put the gold on top of that—"

"Exactly. There are perhaps fifty people who know the whole truth of it. Not even everyone here at Skybowl knows; few of them realize the connection between dragons and gold. The people who supply the Kierstian mine don't know where the gold really comes from, nor does Lord Eltanin. As for who does know—your mother, Tobin, Chay, Ostvel, Riyan—but Sorin and Andry and Maarken don't, and neither does Andrade. We funnel some of the gold to Prince Davvi's crafters at High Kirat, but he doesn't know the source either."

"Not even my mother's own brother?"

"No. Fifty people is too many, Pol. It's not that I don't trust the others, but unless they have a real reason to know, it's better and safer if they don't." He sighed and stretched his shoulders. "And now that you know the background, I can tell you the rest. These caves won't last. The dragons haven't been here in Goddess knows how long, and they won't ever come near the place again. People have swarmed all over it for too long."

"But what about the Hatching Hunts at Rivenrock?"

"That was a single day every three years. These caves have been worked almost every day for over thirty. The other side of the canyon is played out. This side has only a few caves like this one left."

"There's Rivenrock, though, isn't there? We could—

oh!'' Pol sat up straighter. ''The dragons need those caves!''

''And they won't ever return if we do there what's been done here. Ideally, we'll be able to lure them back somehow, and work the caves they use now, north of here.''

''Near Feruche,'' Pol said.

''Yes.'' A handful of sand was clenched in strong fingers. The topaz and emerald ring spat fire. ''Your mother wants me to rebuild the castle there. It looks as if I may have to.''

Something about his tone of voice warned Pol not to ask why he was so reluctant to talk about Feruche. ''But, Father, we can't touch those caves either, or the dragons won't have anyplace to hatch. They won't go back to Rivenrock, and that's the only place with enough caves to make sure of a large population of dragons.''

''So you see, Pol, learning is easy and making things work is hard.'' Dusting off his hands, he got to his feet. ''And now you know all about the dragons and their gold. I didn't want to worry you with it so soon, but. . . .'' He finished with a shrug.

''Are you sorry you had to tell me?''

''No. Better to have one more good brain at work on the problem. Our difficulties aren't immediate, after all. Ostvel estimates another eight to ten years before these caves are emptied. We'll think of something by then.''

''We'd better,'' Pol said, rising. He tossed the shard back into the cave and started for its mouth, then turned back as Rohan cleared his throat. ''Don't tell me there's even more to talk about?''

''No, just a little something you've forgotten.'' He pointed at the thin finger-flame still hovering above the sand.

Embarrassed, Pol dampened the Fire with his mind.

''It's a good thing we agreed not to tell Andrade,'' Rohan added. ''You'd *never* live it down!''

* * *

Far from the caves of dragon gold, Lady Andrade was enjoying the last of a perfect day. The gold she saw around her was a misted glow of sunset that turned the sea to ripples of tawny velvet. She had loosened her hair down her back and shoulders like a young girl's, and the soft breeze through her windows stirred the silver-gilt strands around her face. Like all *faradh'im,* she was a creature of sunlight; winter storms and fog oppressed her spirit. But now, with the wealth of spring around her and the promise of summer in the air, she felt truly alive again.

Leaning one shoulder against the stone framing the window, she folded her arms and sighed with pleasure as the sun flushed warmth through her bones and across her cheeks. Her morbid winter murmurings about age and death were forgotten; she always felt that way when rain-clouds darkened the sky. But the last chills had been warmed from her muscles and blood stirred fresh and strong in her veins again. She chuckled and she swore she'd outlive them all.

It had been an interesting day, and for two people in the keep it would be an even more interesting night. The youth Sejast had been tested that morning for his first ring, and nearly called up a bonfire. But he had neither blushed nor stammered out an apology for his lack of control. He was strong and he knew it. Andrade looked forward to teaching him the fine art of restraint over the next years; she had done it before with young men and women even more gifted than he and even more eager to explore their powers. But she had to admit that his arrogance—that was the only word for it—found its match in Andry alone.

Or in herself, basic honesty compelled her to acknowledge. She chuckled again, wondering how her long-ago teachers had managed to keep from throttling her. She almost wished she was still young enough to have Sejast's man-making night for herself, for she knew she could go a long way toward taming him. But she trusted to Morwenna's skills in the matter. A Sunrunner of eight rings and thirty-five winters, Morwenna had enough Fire in her to scorch even young Sejast quite nicely.

A soft knock at her door turned her head from the vista of sunset over the sea, and she called, "Come in, Urival. It's open." But it was not her chief steward who entered; rather, as if conjured by her thoughts, Morwenna hob-

THE STAR SCROLL 161

bled into the room. She looked vastly irritated and in a
fair degree of pain. Andrade went to her at once, demanding, "What happened? Here, come sit down."

"Thank you, my Lady. What happened? Stupidest
thing in the world." She sank into a chair and slapped a
palm against her thigh in disgust. "I tripped over my own
shadow is what happened. You know that bad step in the
library that everybody avoids? Well, in avoiding it I
stumbled and fell. I'm afraid you'll have to send someone
else to Sejast tonight."

"I hope you've had your injury treated by now."

"Of course, Nothing broken, just bruised. But it hurts
something fierce." She raked black hair from her eyes.
"The Goddess might lend me her spell for the night, but
I doubt even she could disguise this." She hiked up her
skirt to show the livid mark on her dark skin. "Spectacular, isn't it?"

"Very. You're lucky you didn't break anything. Well,
tell me who you'd send in your place."

Morwenna settled her skirt once more and leaned back.
"I regret the lost chance, believe me. He'll be a difficult
one to manage and I was looking forward to it." She
grinned as Andrade gave a snort. Even for a hot-blooded
Fironese, Morwenna's wholehearted enjoyment of making boys into men was nearly scandalous. "Jobyna's too
tame, Vessie isn't quite secure enough in the art for
someone as perceptive as Sejast seems to be. I'd send
Fenice but she's at the wrong point in her cycle. Eridin
would do for him, and I think Hollis is capable, if she
isn't moping about Maarken today."

"Hmm." Andrade sat down and tapped her fingers
against the arms of her chair. "Have you seen Hollis and
Sejast in each other's company?"

"No more than the other *faradh'im* associate with
newcomers. They've spoken, surely. But the Goddess
takes care of secrecy."

"The Goddess," Andrade responded dryly, "trusts us
to use our wits. I don't trust people who know each other
well—"

"Oh, come now! Of the five it could have been for
me, I'd grown up with three of them right here at the

keep, the fourth was my tutor, and the fifth was someone I'd planted the whole herb garden with that spring! And *I* never knew which of them it really was.''

"Point taken," Andrade conceded. "It'll be Hollis then, I suppose. Is the time right for her?''

"She's safe. But I'll admit I'm curious about what kind of children might come of that boy. If he hasn't already left one or two behind him." She chuckled.

"That's a bet not even Sioned would take," Andrade agreed. "Go put a compress on that leg. I'll have your dinner sent up to you.''

Morwenna sighed. "Not exactly the evening I'd had planned. But no matter. Shall I go tell Hollis?''

"I'll do it. You get your weight off that gorgeous bruise." Andrade smiled. "And I promise to have the step fixed.''

"It'd be a help. There's nothing to be done about my clumsiness." She grimaced as she got to her feet and limped out.

Andrade's fingers continued to drum an ever-changing rhythm. If Hollis *was* lost in fancies about Maarken—well, that was too bad. She was not his wife yet. And she was, and would always be, a Sunrunner. She had worked the spell two or three times since her outrageous disobedience in going to Maarken for his man-making night, and Andrade was reasonably sure he knew about those times. But a woman's body was her own, even when her heart had been given. Hollis was not even Maarken's official Chosen yet. The girl knew her duty as a Sunrunner.

As she braided her hair before leaving her chambers to find Hollis, Andrade was aware that it was not so much the girl's suitability for the task that made her Andrade's choice as it was this possibly last chance to remind her of her commitment to Goddess Keep. Andrade was prepared to see another of her *faradh'im* married to a royal lord—but she was damned if she'd see another Sunrunner remove every ring but the one her husband had given her. Hollis would do her duty. She would not be another Sioned.

* * *

Segev volunteered to take Morwenna's dinner up to her. It was the least he could do after engineering her fall.

It had been laughably easy to arrange. She always went to the library for an hour or two of study before the evening meal, preparing her notes for the next day's classes. The faulty step had been his ally; everyone made the same movement to avoid it, and slicking the next one just enough to upset balance had done the trick. He had experimented the night before, careful not to succumb to his own ploy, then wiped the wood clean. This afternoon he had waited for Morwenna's regular visit, and after she limped out, cursing under her breath, had emerged from his hiding place to blot up the traces of oil. The telltale cloth had been thrown down the cliff where the tide would carry it out to sea. No one had seen him, no one suspected that the accident was no accident, and he sat down to dinner with perfect unconcern.

Hollis was missing from her usual seat, and that was a good sign. But neither were Jobyna or Eridin present, and that was bad. Of course, he was taking a chance that someone other than Hollis would take Morwenna's place tonight, but the golden-haired Sunrunner was only his preferred choice. Any of the others would have done just as well, though none were as pretty. It amused him that instinct had turned him to the Chosen lady of Lord Maarken, cousin to the boy who might lose Princemarch by the *Rialla* and who would certainly lose the Desert itself in a few years. Segev was increasingly committed to the notion that he and not his eldest brother Ruval would oust Pol from Stronghold, but it depended on proving himself to Mireva. He went upstairs early, tired of pretending embarrassment at the unsubtle jests of his companions. They were jealous. He had a new chamber all to himself, and a new status signified by the plain silver ring on his right middle finger, earned before any of them had called so much as a fleeting spark of Fire. He escaped their teasing as soon as he could and went upstairs to explore his new surroundings.

He had been too young when Feruche fell to recall the luxuries there, but something in him hungered for beautiful things: silk sheets, thick carpets, tapestries, elegant furniture, and huge rooms to display it all in. His new chamber had none of those things. There was a narrow bed, a small table beside it, an empty brazier, and a small chest for clothes. On the bedside table was a basin for washing and a plain pottery jar he had filled with wine that morning. Now he laced it liberally with *dranath* and sipped a little himself, relishing the unmistakable glow it brought to his body.

Segev lay down naked in bed and mimed sleep. But as time passed he grew impatient, wondering if they'd forgotten about him. How did other youths behave when they knew it was to be their man-making night? He was nervous, but not in the ways they would have been. Every step outside in the hallway quickened his pulse, yet his door stayed closed. The darkness thickened in his windowless chamber and the sheets began to chafe him. He turned onto his left side, then his right, threw the sheets to the floor and dragged them back up again.

Something had gone wrong, he was sure of it. The old bitch Andrade had become suspicious. Someone had discovered traces of grease on the step. His disguise had been penetrated. They were about to drag him out of bed and use all their arts to make him tell everything he knew about Mireva and the stone circle in the forest and—

A crack of light appeared around his door, defining it as a tall rectangle. He sat bolt upright in bed, sweat clogging his hair and skin. Someone entered—no, some*thing,* a glimmering mist without colors, so pallid as to be almost transparent. The door became darkness again, blending into the greater night, but the subtle formless glow glided toward him, casting neither light nor shadow. He tried to still his pounding heart as he felt a gentle finger run softly across his lips. He had not been this agitated with Mireva, nor with the peasant girl to whom he'd lost his virginity at the age of thirteen.

He was on fire.

The hazy light drifted closer and he reached up, his arms closing around a slender female form. Tremors shot through him and he gasped. Pulling her down beside him, he forgot Mireva, his brothers, the reason he was at Goddess Keep—everything. He knew only the dizzying fragrance of her, the suppleness of her, the ancient implicit challenge of her flesh whispering against his own.

Their first coupling spent him quickly. He lay back panting, drenched in sweat, humiliated that he had not lasted longer. A vague memory of Mireva in her youthful guise flickered across his memory; why had she never told him how powerful *faradhi* magic was in this act? The woman, whoever she was, existed only as a faint luminous glow. His fingers could touch her, but he could not identify the shape of nose and brow and mouth, the contours of breasts and hips that would tell him who she was. He could not see the color of the hair cascading around him. He hoped it was golden, and that it was Hollis in his arms, but could not bring himself to care if it was not; her lips were teaching him things not even Mireva had known, bringing him to life again when he had feared the night might be over for him.

He was given longer to recover the second time. Having acquitted himself with better skill, and prepared for the blinding pleasure of her body, he regained his breath and presence of mind sooner. He reached for her hands, trying to feel the number of rings. But there were none, and that frightened him. Shock cleared his head. Real Sunrunners were not even supposed to be curious about who had come to them. He must make no more mistakes. He must remembered what he had to do.

Segev opened his mouth to suggest they have some wine—and discovered he could not make a sound. He knew his own voice had echoed the woman's cries of pleasure, but now his tongue felt strange and thick in his mouth, his lips seemed numb, and his throat closed up, nearly choking him. Truly scared now, he wrenched away from soothing hands and fell to his knees beside the low bed, clutching tumbled sheets in both fists. She was a dream, nothing more than a pale ghost without definition or identity. If *faradhi* powers were this formidable—he reached for the wine and swallowed two large gulps, needing the *dranath* to replenish his courage.

Her fingers closed around his and she took the pottery jug from him. She drank deeply. Segev's hand slipped as she gave the jug back and wine spilled onto his knees. He heard a whimsical, misted laugh from very far away as she coaxed him back up onto the bed.

When the morning chime sounded outside in the hall,

he woke with a spasm of terror. She was gone. He was limp and exhausted, barely able to roll onto his side and sit up. Carefully he called a little Fire into the brazier and by its light inspected the wine jar. Most of the liquid was gone.

Had he gulped down too much? Had she swallowed enough? Anger burned along his tired nerves and he swore aloud. Why hadn't Mireva warned him that Sunrunner arts were so potent?

He drained off the last of the drugged wine and lay back, gradually relaxing as it did its work. Perhaps Mireva had not known; perhaps he was now in a position to learn things she would never know. Perhaps, using such things, he could easily take Ruval's place when it came time to defeat Prince Pol.

Perhaps Segev no longer needed Mireva at all.

Today he would go to the tree circle in the forest and seek his future in the Fire. The original plan had been that he only go through the motions, but he decided that he would indeed summon the magic—for if other things *faradhi* were as powerful as what had occurred last night, he might see things even Mireva could not.

The Sunrunners had taught him all the ritual words and all the correct things to do. He had paid attention for curiosity's sake, for he had never intended to carry out the private ceremony in fact. But now he jumped from the bed and dressed in haste, eager to find out if the *faradh'im* possessed other, equally potent, spells. Combined with what Mireva had taught him he could—

Suddenly he stood still, his hands on the door latch. He would not be going to the forest as a true Sunrunner. In his *diarmadhi* blood throbbed an herb they feared as nothing else in the world. If the spell around the woman last night had been that of the Goddess Mireva had always taught him to deny, then was it possible that there might be vengeance on him for what he had done—and for what he planned to do?

He made himself open the door, shrugging off his superstitious fears. He had succeeded thus far. There was no reason to suppose he would not succeed with everything.

And he began to believe that he could have powers

even greater than those Mireva possessed. He could take Princemarch and the Desert for his own, and become High Prince like his grandsire.

With Hollis at his side? He reminded himself to watch her and Jobyna and Eridin closely today for signs of *dranath* intake. He went downstairs smiling.

Chapter Ten

Sioned frowned with concentration, weighing the flat stone in her palm. Her audience waited nearby— Sionell holding her breath, Pol sorting through his own collection of rocks, and Walvis grinning as he stroked his neat black beard. The Lord of Remagev gestured invitingly to the calm surface of the lake. Sioned angled her arm carefully and sent the stone skimming out over the water.

"Eleven, twelve, thirteen, fourteen!" Sionell cried excitedly. "Can you make it skip that many times, Papa?"

"Easy as sliding down a sand dune," he assured her. He sent a rock flying out across the lake, and his daughter counted off fifteen tiny splashes before it sank. "Best three out of four?" he challenged Sioned.

As they gathered up suitable stones, Pol and Sionell tried their hand at skipping rocks. The older pair exchanged smiles as Sionell made six on her first try and Pol only two.

"Like this," Sionell said, giving instruction that Pol accepted with poor grace. "Watch me do it." A moment later she called out, "Eight! I got eight!"

Sioned turned in time to see Pol's second try. The stone he sailed struck the water three times, then vanished.

"Try again," Sionell urged.

"No, thanks."

The little girl gave him a disgusted look. "How're you going to learn if you won't even try? You can't be good at *everything* the first time you do it, you know."

Sioned caught Walvis' eye and they waited while Pol

engaged in an internal struggle that was plain on his face. Pride won—not unusual at that age. He shook his head and piled all his selected stones into his mother's palms.

"I'll practice some other time."

Sioned and Walvis lined up for their competition. Her first stone skipped twelve times, as did his; her second made sixteen splashes. Walvis groaned as his own second try brought only ten.

"Best five out of seven?" he ventured hopefully.

"A deal's a deal," she retorted, and flicked her wrist. The stone skipped fourteen times and Sionell applauded.

Walvis glared down at his daughter in mock affront. "Whose side are you on?" he demanded, and she giggled. He let fly his third stone. "Twelve, thirteen, fourteen, fifteen—"

All at once a shadow swooped down, wings stirring a ripple of breeze across the water. A blue-black dragon dipped his hind claws into the water, beat the air with powerful strokes, and craned his neck around as he rose into the sky. His snarl of frustration echoed around the crater.

"He thought it was a fish!" Pol exclaimed, laughing. "Look at them all!"

A flight of about forty three-year-old dragons settled in on the far shore for a drink. Wings folded gracefully, long necks bent to the water, they paused as the one who had mistaken a skipped stone for a fish arrived late. He was jostled from side to side and they sang out in derision as he snarled again.

"Walvis," Sioned murmured, "I could swear they're making fun of him."

"I was thinking the same thing. Do dragons have a sense of humor?" He closed one hand on his daughter's shoulder as she moved at his side. "No, you may *not* go closer to look," he ordered.

"But they wouldn't hurt me! They're so beautiful!"

"And they've got teeth half as long as your arm. We'll watch from here and hope they're feeling friendly." He cast a worried glance at Sioned, sharing her thought; they must stay still and not attract the dragons' attention, for stories abounded of people who had been plucked from the ground by dragons when they attempted to run away.

Sionell squirmed. "They've already eaten, Papa. Look at their stomachs."

She was correct; bellies usually lean before a meal were rounded, and a few of the dragons even paused in their drinking to belch. Sioned wondered how many sheep and goats had gone to feed this hoard, and reminded herself to ask Rohan again about cultivating herds for the dragons' sole use.

Thirst quenched, some of the dragons bounded into the air. They flew to a tremendous height, then folded their wings and plunged straight down into the water. Diving, rolling, flinging water at each other with sweeping wings, calling out to the ones onshore, they resembled nothing so much as playful children.

"You see?" Sionell said. "They wouldn't hurt anybody. Besides," she added slyly, "I'm not a princess, and everybody knows dragons prefer princesses!"

"Hush," Walvis said, tightening his grip on her shoulder.

Sioned looked at her son. Enchanted love was in his eyes—exactly the expression that shone on his father's face when dragons were around. The gold mattered nothing to either of them; they loved the dragons as part of the Desert, part of their blood.

Eventually the creatures climbed out of the water to sun themselves. Sioned admired the varied hues of their water-glistening hides, each dragon a different color. She picked out a reddish one, smaller than the rest, who shook diamond-drops from her wings. Sioned watched for a moment, wondering if she dared. Dragons definitely had a sense of fun, and she knew they had thought-colors. She threaded a few strands of sunlight together, cautiously extending the silken gold weave toward the little dragon.

The female arched her neck, fanning out her wings with their dainty golden undersides, and shook her head to clear her eyes of the water still trickling down her face. Her head turned questioningly and she shifted her shoulders, tucking her wings back along her body. Sioned displayed her own colors—emerald, sapphire, onyx, amber—and their pattern, long engraved in her memory. The dragon tossed her head, droplets spraying out as she shook herself all over. Sioned sought a closer contact and the dragon whined through her long nose, shivering a little.

Suddenly the sunlight exploded into a rainbow of color. Sioned cried out at the same time the little dragon threw back her head with a howl of terror. All the other dragons sprang up into the sky, keening a chorus of fear and warning as they fled.

"Mother!"

Pol tried to hold her up as she crumpled, Walvis and Sionell right beside him to cushion her fall. Sioned gulped in several breaths, trembling all over with the shock, and managed a faint smile for her ashen-cheeked son.

"I'm fine," she whispered.

"The dragons aren't," Walvis said grimly. "Listen to them."

The wild music echoed down from the cluster of dark shapes in the sky. Sioned pushed herself upright and winced.

"I was too clumsy. I frightened her."

"What are you talking about?" Walvis demanded. "My lady, what did you do?"

Pol, kneeling at her side, answered. "She used the sunlight to touch a dragon."

* * *

"You did *what?*"

Rohan's eyes blazed down at the woman who sat sipping iced taze as casually as if she'd just returned from an afternoon stroll around the lake.

"Please stop scolding. You can't say anything I haven't accused myself of."

"When I asked if you could touch a dragon, I didn't mean for you to risk your life at it!"

"I'll be more careful next time."

"There isn't going to be a next time." He crossed to the windows of their chamber and looked out at the quiet water. "We heard your scream all the way from Threadsilver."

"Mine, or the dragon's?"

"Weren't they one and the same?" he countered.

That gave her pause. "You may be right," she admitted.

Rohan swung around. "You *faradh'im* talk about being shadow-lost. What if you got lost inside a dragon's colors and couldn't remember your own? It would amount to the same thing, wouldn't it?"

"But that didn't happen."

"This time!"

She set her goblet down and folded her hands in her lap. "You're thinking about forbidding me to try again, aren't you?"

"I'm thinking about having you swear a promise," he corrected.

Sioned bit her lip. "I've never lied to you—"

"But you omit things when it serves your purposes. Oh, you're far too honest to lie—and far too clever to put yourself in a position where you'd have to. After twenty-one years of living with you, my lady, I know you very well indeed."

She said nothing.

"Sioned, there are too many ways I could lose you just in the normal course of things. I won't add another to the list just because of my stupid notion about dragons. It won't do me any good to forbid you outright, and we both know it. I won't make you promise, either. But that means I'll have to trust to your good sense—and to the fact that you want to see your son grow up."

She flinched. "That wasn't fair, Rohan!"

"No," he agreed. "But neither are your little omissions."

She glared at him. "Very well, I'll make you a promise. I won't try it again unless Maarken is with me to back me up and set my colors again if I start to lose them."

"The way you did for Tobin, the night she was caught in the Moonrunning?"

"Yes. I knew her colors and I could bring her back. I promise I won't touch a dragon again without being in the same kind of contact with Maarken. Will that content you, my lord?"

"It'll have to, I suppose." He folded his arms. "You're a dangerous woman, High Princess."

"No more so than you're a dangerous man, High Prince." She smiled a little. "That makes us very well mated, doesn't it?"

Rohan snorted.

* * *

Dragon shrieks woke everyone in the middle of the night. Rohan and Sioned threw on their clothes and hurried to the courtyard, where the entire population of Skybowl had assembled by torchlight, confused and more than a little frightened. Ostvel, sleep-rumpled and worried, shouldered through the crowd to Rohan.

"I've never heard them scream like that at this time of night! What do you think is going on?" He winced as another high-pitched howl split the air. "Goddess! Listen to that! What's the matter with them?"

"I don't know," Rohan replied, glancing around. "Where's Pol? Sioned, do you see him?"

"No—and if he's run outside to watch dragons, so help me I'll blister his backside for him! Walvis!" she called out, catching sight of Remagev's lord. "Have you seen Pol?"

He mounted a few steps and scanned the crowd, then shook his head. "Nor Maarken, either."

Chay and Tobin arrived in time to hear this, and the latter asked Sioned, "You don't think *they* tried to touch a dragon, do you?"

Sioned paled. "They couldn't be so foolish! Pol!" she called out. "Pol!"

"Up here, Mother!"

He and Maarken stood on the gatehouse balcony with several of the Skybowl guard. All eyes turned to them as Rohan shouted, "What are you doing up there? Come down at once!"

"But we're watching the dragons, Father! They're fighting on the shore!"

"I want to see, too!" Sionell squirmed out of Feylin's arms and raced for the gatehouse steps.

Rohan turned to Ostvel. "Get everybody indoors. They can watch if they like, but nobody is to set foot outside the walls until those sires have had it out with each other. They're likely to attack anything that moves."

"At once, my lord. But I've never known them to do battle at this time of night before"

The moons rode high in the sky, illuminating the lake in pale silver. From the thin windows of the gatehouse two dragons could be seen halfway around the lake, highlighted by gleaming teeth and talons. Wings were folded close to lithe shapes as the sires roared defiance, heads lashing out to rip at already bleeding hides. Adolescent dragons lined the crater's lip, watching; in three years they, too, would fight to the death for possession of females.

Pol had helped Sionell up into a window embrasure, steadying her with an arm around her waist. Neither of them noticed the entrance of their elders until Feylin plucked her daughter from her precarious position and held her firmly away from the open casement.

"I wasn't going to fall," Sionell complained. "Pol was holding onto me."

"For which he has my thanks," Feylin replied. "but you'll stay away from the window, my girl."

Pol joined his parents, standing on a stone shelf where, in times of war, archers knelt to loose arrows through the narrow openings. "Which one do you think will win?"

Both dragons were injured now, one holding his left foreleg at an awkward angle, painful to see. They took their battle to the air then, startling the audience of three-year-olds who fluttered their wings in reaction. The fighting dragons circled each other, snapping with blood-darkened jaws and slashing with claws and tails. Grunts of effort and impact resounded across the crater as they pummeled each other. The darker dragon rose high above his rival and for a moment everyone thought he had given up the field. But then he plummeted directly down, all talons and teeth digging into his enemy's back.

The wounded sire bellowed his pain and fury, losing command of the air and his own wings as his attacker's tail slammed across the main bones of his left wing with a crack audible even in the gatehouse. Someone moaned in sympathy. The pair fell toward shore, where the defeated dragon would surely be crushed to death on the stony ground. Yet he retained wit and strength enough to angle his fall, and the two dragons landed with a mighty splash in the water.

The victor stroked upward, calling out his triumph as his vanquished foe rolled in the water, vainly trying to work his shattered wing. The adolescents flew off after the winner, leaving the mortally wounded sire to die.

Rohan was down the gatehouse stairs before anyone but Sioned and Pol noticed he was gone. He was panting for breath when he got to the lakeshore. Pale moonlight shone on water stained dark with blood. The dragon's feeble swimming motions grew weaker. His efforts had nearly brought him to shore, but even if he reached dry ground, he was going to die. Rohan saw in the huge dark eyes that the dragon knew it. Yet he did not give up the struggle, did not cease trying. Rohan's chest ached and he felt the sting of tears in his eyes.

"I'm sorry," he whispered. "I'm so sorry."

He heard the others running to catch up with him, felt Sioned's touch on his arm. "Can we help him?" she asked.

He shook his head. "His wing is gone, and he's lost too much blood."

"Father—please," Pol said softly. "Look at his eyes."

"Can't we at least put him out of his pain?" Sioned held his arm tighter.

The dragon moaned. The sound was echoed by dragon voices, scores of them from beyond Skybowl's rim, mourning him. The night sky was empty of wings, but dragon song swelled and shuddered as if borne on wind created by their beating.

Rohan said thickly, "Bring me a sword."

"No," Chay murmured. "You swore never again, my prince. Never another dragon dead by your hand."

He winced as the dragon groaned again. Walvis took a step forward. "I'll do it," he said softly. "Feylin, tell me where it would be quickest."

"It's not necessary," Sioned told him. "Maarken, you ought to learn this. Come with me."

They went to the water's edge. The dragon cried out, a whimper of pain as his failing body reached the sandy shallows, cool water lapping around him. Sioned crooned to him in a low voice, barely two arm-lengths from the lolling head. With Maarken as her loom, she wove threads of moonlight into a pallid silver weave across the dragon's eyes. The huge body shivered; she and Maarken trembled, too. The dragon's eyes closed. After a time the rigidity of pain left muscles and torn flesh. His face relaxed, the great lungs heaved in a long sigh, and he slept.

Sioned turned. "He's at peace now, I think."

"Mother—did you touch him?" Pol breathed.

"No. I only helped him to sleep."

Tobin nodded slowly. "Andrade used to do the same thing, Rohan—do you remember? When we were little."

Sioned nodded confirmation. "It's something learned with the eighth ring."

"But you—" Chay stopped, frowned, and shrugged. "I'm not going to ask. I've seen you do too many things you shouldn't be able to."

"And some of them things Andrade doesn't know about," Sioned finished. "Did you learn how, Maarken? And did you feel his colors?"

"I understood the weaving sequence," he answered. "I saw a whole rainbow of color. Fading. It can be done, Sioned. It's only a question of when, and which dragon."

Rohan went to the animal's head, stroked the long neck where life beat slower and slower. He had never touched a live dragon before, never been so close to one. The hide was smooth and cool, dark green shading to brown in the moonlight. His fingertips traced the proud lines of brow and nose and angle of jaw. Very lightly he touched the eyelids, feeling how silky-soft they were. Beautiful, even in death.

He looked over his shoulder at his wife and murmured, "Thank you."

* * *

Two days later, Pol leaned over a map spread out on the carpet, desultorily tracing the route his father, Chay, Ostvel, and Walvis were now following to Tiglath in the north. He made a glum face, still disappointed that he had not been allowed to go with them. The reason given had been Tiglath's proximity to possible Merida haunts—but Pol suspected that they all thought him too young. He would be fifteen before winter's end, but they still considered him a child. It was galling.

But he *had* been permitted to attend the planning sessions, as fascinated by the debate on tactics as he had been by the changes in people familiar to him since infancy. Father, aunt, uncle, cousin, and friends vanished. They became the High Prince, a warrior princess, and the *athr'im* of Radzyn, Whitecliff, Skybowl, and Remagev. Even his mother had shed her role of co-sovereign, becoming nothing more than Sunrunner to the High Prince. Enlightening as the military talk had been, Pol had found the assumption of formal roles even more educational. He would have to learn how to do that, he decided—how to submerge his own personality into the responsibilities of his position.

In some ways, Tobin's had been the most startling transformation. Pol's laughing, warm-voiced aunt had spoken with real relish about the possibilities of conquering Cunaxa should that princedom be so foolish as to invade Firon. Lines of advance, probable body-counts, razing the Cunaxan seat of Castle Pine, slaughtering every Merida in existence—Tobin was intimately familiar with all the ways of war. Her cheerful ruthlessness had amused him at first, then scared him when he realized she meant every last word of it. But it finally struck him as being her perfect role in the debate. She was dedicated to the advancement of the Desert's interests—even though her ideas for that advancement were more than a trifle bloodthirsty. She represented her father's point of view; Prince Zehava had liked nothing so much as a good, clean battle that won him added lands as well as added glory.

As Pol listened, it had become clear that his own father was surrounded by people of differing viewpoints who never hesitated to speak their minds. Pol hoped that when it came his turn, he would hear the same advice as freely given. Moreover, Rohan was in complete control of the debate, though he rarely spoke and then only to steer the conversation back to its major concerns. The decisions would be his alone, and everyone knew it. They would argue their own points of view, but it never occurred to any of these powerful people to question Rohan's authority. Pol was awed by this quiet proof of his father's power.

The calling-up of the Desert levies and selected troops from Princemarch had been deliberately casual, designed to alarm no one. Chay explained it as an exercise that would acquaint soldiers from both princedoms with each other's techniques. He proposed that the following year a similar exercise might take place in the mountains so that troops accustomed to the Desert could get a feel for what another kind of warfare might be like.

Skybowl was not equipped to support a large influx of troops, and thus an assembly point had been established at the old garrison below the ruins of Feruche Castle. Pol looked on the map at each Desert holding and the places from which the soldiers of Princemarch would be called, and whistled under his breath at the total of three hundred foot, half that number of archers, and two hundred horse. "Enough to be impressive, but not quite enough to provoke," had been Maarken's conclusion.

Pol could imagine the camp that would soon be set upon the rocky plain outside Tiglath's walls. Tents, cook-fires, the spears and swords of the foot soldiers leaning outside the tents in deadly array; horses picketed within easy reach of their riders; bows unstrung and arrows kept carefully in leather quivers. The double-tailed battle flags of all the Desert holdings would be presided over by Walvis' blue-and-white banner with a golden dragon atop the staff that signified his status as the High Prince's commander in the north. Princemarch's violet would be in evidence, too, with the Desert blue atop it. There would be marching and swordplay, competitions between archers, riders practicing the charges and maneuvers necessary in war. All of it called out to a boy's restless imagination, making him yearn to go and watch even if he could not really be a part of it as a working soldier.

Pol sighed. Almost everyone had ridden out with Walvis and Skybowl's levy. Rohan and Chay would return in ten days or so after showing support for Walvis and meeting with some of the people from Princemarch. Ostvel would be gone longer on a visit to Lord Abidias of Tuath, then swing back by Tiglath and bring word of the camp to Rohan at Skybowl. Only a fraction of the troops available from the Desert and Princemarch would take the field for maneuvers, but Pol desperately wanted just a glimpse of what was going on.

A rebellious part of him said that if he wanted to look,

he could. He was a Sunrunner—not trained yet, of course, but he knew he could weave the light if he tried, glide along its pathways to Tiglath. And oh, how he wanted to—but he didn't let himself think about it too much. He had responsibilities. He could not do it. But he wanted to.

His finger drew little circles on the map as he vowed that once he was older, no one would be able to make him stay put when he wanted to be somewhere else. At least if he was denied the fun and excitement of the summer's encampment, he would be doing something almost as interesting. His finger left Tiglath and touched the little symbol indicating the location of Castle Crag, high in the Veresch on the Faolain River.

There was no definite route planned for the progress. They would wander as fancy took them. The only certainty on their itinerary was that Princess Pandsala expected them at Castle Crag in time for a long visit before going to Waes and the *Rialla*. Pol had seen the Veresch Mountains from a great distance, faraway purple peaks crowned in white snow—an element he wasn't entirely sure he believed in. Dorval's mountainous region never saw snow. He had almost decided that seeing such marvels as pine forests, lakes, meadows, wide rivers, and especially snow was as good as spending the summer soldiering.

"Here you are!"

Pol looked up. Sionell had a positively uncanny knack for finding him. "Good afternoon," he said politely.

"Jahnavi and I are going riding. Do you want to come?"

"No, but thank you for asking."

Sionell gave a shrug and sat in a nearby chair. "Why is Riyan a Sunrunner if his father isn't?"

"For the same reason Maarken is and *his* father isn't."

"Or you and your father," she said, nodding. "Does it always come from the mother's side?"

"Nobody knows where it comes from." He began rolling up the map. "My grandmother's father was *faradhi*, even though he was never trained, and his wife didn't show any signs of it at all. One of their children was Lady

Andrade, who's more powerful than anybody—and the other was my grandmother, Princess Milar.''

"And Princess Tobin is, but your father isn't. And *her* children are, and aren't. It's very confusing!'' She smiled. "You are, though. Do you think you'll be as good at it as your mother is?''

"I hope so.''

"I'd like to be a Sunrunner and touch a dragon.''

"That's not what being a Sunrunner is about.'' He got to his feet, the map back in its case. "Being a *faradhi* is—''

She interrupted, "But you *want* to touch a dragon on sunlight, don't you?''

Pol turned away from the shrewd blue eyes. "None of your business,'' he muttered.

"You do, too. I can tell. I know all kinds of things about you that you don't want me to know.''

"Such as?'' He swung around.

Sionell gave him a pert grin. "I'm not telling!''

"You'd better!''

She jumped up from the chair and ran laughing out the door. Pol dropped the map and raced after her, catching up on the stairs. He made a grab for her elbow but she eluded him.

"Sionell! Tell me!''

"I won't—not until you promise to come riding with us!''

"You are the most impossible brat ever born!''

"I'm not a brat!''

"You are, too. And see if I care about things you probably don't know, anyway.'' He turned to go back to his room.

"Pol—I *do* know something! I know that you want to touch the dragons so you can talk to them and tell them it's safe to go back to Rivenrock!''

He whirled and stared at her. "How did you know that?''

"Because it's exactly what I'd do if I was a Sunrunner.''

He looked down at her pudgy little face, the beginnings of respect sneaking up on him. "Would you? Do you understand about the dragons?''

"My mother's been studying dragons for years and years. She knows more about them than anybody. We talk about dragons all the time."

Pol heard himself say, "There's a lot I don't know about them. Maybe you could teach me."

Sionell glowed with happiness for a moment, then recalled her pride and looked down at her toes, kicking at the step above her. "Maybe I could—if you're nicer to me. You're really a pain sometimes, you know that?"

"Sorry." He tried to think up something else to say. She saved him the necessity by smiling shyly up at him. Someday, he thought unexpectedly, she might even turn out to be pretty. Even more surprisingly, he was about to tell her so when the walls of Skybowl shuddered. "What in all hells is that?" he blurted.

"Listen."

"Are the dragons fighting again?"

"Can't you hear the difference?" she scoffed.

"They don't sound angry," he ventured.

"Of course not. They're mating."

* * *

Sioned and Maarken had spent the last two days with Feylin, who was in the lengthy process of dissecting the dragon. At first the bloody project made both Sunrunners a little ill. Fascination soon replaced squeamishness. And, too, there was something exquisite about the fit of bone to bone, the discovery of how muscles worked, the elegant configurations of flight, that overcame a tendency to queasy stomachs.

Feylin had a sincere respect for dragons and regretted violating this one in death. But her curiosity was stronger. She reported her findings to two scribes, each of whom relied on Sioned's memory to supply what they sometimes missed. Maarken skillfully produced drawings as Feylin dictated to the scribes. His renditions of the delicate interlinking of muscle and bone in the wings were works of art. Other servants were busy building a rocky pyre for the dragon's remains, which were placed there when Feylin was done describing them and Maarken had finished his drawings.

"The brain is twice the size of ours, but without so many curves and ridges to it," she reported, holding the mass of gray material in both hands. "It's also much larger in the back where it meets the spine, and not as developed in the front regions—"

"Wait," Sioned protested. "When did you ever see a human brain?"

Feylin cleared her throat and looked guilty. "Well . . . my mother was a physician. She liked to find out how things worked."

"But how—?"

"One day she found a man lying dead in the hills— there wasn't any way to identify him, no one to claim him—we gave him a decent burning afterward," she finished defensively.

Maarken glanced up from his sketchpad, eyes wide. Sioned gulped, shook her head, and murmured, "I'm sorry I asked. Go on, Feylin."

Brain, eyes, tongue, teeth, nasal structure—all of it was measured and defined for the scribes and then placed before Maarken to be drawn. Over the last two days Feylin had systematically examined the huge corpse—legs, stomach, lungs, wings, chest cavity, and heart. One of the scribes, who had lasted through a detailed description of the dragon's last meal after an exploration of the stomach's contents, finally balked at a lengthy discourse on the eyes. He threw down his parchment and pen, staggered over to the lake, and was violently sick. Sioned took his place, scribbling for all she was worth, and told herself firmly that High Princesses did *not* throw up in public.

"Maarken, you're as green-faced as a pregnant girl," Feylin said suddenly.

"There's blood and then there's blood," he said. "It's different from battle blood."

"Carving up a dragon for study is worse than carving up your enemies?"

"It's different," he maintained stubbornly.

"He has a point, you know," Sioned observed. "How would you like it if somebody sliced *you* up into your component parts?"

"I'd mind plenty if I was still alive! Once I'm dead, what does it matter? I have no more use for my body, after all, once I'm gone from it." Feylin placed the last section of skull on the blanket before Maarken, stretched, and went to crouch beside Sioned. "Anyway, this chance was too good to pass up."

"But it seems so—" She ended with a helpless shrug.

"How else do we learn? My mother wasn't the only physician who investigated human corpses, you know. Does a dead body mind the flames we light around it? Would it mind being poked around in?"

"Just the same, I don't want anybody doing that to me," Sioned told her.

"What if we learn something from this dragon that helps us understand the whole race better?"

"Oh, I'm not arguing with you, Feylin. And I *did* volunteer to help. But I'm afraid I can't look at it quite as calmly as you can."

"I think I know why," Maarken said. "This really isn't any different from carving up any animal we use as food. But Sioned and I have touched dragon colors. The only other creatures we can do that with are humans. And that's what makes it different."

By late afternoon they were finished, and flasks of perfumed oil were poured over the dismembered corpse. Sioned and Maarken together summoned Fire to set the remains alight, and the flames brought forth a spicy-sweet odor. The scribes and workers returned gratefully to Skybowl, leaving Sioned, Feylin, and Maarken to watch the dragon burn.

When the mating howls split the sky, all three jumped. Feylin, whose respect for dragons included a healthy fear of them, turned white; Sioned took her arm in support.

"They're only mating. You've heard that before."

"And it affects me the same way every time. It's ridiculous," she said nervously. "I can study them, count them, watch them—even cut one up to find out how he works. But something about their voices twists me up inside." She gave another start and flinched as a flight of three-year-olds burst over the southern rim of the crater. "Sweet Goddess!"

Sioned's eye was caught instantly by the little reddish female with golden underwings, the dragon she had attempted to touch before. The group had come back to the lake for another drink; neither the mating cries nor the burning corpse seemed to affect them at all. They were not old enough to comprehend or be interested in the former, and as for the latter—it was almost as if with his death, the dragon sire had been erased from their memories. Knowing she was being fanciful by projecting human emotion onto dragons, Sioned still found it incredibly sad.

Her promise to Rohan flickered across her mind and she glanced at Maarken. He returned her gaze speculatively, then nodded. Sioned made certain Feylin was all right, then went to her nephew.

"Back me up," was all she said, and at once felt the powerful sun-weaving of a trained, disciplined *faradhi* mind. His colors of ruby, amber, and diamond created a strong spectrum with her own emerald, sapphire, amber, and onyx, and the separate patterns complemented each other, her own dominant as she'd asked.

But the brilliance of their colors was as nothing to the swirling hues into which Sioned was abruptly plunged with her first tentative brush against the dragon. Rainbows rioted in her mind and she reeled with the impact, each color repeated in hundreds of shades, each carrying a sound, a vision, an impression or memory or instinct— far too much for her to grasp, let alone assimilate into recognizable form. The sheer glut of colors staggered her; the information attached to them nearly shattered her mind. Vaguely, through the rainbow storm, she sensed the dragon's withdrawal from her. Then she fainted.

"Sioned!" Maarken flung his arms around her to keep her upright, terrified by her ashen cheeks and lolling head. Well-honed skills kept her colors in strict pattern, retrieved and reformed before she fainted; there was no danger of her becoming shadow-lost. But this blank unconsciousness unnerved him.

Shaking and white-faced, Feylin helped him lower her to the ground. "Maarken, what the hell happened?"

"I don't know. I didn't see anything or touch the dragon myself—I don't know what she saw or felt." He cupped her head in one hand, slapped her cheeks gently with the other. "Sioned!"

"It can't be too bad, can it? She didn't scream like last time. Neither did the dragon." She unhooked a waterskin from her belt—that item Desert dwellers never forgot to carry no matter where they were—and made Sioned drink. The princess choked slightly, but other than a reflexive swallow she showed no signs of awakening.

Maarken saw a quick shadow and looked up. The other dragons had flown, but the reddish female remained, her underwings gleaming as she circled over the pyre. She called out, a soft whine of distress, and darted down for a closer look before rising to fly tight circles above them, whimpering.

"She's worried about Sioned," Feylin whispered. "Is that possible?"

Sioned stirred at last, shifting groggily. She made a vague warding-off gesture with one hand, then opened her eyes.

"How do you feel?" Maarken asked anxiously.

"I have a headache that goes clear down to my feet. Maarken—"

"You don't remember, do you?"

"Is there something I ought to?" She frowned.

"I don't know. I wasn't close enough with you to see it myself. But you touched that dragon, Sioned. You must have."

"I did?" She sat up and hugged her knees to her chest. "I remember wanting to, and asking you to back me up, but after that—"

"I think we'd better get you to the keep and into bed," Feylin told her.

Sioned groaned as they helped her to stand. "Goddess! I feel as if I've been out in the Long Sand through a whole autumn's worth of storms." She looked up suddenly as the dragon called out. "She's still here!"

They watched the dragon fly low over the lake, sweeping close enough to approach Sioned and look on her with wide, fine dark eyes. She trumpeted again, a single silvery note that echoed around the crater as she flew off into the Desert.

Feylin exchanged glances with Maarken and said, "I heard it in her voice."

He nodded. "I think I even saw it in her eyes. She's glad Sioned's all right, and now she can go back to the others." He regarded his aunt with thoughtful eyes.

"Whatever happened between you, I'd say you've made a friend."

Chapter Eleven

In 701, the year of the Plague, the seaside residence of Waes' lords had been turned into a hospital for the sick. By midsummer it had become a mausoleum. The unburied dead rotted in chambers and corridors for lack of persons brave enough to risk infection by entering the building. One of the last acts of old Lord Jervis' life had been to order his palace burned, both to honor the dead and to prevent further contagion from spreading into the city itself. He had died on the very day of the blaze, and his corpse had been carried from the house in which his family had taken refuge to the fine old residence overlooking the sea, there to burn with his palace and his people.

His widow had moved her surviving family into a home in the city when the danger had passed. Over the intervening years, Lord Lyell had taken over houses on either side of the first one, knocking down walls to run rooms and gardens together, adding new partitions and odd staircases and sloping ramps to connect the various levels. The residence became a habitable if eccentric composition of some thirty rooms on five different levels. It had neither the elegance nor the splendor of the seaside palace, but it possessed a decided advantage in its ugliness insofar as Lady Kiele was concerned. There were more exits than anyone could keep track of, and that suited her very well.

She left by one of them—a side door from what had been a kitchen but was now used for storage—and drew a heavy cloak around her against the evening chill off Brochwell Bay. No one saw her as she glided through the back garden toward the gate that let into an alley. She walked for some distance behind the homes of wealthy merchants and court functionaries, then cut through a park and strode quickly to the portside section of the city. Her destination was an undistinguished dwelling halfway down a foul-smelling back street. The house had been rented for her by her old nurse Afina, and the man who opened the door had been told to expect her.

"Milady," he acknowledged in a voice as salt-rough as his skin. He made an awkward bow and ushered her in. "He's upstairs. Not liking it a bit, milady."

She shrugged, averting her gaze from him, the squalid room, and especially the greasy-haired woman who sat by the hearth ostentatiously counting gold coins. Kiele crossed the filthy floor to the stairs. The man escorted her, and their combined weight on the half-rotted wood sent creaks and groans shivering all along the steps. Heat and smoke from the fireplace intensified the stink; she held her handkerchief to her nose, inhaling its heavy perfume.

"In here, milady." He shouldered open a large door. Kiele pulled in a deep breath to steady her nerves and regretted it as she got a lungful of the man's sweat smell even through the silk held to her nose. "He doesn't know you're coming," he added.

"Good. Leave us. I'll be perfectly safe, I assure you." Her gaze fixed on the tall, lean figure standing in the shadows beyond the candlelight, his back to the door. Rusting iron hinges creaked, and Kiele was shut in the room, alone with a man who might or might not be her brother.

"He's right. I didn't know you'd be here. But it's about damned time!"

She stiffened with fury, then made herself laugh, wadding the handkerchief in her fist. "Impressive! Almost my father's tones. You've got the arrogance down very well. Let's see if you've the looks to match. Come into the light."

"*Our* father," he corrected, and turned, and stepped forward. The feeble glow of the candle on the table struck a face of high bones and sensuous lips. His eyes were like green crystal frosted with ice. Kiele caught her breath and groped for a chair. He grinned without humor and let her find her own support while he took another few steps and loomed over her. She fought back childhood memories of her father doing the same thing, and the terror his rages always provoked. She was not a child anymore, she was a woman grown—and she held the power of this man's success or failure.

"What do you think, sister dear?"

Rallying, she scowled at him and ordered, "Sit down and listen to me. You may be who you claim to be—and then again, you may not. But, by the Goddess, you're going to listen to what I say and follow my instructions. If, that is, you hope to achieve your goal."

He laughed. "Another thing we have in common." He pulled the second chair out from the table and sat down, sprawling long legs.

"Sit up straighter. Legs crossed with the left ankle on the right knee."

He obeyed, still grinning. Kiele unwound her fingers from the silk square and folded her hands on the table. A shrug dropped the cloak from her shoulders, alleviating a little of the oppressive heat. She inspected the young man for some time in silence, hiding her growing excitement. Now that she had recovered from the icy green of his eyes, the resemblance was not quite so shocking. Something about the chin was wrong, and the mouth was too wide. There were other discrepancies. But the height was correct, and the leanness corresponded with descriptions of Roelstra in his youth.

"You'll pass," she said curtly. "With schooling, of course, and with a rinse to bring out red highlights in your hair. Palila's hair was auburn. Yours is too dark."

"Like our father's," he shot back.

"A reddish tint will arouse memories of her—and that's the immediate point, you'll agree. Now explain to me why it took you so long to get here."

"I set out as planned, and on time—according to instructions from some woman who seems to think she's my aunt." He grinned. "She's the daughter of the people who claim to be my grandparents, but I don't own the relationship. Was it her money or yours that was sent to persuade me?"

"Impudence will get you precisely nowhere," she snapped. "Tell me why you're late!"

"There were riders following me."

"Who?"

"I didn't leave them alive to conduct a conversation," he retorted. "They came on me at night, four of them with drawn knives."

"What did they look like?"

"Peasants. One of them babbled something about someone who'd help me challenge the princeling. There was talk of power more potent than the *faradh'im.*" He shrugged. "I don't need anyone's help. I'm ready to take my inheritance *now.*"

"You should have questioned them!"

"What was I supposed to do—ask for information while they cut me to ribbons? I heard them approach and pretended to drowse over my fire, and when they were close enough I started killing them before they could kill me. If that doesn't suit you, sweet sister, then too damned bad."

"Stop calling me that. It's yet to be proved that you're my father's son. And to do that, you need me. You know that, or you wouldn't be here. Who taught you proper speech?"

"Do you want me to use my rustic mountain accent?" he sneered. "Would that help the illusion? I don't need any tricks! I'm the son of High Prince Roelstra and his mistress Lady Palila, born nearly twenty-one years ago just a few measures from here on the Faolain River. Anyone who doubts it—"

"Don't threaten me, boy," she told him. "I don't have to believe in you—all I have to do is decide whether or not to support you. How far do you think you'd get without the backing of one of Roelstra's daughters? Now, how did you learn gentle speech?"

Sullenly, he replied, "A couple of the men at Dasan Manor had been servants at Castle Crag in their young days. They taught me."

"Good. We can say they recognized the highborn in you and tutored you. We can work on your appearance and various mannerisms I can show you. Get up and walk around the room."

He did so, eyes smoldering with resentment. "Do I walk well enough for you?"

She ignored the question, not wanting to admit how

his strong movements distressed her. There was power in that lean, tough body, wedded to a temper that would make him dangerous if crossed. "Lean against the wall. Fold your arms over your chest—no, higher. Good. Now brush your hair from your forehead. Use your fingers like a comb. That's right. Can you hold your own in a sword fight?"

"I've had training. Dasan belongs to a knight retired from service, and he says I'm a natural fighter. I'm good with horses, too. And knives. As I proved on the way here." He gestured to the dagger at his belt. "No worries about that."

"What I'm worried about is your arrogance and your anger. You'll have to control both if this is going to work. You can't just storm into the princes' conference and demand your rights. Let my husband handle that part of it, and keep your mouth shut except to say what we'll tell you to say. Oh, stop glaring at me, Masul! You not only have to prove your claim to Princemarch, but you also have to prove you'll be a prince the others can work with! They'd had quite enough of my father's ways before he died, I can tell you that!"

This was obviously a new concept. He subsided into his chair and blew out a long sigh. "Very well. But you have to understand something first. All my life I've been stuck in that swine-run of a manor at the back end of nothing. Everybody sneaking glances at me, whispering that I couldn't possibly be my supposed father's son, not with my height and coloring, and especially my eyes."

He rose and began to pace. Kiele schooled her expression to coolness. Her father had stalked rooms in just this fashion. But, even more than her memories, Masul's barely leashed strength impressed her again like a physical blow. His pacing made the candle flame flicker as he passed, the light throwing odd shadows onto his face.

"The rumors started when I was about fifteen. Could he be, what if he is, surely he's not, remember the old prince, what really happened that night—"

"*That* is something very few people ever knew," Kiele interrupted. "Palila, Roelstra, Ianthe, Pandsala, Andrade. Of those five, the first three are dead."

"And the two survivors won't welcome me with open arms," he added.

"Pandsala won't give up her power without a terrible struggle," she agreed. "She'll lie her own honor into the dirt before making the slightest slip that could prove you're Roelstra's son. As for Andrade—she's blood-bound to the Desert and she hated Roelstra with a passion bordering on obsession. I don't think she'd lie, no matter what the need, but she's clever as a roomful of silk merchants and won't tell any part of the truth that might support your claim."

"It's up to me, then. I have to look enough like him and Palila, say what you and Lyell tell me, and behave as if I'll be a good, biddable prince once I'm installed at Castle Crag." He grinned again, like a wolf.

She had intended bidding him herself, but it appeared he had a mind of his own. That would help in the process of convincing others, of course, but she suspected that his gratitude for her help would last only as long as it took him to walk inside Castle Crag.

"I'm ready to be educated, sister dear," he said, and sat down once more.

She stared at him for a long time over the candle flame. "Masul, have you ever grown a beard?"

"No."

"Do so, for three reasons. First, many men with dark hair have reddish beards and it would help if that were the case with you. Second, we have to hide you until the *Rialla*, and a beard would do that, make you look older."

"And third?"

She laughed, pleased with her inspiration. "Imagine it! You appear for the first time at the *Rialla*, bearded. All anyone will see is your eyes. They *are* very like my father's, you know. That night we'll shave off the beard—and because they're already primed to see Roelstra in your face, they'll find the resemblance even greater than it is!"

Masul looked startled for a moment, then laughed aloud. "Father of Storms! Brilliant, sister—brilliant!"

"I've not yet decided that I *am* your sister," she reminded him. The words had the intended effect; he looked murderous, then resentful, then determined to win her over to real belief. She rose, satisfied. He would work harder at his lessons in order to prove his identity—and her eventual acquiescence would be all the sweeter to him for having been hard-won. This would give him added confidence in his ability to convince others. Not that he would need much more confidence, she reflected as she settled her cloak around her again. Still, she had established the beginnings of dominance over him through her doubts and her instructions. He would be willing to do as she told him.

"Is this where you're going to keep me until the *Rialla?*" Masul asked.

She smiled, pleased by the phrasing that confirmed her ascendancy. "It won't be too bad after it's cleaned up. But when the city begins to fill later in the summer, I'll have you moved to a little manor we own outside the gates."

"The place you meet your lovers?" he suggested.

She drew back her hand to slap him and he caught her wrist, laughing. "How dare you!" she spat. "Let me go!"

"A woman as beautiful as you must have plenty of lovers—that's the way of things with you highborns, and especially Roelstra's offspring! How many did Ianthe take before she died? I must say it's a pity you're my sister, sister dear!"

She wrenched away from him. "Don't you ever touch me again!" His grin infuriated her, and his mocking parody of a bow. She yanked the door open and slammed it behind her, descending the stairs at a run. Pausing only to order that the house be thoroughly cleaned before her next visit—and tossing another pouch of gold at the woman to pay for it—she left the stifling place for the cool night air outside. It hit her burning cheeks like an ice storm.

As she walked, she calmed down a little and realized that part of her anger was really shock. His suggestion about her lovers and his intimation that he wouldn't mind being one was impudence of the worst sort—he was half her age and possibly her brother into the bargain. Yet something deeper troubled her; she had seen lust in men's eyes before, but recognition of it in Masul's green gaze

brought memories flooding back. Roelstra had looked at
Palila that way, and at many other lovely women. Boldly,
speculatively, arrogant with the assurance that he had but
to beckon and they would be instantly in his bed. Not
because he was High Prince; because he was a man who
enjoyed women's bodies. More than anything else she
had seen or heard tonight, the look in Masul's eyes began
to convince her that he might indeed be Roelstra's son.

Kiele paused for a few moments in the cool darkness
of her garden, looking up at the windows where lights
shone blue or red or green behind thin curtains. Shadows
moved behind some, and all at once white-gold candlelight stabbed out from a fourth-floor window as silk was
pulled aside. Kiele froze, then scurried to the shelter of
a tree. She gasped for breath, then tried to quiet her racing heart. Why should she not take a stroll in her own
gardens if she chose? Still, she stayed where she was
until the spill of light was again covered by green curtains. When she could breathe normally, she slipped back
into the house.

Gaining the main part of the building, she found the
servants in an uproar. She dropped her cloak on the carpet for one of them to pick up, glancing quickly in a
mirror to make sure her hair and gown were tidy before
she demanded to know the cause of the disturbance.

"The Princess Chiana, my lady—she's just arrived,
and—"

"*Princess?* Who told you to call her that?" Kiele
snapped. "Never mind, I know who did. Damn her insolence! She is the *Lady* Chiana in my house, and anyone
giving her royal titles in my hearing or out of it will be
dismissed on the spot! Where is she?"

"With his lordship, my lady, in the Third Room."

Kiele started for the main hall, infuriated anew as she
saw Chiana's baggage strewn about the floor. She ordered
it put in the rooms made ready for her and told herself
that she would have her vengeance on the little bitch soon
enough. For now, she would have to be all honey and
silk. She smoothed her face accordingly and brought a
smile to her lips with the exquisite thought of Chiana's
frantic humiliation at the *Rialla*.

The Third Room was reserved for receiving the most

important guests, being the largest and best furnished.
Differences in the houses that made up the residence made
short staircases necessary here and there, and the steps
leading down into the chamber were perfect for making
an entrance. Kiele always enjoyed the chance those five
steps gave her to pause, observe, and collect all eyes. But
tonight she didn't bother with her usual entrance to the
room where Chiana and Lyell were seated over steaming
cups of taze.

Lyell rose; Chiana did not. Kiele hid her irritation that
her sister had not given her the usual mark of respect.
She smiled sweetly and poured herself something to
drink, then sank into a chair near Chiana's.

"What a precipitous arrival, my dear! But a very welcome one. Was the journey troublesome?"

The two women exchanged polite nothings for some
moments, and Kiele's good humor returned as she imagined Chiana's reaction to Masul. To have both under her
eyes would provide excellent private entertainment during the long summer ahead.

Chiana was definitely and obviously the daughter of
Roelstra and Palila. She had the best features of both,
which created a beauty that at nearly twenty-one more
than fulfilled the promise of her girlhood. Rich, heavy
auburn hair curled enticingly around hazel eyes with startlingly long lashes; she did not have her parents' height
but her figure was in perfect proportion and shown to
advantage by the tight bodice and waist of her dress. Kiele
noted that Lyell was having trouble keeping his gaze from
the full curves defined by that bodice. She made a mental
note to seduce him tonight. She was not quite ready to
have him stray from her bed—certainly not into Chiana's.

As was natural, talk turned to their siblings. "Naydra
is plump and pleased with herself," Chiana said scornfully, "even though she hasn't been able to provide Narat
with a son. I haven't heard from the others in quite some
time. Do you have news of them?"

Kiele ran down the list automatically. "Pandsala sits
at Castle Crag, as ever, being wise and bountiful. Moria
sits in the dower house Prince Rohan gave her, watching
the pine cones fall for all I know—or care. How she can
stand the Veresch the whole year is beyond my compre-

hension. Moswen is visiting Prince Clutha—I think she hopes to snare Halian.''

Chiana giggled. ''That tall, thin drip of water with the mistress and daughters? What would she want him for?''

''His inheritance, of course,'' Lyell said. ''I never met any of Roelstra's daughters who weren't ambitious.'' He said it fondly, with a proud glance at his wife.

''Practical, my love,'' she corrected. ''And interested in survival.'' Her glance was equally loving, but inwardly she cursed him for his unwonted perception. If, however, he understood and was pleased by her ambition, then it would be that much easier to direct him in the matter of Masul. ''Where was I? Ah, yes. Rabia's death has left Patwin inconsolable, it's said. But he'll probably find some charming girl this year and marry again. Danladi is at the Syrene court with Princess Gemma. And that's the roster, Chiana, except for you and me.'' She smiled her most winning smile. ''I'm so glad you've come to help me with the *Rialla* this year. Clutha is so demanding—each has to be grander than the last, and I've run out of ideas!''

''I'm so glad I can be of help to you, Kiele. It'll be such fun! But tell me, what have you heard about this person who claims to be our brother?''

Unprepared for the question, Kiele hoped her sudden confusion would be taken as inability to express her outrage at so presumptuous a claim. Lyell filled the breach, and for one of the few times in her marriage Kiele thanked the Goddess for the existence of her husband.

''It's annoying, of course,'' he said. ''But none of our concern.''

''They say he'll appear at the *Rialla* to claim Princemarch. Could he do that, Lyell?''

He patted her arm. ''Don't worry your pretty head about it.''

But Chiana would, and Kiele knew it. She smiled.

* * *

Prince Clutha had spent his youth and middle age worrying about whether or not his beloved Meadowlord would be the battleground for the Desert and Princemarch. Mountains separated the two princedoms all along their mutual border, but Clutha's broad, gently rolling lands lay smack in the middle between the two; his sire and grandsire had both seen warring armies rage across the wheat fields, leaving burned crops and destroyed villages in their wake. Clutha had never much cared which came out on top, so long as the struggle did not take place on his territory. He had worked assiduously for years to keep first Roelstra and Zehava and then Roelstra and Rohan from coming to blows. But for the fourteen years of Rohan's rule as High Prince and the union of the two lands, his worries on that score had vanished.

No longer concerned about his princedom's safety from without, he had turned his mind to its interior security. Of all his *athr'im,* none had so much potential for both power and mischief as Lyell of Waes. Not that the man was particularly clever, or capable on his own of doing more than running his city with competence; it was Kiele, Roelstra's daughter, who worried Clutha. Lyell was tied to the Desert through his sister's marriage to Lord Eltanin of Tiglath. She and their elder son had died of Plague, but the younger, Tallain, survived as the heir. Clutha had countenanced Lyell's wedding to Roelstra's daughter because it would neatly balance the Desert commitment. He had not counted on the young lord's abandoning the Desert to throw in wholeheartedly with Roelstra in his war against Rohan. Ever since then, Clutha had kept a close eye on the rulers of Waes.

Thus it was that he had left his squire behind after his visit that spring. The youth was not a welcome guest in the residence, but neither Kiele nor Lyell could refuse when their prince offered them his services. Clutha went home to Swalekeep well contented, for this squire was more than just a squire.

Riyan was the only son of Lord Ostvel of Skybowl— and a Sunrunner. At the age of twelve he had gone to Swalekeep for training as a knight, staying for two years before journeying to Goddess Keep to learn the *faradhi* arts. Last summer, at nineteen, Riyan had come back to Meadowlord to prepare for his knighting this year at the *Rialla;* though he had been in effect Lord Urival's squire at Goddess Keep, only a knight could make a knight, and Urival was not. So Clutha would be the one to give him the accolade and a new sword, at which point he would return to Lady Andrade for further education as a Sunrunner.

It was a different plan from the one that had earned Lord Maarken his knighthood and his rings. Training young lords who were also *faradh'im* was a new proposition, and Andrade was frankly experimenting with the best manner of accomplishing it. Soon it would be decided how Prince Pol would be trained. Would he continue at Graypearl with Lleyn and Chadric, or curtail his pursuit of knighthood as Riyan had done in favor of earlier *faradhi* education than Maarken had had? It was yet to be decided.

Riyan knew very well that he was an experiment, and did not mind in the least. He enjoyed both aspects of his training equally and anticipated being the Sunrunner Lord of Skybowl without the slightest qualm. The difficulties that worried Maarken were things Riyan shrugged off. He understood the older lord's problem, but did not share it. In the first place, the power he would have as *athri* of Skybowl was much less than Maarken's as Lord of Radzyn. True, he would have jurisdiction over the gold caves, but others would see to the politics of the Desert and Princemarch. He also felt easier about his *faradhi* status than Maarken. Ostvel never expressed reservations about it the way Lord Chaynal sometimes did. Riyan didn't blame Chay; people who had never lived among Sunrunners often looked on them somewhat askance. But his own father had spent his childhood and youth at Goddess Keep; Ostvel understood *faradh'im*.

Riyan's orientation was service to his prince, not rule on his own. Maarken would have to preside over Radzyn's vast independent holdings, help Pol govern, decide great questions of state, lead armies if necessary. None of that was in Riyan's future. His mother, Camigwen, had been chatelaine of Stronghold, but she had also been Sioned's dearest friend, sister rather than servant. Ostvel held Skybowl for Rohan, not for himself. Rohan had attempted to give him the same arrangement that he had with the most powerful of his vassals: outright ownership of the land. But Ostvel had refused. Skybowl belonged to Rohan. Ostvel oversaw it and served his prince well and faithfully. When it came his turn, Riyan would do the same—both as *athri* and Sunrunner.

These weighty matters were not on his mind, however, as he lounged in his chamber at the Waes residence that night. He was thinking quite prosaically about the chances of getting to know a certain merchant's daughter a little better. The girl and her father had been his escort around Waes his first few days here as he got to know the port city. Jayachin was possessed of blue-black hair, eyes so blue they were nearly purple, and a skin like moonlight. Riyan had a deep and profound appreciation of the opposite sex, especially its members who laughed at his jokes and resisted his advances up to a point. Her father had made certain he had gotten nowhere near that point yet, but Riyan was aware that the merchant was not insensible to the honor of having his daughter courted by the heir of Skybowl, friend to Prince Pol himself.

Riyan intended asking Jayachin tomorrow if she'd care to ride out with him for a day in the countryside. The weather for the past days had been brisk, with a strong wind off the bay savaging the new flowers in the garden to the despair of the groundskeepers. But tomorrow might be gentler. He rose from his bed and went over to the windows, parting the green silk curtains to take a look at the sky.

Recognizing the cloak-wrapped figure down below was easy; Kiele always wore a large gold ring set with diamonds on her right hand, and the thing grabbed even the faintest light. Riyan's brows shot up as she slid into the shadow of a tree. Why hide? he thought. He shrugged, let the curtain drop, and went back to the bed.

Sprawling across the coverlet, he tried to think about Jayachin. But the sight of Kiele tonight combined with his observations since Clutha's departure fit no pattern. Kiele's volume of private letters, some to her half sister Moswen at Swalekeep, some to a woman in Einar, was of interest. She sometimes disappeared all day into the city, saying afterward that she had been shopping—but she never came home with any packages. Once or twice he had followed her out of idle curiosity and discovered that she was remarkably adept at slipping into back streets, where he lost her. And, most puzzling of all, she had invited Chiana here to Waes for the summer.

Everybody knew how much Kiele hated her youngest sibling. Chiana's arrival tonight had been Riyan's cue to vanish upstairs. He knew he ought to have stayed and watched Kiele with her, but Chiana set his teeth on edge. She was beautiful, no doubt about that, and he supposed she could be charming when and if it suited her. But seeing her fawn all over Lyell had been a trifle too stomach-curdling for Riyan's taste that night.

Finally he admitted that Kiele's nocturnal stroll in the gardens bewildered him enough to make him haul on his boots and go downstairs. He had more or less learned the eccentric plan of the residence, and only took the wrong corridor one time out of five on average. Tonight he was accurate, and slipped out into the night.

He went to the place where she had stood, then retraced the steps she must have taken. The groundskeepers were in the process of replacing the white gravel along all the pathways; Riyan was in luck, for the bare dirt had been raked that afternoon. He called up a finger of Fire to give him light enough to see by, and followed her steps. They led directly to the back gate. His brows arched again at that; so it was not an evening meander in the gardens she had been about, but a return from elsewhere in the city. The gate was not fully closed. He opened it, wincing as hinges squeaked softly, and stood in the alley for a few moments, wondering which way she had come and gone. Perhaps this was something Andrade should know about.

Riyan paused, turning his face up to the moons chased by the wind across the sky. He clenched both hands loosely, feeling the four rings that marked him as an apprentice Sunrunner. He could do it on his own, though his technique sometimes left a little to be desired. But these were moons above him now, not the strong and steady light of the sun. The principle was the same; he wondered if he dared it, then smiled.

He closed his eyes, the better to feel the delicate strands of moonlight in his thoughts. With his mind he wove them together, tested them, and was pleased by their easy

suppleness and strength. This was simpler than he'd been
led to believe.

He threaded his own colors of garnet and pearl and
carnelian into the plaited moonlight. They took on a new
luster, shimmering subtly as he cast the weaving across
dark land and star-sparkled water. Following the shining
pathway, he caught his breath at the beauty down below
him and nearly forgot to stop at Goddess Keep.

Someone he did not know was on duty tonight in the
beautiful chamber with three glass walls where at least
one Sunrunner always sat, waiting for any messages that
might come on the light. The windows here were kept
open except in a downpour, when cloud cover prohibited
faradhi communication anyway. Riyan practically danced
through one window and brushed against the unknown
Sunrunner's colors.

Goddess blessing! he greeted cheerfully. *Riyan of Skybowl, with word for Lady Andrade.*

The person's startlement was almost funny. After a
hasty greeting in return there was an apology and a promise to go find the Lady. Riyan hovered in the room, waiting, imagining what must be going on. The duty
Sunrunner would be shouting all over the keep; Andrade
would demand to know what in the name of all hells was
going on. It would take her some time to climb the stairs
from her chambers to the room of glass—

In far less time than he imagined, there was a powerful
presence on the moonlight that captured his weaving and
threaded it through with veritable ropes made of moonlight. *What do you think you're up to, you young idiot?*

I'm sorry, my Lady, but I thought—

*You thought wrong! Can't you feel that the strands are
too frail to get you back safely to Waes? And what are
you doing in Waes, anyway? Why wasn't I informed?*

*Prince Clutha left me here to watch Lady Kiele and
Lord Lyell. And there's been quite a lot to watch. Chiana's here, for one thing.*

Andrade's brilliant colors flared painfully and Riyan
winced. *All right, tell me the whole of it.*

He did so, sensing her astonishment and her suspicions. When he was finished, he heard something like a
hissing intake of breath, and wondered if it was only his

past experience of her that made him imagine it. *You did the right thing by telling me*, she admitted. *Keep watching Kiele when you can—and Chiana, too. But by the Goddess, the next time you'll wait for sunlight or I'll skin you alive and nail your hide to the refectory wall as a caution to all the other young fools who think they know everything!*

Yes, my Lady, he replied meekly.

Do you understand me, Riyan? If you'd tried to return, the moonlight would have unraveled like a rotted blanket—and you would have been shadow-lost. Those four rings of yours do not *allow you to attempt Moonrunning! Now, let's get you back where you started, shall we?*

The moonlight was like a gigantic bolt of silk flung from Goddess Keep to Waes. He slid along it pell-mell, breathless at the speed and the whirl of colors around him. Back in the alley outside the garden again, he watched with his mind as Andrade effortlessly disentangled him from the weave and vanished back along her silken moonlight.

It took him a few moments to recover. But it took him no time at all to promise himself that he would not try that again until he had been properly instructed. The moons might be nearer than the sun, but the light they gave off was thinner, more delicate. He didn't want to think about what might have happened if he'd tried to come back on his own.

* * *

Andrade had not left her chambers, merely woven the moonlight from her windows. On returning she glanced at Urival and Andry, who had joined her after the evening meal to discuss the scrolls again. "It seems interesting things are happening," she said, and told them the gist of her conversation with Riyan.

Urival nodded slowly. " 'Interesting' is the right word for now. I only hope these things don't become 'fascinating.' "

"Or worse," Andry murmured.

Andrade grimaced her appreciation of their remarks. "Well, I don't want to give Riyan too much to worry about. I'll send somebody else to Waes."

"Who?" Andry asked eagerly.

"Never you mind." She eyed him sternly. "You're another one just like him, wanting to know everything, thinking you know it all at your age! Four or five rings, and you believe you understand the universe! Bah!"

Andry stiffened, then bent his head. "Yes, my Lady."

"I've had enough for the night. Leave me."

When he was gone, Urival replaced the scrolls in their cases and went to the door, where he paused and said, "I understand that he needs reprimanding every so often. But not *too* often, or he'll resent you—and be ungovernable."

"You think he's governable now? Did you hear him lecturing us tonight about the scrolls, Lady Merisel, and Sunrunner history he's the first in hundreds of years to know? If he didn't have such a damned talent for translating, I'd take them from him and let somebody else do it. But he's got a quick mind and the will to learn."

"As mind-hungry as Sioned always was, but without Sioned's humility."

"When was that girl ever humble? She and Rohan both have defied me since the day they were wed! She hasn't worn her *faradhi* rings in years! Just that bloody great emerald. Humble?" She laughed bitterly.

"You're in a foul temper tonight."

"I know." She gestured an apology with one hand, rings and bracelet gleaming in the firelight. "What Sioned has is a healthy fear of the power knowledge can give her. Andry's not afraid of anything. Except, for now, me. But not for much longer."

"Andrade—he's like her in that he can be led by love. Not fear."

"I've given him no cause to love me. I never meant to—not with any of them. I don't want them to adore me. It's not necessary."

"If you want them to do your fighting and your work for you—"

"Leave off, Urival!"

"As you wish, my Lady," he said in a voice heavy with disapproval.

Andrade heard the door shut and resisted the urge to throw something. She was too old for this nonsense, too old to be juggling the actions and motives and feelings of so many people. In her youth she had relished power; by middle age she had exercised it with consummate skill. But now she was tired of it. Tired of the responsibility and the scheming and keeping one eye on everyone to make sure they stayed in line.

But more than her weariness, she was frightened. Andry would not stay in line. He would do with the scrolls what she was scared to do: use them.

Chapter Twelve

It was virtually impossible for the High Prince to travel incognito, but Rohan gave it a good try on the journey through Princemarch. No dragon banner announced the identity of the eight riders; no royal badges appeared on the guards' tunics, which were plain and unmatched; no expensive trappings decorated the horses; and no farmer or innkeeper with whom they stayed went without payment, though it was every prince's right to demand free meals and lodging when traveling through his realm.

But though Rohan did not advertise his presence, neither did he deny his identity when people addressed him with royal titles. News of his travels seemed to spread more quickly than *faradhi* messages on sunlight; Andrade would envy the silent efficiency of these people. For his own part, he appreciated their general lack of ceremony. He hated fuss, suspicious practically from birth of those who made a great show in his presence, for show was usually designed to cover substance people did not wish seen. These folk, however, were casual and cordial in their welcome, with nothing to hide from their prince. Rohan viewed this as a tribute to their good sense and Pandsala's good governance on Pol's behalf. Had she been a bad ruler, they would have hated everything to do with him, while trying to hide it with false good cheer.

Accommodations varied. Some nights they stayed in neat chambers at an inn; occasionally they unrolled blankets in a barn; quite often they spent the night in the open

THE STAR SCROLL 203

beneath the stars when evening found them still on the road. Food ranged from tavern fare to farmhouse stews to their packed provisions and whatever half-a-day's hunt could provide.

They rode wherever curiosity took them, investigating local landmarks, seeking deep into remote valleys, riding measures out of their way to visit famous sites recommended by their hosts. There were impromptu races across flower-strewn meadows and excursions into the hills for baths in ice-cold waterfalls. All these side trips were watched over by four guards who, while joining in the spirit of fun, remained on constant alert.

The four were commanded by Maeta, whose presence had not been planned. She merely showed up their third day out, as casually as if the encounter was an accidental one during an afternoon ride. Her explanation that she had always wanted to see the sights fooled no one; they all knew that she had been sent by her formidable mother as an extra guard for Pol. Rohan did not send Maeta back to Stronghold, for not even he felt equal to facing Myrdal's wrath; the old woman was *probably* Pol's kinswoman, but she was certainly the only grandmother he would ever know, and Rohan respected that special relationship almost as much as he respected Myrdal's temper.

Besides, it suited him to add Maeta to the group. Pol had already shown a talent for taking off on his own. The mare Chay had lent him, a streak of lightning compacted into four legs and a pair of roving eyes, liked nothing better than a wild gallop. Pol defended his escapades with the innocent reminder that he had promised to keep the horse in good trim for sale at the *Rialla*. Threats did no good; even the private promise of the application of Rohan's palm against his backside did not impress him overmuch. But his first attempt to bolt off after Maeta's arrival earned him an afternoon riding on a lead rein behind her horse. Rohan heartily approved of his son's discomfiture—while wondering ruefully if he really was so complete a failure as a disciplinarian.

Maarken, too, was glad of Maeta's presence. They talked tactics and strategies most of the day and half the night. She had been in most of the important battles of

the last thirty years, and her wealth of experience was
nearly as great as his father's. Sometimes Rohan and Pol
joined in these discussions, sitting around the campfire
to trade ideas. But more often father and son spent their
time with each other. During the long nights spent talking, Rohan came to understand his son more deeply—
especially the reason why physical punishment was
nowhere near as effective as a judicious dose of public
embarrassment. He should have known, of course; Pol was
just like him in his consciousness of rank, his pride, and
his notions of personal dignity. It was not quite arrogance—and that failing was something to guard against.

The lowlands of Princemarch were a revelation: rich,
rolling valleys of cropland and pasture, a careless abun-
dance that amazed Desert eyes. Farmers gifted the royal
party with the summer fruits of the countryside, proud
of their productivity and grinning as their guests marveled at the bounty.

One midday an incredible array was produced for their
lunch in a farmer's front yard. Rohan asked, "Tell me,
is there anything you people *don't* grow?"

The farmer scratched his chin thoughtfully. "Well, my
lord," he said after due deliberation, "not much."

And it was true. Fruit, grain, meat, cheese, nuts, vegetables—they partook of the plenty and were amazed.

"And you own all of it," Maeta remarked to Pol one
morning, her arm sweeping out to include the fields and
orchards around them.

"All of it," he echoed incredulously. "It must feed
the whole world!"

"A goodly portion of our part of it," Maeta answered.
"You don't remember the old days. Sometimes we had
to give up a year's salt or half Radzyn's horses for food
enough to last the winter. Now that this is ours, we'll
never have to crawl again."

Rohan met her gaze over his saddle as he tightened a
girth strap. "Never again," he echoed. He remembered
very well the year to which Maeta alluded, and the fury
of helplessness in his father's black eyes when Roelstra
had demanded exorbitant payment for food enough to
keep the Desert from starving. More lightly he added,
"But it probably sharpened the wits, bargaining back and

forth. I sometimes miss the stimulation of my first *Rialla* as prince.''

Maeta snorted. ''Nothing wrong with your wits, if what I hear about Firon is true.''

''And what do you hear?''

''That all of this—'' She waved again at the fields. ''—will include most of that.'' One battle-scarred finger pointed northwest where Firon lay.

''It's possible,'' Rohan conceded.

Maarken laughed as he swung up into his saddle. ''Don't let my mother hear you say that! The tapestry map is already being rewoven, you know—she's using it to teach Sionell stitchery. If you change your mind, she'll have your head on a spear.''

''Aunt Tobin knows how to sew?'' Pol was astounded. ''She doesn't seem the type to like that kind of thing.''

''She doesn't,'' Maarken said cheerfully. ''She says it's only good for something to do with your hands when you want to strangle somebody.''

''Strangulation really isn't in her line,'' Rohan observed. ''Knives, arrows, swords when we were growing up—that's more her style.''

''Is it true about her marriage contract with Uncle Chay?'' Pol asked as he mounted.

''No knives in the bedchamber!'' His father laughed. ''Oh, it's true enough. Chay insisted on it.''

''What's in your agreement with Mother?'' Pol teased.

Maeta answered him. ''Sunrunners are much too subtle to go around waving steel. *Her* contract says that the only Fire she'll call up in their bedchamber is the kind that burns the sheets. And that, my lad, is how *you* got started!''

That day, the twenty-fifth of their journey, began the climb into the Great Veresch. Chain upon chain of peaks rose nearly to the clouds, the tallest of them snow-crowned even in high summer. In between were blue-violet depths where, when the angle of the sun was right, thin ribbons of water reflected silver. Conifers ten and twenty times the height of a man grew bunched needles as long as Pol's arm, and bore cones that could be split open for sweet seeds and resin that tasted like honey. Herds of startled deer lifted white antlers to the sky before racing into cover. The water in lakes and streams was the sweetest any of them had ever tasted, as if milked directly from the clouds without touching the ground at all. The number and variety of birds astounded them; the world seemed alive night and day with wingbeats and songs and hunting cries, so different from Desert silence. They sometimes spent whole mornings watching flocks of birds float across a lake or dive for fish or plummet from the sky over prey-laden meadows. And the flowers—narrow trails through the forest would suddenly give way to mountain meadows awash in blue, red, orange, yellow, purple, and pink, the unbelievable profusion of colors enough to make *faradhi* senses drunk.

To the Desert-bred, familiar only with the stark beauty of the Long Sand where nothing grew and few birds or animals made permanent homes, the Veresch was almost frightening. Lowlands that had felt fence and plow were somehow more comprehensible than these mountains, where everything was as it had been since the first trees. People were an afterthought here, and the work of their hands could not begin to match the strength of the forest. In the Desert, people grouped together, the better to withstand the harshness of their place; here, folk lived in tiny settlements of not more than thirty, herded sheep and goats endlessly through the high country, and built lonely cottages deep in the woods. But as alien as their patterns of life were to each other, the two shared a bond that became clearer to Rohan as the days passed. Both peoples had accepted that they could not work changes on the land. The silent power of Mountain and Desert was greater than any fence or plow. People knew what their places would give and what they would not.

Pol turned stubborn about snow. He not only wanted to look at it, he wanted to touch it and make sure it was real. Rohan, secretly sharing his son's curiosity, received directions from a bemused shepherd who obviously thought them all deranged for going to find snow when winter would bring it to them soon enough. The royal party spent two days coaxing their outraged Desert-born horses across frozen crystal fields, and two nights shivering under blankets inadequate for the temperature and the altitude.

"Had enough?" Maarken asked hopefully on the morning of the third day. Pol, clutching a blanket around him on top of every stitch of clothing he had brought with him, nodded emphatically. Pelting everyone with snowballs had been great fun, and the crisp air was literally breathtaking—but he wanted above all things to be *warm* again.

The ride down from the heights showed them ridge on ridge of blue-misted mountains. Startling outcrops of solid granite alternated with hillsides thickly covered in pine. Strange, smooth slabs of rock half a measure wide and punctuated with colossal boulders set their horses' hooves to ringing. They even found some long-abandoned dragon caves, and spent a day exploring. There were, oddly enough, signs of humans nearby; Maarken discovered firepits and the foundation stones of a village-sized habitation, also long forsaken. Of more interest to Rohan and Pol was evidence of a primitive smelter works. They exchanged speculative glances and headed directly back to the caves. But most of the walls had collapsed, and instead of dragons in one of the few usable caverns they encountered a very bad-tempered hill-cat who deeply resented disruption of his afternoon nap. Father and son beat a hasty retreat.

Back below snowline, they began visiting manors and keeps in more systematic fashion. Word of their coming preceded them; they were welcomed with considerably more state than on the early part of the journey. Their first stop was a small keep called Rezeld, where Lord Morlen and his wife Lady Abinor had been preparing for the anticipated visit since spring. Rohan winced inwardly at the boundless enthusiasm of their welcome, but shared the philosophical observation with Pol that Rezeld had probably never seen a prince within its walls—let alone two—and that neglecting personal visits to each *athri* under one's rule was always a mistake.

"The best way of judging a keep or a manor is to visit it yourself," he mused. "Granted, they usually have the place looking its best—except for what they want you to pay to refurbish—but the trick is to look beneath the surface and see what's really going on."

They were seated in Lady Abinor's large, finely pro-

portioned chamber, theirs for their stay. Threadbare tapestries and frayed rugs brightened the room and eased
some of the stone's chill; all the weavings, including the
bedclothes, showed signs of mending inadequate to their
state of wear. The furniture was simple and sparse, and
the glass in the windows needed replacing—but the wine
made from pine cone resin was excellent. Rohan poured
himself another cup and leaned back in a chair, regarding
his son thoughtfully.

Pol looked around him, correctly interpreting his father's last remarks to mean that he was to evaluate Rezeld
and its occupants. Their arrival that morning had been
the greatest event of the past twenty years at the manor;
everyone from the *athri*'s family to the lowliest kitchen
boy had turned out, scrubbed and polished and beaming.
The sons of the house, both a few winters younger than
Pol, had served as squires through dinner and acquitted
themselves nicely for never having had formal training in
a large keep. Lord Morlen's sixteen-year-old daughter
Avaly had shown up in her mother's best silk veil, a-
clatter with wooden and elk-horn ornaments. But Pol saw
Rezeld as a distinctly minor holding, without much
wealth or importance.

"They really did bring out their best for us," he said,
gesturing to the rugs and tapestries. "The necklace Lady
Avaly had on was just carved stuff, not valuable at all.
And from what else I saw . . . I mean, they don't even
have candles, just smelly old torches. I don't think they're
playing poor to get more money out of us, Father. And
they seem glad to have us here."

"Yes, they do." Rohan smiled.

"But why is Pandsala so stingy? There's plenty of
money for new rugs and such, and it's not as if it'd be a
foolish luxury in a climate like this. I can feel the cold
coming up through the floor even with boots on." He
sneaked his toes beneath a carpet for emphasis. "The
sheep and goats are probably all out at summer pasture,
but still. . . . If I was welcoming my prince, I'd want to
have my best animals here so he'd know how good they
are and reward me accordingly by getting good prices at
the *Rialla*."

"That's a very interesting analysis, Pol, based on what

I'm sure were careful observations." The boy's eyes lit with pride until Rohan added, "Unfortunately, all of it is wrong."

"What? Why?" Pol demanded.

"The young lady was indeed wearing row on row of 'carved stuff' in a necklace. Very pretty it was, too. If you'd really been listening to some of the people we've met on the road, you'd know that each betokens a certain number of sheep, goats, cattle, bushels, or other local produce a family lays claim to. Rezeld boasts a rather fine quarry nearby, I'm told, administered by his lordship." He grinned. "But remember, we're only ignorant Desert folk and don't know about that. We think these are her only jewels, poor girl, and not much of a dowry it is to our way of thinking—when in fact she's wearing more dowry than most of our own girls can offer! She also made big eyes at you—yes, I was watching!" he teased as Pol blushed. "Not that I'm surprised. You're a well set-up young man and a prince into the bargain. But she hasn't a hope of attaching you and she knows it—so her probable intention was to make you wistful that so pretty a girl doesn't have more in the way of material wealth. It appears she succeeded, too. Clever girl. His lordship is, in fact, flaunting what he owns and trusting our ignorance to lead us to believe that he's poor."

Pol's jaw had dropped, and his blue-green eyes were as wide as they could get. Hiding another smile, Rohan got to his feet and went to pour himself a third cup of thick, sweet wine.

"Consider the tapestries," he continued, gesturing to the walls. "If their purpose is to keep out cold and damp, why arrange them on rods so they can be pulled aside? They ought to be nailed right to the wall as close as can be. If you'll notice, the rods are new—you can tell not by their polish but by the whiteness of the plaster used to secure so heavy a load. Just to the sides of the fixtures is more plaster, hiding marks where other tapestries used to be. I'm sure there's a whole line of marks beneath, telling us that another weaving does regular duty here. It's the same in all the other chambers we were shown, by the way."

"But, Father, why would they do such a thing?"

"Excellent question. The tapestries these replaced are probably very fine ones that we weren't supposed to see or know about. As for torches, because they can't afford candles—have a look at the brackets. They've been scrubbed clean, but there are still traces of dripped wax. And the size of the sockets is rather inconvenient, wouldn't you say? See how the torch-ends have been whittled to fit. Thus we find that in addition to plenty of sheep, goats, tapestries, and so on, they also possess candles. But we're meant to think they have none of these things."

Settling in his chair again, he gave his son a wry smile. "So we finally have to ask ourselves the point of all this. Why so much trouble to disguise their wealth? Do they want us to cough up a bit? Or is there something else going on here? I tend to think the former, for his lordship doesn't seem quite devious enough to have schemes afoot other than the obvious. But I'll be watching him over the next days—and so should you."

Pol's mouth still hung open. Rohan laughed softly.

"Don't feel foolish, Pol. I'm no magician. Many years ago one of my vassals—long dead—tried to pull similar tricks on me. When I pointed them out to your mother, she looked just about the way you do right now."

"How did you *know?*"

"Well . . . to be perfectly honest, I didn't at first—not until I noticed something else interesting. In a place famous for the quality of its goats, I was served cream made of cow's milk one morning over a dish of mossberries."

Pol suddenly laughed. "Where was he hiding the cattle?"

"Oh, the cattle weren't even the problem. They were only the clue to the private deal he had going with the Cunaxans across the border to supply him with more than just a few cows every year. I won't go into the details, but suffice to say he supplied *me* with excellent cheese until the cows died—as any self-respecting cow does as soon as she can in the Desert." Rohan winked.

Shaking his head ruefully, Pol said, "I never would've seen it! And I would've made a fool out of myself by promising to make Pandsala do more for them! Father, may I ask you something?''

''Whatever you like.''

''I don't understand about being a prince.''

''Oh, dear,'' he murmured. ''Is it things in general, this manor in particular, or something else?''

''All of it.'' Pol sighed. ''We can't trust them for an instant, can we?''

''Of course we can.''

''But you just said—''

''In the important things, we have to trust them. Pol, this matter of tapestries and candles is unimportant. I'll let Lord Morlen know that I know what he's up to—discreetly, of course, to save his pride—and fine him some of his quarried stone for a building project I have in mind. I doubt he'll ever try it again. He'll know I'll catch him at it. But he'll also respect me and trust me, because not only was I smart enough to see through this, but I didn't execute him for it.'' Rohan shrugged self-mockingly. Getting to his feet, he paced to the windows and stood looking out at the mountain twilight.

''He's only doing what his father did, you know, hiding his real wealth from Roelstra. In his time, if Morlen had been caught, he'd be dead. He'll be free to *try* to outwit me again, but my guess is that he won't. People only hide what they fear will be taken from them. I won't take what he can't afford to give—he'll come to trust me for it and appreciate the way I work. Which means he'll fight if I ask him to, so he can keep me as his overlord.''

''And will you trust him?''

Rohan faced him and grinned again. ''As much as I trust any of them—which is to say that I trust my own judgment and wits.''

''You know, I think I'm beginning to understand how we got to be where we are,'' Pol mused, his eyes dancing suddenly. ''Maybe we just outlasted everybody—but maybe we were smarter than all the rest!''

''That's one way of looking at it, and probably as accurate as any other.''

Pol was silent for a moment, then burst out, ''But why do people have to treat us different? I mean, everybody bowing and deferring to us and all—do they do it because we're princes, or because they really think we're special?''

''Why do you ask?''

''Just—the way people react when they find out who I am.''

''Mmm. I see. Makes you nervous, does it?'' he asked sympathetically. ''Me, too. I suppose they have to believe in someone, Pol. We are where we are because people believed in our ancestors for one reason or other. Your grandfather won battles and convinced everyone he could protect them. My ways of protection are different. Morlen will come to understand them in time, if he's smart. He'll trust me and you the way his father never could trust Roelstra. But what all this means is that we have to work very hard to keep their trust and faith.''

''It sounds awfully difficult—and grim.''

''Grim? Not at all. My son, we have to put up with some very tedious people because that's part of the way a prince does business. But it's worth enduring all the fuss because a prince can do so much to serve.''

''You mean serve the Goddess?''

''If you want to think of it that way. Personally, I let Aunt Andrade take care of that aspect of things. I meant to serve the people who trust us to look after the peace they need in order to live out their lives.''

Pol nodded slowly. ''Grandfather did it with his sword. You do it—''

''—by outsmarting everyone I possibly can.'' Rohan laughed again. ''Which I sometimes think is infinitely harder!''

A derisive snort greeted this remark. ''You love it and you know it.''

''I have to admit it can be fun. It's a great responsibility, but a joyful one. To conclude a treaty that gets a better price for sheep, to give a dowry to a boy or girl whose parents haven't anything for them—just knowing that armies won't trample the grain while it ripens—there's goodness in those things, Pol. And if the joy ever goes out of being a prince, then ask yourself who it is you're serving: the people who trust you, or yourself.''

''But you talk about duty as if it really is fun!''

''I never had more fun in my life than the night I gave

Remagev to Walvis. You never saw it when it was nothing but tumbledown walls and old Cousin Hadaan trying to prop them up. Walvis made it into a working keep again. Now he raises more sheep than anybody in the Long Sand, and his glass ingots are among the finest we produce. And there's joy in that, Pol.''

''I guess I understand. But it still seems grim sometimes.''

''Well, I suppose so. But we get so much, Pol—I'm not talking about deference or even the chance to outwit an *athri* who thinks he's outwitted you.'' Rohan smiled again. ''And it's not the jewels and fine horses and things that come of being rich. We get the chance to *do* things. Good things, things that matter and will make this a better place for our having been here.''

He crossed his ankles and stared at the toes of his boots. ''If you and I were, say, a farmer and his son, we'd make sure our wheat grew tall and hearty, so we'd get the best price and feed ourselves—but we're also feeding those who buy our grain. Of course, few farmers look at their crops and say, 'How wonderful that I'm growing such fine grain to feed so many!' But you see my point. All the crafts fit into the weave. So do you and I. Only what we get to do is somewhat more spectacular on the face of it.'' He shrugged. ''And it can hurt more, too. Sometimes you have to lead an army against someone who doesn't see being a prince as the chance to do valuable work, but instead regards it as the chance to make others do as he pleases.''

''The way Roelstra did.''

''Yes. That's when being a prince is a very hard thing. You have the power to order men and women into battle where many of them will die. That's the grimness, Pol. There's no joy in winning a war. There's only grief, and regret that it had to be fought at all.''

''But we have to sometimes, don't we? To get the chance to do the good things, help the people who trusted us enough to follow us and fight for us.'' Frowning, Pol went on, ''But we also have to work hard to make sure we're not cheated by people we have to protect whether they've cheated us or not! It hardly seems fair.''

''Did I ever say it was? Pol, there are many ways of

being a prince. One is to enjoy the material advantages and not worry about the responsibilities. You'll find plenty of examples at Waes. I prefer that type, personally. They're no threat to anything but their own treasuries. Another way is to enjoy your power to order people's lives—not for their beneift, but for your own amusement. You'll see several of that kind, as well. They aren't very fond of me, because I won't let them indulge. And then there's the kind like me, who prefer to exercise their brains instead of their swords. Sheer laziness,'' he said casually. ''I don't like going to war. It involves all sorts of inconveniences and I hate being away from my own home—''

''And Mother,'' Pol added mischievously.

''That goes without saying.''

The boy lounged deliberately back in his chair, legs sprawled and arms dangling. ''I think I'll be your kind of prince,'' he decided, grinning. ''As long as my wife's pretty enough!''

Whatever reply Rohan might have made other than laughter was interrupted by a discreet scratch at the door. Pol straightened up quickly as his father gave permission to enter. A young girl came in, dressed in brown homespun and carrying an empty tray.

''Just here to take away the dishes, your graces—excuse me, please, I won't be but a moment—''

''Of course,'' Rohan said, gesturing to the table where the wine pitcher rested and holding out his cup for her to take.

Pol, primed now to notice everything and draw conclusions, observed the girl closely. Wisps of black hair escaped the severely knotted braids at her nape, and she brushed them back with a remarkably well-kept hand. The dirt beneath her nails was an incongruity somehow, and set him to wondering. As she placed pitcher and cups on her tray, she met his curious gaze quite levelly. Her eyes were a peculiar shade of grayish green, their expression older than her perhaps eighteen winters. He blushed at being caught staring, and rose to stand near his father. The girl bent her knees awkwardly to them before turning to leave, but somehow the gracelessness seemed false as well, fitting her as badly as the brown homespun dress and dull green shawl with its ragged fringe. Her eyes held his again before she went out, and there was laughter in them.

"Father—"

Rohan held up a finger for silence. Pol listened, not knowing what he should be hearing, and then had it. The latch had not clicked. He thought rapidly, then said, "All that wine—which way to the nearest garderobe?"

Rohan nodded his approval and congratulations. "To the left, I think, end of the hallway."

Pol saw no one on his way there and back. He made sure the door was firmly shut when he came back into the room, and his father grinned at him.

"Very nice," Rohan approved. "See anybody?"

Pol shook his head. "Do you really think she wanted to listen?"

"I don't know. It might have been carelessness, leaving the door unlatched. But I think I'll watch Lord Morlen even more carefully. For now, though, I don't want to watch anything but the insides of my eyelids." He turned to the huge bed in the corner. "Do you know, I haven't slept beside anyone but your mother in longer than I can remember. I do hope you don't snore."

"Snore! Mother says that sometimes you rattle the windows!"

"A vile and insulting lie, for which she will pay dearly the next time she kicks all the covers on the floor."

Pol stripped and slid into bed, feeling a bit muddleheaded—not from his father's revelations about Rezeld or being a prince, but from the potent wine. He was gratified that no comment had been made about his taking a cup. Several cups, actually, enough to have made the garderobe really necessary; his ploy hadn't been entirely the inspiration it had seemed. Now, with the torches snuffed and only the soft starlight glowing through the windows, for it was one of those infrequent nights without moons, he felt as if his brain was slowly awhirl inside his skull.

After a considerable time in an unsilent darkness, he turned onto his side and fixed an accusing look on his father's sleeping face. "You do so snore!" he whispered, and got out of bed.

No one stirred down below in the small courtyard. He peered through a broken pane of glass and mused on what else besides tapestries and candles Lord Morlen might be hiding. His father would find it, whatever it was. During childhood Pol had always looked on Rohan as the source of all knowledge and wisdom. Nothing he had seen had ever disabused him of the notion. He simply could not conceive of his making a mistake.

But Pol began to think that he himself had as he saw a single figure hurry through the courtyard, heading for the postern gate. The starlight showed him a bulky dark gown and fringed shawl—and he blinked in surprise. Why would a servant girl be out at this time of night, and leaving the manor? The obvious explanation, a lover, occurred to him. He shrugged. But then the girl abruptly stopped, swung round, and looked straight up at Pol.

A slight, biting breeze came through a broken pane. Pol drew back, his gaze fixed on the woman's upturned starlit face. Not a girl's face; a woman's. Its shape was the same in arch of brows and line of the mouth. But this was the face of a mature woman of fifty winters, probably more. She was smiling, the laughter that had been in her eyes earlier finding expression in a malicious, mocking curve of lips and quirk of brows.

Then she drew the shawl up over her head and melted away, out the postern gate and into the night-dark forest. Pol shivered and turned away, deeply troubled.

"What is it?" his father asked softly, sitting up in bed, the stars glinting off his fair hair.

"Nothing." Pol made an effort to smile. "Maybe Meath is right, and I *am* too young for that much wine."

* * *

Mireva reached the brookside tree where she had left her own clothes, and shucked off those she had stolen from a drying line at Rezeld Manor. Excitement warmed her cheeks and her body; she felt nothing of the night's chill as she redressed in her own garments.

So that was young Prince Pol, she thought. An intriguing face, just like the father's, but with the aura of more than princely power about him. More than Sunrunner power, as well. Mireva laughed aloud as she loosed her hair from its confining braid and shook her head wildly.

She had not been mistaken about the sensation of being with her own that had come at proximity to the youth. She knew it in Ianthe's three sons, and in all others who were of *diarmadhi* blood. But whereas with Ruval, Marron, and Segev, she knew the power had come from Princess Lallante, she had no idea which of Pol's ancestors had carried the gift. Sioned's people were readily traced on her father's side back to the *faradhi* invasion of the continent; no source there. Of her mother's people before the marriage of a Sunrunner to a Prince of Kierst, nothing was known. Perhaps Pol got his doubled talents from her.

But there was Rohan as well. Again, his paternal ancestors were firmly established—but his mother Milar's forebears, who were also Andrade's. . . . Mireva tied her skirt around her waist, grinning. What perfect irony if the Lady of Goddess Keep herself was *diarmadhi!*

Then she sobered. Whoever and wherever it had come from, this second legacy of power was a new wrinkle and possibly a dangerous one. Sunrunner alone was bad enough, but Mireva could have dealt with that. Pol's inheritance of her own kind of power presented several alternatives.

She started the long walk back to her own dwelling, mulling over her choices. Killing Pol tonight had not been one of them; nor was drugging him or interfering in any way with his mind or body. She had only wanted a look at him, to judge what kind of man he would grow into. There was much of his father about him, not only in looks and the way he held himself but in the clear-eyed, intelligent, curious way he had looked at her. No, killing him was not what she had come for, not why she had assumed her guise of youthfulness—and then shed it, knowing he watched. To explore his face with her eyes, to intuit his *faradhi* strength, to set an uneasiness into his mind: those had been her purposes. Killing him would have to wait some years yet.

But this business of his being *diarmadhi* was a thing to give her pause, and perhaps to rethink the future. What if she let it be known and demonstrated somehow that Pol was descended from those Andrade feared so much, those the *faradh'im* had worked so hard to destroy? The other princes were nervous enough about his Sunrunner status as it was; might they object so strongly to having him trained in the arts that Rohan would have to back down on Pol's *faradhi* education in order to save his throne? What if she threw her own support behind the boy, instead of Ianthe's sons, and made him her pupil? That thought held a great deal of charm, but she rejected it with a shake of her head. There was too much in Pol's face of his honorable fool of a father to make Mireva's games of ambition and power palatable to him.

But what if she told nothing about Pol's other gift—and taught Ruval methods the *diarmadh'im* had used to discipline, even kill, their own kind? Their greatest tragedy was that these had no effect on *faradh'im;* while fighting off the Sunrunners so valiantly, they had learned this to their final defeat. Of course, teaching the willful Ruval such potency was a calculated risk; he might use it on his brothers or even on her if she could not control him. She knew Ianthe's sons, and trusted none of them.

Mireva slowed her strides as dawn slid over the mountains, and stopped as she watched the last stars fade before another day of blinding summer sun. Uncharacteristically indecisive, she worried the problems for some time as the air heated around her and made even her thin gown too warm. Then she shrugged. She would wait and see whether Ruval would need such methods against Pol. There were many years ahead to plan the boy's death—and she reminded herself that Sunrunners had their own special vulnerability, one that her people did not share. Pol's *faradhi* blood made him susceptible. It would be an interesting choice of deaths for him—through his proud Sunrunner heritage or through his unsuspected Old Blood. But for the present she had other concerns.

She had not heard from Segev since his departure for Goddess Keep. Soon she would have to reach him on starlight, find out if he was close to successful theft of the precious scrolls. Soon, too, she would have to discover what had happened to Masul, who had killed four of her strongest minions in escaping from what would have been his surest path to triumph. She had heard rumors about him for years, of course; Dasan Manor was only a mountain or two from her home. She shrugged again, irritably. If he was too stupid to grasp at the kind of power she could offer, he deserved to fail. Whether or not he was Roelstra's son made no difference to Mireva; she only wanted to use him to find out what sort of approach would be best when it came Ruval's turn to challenge Pol.

But this led her back to the vexing question of exactly what she ought to teach Ruval. How much she dared teach him. How far she could trust him.

Mireva trudged on through the growing daylight, cursing the necessity of having others do her work for her. At a time when she had been ready to abandon all hope of ever restoring her people to their rightful place, Lallante's grandsons had given her renewed purpose. But still she wished that they were not also Roelstra's get. The man had been impossible to control. She wondered suddenly if that was why Lallante had married him. Her kinswoman had always been a puling ninny, frightened of power and declaring that it was not for nothing that their people had been defeated so long ago. Roelstra, High Prince, most powerful man of his generation—until Rohan had come along—had provided Lallante with a haven utterly safe from any other influences, including those of her own kind. Roelstra, who had been as ungovernable as his grandsons would be if Mireva was not very, very careful.

Chapter Thirteen

Castle Crag had not seen such splendor in more than forty-five years, not since Lallante had arrived to become Roelstra's bride. Banners of all the important *athr'im* of Princemarch snapped in a breeze surging up from the gorge, and the golden dragon on blue was raised to signify that the High Prince himself would soon be in residence. An eager crowd lined the road for half a measure, four people deep. Flowers were strewn, people cheered themselves hoarse, and trumpets blared from the battlements as Rohan and Pol led the way into the courtyard.

Pol whispered to his father: ''I feel like I'm about to be the main course at a banquet.''

Rohan laughed softly. ''They're hungry for a sight of you, hatchling, not a bite of you!''

Rohan had never before visited Princemarch and had resisted all suggestions that he do so. Although nominally it belonged to him, he had made it clear that Pandsala was Pol's regent, not his, and that his son should be considered Princemarch's ruler, not himself. Once the boy was knighted and had learned *faradhi* skills, he would take over here and rule it as an independent princedom until, at Rohan's death, the Desert would also become his. Rohan hoped that years of thinking of Pol as their prince would make the transition smoother when it came time for Pol to govern.

This distinction was pointed up by Pandsala's welcome. She came down the stairway, dressed in blue and violet, and her first bow was to Pol. He followed his father's instructions, taking her hands, raising her from her knees, and bowing over her left hand where she wore the topaz and amethyst of her regency—along with Sunrunner's rings. Only then did she turn to Rohan and bend her knees. Thus it was that in full view of the highborns and other dignitaries assembled in the courtyard, Pol's place was openly acknowledged as being above Rohan's. It was prettily done, and Rohan appreciated it.

Pol had never met Pandsala before, and found her something of a surprise. She did not look her forty-four winters, but was rather more as he recalled Lady Andrade: nearly ageless, anywhere from thirty to sixty. Her face had a sharp-boned, aristocratic handsomeness that conveyed great dignity but little warmth, even when she smiled. In addition to the ring Rohan had given her as token of her charge, she wore five Sunrunner's rings. Her eyes were cool brown, and silver waved from her temples through braids wound atop her head. Her welcome was delivered in a quiet, respectful voice, and everything was done with the ceremony due their rank—and she made Pol very uneasy. Certainly she was pleasant enough. He did not understand his reaction to her; perhaps it was the way she gazed at him, then looked away whenever he tried to meet her glance directly.

"I have messages for your grace from High Princess Sioned," she told him while escorting him, Rohan, and Maarken upstairs to their chambers.

"You do?" Pol asked eagerly, only realizing at that moment how much he missed his mother. Then, because he didn't want to show it, he added, "Have the dragons hatched yet?"

"Not for another ten days or so," she replied, smiling a little. "Probably at about the time we leave for Waes."

"I'm sorry we'll be taking the long way this year, my lady," Maarken apologized with a smile both rueful and charming. "Neither Pol nor I have your enviable ability to cross water without disgracing ourselves."

"It's of no consequence, Lord Maarken. I never much liked the sail down the Faolain anyway." She turned to Rohan. "The High Princess is quite well, my lord, and begs that you will be on time to the *Rialla*. She has much information to share with you about the dragons."

"She and Lady Feylin have discussed nothing else all summer," he said, smiling. "That was a beautiful tapestry on the landing, Pandsala. Cunaxan?"

"Gribain, my lord, and new. I've been encouraging trade with them, as you suggested some years ago. They've improved since their first efforts."

"Mmm. I think we saw a few at Rezeld Manor—clumsy, threadbare things that wouldn't keep out a sneeze, let alone the winter winds they must get up in the mountains." He glanced at Pol, his expression perfectly innocent, and the boy had a difficult time controlling his own. "I was impressed with Lord Morlen, however, and his inventory of livestock. You'll have to fill me in about his quarry, too, while we're here."

"I'm pleased he's done better in the last few years, my lord. He's forever crying poverty." She gestured to a servant who opened a large door of carved pine inlaid with shining black stone. "Lord Maarken, this is your suite. I hope it will be satisfactory."

Maarken was self-possessed enough not to gape at the luxuries within. He merely nodded. "Thank you, my lady. I'm sure it's entirely adequate to my needs. If you'll excuse me, I'll wash off the dirt of the road and attend you later."

Pol did not have sufficient control of his eyes and jaw not to react when Pandsala herself opened the door of the suite he would share with his father. The first room was a gigantic reception chamber, bearing signs of recent redecoration, though not in the manner of Rezeld: here there were new hangings, fresh paint, cushions that had never been sat on, and the tart scent of citrus polish. Blue, violet, and gold were the dominant colors, sumptuous and slightly overwhelming.

The bedchambers were done in similar fashion. Smiling, Rohan watched Pol's face, and when Pandsala had left them he said, "Well? What do you think?"

"It's—it's—"

"Yes, it is, isn't it?" He sank into a chair, relishing its comfort after so many days in the saddle.

"Father—she makes me a little nervous."

"If she behaved a little stiffly, it's because she's anxious for everything to be perfect. Actually, *you* probably make *her* nervous, too."

"Me?"

"Mm-hmm. I may have hired her on, but her real master is you—and she knows it."

"But I don't have any say in what goes on here!"

"Not *yet.*"

Pol digested this in silence, then jumped on the bed, landing with a bounce and a grin. "At least I have my own room and don't have to listen to you snore!"

"I do *not* snore, you insolent—"

"Do so."

"Do not!" Rohan tugged a pillow from behind his back and threw it. Pol responded with an overstuffed bedcushion. Rohan caught it and tossed it back at him. "Not again, or we'll have feathers all over!"

"Dignity, dignity," Pol said mournfully, shaking his head. "I have to behave myself, don't I?" He fell onto his stomach, arms wrapped around the pillow. "Well, when I *do* come to live here, this stuff is going to go. I don't care if princes have to live in state—I'd be afraid to take a bath in case I got the tub dirty! Did you see the size of that thing? You and Mother don't live this way. Why did Pandsala do all this?''

"The whole place is the same, you know. And think for a moment about why she'd want to make this the most splendid suite in all Castle Crag. Don't mistake her, Pol. She's not showing off what she can do with money. Everything she does is for us. When she committed to us against her own father, she risked everything—including her life. There were plenty of people, Tobin and Andrade included, who told me I was out of my mind to make her regent here. She knows that, too.'' He sighed quietly. "Her commitment is all she has. With her royal blood, she could never have been a traditional kind of Sunrunner, attached to a court somewhere. Can you honestly see a daughter of High Prince Roelstra as a court *faradhi?* And since Andrade never liked her much, returning to Goddess Keep was out of the question.''

"Mother wouldn't have her at Stronghold, either,'' Pol observed.

"Uneasiness around Pandsala isn't an uncommon reaction,'' he mused. "I can't say that I'm all that fond of her, but I appreciate her and especially the work she's done for us.'' He paused a moment. "It gave her a life, Pol. She was trained for nothing in her youth except to be a princess, and then after her father's death—'' He shrugged.

"I heard Mother say once that ruling here is her revenge on her father.''

"Perhaps. But she also genuinely cares about you and about Princemarch. We've seen what the results have been.''

"Except that she never figured out about Lord Morlen!'' Pol grinned, then sobered. "But I can't help feeling funny around her.''

"As I said, she probably feels funny around you, too. Stop thinking so much!'' he chided affectionately. "If I worried as much as you do, I'd be bald as a dragon's egg. We're supposed to be having a good time, you know.''

"I *was*—until we had to start getting dressed for dinner. Any chance that there won't be a banquet tonight?''

"You can dream,'' his father replied.

But the banquet was canceled only a short time before

it was due to begin. Rohan was still draped in a bath towel when Maarken came to tell him the information Pandsala had just received on the last of the evening sunlight.

"Inoat of Ossetia and his son Jos went sailing today on Lake Kadar. They were due back well before sunset. But their boat washed up onshore, empty. Rohan—the bodies were found a little while ago. They're both dead."

He sat down on the ornate bed. "Another death—two deaths. Sweet Goddess. . . . Jos is a few winters younger than Pol." He picked at the fringed hangings. "Chale must be devastated. He adored them both."

Maarken nodded. "His only son and only grandson. I met Inoat once or twice—he visited at Goddess Keep while I was there. I liked him, Rohan. He would've made a fine prince." He paused. "I've told Pandsala to cancel everything at once. I hope that wasn't presumptuous."

"No, not at all. Thank you for thinking of it. We'll observe the ritual for them tonight. . . ." He trailed off and raked a hand back through his wet hair. "You know what all this means, don't you? It may sound cold to be thinking politics right now, but—"

"You're High Prince. You have to think politics."

He smiled slightly. "You're very like your father—good for my conscience in all ways. He's soothing when I need it, and kicks me when it's necessary. Promise you'll always do the same for Pol."

Maarken returned the smile. "I'm his the same way my father is yours."

"And Ossetia will be Princess Gemma's. Chale has no other heir."

"Gemma? His cousin?"

"Niece. Her mother was Chale's sister."

Rohan saw Maarken look down at the first of his Sunrunner's rings—a garnet that had belonged to Gemma's older brother Jastri, Prince of Syr, who had died fighting on Roelstra's side against the Desert.

"She's suddenly become a very important young lady," Maarken observed.

"And Waes will be overflowing with men trying to catch her eye."

Maarken gave a start. "Not me!" he exclaimed.

"Have you someone else in mind?"

Blanching slightly, he hesitated and then shook his head. Rohan only smiled. Maarken returned to the main subject, a tactical maneuver not lost on his uncle. "Where's Gemma now?"

"At High Kirat with Sioned's brother Davvi. They're all cousins through the Syrene royal house. Gemma's still a Princess of Syr, of course, and technically Davvi's ward."

"She'll need the High Prince's consent to marry."

"Yes. And what if she chooses someone I can't stomach as the next Prince of Ossetia? Or even worse, what if the man she picks is unpalatable to Chale? He and I don't agree on much."

"If you interfere too much, you'll be accused of trying to control Ossetia through Gemma." Maarken made an annoyed gesture. "And there's Firon! This on top of that isn't going to make you very popular."

"Watch the greedy High Prince gobble up land and power," Rohan agreed bitterly. "We don't need to explore this fully right now, Maarken. Is Pandsala competent at Moonrunning?"

"I'm not sure. She has five rings, and that makes her an apprentice—but I'm not sure how much training she had before she left Goddess Keep. I'll ask."

"Good. If she's capable, then you two can divide up *faradhi* duties for me tonight. I need to get word to Davvi to put a guard on Gemma, if he hasn't already done so. Pandsala can send our condolences to Chale, Regent to Prince. They'll both appreciate that. You'll have to contact Andrade. I don't think she and Pandsala have exchanged a word in fifteen years. And Sioned will have to know all of it after you've finished with the rest." Rising from the bed, he looked at the clothes laid out for him. "Have Pandsala arrange with her steward for gray mourning. Where is the ritual held here?"

"For the dead of other princedoms, the oratory."

"Ah. I'd hoped to see it under more pleasant circumstances. I'm told it's a marvel. Have I forgotten anything, Maarken?"

"Not that I can think of. Do you want me to send Pol in here to you?"

"Yes—do that. Thank you. Then go find Pandsala for me, and we'll get started." Brushing the hair from his eyes again, he said, "And remind me to tell Pol that under no circumstances is he to so much as *look* at Gemma unless he absolutely has to. The only thing I lack is a rumor that their marriage will give us Ossetia. Besides, she's—what, ten winters older than he?"

"Boys grow up fast at nearly fifteen," Maarken commented.

Rohan made a sour face. "I don't think he realizes yet that girls exist."

"Boys grow up fast at nearly fifteen," Maarken repeated, and grinned.

* * *

The candles guttered in neat rows, the warm brilliance of their first burning faded to uncertain glimmers. Rohan stood before them, acutely aware of the darkness behind him. It was long past midnight, the ritual over. He had spoken to the assembled highborns and dignitaries here in the oratory, brief words about the loss suffered in the deaths of Inoat and Jos, fulfilling his obligation as High Prince. The candles had been placed along the back wall, and everyone had gone down to the dinner waiting for them. Rohan told himself he ought to be there, too, even if this was no longer an official ceremonial banquet, for he was hungry and Pol would want him near while everyone took his measure. But Pol had Maarken and Pandsala to see him through any rough patches, and Rohan wasn't ready to join them just yet.

The oratory was an exquisite thing, a half-dome of faceted Fironese crystal projecting out from the cliffside castle, furnished with white chairs covered by white velvet. By sun, moons, or stars, it would glow. But the sky had turned black shortly after moonrise, clouds the color of smoke obscuring all light. Only the candles shone, and they burned low.

Outside the Ossetian seat of Athmyr, the bodies of father and son would be ablaze now on a shared pyre. Old Prince Chale and his *faradhi* would wait and watch through the night until flesh became ash, and then the Sunrunner would call up a gentle breath of Air to carry the ashes over land that had given the two princes birth, land that they would never rule. Candles would burn in honor of that funeral fire here in this oratory and at similar places in each princedom: the small glass-domed chamber at Davvi's High Kirat, the central hall of Volog's court at New Raetia, the *faradhi* calendar room at Graypearl that Pol had described in awed detail. Rohan wondered where Sioned would hold the ritual at Skybowl; Stronghold had a chamber for the purpose, but Skybowl had no such facility. He imagined she would choose a place outdoors by the lake, perhaps even float candles out across the dark water.

The same had been done at Skybowl for his father—of whom Roelstra had spoken here in this very chamber on the night Zehava's body had burned to ashes in the Desert. Rohan doubted that Roelstra's elegy had been heartfelt.

Turning from the candles, Rohan glanced up at the crystal ceiling where flickering lights reflected in the etched panes. Where the clear dome met the stone floor thirty paces from him was a table bearing silver and gold plate and two cups of beaten gold. The chunks of uncut amethyst set into the goblets were said to have fallen from the sky with the first sunset. Only one marriage had ever been celebrated with them, that of Roelstra to his only wife, Lallante. Rohan supposed that sooner or later Pol would stand here to wed some suitable girl. The ruler of Princemarch could hardly avoid being married in his own oratory. Yet despite its beauty, Rohan could not banish the chill he sensed within this room. Roelstra had ruled here too long.

He paced silently down the white carpet to the center of the chamber, directly below the place where crystal met smoothed rock high overhead. The panes were set in delicate stone traceries that must have taken years to carve. He admired the workmanship but wondered why he could sense none of the crafters' joy in creating such beauty. His mother's gardens at Stronghold—her life's work and her pride—had a different feel altogether. She and a small army of workers had transformed the barren wards of the castle into a miracle of grace and growing things: every flowerbed, tree, bench, and curve of the little stream bespoke pleasure in the making. His own refurbishing of the Great Hall had something of the same feel to it—artisans delighting in their skills that produced such marvels. This oratory, despite its magnificence, was a cold and lifeless place that not even the gentle candle-light could warm.

He told himself he would feel differently about it once he had viewed it in full sunshine. He would be able to see across the vast canyon to the opposite cliffs, and down to the rush of the Faolain far below. The oratory would not then feel like a crystal bubble clinging in darkness to the side of a mountain, isolated and chill and redolent of his enemy.

Rohan turned quickly as the doors swung open. Pand-sala stood there, candlelight limning her body and turn-ing her gray mourning gown and veil to dark liquid silver.

"Everyone is asking for you, my lord."

"I'll be down in a moment. How fares my son?"

She smiled, dark eyes glinting with pride. "Charming everyone, of course, just as I expected."

"Don't let his pretty manners fool you. He can be a terror when he pleases, and stubborn enough for six."

"Would he be a boy if he weren't? My chamberlain's four sons have been my pages, one after the other, and each more mischievous than the last." She moved into the room and the doors swung shut behind her. "Because he *is* a boy with those qualities, though, I thought I should warn you. He's heard about the old custom of proving one's strength and courage by scaling the cliffs opposite the castle. I'm afraid he's taken it into his head to try."

"I've heard about it. The idea is to slide back down on the ropes—a little like flying. I can see how that would appeal to him."

"You'll forbid it, naturally."

Rohan chuckled. "Let me tell you something about my hatchling, Pandsala. Forbidding him to do something is tantamount to issuing an open invitation for him to work his way around to doing it anyhow."

"But it's too dangerous!"

"Probably."

"And he's so young!"

"He's older than Maarken was when he went to war. Pandsala, if I forbid it, he'll only go off and do it on his own I could lock him in his rooms and he'd still find a way of getting out and doing just as he pleases. With Pol, you have to use sweet reason and a guile even greater than his own—and sometimes not even *that* works.''

"But, my lord—" she began.

"Let's go downstairs. I'll show you something about our stubborn prince.''

Rohan had only just supplied himself with a plate of food and a winecup when his offspring came through the crowd, Maarken right behind him. "Watch," Rohan whispered to Pandsala, who looked on worriedly as Pol sought permission to test his strength and courage against the cliffs.

"And I was thinking, Father, that it would be good for us politically, too," he finished with admirable if transparent shrewdness.

"As well as terrific fun," Rohan added.

Pol nodded enthusiastically. "I've done some climbing around Stronghold and Skybowl, and Prince Chadric took all the squires to some rocks near Graypearl for lessons. It was right over the ocean, too, so I know all about how to go climbing over water without getting nervous. May I, Father? Please?''

Rohan pretended to consider, though his decision had already been made—prompted partly by Pandsala's automatic assumption that he would forbid this. "What arrangements would you make for this feat?''

"Well, I know it's a little dangerous. But Maarken could come with me if he wants to, and Maeta loves to go climbing—and if we had a group of people who've done it before, then they could take the lead and show us how. It won't be that much of a risk, Father. And if I'm going to be prince here, I really ought to show them what I'm made of.''

Rohan's lips twitched in a smile. "Maarken, how do you feel about this?''

The young man shrugged. "If he's determined to do this crazy thing, then I'll go with him.''

"Hmm. I'll think it over.''

A flicker of disappointment showed in Pol's face, but then he decided to put the best possible interpretation on the words. "Thank you, Father!''

A man approached, was introduced as Lord Cladon of River Ussh, and talk turned to other things. When Rohan and Pandsala were comparatively private once more, he turned to her and smiled. "Well?"

"I think I understand, my lord. He thought up ways to convince you it would be safe in order to win your permission. Had you *dictated* those terms, however, he would have been resentful—and defied you."

"Exactly. A few days from now he'll have researched the problem and presented me with further precautions for his safety—*and* he'll know a great deal more about climbing than he does at present."

"But you'd already made up your mind."

"He's right, you know—it would be an excellent thing if he proved himself at so young an age." He watched as shock widened her eyes, correctly interpreted her expression, and answered it with, "Don't think I'm not afraid for him, Pandsala. But I can't wrap him in silk. I can guide his steps, but I won't prevent him from getting a few bruises. It's the only way he'll ever become a man on his own, a prince worthy of the lands he'll inherit."

"Forgive me, my lord, but—" She hesitated, then went on, "We've all been reminded very painfully today of how quickly a prince's life can be lost. Pol is simply too valuable to risk."

"So was I." He paused, then went on softly, "My parents kept me sheltered until I was thirteen—well past the usual age for fostering. When they did let me go, it was to my cousin Hadaan at Remagev—barely a day's ride from Stronghold. I had a little more freedom there, but not much. By the time my father's last war with the Merida came, I was frantic to prove myself, so I marched out disguised as a common soldier. It was a damned foolish thing to do. I could very easily have been killed. But they'd forbidden me to go as the heir, you see. Maeta's mother, who commanded the Stronghold guard before her, caught me but decided to look the other way. She understood that I'd been more or less driven to it by my parents' cosseting. My poor mother nearly had heart failure and my father was furious with me. But he also knighted me on the field."

"And you don't want Pol driven to the same kind of

thing," Pandsala mused. "Even so, my lord, it's a terrible chance to take."

"Sioned will be livid when she finds out, of course. But I can't help that. I often wonder why I didn't defy my parents much sooner. Perhaps it was lack of opportunity—but I suspect it was really fear of my father." He shrugged.

"It was the same for me," she said, looking anywhere but at him. "We were all terrified of Roelstra. But you never hated your father the way I did mine."

"With us as examples, do you wonder why I allow Pol the freedom to do this? He won't have the need to do anything as foolhardy as I did—"

"Or as wicked as I did. We are indeed edifying examples, my lord." She gave him a tiny smile. "Very well, I understand—but I'll make sure my best people go with him on the climb."

"Thank you. It's all we can ever do, you know—take what precautions we can, and trust to the Goddess' mercy for the rest." He sighed ruefully. "Frankly, the whole idea of this scares me silly. But I have to let Pol be who and what he is. He's going to be, whether I allow it or not—so why fight it?"

"As you wish, my lord."

"Besides," Rohan finished with a grin, "my hatchling quite naturally wants to fly. Pandsala, I'd like to meet privately with each of the vassals tomorrow. Will you arrange it for me, please?"

"Of course, my lord." She paused thoughtfully, searching his eyes. "Do you know, with all the differences between you and my father—both as men and as High Prince—I think it all may come down to one simple thing. My father never said 'please' to anybody in his life."

* * *

Pol was glad of his thick leather jacket as updrafts from the river far below sent chill gusts along the cliffs. Summer was three-quarters over, and whereas in the Desert and at Graypearl the days would still be searingly hot, here in the mountains clouds had formed again last night. Having finally won permission from his father to make the climb—after four days of alternating pleas with detailed plans—Pol had been frantic lest a late-summer rain spoil his chance. They were due to leave for Waes in two days; the climb had to be this morning or not at all.

He looked down for the first time since beginning the upward struggle, and gulped. He hadn't realized how far he'd come, how far below him the river now was. He clung more tightly to the iron ring driven into the rock face and forced himself to lift his head, trying to judge the distance to the top and how long it would take to get there. A tug on the rope around his waist signaled that it was time to make the next move across the cliff. He swallowed hard, refusing to admit that he had been a fool to attempt this climb.

As fingers and toes found holds, his confidence returned. This wasn't much different from scrambling up ragged, wind-sculpted stone in the Vere Hills, except for the distance down. The view was splendid; he really did feel akin to the dragons. He imagined himself equipped with wings, bracing for flight and then soaring out over the gorge, every fiber of his body singing—

"Pol! Pay attention!"

Maeta's command alerted him, and he was reminded that he definitely was not a dragon. He scrambled up to join her on a tiny ledge, breathing hard.

"Some fun, eh?" She grinned at him. "You're doing fine. Give Maarken's rope a tug and let's get started for the top."

"How much farther?" He squinted upward.

"About half the time it took us to get this far. Then we can have lunch, rest, and fly back down."

"I wish we could've flown *up.*"

Maeta laughed and rubbed his shoulder affectionately. "It's the challenge that counts. The privilege of flight has to be earned, you know. Besides, think of the nice, quiet ride back up the canyon when we're done! I'll even let you fall asleep on your horse. See you at the top, hatchling."

She set off again and Pol watched her find the handholds near the next iron ring. Maeta threaded the rope through and tied it off to provide Pol's support for the next part of his climb, just as she was linked to the man above her for safety. Soon Maarken had joined Pol on the ledge, panting to catch his breath.

"I must've been crazy to agree to this!"

"You and me both," Pol admitted. "I'm running out of fingernails." He held out hands scraped and bloodied by gripping sharp stone, and grinned at his cousin. "But it's worth it! Take a look!"

Maarken seemed to inhale the sky and trees and cliffs, his gaze lingering as Pol's did on the multicolored wild-flowers clinging to the rocks. "Wonderful!" he exclaimed. "But I don't dare look down—last time I did I nearly lost my breakfast. I don't think I'll be able to climb my way out of bed tomorrow! But you're right, it's worth it." He peered across the canyon, and pointed. "Is that your father and Pandsala?"

Pol waved and nearly lost his balance. Maarken steadied him with a firm grip on his shoulder. "Thanks," he said shakily. "D'you think they can see us?"

"That blue jacket of yours must be visible for half a measure."

"As if you're inconspicuous!" Pol scoffed, flicking a finger against his cousin's bright red. Another tug on the rope alerted him, and he set off again. After half a morning of this he was sure of what he was doing, but the ridges cut into the stone had been made for a full-grown person, not a boy coming up on his fifteenth winter. He had to stretch quite a bit sometimes to reach the holds, and his shoulders and legs were beginning to ache in earnest. "When the hell am I going to *grow?*" he muttered as he scrabbled for a niche and barely reached it.

He was also eager to grow in ways other than height. Over the past few days Pol had sat in on talks with men who were nominally his vassals, and the ambassadors and emissaries from other princedoms. Rohan's warning that a prince must listen to some very tedious people had been forcibly demonstrated; at times, Pol could barely keep his eyes open. But it was amusing to watch these people look back and forth from him to Rohan—one the real owner of Princemarch and the other its real ruler. They couldn't seem to decide if they ought to be seriously concerned with Pol's opinions or treat him with a kind of half-amused indulgence: the boy pretending to be a

prince. It would be nice to be older, he mused as he
sought for the next toehold, to be Maarken's age and
Maarken's height, with Maarken's easy authority.

He had just secured himself to the next ring when a
metallic clang hit rock. His head turned, and something
gray and slightly rusty flew past him down into the canyon. Looking up, he saw Maeta frozen on the cliff face,
arms and legs outspread.

"Maeta!"

"Check the ring, Pol. Hurry."

He inspected the iron circle and terror stopped his heart
for a moment. The spike anchoring the ring had worked
loose. If stressed, it probably would hold no weight
greater than his own, and might not even support *him* for
very long.

"It's coming out, isn't it?" Maeta called softly, her
voice slightly breathless.

He explored the joining of spike and stone. "Somebody's picked at it!"

"I thought as much." She hesitated, then said, "My
rope's frayed, too."

"The man ahead of you must've—"

"I don't think so. Not and risk his own life in the
process. Pol, untie the rope connecting us."

He realized what she was asking. "No! If you lose
hold, you'll fall!"

"And if I fall with the rope tied to the ring and to you,
I'll take you with me. Do as I say."

"Maeta—I can climb up to you—"

"No!" The force of her exclamation shifted her body,
and pebbles trickled down from the slender purchase
gained by her left boot. "Listen to me, kinsman," she
said more softly. "This is no accident. The ring that just
fell had been dug loose. I was a fool not to see it before.
I apologize, my prince."

"Maeta, just hold still. I'll come up to you. Neither
of us will fall—"

"Damn it, untie the rope! I don't intend to fall! But if
I do, you and Maarken won't be able to hold me, not
with that ring ready to come out of the rock! Do it, Pol!
The longer you take, the longer I have to stay as I am."

He choked back another protest and did as told. Maarken, still on the ledge below, called up, "Stay put, both of you! I'll get the rope around the rocks!"

"Maarken—don't let her fall!"

Although what he thought his cousin might do was beyond him. His gaze fixed on Maeta, willing her to find a more secure grip. She found a crevice, then another, groping for holds that would take some of the strain from her muscles.

"Pol, don't move." Maarken was just below him. "I've lashed the rope to some rocks and alerted everyone below us. Let me past you and I'll tie the other end to Maeta."

Pol flattened himself against the cliff as Maarken maneuvered past his legs, finding holds where none had been carved into the cliff. "She's more secure now," the boy said, amazed at the calm voice he didn't recognize as his own. "What do you want me to do?"

"Climb back to the ledge, get a grip on the rope, and brace yourself." Maarken paused to pat his leg reassuringly, then slid by and started for Maeta.

It had been much easier to stretch upward with his arms than it was to grope downward with his feet while his fingers dug into the crevices. He was nearly to the narrow ledge when he heard a thin hissing sound that made him flinch with reaction. The steel tip of an arrow struck a spark off stone an arm's length from his head.

"Maarken!" he yelled.

"Get behind the rocks!"

Another arrow brought a flash near Maarken's feet. Pol scrambled to safety and stared across the gorge at Castle Crag. The arrows had to be coming from there, loosed by a viciously powerful bow to reach all the way across. But the towers were too far away for him to see the bowman, who might have been hidden in any one of a hundred windows. Pandsala, he thought irrelevantly, was going to be furious.

Maarken was right below Maeta now, his fingers within reach of her ankle. The climbers above her had tossed down a fresh rope, and she tried to grab it as they swung it closer to her hands. Maarken shouted to her to keep still. Another arrow and then another hit the stones with faint ringing sounds. Pol curled as small as he could get behind an outcropping of stone, fists clenched, salt sweat burning in his eyes. "Come on, come on," he whispered. *"Please—"*

Maarken pulled himself up nearly beside Maeta, his arm reaching for her waist. She coughed and gave a start of surprise. Very slowly her hand reached back to fumble at the arrow embedded next to her spine, an arrow fletched in brown and yellow. Merida colors.

Her fingers loosened. Her tall body arched over backward, giving Pol a view of her already dead face, her sightless black eyes. It took forever for her to fall away from Maarken's desperate grasp, away from the gray cliff, past Pol, drifting down to brush against jagged stones and finally disappear into the dark depths of the canyon.

There were no more arrows. Pol turned tear-blurred eyes to Castle Crag and saw a bright flame rising from the upper battlements. Like a torch flame at this distance, a single light against the shadowy bulk of the keep—but a flame that grew arms that thrashed in futile agony as Sunrunner's Fire immolated human flesh. The torch flared, then sank out of sight.

He felt Maarken's hands on his shoulders, heard sobbing breaths. "Pol—are you all right? Not hurt? Talk to me!"

He looked at Maarken without comprehension. Sweat and tears streaked his cousin's face, and there was a gash circled by a swelling bruise on Maarken's forehead. "I'm not hurt," he heard himself say. "But you are."

"Just a scratch. Never mind me. We'll stay here for a while until you stop shaking." Maarken's strong arm went around him.

"I'm not shaking," Pol said, then realized he was. He buried his face against his cousin's shoulder.

"Shh. She's worth more than our tears, Pol, but that's all we can give her right now. Even though she'd scold us for it."

"If—if she hadn't made me untie the rope—"

"Then we would've lost you, too," Maarken said thickly. "Sweet Goddess, to have that woman's courage—"

After a time they quieted, and Maarken's embrace relaxed a little. "All right now?" he asked, wiping his own cheeks.

Pol nodded. "I'll find who did it, and I'll kill him."

"Pandsala already has. You saw the Fire. She killed with her gift."

Shock warred with fierce joy that the archer was dead. But stronger than either, outrage stiffened Pol's spine. Pandsala had acted peremptorily, killing the assassin before he could be questioned.

"She'll answer to *me*," Pol corrected. "I am prince here, and I'm the one they wanted dead. If the loosened rings didn't do it, then the archer was there to finish me off. Why didn't Pandsala order the man subdued and held?"

"I'm sure she'll have a good explanation." He waved to the rest of the climbers, who were making their way swiftly to the ledge. "Meantime, it seems we're arguing with her for saving our lives. Would you rather be dead?"

"No. But she didn't have to kill him—especially not that way."

"Remember whose daughter she is."

"And whose son I am." Pol knuckled his eyes and took a deep breath to steady himself. "Did you see the arrows, Maarken? Brown and yellow. Merida."

"Who else?"

* * *

Pandsala was not merely furious. In her father or her sister Ianthe, this rage would have brought further executions. She wanted to find someone else to punish, someone on whom to vent this terrible fury of shame and fear. She watched the Merida burn down to ash in Sunrunner's Fire and only the presence of the High Prince prevented her from calling the captain of her guard and killing him, too, for allowing a traitor to invade Castle Crag.

Rohan, set-faced, turned away from the writhing, stinking flames. His gaze sought the cliffs opposite, where Pol and Maarken were being helped up to the clifftop. He walked around the smoldering corpse and stood with his hands flat on the wall, the stone cool and gritty beneath his palms. The canyon gaped below him, magnificent and lethal. The Faolain River seethed white foam against the rocks. Had this been the Desert, scavenger birds would already be circling. But this was not the Desert, and they would find Maeta's broken body far downriver or wedged among the crags—if they found her at all. Death in dark water was not suited to a woman of bright sands and endless skies.

He was aware of Pandsala's presence behind him. Her rage made him marvel at his own deadly calm. He ought to be roaring out his fury, ordering reprisals against the Merida hidden in the valleys of Cunaxa. Twice now they had attempted Pol's life; by rights he should be claiming a hundred Merida lives for each threat against his son. His northern levies under Walvis' command were already near the border. He had only to send word to Sioned via Maarken on the sunlight, and the invasion would begin.

He knew why he would not. All the evidence was gone: arrows with their telltale colored fletching, face with its probable chin-scar, mouth with its secrets of identity and infiltration silent forever. The law was the law, and to act without evidence would be to become like Pandsala's father Roelstra, a High Prince who did as he wished and shrugged at the law.

Rohan saw Pol and Maarken safely hoisted up to the clifftop, knowing they would rest for a time before making their long way around to the path to the crossing upriver. It would be past nightfall before their return to Castle Crag, before he could look on his son's living face again.

"My lord," Pandsala began.

"No." He glanced briefly at her, then at the pathetic heap of gray-black ash on the stones. "Not now." He walked slowly down the spiraling stairs to the main part of the castle, his goal the crystalline oratory sparkling in the sunlight. The etched and faceted glass threw rainbows over the white carpet and furnishings, across gold and silver on the table. Rohan went to the far wall and sank to the floor, legs folded up, spine pressed against the stone where it merged with clear crystal. From here he could see the cliffs and watch his son's progress down the canyon road and know that Pol was safe.

For how long?

Rohan bent his head, covering his face with his hands.

What good was all his power if he could not protect his son? He ought to crush the Merida now, and Prince Miyon of Cunaxa as well for giving them shelter. Tobin would see this assassination attempt as the perfect excuse for invasion, even better than a Cunaxan encroachment onto Fironese soil. Why couldn't Rohan do it?

And there was more he ought to do. Accept the Fironese invitation and claim the princedom now. Order his wife's brother Davvi to have the heiress Gemma instantly married to either of his sons, thereby securing part of Pol's future through his kinsmen. No, Rohan reminded himself dully. Not kinsmen. Sioned was not Pol's blood mother.

Ianthe was. Ianthe, daughter of Roelstra, High Prince and tyrant. And here in the environs of Castle Crag, Pol had nearly died. Did Roelstra's malignant spirit linger here, as Rohan had vaguely sensed the other night?

He turned his face to the sunlight, felt its warmth on his body. Neither Roelstra's presence nor Roelstra's example would taint Pol. Rohan would not order the invasion of Cunaxa; neither would he seize a princedom, nor play politics with a young girl whose only crime was to be born a princess. He had watched Roelstra use his daughters as bargaining points, seen Roelstra's armies on Desert soil during a war based on flimsy pretext. He would not be the kind of High Prince Roelstra had been. If this was seen by some as weakness—he shrugged, for he cared about very few opinions in this world.

He looked around at the rainbows on the white carpet, smudges of color against colorlessness. The oratory was finer for the sunlight, for the colors that spoke of its Sunrunner prince. But the things with which Roelstra had filled this oratory would have to be replaced.

Rohan got to his feet, walked slowly around the perimeter of the glass cage to the table with its rich ornaments. His fingers clenched around one gold-and-amethyst goblet. An instant later a crystal pane shattered, and the priceless trinket vanished down the canyon to the dark water.

* * *

Pol held himself with the stiffness of abused muscles and utter exhaustion. His body was reluctant to obey the order of his pride to stand straight and behave as the son of his father and mother ought. He walked into the huge banqueting hall without looking at any eyes other than those that were so like his own in a face as sternly controlled.

Relieved murmurings chased each other through the assembly of vassals, ambassadors, and retainers. Pol was dimly aware of them, but most of his attention was focused on his father and on controlling a shameful need to be folded in strong arms. At this moment when he must conduct himself as a man, he had never felt more like a boy in need of his father's embrace.

Rohan descended the four steps from the high table and met Pol with a hand on his shoulder and a slight smile. The gesture and expression appeared casual, but Pol felt the long fingers tighten with fierce possessive love. Then Rohan looked over Pol's head to the crowd. Then they both turned and faced the gathering.

"We thank the Goddess and the good people of Castle Crag for the safety of our beloved son. With such protection, he will surely govern long and well over Princemarch."

A cheer went up, and Pol felt his father tense as if trying not to hug him close. He understood; they were not father and son right now but High Prince and Heir. He looked around him, surprised at the real joy and relief on most faces, intrigued by the careful smiles on others. No one here wanted his death, he was sure of it. But there were those who would not mourn too long.

He and Maarken followed Rohan up to the dais, where Pol took the chair between his father and Pandsala. Her face was pale and expressionless; she would not look at him. Maarken sat on Rohan's other side, as weary and aching as Pol but just as determined not to show it.

The hall was silent. Rohan said, "Tell us what happened."

Pol did. They had not stopped to wash or change clothes; he wanted everyone to see their bruises and dirt. He made especially certain that all knew of Maeta's sacrifice, and if there was a catch in his voice as he spoke, no one blamed him. When he told of the colors on the arrow that had killed her, a low rumble went through the hall. His account ended with praise for those who had helped him and Maarken to safety; he had made sure on the way back to learn their names. He paused then, ending with, "I'm grateful for your care of me today, and I'm sorry I didn't complete the climb and failed in my—"

They did not let him finish the sentence. "Failed?" someone cried. "We were the ones who failed you!" And above similar protests another called out, "It's a stupid custom that nearly cost us our prince!"

"I'm going to try again," Pol insisted. "And next time I'll make it to the top and earn the flight back down—and I'll do it all on my own, too!"

"Not if I have anything to say about it!" The large, burly form of Cladon, *athri* of River Ussh, stomped forth from chair to aisle. "You proved your courage and that's what the climb is for! We'll not risk you again, young prince!"

"But it's the closest I'll ever come to flying like a dragon!" Pol was instantly aware of how childish that sounded, and felt his cheeks burn. But though laughter rippled through the hall, it was kind, understanding, even admiring. He was confused until he heard his father whisper, "Well done! You have them now, my hatchling." And he realized that without meaning to, he had done something very clever. The highborns of Princemarch would have been duly impressed with a completed climb—but the attempt on Pol's life had done more to increase his value in their eyes than anything else could have done. And he had sealed their commitment by vowing to do the climb again. He was theirs now, claimed by them all as their prince.

It was an odd feeling, vaguely reminiscent for a moment of his reaction on arrival, a little like being offered up on a golden plate. But then he understood. In claiming him, they had also given themselves. His father was right. He had them. If he was theirs, they were also his.

"We'll discuss it some other time, Lord Cladon," Rohan said, with a sidelong glance for Pol that combined paternal firmness and princely order. Another chuckle went through the assembly and Cladon bowed, satisfied as to Rohan's cautionary instincts. "For the moment," the High Prince went on, "we're happy to have him back safe and sound."

"I—I have something else I'd like to say." Pol was amazed when the sound of his voice commanded instant silence. "When we find Maeta—she told me how beautiful she thought this land. I'd like to hold her ritual here, so that a little of her will remain in Princemarch, before her ashes are returned to the Desert."

"Well said, your grace!" Lord Dreslav of Grand Veresch stood, his cup lifted high. "To our young prince!"

Later, when the royal pair were alone in Pol's chamber and they were only father and son again, Rohan clasped Pol tight to his chest. Pol clung to him, trembling with weariness. After a time he calmed down and pulled away.

"You don't mind, do you? About Maeta's burning?"

"No. It was a good thought, politically as well as personally. I know she'd like becoming part of this land you'll rule one day. They say here that the ashes of the dead become flowers." Rohan sat heavily in a chair and rubbed his eyes. "But I want the wind off the Long Sand for myself, Pol. Promise me that wherever I end, you'll bring me back home."

"Father—you can't die! Don't talk that way." He knelt beside the chair and grasped his father's arm.

"I'm sorry." Rohan smiled fleetingly. "I'm very tired, and watching you on that cliff wasn't calculated to add years to my life."

"I shouldn't have gone. Maeta would still be alive."

"And there would still be a Merida here to threaten you. Don't ever second-guess life, Pol."

He rested his cheek on Rohan's knee. "Mother's not going to be happy," he murmured.

"Maarken will know how to explain it to her. She'll understand."

"Even the way Pandsala killed the archer?"

"Your mother . . . has done similar things. She'll understand that, too."

Pol tried to imagine his mother doing what Pandsala had done—and it was only too easy to see her green eyes blazing as she called down Fire in defense of what she loved.

"That's why she and Lady Andrade don't get along,"

Rohan said suddenly. "Speaking of whom, she'll have quite a bit to say about this and I don't think Pandsala will enjoy any of it. But I doubt Andrade will even attempt to punish her. She broke the vow, but she also saved your life."

"Father, do you approve of what she did?"

"The man should have been taken alive and questioned. He might have given me the excuse I needed—in front of witnesses—to invade Cunaxa and destroy the Merida once and for all." He stared at the dark, empty windows.

"But you're tempted to do it just the same?" Pol ventured.

"Without justification, I can do nothing." He looked down at Pol. "Do you understand? Do you see that dearly as I love you, and afraid as I am for you, I can't go against the laws I myself helped to write?"

"Of course I understand," Pol said, hiding astonishment that his father should be saying such things to him. "Besides, it might not've been the Merida behind this at all. It might be the man who claims to be Roelstra's son."

"Perhaps." Rohan rubbed his eyes. "It'll be worse at the *Rialla*."

"I'll be careful."

"I doubt there'll be another attempt before then. They'd have to be more subtle. Not everyone is happy that one day you'll rule two princedoms and probably a goodly chunk of Firon as well. I don't mean to worry you with it, especially at your age, but you must know what we're up against."

Pol said softly, "Thank you for saying 'we.' You never have before."

Rohan blinked. "Haven't I?"

"No. It's always between you and Mother, or Chay, or Maarken—never me included as an active partner."

His father looked bemused. "It seems as if you've impressed *me* as well as everyone else today with the fact that you're growing up. Very well. *We*, meaning you and I, have a great deal to talk about. But *we* also need to sleep until at least noon tomorrow. And that is an order that *we*, as the High Prince and your father, will hold you to obeying."

Pol made a face, then laughed. "I'm going to climb that cliff and fly down one day. I'm not the Dragon's Son for nothing!"

"But still a hatchling. Fly over to your bed and get some sleep."

Chapter Fourteen

Andry surveyed his audience, trying to banish a sudden attack of nerves. He'd used up his full quota of reassurances getting Andrade to agree to let him rather than Urival experiment with a formula from the Star Scroll. He *knew* it would work. He had fretted with excitement all day long at the imminent prospect of proving his theory. But all at once the idea of working an ancient sorcery unnerved him. He gulped down the peculiar lump in his throat and composed himself.

He had chosen the little kitchen in the library wing for his demonstration. Not only was that whole section of the keep quiet and deserted at this time of night, but there was a necessary supply of running water and a hearth over which to concoct his potions. This was also the oldest part of the castle—he'd found its plan in one of the historical texts—and if Lady Merisel's spirit lingered anywhere at Goddess Keep, it would be here.

Urival and Morwenna were to be his subjects while Andrade observed. Hollis was with them as well, looking a little strained around the eyes as she gave him a slight smile of encouragement. She believed in his interpretation of the scroll, and thus could not be part of the experiment. Instead she would help him and provide extra witness to what happened.

"I've chosen an ointment whose properties I won't tell you about just yet, so your reactions will be spontaneous," he began. "I've mixed two versions, one according to the recipe as it stands and the other following the indications of the manuscript code."

"I hope it's something you can counter with medicine

of our own making," Morwenna said casually, though her suspicious gaze flickered to the pots on the table.

"Of course." He glanced at his great-aunt, whose face was perfectly expressionless. But her fingers beat slowly, arrhythmically, on the arm of her chair. Andry swallowed and attempted a smile. "It's nothing serious, believe me, and nothing we can't cure in an instant."

"Get on with it then," Urival said.

Andry directed them to chairs facing the door, backs to the hearth and the table where he would work from two small cauldrons. Hollis stood beside him, ready with clean cloths and a bucket of water. Andrade positioned her chair so she could watch everything, including Urival and Morwenna.

"I'm going to give you several doses each. You won't be able to see which pot I'm taking them from. They might all be the real thing, they might all be fake, or they might be any combination in any order." When all was ready on the table before him, well out of view of the subjects, he chanced another look at Andrade. She lifted one elegant brow in silent challenge. She wanted him to fail, to be proved wrong. The implications were too dangerous. Andry knew very well it was going to work, and at this moment gave not a damn about the implications.

"Please hold out your right hands," he said. Taking a spoonful of thick, warm paste from one of the copper pots, he smeared a little on each upturned palm over the heel of the thumb. A few moments later Urival half-turned in his chair.

"So? Nothing."

"I know. That was made strictly according to the recipe. Hollis, can you wash off their hands for me, please?"

He dipped the spoons into both mixtures this time, placed a little of one on Urival's hand and the other onto Morwenna's. She tensed, expecting she knew not what— but it was Urival who gave a gasp of surprise and pain.

"God of Storms! My hand's on fire!" His fingers were trembling and the muscles of his hand cramped, drawing the thumb into the palm with a contortion as agonizing to see as it was obviously painful to experience.

"Wash it off, quickly," Andry said to Hollis. When

she had done so, the muscle slowly relaxed, and some of the tension left Urival's face.

"I take it that was the real thing," Andrade observed in her coldest voice. The fingers of her left hand drummed the tabletop.

"Yes, my Lady," Andry said. "Morwenna, please dip your hand into the water. Thank you. Any aftereffects, Urival?"

"It aches a bit, but the pain's gone." He inspected his thumb, prodded the heel gently. "Leave it on longer next time. I want to see if it'll spread to the rest of my hand."

Andry said nothing, feeling Andrade's eyes on him like blue ice while he smeared the different ointments over his subjects' thumbs. Urival cursed, sweat springing out on his forehead. The deep lines on his face drew taut with pain as his hand began to cramp around itself.

"No—leave it on," he gasped. "It's spreading all through my palm—*Goddess!*"

Andry winced in sympathy as his fingers knotted together, muscles contracting to draw bones out of alignment. Urival's other hand gripped the arm of his chair forcefully enough to splinter the brittle wood. Hollis reached over to wash his hand clean, but he shook his head, teeth gritted.

"Enough!" Andrade exclaimed as his wrist began to contort. Hollis bathed Urival's hand in cool water and his head fell back, his eyes closed and his face ashen. Andrade fixed Andry with a hard stare. "You proved your point."

"But it's not fair to let Urival be the only one." Morwenna turned in her chair and held out both palms. "Make one the fake and the other real. I don't know which it is from your little pots there."

Andry looked to the Lady; she nodded curtly. He applied the pastes to Morwenna's hands, and the fingers of the left began to curl up at once. Her breath hissed between her teeth. "Sweet Mother! He was right—my whole hand's afire!"

Andrade rose, grabbed the bucket of water, and plunged Morwenna's hand into it. "Congratulations," she snapped at Andry. "You were correct. Now destroy that terrible brew at once!"

"But—"

"Destroy it!" she thundered. "And you're lucky I don't order the Star Scroll burned as well! If this is the kind of knowledge it contains, then it *ought* to be burned!"

"No!" Andry exclaimed, unable to help himself. Hollis put a warning hand on his arm and he subsided.

"Hold your tongue," Andrade told him. "And say nothing of this to anyone. Do you understand me, Andry?"

"Yes, my Lady," he muttered.

When Morwenna had recovered, she and Urival left the little kitchen with Andrade. No one had said another word. Andry slumped into a chair by the glowing hearth and stared into the flames, grim silence like a too-heavy cloak on his shoulders. Hollis stood beside him, hands deep in the pockets of her trousers.

"She's blinded by fear," Andry muttered. "She doesn't understand."

"Perhaps you chose the wrong sort of demonstration," Hollis suggested. "It was dramatic, I'll grant you, but something that causes such pain wasn't the wisest choice you could have made."

"What else could I do? I couldn't very well make somebody sick and then cure it with something else from the Star Scroll, could I?" He rose and began to pace the tiled floor. "But I was right, Hollis. I was *right*. She just doesn't want to admit it. Do you know what it says about *dranath?* That it cures the dragon sickness, what we know as the Plague. Lady Merisel wrote in the scrolls that *dranath* can cure the sickness, and we know that's right because we saw it happen. If we'd known sooner, if we'd had the scrolls, then maybe my brother Jahni and my grandmother and Lady Camigwen and all the others would still be alive! And *she* talks of burning the Star Scroll!"

The usually soft-spoken Hollis rounded on him in sudden fury. "Can't you see why she's afraid? She's seventy winters old, Andry! The scroll threatens her—not because she's set in her ways, but because she's *old* and may not have time enough left to control the danger you've shown her! Can't you understand that?"

He stared at her. In all the times he had secretly put himself in Andrade's place as ruler of Goddess Keep, he had never considered that one day he, too, would grow old, that time would grow short, that he would not be able to make plans and see them through. That he would die.

Hollis evidently found something in his face that satisfied her. In quieter tones she continued, "It's not that she doesn't want to know what's in the Star Scroll. She's frightened of a future she may not be around to shape. She's spent her whole life at it. Do you wonder that it scares her?"

"But she can't order me to burn it. She *can't.*"

"I don't think she will. She knows how important it is. But she also sees dangers you don't." Hollis rubbed her forehead wearily. "And forgive me for saying that you'd better learn to fear those dangers yourself."

Silently he took the two small copper pots from the table, went to the fire, and scraped out their contents onto the coals. A sickly stench rose and he coughed, backing away hastily as his nose began to burn. Hollis, who had also gotten a faceful of the smoke, staggered over to a chair and slid into it, choking. Andry glanced around frantically, barely able to see through the tears clouding his eyes, and snatched up a cloth to soak in fresh water at the sink. He ripped the cloth in two, placed half to his own nose and the other against Hollis' white face.

"Breathe!" he ordered.

After a moment the burning sensation faded, soothed by the droplets of water they both inhaled. But their eyes teared and they coughed for some while afterward. When each had recovered, Andry crouched beside Hollis' chair and looked anxiously up at her.

She wiped her eyes and tried a smile. "It seems we haven't translated far enough into the scroll to learn *that* one. Believe me now?"

Andry bent his head. "Yes. I'm sorry, Hollis."

He felt her fingers tousle his hair fondly. "Listen to me, little brother—for I hope that soon you *will* be my little brother. You're brave and clever and more intelligent than you have any right to be, and your gifts are far greater than you realize just now. I love you for yourself, Andry, and for Maarken's sake.''

"But?'' he asked in a muffled voice.

"You're young. It takes years to learn how to be patient, how to be wise and cautious. Don't let your powers and your intelligence blind you to the fact of your youth.''

He looked up, about to reassure her that he would be cautious and wise. But the deathly weariness of her face swept all other thoughts from his head. "Hollis—are you all right? You look awful.''

She chuckled softly. "Another thing you'll learn with age is how to talk to a woman. The proper words would be, 'You look a little tired, why don't you go rest?' But never mind. I'll find Sejast and get him to brew me a cup of that special taze of his. It works wonders.''

"I feel in need of a little, myself,'' Andry admitted.

"He swears the recipe was given to him in secret by an old witch in the mountains,'' she said smiling.

Andry grinned and got to his feet. "Who made him swear never to reveal its contents, or she'd pry out his eyes with her fingernails and draw his veins from his living body—''

"Andry!'' she chided. "Don't make fun. Maarken told me you were terrified of lizards when you were little, because you thought they were baby dragons that had crawled out of their shells to breathe fire on you!''

"A perfectly natural assumption! But I suppose it really doesn't do to make fun of witches.'' He glanced significantly at the door where Andrade had disappeared. "You go to bed. I'll clean up in here. And you really do look awful, you know.''

She pushed herself to her feet. "What happened to your share of your father's infamous charm?''

"I'm saving it for a girl who's not already promised to one of my brothers!''

* * *

It was very late, and Riyan had to keep pinching himself to stay awake. Following Lady Kiele on her nocturnal excursions in and around Waes was usually very dull. Tonight looked like no exception.

Riyan had made quite a few friends in Waes through the natural inclinations of a sociable nature, through ulterior motives, and through sheer boredom. His informant, the servant of Jayachin's father and sometime drinking companion at a local tavern, had heard from a footman, who had heard from an undercook, who had heard from Lady Kiele's maid (whom the undercook was courting) that she had ordered a horse saddled for an evening ride. A groom had accepted Riyan's help in readying the horse, and it had been child's play to cut a deep groove in the mare's off hind shoe. The mark would show up very clearly on ground still moist after the previous night's light rain, making it simple to follow Kiele.

Riyan had done just that after posting another servant outside his door with orders to answer all inquiries with the news that he was abed with a summer chill. Slipping out by one of the multitude of doors was easy. And now he huddled beside a bush, watching a small manor house tucked into a stand of trees.

The windows had been hung with black curtains, but jagged lines of light seeped through here and there, tempting him closer. He resisted, not knowing how many people might be within. He had no intention of being caught; he'd seen no guards thus far, but there was always a chance.

Over the spring and early summer he had followed Kiele whenever he could manage it. Most times she went to the homes of various notables in the city—including that of Jayachin's father. The visits were undoubtedly connected with plans for the *Rialla*, but every so often Riyan strongly suspected that Kiele's arrival was a complete surprise to her hosts. She went out every eight or ten days, and once he had traced her to a dockside house. Investigation the next afternoon had revealed only a very large sailor and a very ugly servant woman, neither of whom he could imagine being of use to the Lady of Waes. Riyan had not seen her go to the house again, and cursed himself for scaring her away. His own visit had doubtless been reported, and she had not dared go there again.

But tonight the marked horseshoe had led him from the city gates to this country manor. Riyan had lost her in a wood, not being overly familiar with the paths around Waes despite interesting excursions with Jayachin. (They usually had more to do than conduct a comprehensive walking tour—although Riyan had thus far enjoyed little romantic success.) But the nick in the horse's shoe had served him well, and he had only to conjure a wisp of Fire as needed in order to know where she had gone.

Kiele's journeys might be nothing more sinister than meetings with a lover—Riyan wouldn't have blamed her, Lyell being the dullard he was—but Kiele had struck him as a cold woman whose passions would be reserved for power and hate. He'd heard the stories about her father and her sister Ianthe.

And there was an odd feeling slithering around the residence these days. Chiana, after being rebuffed more than once by Riyan, had at last left him alone and concentrated on Lyell. Kiele didn't even seem to notice. She spent a great deal of time away from the residence, saying she worked on arrangements for the *Rialla*. But sometimes Riyan saw her sitting with plans spread out before her, staring into space with a secret, feral smile on her lips.

After waiting what he considered enough time to make certain no one would come marching around the side of the house with sword in hand to guard whoever was inside, Riyan moved closer. He was sufficiently familiar with the mare tethered outside so that the animal did not sidle nervously or whinny at this appearance; he patted her neck in thanks and crept up to the windows.

He could see a slice of the room through the chink in the curtains. Clean, neatly but not luxuriously furnished, blazing with light that made him blink, it was the home of comfortable but not wealthy people. Kiele walked past and he started at her closeness to the window. She was wearing a light summer gown of green silk and he could almost hear it swishing with the angry swiftness of her steps. Riyan squinted, trying to bring into focus a figure standing just out of his range of vision.

A steely hand clamped own on his shoulder. "What in all hells are you doing here?" a voice hissed in his ear.

He nearly yelped with fright. Another hand grabbed his jaw shut to prevent just that. Riyan considered struggling, abandoned the idea as too noisy, and was just about to go for his boot knife when he realized the hand over his mouth wore rings. He relaxed completely and lifted his own hand.

"So," the voice breathed, and let him go.

Riyan followed the man away from the house. Safe in the cover of the trees, he saw a little finger of Fire dance delicately atop a waist-high bush, and nearly yelped again.

"Kleve?" he whispered. "What are you doing here?"

The older man grinned tightly. "What I've done for most of my life, of course—following Lady Andrade's orders."

"So am I! She told me to watch Kiele—"

"But not, I think, to follow her all over Waes and beyond." Kleve sank down in the dirt, shaking his head, and Riyan crouched beside him. "I can't tell you how many times I've had to hide from you as well as from her when she takes her little jaunts in the night!"

"You mean you—and I didn't *see* you?"

"Of course not. Count your rings, Sunrunner. And then count mine." Kleve gave him a genial slap on the shoulder. "You've grown since last I saw you at Sky-bowl."

Kleve was one of a few itinerant *faradh'im* who traveled the princedoms at Andrade's behest, observing and reporting things that Sunrunners attached to specific courts did not usually hear about. He had been instrumental in certain maneuverings during the war the year Prince Pol was born, and during Riyan's childhood at Skybowl had sometimes arrived for a few days of relaxation, companionship, and good food. Ostvel set great store by Kleve, and a running joke between them was the *athri*'s attempt to persuade Kleve to become his court Sunrunner. Kleve hated walls of any kind, be they around a city or a small keep; he was happiest traversing the rugged lands around Cunaxa, Princemarch, and the northern Desert.

"Why so far from home?" Riyan asked now.

"I could ask you the same. Has Clutha given up and thrown you out of Swalekeep in despair at your ever becoming a knight?"

"He doesn't trust Kiele or Lyell, either," Riyan answered, grinning. "And I'm to be knighted at the *Rialla*.

Father will be here, I hope—say you'll stay long enough to see him.''

"Wouldn't miss it. Do you know what Kiele's up to?"

"I know about the house by the docks," he began.

Kleve snorted. "You mean the one you scared her away from? I could have throttled you for that!" He doused the finger-flame with a gesture and peered out at the house. "Get back to the residence now, Riyan. I can take it from here."

"Lady Andrade told me to watch," the youth said stubbornly.

Kleve gripped Riyan's shoulder. "Andrade would half-kill me and your father would finish the job if I let anything happen to you. So far you've been safe enough—you haven't seen anything or learned anything important. But if what I suspect is true, then it's more dangerous than you know to be here tonight."

"What have you found out?"

"A few things," he evaded. "I hope to know for sure tonight. You did me quite a service, by the way—by following you, I found Kiele. She's given me the slip the last few times out." He got to his feet. "I'm going for a look and a listen. You can help me best by returning to town. There's a goldcrafter named Ulricca who lives on New High Street. Meet me at her place tomorrow morning. Now, move."

Riyan looked rebellious. "Kleve—"

"Sunrunner you may be, and nearly a knight—but this isn't work for you. Do I have to number my rings and quote the authority they give me?"

"No, but—"

"So do as you're told. You'd better get started. It's a long walk." Kleve softened the command with an affectionate nudge. "I'll tell you the whole thing tomorrow."

"You'd better," Riyan muttered.

* * *

Andry could not sleep. He almost went to Hollis' room to ask her to work the spell she'd been learning from Urival, but basic decency demanded he let her rest. With or without Sejast's witch's brew, she had been exhausted recently. He shook his head as he pulled on his clothes, glad he'd grown up in sophisticated places where witches and the like were tales to entertain children.

And yet—he was brought up short on the stairs as a thought hit him. Some of the things in the Star Scroll could definitely be considered witchcraft. Its very title was evocative: *On Sorceries*. What if Sejast really had run into one of the old folk? He was more inclined to think the boy had encountered a sage who knew odd herbal remedies, rather than a sorceress of the old ways. But someone had been watching the night Meath had delivered the scrolls—watching not on sun or moons, but the faint thin glow of stars. Andry continued down the stairs, shivering slightly, and resolved to find out more from Sejast about his witch.

He made his way to the library wing through the silent halls of the keep. He was nearly at the locked door of the chamber where the scrolls were kept when he realized Hollis had the key. So much for spending the night in soothing research, Andry thought ruefully, and wondered what else might ease his restlessness. A brisk walk around the gardens? Perhaps he could visit the stables to check on his horse. Maycenel had been sadly neglected while he worked on the scrolls, and he felt guilty about it. His father had given him the young stallion when he had become Prince Davvi's squire—a mount fit for the knight Andry would never become. Sorin had been gifted with Maycenel's twin brother on his departure for Prince Volog's court that same year—a nice piece of work, twins for twins. But Sorin had put his Joscenel to the use their father had intended, and would be knighted this year. Andry wondered suddenly if Chay was terribly disappointed that he had not done the same. And, if he was, whether he would ever show it.

The courtyard was empty but for cats on the hunt. Andry crossed the flagstones to the stables, expecting to hear only the drowsy sounds of horses in their stalls. The clink of a bridle startled him. He followed the sound to the far end of the building, stepping noiselessly on fresh straw.

"Hollis!" he blurted, unable to prevent the exclamation when he saw her long tawny hair. "What are you doing here?"

She whirled and dropped the bridle in her hands. A
saddle was propped in the straw near a fleet little mare
that had been his father's gift to Andrade a few years ago;
old as she was, the Lady of Goddess Keep could still
appreciate a fast ride on a good horse. Hollis stared for
a moment, then bent to retrieve the bridle. The metal
clanked with the shaking of her fingers.

"I just—I thought I'd go riding—"

"At this time of night? Have you slept at all?"

She shrugged, back to him as she fitted the leather
straps over the mare's head. Andry leaned his elbows on
the half-door of the stall and frowned. Hollis loved horses
and riding—she would hardly have been a suitable wife
for the next Lord of Radzyn Keep if she had not—but this
was more than a little strange.

"Want some company?" he finally asked, a deliberately casual offer.

She shook her head violently, untidy golden braids
whipping around her shoulders. Her fingers were wound
in the mare's black mane, and her body began to shake.
Andry's jaw dropped when he heard a tiny sob claw up
from her throat. He hauled open the door and went to
her, patting her back awkwardly, wishing Maarken were
here to comfort her. *He* must be the reason she wept,
Andry told himself.

When she stopped crying, she faced him and attempted
a smile. "I'm sorry. I'm not usually so silly."

"You don't have to worry about the *Rialla*, you know,"
he said, trying to explore his surmise about Maarken.
"My parents will love you, just as Maarken does."

She blinked, and he realized that his brother was the
farthest thing from her mind. She didn't even bother to
cover the reaction, and that startled him even more.

"You're tired," he went on, floundering for excuses to
explain her behavior. "You haven't gotten any sleep. Go
back upstairs, Hollis."

She nodded feebly. Andry took the bridle from the
mare's head, hung it on a nail, and heaved the saddle
back up onto its stand. When he turned, Hollis was gone.

He caught up with her in the courtyard and touched her
arm. She gave a little cry and started away from him.

"Oh! Don't sneak up on people! What are you doing out this time of night?"

It was as if the moments in the stables had never occurred. He could find nothing in her face or her eyes to indicate she was not seeing him for the first time that night. "I couldn't sleep. I went to the library to work on the scrolls, but you've got the key."

"It's up in my room." She cast a glance back over her shoulder at the stables, almost desperately.

"I know," he said, more mystified than ever at her strangeness. "I'll just go back to bed and pretend I can sleep."

"Maybe a book would help," she suggested, sounding more like herself. "I know several guaranteed to have you snoring in two pages." She laughed, but there was a wildness to the sound that canceled any relief he might have felt at the return of her sense of humor. She was fey and skittish as an untamed filly—not at all the sensible, practical Hollis he knew.

* * *

Kleve slid up to a window, hoping Riyan would do exactly as told. Bother the boy, anyhow—and bother Andrade, for setting Riyan to do what Kleve was perfectly capable of doing all on his own. Still, he had to admit that the young man's presence had been useful tonight. He would never have found Kiele if not for Riyan.

He moved around the side of the house, trying to find a partially open window that would allow him to hear what was being said inside—and nearly got hit in the face by a window suddenly flung wide. He flattened himself against the wall, clamping his teeth shut over an exclamation of surprise, and froze until the curtains dropped again to guard the light inside.

"It's an oven in here, damn it! Hotter than the Desert in high summer!" a man's voice grated. "If I have to try these damned clothes on, then at least save yourself the trouble of washing my sweat from them afterward!"

"You have absolutely no sense of caution! I'm sure I wasn't followed, but if you think we're safe, then think again!"

"Shut up, Kiele!"

"How dare you give me orders! And whatever possessed you to come into the city today? Of all the stupid, foolish things—!''

"I was bored! You've kept me out here for longer than I can remember! And no harm came of it—who'd recognize me?''

"Someone recognizing you is exactly the point!''

"If my former jailer hadn't been out drinking, no one would have been the wiser. But no, he had to be half-drunk and, of course, he *had* to run to you and tattle!''

There was the sound of something, a chair perhaps, crashing to the floor. Kiele gave a little cry and then a curse, and the man laughed.

"Calm yourself. You came here to lecture me, and I'm not interested. Let's get on with the clothing, shall we?''

"You'll learn to keep your mouth shut and do exactly as I say—or you'll ruin us all, Masul!''

When he spoke again, his voice was savage. "I'm sick of being caged, and I'm sick of you telling me what I should and shouldn't do, and most especially I'm sick of your doubts! When are you going to admit that I am who I say I am, sister *darling?*''

Kleve dug his fingers into the weathered wood of the house as his knees wobbled with sudden shock.

"Try on the tunic,'' Kiele said with the inexorable ice of a mountain glacier.

Kleve shifted so he could peer through the tiny gap in the black curtains. His muscles creaked a protest at the awkward stance necessary to avoid rustling a flowering bush, but his reward was a view of Masul's head poking through the neck of an elegant dark violet velvet tunic.

Once, a very long time ago, Kleve had traveled to Einar on Andrade's business. Midjourney, he had nearly been trampled on the road by a group of highborns out for a day's hunting. No apology had been offered; indeed, their young leader had told him to get his filthy Sunrunner carcass out of the way or regret it. Laughing, they had ridden on. It had been Kleve's distinct pleasure to follow them in secret and scare off a prime stag by calling up a judicious gust of wind across its hindquarters. He'd amused Andrade with the story on his return to Goddess Keep. Her satisfaction had been all the greater when he had conjured the leader's face in the fire. She had identified him instantly.

The face he saw now—green-eyed, high-boned, sensuous, sullenly handsome—would be, without the beard, nearly the living image of that arrogant youth, High Prince Roelstra.

He slid down the wall to the grassy ground, stunned. So the rumors were true, and his suspicions justified. The pretender existed and Kiele was sheltering him. She had probably coached him in her father's mannerisms and the like, rehearsing him for an appearance at the *Rialla*. And Chiana was at the residence in Waes—Kleve understood that very well. Kiele's delight in Chiana's humiliation would be the final spice in the taze. The Father of Storms himself could not have created the uproar this Masul would cause, with Kiele's help.

He could still hear voices from within the house, but paid them little mind. Masul was trying on clothes, half a dozen garments designed to make him look as regal and as much like Roelstra as possible. Kleve leaned his head back and squeezed his eyes shut, bringing both faces to mind again. The resemblance was there, no doubt of it. But was he truly Roelstra's son? And if so, what then? Had he a right to his father's princedom? Strictly speaking, Kleve supposed he did. But Rohan had defeated Roelstra years ago and claimed Princemarch by all the rules of war. And none of that would matter, for even if Masul was not who he claimed to be, many of the princes would choose to believe—if only to make trouble for Rohan.

Political complexities were beyond him, Kleve told himself. He would convey this staggering news to Andrade and she would make the decisions. She was very good at that. He pushed himself to his feet, bones aching a little with the dampness of yesterday's rain. He needed quiet, seclusion, and moonlight. He crept away from the house, not needing to see or hear anything more, heading for the trees where he'd left Riyan.

Something warned him, some muted whisper at the edge of his perceptions, half an instant before he heard the voice.

"So you were right after all, Kiele. We *were* being watched."

A long, hard hand circled Kleve's wrist, fingers that dug all the way to the bones. The Sunrunner wrenched away and cursed, lunging for the mare tethered nearby. Masul only laughed as Kleve grabbed the reins, fit his boot into a stirrup, and lurched up. The fist that slammed into his lower back made him spasm with pain. He lost his balance and sprawled to the ground.

"I told you I heard something!" Kiele cried, her voice thin and shrill. "Masul, what are we going to do with him?"

"First, we'll find out what he knows."

Kleve knew what would happen after that. He struggled to his feet, hanging onto the saddle for support, and lifted one hand. "You'll answer to Lady Andrade! I'm *faradhi!*"

Into the darkness he spun a flaring weave of Fire, called up in desperation—for by its light he saw his own death in Masul's green eyes. The young man was laughing at him, a deep and mellow laugh that congealed his blood.

"I've always wanted to meet one."

Kleve fought a small, incoherent war with his lifelong vow not to kill using his gifts. Self-preservation and the need to get this information to Andrade battled against his training, his ideals, his vocation, and his morals. He turned his face to the moonlight, staggering back against the horse's flank as Masul kneed him in the groin. The Fire guttered out, and instinct spun other threads with frantic speed. Power flushed through him with dizzying strength in his need as he completed the weaving. The iron grip twisted his arm. He fell to his knees, tangled in moonlight. Sorting threads with frantic bursts of power, he struggled against Masul's physical hold and made a mighty effort to pattern the moonlight into fabric that would reach to Goddess Keep.

There was an icy chill at the base of his left little finger, quickly replaced by a searing pain.

"Finger by finger," Masul said.

In his youth, when he'd delighted in invigorating battle with mountain raiders who respected profits more than Sunrunners, he'd known his share of wounds by knife and sword. But when Masul's steel blade slashed off his finger, he felt as if his entire body had been cut open, every nerve severed. Threads of moonlight turned to spun silver glass around him and shattered. The shards lacerated his mind. He screamed, the sound becoming colors that were additional knives in his head, in his flesh. The thumb was carved from his right hand and he screamed again.

"Don't kill him! We have to find out what he knows and if he's told Andrade!"

"It's only two fingers. He won't die of it. What a coward he is—just listen to him yelling!"

Kleve was incapable of fighting the appalling agony that butchered him from inside out. Another finger dropped into the blood-washed dirt. He died before they could ask their first question: died not from loss of blood or physical shock, but from the steel that repeatedly pierced him while he tried to use his *faradhi* gifts.

* * *

Segev heard voices in the library just as he located the Star Scroll on the shelf. He froze, fingers extended, nearly touching his prize. A flicker of his mind darkened the tiny flame he had conjured to see by. He told himself to wait it out, stay calm, remember how close he was to success. Whoever had entered would soon be gone. He had waited earlier behind a row of shelves for Andry to leave, and he could wait again.

But it was Andry's voice he heard. "If you think Wilmod's essays are boring, you should try Dorin's. At least Wilmod knows how to construct an argument. Dorin's just plain awful at everything!"

They were down the room from the small chamber where the scrolls were locked away with other important records. Segev rapidly reviewed the layout and breathed a sigh of relief as he recalled that the books Andry talked about were on the other side of the library. But then he tensed again when recognition of the second voice destroyed all his plans.

"I was thinking along the lines of farming manuals as a soporific," Hollis said teasingly.

Segev heard their footsteps fade down the long row of shelves and moved quickly. He had touched nothing but the lock on the door, so there was nothing to put back as it had been. He let his fingers brush longingly against the leather case containing the Star Scroll, then went to the door. He slid through and the lock worked with a faint click. Pocketing the key, he cursed Andry for ruining it all. Hollis, obedient to a suggestion he had made tonight while serving her *dranath*-laced taze, had gone to the stables as planned to saddle a horse for his swift, unnoticed departure. But Segev dared not chance now that the mount had been left for him.

He used the shadows to conceal his progress toward the main door, but froze again as he heard them coming back in his direction. There was an alcove nearby with a study table and a chair. Segev sat, opened a book left there, and put his head down on his folded arms.

"Oh, Andry—look," Hollis said softly from nearby. "I didn't see him earlier. Poor boy!"

"He certainly is devoted to his studies," Andry whispered. "Should we wake him?"

"He'll have a terribly stiff neck tomorrow if we don't."

A gentle hand touched his head and despite himself a shiver of excitement went through him. He had never forgotten that night with her and doubted he ever would. He used the startlement to mime abrupt awakening from sleep, and mumbled, "I'm sorry, Morwenna—I forgot the answer—oh!" He blinked and sat up. Hollis wore a fond, amused smile, and Andry was grinning over a scroll clasped to his chest. "What happened? Did I fall asleep?"

"Yes, and quite some time ago, I'd wager." Hollis ruffled his hair. "Come up to bed, Sejast."

He gave the perfect impression of being fuzzy-headed with too little sleep as he got up and yawned. Andry's sharp gaze had gone to the open book on the table, and his brows lifted exactly the way Andrade's did.

"Magnowa's treatises? That's pretty advanced stuff."

Segev was thankful that he actually knew about the book, and managed a bashful shrug. "Some of the words are hard, but it's interesting."

"A good deal of it is closely related to the old language," Andry observed. "Are you having much trouble?"

"Some, my lord. but it gets easier." Boldly he added, "I guess it must be the same way with the scrolls."

Hollis answered Andry's astonishment with, "He comes from the mountains. The dialects there are closer to the old tongue than what we speak. He's interested in history and has helped me several times."

The young Sunrunner nodded slowly. "Maybe you'd like to give me some advice on a few translations.

Segev nearly yelped in delight. "Could I, my lord?"

"The histories are tough going in parts, and there are a lot of words I can't figure out. I'd appreciate the help."

"Oh, thank you! I'd love to work with you and Lady Hollis—" He cast a look of calculated adoration at the golden-haired Sunrunner, who smiled back at him, her dark blue eyes alight.

Andry's lips twitched at the corners, for he had seen precisely what Segev wished him to see: a boy infatuated with an older woman. "I'll talk to Lady Andrade about it tomorrow. Meantime, I think we all ought to go back upstairs, don't you?"

Having impressed Andry with his admiration for Hollis, it was an easy matter to include himself in escorting her back to her chamber. He pretended to be drawn to the view of the sea from her windows, and on the way back to the door dropped the key soundlessly into the little silver bowl on her desk where he'd found it. He lingered as long as he could in telling her good night, then returned to his own small, windowless room.

Reaction set in after he had closed the door. He sat down on his bed, the chamber lit by the glow of the brazier—necessary for light but also for keeping some of the damp from the walls, even in summer. Bemused, he held out both hands and watched the fingers tremble. He had nearly been caught tonight. He didn't want to think about what Andrade would have done to him had she discovered his true identity and purpose here, let alone what he'd done to Hollis by addicting her to *dranath*.

But he had not been caught. True, the Star Scroll was not in his possession, and he was not galloping north to Mireva. But something even better had happened, if Andry followed through with his notion of having "Sejast" help with the scrolls. He could work his way to free access to them, and learn more than Mireva had ever guessed—certainly more than she would ever teach him of that dangerous knowledge. Ruval was the one she'd chosen to educate in the finer points of the craft; Ruval, whose only recommendation was that he was Ianthe's firstborn son.

Her thirdborn sat hugging his knees and grinning. He was glad he'd been unable to steal the scrolls, glad he would be staying here. If he played his part correctly, he would learn what the Star Scroll could offer along with all the *faradhi* secrets being taught him daily. He might even be taken to the *Rialla* as part of Andrade's suite. Hollis liked him, could not do without him. She would ask Andrade for permission to bring him along.

Why wait? Once there, he would challenge the High Prince himself.

* * *

Riyan flattened his back to a tree as Kiele galloped past on her mare. He'd heard the screams, faint but clear in the night stillness, and had barely slid into the woods in time to avoid her as she ran back to the manor house.

By the time he arrived, the place was silent and deserted. Riyan watched for some time from shelter, tremors shooting through him, before he finally approached the dwelling. The door was unlocked. He entered cautiously to find the interior empty. There were signs of habitation—and also of hurried leavetaking.

Outside again, circling the house for a clue as to what had happened there, he found nothing. Dirt and grass had been scuffed along one wall, but that could have been the work of the mare. Of Kleve there was no sign at all.

Riyan inspected the house once more in growing perplexity. He discovered food, used crockery, a rumpled bed, and a few clothes that would fit a tall, athletic man. Returning outside, he glanced up at the moons, tempted to use their light to cast about over the countryside for Kleve. Memory of Andrade's warning dissuaded him— that, and Kleve's promise to meet him tomorrow at the goldcrafter's. Riyan looked down at his four rings with a sense of betrayal. Knowledge enough to weave the sunlight, but not the moons he needed so much right now.

He returned to the residence, slipping into his chamber

as dawn first touched the sky. Despite his unease, he slept soundly for several hours and was up in good time to keep the appointment at the goldcrafter's.

But Kleve did not.

Volume Two

...

PART TWO

Sorcery

Chapter Fifteen

Sioned crouched atop a knoll in the tall summer grass, a breeze off Brochwell Bay ruffling her loosened hair. The sunlight came from behind her, making her an unidentifiable shadow—a trick her Desert-bred husband had taught her—as she watched the activity in the encampment below, where nearly ninety tents formed eleven neat little enclaves of color. Each group followed roughly the same pattern: the prince's large pavilion in the center surrounded by smaller tents for vassals, aides, and servants. Her own pavilion, an immense thing of blue silk that had been Prince Zehava's last extravagant purchase before his death, occupied the best site on a rise just above the west branch of the Faolain River. The dragon banner was unfurled, for although Rohan had not yet arrived she shared his sovereignty. The dragon was as much hers as his. He had made that quite clear at their first *Rialla*. She smiled to herself, recalling the slack-jawed amazement of the other princes when Rohan had broken all tradition and brought her into a banquet at his side. Since then other wives had demanded—and by and large had received—the same privilege. None of them, however, shared their husbands' authority as completely as did Sioned. The dragon was proof of that, too, holding a gold *faradhi* ring set with an emerald in his claws.

The other princes had followed Rohan's lead as well in the use of personal emblems to identify their people and belongings. In the last ten years all had chosen devices of their own, though Chay remained the only *athri* with his own symbol. The encampment was gaudy with colored tents and seethed with pennants flying above them that depicted all manner of devices. Some were beautiful, others merely appropriate. Fessenden's silver fleece on sea-green fluttered on tall silver poles; Gilad's three silver moons on blushing pink wafted above tents of the same ridiculous color. Dorval's white ship on a blue field

waved a full arm's length higher than Grib's white candle
on red, sure to irritate proud Prince Velden, who would
doubtless order taller flagpoles next time. Above her cousin
Volog's tents the breeze fingered scarlet banners with elegant silver flasks thinly outlined in black. Ossetia's wheat-
sheaf on dark green was beribboned with mourning gray
to remind all of Prince Chale's loss of son and grandson.
Sioned noted the quiet of his camp, sad contrast to the
bustle elsewhere. She pitied the poor old man, forced to
attend the *Rialla* when his grief was so new.

Three colors were missing from the array below her,
and there were corresponding gaps left for those who had
not yet arrived. Her brother Davvi was due sometime
today, and by evening his turquoise tents would rise near
her own blue just as his princedom of Syr bordered the
Desert. Princemarch's violet would be established on the
other side when Rohan, Pol, Maarken, and Pandsala rode
in tomorrow. They had not taken the usual route down
the Faolain to the *Rialla,* prohibited by the fact that neither Pol nor Maarken could set foot on anything that
floated. Pandsala had no such difficulty, and it remained
one of the curiosities of her Sunrunner abilities that she
had no qualms about crossing water. Andrade and her
suite—including Maarken's intended wife—would arrive
whenever Andrade felt like arriving. Her white tents
would be set up apart from the rest. Sioned had made
certain that several prime locations were left open for
her, but just where the Lady would choose to make her
camp was, as ever, her own affair.

Sioned sat back on her heels, lips pursed as she considered the meetings that would constitute the working
portion of the *Rialla* for Rohan. The last three assemblies
had been rather tame affairs compared to the first one she
had attended. Trade agreements, boundary agreements,
marriage agreements—nearly everyone had agreed on
nearly everything. Sioned ascribed much of this amity to
Rohan's statesmanship and skill at weaving so many different personalities and aims into a more or less cohesive
group. But though she knew his acumen was responsible
for much of the concord between princes, other factors
were involved. The *Riall'im* of 701 and 704 had been
canceled; Plague had stunned the continent before the

first and three years after that, Roelstra's death had dealt everyone another shock. Sioned's mouth tightened to a bitter line as she reflected that almost no one had believed Rohan could prevail over the powerful and cunning Roelstra. Memory of their final combat, a fight to the death beneath a dome of starlight woven by Sioned herself, could still make her shiver. Roelstra's planned treachery had failed; Rohan had killed him in a fair fight. But the remembrance of the strain as she used forbidden starlight at an impossible distance was the stuff of nightmares.

In the years since then, the older princes had bided their time, waiting to see what kind of High Prince Rohan would become. The younger, less experienced ones had waited, too, watching for strengths and especially for weaknesses. By now they all had his measure as a man and as a prince. Despite his obvious power, they were anxious to test him.

She combed her fingers through the long grass, judging its moisture as a daughter of a farming lord had been taught to do. No grass grew in the Desert that had been her home for nearly half her life now, but the old habit was in her and, recognizing it, she smiled. Her childhood at River Run seemed very far away. The holding now belonged to Davvi's younger son Tilal, who for eight years had been Rohan's squire. Tilal was twenty-four and looking for a wife. Sioned reminded herself to get a wager going with her brother on how many young ladies would lose their hearts to the young lord's black curls and brilliant green eyes. She anticipated a tidy profit from Davvi's modesty regarding his offspring's attractions.

If only family matters were all she need worry about. . . . She saw her fingers curve into dragon claws and consciously relaxed them. In a way, this purported son of Roelstra's *was* a family matter. Her gaze raked the encampment and she totaled up the princes likely to favor the youth's claim, if only to make trouble for Rohan. Miyon of Cunaxa was the prime candidate; a tall, thin, haughty man of thirty winters, he had finally managed to wrest control of his princedom from advisers who had ruled in his name for many years. He had executed them all, reportedly with his own sword. But though control of Cunaxa had changed, its policies had not. Miyon coveted the northern Desert and gave shelter to the Merida whose land it had long ago been. The Desert city of Tiglath, while not a port by any means, offered the only relatively safe harbor north of Radzyn. Cunaxan goods—wool, carpets, clothing, and the finest swords and metalwork in the princedoms—were mostly sent overland, for Lord Eltanin of Tiglath loathed the Merida even more than Rohan did and charged the Cunaxans huge sums for the right to load ships off his coast. More often than not the merchants chose caravans rather than ships, despite the expense of overland transport. Miyon was realist enough to keep from setting his sights on Radzyn to the south, where Prince Lleyn's great cargo ships found anchorage, but he would always look hungrily at Tiglath. He would support the pretender's claim whether he believed in it or not; anything to put pressure on Rohan to change Eltanin's crippling port fees.

Cabar of Gilad and Velden of Grib were two more young princes aching to test Rohan's authority. They had behaved themselves for quite a long time now, but there had been indications at the last *Rialla* that they were only looking for a convenient excuse for a challenge. Saumer of Isel might go either way, depending on his current desire to irritate Prince Volog, with whom he shared an island and a grandson. Likewise Prince Chale was questionable; he and Rohan were often opposed because Chale had cordially loathed Prince Zehava, Rohan's father. Sioned suspected that Chale had supported Roelstra in his war against the Desert, but whatever proof might have existed had long since been ignored in the interests of princely amity. Rohan was very generous when it suited him. Still, Chale's grief over the loss of his son and grandson might make him apathetic—which could be help or hindrance. Sioned had no way of knowing.

Those who would support Rohan were Lleyn, Volog, and Davvi. Of the remaining four princes, Clutha of Meadowlord would in all probability revert to his traditional position of neutrality. It was an old habit that died hard; Clutha had spent too long with one eye on each of his borders, wary lest his land become their battlefield yet again. As for Princemarch itself—Pandsala's voice as regent would be raised against the pretender, but her influence would be negligible. If it was decided that this man was who he said he was, Pandsala would be out of a job. Pimantal of Fessenden could, quite simply, be bought with a few hundred square measures of leaderless Firon, whose representative would have no vote in the matter at all. Neither would Rohan or Pandsala.

It was interesting that the tents below were grouped pretty much along political lines. Those of Cabar, Velden, and Miyon were to the west; Lleyn and Volog were near Sioned's own blue tents and the spaces left for Davvi and Pandsala; Clutha, Pimantal, Saumer, Chale, and the black pavilion housing Lady Eneida of Firon were to the east. Three to be watched, three to be sure of, and four to be swayed if possible. She wondered what Rohan might offer to win the doubters—and which of their nervous fears Miyon would play on to gain their support for his side.

All this was assuming, of course, that conclusive proof either way could not be offered regarding this pretender. Sometimes Sioned believed that Andrade and Pandsala would be able to convince everyone straight off that Chiana was the child born to Roelstra's mistress, Lady Palila. But she was also a realist, and as she gazed moodily down at the tents where ambitious princes plotted for their own advantage, she knew that she and Rohan had to be prepared for the worst.

She got to her feet and stretched, glancing automatically to the north, where Rohan and Pol were even now riding toward Waes. She had much to tell them of the detour she had taken with Chay and Tobin back to Radzyn to collect horses for sale; their progress through Syr and Meadowlord had had all the grace and dignity of a threatening stampede. But she was more concerned with hearing the details of their summer. Maarken had kept her informed on the sunlight, and she had done some judicious observing herself at various times—most especially to reassure herself that Pol was unharmed after the disastrous climbing expedition at Castle Crag. But she wanted to hear it all from her husband and son, and most of it from Rohan—preferably in bed.

That reminded her of certain arrangements she wished

to make. She ran back down the hill, arriving breathless at her pavilion. Tobin had helped herself to Rohan's large desk, going over her notes for the breakfast she always served to the princes on the fourth morning of the *Rialla*. The princess looked up as Sioned entered, and smiled.

"Do you know, even after all these years, I can't find a single improvement to make in Camigwen's plans? She was an absolute marvel of organization."

"Stronghold still runs according to her orders. Can you imagine what she would have made of Skybowl if she'd gotten her hands on it? Although I must say Ostvel hasn't done too badly."

"What are you doing?" Tobin asked as Sioned opened a chest and rummaged through its contents.

"Collecting a few things. I'm planning a surprise for Rohan."

Tobin laughed as Sioned held up two familiar wine goblets. "Those *can't* be the same ones you bought at the Fair twenty-one years ago!"

"Of course they are. And when Davvi arrives I'm going to steal a bottle of his best mossberry wine, and— what's all that racket outside?"

Both women left the private area of the pavilion and poked their heads outside. Sioned asked the guard on duty what all the fuss was in aid of; he saluted casually and replied, "I think it's his grace Prince Davvi arrived, my lady. Shall I send a squire and ask him to attend you here?"

She was already running to meet her brother, dodging past horses, baggage wains, and servants clothed in turquoise. Davvi had become Prince of Syr after the death of their close kinsman Jastri in Roelstra's war against Rohan; though not born to the honor, Davvi had proved a capable ruler and an ally for reasons of friendship and philosophy as well as blood bond.

He turned from ordering the arrangement of his tents when his sister called his name. He was very little like her in appearance, except for the green eyes that flashed as he swung her up in his arms. "Look at you—High Princess, indeed! Dressed in your oldest riding leathers, your hair a wreck, boots scuffed—what a disaster you are, Sioned!"

She made a face at him. "That's hardly the way to address the High Princess! You're looking well, Davvi—there's a bit more of you than there used to be, but it's very becoming." She poked him playfully in the stomach.

"Oof! I resent that!" He pinched her chin and laughed again. "But look who I've brought with me, Sioned."

She turned and found Kostas and Tilal nearby. After hugging them both, she stood back to look them over. "Davvi, how did you ever manage to produce such gorgeous sons? Goddess knows, *you're* nothing to look at. Kostas, you get more princely every time I see you. And Tilal—have you gotten taller *again?*"

"Not unless you've gotten shorter," he replied. "I know for a fact you've gotten more beautiful. Hasn't she, Kostas?"

"Unfair to every other woman at the *Rialla,"* the elder of the brothers replied, shaking his head with regret.

"Save your pretty speeches for the girls whose hearts you'll be breaking," she retorted.

They were indeed a handsome pair. Tilal was slightly taller, his striking green eyes set in a face crowned by glossy black curls. Kostas conceded nothing to his brother in looks; his waving brown hair was smoothly swept back from almost black eyes, and his solidly muscular body was broader through the shoulders, though just as lean through the waist and hips. Sioned revised her plan of wagering on Tilal's conquests to include Kostas as well. Between them they would have every unmarried female in fifty measures aflutter. Sioned grinned and told them so.

Davvi snorted his opinion. "They're quite conceited enough, thank you. Don't encourage them! Let's go for a walk while they do a little honest work for a change and help get everything put together. We can catch up on all the news."

She took Davvi's arm and they set off toward the river. Parental pride kept them talking about their children for quite some time as they walked along the riverbank. A family dinner was agreed on for that evening at Davvi's tents and at his insistence. "You have enough to worry about without watching half your food stores inhaled by my two gluttons."

"Oh, very well. But I'll bring the wine. Now tell me what's troubling you."

"That obvious? All right. I need your opinion and your advice, Sioned."

"It sounds serious."

"It is. You know Wisla always meant for Kostas to marry Gemma, and they've both resisted it. At first I think it was because of what happened to her brother Jastri. But I've made sure she's treated as a Princess of Syr, and she's continued to live at her childhood home. We've done everything possible for her, including a dowry if she chooses someone other than Kostas."

"But now she's dowered with all of Ossetia as Chale's heiress. I begin to see the problem—but go on."

"It's fairly plain. Gemma's mother was Chale's sister, and whoever she marries will become Prince of Ossetia. Goddess, all this tangle over inheritances—is it my imagination or is it worse than anything that's ever happened before? Which reminds me, what about this supposed son of Roelstra's?"

"Later," she said, shaking her head. "Tell me about Gemma."

Davvi pushed a willow branch aside for her. "Kostas is handsome, charming when he pleases, capable enough in governance—and a fool. Once word came that Inoat and young Jos were dead . . . well, he couldn't have handled it worse. He's ambitious without the cleverness to disguise it, Sioned. If he'd been smart, he would have used the opportunity to comfort Gemma, be the one she turned to in her grief. She was very close to her Ossetian cousins, for all that Inoat was so much older than she." He paused thoughtfully. "Gemma's a girl of deep and rather stubborn feelings. The kind who decides and then never wavers from the decision no matter what."

"Not the best quality in a ruler, but—no matter. Go on."

He smiled briefly. "I hear the High Princess talking. Let's see, where was I? Oh, yes. Kostas couldn't hide his excitement and announced to everyone that they'd be married here at the *Rialla*. She reacted the way any proud and high-strung girl would. She positively won't have him, Sioned, and he's equally determined to marry her so he can add Ossetia to Syr when I'm gone.''

"Oh, dear,'' Sioned murmured.

Davvi bent and picked up a few loose pebbles from the riverbank, throwing them idly into the water. "I'm fond of the girl. She came to replace Riaza, the daughter Wisla and I lost in the Plague. But I like her for herself, too— and I'll admit that it's partly because she's shown no interest in marrying Kostas just to make herself Princess of Syr.''

"He can be a little difficult at times,'' she observed diplomatically.

Davvi snorted. "He can be a damned idiot, as his recent actions indicate! Gemma was in no hurry to find a husband—but now I'm afraid she'll take anyone rather than Kostas. I want her to be happy. She was a great comfort to me when Wisla died two winters ago. She and Danladi—that's Roelstra's daughter by Lady Aladra—they brighten up life for an old man like me.''

"Danladi?''

"Quiet child, blonde hair, very shy. It's an odd friendship, because Gemma's so strong-willed.''

"Even odder—Roelstra was the one who led Jastri into the war that cost him his life.''

"I told you Gemma's impulsive in her likes and dislikes. They're the same age, and were only children when Roelstra and Jastri died—and they're both exiles of a sort, I suppose. They're like daughters to me, Sioned.''

She crouched down on the gravelly bank and began sorting pebbles. "Kostas can't drag Gemma kicking and screaming to the Lastday marriages, you know.'' Her brother made no answer, merely sat on his heels at her side, and she glanced at him, startled. "Don't tell me he'd dishonor her and force her into marriage that way? The laws about rape would make that very risky.''

"I'm sure it's occurred to him,'' he replied grimly. "I thought you and Rohan might have an idea or two. The truth is that I don't want Kostas to have both Syr and Ossetia. He's my son and I love him, and he'll do very well with what I'll give him—he's a good man. But—''

"But you don't entirely trust him?" she suggested gently.

"Awful thing to admit about a son, isn't it? If it was Tilal, I wouldn't hesitate an instant. You and Rohan made a fine man of him, Sioned."

"We had excellent material to work with, thanks to you and Wisla."

Davvi shrugged. "Do you ever—I mean, Pol's still very young—"

"I think the difference is that Pol's being trained to the responsibilities of two princedoms, not just one. Kostas probably sees taking Ossetia as the fulfillment of ambition, not a responsibility."

"And Pol will be a *faradhi,*" Davvi said softly.

Sioned was so startled she frankly stared at her brother. "Are you telling me that part of Kostas' ambition is to have Sunrunner children with Gemma?"

"I suspect it. It's not unknown in the Ossetian line, you know. That's another reason I don't want him to have both princedoms. But discounting that, he doesn't much like Pol's potentials. Don't look at me that way—you know very well there are others who feel as he does. Pol will be High Prince and a Sunrunner. That's a combination that makes a lot of people nervous."

She flung the stones into the river and sprang to her feet. "Father of Storms! Will it stop only when all princes are also *faradh'im?*"

"I don't know," he told her frankly. "Again, if it was Tilal, I wouldn't be worried. He spent a long time with you. He's not envious or resentful or fearful of what you are—and what Pol will become." Davvi sighed deeply and shook his head. "Sioned, at times I wonder what our parents would have said about our lives."

Sioned put a hand on his shoulder. "You have more memories of them than I do. What do you think they would have said?"

He shrugged uncomfortably. "I think perhaps I never would have married Wisla, and if I had not, then you never would have been sent to Goddess Keep."

"And I never would have married Rohan, and you never would have become Prince of Syr. Don't be silly, Davvi."

"You were so little," he muttered, looking anywhere but at her. "I didn't know what to do with you, how to raise you. And Wisla—"

"She wanted to be lady in her new home. And I wasn't exactly an easy child to deal with," she added wryly. "There's nothing to forgive, my dear. Things happen as they happen. We make the choices and do the best with what comes of them. Not very original, I know, but true just the same."

At last he smiled a little. "Yes, but we can also nudge things a bit."

Sioned returned the smile. "Then nudge Gemma in the direction of Chale's tents for the duration. He probably wants her there anyway, as his heiress."

"You would have been wasted as anything other than High Princess."

"So I keep telling my husband."

"I'll remind him the next time I see him." They started back toward the encampment. After a moment he took her elbow and they stopped beside a willow tree. "What can you tell me about this pretender?"

"Not much," she admitted, running her fingers along slender green leaves. "He'll show up here and try to establish his claim, of course. The trouble is that there was so much confusion the night Chiana was born."

"I'll bet she's tearing her curls about now."

"If that's all she does, we'll be lucky. We had dinner at the Waes residence the night we arrived and she was all over Chay, trying to seduce him into supporting her— as if *he* might believe in this man's claim!" She giggled suddenly. "I thought Tobin was going to burst!"

"From jealousy?" Davvi asked, his tone incredulous.

"From trying not to laugh in the girl's face! Still, you can understand Chiana's position. If this pretender is convincing, all her pretensions go sailing out to sea. She's frantic. And her behavior is going to cause doubts where none existed before." She shrugged in annoyance. "If she had any wits, she'd act as if it was all beneath her notice. But no, she must solicit support everywhere, using her smile and her body."

"It's a good thing Pol's so young," Davvi said, grinning.

"Yes, but she'll start in on Rohan, naturally. There's no logic to the way she thinks, Davvi! Why would Rohan believe this man?"

"Perhaps she has ambitions of her own."

"Mmm. Like Ianthe, the *Rialla* of 698. *She* tried to seduce Rohan, you know."

"No, I didn't. I can't see her succeeding."

Sioned pushed away a memory fifteen years old: Rohan at Feruche, injured, drugged with *dranath*. Pol was the result of that night.

To her brother she said, "Of course not. But she and Chiana are the same type—they keep on trying, even when the man in question pushes them away with both hands. Come, let's go back so you can order our dinner and get some rest. Be sure to send a note to Chale offering to lend him his heiress. Gemma will be guarded in his camp as closely as Pol will be in ours—and probably like it just about as much."

* * *

When Sioned returned to her pavilion she found preparations being made for an impromptu party. Ostvel looked over her battered riding clothes and pulled her into the private section of the tent, where he had laid out a gown suitable for the High Princess. "Have you forgotten that you're giving a little welcome-to-the-*Rialla* party?" he asked. "Get dressed and comb your hair."

"Oh, do I *have* to? Tomorrow's soon enough to talk to these people."

"What you might learn today is more important. Change your dress and be quick about it—they'll be here any time."

"You think these things up to torment me," she complained, and resigned herself to the deep blue silk he had chosen. Sioned served as her own maid—a thing that had shocked Rohan's mother when Sioned had first become his wife. But there were very practical reasons for it: her clothes were kept simple enough so she could dress herself quickly if need be, and she insured that the only people who entered their quarters were herself, Rohan, and his squire. Privacy was desirable for the High Prince and High Princess; for Rohan and Sioned personally, it was essential.

She emerged from the tent holding a scrap of loosely woven silk whose purpose defeated her. "Ostvel, this is lovely, but what do I do with it?"

"That's the latest thing—or will be, once all the women see you wearing it." He draped the cloth over her head, arranged it across her shoulders, and finally folded it back to leave her face visible. "It's called 'lace' and you're not only going to set a new fashion, you're going to establish a new industry."

"How clever of me," she said wryly. She fingered the delicate weaving of blue silk cobwebs that formed a pattern of interlocking flowers. "Whose industry?"

"Yours, by spring. I found a weaver this morning who makes piles of this stuff, and bought about a quarter of it. On my advice, he'll hike his prices up for the Fair. In gratitude for your patronage, he's decided to move from Grib to Princemarch and teach others how to do this." Ostvel gave her a smug grin.

"Why, you conniving man!" she exclaimed in admiration. "Since we have exclusive rights to the silk trade, we'll make a fortune."

He bowed. "My fee for this brilliance will be modest—say, fifty percent of the profits."

"Fifty!"

At that moment her guests began to arrive, eager to sample the wines, breads, meats, and cheeses set out on long tables in the open air. Tobin and Chay showed up a little late, the princess wearing a similar veil of dark red silk lace that framed her delicate features like woven rays of sunset. The envious glances of the other ladies present confirmed Ostvel's cunning; they would soon be clamoring for the beautiful stuff.

It was a casual party, but not entirely congenial. Too many tensions and rumors chased each other from group to group. Everyone was there, naturally. Lleyn, leaning on the dragon-headed cane Rohan had sent him, held a small court of elders beside a tree, Clutha and Chale joining him; the old princes left it to the younger folk to circulate and chatter, content to observe and comment with the asperity that was the privilege of their years and experience.

Miyon of Cunaxa complimented Sioned on her veil

with as much charm as if a Desert army was not right across his border, then excused himself to talk with Cabar and Velden—rather unsubtle of him, Sioned thought, but exactly the configurations of allies she had envisioned. Davvi spent his time entertaining their cousin Volog of Kierst, who had Saumer of Isel in tow. The latter was looking mellow; perhaps he would be in a mood to support Rohan and reject the pretender's claim. Sioned blessed her brother's tact and turned her attentions to the *athr'im*.

There were more of them here than in previous years, many in search of wives. Patwin of Catha Heights, still a widower after the death of Roelstra's daughter Rabia; young Sabriam of Einar; Allun of Lower Pyrme; Tilal of River Run—there were hands and fortunes enough among them to keep the young highborn ladies busy. And that wasn't even counting the heirs to princedoms, like Kostas, who were also in need of brides.

Sioned welcomed them all, saw them provided with fine wines from Gilad and Ossetia and Syr, and thanked the Goddess for Stronghold's isolation. She knew she would long since have gone mad if forced to have this constant parade of people around her, watching, judging, waiting for a slip, jealous of a smile that might indicate preference. Tobin and Chay, however, were in their element. Charm and good humor positively oozed from them both. Tobin was engaged in putting young Milosh of Fessenden, Pimantal's youngest and favorite son, at his ease; the boy was barely twenty and obviously dazzled by her. Sioned silently saluted her sister-by-marriage's political acumen. They needed Fessenden. Chay had drawn Velden, Miyon, and Cabar around him and was talking swords and horses—conversation nicely calculated to appeal to three proud young men eager to impress this great lord with their knowledge. Young people flirted, older people drank and talked, and by sundown most of the wine was gone and Ostvel ordered another few casks broached.

Yet as Sioned discussed Pol's training with Princess Audrite, she noted that three faces were missing. Audrite was quick to catch her frown, and asked its cause.

"We're lacking a few celebrants," Sioned commented.

Audrite's thick dark lashes lowered slightly as she scanned the crowd. "Ah, yes. Our friends from Waes and the Lady—excuse me, the *Princess*—Chiana." Audrite's mouth twisted as if the name soured her tongue, and Sioned chuckled. "They'll have the excuse of last-minute preparations, of course, but it's rather rude of them not to put in an appearance."

"In a way, I'm glad they're not here. The young ladies ought to be glad, too. Chiana isn't exactly subtle."

"Why, cousin!" Audrite pretended to be shocked, and both women laughed. "Seriously, it's not Chiana anyone should be concerned with. I heard some disturbing things about Kiele today. She's put it about that Lyell has had this pretender researched, and the information is all to the young man's advantage."

Sioned frowned. "So that's why there was more than the usual chill between her and Chiana the other night. Like frozen sugar."

"You can count on our support, of course. This man is an imposter, certainly—but even if he were for real, neither my husband nor his father relish the idea of another Roelstra. Besides, Rohan won Princemarch by all the rules of war, and was confirmed by the princes."

"Except Miyon, whose advisers kept him at Castle Pine." Sioned glanced at the tall, dark figure, frowning lightly.

"I wouldn't worry too much about him. He's inexperienced. He's bound to make some sort of mistake."

"I agree—but we can't count on the errors of others to promote our cause." She sighed. "I know that you and Chadric and Lleyn will do your best for us—and I thank you for it." She excused herself and stood a little apart from her guests, waiting until the servants had placed ten tall poles around the area and secured unlit torches atop them. Sioned concentrated for a moment, gestured, and the torches sprang to life. There was a slight murmur of surprise and all gazes turned to her, just as she had intended. She smiled sweetly. It never hurt to remind them that their High Princess was also a Sunrunner.

Ostvel brought her a fresh cup of wine. "Exhibition-ist," he accused.

"You're getting stuffy in your old age. What's the use of being *faradhi* if I can't have a little fun every so often? Did you see Miyon's face when that torch lit right over his head?"

Ostvel stepped back and bowed to someone who was approaching Sioned from her left. "Princess Naydra," he said, bowing slightly, and after murmuring a polite excuse left them alone.

"Good evening, your grace," Naydra said. "I've been admiring your veil. It's very beautiful."

"Thank you. I must compliment you in return on your pearls. I've never seen that exact shade of pink before. They're exquisite."

"My lord is very generous to me." Her dark eyes found and caressed her husband, Lord Narat of Port Adni, a bulky and cheerful man currently engaged in lively conversation with Prince Saumer.

Sioned beckoned a servant over and asked him to fetch Naydra another cup of wine. As the two women exchanged the meaningless pleasantries required of princesses, Sioned regarded her companion thoughtfully. Naydra was the eldest of Roelstra's daughters, the only one besides Pandsala of his legitimate offspring now living, and thus the only other one with the right to be styled "princess." She did not much resemble her two more notorious sisters. Her eyes were the same shape and color as Ianthe's, and she had much of Pandsala's dignity, but there the similarities ended. Naydra was quiet, subdued, and utterly without fire or ambition.

"I wanted to tell your grace that I'm more grateful every day for your goodness to me."

Sioned smiled uncertainly. "I'm afraid I don't understand."

"I regret that I'm unable to give my lord an heir, but beyond that I have nothing to wish for. I have a life that pleases me, and it's thanks to you and the High Prince that I am happy." She looked down at her hands. "Your generosity in dowering me—"

"Oh, Naydra—please, don't. I'm only sorry we weren't able to do the same for all your sisters."

"Yes—marriages that would have come to Rusalka, Cipris, and Pavla, had they lived. There are few of us left now. Myself and Pandsala, Kiele, Moria, Moswen, Danladi. . . ." Naydra glanced up and shrugged. "The latter three have avoided marriage, you know. Not because they lack suitors or dower, but because betrothal seems to be dangerous for Roelstra's daughters. And Rabia's death in childbed after two normal birthings was a shock. I nearly died, too, you know, miscarrying my poor baby." The princess looked directly at Sioned for a long moment, then away. "It's almost as if there's a curse on us and our children."

The servant came then with Naydra's wine, giving Sioned time to mull over the catalog of sisters and the strange conclusion Naydra had drawn. When the servant had left them, Sioned asked carefully, "What are you trying to tell me, my lady?"

"Nothing, your grace. It only makes me sad." But again Naydra met her gaze in uncharacteristically direct fashion. "With your permission, I will attend my lord." With a small, graceful nod, she moved away.

Sioned smoothed the frown from her forehead but could not stop thinking about what Naydra had said. Perhaps the princess was still grieving over the loss of the only child she would ever carry—Sioned understood that only too well, for her own miscarriages still haunted her. But Naydra had seemed to imply something else. A curse on Roelstra's daughters and their children—ridiculous, the kind of thing reasonable people knew to be mere superstition. Rabia's three daughters were perfectly healthy, and Kiele had a fine son and daughter. And Ianthe— Sioned sipped at her wine to wash away the bitter taste that always came with the thought of Pol's mother. A curse; what nonsense.

Still, she mused as she joined Lleyn, Chale, and Clutha, out of eighteen daughters born to Roelstra and his various ladies, only seven were still alive.

It was only then that she realized that in her catalog of sisters, Naydra had not included Chiana.

* * *

Sioned was awakened early the next morning by shouted greetings, clanking harness, and her husband's demands to know why his lazy wife was so late abed. She barely remembered to grab a robe and fling it on as she went flying out of the pavilion and into his embrace.

"Rohan—oh, love, I've missed you!" She locked her arms around him and buried her face in his neck. He smelled of healthy sweat, leather, and horse—a lovely stink as far as she was concerned.

"Father of Storms, woman, let me breathe! And get some clothes on, you're making a spectacle of yourself!" He laughed, hugging her tighter to his chest.

"Oh, shut up," she said, and effectively prevented further scolding by claiming his lips with her own. When she considered him to be thoroughly greeted, she drew back and asked, "Now I've made a spectacle of us both— as if you cared!"

"I'm surprised the whole camp hasn't lined up to watch." He kissed her again.

Maarken nudged Pol. "Hurry, get everybody here and we can sell tickets—two coins a head and split the profits fifty-fifty!"

Rohan released her and she turned to her son. There was something older about his smile, reflecting what had happened to him during the summer they had been apart. And surely he was taller. She held out her arms and he came forward, and she pressed her cheek to his sunny hair. When he wriggled slightly—young enough still to want a hug, but old enough to be conscious of his dignity—she let him go and saw Pandsala standing silent and watchful nearby. Sioned smiled at the princess.

"What in the world have you been feeding him at Castle Crag? He's gotten taller—grown right out of his tunic!"

Pandsala's eyes lit with humor and she came forward to touch hands with Sioned. "Fresh mountain air and sunshine will do that, your grace. I'm pleased to see you."

"And I you, and looking so well—especially after hosting my hatchling." She eyed Pol. "Have you caused her grace any trouble?"

"He was a joy to have with us," Pandsala said softly. "All of Princemarch was reluctant to part with him."

Pol looked so smug that Sioned decided his dignity

required a little salutory teasing. "No pranks, no escapades, no disobedience? I don't believe it! You must tell me your secret for turning him into a rational being with manners, Pandsala."

"Mother!" Pol protested, and Sioned laughed. "I was a very good guest!"

"He was indeed, your grace," Pandsala seconded.

"She can tell you all about it once we've been made comfortable," Rohan said pointedly. "I assume you're about to offer everyone a bath, a bed, and breakfast while Pandsala's tents are set up?"

"All begun the instant you finally showed your noses," she assured him, then turned to the regent. "Princess Tobin has offered her tent for your comfort. You'll probably want to rest while Ostvel and your steward supervise your camp."

"Thank you, your grace. That would be most welcome." She bowed and withdrew, accompanied by a waiting-woman who hovered at her side.

Maarken then came forward to greet Sioned. "Has Andrade arrived yet?" he whispered in her ear.

"Later today, perhaps tomorrow. And I haven't forgotten our wager." She drew away and smiled at him. "Your parents will want to see you at once. And Sorin's been by several times from Volog's tents, asking when you'd arrive."

"Sorin? Oh—of course! He's to be knighted in a few days." Maarken turned to a squire. "Find my brother at the Kierstian tents, please, and tell him I'll be with our parents." To Sioned, he went on, "We'll all dine together tonight?"

"Naturally." Maarken strode off and Sioned waved her husband and son into the pavilion. "Baths and food for both of you, and then a rest."

"But I'm not tired, Mother."

"You will be."

A short while later, the promised hot bath and breakfast proved her correct. Pol yawned his way into the portion of the huge tent sectioned off for his bedchamber, and Rohan shared a smile with his wife.

"Are you always right?"

"Not always—but I'm *never* wrong."

He snorted. "And if you are, you don't admit it."

"Neither do you." She refilled their cups with steaming hot taze and leaned back in her chair, set opposite his at the desk. "Maarken kept me informed, of course, but I want to hear it all from you."

Rohan smiled. "Pandsala wasn't just being polite, you know. I think everybody who met Pol wanted to take him home!"

"Just as I expected. Tell me about the vassals."

"There aren't many. Roelstra took most of Princemarch into his own hands, so the holdings are run by glorified stewards, not *athri'im*. There are four exceptions. My favorite is Lord Garic of Elktrap Manor. He's a crafty old soul—waited out Roelstra, hiding most of his wealth, with the result that his two pretty granddaughters are dowered like princesses."

"Mmm. Speaking of princesses and dowries. . . ." She told him about her conversation with Davvi and her solution to his problem.

"Very astute of you, love. Chale can probably use the comfort Gemma's presence will give him." He rubbed his forehead wearily. "What news should I know about?"

Sioned detailed what she knew, what she suspected, and what was currently rumored. Rohan listened in impassive silence to the long recital, and at last nodded slowly.

"Something interesting happened the day before we left. Pandsala has been scouring Princemarch since spring for any word about this pretender. As it happens, he grew up at Dasan Manor, and his name is Masul. Lord Emlys of Dasan was long gone from Castle Crag with the other vassals and stewards by the time word came, so we couldn't question him. Pandsala's informant says that Masul vanished about the end of spring with a little money, the clothes on his back, a sword, and Emlys' best horse. The horse turned up in Einar, of all places. But Masul is already in Waes, I'd bet anything on it."

"What do they say about him? Is it possible he's Roelstra's son?"

Rohan stretched the tension from his shoulders and Sioned went to stand behind him, rubbing the strong, taut muscles. "Ahh . . . that's wonderful. They say the boy is tall, with dark hair and green eyes. Lived with his grandparents at Dasan. Their daughters were in service at Castle Crag, one of them as nursemaid to Kiele and Lamia. And now you tell me Kiele is circulating word that this Masul just may be her brother. An interesting connection, don't you think?''

"Her invitation to Chiana becomes clear, too. You know how we wondered about that all summer. They've never been fond of each other, especially since Chiana tried to seduce Lyell. Kiele's going to pay her back with public humiliation.''

"Roelstra's daughters are such delightful women.'' Rohan murmured.

"Now, I've always liked Naydra and so have you. I was talking to her last evening, and she said the oddest thing. We spoke of her sisters and—''

"Sioned? Rohan?'' Tobin peeked around the partition. "Your son claims he's about to expire of starvation and asks can we please eat now? I must say I agree with him. It's noon.''

"Have we been talking that long?'' Rohan asked, surprised. "And when did Pol sneak out of here?''

"After lunch, you're going to bed,'' Sioned told him.

"All alone?'' He pulled a forlorn face.

"You don't have the energy to do me justice,'' she said, laughing. "Besides, I've got a surprise planned for later. Get what sleep you can, because you won't get any tonight.''

"You have a way of making a threat sound absolutely delightful.''

Late that night they saw their resentful but obedient son tucked up in bed and left the pavilion. Guards trained by Maeta in the arts of protecting irreplaceable princes were on duty; Pol was safe. The family had drunk to Maeta that night at dinner after Maarken and Pol had told them of the manner of her death. When they returned to the Desert, the rest of her ashes would be scattered on wind summoned by the *faradhi* princess she had served— and the young, untrained *faradhi* prince she had given her life to protect. Pol's education would begin early so that he might perform this service for his kinswoman.

Sioned would teach him, and she cared not a damn what Andrade thought of it.

"Where are you taking me?" Rohan asked as they strolled the riverbank past the bridge.

"Back twenty years," she replied, leaning her head on to his shoulder. "You've just done something dreadfully heroic by saving me from the evil clutches of an infamous seducer—"

"Heroic, eh?" Rohan laughed. "And we're about to anticipate our marriage vows by several days, is that it?" He held her closer to his side. "I thought I loved you then. It was nothing compared to now."

"You haven't lost your romantic impulses," she approved, and conjured up a tiny flame on the damp grass ahead of them, gentle light that limned the shape of a willow tree. Parting its branches, she revealed the snug den she had created the afternoon before, over which a bemused guard had kept watch until tonight.

Rohan slid inside and Sioned followed after damping the little Fire. "It's considerably more welcoming than last time," he commented, patting the blankets spread on the ground. "As I recall, we had to use your skirt for a bed." He reached over and fingered the two glasses and bottle nestled against the willow's trunk. "And you accused *me* of being a romantic!" The faint light of moons and stars filtered through the silver-green canopy of leaves around them, touching his face with cool, soft fire. Sioned took his hands, held them to her cheeks, turned her head to kiss each palm.

"I love you," Rohan said.

Their lips met and they sank down onto the blanket, content for a long while simply to kiss one another. Sioned lost herself in the warmth of his arms, the wine on his tongue, the delicate nuances of his mouth on her own. Bones melting, sweet weakness stealing through her veins, cherished familiar ache growing in her body, she glimpsed in memory the shy youth who had first made love to her beneath this willow tree, and smiled against his lips.

Chapter Sixteen

Prince Volog of Kierst was Sioned's cousin, a fact no one would have cared about had she remained an obscure Sunrunner at Goddess Keep. But she had married Rohan, who had become High Prince; events had made her brother Prince of Syr. Thus Volog found himself blood-bonded to some very important people.

He was wise enough—and proud enough—neither to ask favors nor to trade on the relationships. There was no need to do either. His position and his possessions made the bond one Rohan was pleased to acknowledge to their mutual advantage. In his turn, Volog found Rohan a pleasant friend and a helpful kinsman. He did not resent the chance that had given Sioned their grandmother's *faradhi* gifts instead of himself, for he was that rare man who held onto what was his, appreciated what life gave him, and did not extend himself beyond his known limitations.

To be sure, he gloated over the eventual union of Kierst with Isel into a single princedom. But he did so in private, not wishing to stir up trouble that Saumer of Isel was perfectly capable of causing until their grandson came of age. At Rohan's strong suggestion, a marriage had taken place between Saumer's only son and Volog's eldest girl. Volog's heir had later wed Saumer's favorite daughter. The latter union had produced a son who became sole heir to both princedoms when Saumer's heir died without issue. The child would be brought up at both courts until his twelfth winter, at which time Volog intended Saumer to agree to the boy's fostering at Stronghold. He did not require Saumer's approval, but he was smart enough to know that they ought to be in accord over the education of their mutual heir. Volog enjoyed his triumph in private, and in public was the soul of friendship to Saumer. Each man conveniently forgot about the hundreds of years their forebears had spent encouraging land-thievery and cattle-stealing along their mutual border.

Volog had another daughter, his youngest child and his

favorite. Alasen was a charming girl, twenty-two winters old, with gold-lit brown hair and green eyes the color of the sea off the Kierstian coast. Delicate arching brows and a sweet, serious mouth completed her beauty; her intelligence was evident in her face and her conversation. She was Volog's pride and joy.

But she was not looking her best when he presented her with gruff pride to Sioned on the first morning of the *Rialla*. Her cheeks were pallid, her eyes dark-circled, and there was a pinched expression about her mouth. Sioned knew that none of it was due to trepidation at meeting the High Princess. She knew the signs of a protracted recovery from crossing water when she saw them.

"The journey from Kierst was not one you enjoyed, I think," she observed wryly. "Volog, it seems our grandmother's influence hasn't entirely missed your line after all."

"I'm not *faradhi*-gifted, your grace," Alasen said quickly, and with such firmness that Sioned's brows shot up. "Others besides Sunrunners are ill in ships."

Volog shrugged. "Whether she's gifted or not remains to be seen, Sioned. I thought you might like to meet her just the same."

Sioned correctly interpreted this to mean she was to find out whether or not Alasen was indeed *faradhi*. It hovered on her lips to ask why Volog had not taken her to Andrade long ere this, but the glance of loving indulgence he gave his daughter explained all. Alasen denied the possibility; her father could not bring himself to submit her to Andrade's testing against her will. Sioned was his next best solution.

"I'm delighted to meet her," she said, smiling. "If you're feeling up to it and you've nothing else to do, would you care to accompany me to the Fair today? My husband has strictly forbidden me to buy my son presents to spoil him, and naturally I have no intention of obeying."

Volog rumbled with laughter. "The rights of a mother supercede the commands of a husband, and rightly so! Goddess knows, her mother and I have spoiled Alasen shamelessly."

"Rohan's father once told him that daughters are to be

indulged, for it's a husband's problem to discipline a woman.'' Sioned laughed softly, but did not miss the tightening of Alasen's lips at the mention of husbands. ''I can't say that Prince Zehava ever took his own advice, for he indulged both daughter and wife until the day he died. Rohan never believed him, anyway!'' She turned to the girl. ''I'd be glad of your company today, Alasen.''

The banter had relaxed her, and she gave Sioned an enchanting smile. ''I'd love to join you, your grace.''

''Then I'll leave her in your care,'' Volog said, and departed.

Sioned took the girl's arm. ''If you feel you can't use my name just yet, then please call me 'cousin.' Between the two of us it's actually true, not like most of the others I have to address by that term.'' She wrinkled her nose and Alasen grinned.

''I know exactly what you mean. Every time I have to use it with Prince Cabar, I'm reminded how grateful I am that it *isn't* true.''

''Our dear cousin of Gilad is a bit on his dignity, isn't he?''

''He's pompous, arrogant, and unbearable,'' Alasen summed up tartly, then blushed. ''My father's right—I've been so spoiled I forget to speak with proper respect.''

''Speaking it and feeling it are different things. We're family, Alasen. Say whatever you like.'' Sioned winked at her. ''Goddess knows *I* do!''

The two women were dressed casually, and as they joined the queue at the bridge there was nothing to distinguish them from anyone else going to the Fair that day. All rank and privilege were set aside, a relief from the ceremony of other occasions. The vendors addressed everyone from serving maids to princesses with exalted titles; the prettier the lady, the more outrageous the form of address. Men, be they lords or grooms, were always ''Your Excellency'' at the Fair. Plain garments and a leveling of rank were the rule.

Nevertheless, Sioned's red-gold hair was well-known, even though the huge emerald on her finger was hidden by thin leather gloves. Attempts to defer to her were discouraged with a smile and a shake of her head, which only led to more deference. She politely refused a place at the head of the queue waiting to cross the bridge; a path opened up for her anyway. On the other side of the river, merchants forsook the rest of their customers to wait on her. She pointedly moved away when it happened, and after a time word spread that the High Princess was in the crowd but did not wish to be recognized. Things settled down, and she was able to do some serious shopping.

"Is it always like this for you?" Alasen asked.

"For the first little while, yes. Long gone are the days when I could walk here unnoticed. This is your first *Rialla,* I take it?"

"Yes—and it's wonderful! I've visited Port Adni, of course, and the markets there. But it's nothing like this!" She gestured to the happy chaos of merchants' stalls, customers, squires and pages running errands, apprentices carrying fresh wares to replace those already sold. The Fair was bright with colored awnings and noisy with a milling crowd in a holiday mood—and, at the far end of the huge field, smelly with pens full of sheep, goats, calves, and young elk. Their bleating was nearly as loud as the chatter of the bargaining going on. The two princesses went to inspect them.

"Look at that little calf with the white splash on his face," Sioned told Alasen. "He's going to be an absolute monster when he's grown, and sire many generations just like him."

"How do you know about such things?"

"I grew up on a working farm, not in a palace," Sioned replied, smiling. "That little fellow is descended from stock I tended as a child. His bloodlines are quite as grand as any of Lord Chaynal's stallions." The calf, as if sensing himself the object of discussion, ambled over and snuffled at Sioned's outstretched hand. "Davvi's going to make a fine profit from you, my lad."

"Why should a prince concern himself with livestock?" Alasen wondered.

"A prince should involve himself in everything that happens within his borders. Actually, Princess Pandsala thought this up. It's her idea that the stock of all princedoms can be improved by mixing bloodlines. At a price, of course," she added, chuckling. "Cattle-breeding may not be as glamorous as Chay's horses, but it's a great deal more practical.''

"My father says there are hawks for sale this year, too. Were they the regent's idea? May we go look at them?''

"I was headed there next. And they're *my* idea,'' she continued as they started up a hill to the woods. "We could never afford good hawks when I was a girl. The best are bred in Princemarch and kept only for the very rich. They're still expensive, but most people should be able to afford them.''

The caged hawks were in the cool shade of the trees. A few wore hoods despite the distance from the noise and bustle of the Fair. Sioned surveyed the results of her little scheme with satisfaction. The falconers were doing a brisk business, evidenced by little tags on many of the cages that indicated the birds had been sold. The tags were color-coded to individual princes and *athr'im*. She was pleased to note that people had done their buying early.

Alasen gazed in awe at a preening amber-faced hawk. One long wing stretched the limit of the cage to show bronze and green and gold pinions. "Isn't she beautiful?'' the girl whispered.

"I always wanted to fly,'' Sioned murmured. "Especially watching the dragons over River Run when I was little.''

"It must be the most wonderfully free feeling in the world,'' Alasen said dreamily. "To know that all you need is the sky and the sun.''

"It's something like being a *faradhi*,'' Sioned remarked, and received the reaction she had expected. Alasen's shoulders stiffened and she turned away from the hawk. Sioned pretended not to notice. "I'm about to spoil my son by purchasing one of these birds. Help me pick out the best.''

"But he owns them all, doesn't he?''

"He owns the right to breed them, which we sell at a nice sum to these good falconers, who reap the profits of their labors.''

A bearded young man approached them, bowed low, and swept out a hand to indicate his wares. His full sleeves made the gesture reminiscent of flight, an impression accented by the sharp curve of his nose and two small, bright eyes.

"A hawk for Your Magnificences? None finer than mine! A personal grant from the high and mighty Prince Pol himself, given with his own royal hands. Modesty aside, my hawks are born of matings much like the one that produced the young prince himself—fabled lady mother and powerful princely sire that he has, and my hawks the same. Allow me to show you birds that the High Princess herself complimented me on only this morning, excellent judge that she is of all things in this world including hawks, and told me the famous emerald on her hand would be a fitting price for any one of these beauties."

Sioned stuck the gloved hand wearing the famous emerald into her pocket. "That's as may be. But how much are you willing to sell one for?"

He named a price that made her blink. Pandsala had set strict limits on the amount to be charged; even taking into account the bartering that would bring the price down, the final sum would be considerably above that limit. The idea was to make the birds available, not to make stupendous profit.

To Sioned's surprise, it was Alasen who began to bargain the price down. Her expertise was an education to Sioned, who had never been much good at such things. When she saw something she wanted, she could never bring herself to haggle and possibly work herself into a position where pride would compel her to walk away. Most merchants saw this in her face with the first half-hearted exchange. But Alasen was a true artist who obviously loved the game, and soon had the falconer clutching at his tousled hair and clawing at his beard in pretended agony. Sioned kept silent and enjoyed the show.

At last Alasen turned to Sioned. "You'd best go look at the other hawks. I'll join you shortly, I think—this man's skull is as thick and hard as an unhatched dragon shell."

Willing to play her part, Sioned strolled among the other cages. She asked about prices and found equally outrageous starting sums. She counted colored tags, made a rapid mental calculation, and returned to Alasen, who had bargained the price down to where it should have started.

After catching the falconer's gaze with her own, Sioned slowly and deliberately drew off her gloves. With the emergence of the emerald, the man's eyes popped. He looked at hair, eyes, and emerald again to confirm her identity, then gave a howl of dismay that brought the other falconers running. For a moment Sioned thought he would prostrate himself and throw dirt over his head in penance. To his fellows, he shouted, "Her Most Noble and Exalted and Gracious Royal Highness, the High Princess!"

Sioned looked them all over, hands on hips. "Goddess greeting to you," she said sweetly. "I'm very happy to see things proceeding so well, and at so handsome a profit." She smiled, and guilt appeared on every face. Alasen hid a grin behind her hand.

"If memory serves," Sioned went on in a tone that indicated her memory was faultless, "a specific price was set for these hawks. Now, I have no objections to a modest markup. That's economics. But my son will be grieved to find that his generosity to you has not been matched by your generosity to your customers. A simple calculation of the probable sale prices of these birds tells me that each of you has made additional profits amounting to the price of one hawk each. There are five of you. Therefore," she concluded with another smile, "you owe my son five hawks." A meaningful pause. "Thus far."

"But—Your Excellent Royal Highness—"

Sioned ignored him. "My cousin fancies the amber-faced one over there. I rather like the one wearing the green hood, myself. That's two. I'll trust your judgment to choose the best you have and tag them as belonging to my son. Do we understand each other? Marvelous! I think I need not add that I have counted the number of unsold birds, and at a similar rate of unauthorized profit you'll end up owing my son eight more hawks—if you continue your current practices, that is."

"But—the scandal if our prices suddenly drop!" one man protested.

"Our first customers will be furious! I beg Your Worshipfulness to reconsider—"

Alasen spoke up. "They're right, cousin. As I see it, there are two solutions. Our good friends here can refund the difference when buyers come to collect their hawks—" She paused as they moaned. "—or they can stick to their prices and make their next customers believe themselves prodigiously clever bargainers."

"There is merit in what you say," Sioned replied thoughtfully, sternly repressing a grin at the girl's cunning. "It would indeed be embarrassing for these honest merchants to admit they overcharged their first customers, after all. What do you say, my friends?"

The bearded falconer gulped. "Her Graciousness is all perception and genius. We will allow future customers to—to—" He choked slightly and one of his fellows poked him in the ribs. "The bargaining will continue until prices are what the regent specified," he finished, every word obviously tasting of vinegar.

"Splendid!" Sioned beamed. "So the five hawks—the two I mentioned and three to be chosen by yourselves— are all you owe my son. By the way, the birds are to be tagged for myself, the High Prince, my son, Princess Tobin, and Princess Alasen of Kierst—with whom you have just had the honor of speaking."

Alasen's eyes rounded in astonishment at the gift. Sioned took her arm and with a last smiling glance at the falconers led the girl back down the slope. They were barely out of earshot when Sioned could no longer contain her laughter.

"I haven't had that much fun all year! Can you believe what they were asking for those hawks? Pandsala will be furious."

"My lady—I really can't accept—"

"Why ever not? You earned it. And in case you hadn't noticed, those five hawks didn't cost me a thing. You said you loved to watch birds in flight, Alasen, and I can't think of anything lovelier than that golden-faced hawk with her wings spread to the sun. Not another word on the subject."

Alasen hesitated, then smiled. "From me, no—and

thank you! But you'll hear plenty of words from people who think they're terribly clever in striking a bargain!''

They returned to the Fair, heading for the food stalls. Delectable scents competed with each other in a riot of temptation, and Sioned gave in gleefully. From meats, cheeses, cakes, vegetables, pies, fruits both fresh and preserved, and hundreds of bottles of wine, she chose an elegant luncheon.

''We'll take this down to the river so we can eat in peace,'' she said, handing Alasen a crock of fresh berries soaked in honey and herbs. She juggled the rest of the food while trying to avoid a tribe of young pages out for a day's fun. ''Then I have to come back and find something else for Pol, and—oh!'' She caught her balance and turned to the person who had jostled her, a handsome woman of middle years with a curiously intense gaze.

''Your pardon, noble lady,'' the woman murmured.

''No damage done,'' Sioned replied cheerfully. ''It's quite a crush here, isn't it?''

''Yes. But I see you have no bread for your meal. I can recommend the baker from Waes, just down this aisle.''

''Thank you for your suggestion, but—''

''His goods are not to be missed,'' the woman interrupted.

Sioned was about to smile another polite refusal. But something urgent, almost desperate, about the woman's eyes stopped her. ''Indeed?'' she asked cautiously, wondering how far the woman would go in her insistence.

Far enough to whet Sioned's curiosity. She plucked at the High Princess' sleeve and whispered, ''Please, your grace.''

''Show me.''

She and Alasen followed the woman down the row of stalls to one with a bright red-and-yellow awning—Waes' colors, displayed by that city's merchants as all at the *Rialla* Fair showed their lord's colors by law. Rounds of unleavened bread were piled in baskets, sorted according to size and flavoring. All bore the baker's mark on top, an impression much like that made by a seal into wax. This baker had chosen a stylized ocean wave as his hallmark, which also appeared in white paint on the wooden stall.

The angular old man behind the counter turned from completing a sale, and his gaze narrowed at the sight of Sioned's escort. "Ah. Ulricca. Found me another customer, have you?"

"Only the best for this lady," Ulricca said.

"I have eyes," the old man grumbled, and pushed aside a yellow curtain at the back of the booth. "Mind that nobody steals while I'm gone," he admonished, and disappeared.

"The best?" Sioned murmured to Ulricca, who pretended not to have heard. Alasen looked a question at her, and Sioned gave a little shrug.

A moment later the old man was back. In his hands was a large round of bread wrapped in a clean though somewhat floury cloth. Sioned had coins ready, but the old man shook his head. "No money necessary. I know whom I serve."

"Even a highborn pays for her meals. I'm sure I shall value your best." She pressed two gold coins into his hand—a hundred times the cost of a loaf of bread.

"I trust so, noble lady." He bowed and went to help another customer.

"Sioned—where did that woman go?" Alasen glanced around, frowning. "I didn't see her leave. Who was she?"

"I've no idea." Sioned looked around for Ulricca and found not a trace of her. Shrugging, she took Alasen down to the riverbank and chose a seat beneath a trellis covered in flowering vines. She set out their meal with deliberate casualness and last of all unwrapped the bread. It was cool, and had been a long time from the oven; the cloth was not to protect Sioned's hands but to hide something about the bread that might arouse suspicion. It was Alasen who spotted the mark on the bottom of the loaf: not the baker's ocean wave but the rough outline of a dragon in flight, drawn in the dough with a knife.

"Is it a message?" Alasen asked, wide-eyed.

Sioned shook her head. "Identification." She pierced the edge of the round with her thumbnail. "I'll open this as if we're going to put our cheese inside. And if you move just a little to your right, those people eating over there won't be able to see a thing. Thank you. Aha!" She extracted a folded piece of parchment about the size of her palm, its surface sticky with oil. As she brushed it off, a golden circle fell out and she caught her breath.

"A ring?" Alasen breathed, then gave a start. "A *faradhi* ring!"

Sioned put the note and the ring into her pocket. "Yes," she answered. "Open the wine and let's eat."

When they had finished lunch they gathered up the leavings and walked down to the river, distributing crumbs to the birds. It was only then that Sioned took out the note. "This had better be worth the gold," she muttered. Alasen was nearly dancing with impatience as Sioned scanned the terse message and replaced it in her pocket. "There's only one way to separate a Sunrunner from his rings—which this note confirms."

"What does it say?"

"Forgive me, Alasen. I can't tell you. But I can let you know that you're right about its being a *faradhi* ring. It's the color of the gold—slightly reddish, as you saw."

"And the Sunrunner who wore it is dead."

"Yes. Otherwise it would still be on his finger." She looked down at her own hands. "I'm the only one who ever had her rings stolen from her and lived . . . never to wear them again."

"But the note—"

"I can't talk about it, Alasen."

"You think I'm too young and sheltered, don't you?"

"I was younger than you when I became Rohan's princess, so it'd be pretty rotten of me to hold your years against you. But there are certain things you *should* be sheltered from, because honest innocence is the best defense against awkward questions. Right now you know that a Sunrunner is dead and that I received a message. If you don't know any more, you'll be safe. Not even princesses with Sunrunner gifts should know everything."

"*You* do," Alasen muttered.

"Oh, my dear! If only!" She paused a moment. "You didn't jump just now when I named you *faradhi.*"

Alasen broke cheese into bits she tossed in the water for the fish.

"Have you ever heard the story of Siona, the grandmother your father and I share? She was a Sunrunner at Goddess Keep who met Prince Sinar at a *Rialla*. They fell in love. It was a terrible scandal, because at the time princes and lords did not marry *faradh'im*—not formally trained ones, at any rate. It was feared that the gifts would emerge in the next generation of rulers, trained by *faradhi* parents without the supervision of Goddess Keep.''

''Times seem to have changed,'' Alasen said with a furtive glance at Sioned.

''Andrade changed them to suit herself. It wasn't until me that the gifts showed up in the Kierstian line—and now you. It's not so terrible a thing, you know, being a Sunrunner and a princess.''

''But it makes me valuable, doesn't it?'' Alasen burst out. She flung the rest of the cheese into the water. Silver-green fish converged and the water roiled as they fought over the food.

''Ah,'' Sioned murmured, understanding. ''If not for me and my rule-breaking marriage to Rohan, then you could have admitted your talents, been trained, and lived only as a Sunrunner if you chose. But because of me, you're an important young lady when it comes to marriage.''

''It's not your fault,'' Alasen said quickly. ''You're right, I know I have the *faradhi* talents. I've always known it. I didn't think it was possible to be a princess and a Sunrunner both. And I'm a Princess of Kierst—I have duties. Even if I had been trained at Goddess Keep, my position demands that I marry a prince or a lord. So you see that it's better this way. I don't really have any choice.''

''But there's a part of you. . . .'' Sioned prompted.

''Yes—a part of me that says if I don't learn those things, then I'll live my life knowing I'm only half of what I could have been. But I don't want to become like those calves or sheep, valuable for my *faradhi* bloodlines instead of for myself. It's bad enough being a princess with the kind of dowry my father will give me. But at least I've been trained for that kind of life.'' She glanced up at Sioned. ''I don't think there's any training for being a Sunrunner princess *except* life.''

"Even so," Sioned reminded her gently, "you want to fly."

Alasen nodded curtly. "I can't help it—but I don't have to give in to it, either." She dusted her hands clean and shrugged. "I'm sorry—I shouldn't be bothering you with my problems, especially after that note."

"What I faced was the opposite, you know. I knew how to be a Sunrunner, but I'd no idea what would be demanded of a princess. Come, we ought to be getting back to the encampment."

Sioned left Alasen at Volog's tents and went to her own pavilion, where Rohan was taking a midday break from his princely pursuits. She kissed him a greeting and told him first about the hawks, which had him chortling.

"You're right, Pandsala will be livid! We'll have to warn her. Alasen sounds a very clever girl."

"It's a pity she's too old for Pol."

"I thought you had your heart set on Sionell—and Goddess knows she has hers set on him."

"Every prince should have a choice," she told him sweetly. "Just as you did."

"Mmm—as long as the choice coincides with what *you* want, you mean." He tugged playfully at one of her braids. "My morning wasn't half so entertaining. Everybody bartered back and forth, Lleyn sat there silent and amused, and no one mentioned the real business of the *Rialla* at all."

"Firon and Masul, but mostly Masul," she supplied. "Not even a hint?"

"None. But Lyell has asked to address the princes tomorrow. I can't say I'm looking forward to it."

"Then think about this instead." She produced the ring and the folded parchment, and told him how she had acquired them. "A little oblique toward the end, don't you agree?"

He read the note aloud. " 'This ring belonged to Kleve, who is dead. His other rings are gone, as are the fingers they circled. His body was being readied for the pauper's fire when he was identified and given decent burning. His murderer is unknown. But take warning: Word in the city is that the father of a son is in danger usually meant for the Desert.' " Rohan chewed his lip for a moment, then said, "Kleve was a good man. A good friend to us. Was he here for Andrade's purposes, do you think?"

"Yes. I didn't want to attract attention to the baker, so I didn't go back to his stall. But I could find him again if you like."

"And place him in danger? No. He or this woman evidently consider this note all we need to know." He clenched his fist around the gold circle. "Goddess—poor Kleve. It's barbaric. They cut off his *fingers*—left him to die and be burned in a common pyre—"

Sioned placed both her hands around his. "Kleve was here in Waes. Kiele's city. The woman who's championing Masul. Whatever he found out cost him his life. There's no other way to read it."

Rohan moved away from her, still grasping the ring. "It's not me they're after—'usually meant for the Desert.' That implies the Merida, of course. But 'the father of a son'?" He swung around suddenly. "Whose son are we concerned with here? Roelstra's! But he's already dead—so the threat—"

"Wait, you've lost me," Sioned protested.

"—must be to Masul's real father! Don't you see it? Who could provide the most damaging evidence? A man who looked and spoke and moved like Masul, and who isn't anywhere near dead!"

Sioned's brows quirked up, then down. "You're reaching," she said flatly. "There are dozens of fathers here who have sons—"

"And only one we're really concerned with," he reminded her. "But how do we go about finding him?"

"Well, who would *he* want to find?"

"Presumably the people who'll pay him the most money—either to talk or not to talk. He hasn't come to us, so I think we can assume he's looking for the latter. Who would he go to? Kiele? Miyon? Masul himself?"

"If Kiele ordered someone to murder Kleve—and I think she did—then she wouldn't hesitate to kill this man, too. Permanent silence." Sioned began to pace. "Who would he talk to? How familiar is he with the politics of this?"

"I don't—"

He was interrupted by the entrance of a guard. "Your

pardon, Highnesses,'' the woman said. ''The Princesses Pandsala and Naydra request a moment of your time.''

''Yes, of course,'' Rohan said distractedly. Then he stared at Sioned. ''Do you think—''

The sisters came in, and Pandsala's first words confirmed their suspicions. ''My lord, my lady, I'm sorry to disturb you, but a man came to Naydra this morning—''

''Let me guess,'' Sioned told her. ''He claimed to be the real father of this pretender, and wanted money to keep silent about it.''

Naydra's eyes widened. ''How did you know?''

Pandsala turned very pale and whispered, ''What a fool I am!''

''You couldn't have known,'' Rohan said. ''And you came to me as soon as you learned of it. Princess Naydra, please tell me what happened.''

''He said that as my father's daughter, I should want you and yours out of Princemarch, and if I didn't pay him—''

''You sent him away, didn't you?'' he interrupted. ''I appreciate your loyalty, my lady, but I wish you'd gotten word to me at once.''

She wrung her hands together. ''My lord, I'm sorry, I didn't think he was—that all he wanted was money—''

''You were right about that part of it,'' Rohan said more gently. ''I don't blame you, my lady. Please tell us everything he said.''

''He told me that he'd fathered a child on a woman married to another man, all of them servants at Castle Crag. He was part of the barge crew—I don't remember him, but that doesn't mean anything, really. I listened to him as long as I did only because I was so astounded at his impudence.'' Naydra pulled herself together with admirable aplomb and told them as much as she knew.

The man had been tall, dark-haired, and green-eyed—as Masul was reported to be. After the barge had burned that night, he had settled for a time in Waes, then worked on various ships. Rumors this spring had brought him back, where he had been waiting for the *Rialla* to see what his information could get him.

''I went to Pandsala soon after he left, my lord—I was

so insulted that he would think I would betray you and Princess Sioned, who have been so good to me—''

"Could you find him again?" Rohan asked. "Tell him you've reconsidered?"

Naydra shook her head. "I'm sorry, my lord," she said miserably. "After I recovered from the shock of his impertinence, I sent him on his way with no doubts about my loyalties. Then I went to tell Pandsala about his lies, in case he came to her next."

Sioned sighed quietly. "Well, where *would* he go next? Not to you, Pandsala, certainly. Kiele is a possibility I don't want to think about. He wouldn't live past his first few words."

Naydra turned pale. "My lady—you don't think she would—"

"I'm almost positive of it." She turned to her husband. "If I were he, I'd go to Chiana next. She doesn't have much money, but she's got the most to lose."

What Chiana lost was her temper. She was summoned to the pavilion and told the essence of what had happened, and turned furiously on Naydra. "You stupid fool! Why didn't you keep him with you and send for the rest of us?"

"That's enough," Pandsala snapped.

"Not by half, Princess-Regent!" Chiana spat, fiery-eyed. "You and Ianthe and your stupid schemes—if not for you, none of this would ever have happened!"

"My lady," Rohan said with deceptive mildness, "your opinion is not necessary right now. Your intelligence, however, is. Calm yourself and think."

"Oh, yes, you can order me to be calm and cool—it's not *your* identity at stake here, is it, High Prince?"

Pandsala took a threatening step toward her half-sister. "Be silent!"

"Don't you dare presume to give me orders, you treacherous bitch!"

Rohan muttered a curse under his breath. "Stop it, both of you. Chiana, return to Kiele's tents—yes, I know it's the last place in the world you want to be, but it's the only place you can be of use to yourself."

She gulped in a deep breath, shooting a poisonous

glance at Pandsala, and nodded. "Yes. Please excuse me." She bowed to him and withdrew.

Pandsala said in a wooden voice, "I beg pardon for her manners, my lord."

Sioned smiled faintly. "Pandsala, the girl *has* no manners."

Closing her eyes, the regent murmured, "Yet she's right. If not for Ianthe, and Palila's stupidity in heeding my revision of her plan, none of this would be happening."

"You were young and desperate," Naydra said softly. "Like the rest of us."

Sioned nodded. "I don't condone what you tried to do. But I understand it."

Pandsala met Sioned's gaze, and suddenly it was as if they were alone. "Even though it was all in pursuit of Rohan?"

"He was only a symbol for you both. Freedom, in the form of one man. But I think you've learned what Ianthe never did—that we make our own jails."

Pandsala hesitated, then murmured, "I've never said this before to anyone, but—he chose wisely in choosing you." Her cheeks colored and she glanced nervously at Rohan, abruptly recalling his presence. "Forgive me, my lord. With your permission, Naydra and I will leave you now."

When the pair had gone, Rohan heaved a sigh and flung himself into a chair. "Come here to me, Sioned."

"How can you sit there and—"

"There's not much I can do about any of this right now, is there? Come over here." When he had pulled her down into his lap, he sighed again. "The day becomes more and more interesting. But remind me when I choose a mistress to pick a lap-sized one. Those long legs of yours—"

"I regret my oversufficiencies, my prince. And I still want to know—"

"Sioned, if I order a search of every tent and all of Waes, I'll alert our enemies to the fact that I consider this man to be of vital importance—thereby killing him more effectively than if I'd run him through with my own sword. So I intend to wait and see what happens, which is all I *can* do for now—other than reacquaint myself with my wife after a whole summer's absence.''

A few moments later the voice of Rohan's squire came from the other side of the partition. ''Your Royal Highnesses?''

''Damn,'' Rohan muttered, and Sioned rose from his lap. ''Yes, Tallain, come in,'' he called.

Tallain, only surviving son of Lord Eltanin of Tiglath, was wheat-blond and dark-eyed, a well-built young man of nineteen winters only a year or so away from being knighted. Rohan had been fortunate all his life in his choice of squires, and Tallain was no exception. Walvis, younger son of a minor landholder, had become an accomplished battle commander, a trusted *athri*, and a good friend; Tilal, Sioned's nephew, was now an important lord in his own right and remained close to them. Tallain would one day rule over the walled city in the north, important bastion against the Merida and the Cunaxans across the border, and he was being trained with this in mind.

He bowed, brushed his ever-unruly shock of hair from his eyes, and said, ''I'm sorry, my lord, my lady. But someone left this outside the pavilion. All I saw of him was a plain dark tunic—no emblem, no colors I recognized.''

Rohan accepted the pouch of rough brown wool and undid the drawstrings. ''Ah,'' he said softly as he extracted a fine glass knife. ''Merida.''

Tallain stiffened, but it was Sioned who spoke. ''The death usually meant for the Desert?''

''I presume so. Another warning—more and more interesting,'' he repeated. ''Thank you, Tallain. And don't worry. This really isn't meant for any of us.''

''I'll double the guard anyway, my lord.''

''No, you will not.''

Tallain bowed and looked unhappy. ''As you wish, my lord.''

When the young man was gone, Rohan stroked the sharp blade of the knife with one finger. ''I've seen too many of these, plenty of them directed at *me.*''

''What do you think they mean by it?''

''They want me to know they're here. They want me

to worry about Pol—but not about this father of a son
our baker friend warned us of.'' He looked up at her.
''Sioned, if I truly were the hero you accused me of
being last night, I'd scour the encampments and give no
one any peace until I found the man—and he'd be found
alive. Heroes are supposed to act on impulse, do things
they haven't really thought through. And for heroes, such
things always work. That's what makes them heroes.''
He paused, turning the knife over in his hands. ''When
I was young, I had all the impulsive power of youth and
unimportance behind me. Oh, I had a princedom and that
made me someone to reckon with, but I wasn't High
Prince. I didn't have to be concerned with everything and
everyone. Now, I have to be. The power of being High
Prince limits me.''

Sioned nodded slowly. ''Back then, the only limit was
what you *could* do. Now it's what you *shouldn't.*''

''Exactly. And there's no other person in this world
who'd understand what I mean. What would I become if
I ran roughshod through everyone's lives simply because
I'm the High Prince and have the power to do so? If I
were still only Rohan, who ruled the Desert, then I could
try pretty much whatever I liked—because there'd be
someone more powerful than I to stop me if he could.
But there's no one like that now.'' He finished with a
self-mocking shrug. ''And it's not in the description of a
hero to be shy about using power.''

''My description of a hero is very different,'' she said
quietly. ''I'm looking at him.''

''You, my dearest love, are prejudiced.''

''Of course,'' she agreed readily. ''But take a look at
those around you sometime, who look to you for guid-
ance. Take a look at your son, who worships you. Rohan,
if being a hero is having the courage to resist using power
arbitrarily, then you *are* a hero, beloved.''

He shrugged again. ''What you call courage looks like
cowardice from here. And it doesn't get us any closer to
locating Masul's father.''

''Is that what we're really talking about?'' she asked
softly.

He gave her a tiny smile that vanished almost before it
touched his lips. ''I suppose not. What we're really talk-

ing about is finding and executing Masul before he can say a single word. Before we have to use this father of his to destroy him.''

He looked down at the knife—a Merida knife, from which the ancient league of assassins had taken their name: ''gentle glass.'' Suddenly he threw it viciously through the air. An instant later the shining blade hung quivering from a wooden support on the other side of the tent.

''To all hells with debates about power! Sioned, even if I have to break my own laws, I'm going to root out every one of those murderous vermin and execute them— with my own hands, if necessary. Pol is *not* going to spend his life looking over his shoulder for a Merida blade!''

Sioned stared at the knife for long moments. It took great effort to pry her gaze from it and look at her husband. ''Then make it profitable for Miyon to expel them from his lands.''

''What would you suggest?'' he asked bitterly.

''Give him something in exchange for the Merida— and, incidentally, for his support against Masul.''

''Such as?''

Calmly, she drew the Merida knife from the wood, held it so the light glinted off its glass blade.

''Set Chiana on him,'' she said.

Chapter Seventeen

Like her father, Pandsala did not believe in talking about power. She believed in using it.

Pandsala waited at Lyell's garish red-and-yellow striped tent, growing angrier by the moment as Kiele kept her cooling her heels in an antechamber. When at last admitted into her half sister's presence, Pandsala was seething. That she was forced to conceal her fury only added to her hatred of this flaunting beauty who received her with the widest and most insincere of smiles. Of all her sisters and half sisters, Kiele was the one who should have been dead. Pandsala regretted not having killed her years ago.

"Pandsala! I hope you weren't kept waiting too long. My squires told me only a moment ago that you were here—they do so hate to interrupt Lyell and me when we get a little time alone." Kiele kissed the air beside Pandsala's right cheek. "You're so fortunate not to be married, you know—one always worries about not spending enough time with one's husband and children."

Pandsala bore the embrace stolidly, not missing Kiele's barb about her husbandless, childless state. "I regret disturbing you," she made herself say.

"Think nothing of it. It's been so long since we had a good long talk together—why don't I order a couple of horses and take you into the city? I'll give you a tour of the residence, and we can have a snack. It's an eccentric place, but I've managed to make it livable if not logical."

Pandsala debated for a moment about letting Kiele stew in surmises about this visit, then decided she hadn't patience for it. "I'm afraid I'll have to defer the pleasure of seeing your home, Kiele. I have something rather distressing to discuss with you."

"Oh?" Kiele gestured to chairs. "How may I help you, Pandsala?"

"Naydra came to me today with the most astonishing story."

With a whisper of silk skirts, Kiele sank into a seat. "I haven't had the chance to speak to her yet. How is she?"

Pandsala gave her full credit for ability to contain her curiosity about this conversation with a sibling she cordially loathed. The feeling was mutual and they both knew it, and Pandsala began to feel a certain relish for the game.

"Oh, fine. But her tale was quite amazing. It seems—" She hesitated just the right amount of time, then went on in a low voice, "Kiele, there's some man in Waes saying he's the true father of this pretender."

Kiele's eyes went wide, but she cheated Pandsala of

most of her real reaction to this news. "Incredible! What can this mean?" she breathed.

"It means everyone is looking for him. Naydra was approached for money to keep him quiet—that as our father's daughter, she'd naturally wish Rohan out of Princemarch. How could he think any of us would want that? Father gave us nothing—and Rohan has given us everything."

"Oh, yes, he most certainly has," Kiele said earnestly, and again Pandsala was forced to admire her for keeping a completely straight face.

"I came to you, as another loyal servant of the High Prince, to ask if you'd set your people looking for this man. They know Waes much better than mine do. If he *is* the real father of this pretender, then his truth must be heard. And if he's not—" She shrugged. "If he's not, he'll have to be taught a lesson for lying about such serious matters of state. Will you help, Kiele?"

"With all my heart, Pandsala. It's shocking, isn't it, this whole tale of Father's possibly having a son. And now this man with his story—" Suddenly Kiele dimpled. "Oh, what if it's true? What if Palila really did get herself pregnant by a groom or a cook or some such, in hopes of giving Father a son?"

Pandsala gave her a genuine laugh. "I wouldn't have put anything past that bitch, would you? Goddess, do you remember how much we all hated her? To tell the truth, my dear, I'm rather astounded to find you giving house room to her daughter." She laughed again as the shot struck home.

"That little—" Kiele bit her lips shut too late. Pandsala nodded slowly, smiling. "Chiana is my guest here, and has been a great help to me in planning the *Rialla*," she went on in a desperate attempt to recoup.

"I lived with her for six long years at Goddess Keep," Pandsala pointed out. "Frankly, my dear sister, it would almost be worth it to find out that this pretender really is who he says he is, if it would humiliate Chiana!"

Kiele sat back in her chair, hands and arms limp at her sides, her mouth open. Pandsala laughed softly.

"Can't you imagine it? Disgraced, deprived of status, revealed as the daughter of a servant. It's what Ianthe and

I planned for her at her birth—and she's the reason I was banished to Goddess Keep in the first place. I have to admit I'd dearly love the sight of a daughter of her insufferable mother earning her keep as a scullery drudge!''

''It presents an interesting picture,'' Kiele acknowledged with a sudden smirk. ''Actually, I invited her here in hopes she'll find someone to marry her and take her off all our hands. I know Naydra has had enough of her, and I'm growing more than a little weary of her airs and graces, myself.''

''In a way, it's a pity this pretender's claim *isn't* true.'' She watched that one sink in, and waited for the questions. They were not long in coming.

''It was the oddest night, wasn't it? Of course, you were there,'' Kiele said casually. ''But you know, I can't help but wonder, what with all the confusion—what *really* happened, Pandsala? Only you and Ianthe ever really knew.''

''And Lady Andrade,'' Pandsala added smoothly. ''You're right about the circumstances. Sheer chaos. But I *was* there, Kiele. And I know. That's why I can't allow the issue to be obscured. Will you do me the favor of having your people look for this man in the city and at the encampment and the Fair? They ought be able to find a stranger of a certain description, even with all the other strangers around. He may adopt the colors of some lord or prince, but I doubt it, as anyone legitimately in service would know all his fellows. He'd be in danger of challenge.''

''He has no master of his own, then?''

''Not that I know of. He was wearing plain clothing when he spoke to Naydra. Will you do it, Kiele? I'd be in your debt.''

''I'll be glad to help,'' Kiele said fervently. ''What does he look like?''

She gave every detail Naydra had been able to recall under Pandsala's questioning, which had been a great deal fiercer than Rohan's. Kiele then escorted her out, all sweetness and cooperation, and the two women parted on the best of terms. Pandsala walked back to her own tents, where twenty servants waited for her as ordered.

They had abandoned the colors of Princemarch and were dressed in plain tunics.

"Watch every servant leaving Lady Kiele's tent. They will be looking for a tall, green-eyed man. Now, heed me carefully: this man is *not* to reach my sister. Secure him and bring him to me at once, safe and unharmed. Not a word to the High Prince's people or anyone else. Most especially do not let Kiele's people know who you are. There will be substantial reward for your success. Are there any questions? Good."

* * *

Rohan couldn't quite live up to his words about letting things happen as they would. He snatched a moment to confer with Tallain, instructing him to alert all the guards and servants to the description of a certain man Rohan wished to speak to. If they saw him, he was to be brought to the pavilion at once.

"But tell them not to be obvious about it," he finished. "No fuss, and no searching tents or questioning everyone they meet."

By late afternoon Rohan had abandoned the parchments that demanded his attention in favor of a meander outside by the river. He excused dereliction of duty by reasoning that he needed fresh air to clear his head. He had never been very good at lying to himself.

As casually as he had left his pavilion—and with the same excuse he'd given Tallain—Sioned appeared at his side. "Lovely afternoon for a walk, isn't it?" she asked.

"Lovely," he echoed.

"Everything's arranged for our various parties," she went on idly as they neared the riverbank. "Food enough for an army, and enough wine to float half Lleyn's merchant fleet."

"That's good."

"Pol tells me he's giving me a present to wear to the Lastday banquet. But he won't say what it is."

"First I've heard of it." He plucked a flower from a bush and began shredding the petals.

"Confess, Rohan—what you'd really like to do is go through every tent and house and cottage within a hundred measures."

"If I admit to it, will you?" He smiled at her.

"There's not really much chance of finding him, is there?"

"Not much."

They continued along in companionable silence for a time, heading for the bridge that crossed the Faolain. People were returning from the Fair loaded down with packages and satchels, discussing purchases and current rumors. Rohan and Sioned went mostly unnoticed in the crowd, for both were plainly dressed and kept their hands with the telltale rings in their pockets. Some few recognized them, but at a slight shake of the head from either merely bowed slightly and went on their way.

"Plenty of people here this summer," Rohan observed.

"More than enough to blend in with, wouldn't you say?"

"Except if you happen to be a young prince with two zealous guardians. Look." He pointed to where their son walked along the river, Maarken and Ostvel in close attendance.

"It seems none of us can stay put for the afternoon," Sioned murmured with a wry smile.

"I can't say I blame us." He led her out of the crowd and toward Pol. "I wonder where Riyan is," he asked suddenly. "Clutha's here, but Riyan hasn't come by to greet Ostval yet."

"I expect he's been too busy. He was in Waes this summer, you know, keeping an eye on Lyell for Clutha. But he wasn't at the residence when we had dinner there. Chiana said he'd ridden to the Faolain crossing to meet Clutha's party." She waved to Pol as he hurried up the slope toward them. "She seemed rather put out, probably because she didn't get anywhere with Riyan."

"My love, the boy has *taste!* But I'd like to talk to him. Perhaps he's heard something."

"I'll ask Clutha to send him by tonight." She smiled as Pol approached and gave them a courtly bow and a mischievous smile.

"Have you been over at the Fair?" Pol asked. "I actually got to see it for a little while," he added with a half-teasing, half-resentful glance over his shoulder at Maarken and Ostvel. "I had some business to settle."

"My present?" Sioned hinted.

"Could be!"

"Whatever it is, I hope it fits," she replied, rumpling his blond hair. She turned to Maarken then and added, "I assume you took a little time for yourself and spoke to at least a dozen goldsmiths about wedding necklets."

The young man made a face at her, and Ostvel chided, "Now, Sioned. Don't fuss the boy. Besides, it was only half a dozen. I counted."

They were just about to start back to the Desert tents when someone in the crowd nearby shouted a warning. There was a scuffle on the bridge and people scattered from the steps, screaming. A tall, ill-dressed man lurched against the railing. Gouts of blood spurted from his neck.

"Sweet Goddess—someone's killed him!" a man's voice cried.

"There they are! Grab them, don't let them get away!"

Rohan and Ostvel were already running for the steps. Pol would have done the same but for Sioned's firm grip on his shoulder—and it took all her strength to hold him. Maarken stood between them and the bridge, scanning the crowd warily with sword drawn, ready to defend them if necessary.

But it was Rohan who needed a sword—a weapon he had not carried for the length of Pol's life. A man wearing yellow and brown surged from the knot of frightened people and leaped for him, blade gleaming. Rohan's boot-knives were in his hands instantly, and he fought with all the swift grace and skill of one born to wield a blade. Ostvel grappled with a second man in Merida colors who jumped him before he had the chance to draw his sword. They rolled down the slope and splashed into the river.

"Father!" Pol cried, struggling against Sioned's grasp.

The battle was over quickly. Very few were a match for Rohan in a knife-fight; this man was not one of them. He was forced up the steps of the bridge, bleeding from a dozen gashes. At last he turned, wild-eyed, and flung himself over the rails into the swift-flowing river. He surfaced once, arms flailing. Hurtled downriver by the vicious current, caught in an undertow, he screamed and vanished.

Ostvel had meantime managed to prevent his attacker

from drowning him and was instead encouraging the man
to breathe water by holding his head under in the sandy
shallows. Rohan helped Ostvel drag the man out of the
river. They shook him, slapped his face, and after a time
he choked and vomited.

Sioned allowed Pol to escape her grasp, and Maarken
followed him down to the banks. The crowd huddled
nearby, murmuring and amazed. No one but Sioned remembered the dying man on the steps.

She went to him, and saw at once that nothing could
help him. His throat had been sliced clean through, the
whiteness of bone visible through a gaping slash that had
ceased to gush blood with the ending of his heartbeat.
His sleeve had caught on a nail and he hung limply, his
open green eyes seeming to stare right through her.

As she descended the steps a woman pushed through
the crowd, dragging a reluctant captive with her. Sioned
tensed, for the woman wore no identifying colors or
badge of service.

"Commander Pellira, your highness, of the regent's
guard," the woman said, bowing. "I regret we weren't
fast enough to catch the others."

"Who's this?" Sioned asked softly.

"I'm not a murderer!" The captive had stopped trying
to get away. "I was only coming back from the Fair when
she grabbed me!"

"Tell her grace the truth!" Pandsala's guard snapped.
"He was following the dead man over there. I know,
because *I* was following *him.*"

"Take him to our pavilion and watch him," Sioned
told her, suddenly very tired. "We'll question him later."

She stood beside Pol and Maarken as Ostvel worked
on the second assassin. Rohan propped him up as he
shuddered and gulped in air, his gratitude at being alive
warring with sheer terror.

Rohan stood up, blood streaking his jaw from a knife-
graze, and met Sioned's gaze. She shook her head, and
he sighed quietly.

"This one will live," he told her.

"Merida colors," Ostvel grated, his voice sounding
bruised.

"No," Pol said. "Father, look at your hands, and Ostvel's." He gestured to Rohan's fingers, stained brown and yellow from the man's tunic. "He's not Merida. The colors were dyed into them only recently—and not very well. See how it's run all over your hands? And why would they so obviously wear their own colors, anyway? That's not the Merida style."

"You've sharp eyes," Ostvel acknowledged. "But if not Merida, then who?"

"Why don't we ask him?" Rohan prodded the man in the leg with the toe of his boot. "Have him brought to our camp and dried off. And I think you're due for a change of clothes, Ostvel, before you catch your death of a chill. Have the dead man brought along as well," he added.

"Dead?" Pol glanced over to the bridge.

"Yes. Very." Sioned felt an irrational desire to hold her son to her heart, protect him from all that was ugly and foul in this world. She contented herself with brushing her fingertips against his shoulder. "Will you help me up the slope, Pol?"

He put his arm around her waist and she was comforted by his closeness, his warmth, the living strength of him next to her. Untested, untried, unblooded—but he had grown nearly as tall as she over the summer, and would soon be a man. One did not try to protect men from life. Especially not princes.

She heard Maarken order that the drowned man's corpse be recovered if possible from downriver. She heard Ostvel's cough, the assassin's whining protests, the murmurs of the slowly dispersing crowd. But she did not hear her husband's voice, and when she had gained the top of the riverbank she turned to look for him.

He was standing motionless by the bridge as several men heaved the corpse upright and carried it from the steps. Rohan glanced up and Sioned caught his eyes that mirrored there own weary, helpless anger.

He joined her and Pol, who at last broke the uneasy silence among them. "I've never seen you use your knives before, Father."

Rohan barely looked at him as they started for their tents. "Good at it, aren't I?" he asked in a bitter tone that Sioned understood and Pol did not. The boy's cheeks flushed and his lips tightened. Rohan shrugged. "Any idiot can use a knife, Pol. It's very direct and—heroic. But the results are usually not worth the trouble."

* * *

Maarken had never had much use for liquor as a cure for jangled nerves, and vaguely disapproved of people who turned to a bottle in times of stress. But that evening he learned the value of a winecup's companionship. He sat alone in the growing darkness and welcomed the spurious strength of the Syrene vintage through his veins. After viewing the murdered man, Maarken felt in need of a restorative.

It was not that the corpse had been messy, he told himself as he refilled his cup. The knife had sliced through the man's throat with incredible skill, and death had been swift. Maarken had been younger than Pol when he'd seen far worse in war—whole battlefields of men and women hacked into pieces barely recognizable as human. He had seen far more unpleasant deaths.

He rose, pacing the private tent he merited as the almost official Lord of Whitecliff, aware that his knees were not what they should be. He drank more wine. Somehow the murder had shaken him even more than the tragedy of Maeta's death at Castle Crag. All spring and summer he had known about the problems facing his uncle, but the sight of that green-eyed corpse had made the dangers immediate. His private concerns were trifling compared to the threat posed by the pretender.

Maarken knew how precarious Rohan's position was. The real difficulty was not even this man's claim. What it came down to was *faradhi* power. Pol's personality would go far toward convincing all that he did not have the makings of a tyrant, would not use his Sunrunner gifts in combination with the powers of the High Prince to crush all opposition. But if he was the son of his royal father, he was also the child of his *faradhi* mother. No matter how winning his ways, many feared the two powers combined in one man.

Maarken sat down again and closed his eyes. A picture of the corpse was burned onto his lids: tall, dark-haired, with green eyes wide open to the last of the sunlight. They could hardly display the dead body as evidence against the claimant; there were plenty of green-eyed men in the world. Who was to say that this one had fathered the pretender?

"Damn," he muttered, clenching his fist around his winecup. There had to be something they could do, some way of convincing people—

"Why all alone in the night, my lord?"

The feminine voice startled him so violently that wine sloshed out of his cup.

A slim shadow moved toward him in the gloom. "You shouldn't be solitary and sad, my lord. Share your trouble with me."

Without thinking he called Fire to the wick of a candle. "Chiana?" he asked incredulously. "What are you doing here?"

"You *faradh'im!* Always startling a person!" She laughed lightly and came closer. Her fingers rested on the back of his chair beside his shoulder, and somehow the gesture was more intimate than if she had touched him. "I came to ease your loneliness, my lord."

"Thank you for the thought, my lady," he said, remembering his manners at last. "I mean no offense, but I would prefer to be alone. I'm no fit company for a lady tonight."

She laughed again, low in her throat this time. "I'd wager you're always excellent company for a woman—especially at night."

Cool, soft fingers brushed his nape. It had been a long time since he had received caresses from a beautiful woman, but this was the wrong woman. He got to his feet, cursing the wine that had made him light-headed. Chiana gazed up at him, candlelight making her face all soft lips and shining, excited eyes framed by artfully tumbled hair.

"Forgive me, my lady, but—"

"You're too modest," Chiana said playfully. "But I can tell, my lord." Her gaze roamed over his face, down his chest and arms. "Yes, I can definitely tell. . . ."

Even with the chair between them he felt as if she had her hands on him. The wine had not so befuddled him that he gave in to her. Neither had it dulled his powers of reasoning. He knew why she was here, and it was not because of his charms. She was terrified of the pretender and groping toward any man who, by marrying her, would provide her with a noble title to replace the one she feared she was about to lose. But one did not tell a lady she was a scheming little bitch. "I thank you for the compliment, Lady Chiana. It's as unexpected as it is flattering, coming from a lovely woman. But—"

"Maarken! Maarken, they're here!"

He sent up brief and heartfelt thanks to the Goddess for providing him with a cousin who occasionally forgot his manners. Chiana backed off as Pol came running into the tent. The boy's jaw dropped halfway to his knees at the sight of her, but he made a quick recovery.

"Lady Andrade is here, and Father says to hurry," he said after making a slight bow to Chiana. "I'm sorry to interrupt—"

Chiana's voice was cool and distant. "I should return to my sister's tent. I have enjoyed our conversation, Lord Maarken. Nothing would give me more pleasure than to continue it another time." She bent her knees to Pol. "Your Royal Highness."

"My lady," he said as she swept past him. Then he whistled soundlessly. "Maarken, I really am sorry—"

Maarken pinched the candle out. "Being alone with a pretty lady is desirable only when you *like* the lady."

"If you tell me it's something I'll understand when I'm older, I'll kick you," Pol replied, grinning. "Come on, Lady Andrade is asking to see you."

Though Maarken didn't care much about seeing Lady Andrade, it was difficult to keep his strides from lengthening as he accompanied Pol to the blue pavilion, and even more difficult to keep his expression under control as he entered and his eyes found Hollis. But Pol again forgot his manners.

"He wasn't with Aunt Tobin and Uncle Chay," the boy reported. "He was in his own tent with Lady Chiana."

Maarken turned red. Grateful as he had been to his cousin earlier, now he could cheerfully have strangled the brat. Rohan's lips twitched with barely suppressed mirth, and Sioned coughed to hide her laughter. Andrade looked him down and up, with a brief stop below his belt. But Hollis reacted not at all. She stood to one side with Andry and a tall, black-haired youth Maarken didn't know. Her dark blue eyes were circled beneath with bruises of weariness. She looked thinner, and the supple energy that usually shone from her seemed tarnished somehow.

"Well," Andrade said, breaking the awkward silence. "Your own tent now, eh? Chay must have given you Whitecliff, and about time, too."

"He has, my Lady." Maarken bowed to her.

"Isn't somebody going to ask me to sit down?" she complained. "And I could do with something to drink."

Maarken and Andry performed squire's duties as Pol and the black-haired boy brought extra chairs. Hollis sank into hers with a long sigh, and the boy hovered behind her with an almost proprietary air.

"Pleasant trip?" Maarken whispered to his brother as they poured out cups of wine.

Andry grimaced. "Hell on horseback. Remind me not to tell you about it."

They finished distributing the wine as their parents entered. Andrade waited while they greeted Andry, then directed them to chairs as if this were her pavilion, not Rohan's. But they were all long accustomed to her ways.

"Sorin has duty tonight with Volog and can't come," Chay said as he sat down. "Goddess! Do you know how depressing this is? All my sons can look me straight in the eye! It's not fair. They started out so short!"

"Perhaps you're only shrinking due to rampant decrepitude," Andrade commented. "I hope the rot doesn't extend to your brains, any of you. What are you going to do, now that Masul's real father is dead?"

Rohan leaned back in his chair. "You don't miss much, do you?"

"My eyes and ears may be old, boy, but they still function. What are your plans?"

"I'd rather hear about yours. Your Sunrunner Kleve was keeping an eye on Kiele for you, wasn't he? What did he find out?"

It wasn't often that anyone managed to startle the Lady of Goddess Keep. Maarken glanced at Hollis, prepared to share an amused glance at Andrade's astonishment. But Hollis was staring into her untasted wine, and the black-haired boy was hovering even closer.

"How did you know about Kleve?" Andrade demanded.

As gently as possible, he said, "We received word today—and proof—that he's dead. They cut the rings from his fingers by taking the fingers themselves, Andrade. He probably died for something he knew. Do you have any idea what it was?"

Andrade's face was immobile. After a few moments she whispered, "No. I—I knew he was dead. Riyan told me. But he didn't say how it happened." Rallying, she took a long swallow of wine. "Kleve is dead, and his information with him. Masul's real father is dead, and his testimony with him. You haven't managed this very well, Rohan."

Pol had been standing between his parents' chairs, listening wide-eyed. But at this point he stiffened and took a step forward, frowning at the implied insult to his father. Maarken could have told him to save his indignation; Andrade spoke that way to everybody.

She noticed, as she noticed everything. "Meath tells me you can call Fire," she said abruptly to the boy.

"I can, my Lady."

"What else can you do without ever having been taught?"

"I don't know," Pol replied boldly. "I've never tried."

She gave a bark of laughter. "You're the son of your father, all right."

"And of my mother," Pol added. Maarken hid a slight smile. If Pol was awed by their formidable kinswoman, he was determined not to show it.

"Mmm, yes. And of your mother," she said. "Tobin, take your husband and sons to your own tent. I have no time for family news right now. Pol, you may go with them. Hollis, Sejast, go tell Urival to hurry up. I'm tired and I want to rest in my own bed sometime before midnight."

Andrade watched them obey her orders, not missing the look Pol gave his parents as if asking whether or not he had to do as Andrade told him. She approved the boy's spirit, but it also made her feel very old. It would take all her energy and authority to make a good, obedient Sunrunner of him. If anyone could.

"I want to know your plans," she said to Rohan again when the others had gone. "And don't tell me you're going to trust to the truth. This isn't a game played by nice rules."

"What would you suggest?" Sioned asked coldly. "Buying cooperation would certainly be effective—it would convince everyone that we doubt our own position!"

"Truth may be an excellent defense," Andrade snapped. "But what we need right now is a plan of attack."

"I thought you'd have everything all plotted out for us," Sioned retorted. "And all we'd have to do is speak our lines. You're the one who hasn't managed this very well, Andrade."

She was silent for a moment, searching the face of her most beloved student. "When will you believe that I never wanted mindless obedience from any of you? If you had been an idiot, I would not have chosen you for Rohan."

"I'll believe it when you prove it. You've just done the opposite again by calling it *your* choice, not ours."

It was an old debate between them and one that suddenly wearied her. "I put you both in the way of choosing. But I don't give orders to anyone but my Sunrunners. And you'll note that I no longer give *you* any orders at all. I've learned that it does no good."

"And do you tell everyone that I'm no longer a Sunrunner?"

"Stop this," Rohan said quietly. "Andrade, you asked my plans and answered your own question. The only weapon we have is the truth. I can't bargain or cajole or command my way out of this. Masul must be repudiated or Pol's claim to Princemarch will never be secure. The only thing I can trust is the truth."

"And not me," Andrade whispered, feeling very old again, telling herself it was only fatigue. "*My* truth is suspect." She wrapped her fingers around the winecup, staring at the bracelets on either wrist, linked to her rings by thin chains. "It galls me. Nothing to do with Roelstra ever happens in ways I can control." She gave in to impulse and flung the goblet to the floor. "Goddess! Why could he not have died forever and left us all in peace?"

An instant later, humiliated by her outburst, she shrugged irritably. "Your pardon. I'll see you get a new rug to replace the one I just ruined."

Sioned spoke, her voice soft, almost apologetic. "My Lady—though I no longer wear any ring but my husband's, the ones you gave me are still on my hands. Tell us what you think we ought to do."

More moved than she would admit, Andrade shook her head. "I'm tired. We'll talk tomorrow." She pushed herself to her feet and muttered, "Hasn't Urival raised that damned tent yet?"

Urival had, and was now ordering it furnished with carpets, tables, chairs, beds, and other amenities from the baggage wains. Segev assisted him and the other Sunrunners after finding a chair for Hollis to rest in. He had had no opportunity today to give her more *dranath* and she was showing the effects of withdrawal. Segev hurried about his tasks and at last escaped with the excuse of finding some wine. He paused in a shadow in the growing enclave of Andrade's white tents and pulled the stopper from the bottle. Not trusting his abilities at sleight-of-hand to get the herb into only one cup, he sprinkled the *dranath* into the bottle itself. One drink of it would cause nothing more than a headache for someone not previously dosed.

The white pavilion was fully furnished by the time he returned. Lady Andrade reclined in a soft upholstered chair, attended by the High Prince and High Princess. Hollis sat nearby. Segev poured wine for them and for Urival, bowing low to each as a good one-ringed Sunrunner should in the presence of the High Prince and such exalted *faradh'im*.

"And that's the tale of our evening," Prince Rohan was saying. "Naydra has identified the corpse as the man who came to her earlier today. Pandsala had a little scheme of her own going, by the way—no one of her blood was ever able to resist playing with events."

The High Princess nodded thanks as Segev poured her wine. "It seems she had a little chat with Kiele, who set her people to scouring Waes for this man—while Pandsala's own servants followed them like dragons after a doe.''

"Well? What of it?" Andrade asked.

"They traced Kiele's people to the Fair, where it seems everybody who wanted to find this man found him indeed." Sioned gave a little shrug. "Rohan believes in letting things happen. Well, they happened, all right."

Segev marveled that they spoke so freely in front of him—but then, he was supposedly one of them, a Sunrunner, a member of Andrade's personal suite. He grinned to himself and took up a position in the shadows behind Hollis' chair.

"We let Kiele's man go," Rohan added. "There's nothing to accuse Kiele of, after all. She was only acting on Pandsala's orders. It doesn't matter that we know damned well she would've had him killed if she'd gotten her hands on him."

"Granted," Andrade muttered. "What of this Merida who isn't a Merida?"

"We thought you might like to interview him with us," Rohan said almost casually. He gestured to Segev, who stepped forward and bowed. "Tell my squire outside to fetch this man, please."

"At once, your grace."

The man was being held in the High Prince's encampment, damp clothes nearly dry as he huddled by the fire with his arms tied behind him, dark head hanging. Rohan's squire, Tallain, nodded to the guards, who nudged the captive to his feet. His head jerked up and Segev nearly gasped. One of Mireva's people, here! He sorted through what he had heard since arriving tonight and gulped down his panic. She must be told at once. This man must not live long enough to blurt out anything that might identify Mireva or her aims—or, worse, Segev himself. He moved more deeply into the shadows beyond the watchfire and bit his lip. The man had not seen him, and with a little luck Segev should be able to escape without being recognized.

"Clean him up," Tallain was saying. "The High Prince and Lady Andrade are waiting."

Segev paused until he was sure the pounding of his heart would not sound in his voice, then said "Would you make my excuses to Lady Andrade, please? I—I guess I'm more tired from the journey than I thought."

Tallain glanced over with a brief smile. "I've heard travel with Lady Andrade can do that. I'll tell her you've gone off to bed."

"My thanks," Segev replied, bowing, and made his escape.

Away from the tents, he took several deep breaths of chill night air to calm himself. Realization of who had sent the assassins to kill the pretender's father had startled him badly but, more than that, kept his heart racing as he walked down to the river. He had grown used to living around *faradh'im,* and was even accustomed to Lady Andrade by now. But something about the High Princess made him nervous, and he would much rather not be in company with her again.

He shook off the feeling as he reached the river and spent a few moments admiring its silent, star-strewn flow. There had been no water to cross on the road to Waes, so he had been spared the inconvenience of miming the appropriate sickness. Mireva had taught him how to simulate the usual *faradhi* reaction to water, and he was grateful he had not had to resort to the rather unsavory trick. Mireva had taught him much, but Andrade and his growing ambition were teaching him more. The tension of fooling both women at the same time exhilarated him. He was the first descendant of the ancient blood to learn the old ways *and* those of the *faradh'im;* he knew he could use both with equal skill. The *Rialla* presented endless fascinating opportunities, once this dangerous man had been dealt with.

Well away from the encampment, he found a bend in the river and went as far out as he could, boots crunching in the fine gravel. He stared up at the expanse of starry sky above the river, finding comfort in its brilliance. He adapted Sunrunner methods to the weaving of thin, delicate filaments of silver light as no *faradhi* but Princess Sioned had ever done. There were no colors on this weaving, only the shining pallor of the stars. He had never dared contact Mireva this way while at Goddess Keep— which, considering his unauthorized alteration of her plans, was for the best. As he followed the glittering path of plaited light north to the Veresch, he buried his secrets beneath layers of obedience—and temporarily forgot where he put the shovel.

She stood alone in the middle of the stone circle. She might have been there for moments or days in that same position, waiting as she had said she would wait every night of the *Rialla*. Segev wrapped his rope of starlight around the rock cairn and saw it begin to glow silver.

Very impressive. Andrade has taught you well.

Was there the faintest hint of suspicion in her voice? Segev cursed himself for showing off his abilities.

You sent me to learn, my lady. And I have much to tell you. Rapidly he gave her news of the present danger, ending with a plea to be rescued from possible discovery. It would please her, his total dependence on her to save him.

He could almost hear the breath hissing between her teeth. *By all Hells! How could they be so stupid? My orders are to be obeyed, not anticipated! They were to watch, not kill! But now this fool will die. He was prepared by me before he left. As were you, Segev. Learn well from this.*

He blanched. Prepared? The warning slid through his veins like an icy mountain stream beneath its winter covering of frozen snow. *Yes, my lady,* he replied humbly. *There is more—do you wish to hear it now?*

She made no answer. He saw her begin to sway lightly back and forth before the cairn, arms outstretched, her face carved into terrible lines. A few sick thuds of his heart later, she spoke again.

It's finished. Tell me now.

He did so, detailing his acceptance by Andrade for *faradhi* training, the abortive attempt to steal the scrolls, his success in addicting Hollis to *dranath*. Mireva's eyes lit as she listened, and she laughed when he told her of the Sunrunner Kleve's death.

Wonderful! Assist this pretender any way you can—for all that he was too foolish to recognize our offer of assistance in the spring. What about the scrolls?

Here, with Urival. They don't know I know. But I had access to the place they were kept, and the day we left, they were gone. Urival's saddlebags never leave his sight. But I'll secure the scrolls by Rialla*'s end.*

Excellent! Her gray-green eyes sparkled and for an instant she looked like the beautiful young girl who had taught him what it was to be a man. *I'll be watching by starlight, Segev, and on the next moonless night when no* faradh'im *can weave.*

He sped back to the banks of the Faolain, shaking with relief. He had survived a test much more formidable than any that Lady Andrade could devise. And he had also rid himself of a threat—though exactly how Mireva had disposed of the man did not bear thinking about. He reminded himself that she possessed powers beyond his experience and possibly beyond his imaginings. He gulped as he heard again the fatal word *prepared.*

But when he thought of the Star Scroll again, a smile teased his lips. When it was finally in his hands, he would not give it to Mireva. He had earned it; it would be his.

* * *

While waiting for the prisoner to be brought to them, Urival gave Andrade a long, level stare. He said nothing, merely looked at her until she grimaced a reply.

"What's being so subtly debated here," she told Sioned and Rohan, "is the subject of the scrolls Meath brought us from Dorval this spring. I have my little surprises, too. Hollis, you've worked on the damnable things. Tell their graces."

"The scrolls are histories, mainly," Hollis explained. "Andry has done most of the translating—it's been difficult because of all the false trails and little cues we sometimes miss until something much later on doesn't make any sense. And we're nowhere near finished yet with them all. But they tell about the Sunrunners who abandoned a huge old keep on the island and came to the continent to oppose a group of sorcerers."

"Sounds more like tales for children at bedtime," Rohan said.

"Oh, but these people were real, your grace! Lady Merisel in particular—there've been times when Andry swears he can feel her presence at Goddess Keep." She hesitated, then went on, "And those others, the ones the *faradh'im* came here to defeat—they were real, too. Some of what they could do was very similar to our *faradhi* techniques, but—''

"But without our ethics," Andrade finished mockingly.

Hollis didn't seem to know how to respond to that. "They seem to have taken control of a great many people and places on their way to complete power over the continent, and the ancient *faradh'im* left their isolation on Dorval to fight against them. The scrolls are quite impressive, your graces."

Andrade grunted at the understatement. "I should have known talking about her pet project would liven her up," she said to Urival. "Not two words to say for herself the whole trip, and now we can't shut her up."

The young woman smiled. "All I needed was a little rest, my Lady."

"And a sight of Maarken, hmm?" Sioned chuckled. "Forgive me—but he's not very subtle, is he? And no more of this 'your graces,' if you please. Hollis, if you've no other family and if you will permit, I'd be proud to stand with you as a sister *faradhi* when you marry him."

Her blue eyes widened. "Your grace! I—"

Rohan winked at her. "Nothing much gets past the High Princess, either."

"I have a bet with Maarken that I could identify his Chosen lady at first sight," Sioned explained, smiling. "It wasn't difficult!"

Hollis looked from one to the other of them, completely at a loss. At last she managed to murmur her thanks.

"That's settled, then," Andrade sighed, "even if nothing else is. Go to bed, Hollis. I want to talk with Rohan and Sioned. And this captive of yours ought to be showing up soon, yes?"

Hollis bowed and left them. Sioned nodded to herself. "She's going to make Maarken very happy."

"You're learning my tricks," Andrade accused with gruff fondness. "How did you know? Did he tell you?"

Before Sioned could do more than look smug, Tallain appeared in the doorway of the white tent. "My lord, he's here. Not too willing about it, either, when he heard who he'd be seeing."

"Afraid of the old witch, is he?" Andrade asked. "Well, bring him in."

But the guards got him no farther than the threshold. The man's dark hair and pallid face suddenly seemed to glow with the chill radiance of the stars behind him in the night. Horrified eyes fixed on Andrade, he groped out with stiffened, white-boned fingers, then slumped to the carpet.

Tallain fell back in shock. "My lord—what—"

Rohan knelt beside the prone figure, searching in vain for signs of life. The slack-jawed guards could have dealt with an escape attempt, threats of violence, shouts of defiance—but not with this. "M-my lord," one of them whispered, "we did him no hurt, none!"

Rohan nodded slowly, fingers resting lightly on the man's chest. "His heart has simply stopped," he murmured.

Andrade stared at the corpse with a stony glare more frightening than anger. "So," she said at last. "The sorcerers still live after all."

Rohan's head snapped around, a scowl darkening his face. "What do you mean?"

She paid him no heed. "Get this—" she pointed to the dead man, "—out of my sight at once. Throw it into the sea for all I care. But it shall not know Fire. Nothing touched by such foulness could ever be cleansed."

After the corpse had been removed, with Rohan's caution that nothing be said of this to anyone, Sioned faced Andrade. "What do you mean, sorcerers?" she asked, repeating Rohan's question.

"Just what I said." She sighed heavily. "Sweet Goddess, to be able to kill at a distance, using starlight. . . ." A shudder coursed through her and she drew her cloak tighter around her breast. "There's a scroll Hollis didn't mention, but it seems I must tell you about it now. We've called it the Star Scroll for the design on its first page. And it deals with sorceries. Probably with things just like this."

"Has it been fully translated?" Rohan asked.

"Not yet. And I don't know that I want it to be. Not if it contains knowledge like this. Oh, Andry is full of reasons why we should learn all that the Star Scroll can offer, and use their own weapons against them—including *dranath*—but what would that make of us?''

Despite the bitterness in her voice, Rohan almost smiled at her. "It seems you and I agree on one thing, at least."

Sioned nodded thoughtfully. "Now I know why you asked Tobin to have me bring along this packet." She produced, to her husband's astonishment, a small piece of folded parchment and handed it to Andrade. "It's very old, though. Rohan took it from Roelstra over twenty years ago. Will it still be good?"

"Nothing about *dranath* is good, except its use against Plague," Urival muttered, absently rubbing the rings on his hands as if they pained him.

"It ought to be potent still," Andrade mused. "It's all we have access to, so it had better be. I didn't want to ask Pandsala to bring me some from the Veresch. She's not someone I'd trust with knowledge like this."

"I think you're wrong about her," Sioned replied mildly. "But it doesn't matter. What do you plan to do with it?"

"Conduct a few experiments of my own, the way Andry did. Urival, stop looking at me like that. Who's more qualified to investigate sorceries than an old witch like me?" She smiled humorlessly, turning the parchment square over in her hands. "You used a little of this to help you over some rough spots on the way home that year, didn't you, Sioned?"

"Only a little. A pinch in a glass of wine, less as the days wore on. Roelstra gave me quite a bit that night. The same happened after the dose that cured the Plague." Her shoulders shifted to shrug off the memory. "Be careful with it."

"She will be," Urival stated, his face grim.

"Do you think Roelstra knew about the old sorceries?" Rohan asked.

"If he had, he would have used them—not just the *dranath* to addict poor Crigo." Urival shook his head. "I've talked myself hoarse with warnings that no one listens to."

"Would you rather see Andry at his little demonstrations again?" Andrade snapped. "What frightens me about him is that he's not as frightened of the Star Scroll as he ought to be.'' Andrade eyed the royal couple. ''I hope you've instilled a little respect in that hatchling of yours. Andry has been a handful, but Pol's stubbornness might be the death of me.''

Sioned hesitated, then said, ''Andrade—I don't want Pol coddled or given special treatment, but promise me you won't bully him too much. He's not like any of the others, not even Maarken or Riyan. Who he is, what he'll become one day—promise me you'll keep those things in mind.''

''We can hardly escape them,'' she responded in dry tones. ''Leave me now. I won't be drugging myself tonight, so stop scowling. All I want is some sleep.''

Rohan and Sioned were silent as they returned to their pavilion. He sank wearily into the chair at his desk.

''So that's why Meath was attacked on his way to Goddess Keep. Today has been hellish all the way around. And the way she talked about Andry—''

''He's not a little boy anymore.''

''No. But I can't share her apprehensions about someone I used to play at dragons with. What an *interesting* family we have,'' he added wryly.

Sioned began taking off her clothes, pausing only to throw a bedrobe at him. ''Here. If you're going to be up half the night, at least be comfortable.''

''What do *you* think about the Star Scroll?'' he asked as he shrugged out of tunic and shirt before wrapping himself in the blue silk.

''I think the potentials for danger and knowledge are just about equal,'' she mused. ''The old sorcerers *are* still around. What happened tonight—'' She shivered. ''Tradition generally confirms Sunrunners on the continent for at least three hundred years. That's a long time to be in hiding.''

''But where? Why? What are they waiting for?'' When she only shrugged, he said, ''You're awfully calm about this. Is it because you, too, know how to use the stars?''

She would not look at him, only stood smoothing the folds of her bedgown with fingers that trembled a little. ''I'm scared to death,'' she whispered. ''What I did was instinctive. There was no other light to use. I had to know where you were. . . ." At last she met his gaze. "Rohan, what if I'm—"

"One of them?" He shook his head. "Don't you remember what we were saying about power? It's not power of itself that's good or evil, Sioned. It's the person wielding it. You're wise enough to know that."

"If you say so." She shrugged again, and in a steadier tone went on, "To the Sunrunners, these people are a threat. To the other princes? I don't know. But Pol is both Sunrunner and prince. That makes him dangerous to them in new ways, it seems. They went to a lot of trouble to kill the only witness who could challenge this Masul's claim and make it seem as if Merida were responsible. So they're still hiding." She sighed and extinguished the bedside candle. "Make sure your feet are warm before you come to bed."

"Prosaic advice. Are you so certain I'll be awake that late into the night?"

She stretched out and drew the blanket over her shoulders, replying unanswerably, "I know you, my lord *azhrei.*"

Chapter Eighteen

Everyone knew that no serious business would be transacted by the princes in the time before Lyell of Waes addressed them that morning. Rohan spent half the night wondering how he might save himself the embarrassment of trying to conduct what were bound to be fruitless discussions. He resigned himself to a morning that would reflect badly on his leadership through no fault of his own—while cursing Kiele's cunning that had deliberately arranged the time at which her husband was scheduled to speak.

But Prince Lleyn spared him any awkwardness. The old man insisted on making an uncharacteristically garrulous report on the current state of shipping throughout the princedoms. Everyone used Lleyn's merchant fleet, so everyone was compelled to pay attention. Rohan blessed him and kept an eye on the water clock.

It was a new device, more reliable than the old sand-glasses. Sand eroded crystal as it passed through, shortening the days. Time in the form of water dripped from a sphere through a hole cut into a flawless ruby, down to another sphere marked off in regular increments. The hinged, airtight lid of the upper crystal was a golden dragon with emeralds for eyes. Rohan had ordered it made for him two years ago after a Fironese crafter had written to him about its principles, and one of his goals was to establish the manufacture and trade of such clocks. But as Lleyn droned on, and there was no discernible difference in the level of water in either sphere, Rohan began to doubt that accurate measurement of time was such a good idea after all. Waiting was waiting, no matter how one counted off the time.

At a little past the fifth level of the clock a guard in Desert blue slid into the tent and around to Rohan's chair. Lleyn immediately gave over the meeting without a single indication that he had rambled on at great length to very definite purpose. Rohan thanked his grace of Dorval for his valuable information, then addressed the other princes.

"Cousins, yesterday Lyell of Waes requested a few moments of our time. As all of us know, it's not unusual for an *athri* to have something to say." He smiled slightly to imply that Lyell's words had about as much importance as the customary whining of a dissatisfied vassal. "Shall we hear him out?"

"If it doesn't take too long, then why not, my lords?" Cabar drawled, and won a few half-hidden grins of anticipation from around the table.

Davvi said pleasantly, "Perhaps we might admit our heirs to observe. Our sons are trained at home and they're well-schooled by their fostering lords, but there's no substitute for observation of ruling princes at work."

"Excellent notion," Clutha said. "It'll give my boy a chance to see how princes conduct themselves. A lesson he needs," he finished grumpily.

There were no objections, although there were only four heirs present at the *Rialla* this year. Volog and Pimantal visibly regretted not having brought their eldest sons; Velden's and Cabar's were still little boys. Miyon was not married, but it was rumored that several children could claim him as father.

Rohan met Davvi's gaze, seeing a familiar look of innocent cunning in green eyes very like Sioned's, and silently conveyed his approval of the ploy. Pol was the heir who needed to be where all could see and compare him to the man Lyell would undoubtedly produce at the climax of his speech. There was a brief interlude while squires were sent to collect Chadric, Kostas, Halian, and Pol. Rohan used the time to give a casual explanation of the water clock with an eye to creating a demand for them when Firon became his. Saumer of Isel made the wry observation that although the device could not be much use in the Desert, where the sun shone constantly and sundials were common, he could certainly use one at his own rainy castle.

Prince Chadric arrived, bowed to all, and took the seat placed for him behind his father's chair. Lleyn murmured something to him and Chadric's lips quirked with amusement. Soon Kostas, Halian, and Pol were present, the latter with his cheeks still pink from a hasty scrub and his hair slicked back by a damp comb. He gave them all a sunny smile, obviously excited to be included, and from around the table kind nods were given—some reluctantly, to be sure. But Pol was hard to resist.

Rohan was about to order that Lyell be admitted when the tent flaps parted to admit an unexpected quartet. Three were princesses; one was the acting representative of her princedom. Sioned and Pandsala flanked young Gemma and Lady Eneida of Firon, and the men frankly stared. With all her outrageous assumption of co-sovereignty with the High Prince, Sioned had never sat in on any *Rialla* meetings before. Women were simply not allowed in formal conclaves, and not even she had dared flout tradition. But Davvi's suggestion that heirs be included made this an informal meeting. Rohan knew he should have expected his wife to take advantage of it.

"My lords, good morning. I was with my son when your summons came, and took it upon myself to bring the Princess Gemma from her tent. Along the way I encountered Lady Eneida of Firon with the Princess-Regent." She smiled as if this happy coincidence had indeed been a coincidence. Her eyes didn't bother challenging them to object; they wouldn't, couldn't, and she knew it. "Cousin," she gently prompted Chale, "your heir needs a place to sit down."

Four drops of water fell from the clock's upper crystal to the lower one while the old man looked torn between indignation that women had invaded this princely gathering and smug approval of Sioned's coup. Tradition lost—as usual around Sioned. He waved Gemma to him and placed her chair himself.

Sioned continued, "I regret I cannot stay. Your ladies are joining me in only a little while, and there is much to be done." She gave them all another sweet smile and, after bowing to her husband, withdrew.

A lifetime of discipline kept Rohan's face straight. Sioned had instituted her luncheons three *Riall'im* ago, and princes grew nervous when they considered what their wives, sisters, and daughters said during private chats with the High Princess. Women said to other women what men often scorned to hear; Rohan usually got a clearer idea of what was going on from Sioned's reports of what the ladies had said than he got from the princes themselves.

Lady Eneida, thin and straight as a sword, stood beside the chair placed for her. "My lords, though Firon is without a prince, her grace asked me to join you as my land's representative." With that she sat down, the action fairly trumpeting her right to be there.

Pandsala had already taken her seat behind Pol, who sat directly at Rohan's side and not behind him. This, too, startled the other princes slightly, but he had been acknowledged by them all shortly after his birth as possessing Princemarch in his own right. Legally, he could have sat in on their formal talks as well. As his regent, Pandsala technically had no right to be present, but no one had the courage or the bad manners to protest. Besides, many were eager to see her face when confronted with the man who could be her brother.

Rohan gestured to Tallain and leaned back casually in his chair. It was a deliberate pose expected of him under the circumstances; he did it anyway. A glance at his son's profile polished his wits to a sharp gleam. Pol would not lose Princemarch before he ever had the chance to rule it.

Lyell came in, and not alone. A tall, bearded young man was with him. His dark hair had a faintly reddish tint that was stronger in his neat beard, and was trimmed to frame very green eyes. He wore a plain tunic of finest blue silk so dark as to be nearly violet. Tan leather trousers clung to muscular legs above soft boots dyed to match the tunic. A heavy silver ring was on one finger, a thin gold circle on another, and an amethyst earring swung close to his cheek. His gaze moved slowly from face to face in the stunned silence, lingering a moment on Pol before he stared straight at Rohan. He did not bow.

No one breathed for several seconds. Then Pandsala surged up from her chair, white to the lips and trembling with fury. "Bend your head and your knees to your betters, peasant!" she spat.

"And greetings to you, dearest sister," Masul replied, smiling.

"That relationship has yet to be proved," said Prince Lleyn in mild tones, a calm reminder that broke the tension holding everyone in thrall. Rohan blessed the old man again and touched Pandsala's arm. She sank back into her seat, glaring.

"Lord Lyell, I assume you have an explanation," Rohan said quietly.

"I do, your grace." Lyell bowed, as Masul still had not. "Of all the things I might have said, none would impress your graces so much as the simple sight of this man. My wife, Lady Kiele, has questioned him at great length, and she is satisfied that he is indeed her brother, born of the late High Prince Roelstra and his mistress, Lady Palila. I have spoken with Lord Masul as well, and I, too, am convinced."

Pandsala's breath hissed as Lyell gave Masul the title, but she neither spoke nor moved. Rohan hoped she would continue to hold her tongue, and regarded Lyell with one brow slightly arched.

"I ask your pardon for my boldness," the Lord of Waes went on, "but—"

"But you required our complete attention," Rohan said dryly. "Proceed."

Lyell's pale cheekbones acquired a ruddy stain and he licked his lips nervously. But no one was looking at him. He faded next to Masul's vivid presence.

The pretender stepped forward. Cabar and Velden moved their chairs apart so he could stand at the table between them. "I can tell my own tale, my lords," he said.

"Your own lies," whispered Pandsala, but only Rohan and Pol heard her.

"I was born here at Waes twenty-one years ago on the sail barge belonging to High Prince Roelstra—a fact I have known all my life, verifiable in city birth records which will be presented for your inspection. On that same night other children were born in the same place, and their names also are listed." He hooked his thumbs in his belt; Roelstra's gesture. Kiele had taught him well, Rohan thought.

"The Princess-Regent can testify to the confusion of that night, brought about by her own efforts and those of her sister, Princess Ianthe." He smiled mockingly in Pandsala's direction. "Should Lady Palila produce a male child, the boy would take precedence over them—a thing most undesirable in their eyes. So they brought along other pregnant women, induced labor in them when Palila began her own, and hoped that at least one of the women would bear a girl who could be substituted for the male heir if such was born. This was the plan outlined by Princess Ianthe to her sister. But Princess Pandsala then went to Lady Palila, told her of the plot, and promised that if a *girl* was born to her that Pandsala would exchange this eighteenth worthless daughter for a boy-child who—they hoped—would be born to one of the other women.

"A risky plan, you will agree. There was chaos that night—babies being born, people milling about, the two princesses running back and forth from Palila's suite to the lower hold. Yet some things were seen and heard by all.

"First, Lady Palila was heard to shout in triumph that she had borne a son to Roelstra. Second, when the happy father arrived, there were two children present. One was Chiana. The other—'' Masul again fixed his jeering gaze on Pandsala. ''The other was a boy. Roelstra's true son. Me.''

"Liar!" Pandsala snapped. "Both children were girls! The infant boy hadn't been born yet!"

Rohan stifled a sigh. It would have been better for Pandsala never to have admitted that she had seen a male child at all. But he supposed she was past her limits now. He couldn't much blame her.

"Look at me, sister! Haven't I our father's eyes, his height, his bearing? Doesn't the color of my beard suggest the color of Palila's hair?'' He addressed the others once more. "The woman who called herself my mother was blonde and dark-eyed. Her husband was of the same coloring. Both of them were of less than medium stature. How could two small, fair, dark-eyed people produce a tall, dark, green-eyed son?''

It was Davvi—loyal, earnest, one of the architects of Rohan's power and Pol's inheritance—who rose in their defense.

"I have two sons taller than I, and my late wife was small enough to fit beneath my chin. Posture and gestures may be learned. As for green eyes—many people have them. Prince Pol's eyes are quite green in certain lights. Does this mean that he, too, may be Roelstra's son?''

Davvi, who believed the lie Sioned had started and Rohan had let stand because every good barbarian prince desired a son to rule after him. Rohan sat with an impassive face, dying a little inside.

"I respectfully ask our cousin of Syr what evidence there is to the contrary?'' Velden of Grib got to his feet beside Masul, hands planted aggressively on the table before him. "Can the Princess-Regent say for certain which child was which? Who else was there that night to witness the birth of Palila's child?''

Pandsala spoke in a voice that would have iced the Long Sand in midsummer. "My sister Ianthe was the only attendant at the birth. And she is dead.''

Velden spread his hands, dark eyes wide with pretended bewilderment. "I ask you, my lords. Is it possible that this man is Roelstra's son? There are no living witnesses to the contrary. But there is the evidence of our own eyes."

Miyon rose to his feet on the opposite side of the table. "Look at him, cousins," he said in silken tones. "Some of you knew the late High Prince very well. Is there a resemblance?"

The older princes stayed silent. Pandsala did not.

"I am Roelstra's unchallenged daughter, and I say this man lies!"

"But does he look like Roelstra?" Miyon pressed. "Enough like to be his son?"

"Tall, dark-haired, green-eyed—I could find a hundred fitting the description! It proves nothing!"

"But *this* man's birth is recorded in the registers of Waes for that particular night."

"Are you telling me I would not know my own flesh and blood?" Pandsala exclaimed, rising half out of her chair. "Are you daring to call me a liar?"

"Never, my lady!" he protested, eyes wide. "But . . . perhaps your position does not encourage you to look on what may be the truth with clear eyes."

Madness, Rohan told himself. None of this had anything to do with Masul's claim, but with Pol's.

Cabar of Gilad took up Masul's cause. "My lords, consider. If this man is indeed Roelstra's son, then we must think very carefully whether or not we shall deprive him of his birthright as a prince. *As one of us.*"

It was not that Miyon and his faction wished Masul to take up residence at Castle Crag, but that they wanted to prevent Pol from ever doing so.

"It is true that High Prince Rohan defeated Roelstra in war, and claimed all of Princemarch on his son's behalf," Cabar went on. "But if this man's words are indeed true, then he *is* one of us. A prince."

"Look at him," Miyon said. "Weigh the evidence of your own eyes against the lack of specific information about that night."

Rohan slanted a look at Pol from the corner of his eye. The boy sat very still, his wary, fascinated gaze on Masul. Rohan wondered what Pol was thinking. He tried to ignore the questions rampaging through his own mind—was the man really Pol's kinsman, his uncle? Did it matter? If what they wanted was for Princemarch to continue in Roelstra's line, then Pol would fit the requirement perfectly. But Pol ruling both Princemarch and the Desert was exactly what they did not want.

"The coincidences are too many," Miyon said. "I have spoken with Lady Kiele—another of Roelstra's daughters—and she has concluded after interviewing this man that he is indeed her brother."

Turn Chiana loose on him, whispered Sioned's voice in his mind. Rohan looked down at his ring, the huge topaz gleaming in the circle of emeralds like a dragon's eye—watching, waiting. Dragons knew how to attack with exquisite cunning. Rohan was the son of one dragon, father of another.

Clutha and Saumer were questioning Masul about his life at Dasan Manor, his training in arms, his views on everything from the silk trade to the new port a-building at the mouth of the Faolain. Masul pleaded ignorance of many princely matters, but that would flatter the others into thinking he could be influenced. The answers he did give were forthright and cleverly thought out: guileless honesty disguising deliberate cunning, and designed to present him as a worthy prince. But, more importantly, an unthreatening one.

Rohan felt as if the ground was crumbling beneath him like sand over a sinkhole. If only the past could be conjured up to exhibit the truth as clearly as Masul's form and features visibly exhibited a lie. . . .

Conjuring.

Powerful Sunrunners could glimpse bits of their personal futures. Sioned had known that Rohan waited for her from the time she was sixteen winters old. Years later she had seen and shown him herself holding an infant with Rohan's blond hair; they had known that although she was barren, she would somehow give Rohan a son. *Faradh'im* could sometimes conjure up visions of the future. But could they do the same with the past?

Andrade had been there that night. So had Pandsala. Their verbal testimony was worthless because of who they were to Rohan: his aunt, his regent. But if either or both could provide a clear vision of what had happened that night—

Rohan got to his feet and glanced at the water clock. All conversation ceased; he drew attention away from Masul effortlessly. The young man recognized and resented it. *He* was supposed to be the focal point and it visibly galled him to be so easily upstaged by this slight, quiet man who was twice his age.

"My lords, my ladies," Rohan said, "it grows late and I'm sure we are all in need of time and privacy in which to consider this matter. There is evidence still to be presented. Lord Lyell, be so good as to hold yourself in readiness for such time as we may call upon you again." He pretended to consult his notes. "Cousins, this afternoon we will take up matters of trade between Cunaxa, Fessenden, Isel, and Ossetia. Until then, we are adjourned. I thank the heirs and representatives present for their attendance and attention—and I trust the experience has been edifying."

Masul did not bow on his way out, either. He left in company with Miyon, Cabar, and Velden, with Lyell, forgotten, trailing along behind them. Chadric took a few steps toward Rohan as if he wanted to say something, but then seemed to think better of it and helped his father leave the tent. Soon Rohan was alone with Pol, who was staring into the empty air. To give the boy time to marshal his thoughts and questions, Rohan made a slow circuit of the tent, halting before the water clock. He ran one finger over the carved dragon, watching water drip inexorably through the ruby.

"Father?"

"Yes, Pol."

"Why aren't you going to let them discuss the evidence this afternoon?"

"Think about whose trade we'll be reviewing."

There was a short pause. "Miyon's, so he has to come and pay attention and you can keep an eye on him. But the others haven't really declared for either side, have they?"

"No. And by listening to how they conduct themselves with Miyon over trade, I may get an idea of where they might jump on this other matter."

"Oh!" Another moment, and Pol said excitedly, "And if he's nasty over his wools and metals, they might get irritated and lean toward us!"

"Maybe." Rohan turned and asked, "How do you read all this?"

"Miyon looks pretty easy to twitch," Pol said shrewdly. "I think he thinks he's very clever. But he's also stubborn and proud."

"A dangerous mixture. Why should I—what did you call it? Twitch him?"

"To get Chale and Pimantal and Saumer mad at him."

"And would it be wise of me to do it openly?" Rohan shook his head. "Roelstra did that, you know. He created dissension deliberately, so he could solve problems he himself made by exercising his power to get what he wanted to begin with. That's not how I work, Pol. If Miyon antagonizes them on his own, fine. I must be more subtle, and let him know what real cleverness is." He smiled. "He's eager to try his strength against me, and my army along his border this spring and summer hasn't made him love me."

"But what about Kiele? She's the one who made all this possible for Masul."

"An interesting woman," he admitted. "Presumably, she didn't balk at murdering a Sunrunner. By the way, I wouldn't be at all surprised if Masul had done that himself. He seems to have all the right killing instincts. Look at how well he played off Pandsala." Rohan sighed deeply. "Pol, there's a vast difference between wanting power and wanting what power can accomplish. *Faradh'im* inherit power and are trained in its uses. But sometimes a prince or *athri* comes along who doesn't understand it at all. He wants the fact of it, but cares nothing for its substance. Roelstra was like that. He enjoyed power for its own sake. Am I making any sense?"

"I think I understand," the boy said slowly. "He opposed you because you had power and Mother. It wasn't that he wanted to do the same kinds of things you did with your power. He just couldn't stand that you had it." Pol hesitated, then said, "From what I've heard today, Princess Ianthe was like that, too, wasn't she?"

Rohan kept his expression calm. "Yes. She was like

that, too." He stretched and said, "Come on, we should get something to eat. I have a long afternoon ahead of me. I assume you'll return to the paddocks to exercise Chay's horse?"

"How did you know that's where I was?"

Rohan was glad of the chance to laugh. "Your mother—or was it Tobin?—made sure you were washed and combed before you got here, and you even cleaned your boots. But you forgot to remove that hoof-pick from your back pocket."

Pol made a face. "It was Aunt Tobin. I thought you were going to say something magic, like Mother usually does when she figures out what I don't want her to know."

"Start practicing the art of observation. It can be very useful—and not just when you want to astonish your son."

* * *

Another father and son spoke alone together in another tent, but this time it was the son who astonished the father.

"Why didn't you come to me with this earlier?" Ostvel demanded of Riyan. "Has Clutha kept you under lock and key?"

"Just about," the young man replied. "I'm sorry, Father, but this is the first chance I've had to get away. I'm only here now because Sioned made a direct request to Clutha this morning. Halian demands my constant attendance, for all that I'm supposed to be Clutha's squire."

"Couldn't you have—"

"No," Riyan stated flatly. "I couldn't disobey Halian or do anything out of the ordinary. And I didn't dare tell anyone but Lady Andrade what I saw. If Kiele and this Masul murdered Kleve—"

"They'd have no qualms about doing the same to you." Ostvel surprised his only offspring by pulling him into a rough embrace. "Forgive me for snapping at you. You did the right thing." He released his son and sank into a chair. "So we have proof of a sort."

"Of a very poor sort. Kleve never actually told me his suspicions. And I never got close enough to the house to see who was in it besides Kiele. I didn't see Masul. I didn't see him kill a Sunrunner." His hands clenched, his rings bright arcs between whitened knuckles. "Father, for all I know Halian is in league with Kiele, and has been keeping me away from you on purpose. I don't trust anybody and that scares me." He paused, shaking his head. "The most we can do is tell Rohan and Sioned. Maybe they'll be able to confront Kiele with it and frighten her off somehow."

"It would only put you in danger by letting her know that you saw something you shouldn't have. I can't risk you, Riyan. I won't risk you." Looking directly into his son's eyes, he said, "You're all I have left of your mother."

Rarely had he heard Ostvel even mention the woman Riyan barely remembered. He swallowed the ache in his throat. Standing beside his father's chair, he studied the worried face, the cloud-gray eyes. "What do you think Mother would have done?"

Ostvel shrugged, uncomfortable with the emotion. "If you knew how many times I've asked myself that over the years since she died. . . . She probably would have said exactly what you have." He shifted position and went on, "We—Maarken and I—took Pol over to the Fair again for a little while today, and only had to keep our ears open to hear all the latest rumors. Masul is, he isn't, he couldn't be, he ought to be, how long will Rohan let him live. . . ." Ostvel slammed his fist on the arm of the chair.

"It seems to me that the length of Masul's life depends entirely on Masul himself," Riyan murmured.

"Try convincing others of that. They don't know our High Prince the way you and I do. He'd cut off his own arm before he'd make a surreptitious or dishonorable move against this pretender."

"And tell us it's practicality that stays his hand, not any particular nobility on his part."

"Accuse him of being noble and he'll laugh in your face. It has to do with freedom."

"Whose?" the young man asked, bewildered.

"His. Don't worry," he added in sympathy. "I don't completely understand it either. What he says is that when you take action, you trap yourself into that action. But by waiting and seeing how things develop, you keep your options open. You're free to choose what to do—or what *not* to do.''

"You're right. I don't understand at all.''

"I think it goes back to his first *Rialla*,'' Ostvel mused. "He did certain things that trapped people into doing certain other things. But he got trapped, as well—and he didn't much like it, I can tell you. What you have to understand about him is that he'll never use us. He knows exactly what we're made of, our strengths and weaknesses, and makes his own plans accordingly. But he'll never trap us into doing things. It was done to him and he hated it. With Rohan, you'll never do anything for him that you wouldn't have done of your own will. He won't twist you all awry getting you to do what he wants. But because he knows who and what you are, you'll do it anyway.''

"He really is the *azhrei*,'' Riyan said, half in wonder. "A dragon waits to see which way the herd will run before he begins his hunt.''

"I suggest you do the same,'' his father warned. "You've not been away so long that I can't still tell what you're thinking. You've your mother's eyes, you know. She never could hide much from me. Don't even consider it, Riyan. Rohan and Pol must meet this man in public and discredit him in public, or Pol's claim will never be secure.''

"Pity,'' Riyan said briefly.

"Whatever you're thinking, I forbid it,'' Ostvel warned.

"I wasn't thinking anything, Father.''

"Good. See that you continue not thinking it.'' The storm clouds in his eyes cleared a little. "Sit down and talk to me of other things. I'm sick of plots and politics. How did you like returning to Clutha's service? Has he treated you well?''

Riyan answered with stories of his time at Swalekeep, finding relief equal to his father's in discussion of matters no more weighty than the best method of saddle breaking a horse or the antics of Halian's illegitimate daughters. But though much of him relaxed into easy conversation, a deeper part of his mind was working out ways he could continue to observe Kiele—as his fostering prince had, after all, commanded.

He found his opportunity later that day. Lady Chiana required certain things at the residence in Waes, and had enlisted Prince Halian as escort on the ride. This was a piece of rather transparent guile on her part, for if Halian was with her, he could not be elsewhere listening to persons who doubted her royal birth. Riyan, whom Halian had once again appropriated from Clutha, went along with them and listened stolidly to their flirtation. All the arch comments and teasing laughter Chiana lavished on Halian were things long since directed unsuccessfully at Riyan; he was privately amazed that she varied her technique not at all from man to man. But Halian swallowed all of it as if he was the very first ever to rise to her bait. Riyan felt rather sorry for him, but he was contemptuous, too. The prince was welcome to her, and much joy might she bring him if he was fool enough to make her his wife.

On arrival at the residence, she tossed her reins to Riyan as if he were nothing more than a groom and gave him casual permission to attend to his own pursuits. Halian waved him away, intent on Chiana.

Riyan watched the pair mount the steps to the main doors, thinking sardonically of Kiele's probable reaction to having her home used as a whorehouse. Chiana was no idiot, he'd give her that; there were servants aplenty inside to witness the amount of time she and Halian would spend alone, probably locked away in an upper chamber with access to a bed. If Halian thought he'd be getting Chiana for free, he was in for a shock. Riyan shrugged and helped stable the horses, exchanging idle chat with a friendly groom who knew him from his stay here.

After a brief debate with himself, he rode to the manor house outside town where Kleve had been killed. He reined in before it, lips pursed and brow furrowed. Sunlight poured down the roof like a glaze of warm honey; wildflowers sprang up from the surrounding grasses; it did not look like a place of death. Tethering his horse, he opened the door cautiously and went inside.

The rooms were as empty as when he'd inspected them the night of Kleve's death. Nothing had been touched—the bedclothes were still tumbled and the used crockery stank of rotted food. Riyan shook his head over the fool's errand he was engaged in. If no one had returned to tidy the evidence, chances were there was no evidence to be found. But he had to try.

The afternoon yielded faint dark stains on the floor that might have been blood, and other signs of hasty abandonment he'd missed last time—a shirt kicked under the bed and forgotten, a woman's earring under the table where candlelight hadn't caught it but sunlight did. It had to be Kiele's. But short of ransacking her jewel coffers for the other one, there was no way to prove it. Besides, she would have disposed of the matching earring the instant she'd discovered she'd lost this one. But evidence was here, all right—which made him revise his original interpretation of the disorder. No one had returned because no one dared. Perhaps he'd disturbed something in his search that night, warning the occupant to flee at once. Perhaps he had even been seen entering or leaving the house—and if that was true, he marveled that he was still alive. Riyan pocketed the earring and continued the hunt.

Toward dusk he found usable evidence stuffed into a closet at the back of the house. Riyan's active imagination prompted speculation that a piece of clothing or some other article belonging to Kleve had, like the shirt and earring, been forgotten in a panicky departure.

But he was not prepared for the bundle of heavy wool in the closet, stiff with dried blood, wrapped around a towel that contained three severed fingers.

Riyan dropped the grisly bundle, backing away in horror. A cry clotted in his throat. Stumbling, half-blind, he ran for the sink and vomited up everything in his stomach. When he was empty and exhausted by the violence of his reaction, he pumped water to wash his face. Sight of his own water-polished rings made him gag again.

It seemed forever before he could make himself go back. The blanket lay where he had flung it, the pattern of red and yellow crusted over with dried blood. As for the towel—Riyan knelt, trembling, and forced himself to touch a finger, to begin removing its ring. Andrade would want them, he told himself over and over. Andrade would want them as proof.

But then he stopped, staring at the plain circles around the severed fingers.

Kleve had worn six rings, marking him as adept at using both sun and moons. But on the bloodied towel before him were three fingers wearing only two silver rings.

He sucked in a great lungful of air, steadying himself. His father had told him that Sioned had somehow recovered one of the gold rings; it was how they learned of Kleve's death. It must have been from the left first finger—missing from this grim collection. The other gold was gone from the right thumb. It was the proudest ring of all, the fifth that signified full Sunrunner status. He could see the white circle on dead skin where the ring had been worn for most of Kleve's life.

Where was that fifth ring?

Riyan pushed himself to his feet and went to the window, flinging it wide to let clean air in. Then he got a fresh sheet from the stack in the linen cupboard and used it to wrap the evidence. He took another sheet and folded the blanket in it—thick red-and-yellow wool, Cunaxan weave, that had undoubtedly shrouded Kleve's corpse while it was carried away. Masul was said to be tall and strong, with broad shoulders and muscles enough to make the burden a relatively light one. And Riyan felt sick again at realizing that while he himself had been poking around the manor house, Masul had been depositing Kleve's body somewhere for the scavengers to find. Why couldn't Masul have returned while Riyan was still there? He bitterly cursed the missed chance—then gulped and acknowledged that the Goddess had been watching over him that night.

But why had Masul not sliced off Kleve's hands completely? Even if he'd taken all the rings, there would have been marks around the fingers left by the sun. Without hands, nothing could identify him as *faradhi*. An instant later the answer was obvious. A corpse with missing hands could point in only one direction: the murdered Sunrunner.

Still, Masul had neglected to dispose of the severed fingers; a stupid mistake. No, a fatal one. Had he trusted that after once finding nothing, no one else would come and make as thorough a search as Riyan had just done? Had haste made him careless? Had he not dared come back here or had his own arrogance betrayed him?

Riyan wondered what poor terrified person had found Kleve's body. But he knew why no one had come forth with the information. Who wanted to be connected with the death and desecration of a Sunrunner? How the gold ring had found its way to Sioned was a mystery he gnawed at while stuffing the sheets into his saddlebags. Perhaps someone had gone looking for Kleve or heard a rumor, or the remaining rings had been taken from his fingers for sale. It didn't matter much, and Riyan told himself to stop questioning the Goddess' good will. She looked after her *faradh'im;* that was all he needed to believe in. What was important was the terrible evidence lashed securely into leather pouches.

He returned to the house and washed his face and hands again, shivering. It was dusk; Chiana and Halian would be impatient for his return. He stuffed the sheets with their terrible contents into his saddlebags. A gallop through the crisp evening air blew away the horror and fanned his anger. He would see Masul dead for this, and Kiele with him. They had murdered a Sunrunner. He hoped Andrade would match their viciousness when she decided the manner of their deaths.

Halian and Chiana had ridden back without him. Riyan shrugged, caring nothing for any punishment the prince might decree for his dereliction of duty, and stayed at the residence long enough to down two large cups of wine before riding back to the encampment. He did not stop at Meadowlord's light green tents, but instead made straight for the High Prince's pavilion.

Riyan went past Tallain without a word. He bowed and swept a grim gaze over his father and Rohan, who fell silent as he threw the saddlebags on the desk.

"Proof," he said curtly.

Ostvel opened the leather bags and caught his breath. Rohan said nothing as the contents were placed before him. He studied them for a long time, then met Riyan's eyes.

It took only a few moments to tell the story of his afternoon. His father looked murderous. Rohan's eyes kindled with a slowly gathering fury that, if unleashed, would destroy everything in its path.

"One of them has the other ring," Riyan finished. "I'm sure of it. My guess is that it was the fifth, gold for the right thumb, the Sunrunner's ring."

"Too big for Kiele," Rohan murmured. "But Masul's size. Yes."

"If he dares to wear it, we have him."

"Perhaps. Perhaps." Rohan folded the sheets over and replaced the bundles in the saddlebags. "Your father has told me the rest. But I must give you an order now as your prince, Riyan—something you may find difficult to obey as a Sunrunner." He held Riyan's gaze with his own. "Say nothing to Andrade of this. Nothing."

He felt no conflict. "I was your man the day I was born."

The blond brows arched slightly. "Not even a fleeting qualm? Andrade won't be pleased by that. Whatever you may be to me, you are partially hers."

"*All* that I am, my prince, is yours," Riyan said with simple dignity.

Rohan nodded slowly. "You honor me, Riyan. Have Tallain return with you to Clutha's camp. If anyone asks, he is to say you were summoned by me when you rode in. That should excuse you from any difficulties with Halian. As for your absence today—"

"I'm answerable to Prince Clutha, my lord. Not Halian."

"I understand. But let me know if there's any problem."

"Yes, my lord." He bowed and started for the door, then paused and turned. "I have a favor to ask. Will you make sure they take a long time to die?"

Ostvel made a sound low in his throat. Rohan merely nodded. "Yes, Riyan. Both Masul and Kiele will be a very long time dying."

"Thank you, my lord." Riyan bowed again, satisfied, trusting his prince as implicitly as he trusted his father, and left them.

Ostvel picked up the saddlebags and held them to his chest. "You know what the penalty is for murdering a *faradhi.*"

"Yes. But not yet. Not until he's been disproved in his claim. That ties my hands, Ostvel." His fists clenched as if tightening around Masul's throat. "Sweet Goddess," he whispered, "how dearly I'd love to kill him *now*." Then he looked up. "Riyan must be watched very carefully. If Masul suspects anything, his life will be worthless. Have you friends among the Sunrunners Andrade brought with her?"

Ostvel nodded. "I'll make it a personal favor, nothing that Andrade need concern herself with."

"Good. It will turn out as we need it to, my friend. We haven't come this far and done so much to see it all ruined now."

Ostvel bowed slightly. "I never believed any differently, my prince," he said softly.

After he had gone, taking the saddlebags with him, Rohan murmured, "I wish I could believe with you, my friend."

Chapter Nineteen

Princess Alasen was a past mistress of the art of escaping any escort her father chose to set over her. Simplicity itself in and around the castle of New Raetia on Kierst, freedom was even easier to arrange in the crush of people on their way to the races. Among them, Alasen became only a young girl in a plain dress, anonymous unless one noted her father's silver-flask emblem stitched on the tiny leather purse at her belt.

A canopy of green silk had been raised above the royal enclosure, and the stands were filling rapidly. Much of the crowd veered off to find good seats, but Alasen continued on to the paddocks, where young men soon to be knighted were to demonstrate their horsemanship before the racing began.

She found a place at the rails and propped her elbows on the painted wood to watch. Her father's squire, Sorin of Radzyn Keep, led fourteen highborn youths on mag-

nificent horses into the grassy meadow, pausing to acknowledge the cheers of friends and relatives assembled
to watch. They began a formal ride around the enclosed
area, changing gaits and directions with invisible signals
to their mounts, cutting diagonals and riding intricate
patterns in perfect formation. Sorin rode one of his father's horses, an elegant dapple-gray mare with a black
mane and tail; Alasen wondered about the chances of
convincing her father to purchase the animal for her and
decided they were fairly good. Volog was in excellent
humor despite the scandal of Masul's appearance, and his
private talks with the High Prince had been much to his
liking. He was pleased, too, that she had formed a
friendship with Cousin Sioned. It might be possible for
her to coax him into buying the mare, even without its
being a wedding present.

Alasen was under no illusions as to why her father had
brought her to Waes this year. Young men had been presented for her inspection at New Raetia for two years
now—rather late for a princess, but then she was Volog's
last and favorite child, whom he wanted to keep with him
as long as possible. But she would be twenty-three this
autumn, and it was time she married. If she was disinclined to accept any of the young men who came to Kierst,
then Volog was determined that she look the rest of them
over at the *Rialla*. But he expected her to choose a husband, and she knew it.

Sorin rode into the center of the paddock by himself,
showing off more fanciful maneuvers—curvettes and flying leaps designed to flaunt a rider's skill and impress
potential customers with the horse's quality. Lord
Chaynal stood a little way down the railing from Alasen,
critical eyes noting every nuance of his son's performance. Many of the other horses being ridden today were
his as well, the rest belonging to Lord Kolya of Kadar
Water—Chaynal's only serious rival in horse-breeding.
The two holdings had enjoyed generations of friendly
competition, scorning and degrading each other's horses
with cheerful predictability at each *Rialla*.

Alasen applauded her approval of Sorin's skills and
waved as he rode past the railing to collect well-deserved
accolades. He grinned and winked at her. He certainly

was the best-looking of all the young men—long and lanky, with his father's chiseled features. He was the best rider, too. Alasen's pride in him was that of an elder sister, and it was a relief to them both that the warmth of their friendship was untouched by Fire. Their parents had once or twice discussed the possibility of a match, but nothing had ever come of it. She and Sorin laughed heartily at the very notion. He would make a wonderful husband for some woman, but not her. For all his twenty winters and many knightly accomplishments, Sorin was like a great playful colt who still bumped his knees and nose. Alasen was a little surprised to see him so self-possessed and grown-up today.

She wondered suddenly what his brother Andry was like, the twin who had rejected the usual nobleman's training in order to become a Sunrunner. The seriousness of his goals was probably reflected in his personality, she mused—all the playfulness and humor she liked so much in Sorin schooled out of Andry during his years at Goddess Keep.

Other young men were taking their turns now, and Alasen's eye was caught by a splendid Radzyn sorrel ridden by a youth wearing Meadowlord's light green. The squire made his mare dance delicately across the paddock at an impossible angle, and the onlookers gasped with pleasure as the horse changed directions with the airy grace of a feather in a wayward summer breeze. The young man was of middling height with the dark coloring of Fironese mountain folk, and not half so handsome as Sorin. But as he rode past her, one sight of his eyes reversed her opinion of his looks. Fringed by long, thick black lashes, his eyes were a deep velvety brown with bronze glints, shaped wide and long beneath straight, heavy brows. These astonishing eyes changed his face from merely pleasant to nearly beautiful. He reined in the mare directly in front of her, shifted not a breath in his saddle—and the horse suddenly reared back, gathered herself, then came down on forelegs with rear hooves lashing out. It was a warhorse's move, precise and deadly, and the crowd burst into applause.

"Oh, well done!" Alasen cried along with the cheering audience.

"Do you think so?" a man's deep voice said at her shoulder.

"Oh, yes," she answered without turning, enthralled by the young man's ride. "Just perfect! Do you know who he is, sir? He wears Meadowlord's colors, but then every squire is still in his fostering lord's colors."

"His own are blue and brown, for Skybowl. His name is Riyan, and he's my son."

Alasen looked up then into a pleasant, smiling face. There was a family resemblance about the brow and nose, and she realized that with maturity the son would become nearly as distinguished as the father. But their eyes were very different; the ones gazing down at her now were gray, shaded by dark lashes and a shock of tousled brown hair showing threads of silver. "You must be Lord Ostvel," she said, returning his smile.

"The same. I thank you for the compliment on my son's behalf. A father's pride is one thing, but to hear a young lady's praise confirm it. . . ." He gave a self-mocking shrug. "And you must be Princess Alasen of Kierst."

"How could you know that? I purposely wore my oldest and plainest dress today, and I'm trying to blend in with the rest of the crowd!" She laughed up at him.

"I doubt you could ever succeed in that, my lady. As for knowing who you are—I met your mother once and you've the look of her. But the green eyes confirm it. They're precisely the same color as Prince Davvi's, and the same shape as Princess Sioned's."

"Really? I know I look like my mother, mostly, but do you think I resemble the High Princess even a little?"

"You sound as if you'd like to. But I'd say that looking like yourself is quite enough. You've certainly impressed that young man over there." He nodded to where Lord Chaynal stood with a youth whose blue eyes were indeed studying her most intently. "Obviously he finds it more rewarding to look at you than to watch his brother ride."

"His brother?" Alasen repeated blankly.

"Sorin. Your young admirer is Andry of Radzyn, and lately of Goddess Keep."

She forgot the dignity of her twenty-two winters and

stared. So that was Sorin's twin! "They're not very much alike, are they, my lord?"

"It used to be almost impossible to tell them apart. But they've grown up quite differently in the last years." His voice was suddenly expressionless and she glanced up at him, startled. He noted the look and smiled once more. "But I'm keeping you from watching the rest of the show. They're about to ride toward each other at a full gallop—Sorin's idea, the madman. I just hope Riyan doesn't disgrace himself by falling off."

"I doubt he's done that since the first time you put him on a pony," she chuckled.

The line of riders formed again, then broke in two at the middle. They cantered to opposite ends of the meadow, wheeled in place, and at a signal from Sorin thundered toward each other with a speed that promised to annihilate them all. Yet somehow each found a space to gallop through, and in the next instant they had all lined up again to enjoy the crowd's applause.

"Excellent," Lord Ostvel murmured. "But don't tell my son I said so," he added.

"But he deserves to be told, my lord. Next to Sorin, he's the best rider here."

Laughter rumbled up from deep in his chest. "No more syrup for my paternal pride, my lady! Tell me, what do you think of the mare he's riding?"

"As a warhorse, perfection. As a casual mount—" She shook her head. "That mare would fret herself to skin and bones if she wasn't given anything more than a good gallop every other day."

"I agree. She's too high-strung. I need to gift Riyan with a proper knight's mount, though. Which horse would you favor?"

She hesitated, then had to answer honestly. "Sorin's gray, without a doubt."

Lord Ostvel gave a long sigh. "I was afraid we'd agree on that, too. Chay's going to demand half a year's income for that horse—and he won't knock the price down for the sake of friendship, either!"

The crowd was breaking up now, heading to the stands to watch the first race, and Alasen was jostled against the rails. Ostvel took her arm to steady her. "I'm all right," she assured him. ''But I think I'll wait here until the crowd thins a little.''

''No need. I'll escort you, if you'll permit. Would you like to go congratulate Sorin?''

''Yes, please!''

Together they made their way to where Lord Chaynal stood with his sons and Riyan. Ostvel ruffled his own son's dark hair as if he was still ten years old instead of two days away from formal knighthood; Riyan bore with it, grinning, and gold sparkled with the bronze in his eyes. Alasen was introduced and noted that Riyan was not another such as Sorin—though just as accomplished at the arts of being a knight, he also possessed social skills enough not to blush in the presence of a pretty girl. He gave her a bow and a smile, and again she saw his father in him.

Sorin then claimed her attention with a demand to be told how wonderful he was. Alasen laughed at him. ''You stayed in your saddle, which is more than I expected!''

He turned an aggrieved face to his father. ''Allow me to thank you, my lord, for never giving us any sisters! Andry, this is the girl I told you about, who's made my life misery for nearly eight years. Princess Alasen of Kierst, my brother, Lord Andry.''

Alasen was in for a surprise. She received a very elegant bow, a very direct stare, and a very composed pronouncement of her name and title in a voice that made *her* complexion change color, not his.

''So you're Volog's youngest,'' said Lord Chaynal. ''Happy man, to have such a treasure in his castle. I even hold you excused from never having taught this hopeless whelp of mine any manners during his time at New Raetia.''

She met his grin with sparkling eyes and her lips tucked into a rueful line. ''Indeed, my lord, I am sorry. We tried everything, but to no avail.'' His eyes were gray like Lord Ostvel's, but like sunlight on moonstones where the other man's were silver in shadow.

''She means,'' Sorin said, ''that she used to throw books at me in the schoolroom. Don't try to deny it, Allie, you know you did. I still have the scars.''

"And the addled wits, if her aim was good enough," Andry teased.

Lord Chaynal moaned. "Mannerless, impudent, fractious—Ostvel, what did I ever do to deserve such offspring?"

"Something dreadful, I'm sure. We ought to get out of the sun, Chay. Desert folk don't mind it, but I'm sure Princess Alasen would prefer to be in the shade."

"Is the heat in the Desert as terrible as they say?" she asked.

Lord Chaynal smiled, and once more she could see a son's maturity in a father's face. "It would burn forty freckles onto your charming nose before you could draw a breath."

"Stop flirting or I'll tell Mother on you," Sorin threatened, grinning.

"Indeed?" The Lord of Radzyn drew himself up to his full height—only a fingerspan or so greater than his sons', but he also outweighed each by a silkweight of solid muscle and out-shouldered them by the breadth of a hand. "I compliment pretty girls just as I please, boy, and the day I stop—"

"Is the day Maarken inherits," Andry interjected slyly, "because you'll have been dead at least three days!"

His lordship gave a martyred sigh. "Alasen, my dear, if you ever have sons, have them only one at a time. They're bad enough singly—as Ostvel and Rohan can attest. Twinned, they're more than any rational person should be called on to endure. If you'll excuse me, I should be seeing to my entries in the first races. And if you've a mind to a wager, I recommend my black mare in the fifth." He bowed, smiled, and strode off.

Alasen was a little amazed by the playful bantering between fathers and sons, so different from the relationship between Volog and her brothers Latham and Volnaya. The scrupulous respect and politeness they showed each other were quite the opposite of the affectionate abuse she had just heard. But she liked their easy manners and knew instinctively that their teasing came in direct proportion to their love for each other.

She was also surprised at herself for joining in. But she had probably picked up the ability from an indulgent father and Sorin's constant teasing. She would miss them when she married. The reminder of the reason she was at Waes took some of the brightness from the day. She deliberately turned her thoughts elsewhere as she started back to the stands.

Sorin, Riyan, and Lord Ostvel took the lead, leaving Alasen and Andry a pace or two behind. They walked in a silence she found embarrassing after the preceding chatter. At last he spoke.

"You have no attendant with you today, my lady?"

"I like to escape sometimes," she confessed. "My father has a tendency to watch over me as if I'm made of Fironese crystal."

"Anyone looking at you might say that you *are*," he mumbled.

Alasen gave him a startled glance. He was looking anywhere but at her. She had heard compliments from her cradle, yet Andry's words sounded more like a grudging admission of an inescapable and somewhat uncomfortable fact than a bid for her favor. All at once he looked exactly like Sorin did in the presence of other pretty girls, his cheeks red and his steps a bit too long. She smiled indulgently. Boys were amusing creatures, but she was old enough to know that she preferred grown men. Still, Andry was rather sweet, and though the set of his features was different from Sorin's he was just as good-looking. With the exquisite Princess Tobin and the dashing Lord Chaynal for parents, none of the brothers could possibly have turned out ill-favored. And Alasen approved wholeheartedly of handsome young men.

It seemed to Sioned and Tobin, sitting in the royal stands, that there were more young people at the *Rialla* than ever before, most of them looking for suitable spouses, as Alasen was supposed to be doing. The High Prince's liberal rules about who could attend had swelled the ranks of each prince's retinue with highborn youths and maidens, their servants, and guards for their material wealth. For their persons, no guards were necessary; Rohan held each prince personally responsible for the safety of the young people in his charge, and no one wanted to cause a war over any outrages perpetrated on or by those whose innocent purpose here was to get married.

Sons and daughters not heir to their parents' lands usually had little other than their charms to recommend them. Rohan and Sioned, wanting to even up the matrimonial stakes a little, had once considered providing all with enough gold to make a decent start in life. Tobin had ruthlessly quashed this notion by saying that if they really wanted to advertise the dragon gold, why not just take everyone on a tour of the caves? Ways were found of dowering the worthier and poorer young men and women just the same, principally through the races. Formerly, only the winning riders had come away with prizes, but now those who came in second and third received small purses of silver. It was said that some of the young men lost on purpose to win useful cash instead of the gems that came with victory—gems they could not afford to have set and which did not fetch their true value at the *Rialla*.

Heirs and *athr'im* had no need of anything but their positions to attract young women to them. There were many unmarried men present this year—Miyon of Cunaxa being the greatest prize as a prince already ruling. Sioned thanked the Goddess that Pol was still too young for the flirtatious follies going on all around her in the stands, and she and Tobin amused themselves between races by commenting on pairings that seemed to change every other moment.

Halian of Meadowlord and Kostas of Syr were much in demand and obviously enjoying themselves hugely. Patwin of Catha Heights, widower of Roelstra's daughter Rabia, was another excellent catch, judging by the cluster of females around him; in addition to his wealth and caressing brown eyes he possessed a gorgeous hilltop castle legendary for its gardens. Young Kolya of Kadar Water, Allun of Lower Pyrme, and Yarin of Snowcoves were all besieged.

"I'll bet the next winter's snowfall that Clutha's granddaughter Isaura marries Sabriam of Einar," Sioned whispered to Tobin, nodding to the pair who were trying to hide their clasped hands beneath the cover of the girl's skirt.

"Every grain of sand in the Desert says that Allun finally gives in to Sabriam's sister," Tobin replied. "Look at Kiera over there, using those big eyes on the poor boy! It'd make for an interesting alliance, I must say.''

''Mmm. I'm more interested in who goes after Tilal. Where'd he vanish to, anyway? And just look at Chale, glowering over there—he's scaring off anyone who even comes within speaking distance of Gemma! How's the girl ever going to provide the next Prince of Ossetia if he doesn't let her talk to anybody?''

''Who's that with them? The blonde girl who looks as if she'd been washed once too often and hung out limp on a line?''

''I think it's Danladi—yet another of Roelstra's daughters. You know, the one he had with Lady Aladra.''

''Oh, Sioned, quick! Chiana's cornered Miyon! And there's Halian near them, looking like a storm over the Veresch! Now, *that's* interesting!''

The next race began, and they concentrated on cheering a Radzyn stallion to victory. Most of Chay's horses were being ridden by younger sons with hopes of winning prizes. Chay was generous, but only youths he trusted personally were allowed to ride his entries. The approval of the powerful Lord of Radzyn was enough to keep many young ladies avidly watching to see who he honored with a ride on one of his horses.

Tobin applauded immodestly. ''We won again! Marvelous! Who's up, Sioned? I can't see that far.''

Rohan slid into the seat beside his wife and announced, ''Our own Tilal. I'm going to have wonderful fun pouring a river of garnets into his hands. Have you ladies decided yet who'll wear the wedding necklet he'll have made of them?''

''Who's applauding loudest?'' Sioned countered.

Many cheered him as he rode past on his victory lap, but Sioned's eye was caught by something that puzzled her deeply. Kostas, despite a smile and a wave for his younger brother, did not take his gaze from Gemma very long. She had her nose buried in a book, ignoring everyone and everything. Pale, delicate Danladi's blue eyes were narrowed with worry. Sioned sat back with a frown.

One of Lord Kolya's entries was the victor in the next race. The young man danced with pride and excitement as he went down to congratulate his rider, and actually flung his arms around the mare's neck. The royal trio laughed, then paid close attention as the next race was called—for Maarken was riding.

"I do so want him to win," Tobin said with a casualness that fooled no one. "I can't afford to part with any of my own jewels when he finally needs a necklet for his bride."

Rohan snorted and exchanged a half-hidden grin with Sioned. A short time later Maarken had ridden to an easy win. Tobin forgot herself and leaped up, cheering raucously for her son. This time Rohan and Sioned burst out laughing, and her sternest reprimands could not shut them up.

A vendor selling fruit ices came up the aisle, and Rohan tossed him coins enough for three cups. Tobin appropriated the apple ice right out of her brother's hands.

"I wanted that one!" he complained. "I paid for them, I should have first choice."

"Hush up and behave yourself," Tobin admonished, handing him the mossberry ice he had given her. "Anyone would think you're still twelve years old."

"You're a selfish and unnatural sister," he grumbled. "Look, there's Sorin!" When her head turned, he snatched the cup from her and replaced it with the mossberry ice.

"Rohan!" She elbowed him in the ribs.

Sioned laughed. "In another moment you two will revert to childhood and start playing at dragons. High Prince and the Lady of Radzyn, indeed! Now, tell me the name of that beauty Sorin's riding. He looks like one of Pashta's get."

"He is. That's Joscenel, twin to Andry's Maycenel. We gave them both a good horse when they became squires. Rohan, give that ice *back!*"

He held the apple cup out of her reach. "A good horse? That one looks like solid muscle covered in sunlight. I give him three lengths and a tail."

"Pashta never sired a finer pair," Tobin said. "No bet, little brother." She licked at the dripping ice in her hand, making a face at him. "This is better than the apple, anyway."

"It is?" He tried to switch cups again, and they giggled like children.

Sioned, safe with her snow-cherry ice, lost her grin when another horse came into view. "Rohan . . . look who's riding the Kadar horse."

He glanced around. All mirth faded and the light left his eyes.

"Well?" Tobin prompted. "I'm a victim of old age and my eyes aren't any good at that distance. Who is it?"

"Masul," Rohan replied colorlessly.

It seemed that everyone saw him at the same time. Quiet descended like a cloud over the animated conversation in the stands. One last nervous giggle sounded from somewhere, and then all was still. Masul bestrode a magnificent bay stallion, the characteristic white blaze and feathery white tufts at each hoof marking the horse as one of Kadar Water's breeding. The young man was not wearing Lord Kolya's colors, however—and Lord Kolya was in shock at the sight of the pretender riding one of his horses. Masul was dressed in a silk shirt the deep violet color of Princemarch.

He had shaved off his beard, a ploy not lost on anyone with half a brain. The clean, harshly handsome lines of his cheeks and jaw were visible now below the startling green eyes. As the horses paraded past the stands, Sioned met his gaze for an instant and saw the sheer glee in his grin. Fury gripped her that he dared wear Princemarch's color, swiftly followed by profound gratitude that Pandsala was safely in her tent. Rohan had told her about the regent's mood and actions yesterday, and Sioned was certain that had Pandsala been here she would have ripped the violet silk right off Masul's shoulders.

She darted a look at her husband, who appeared to be contemplating some similar act of mayhem. Tobin's black eyes were snapping with rage and her cheeks were deeply flushed, but Rohan's anger was as pale and cold as if his face had been carved from snow.

Lyell was the official starter. He toyed with the fringe of a large red-and-yellow flag as the dancing, restive horses lined up. Sioned's gaze traced the measure-round course and saw to her horror that this was the race to Brochwell Bay and back. The jumps were in position; a section of railing had been removed where the horses would leave the track for the cliffs. Anything could happen along that unwatched course. She knew that only too well. Rohan had ridden the same race twenty-one years ago to win her emeralds, and had nearly been killed along the way.

Sorin patted Joscenel's sleek, sunny neck, and a white-tufted ear swiveled back to listen to whatever he was saying. Sioned glanced over the other horses. Sorin was definitely the entry to beat. Two riders were on Lord Kolya's horses and wearing his russet-and-white; two more entries bore the plain red of Prince Velden of Grib. Another of Chay's horses was down the line from Sorin. Both young men were in his red-and-white silks. The eighth horse was Lord Sabriam's, distinguished by the orange and yellow of Einar, and a ninth belonged to Lord Patwin, the rider his younger brother dressed in garish red and blue stripes. These would battle it out for third place, for it was obvious that the contest for first would be between Sorin and Masul.

Tobin, recovering from her initial shock, was now the picture of composure to anyone who did not know her. Sioned, who knew her very well, saw a telltale pulse pounding in her throat as she bent to place the uneaten ice at her feet. Small, delicate fingers were then laced together in the princess' lap, knuckles white with tension. Tobin would show nothing more than a mother's justifiable pride when her son rode to victory. And Sorin must win, Sioned told herself, looking at Rohan's frozen, expressionless face. He must.

Lyell swept the flag down and the horses shot forward like arrows from nine warrior bows. Clods of dirt were flung up as they pounded past the stands and through the opening in the fence. The crowd gasped once, and then the strange, unsettling, whispering silence descended again.

As she had done years ago when Rohan had been up on Pashta in the same race, Sioned swiftly wove a thin plait of sunlight and sent it after the riders—thanking the Goddess that the sunlight was on her face and she did not have to draw attention to herself by moving. As she watched the nine horses separate on their way to the wood, she had the distinct impression that someone else was observing on the sunlight as well. Maarken, perhaps, or Andry, anxious for their brother. Careful to keep her own weaving distinct and separate, she glided toward the cliffs, waiting for the riders to emerge from the trees.

Masul was in the lead, Sorin just behind, the others trailing by at least two lengths. Joscenel was a streak of pale gold against the dark gravelly ground. Sorin rode close to his horse's neck, so much in harmony with the stallion that every stride seemed to find response in the ripple of muscle beneath Sorin's shirt. Sioned had never seen anyone ride this way, not even Chaynal, who was the best rider in living memory. Chay sat his horses with easy authority; Sorin became one with his mount.

Masul approached the sharp, dangerous turn at the cliff with rocks flying from beneath his bay's white-feathered hooves. He had to haul the animal's head cruelly around to avoid plunging over into the sea. Sorin judged the angle better, slowing Joscenel for an easier turn, and made up ground as Masul's outraged horse faltered, nearly stumbling, before finding his stride again.

Behind them, one of Velden's riders miscalculated and his terrified horse pulled up short, skidding to a halt on his haunches a man-length from the cliff edge. His rider went flying and vanished over the jagged rocks. The horse, trembling all over, limped away.

Sioned did not wait to see if the rest negotiated the turn safely. She raced back on the sunlight and saw Rohan and Tobin staring at her, only now realizing she had not been entirely with them.

"A rider went over the cliff," she said. "One of Velden's. He needs help—if he's still alive."

Rohan nodded curtly and left them, shouldering his way down to the track. Sioned felt Tobin cling to her hand, but had no time to reassure her. She rethreaded the sunlight and sped along it, hoping to catch Sorin and Masul as they emerged once more from the wood.

But the two horses were even faster than she'd thought. Both were well away from the trees. Masul's stallion was lathered, ears laid flat, teeth bared; only his rider's iron grip kept him from giving in to deeper instinct and turning to attack. Blood welled along the bay's hindquarters where the golden stallion had evidently gotten in a vicious bite. Sioned was astounded that the two warhorses still obeyed their riders.

Sorin was pressed even more tightly to his horse's neck now, his shirt cut to ribbons by low branches in the wood. His gloved hands held the reins almost at the bit. For three strides the pair hurtled along neck and neck, and then Joscenel began to pull ahead.

Suddenly Fire blossomed before them to the right, directly in Sorin's path. His horse swerved madly, eyes showing white with terror. Joscenel plowed into Masul's bay and the big horse stumbled. Recovering in a stride, they still ran so close together that sparks struck by iron-shod hooves on stone flew up simultaneously. Sioned saw the prong end of Masul's whip flash, and Sorin's back arched as steel cut into his shoulder. Joscenel struggled to maintain his balance as the young man lurched in the saddle. Masul kept his bay stallion right beside Sorin, riding for the edge of the Fire, forcing Joscenel directly into the chest-high flames.

Sorin righted himself and signaled his horse. Muscle bunched beneath the sweat-darkened hide and Joscenel soared over the Fire, landing a long stride beyond it with his belly singed and his white saddle blanket smoldering. The flames vanished, leaving a thin blackened line in the dirt that was quickly obliterated by the hooves of six other horses.

Sioned gave a violent shudder as she slid back down the sunlight. Staggering to her feet, her vision cleared just in time for her to see the two stallions thunder onto the track toward the first jump. Masul used his whip on his stallion, the shine of the silver prong sullied now with blood. The first jump was cleared, and the second. Sorin was on his heels by the third. One of Lord Kolya's horses foundered after the first obstacle, his thrown rider rolling quickly out of the way. Nobody seemed to notice.

Had Tobin's fingers been knives, they would have sliced Sioned's arm to the bone. Someone cried out in the silence, echoed by another shout from the commoners' stands, and sound rippled through the crowd—not cheers of encouragement but release of unbearable tension.

Sioned heard a low moan claw up from Tobin's throat, knowing that the princess' control was nearly gone.

Bay stallion and golden stallion cleared the last jump together. The former's ribs and mouth were coated with blood-red foam; still the whip dug into his sides. Under its assault he used up the last of his great heart and crossed the finish-half a stride in the lead.

Tobin dragged Sioned down through the crowd to the railings, and Sioned finally succeeded in getting in front of her tiny sister-by-marriage to protect her from the wildly screaming throng.

"Make way!" she shouted. "Let me pass! Make way for the High Princess!"

"Sioned!" came a familiar bellow. "Over here!"

She shouldered her way to Ostvel, gripping Tobin's hand. He was at the rails, keeping a place clear for them to duck through. "Get everyone to the paddock, quick, or there'll be trouble. Chay's got murder on his face."

"Can you blame him?" Tobin snapped before climbing through the rails.

Rohan was already on the track, waiting for Sorin to canter his blown and trembling stallion back to calm. He grasped his sister by the shoulders when she would have hurried to her son. "No! You'll get trampled. Tobin, stay here."

"I'll pull that lying bastard off his horse and feed him to the dragons!" she hissed. "Let me go!"

He bore with her struggles for a moment, then rapped out, "Stop it! Do you want everyone to see you?"

It was not something that would have mattered to Sioned, but Tobin, born and bred to princely station, had been trained to present a certain face to the outside world. She shook her brother off and smoothed back her hair. "No need to rattle my bones loose," she said acidly.

Rightly interpreting this as a sign of recovery, Rohan nodded. Sorin was riding closer now, and Sioned feared for a moment that Tobin would explode anew. She could tell the difference between marks left by slashing branches and the torn and bloodied shoulder caused by the lash of a whip. But though rage burned even hotter in her long-lidded eyes, she said nothing.

Sioned felt someone pluck at her sleeve, and looked

around. Alasen stood at her side, ashen-faced. "Is Sorin all right?" the girl whispered, and Sioned recalled that the two had grown up together at Volog's court.

"He'll be fine, with only a scar to show for his trouble."

Sorin rode up then, Joscenel having settled down. He gave Alasen a tight smile. "I'm not hurt, Allie. Just get me the hell out of here before I kill that pig. I don't trust myself nearer to him than a measure."

"You *or* your father," Rohan said mildly, though his eyes flashed. "But I see no need to insult pigs, Sorin. They're certainly much better bred than Masul. Let's get your horse to the paddock and cared for, shall we?"

Tobin turned on him with a look of furious betrayal, still wanting nothing more than to confront Masul with what he had done. But she obeyed Sioned's warning look and took Joscenel's bridle in one shaking hand. "Let's get out of here," she muttered, leading them to where Ostvel had waylaid the livid Chaynal.

Rohan was looking at Alasen. "With those green eyes, there's only one person you could be. Princess, would you be so kind as to stay here and watch certain people for me?"

She understood instantly. "Of course, your grace. It'll be a real pleasure."

Sorin gave a short laugh over his shoulder. "Go flirt with Masul. He'll be so dazzled he won't see that what you really want is to scratch his eyes out."

"If I decided to soil my hands by touching him, I'd aim a good deal lower down," she retorted, and set off toward the group clustered around the victor.

Rohan blinked in startlement, then grinned, and then scowled as Chay finally eluded Ostvel and stormed up. "Not here," he ordered sharply before Chay could do more than open his mouth. "This horse needs attention."

Chay turned scarlet and for a moment Sioned thought he would defy Rohan. But then he swallowed hard, nodding.

"Just as you say, my prince." He ran his fingers gently over the stallion's singed belly and legs, then met his son's gaze. "You'll have to explain this. I trust you *can.*"

"Not here," Rohan repeated, and they started for the paddocks.

They were joined along the way by Pol, Maarken, and Andry. Sioned searched the brothers' faces, but saw only anger. Unable to convince herself that it had been one of them she had sensed on the sunlight, she drew Maarken to her with a glance.

"Did you watch the race?" she whispered. "By *faradhi* means?" When he looked surprised and shook his head, she called Andry over and received the same answer.

"Did *you?*" Maarken demanded. "What did you see?"

"I want to talk to Sorin first."

She appropriated him from his father once they had reached the paddock. Rohan distracted Chay by asking what treatment they would give the injured horse, and they led Joscenel away. Sorin submitted to his mother's inspection of his back and shoulder, wincing as she cleaned the scrapes with fresh water brought by a groom. As Tobin worked, Sioned glanced at Ostvel. He nodded and led the unwilling Pol off to help Riyan get ready for the next race.

"Sorin," she said at last, "tell me exactly what happened from your point of view."

He was seated on an overturned bucket as his mother dressed his wounds. He regarded Sioned thoughtfully, blue eyes narrowing beneath the untidy shock of brown hair. After a moment he nodded. "*My* point of view means you had one as well. I should've guessed. It was a clean ride until we got out of the wood on the way back. All at once flames shot up in front of me. Joscenel was startled and slammed into Masul's horse. That's when he got me with his whip."

"Andry," Tobin said through gritted teeth, "make a bandage from what's left of Sorin's shirt."

Red and white silk ripped as Sorin went on, "Masul went around the Fire, but I had to jump right over it. The bastard maneuvered me right into it. That's how Joscenel was burned. Then I just kept riding—and lost, damn it to all hells!"

"It could have been your life you lost," Maarken said.

Then, with an effort at easing the grimness, he added, "Or your looks, if he'd laid your face open with that whip."

"Fire," Andry murmured, holding the makeshift bandage to his twin's shoulder while Tobin tied it. "Sunrunner's Fire?"

Sioned nodded. "That's why I asked if you or Maarken had been watching. I felt someone else. If it wasn't either of you—"

Tobin looked up, her voice dangerously soft. "Do you mean a *faradhi*, one of our own, is responsible for this?"

Andry held Sioned's gaze as he answered his mother. "We aren't the only ones who can call Fire. It you don't need me, Mother, then I'd better go tell Andrade about this."

"I'll go with you," Maarken said. "Sorin, not a word to anyone."

He nodded unhappily. "But you'd better explain this to me, Andry."

"I'm just glad you're still here to explain it to," his twin replied, and left with Maarken.

"And just what is it that needs explaining—and to *me*, I might add?" Tobin demanded.

"Whatever it is," Sorin said as he got to his feet, "we can't talk about it now. Look." He nodded to the new arrivals in the paddocks: Lyell, Kiele, and Masul, the latter leading his exhausted stallion. "If Father safely occupied?"

"Yes. And I'm leaving," Tobin said. "Sioned, deal with them. I don't trust myself." She turned on her heel and stalked off, a deliberate snub to those now approaching.

"Follow my lead," Sioned whispered, and Sorin frowned. "I mean it. You already know they're dangerous. Let me handle this."

Kiele got to them first, polite concern the thinnest of masks over her triumphant excitement. "Your grace—my lord, what a relief to find you unhurt! How is your horse?"

"Recovering," Sioned observed, "as that one obviously needs to do. Lord Lyell, should you not be seeing to the comfort of your horse?"

"How did you know he's mine?" Lyell asked, then tacked on a hasty, "—your grace."

"Your colors edge his saddle blanket—and this young man can hardly possess the funds to purchase such an animal." Nor does he know how to treat his prize, her eyes added as she gestured to the stallion's hanging head, the blood at ribs and mouth.

"An excellent race, my lord," Masul told Sorin with a condescending smile.

Sorin nodded curtly. "Interesting, certainly."

Masul turned to Lyell. "You ought to take the High Princess' suggestion and see to the horse. I'm sure you'll want to go with him, sweet sister."

Kiele's smile was strained around the edges, her eyes hinting at harsh words for Masul later on for commanding them like common servants. But she turned the moment to advantage by saying, "Of course. We'll meet you back at the royal enclosure for the final contests, your grace."

A corner of Sioned's mouth lifted in a mocking smile as Kiele gave Masul the title he did not merit, but she said nothing as Kiele and Lyell led the horse away. Masul was direct about his attack, as she had expected; if nothing else, his lack of subtlety marked him as someone else's son, not Roelstra's.

"I thought you might like to know, Lord Sorin," he said, "that I have no intention of filing a complaint for what happened on the course."

Sioned had been expecting something of the sort. Sorin had not. Thick dark brows slanted down. "A complaint? Against *me?*"

Masul shrugged. "Your reputation as a horseman suggested you could control your mount. I'll have bruises for days after being slammed into like that, and it's a wonder we both weren't thrown. Had it occurred on the track where the judges could have seen it, I would've had no choice but to lodge a formal protest. But since no one else saw. . . ."

Sioned knew how close Masul was to losing several teeth from the temper Sorin had inherited from both volatile parents. She said, "I'm sure Lord Sorin is similarly inclined to generosity, though I would say he'll bear the scar on his shoulder long after your bruises have healed. But I'm pleased to see you young men in agreement. We wouldn't want any difficulties to arise over the race, would we? Such things have a tendency to flare like Sunrunner's Fire."

Masul could not hide his reaction. Green eyes—nearly the color of Roelstra's, she noted now that she was staring directly into them—narrowed and a muscle in his cheek twitched. His voice came from a clenched throat. "I have no experience with *faradhi* matters. No offense meant to yourself, High Princess, but I have no wish to learn about them, either."

"I am neither offended nor surprised. Fire of any kind is dangerous, don't you agree? One so often burns one's fingers." She gave him a small, chill smile. "You have my permission to withdraw."

Masul froze for a heartbeat, then inclined his head an insulting fraction and strode off. Sorin spat into the dirt where he'd stood.

"My sentiments exactly," Sioned murmured. "But he took the hint, which is what I wanted."

"What hint?" Sorin exclaimed. "That slimy son of a—he had the *balls* to accuse me of riding into him on purpose!"

"And did not mention the real source of the incident," Sioned pointed out. "Sorin, I only want to tell this once. Tonight, after the prizes are given, we'll all meet in Andrade's pavilion and talk this out. But for now, say nothing. And smile—there are some pretty girls coming to comfort you."

"The only thing that could comfort me is redoing Masul's face with my fists," he muttered. "His features please me very little."

"Yours seem to be in favor," she told him. "Relax until tonight, Sorin—and if you don't end this afternoon with at least five of those girls in love with you, then you're not your father's son." She winked at him.

He gave a short laugh in spite of himself, and turned his attention to the young ladies—reluctantly at first, then with more enthusiasm as he realized that being a good-looking young lord with a romantically wounded shoulder could be a most entertaining experience.

Chapter Twenty

Andrade's white pavilion filled slowly at irregular intervals that midnight. Sunrunners on casual guard wore thin leather gloves against the autumn crispness in the air, neatly hiding the fact that not all of them were in fact Sunrunners; cloaks in various shades of blue, brown, and black concealed any telltale badges of service to Rohan, Chay, or Pandsala. A careful investigation of a few other tents might have given a good idea of who met with the Lady of Goddess Keep in secret that night. But two things counted against the presence of any prying eyes: the extreme lateness and the lavish banquet that had ended only a short time earlier. No one cared about anything more important than getting to bed and avoiding the headaches sure to attend upon the morning. Ostvel had given strict instructions that the High Prince's guests were never to sit more than an eyeblink with empty winecups.

Rohan arrived first with Pol and Pandsala. All three were still fuming at the manner in which Masul had collected the jewels he'd won in the race—Princemarch's own amethysts, the reason he'd chosen that race to enter, of course. His bow to Rohan had been barely respectful, his grin openly mocking. Though relegated to a lower table with Kiele and Lyell, he had practically held court both before and after the meal. So great was Pandsala's fury that she had eaten nothing. Rohan had hidden his anger better, and Pol had followed his father's example rather than his regent's. Sioned had been the only one to disturb Masul's triumph, for reasons none of them understood; he was seen to jerk back in startlement when, with oncoming dusk, she had risen from her chair to gesture the candles and torches alight. Her smile in his direction had been perfectly poisonous.

Chairs were arranged in Andrade's pavilion around a small brazier where glowing coals kept out the chill midnight air. Urival sat next to Andrade on one side of the circle, Pol between his father and Pandsala opposite. No one spoke. Tobin and Chay arrived with all three of their sons a short time later; Ostvel and Riyan joined the group soon after that. At last Sioned came in with Alasen of Kierst. The girl's hands were folded tightly together and she did not raise her eyes as she was introduced formally around the circle. Andrade looked a question at Sioned and touched her own rings. Sioned nodded confirmation. The Lady of Goddess Keep turned a speculative eye on the young princess, who took the seat beside Sioned and next to Andry.

"Hollis should be here," Sioned commented, her gaze finding Maarken.

The young man flushed. Meeting his parents' puzzled gazes, he drew a deep breath and said, "I ought to have told you before this. I hope to make her an official part of the family in a few days."

Tobin sank back into her chair, stunned. Chay simply gaped. Sioned whispered a request to Andry to go find Hollis, then said, "I'm sorry, Maarken, but I didn't know any other way to include her without its seeming strange to those who didn't know."

"Sioned, my love," Rohan murmured, "you are about as subtle as a dragon spotting an unguarded herd."

Maarken was still watching his parents. "I just couldn't seem to find the right time to tell you. I know you haven't had a chance to get to know her yet, but I'm hoping you'll approve."

Tobin smiled at her eldest. "I was prepared to love whomever you chose, darling—and you've made it wonderfully easy. Although I'll never forgive Sioned for knowing it first!"

"It wasn't me who told her," he explained, beginning to smile. "We had a bet going that she'd guess."

Chay reached around Sorin to grasp Maarken's arm. "If she's as clever as she is beautiful, you're a lucky man. A Sunrunner, too—how many rings is it?"

"Six, like mine."

"Your grandfather Zehava always said he wanted good-looking descendants," Rohan teased. "I think his ambition is safe into the next generation."

Andrade sat quietly, smiling, while the others added their congratulations. Finally she said, "I had nothing to do with it this time, Sioned. As a matter of fact, they managed it in spite of me. Someday you'll have to get them to tell you how it came about."

"My Lady!" Maarken protested automatically, red to his earlobes.

"If you don't, I may tell them myself!" she threatened with a grin and a wink—startling those in the group who had experience only of her more caustic humor, or who had no experience of her at all.

Andry returned to the tent alone and bewildered. "Maarken—I told her she was to come here, and why, and she said—"

"Something self-effacing, I trust," Andrade remarked, but her gaze had sharpened.

Andry shook his head. "She said she couldn't in conscience join us because—because it would be under false pretenses."

Maarken gasped as if someone had hit him in the gut. He shoved back his chair and strode from the tent, leaving a shocked silence behind him.

Rohan had to clear his throat twice before he could say with reasonable calm, "Andry, why would she say such a thing?"

"I don't know. Maybe she's just tired. She hasn't been all that well most of the summer. And it would probably scare me, too, being summoned to a conference like this. After all, none of us is exactly nobody."

"Succinctly if inelegantly put," Andrade said. "Alasen, I trust we do not intimidate you too much? Good. Andry, sit down. There's nothing we can do that Maarken can't do for himself, so we'd best get on with this. Sioned, I assume you're the one with the explanations. You'd better begin them before curiosity kills us."

"Yes, my Lady." Sioned looked around the circle once, then began. "Someone called Fire down onto the course today, threatening Sorin but not Masul. Afterward, Masul approached Sorin and they exchanged words—"

"As they're both alive and intact," Andrade interrupted, "I may assume that the words were at least marginally polite."

"You may. But when I hinted at Sunrunner's Fire, Masul reacted very oddly. He knows as well as Sorin and I what happened. Only I led him to believe it was one of us who had done it.''

Sorin gave a muffled curse. "You wanted him to think the flames had been meant for him, not for me!''

"I thought he might sweat a little. Anything that unbalances him works in our favor.''

"Good thought,'' Rohan said. "But the problem is that *we* know the Fire was meant for Sorin.''

"It rose up right in front of me,'' the young man confirmed. "It was easy for Masul to avoid it.''

Chay leaned forward, elbows on his knees and hands clasped between them. "Do we have another renegade Sunrunner, then, like the one Roelstra corrupted?''

"I doubt it very much,'' Urival replied quietly. "For reasons I will explain shortly. Sioned, did he admit to having seen the Fire at all?''

"Not out loud, no.''

"Then there are three alternatives. First, he didn't expect it but now believes that someone wishes to help him, and doesn't wish to jeopardize that person by admitting he even saw the Fire. Second, he knew in advance and is certain it was meant for Sorin, and doesn't wish to admit that someone with *faradhi* gifts is working for him. The third alternative is suggested by his reaction to your mention of Fire, Sioned. He may believe that a Sunrunner did indeed do this, and will do something even more deadly if he complains of it. Do you think he's honestly frightened of us?''

Sioned frowned, then nodded slowly. "He's extremely wary, at least, of what he believes we're capable of. Sorin, did he look frightened to you?''

"It seemed as if he resents *faradh'im* more than he fears them, although you made him really nervous tonight when you lit the candles.'' He grinned suddenly. "I think Masul's just started to realize that Pol's surrounded by Sunrunners.''

Chay said, "Whichever of Urival's alternatives holds true, he'll be worried about us.''

"*Us?*'' Tobin asked, surprised. "Do you know that's the first time you've ever included yourself with the Sunrunners?''

He shrugged. "I have a wife, two sons, a sister-by-marriage, and a nephew who're all *faradh'im*. My eldest son is about to marry one. We're sitting here with the Lady of Goddess Keep, the whole place is lousy with Sunrunners, and you object to my saying 'us'?''

"How nice to know the Lord of Radzyn finally accepts us," Andrade said dryly. "The question is, how can we turn events to our advantage?"

Rohan looked thoughtful. "If we assume Masul was as surprised as Sorin and doesn't know there's somebody helping him, then it might be possible . . ."

"To do what, Father?" Pol asked.

"To encourage this belief and present him with a somewhat stupefying source of help." He turned to Pandsala. "Could you swallow your hatred long enough to convince him?"

She hesitated, then shook her head. "I've been too vehement. Had this come several days ago, after my talk with Kiele—she and I are agreed that Chiana's humiliation by whatever means would be most satisfying. But after yesterday's encounter with Masul. . . ." She lifted her hands, let them fall back into her lap. "I'm sorry for it, because the idea is an excellent one. But a sudden conversion to his cause would be suspect. If there were others of my sisters who had the gifts, it might be possible. But I cannot even think his name without wanting to spit."

"You're not the only one," Tobin muttered. "Sorin, how's your shoulder?"

"Healing, Mother. Don't worry."

"Well, so much for that idea." Rohan sprawled his legs out in front of him and stared at his boots. "We can discount the assumption about the Fire being meant for Masul, because we know this to be untrue. We have to work with what *we* believe to be the truth, which is either that he didn't know and welcomes the help, or that he knows very well indeed." He paused, then slowly lifted his gaze to Urival. "I'd be interested to hear your reasons now, my lord, for thinking that there is no Sunrunner corrupted to causes other than our own."

Urival's golden-brown eyes darkened, the angles of his face like rough-hewn stone. He looked around the circle as Sioned had done, but not to collect their attention. He judged each face in turn, from the prior knowledge in some to the frank bewilderment in others. At last he spoke, having satisfied some inner criteria for each person present.

"I suspect none of the *faradh'im.* I trained them all; I know them. The person I suspect is an unknown, and adheres to the old ways of sorcery, which the Sunrunners left Dorval to oppose. It is a shock, but not really a surprise, to know that some of the descendants of those sorcerers still exist."

"But they work with starlight, not the sun," Andry protested. "What went on today happened in broad daylight!"

Ostvel's gaze was focused on the glowing brazier, his gray eyes lit almost to rubies by the coals. "My late wife was from the Fironese mountains, as her dark coloring made obvious. The legends of sorcerers were more than legends where she grew up. There were two kinds of gifts—one kind we see in the *faradh'im,* and the other very similar but of a different emphasis. They could use sunlight if they chose, but preferred the stars, believing that power more potent and moonless nights the best time to work. Camigwen always thought that the reason Sunrunners were forbidden the starlight was because these others had used it. The ancient *faradh'im* did not wish to be mistaken for their enemies."

Sioned murmured, "She told me some of the tales when we were very young. I never believed them."

Andrade's fingers beat a slow rhythm on the arm of her chair, her jeweled rings catching the light in a rainbow of colors. "The prohibition regarding use of the stars is as adamant as that regarding use of the gifts to kill."

Ostvel's gaze now lifted to Sioned across the circle. "Yet it cannot be intrinsically evil to weave light from the stars. Sioned has done it—the night Rohan battled Roelstra in single combat. Others were caught up in it— Princess Tobin, the regent, Urival, Lady Andrade herself. No one could suspect any of you of being sorcerers. So it must have been forbidden simply because the old ones did it. What could be evil about starlight, except in the way one uses it?" He paused a moment, then bowed to Andrade. "Forgive me for presuming to interpret *faradhi* matters, my Lady."

"Presuming?" She snorted. "You are as much one of us as if you wore the rings."

"Thank you. Then I will further say that because Sunrunners can use starlight, as Sioned proved, Andry is mistaken in his assumption that it is the only sort of light with which these sorcerers work. They may prefer it, but. . . ." He shrugged. "All this leads to a conclusion I don't think any of you will like. There is no reason to assume that these people cannot call Fire or use the light of sun or moons. Therefore there is no reason to assume they cannot become *faradh'im.*"

Urival's spine became a swordblade. "Are you telling me I might have trained the descendants of our enemies?"

"You have undoubtedly trained people, my lord, who aren't aware of the real source of their gifts. The power is the same. The uses are not." He turned to Andrade. "Is there any way to tell the two apart?"

Andry was the one who answered. "I haven't got all the scrolls translated yet, my lord. It may be that there are clues within—"

"Scrolls?" Alasen instantly blushed and shrank back into her chair, having startled herself with her one-word question. "Forgive me, I'm sorry—"

Andry smiled kindly. "No, I'm the one who ought to apologize. I forgot that not everybody here knows about them. They're histories, mainly, of how the ancient Sunrunners left Dorval to oppose the sorcerers on the continent." He turned to Ostvel. "Did Lady Camigwen ever say anything about the old language?"

"Not that I recall. Dialects vary widely in the remote mountains, you know."

The young *faradhi* sat forward eagerly. "That's where the scrolls say the sorcerers fled after they were defeated!"

"And so every person with the gifts who comes from the mountains is probably of the Old Blood? Bah!" Urival flung up his hands. "I'll have you know that my grandsire was born at the highland source of the Ussh

THE STAR SCROLL 379

River, and his fathers before him back as far as anyone knew. Does that make me a sorcerer?''

"No, my lord," Ostvel said calmly. "But it might make you part of the remnants of their blood.''

Pandsala said, "My mother was from a place called only The Mountain."

Sioned's eyes met Rohan's for an instant before she said, "This is all speculation, Ostvel. Interesting, I'll grant, but what has it to do with our present circumstances?''

"I think it has a lot to do with them, Sioned," Tobin interjected, having understood the look that had passed between the pair. Pandsala's mother was Pol's grandmother; if she had been of the Old Blood, then so was he. "If all this is true, then there could be descendants of sorcerers who aren't about to be commanded by their ancient enemies. And we would never know who they were, because their skills would be exactly the same as ours.''

Riyan had been chewing his lip this whole time. At last he burst out, "Father—is that what my mother was? Is that what *I* am?''

"You and she are proof of the nature of the gifts," Ostvel said firmly. "Rohan, you hold the same kind of power Roelstra did. Is it power that produces evil, or the man?''

"We know the answer to that," Andrade snapped. "Not to spare your feelings Pandsala, but Roelstra would have been a tyrant in a pig-wallow."

"My feelings about my father are roughly comparable to yours, my Lady," the regent reminded her. "I believe Lord Ostvel's comparison to be valid. Certainly I would prefer it to be so, if my mother was indeed of the Old Blood. But there may be a way to tell the two apart. There is no hint of Sunrunners in Roelstra's line. Yet I have become a Sunrunner. You yourself theorized, my Lady, that the gifts must come from my mother. And I am different from other *faradh'im*. I can cross water without difficulty.''

Sioned was amazed by Pandsala's courage in pointing this out. It was tantamount to admitting she came of a line of sorcerers. "So," she heard herself say, "we have only to conduct that test?"

"Perhaps," Pandsala said softly. "It might be useful. But if Lord Riyan is also of the Old Blood, and he has the usual problems crossing water, the test may not be valid."

"I get sick," the young man told her, "but not very. Does that mean anything?"

"Who can say?" Urival shrugged. "But word of this goes nowhere," he added in warning. "All we lack is some fanatic demanding proof of pure *faradhi* blood through a test! And it wouldn't signify, anyway, because whoever's clever enough to have learned Sunrunner arts would be smart enough to fake the usual reaction. So that leaves us nowhere."

Andry cleared his throat. "Every piece of knowledge helps, my lord," he said in quiet tones.

Riyan was still looking troubled, but not, Sioned thought, because of his possible ancestry. "What is it, Riyan?" she encouraged.

"My lady . . . I think it's likely that this person is among us, someone we wouldn't begin to suspect. If they gave one of their own to be Roelstra's wife, then isn't it possible that they wanted a son born of the marriage to become High Prince? That way, they could come out of hiding and openly challenge the *faradh'im.*"

Sioned tried not to, but could not keep from glancing at Andrade—who had wanted *faradhi* princes born of herself and Rohan. *Are we so different from them after all?* her eyes asked Andrade, who looked away.

Urival said, "And failing this, Masul is an opportunity to break the power of the present High Prince, who is so closely tied to us." He looked down at his nine rings. "I wonder if Roelstra ever know."

Shifting slightly in his chair, Rohan said to Alasen, "You were going to tell us what you observed this afternoon, my lady."

"Yes, your grace," she said promptly. "Those with Masul after the race were Kiele and Lyell, Prince Miyon, Prince Cabar, and Cabar's wife Kenza. Prince Velden joined him a little later, as did Lord Patwin—who addressed him as 'brother' on behalf of his late wife, Lady

Rabia. Prince Saumer watched from nearby, looking as if he'd swallowed a vat of bad wine. Prince Clutha's heir Halian was just as unhappy, but he was staring mostly at Chiana.'' Alasen gave a faint smile. ''*She* was hanging onto Miyon and didn't realize until too late where he was going. Masul gave her the nastiest smile and said he'd be pleased to share the prize with her, as he wished to be known as a prince who saw to the dowering of his common folk. I thought she'd tear his throat out.''

''I can imagine,'' Ostvel said dryly. ''The lady is in a rather awkward position. I must say I'm enjoying it.''

''So is Kiele,'' Sioned pointed out. ''And that worries me.''

Rohan got to his feet and began to pace as if he could no longer sit still. ''What have we got, then? Patwin following his overlord Velden by going over to the pretender. Saumer jumping any which way. Halian may be able to influence his father if he wants Chiana badly enough—Clutha wouldn't marry his son to a servant's daughter. But I'm not going to count on it. Thank you for your work, Princess Alasen. You've been very helpful.

''But we still have the matter of this unknown who's helping Masul. He was raised in the Veresch, so he may know all about this and be playing ignorant to protect the source of his aid. We have proof that sorcerers exist—the attack on Meath as he carried the scrolls to Goddess Keep, the scrolls themselves, certain other incidents—yet we have no idea who or where these people are. All in all, it's quite lovely, isn't it?''

He rubbed the back of his neck and sighed. ''Andrade, I need to discuss something with you in private. I thank the rest of you for meeting me here. You may go to your beds—and start watching for anyone who might be our culprit.''

* * *

Maarken stood outside Hollis' tent, irresolute for one of the few times in his life. A brisk wind made his silk shirt a sheath of ice, but his trembling came from much deeper inside. As he stood there shivering he gradually realized that no amount of waiting would settle the chaos of his feelings. Only Hollis could do that by explaining herself.

There was a single lamp lit within, turning the tent into a large white lantern. He could see her shadow on the fabric wall: shoulders rounded, head bent, pacing like a caged animal. He pushed aside the tent flap and went in.

"Hollis—" Her name caught in his throat as she swung around to face him. "Hollis," he said again, his voice thick. "Tell me why. Tell me what's changed."

Terror and tears filled her eyes. She shook her head, long bright hair undone down her back.

Maarken tried again. "I told my parents tonight. They're waiting to welcome you. When Andry told me what you'd said—"

"I've shamed you," she whispered. "Maarken, I'm sorry, I never meant : . ."

"Then what *did* you mean? You haven't spoken to me, you haven't tried to see me, you haven't even *looked* at me! Not even now, when your eyes are right on me!" He heard his voice roughen with emotion, saw her flinch. "Hollis, *look* at me!"

She faced him, her eyes incandescent with fury. "You have others to look at you—I heard what Prince Pol said about Lady Chiana in your tent! Go feast your eyes on *her!*"

"Chiana? Oh, Goddess! She came unbidden and unwanted, Hollis—you can't possibly be jealous of her!"

"Doubtless with her royal lineage you're working so hard to uphold, she's better suited to your royal self than I!"

He took the three steps that separated them and grasped her shoulders. "You're going to talk to me. Do you understand? Tell me why, Hollis. Now!"

"Let me go! Damn you, Maarken, if you don't get your hands off me—"

He stopped her words by taking her mouth. She struggled frantically in his arms like a wild, frightened thing. Then, with a low sobbing moan, she clung to him and her lips parted to his kisses. Rage melted from him, along with the terrible ice in his heart. Maarken lifted her and carried her to a cot in the corner. Her hands fumbled at his clothing and he chuckled against her mouth, amused by her awkwardness and haste.

"Can this be the woman who came to me in the guise of the Goddess to make a man of me?" he whispered teasingly. "Have you forgotten everything you ever learned, my clumsy Sunrunner?"

"Do something with your mouth other than talk," she ordered, becoming the Hollis he knew so well. He laughed again and obeyed.

It was the change in the shadows that warned him, a blurring of his image on the tent wall as he sat up to remove his shirt. His head turned and he saw a candle held in the shaking hand of the black-haired boy. A small voice observed wryly in his head that he ought to be getting used to having private moments with beautiful women interrupted by children.

"I—forgive me, I'm sorry, I didn't know you weren't alone, my lady—" The youth was holding a steaming cup of taze in his other hand, and the violence of his trembling put him in danger of spilling the hot liquid. "I only thought you might like some more—I didn't know—"

Hollis sat up and pulled her clothes together. "Thank you, Sejast," she said with admirable calm. "That was very thoughtful of you."

"Leave it and go," Maarken added, and the boy nearly dropped cup and candle both in his haste to obey.

"I'm sorry my lord, my lady—"

"Forgiven," Hollis said kindly, and he gulped. But as Maarken put an arm around her, something flickered in the boy's eyes, something older than his years and very dangerous. "It's all right, Sejast," she said, and he fled.

Maarken felt her draw away from him, watched her do up her bodice with a finality that made his heart plummet. The mood had been broken and there was little hope of salvaging it. He had an intense urge to throttle that stupid child, but instead rose from the cot and brought Hollis the cup.

She sipped and met his gaze over the rim. "He makes a special brew and brings it to me every night about this time. I was just finishing the first cup when you arrived. It helps when I'm tired."

"I suppose I ought to be grateful for his care of you.

Andry tells me he's become your shadow. But I must say I admire his taste more than his timing.''

''He's just a sweet boy who thinks he's in love with me. Affection isn't so plentiful in this life that any of us can afford to reject it when it's offered, whatever its source. Besides, I don't want to hurt him, Maarken. He'll grow out of it.''

''He'd better hurry up about it.''

''Oh, stop being so silly.'' She gave him the cup as a gesture of peace.

He took a long swallow that burned his tongue, then another, and handed it back to her. ''I should return to Andrade. Unless you want me to stay.'' *Please want me to stay,* his eyes told her.

She was staring into the empty cup. ''No, you're right. You ought to go back.'' She paused, drawing a long breath. ''I didn't mean to upset you. It's just—I don't know any of them and they don't know me. There's so much power in your family, so many different *kinds* of power. Can you understand that it's difficult for me to see myself becoming part of them?''

''All they need is a chance to know you, and they'll love you as I do.''

''Please don't push me,'' she whispered helplessly, still not looking at him.

He wanted to take her face in his hands and force her to *see* him. ''Very well. But we belong to each other, Hollis. We Chose each other.'' He pressed a kiss to the crown of her head and left her.

He did not return to the white pavilion. He strode down to the river and sat on a large rock, gazing blindly into the dark water, his body clamoring plaintively for Hollis' body, his head aching as if he'd swallowed two bottles of wine rather than half a cup of harmless taze.

* * *

When everyone had left the white tent, even Sioned, Rohan finally sat down again. The tension of the day had exhausted him, wound his muscles into knots, throbbed through his veins. And if he was tired, Andrade looked haggard. The brazier's glow highlighted the deep crevices around her mouth and across her forehead. She had

shaped so many lives, influenced so many destinies—
including his own. She had brought him Sioned.

Urival sat beside her, golden-brown eyes nearly the
color of mud beneath the heavy shadows of his brows.
Both *faradh'im* looked terribly old.

"Sioned can conjure pieces of the future in Fire," Rohan said abruptly. "Could you conjure up the past?"

The breath left Andrade in a rush and Urival's eyes
turned black. Her fingers groped toward his and clung
tightly. Rohan wondered very suddenly why he had never
before realized that the pair were lovers, and had been
for more than the length of Rohan's life.

"I've often wondered if you picked up that little trick
from me, or learned it on your own," Andrade remarked
at last, her voice as cool as ever. "Never smear it with
honey when you can shove it down their throats, eh?"

"We're all tired." Rohan folded his arms to hide the
trembling of his hands. "None of us has time to scrape
off any sugar-coating. Can you or can't you?"

"To quote your son—I don't know. I've never tried."
She let go of Urival's hand and laced her long fingers
together. "I assume it's a particular night you wish seen
in the Fire."

"Andrade—" Urival began, but her lids had already
drooped over her blue eyes and the coals in the brazier
flared in response to her silent call.

Rohan held his breath. She brought her folded hands
to her lips and squeezed her eyes shut, face drawn into a
taut mask, proud bones stark beneath aging skin. Fire
leaped up in the bronze cauldron, wavered, steadied,
jumped toward the ceiling. Hazy pictures began to form
in the flames.

Lanterns were lit on Roelsra's barge, swaying gently in
the night with the motion of the river. Sailors milled
about nervously on deck. There was a narrow staircase,
a tiny, dim room where three women writhed and shuddered in their labors, watched over by Princess Pandsala.
The scene abruptly shifted, and women clustered in a
paneled corridor. Andrade's ringed hand pounded without sound against a closed door. And that door opened.

The Fire blazed wildly and died with a sound like a
sword hissing back into its sheath. Andrade gasped, her

forehead slick with sweat, and sagged against Urival. He held her close, glaring in fury at Rohan.

"Satisfied?" he spat.

Rohan knelt before his aunt, taking one of her hands, frightened by her sketchy breathing. "Andrade—I'm sorry—"

"No," she whispered hoarsely. "Be still." She sucked in a huge lungful of air, then another, and straightened. "I'm only winded. Now I know why such things are forbidden." She held out her free hand and watched it quiver, bemused. "Sweet Goddess. That's never happened to me before. It felt like falling into an endless well, into the dark—" She broke off and tossed her head to clear sweat from her eyes. "It's possible. I might be able to do it."

Urival gave a lurid curse. "You'll do no such thing because he's not going to ask it of you! Don't be a fool!"

She ignored him. "Did you see anything useful, Rohan?"

"The barge, the room belowdecks, a few women in a hallway, your hand knocking on a door. That's all."

"I didn't take it far enough," she fretted.

"Any more and you would have fainted—at the very least!" Urival rasped. "Are you out of your mind?"

"No more than usual. Peace, my old friend. Rohan, I'll do as you wish if it becomes necessary. When would you like to schedule my performance?"

"If you think you can manage it, in two days' time. But—"

"But nothing. Only—you won't be able to get the same from Pandsala. It took everything I had just to get the little you saw. She's not up to it either in talent or training." Her hand tightened around his. "Try everything else first. I'll do this if I must, for Pol. But only if I must."

"Only if there's nothing else I can do," he promised. "You scared me half to death."

"It wasn't exactly a pleasure for me, either," she responded with the old acerbity. "Go on, get to bed."

Rohan pressed her fingers to his cheek, then to his lips. "Forgive me, Aunt," he said. She smoothed back his hair almost tenderly, one of the few gestures of affection she had ever given him. It brought a lump to his throat. Before he could embarrass them both, he rose and left the tent.

Just as the white silk fell closed behind him, he heard Andrade say, "Urival—bring me the Star Scroll."

Rohan walked very slowly back to his own pavilion. He had what he wanted. And it terrified him.

Chapter Twenty-one

At Pol's age, being bored was bad enough. But when combined with the certainty that strange things were brewing, important things that concerned him but that no one bothered to tell him about, boredom became a grim determination to *do* something. Almost anything.

His Aunt Tobin always gave a breakfast party on the fourth morning of the *Rialla*. Absolutely everyone was there, feeding like half-starved dragons. Pol wandered from group to group spread out between tents in the new sunshine, sulkily chewing on a biscuit stuffed with sausage and fruit preserves. All the princes and *athr'im* and ladies and squires bowed when he passed, but they were caught up in their own converstional pursuits. They were, in fact, ignoring him. Even his own family was too busy to do more than smile in his direction. His father was in deep consultation with Lleyn and Chadric; his mother chatted with Miyon while Tobin gradually maneuvered Chiana over to them and left her there; Chay and Sorin talked horses with Lord Kolya; Andry stood tongue-tied and grave near Volog and Alasen of Kierst; and Maarken hurried back and forth from the trestle tables to where Hollis sat with Andrade and that intense black-haired youth, trying to find delicacies to tempt her appetite. Pol looked on them all with a sense of betrayal. He wasn't stupid, he wouldn't have blurted out any secrets, and he would be High Prince one day—and yet none of them had thought to include him in the great doings and schemes hatching around him like dragon eggs. He would

even have welcomed Sionell's irritating company right
now; at least she paid him some attention.

He strayed over to where Ostvel crouched before the
central firepit, where still more food was being cooked.
Lord of Skybowl though he was, still he took upon himself his old duties of chief steward of Stronghold while
at the *Rialla*, and swore softly as he built up the fire.
New wood had been stacked to replenish the flames, but
the logs were slow in lighting. Pol had a sudden, perverse
idea, and gestured casually with one hand. Flames surged
up, immolating the wood and startling Ostvel into another curse.

Pol suddenly knew that people were staring; some even
backed away from him, wide-eyed. He gave everyone his
sunniest smile. Let them ignore *that*, he told himself.

"Does that help any?" Pol asked Ostvel in his most
innocent tones.

The Lord of Skybowl rose, scowling at him. "Don't
you ever dare do that again," he said through gritted
teeth.

Any pleasure in his trick evaporated. Ostvel had never
used that tone of voice to him in his life, let alone looked
at him with such dark disapproval. Pol tried to shrug off
his discomfort, and turned to go back to the main party.
But whispers had run through the gathering, and now
everyone was looking at him—including his parents,
whose eyes shone cold green and even icier blue.
Abruptly Pol was the cynosure of all attention, and he
felt his cheeks grow hot as first his father and then his
mother turned away.

But then he happened to see Masul, over by a tree with
Kiele and Lyell and Cabar of Gilad. The pretender's complexion had gone as white as Pol's was now crimson. The
boy slid his gaze around the rest of the assembly as people resumed their former conversations or, more likely,
spoke of him in hushed tones. The stinging blush faded
from his cheeks and he realized that whatever his parents
might think, he had succeeded in reminding Masul that
it was more than a prince he challenged; it was a Sunrunner.

Pandsala came over to him then, and for the first time
he felt a glimmer of real liking for her as she rescued

him from solitude and silence. She talked quietly about the weather, and gradually Pol relaxed. Then she led him over to where Gemma stood beside old Prince Chale, who was barely tolerating the presence of Pol's cousins Kostas and Tilal. The latter grinned at him while Chale said something conventional about the excellence of the meal. Then, with a bow to Gemma, Tilal took Pol's arm and coaxed him off for a private talk.

"Not the wisest thing you ever did, cousin," the young man told him. "But I don't think your mother will complain too much."

"Did you see Masul's face?"

"No, I was watching Clutha." Tilal snatched up a pastry from a tray borne by a passing servant, and munched on the tidbit as he went on, "He's got an easy face to read, you know. Riyan tells me Halian's been after Clutha to commit to your side, because he wants to marry Chiana—Goddess help him! But the old man's balking. I think what you just did was remind him what manner of prince you're going to be. If Masul gets hold of Princemarch, Meadowlord's right in the middle again. And the last thing Clutha wants is to provide your battleground—especially with a Sunrunner prince on one side of him!"

Pol sighed softly in relief. "Thanks. I'll use that information when Mother and Father start yelling at me."

"Oh, they'll have forgotten all about it by this afternoon."

"Only if I disappear for a while. Listen, do you want to go over to the Fair? I have a couple of things I have to check on. Do you have time?"

"Ask permission first. I don't know if my sword is enough in their eyes to protect you."

"I'm sick of asking permission, and I'm sick of not being told anything!"

Tilal grinned again, and it was impossible to sustain resentment in the vicinity of those merry green eyes.

"I sound like a spoiled brat, don't I?" Pol asked diffidently.

"You sound like every boy who's coming up fast on being a man. You should've heard *me* until I really got to govern River Run. I'll meet you outside my tent after this party breaks up, all right? I'll go ask your parents right now for permission—that way you won't have to go near them until this afternoon, if you're lucky.''

Pol nodded grateful thanks. He found a convenient tree and leaned against it, watching the highborns and thinking how fond he was of Tilal. He had known his mother's nephew since birth, when the young man had been Rohan's squire. Tilal had been knighted during the celebrations of Pol's eighth birthday, and giving Tilal the traditional loaf, salt, and gold belt buckle was one of the best memories of Pol's childhood. Tilal had left Stronghold that next spring to live with his parents at High Kirat, the Syrene seat, and a year later had taken possession of the combined holdings of River Run and River View. The former was his birthplace, and Davvi and Sioned's as well; the latter had become part of River Run through Davvi's marriage to its heiress. Thus Tilal ruled a considerable stretch of land along the Catha River, some of the best farming and grazing country in the princedoms.

At the Syrene enclave, Tilal's pennant of green and black fluttered above his small turquoise tent. A squire younger than Pol bowed nearly to the ground on seeing him. Tilal, emerging from the tent with a large leather purse jingling in his hand, smiled a greeting and waved the squire away.

"I think Aunt Sioned is glad to give you something to do today," he confided. "She's not all that pleased with you, but I don't think there'll be any punishment. All her time and imagination are busy elsewhere." He tied the purse to his belt, checked his sword, and said, "All right then, we're off. If we hurry we can get to the Fair before the crowds."

"But I'll bet the girls still follow you, all the way over there," Pol teased. "I was watching at breakfast this morning, before you and Kostas started talking with Chale.''

"Oh, most of the girls will be staying here today, planning their finery for the next few days. I'll let the other men have a chance," Tilal replied, a breezy note in his voice, his eyes self-mocking. "There's a Cunaxan vendor Kostas told me about yesterday who makes the most amazing swords. I want to get one for my father."

"Do you think Sorin and Riyan would like something from him?" Pol asked as they walked. "I want to get them each a present, and I brought a lot of money. Oh, and I have to stop by a certain silk merchant's, and I need the best Fironese crystaller."

The Cunaxan proved to be a true artist. The sword Tilal purchased from him was a marvel of gleaming steel decorated with engravings of apple trees heavy with fruit. He etched Syr's emblem while the cousins watched. The grip was adjusted to Tilal's specifications to make it comfortable for his father, and while Pol selected two fine knives for Sorin and Riyan in celebration of their knighthood, Tilal produced a handful of small garnets to be set in spaces left by the crafter for the purpose.

The work took a long time, but the result was magnificent. Noon sun slid down the long blade and smoldered in the dark jewels, found its echo in the gold-chased hilt. Tilal wrapped the sword carefully in a length of softest wool, paid for his prize, and sighed happily as they walked away from the booth.

"Were those the garnets you won in the race?" Pol asked. "Aren't you going to have the rest of them set into a necklet?"

"Perhaps."

The boy eyed his cousin sidelong. "Oh. I see. No lady has struck your fancy to make a bridal necklet for."

To his astonishment, Tilal's jaw hardened and his eyes were fierce as he said, "Prince you may be, but that's none of your business."

Pol nearly stumbled over his own feet. It seemed to be his day for provoking furious looks from family and friends; he kept his mouth shut as they searched the aisles of booths and finally stopped before a collection of crystal that seemed blown of soap bubbles, all soft pink and green and blue iridescence in the sun.

Tilal relented, becoming once again the cousin and good companion. "Who's this for? Your mother?"

"No. Another lady." Pol laughed as Tilal's black brows shot up in surprise. "As everybody keeps telling me, I'm too young for *that* yet! I broke a glass belonging to an innkeeper's wife in Dorval, and I need to replace it." He pointed to a fragile goblet in the shape of a fantastical yellow flower, footed in green leaves and rising on a stem where tiny crystal pearls imitated dewdrops. "I think I'd like that one, please."

"A wise and brilliant choice, exalted lord," the merchant enthused.

"How're you going to get it all the way back to Graypearl in one piece?" Tilal asked.

The merchant snorted. "I'll wrap it so fine and safe that the worst winter storms couldn't even make it tremble. A moment only, most gracious lord."

When the wooden case was readied—twice the size of the goblet and packed with lamb's wool—Pol asked that it be sent on to his father's pavilion. On realizing who his customer was, the merchant blanched, abased himself, and with reckless speed snatched up another goblet and presented it to Pol. This one was a gorgeous creation of purple glass shading into blue at the rim, darkening down the stem to a foot of opaque black. The whole of it was supported by three thin wires of gold that swirled up and around to circle the rim.

"My prince," the merchant said humbly, and bowed again.

Pol blushed, and wondered if his complexion would learn to behave itself with age. "I really can't—"

"Please," the Fironese said. "I speak for my guild and for all my people when I say that we eagerly anticipate coming under the benevolent governance of so noble and powerful a prince."

"That's very kind of you, but—"

"Please, your grace." The man's dark eyes met his, and Pol remembered Lady Eneida's fears of being invaded by Miyon of Cunaxa. It seemed the Fironese really wanted him as their prince. He'd have to tell his father that.

"I accept, with great thanks," Pol said. The goblet was wrapped and added to the first one, to be sent along with it to the High Prince's pavilion.

"Well, well," Tilal murmured as they left the Fironese.

"I can't help it," Pol replied, shrugging. "They're determined to give us their princedom. Better us than the

Cunaxans.'' He stopped abruptly, aware that Tilal had a claim to Firon, too.

His cousin was grinning at him. "Better you than me!''

"Really? You don't want it?''

Tilal gave an exaggerated shudder. "Me, up there in all that snow? Do you want to kill me off?''

"It doesn't snow *all* the time,'' Pol reminded him.

"It snows enough. I don't want Firon, Pol. I've told my father so. It's too far from—from everything.''

What Firon was too far from had been amended, but Pol didn't press for a correction. "Well, if that's how you feel about it . . . but I don't know too many men who'd turn up their noses at a princedom. Come on, let's get something to eat and then visit the hawks. Mother says she bought me one, and I haven't had the chance to see him yet.''

They selected various snacks and ate as they walked up the hill to the wood. Pol wanted to explore—out from under the stern eyes of Maarken and Ostvel—and so before turning for the caged and hooded birds, the pair slid through the trees and underbrush. Tilal made a game of it, teaching Pol some of the tricks necessary for hunting in a forest, which this son of the open Desert had yet to learn.

"You'll have to come to River Run some autumn and I'll show you what *real* hunting is,'' Tilal chuckled after Pol had stepped on yet another twig, its loud crack startling him.

"My lord Chadric lets us come with him sometimes, but it's always on horseback, hunting deer. Show me again how to walk without any noise.''

Tilal obliged, and Pol imitated him with growing skill. Each foot was placed softly, carefully; every muscle in the body controlled; all senses aware of scents and textures and breezes and sounds—

"Come any closer and I'll scream,'' a woman said quietly.

Tilal grabbed Pol's elbow and they both froze. The voice had come from beyond a stand of berry brambles, its owner invisible and unknown to Pol—but the tense anger on Tilal's face revealed that he knew the woman's identity.

"I mean it, Kostas! I'll scream and bring everyone running to witness this shameful—"

"No, Gemma. You won't scream. Above the noise of the hawks and the noise of the Fair, who would hear you? Besides, I mean you no harm, my lady. Only come to me, be with me—"

"No!"

Tilal's fingers put bruises onto Pol's arm to stop the boy's intended rush into the woods. "No," he breathed. "Wait."

"But he's going to—"

"Not even Kostas would do that."

Pol considered. Rape was a heinous crime. If found guilty, the accused man was deprived of the physical equipment that would enable him to repeat the offense. If the woman made a false accusation, however, her dowry was forfeit to the man and her overlord had to pay a hefty fine for her lies. Kostas and Gemma both knew the law; neither would be so foolish as to risk rape or an accusation of it.

Gemma was stating this very fact to Kostas as Pol and Tilal listened. "I'm sure you eventually want children! But be assured, my lord, that they will not come from me!"

"If you accuse me I can prove my innocence—and then you would lose Ossetia, for that's your dowry. I would be Prince of Ossetia with or without you, my lady. I would much rather it be with you at my side, in honor."

"Honor!" she spat. "And how would you prove your innocence? What makes you think my uncle Prince Chale would even let it come to trial? I have only to accuse you, and he'll kill you!"

"With *my* uncle High Prince Rohan standing by? I think not, my lady. There are four witnesses of impeccable repute ready to swear I was with them all day. Come, Gemma," he said, his voice softening. "Stop this nonsense. We have always been intended for each other, even before you became Chale's heir. Accept me, and I'll make you happy, I swear it, and be a good and wise prince for both our lands—"

By now Tilal's hand was white around the wrapped sword. He had heard enough. He let go of Pol and slipped through an opening in the bushes. Pol followed, trembling with fury, and stood watching as the brothers confronted each other in the little glade.

"Four witnesses more impeccable than your own brother and the High Prince's son?" His voice was a swordthrust into Kostas' spine; the elder brother whirled, rage blazing in his eyes. "How dare you?" Tilal hissed. "Damn you, Kostas, leave her alone and before I forget you're my brother!"

Kostas' answer was to unsheathe his sword. Tilal tore at the wrappings of the weapon he'd bought for his father. Gemma had the good sense not to scream; instead she flung herself between the pair, a courageous move that nonetheless irritated Pol. He went forward, grasped her arm, and hauled her out of the way.

"They won't fight, my lady," he told her in a clear voice meant not so much for her as for his cousins. "If they do, everyone in all the princedoms will hear about this from *me*. Put up your weapon, Kostas. *Now*. Tilal, if you untie one more of those knots—"

Enraged, the brothers turned on him with snarls. Pol found that his shaking had retreated deep within his body. His hands and voice were steady, his knees secure. He felt at once powerful and vulnerable: his will and personality battered strongly at their anger, but he was vulnerable to his own strange inner trembling, a warning he could not understand. Did his father ever feel this way? Was this what it was to experience the power of being High Prince?

Power he had, and it was exhilarating as well as frightening. Kostas slammed his sword back into its sheath. Tilal's fighting stance relaxed a fraction. Gemma was the one trembling now, her breath coming in little gasps.

"Do you wish to charge this man with rape, my lady?" Pol asked coldly.

She shook her head, bright auburn hair straggling down her neck and cheeks. "No, your grace. I do not."

"A wise decision, my lady." He eased his grip on her and looked at the brothers. There was nothing more pathetic than two otherwise rational men fighting over the same woman. "You both want her."

Tilal glared at him, then turned away. Kostas looked

as if he would draw his sword again and use it on Pol. The heady feeling of pitting his will against theirs grew—along with an equivalent fear of what might happen if he failed to dominate them.

"Did either of you ask Gemma what *she* wants? Gentle Goddess, what a pair!" Pol snorted. "My lady, do you want either of these fools?"

She freed her hand from his and pushed the hair from her face, pulling herself straight and proud. "The truth, your grace? Yes. And it is not Kostas I want for my husband."

"And Prince of Ossetia," Pol reminded her. "Tilal, are you listening? Face me. Ask her."

"No!" Kostas shouted. "I won't allow it!"

Pol sighed. "Tilal, I'm waiting."

The young Lord of River Run swung around, still furious. "I hope you're enjoying this, your grace!" he said viciously. "Yes, I want her! I've always loved her—but I wouldn't marry her now if—"

Why were supposedly grown men so colossally stupid? "You're about to lose your chance, Tilal. Ask her now or not at all."

Kostas gave an inarticulate bellow and lunged for his brother. The pair rolled on the ground, not even remembering swords and knives, intent on the more direct satisfaction of pummeling fists, broken bones, and smashed jaws.

Pol watched for a moment, thoroughly disgusted. They probably would not do each other any serious damage, being evenly matched physically and too furious to be really effective in their battle. But as Kostas got in a decent kick, Gemma cried out Tilal's name, clinging to Pol's shoulder.

He shook her off and concentrated, calling Fire. Not much—just enough to get their attention. A respectable gout of red-gold flames rose from a stone to the height of the nearest bush. Gemma gave a little choked scream. Tilal and Kostas reacted more violently, breaking apart from each other and scrambling to their feet. The tense knot of power inside Pol uncurled, sending tendrils of excitement through him—still countered by the apprehension. He was beginning to cherish that chill little warning, and to understand it as an essential part of wielding power.

"Now," he said softly, in the way he thought his father would, "shall we behave like civilized people? Good. Tilal, the princess and I are still waiting."

* * *

After Tobin's breakfast party—which had left Sioned satisfied with Chiana's progress in claiming Miyon's attention, if not with her son's little performance—she returned to her pavilion intending to spend a few quiet moments alone in her private quarters. But Andrade and Pandsala had arrived before her.

"Please don't start," Sioned warned as she sank into a deep chair. "Rohan didn't sleep very well last night, which means I didn't either. And I'm trying to think up a really good excuse to avoid blistering Pol's behind for him."

"Oh, that." Andrade waved away the boy's lapse with one hand. "I was impressed by his control, actually. Sioned, we have things to discuss that can't wait."

"I'm sorry, your grace," Pandsala put in quietly.

"Apologize some other time," Andrade interrupted. "Sioned, over the years you've reasoned out most of my plans. But now the time is perfect for the culmination of everything I've worked for—and everything you and Rohan have wanted as well."

Sioned felt herself go rigid with suspicion, and tried to relax. "The two are not necessarily the same," she commented warily.

"Nonsense. We all want the same thing in the end. And there'll never be a better chance for it. You can't consolidate everything under your own banner this year, of course, but the makings of it are right under your nose. Rohan started it himself when he encouraged Kierst and Isel to join in marriage. When Volog and Saumer are dead, that boy—what's his name? Arlis—he'll inherit both princedoms. And he's Pol's kinsman, which makes it perfect. Pol might just as well be ruling Kierst-Isel himself."

Sioned murmured, "Go on."

"As for Ossetia—if we marry off Gemma to Kostas,

then Ossetia and Syr are united as well under Pol's kinsman. What could be better?"

"Is there more?" she asked softly.

"Yes, your grace," Pandsala replied. "There is Firon.
If it becomes part of Princemarch, then the crystal trade
will be yours, as well as another princedom. And there
is Port Adni. Lord Narat has no heir. His holding will
revert to Volog on his death, and become part of Arlis'
wealth. And there is Waes, as well. Once this pretender
is exposed as a fraud, Kiele and Lyell can be dealt with,
and Waes will become Clutha's." She hesitated an instant, then went on determinedly. "I suggest the same
for all the others who support Masul. If they are allowed
to retain their princedoms after opposing Pol's claim, they
will always be enemies and not to be trusted. There are
enough loyal young men within your own family and
those of your allies to provide princes for Cunaxa, Gilad,
Grib, and Fessenden, which look to be the main sources
of opposition."

"Do you agree with this?" Sioned met Andrade's cool
blue eyes.

"I do," she answered, nodding.

"So," she said. "If I understand you correctly, our
goals should be as follows. First, obliterate Firon to our
own profit, no matter what anyone else might say about
it. Second, arrange for a marriage that will combine two
princedoms under my nephew, no matter what the two
young people involved think or feel. Third, oust the Lord
of Waes and his wife for the crime of being mistaken, so
that Clutha may have the city as a present with our good
wishes. Oh—and replace all those others who opposed
us with persons of our own choosing. Are these the general ideas? Am I accurate in my interpretation?"

Pandsala compressed her lips for a moment, then said,
"Yes, your grace."

Andrade frowned slightly, then nodded. "Reluctantly,
yes."

"*Reluctantly!* Sweet Goddess! You, Pandsala, I might
excuse, for you know me little for all that you've been
Pol's regent so many years. But you, Andrade! You've
known Rohan and me since we were children! You can
propose such things?"

"On behalf of the dream we share—yes!"

"We share *nothing!*" She stood, fists clenched, glaring at the two women. "How dare you suggest this! As if Rohan would destroy princes and princedoms to create new ones more to his liking! As if you and we shared a dream!"

Andrade sat forward in her chair, white with fury. "And will you let this go on and on—all the petty rivalries, the threats to Pol? What I dream is a consolidation of *all* princedoms under your son as High Prince!"

"The *Sunrunner* High Prince!"

"And why not? Rohan started it by taking Princemarch and setting up the unification of Kierst and Isel! What was he aiming at, if not what I've outlined to you? When will there be a better time to achieve it all? When Masul is seen as the liar he is, all those who supported him *must* be punished! What cleaner way to rid yourselves of enemies and unite their princedoms under Rohan? Or do you want him to do it in the field, with blood soaking into the lands Pol will rule? Rohan, who long ago put up his sword and swore never to wield it in battle again! You can balk with pretty questions of conscience at this chance to do everything at one stroke?"

Sioned took the few paces that separated them and bent, gripping the arms of Andrade's chair, until their faces were only a breath apart. "His dream and mine is a union of princedoms under laws agreed to by all, enforced not by the sword but by honor and belief that those laws are *better* than the sword! *Your* dream is to arrange the world to your liking, with Rohan as the figurehead!"

"Not him, your grace," Pandsala said clearly. "Pol."

She whirled on the regent. "You'd give him a legacy such as this? Lands seized, holdings absorbed, princedoms smashed together without regard to laws or the people those laws were meant to serve, princes thrown out of their castles—or were you planning to kill them all?"

"And what legacy will come otherwise?" she countered. "Opposition from all corners, princedoms up for sale to the strongest sword!"

"Lands held together by consent!" she snapped. "Not by some unholy patchwork—with a pack of embittered former princes plotting to regain their lands, the Merida multiplied tenfold!''

''Then kill them,'' Pandsala said simply. ''There will be time for laws later, after your rule is consolidated.''

''After my husband has lost the trust of *all* princes!''

''They'll agree with whatever he says, and live by it!''

''You mean they'll live with his sword at their throats! I won't live that way, Pandsala—and that's not the world we're going to leave our son!''

''But you're going to take Firon, aren't you?'' Andrade interposed shrewdly.

Sioned drew back. ''If the Fironese wish it, and if the other princes agree according to law—''

''A nice salve to Rohan's tender conscience! You sound more like him than yourself, Sioned. I taught you to be more practical.''

''You taught me many things, Andrade—some of which I know you wish I'd never learned. But my husband has taught me much more. Yes, we'll take Firon, within the law. Don't you understand? I know you scorn his need to make all of it legal and proper when he could simply grab what he wants and have done with it. But don't you see? What would that make of him, and the laws he helped to write? If he doesn't abide by the law, then who will?''

''I'm trying to show him there's a chance to extend his rule of law from one end of this continent to the other! He can do it all *now*, things that would take the rest of his life to accomplish if he plays the honorable and noble-minded prince! Goddess, why can you not *see?* Zehava had the sword for it, but not the cunning. Rohan—''

''You'd make him into another Roelstra,'' Sioned told her icily. ''If that's what you want, give your support to Masul!''

Andrade pushed herself to her feet, white-faced and trembling with fury. ''You fool! You told me you still wore your rings! I gave you a world wrapped in a silver ribbon, and you—''

''You gave me nothing but the rings I indeed no longer wear—that are like scars around my fingers and my mind!''

Sioned was trembling, too. It was the old battle between them, Sioned's heart-deep commitment to Rohan battling Andrade's adamant demand for obedience. They had thrown the words at each other before, but never this openly, never with Sioned's defiant disobedience confronting Andrade's imperious verdict of betrayal.

"You're like me, Sioned." The Lady's voice scathed like a whiplash. "Your schemes are only variations on my own. Yes, I've known you and Rohan since you were children. I made you what you are, both of you. And I made your son, too, through you."

"You're a spider!" Sioned retorted. "Weaving sunlight and moonlight like a web to trap and poison us all! You want everything to belong to you, because you've never belonged to anything! I'm not yours! Neither is Rohan, and neither is Pol!"

"You're the one who doesn't understand. What can be your goal, if not consolidation of all princedoms under him? As both High Prince and *faradhi,* trained by me—"

"Never."

That was the single word that could break Andrade, in this battle she could only lose. Sioned saw it in her eyes, the sudden shattering of her anger, leaving only a pitiable plea; she saw it, and felt vicious satisfaction.

"I will be the one to teach him," she went on. "Not you. And you'd better hope you made Rohan and me as well as you believe you did, Andrade—for what Pol will be, *we* will make."

"No!" she gasped, betrayed into the cry by panic. "You cannot!" But pride flooded back almost at once, flushing color into her ashen cheeks. She swept from the tent in a furious rush of silk skirts. After a moment, Pandsala followed.

Sioned stood alone, quivering, ashamed to realize that Andrade had been right about one thing: the words were Rohan's, not hers. And she admitted to herself how close she had been to casting aside her husband's honor and agreeing wholeheartedly with Andrade.

All during childhood and youth she had been taught to obey Andrade without thought or question. Rohan had been raised a prince to rule and to give orders, not to obey as Sioned had been taught. It had been so easy, so safe to do as bidden and not ask why. But the power of a High Prince and his Sunrunner Princess necessitated constant questioning. Sometimes Sioned wished she could simply give over the responsibility and obey the orders of others. But she could not. Rohan had shown her that it was impossible.

Tobin had no such scruples. But then, Tobin had nowhere near the power Sioned possessed. Chay evidenced no conflicts. But however high his station, Chay was a vassal of the High Prince, sworn to obey him in all things. Chay had absolute faith in Rohan. He might question, but he trusted totally, and obeyed.

Sioned did not have the luxury of such obedience. Rohan wanted her to agree with him intelligently or not at all. If she nodded placid acquiescence to everything he said no matter what she really thought, he would despise her for a fool. If he ever dictated that he was right and that was that, and she let him, he would hold her in even greater contempt for abrogating the responsibility inherent in the possession of a mind.

She went into the bedchamber area and stretched out, arms folded behind her head. The difficult times came when her mind agreed with Rohan and her feelings could not. The mind educated by over twenty years of ruling according to law—the mind that had always leaned in that direction anyway—had been horrified at Andrade's and Pandsala's proposals. But the feelings for her son, for his safety and his prosperity as High Prince, clamored that the two women were right. Take what was offered, seize the chance to be rid of obstacles like Miyon and Kiele, and leave law to a time when they could afford it.

Sioned could almost see her husband's elegantly arched brows. "How very expedient of us that would be," he would say, and smile—for he knew that whatever her emotions, she would no more give in to the demands of the barbarian than he would.

No one disturbed her for a long while, and it was well after noon before she roused herself. Princess Audrite would be coming by soon to discuss the latest rumors of who was on whose side. And then Rohan would come back from the afternoon meeting, tense and restless as he had been ever since the *Rialla* began. Sioned would not tell him about Andrade and Pandsala. The less he had to worry him, the better.

Going into the main part of the pavilion, she was surprised to see Pol had returned from the Fair. Sioned hadn't the heart to scold him for the offense of the morning, not when he slouched wearily in his chair like this, arms dangling at his sides.

"So you're back," she said. "Have a nice time?"

He looked up at her, his face uncannily like his father's as the dark blond brows lifted. "Oh, yes. Just lovely." The tone of voice was Rohan's, too: sardonic, with a faint edge of bitterness.

"What happened?"

One hand lifted, fell again. "Not now, Mother. Please."

Sioned stared at him, nonplussed. She was spared the necessity of thinking up a reply by the entrance of three young squires with two enormous wooden boxes and a huge package wrapped in fine silk. Pol directed them to set the parcels on a nearby table.

"I presume you're not going to tell me what those are," she said at last.

He glanced up again, as if he was truly seeing her for the first time. A slight smile tugged at the corners of his mouth. "Well, the biggest one's for you," he said.

"My present?" she asked, feeling strange. He no longer looked anything like the little boy he had been at the beginning of the summer. "May I open it?"

"You'll have to, to be sure it fits. You didn't notice being followed the other day when you were at the Fair, did you? The merchant crept along behind you, taking your measurements with his eyes!" Pol laughed, but still the boy made no appearance. "He said today that if it weren't for your red hair to identify you, he never would have guessed whether you or Alasen was the older!"

"Merchants are lying thieves—but do tell me what else he said about me."

Finally the strained expression left Pol's eyes, and he was a boy of nearly fifteen again, not a man twice that age. Sioned laughed with relief as she tore open the silk wrapping. Then she gasped.

"Pol!"

"Don't scold," he pleaded, eyes alight with excitement. "You remember what I told you about the inn below Graypearl? A couple of silk merchants there insisted on rewarding me with enough silk for gowns for you and Aunt Tobin. The red and silver one is hers—they've made clothes for her before, so they already knew the size. The other one—"

Sioned held the gown up, listening to the delicious rustle of richly embroidered green silk. "This is absolutely beautiful—and absolutely scandalous! No lady wears anything fitted so tight and cut so low!"

"Not many ladies *could*," her son pointed out. "But you can."

She eyed him narrowly. "Are you learning your father's ways of sweet-talking me, or did you borrow that from the merchant?"

"Mother! It's only the truth!"

Sioned disappeared behind the partition and hauled off her plain summer gown. "Goddess, I hope it fits!" A few wriggling moments later she emerged and twirled around on her toes. "Well? What do you think?"

Another voice spoke from the doorway. "I think my son has definitely inherited my exquisite taste," Rohan said. He came in and ruffled Pol's hair playfully, smiling. But neither gesture nor smile could disguise the exhaustion and anxiety in his eyes.

"You're back early," Sioned ventured.

"And a good thing, too—if I'd seen that for the first time before the banqueting, you'd have to spend half the night reviving me. Is this your design, Pol?"

"It's like dresses the village girls wear on Dorval. I guess the merchant thought the style would suit Mother."

"I'd say he was right. Although you'll never be able to wear it in daytime at Stronghold, Sioned. With that low front you'd get sunburned instantly."

"Front? Take a look at the back!" She spun around to show him how much of her spine was revealed. "And you can't tell me that any modest village maiden on Dorval wears anything like this!"

"Well, there's more material to their dresses, of course," Pol said, grinning. "But they aren't princesses, either."

Sioned smoothed the silk down her ribs, over the dropped waistline and tightly fitted yoke at the hips. "I won't be able to eat a thing from now until the Lastday banquet or I'll never get back into this," she mourned. "And if I eat that night, I'll pop all the stitches."

She disappeared to take off the gown and fold it into its silk wrappings again. When she rejoined them, Rohan had lowered himself into a chair with his head leaned back, eyes closed. She exchanged a worried glance with Pol.

"Father, is it true that you helped arrange things between Aunt Tobin and Uncle Chay?"

One blue eye opened to regard Pol. "Well, in a manner of speaking."

"And Walvis helped you and Mother?"

"Yes."

Sioned poured cool drinks, asking. "What is all this in aid of?"

"Well . . . I think I've done something similar, in a way." Pol's face was pensive, but there was a telltale gleam dancing in his eyes.

"For whom?" Rohan opened both curious eyes.

"I hope it's all right—there's not much anybody can do about it now, anyway. It just sort of happened today."

"Who are you talking about?" Sioned asked. "We know about Hollis and Maarken, but they're the only ones of our immediate family who're—"

"It's not Hollis and Maarken," Pol said.

"Then *who?*" Rohan demanded.

"Tilal and Gemma." Pol shrugged, keeping an admirably straight face as his parents gaped. "It took a while, but I finally got them to see the obvious. I hope nobody minds too much. I mean, Kostas does, but that's his problem, not ours, right? And what he really wanted was Ossetia, not her. Tilal was pretty stupid about not wanting to ask her now that she's Prince Chale's heir, but I persuaded him to start talking." Pol sighed. "Once he did, he didn't shut up. They've loved each other all this time, can you believe it? She was too proud to say anything to him, and he wanted to make River Run the richest holding in all Syr before he asked her. And neither said a word about it. But that's not the problem now. For all

I know, they're still out there talking each other's ears off!''

"Tilal?'' Sioned managed.

"And Gemma?'' Rohan was still staring.

Pol began to laugh. "They were so funny! Promise me that when I fall in love with a girl, if I start acting that stupid you'll tell me before I make such a fool of myself!''

Chapter Twenty-two

No one said a word about Tilal and Gemma. No one had to. The couple's appearance at Clutha's outdoor feast that evening fairly trumpeted their Choosing of each other. Inseparable, insulated from everything by their own private weave of happiness, it was doubtful they knew anyone else existed.

Davvi looked utterly blissful in his relief. Chale seemed to be getting used to the idea. It was remarked on—quietly—that Kostas was conspicuous in his absence.

The tables were packed with highborns, some of them in nearly Tilal's and Gemma's state, for over the last days understandings had been reached between many couples. One pair, however, sat apart from each other, the man's face grim, the woman's pale and strained. Beside him were his younger brothers—and beside her was a black-haired youth with eyes the color of new leaves in shadow.

Andry worried about Maarken and Hollis, but someone else took up most of his attention. Princess Alasen was four tables away from him, surrounded by eligible young men whose enthusiasm for her company was strictly observed—and occasionally quelled—by her father. Glimpses of her through flowers and chattering faces did unaccountable things to Andry's heartbeat and respiration. He did not understand what was wrong with him that he had so little interest in the dishes set before him—not even the gorgeous tower of spun sugar and pastry studded with candied fruits that was presented for dessert. Maarken, deep in his own melancholy thoughts, did not notice, but Sorin did—and found his twin a dull companion indeed.

Chiana's laughter dominated her table. She had good reason for high spirits. Halian sat on one side of her, Miyon on the other, and Masul was way over on the other side of the gathering, seated with Kiele, Lyell, Velden, Cabar, and Cabar's disgruntled-looking wife, Kenza.

Presiding over a quiet table of older princes was Lady Andrade, Urival at her side as always, her austere demeanor softened a little by being in relatively undemanding company. Prince Lleyn even made her laugh a few times. Nearby were Ostvel, Riyan, Chay, and Tobin, trading tales of Pol with Audrite and Chadric. The boy himself sat between his parents at a table with Pandsala, Milosh of Fessenden and Lord Kolya; the two young men scarcely dared to breathe in the presence of the High Prince. Other highborns were scattered about, the conversational level rose and fell with innocuous regularity—and no one said anything about what was on all minds.

The whole evening was driving Sioned just the slightest bit mad.

She knew what the faces were hiding. Rohan's early adjournment of the princes' meeting had come because Velden had insisted on a vote regarding Masul's right to Princemarch. It was Saumer of Isel who had proposed another day of waiting. The prince was genuinely troubled, but there was no way of knowing whether he wanted time to be persuaded or if he wished to marshal his arguments. Rohan was distracted with worry that Volog had not been able to convince Saumer—or, worse, that his grace of Kierst had somehow offended his grace of Isel, and the latter would vote for Masul just to spite the lifelong rival he had been forced to work with these last years.

The decision would be rendered the next day. Everyone knew it. And no one said a word about it.

Unbeknownst to her son, who would have stared open-mouthed if he'd realized it, Sioned's mood was a fair approximation of what had that morning prompted Pol to give his little demonstration of *faradhi* skills. There was a growing need in her to do something, anything, to take those polite masks off princely faces. She wanted to remind them of the powers she and Rohan held between them, powers that Pol would wield on his own. She craved their widened eyes, their awe, and even their fear of a Sunrunner Princess—and the Sunrunner who would one day be High Prince.

Goddess be thanked, the dinner ended early. After the morning wine-heads that had followed on Rohan's dinner the night before, no one was willing to repeat the experience—especially not with such an important vote coming on the morrow. Sioned herself wanted nothing more than sleep—a thing she knew would be in vanishingly short supply. So when Tobin asked her company for a cup of hot taze after the meal, they both knew it was really an excuse for staying up all night talking.

Rohan returned alone to the pavilion, leaving Pol under the watchful eyes of Maarken and Ostvel. Along with Riyan, Sorin, and Andry, they had accepted Volog's invitation to listen to a little music before bedtime, and as Rohan settled in at his desk he could just catch the sweet sound of a flute. He enjoyed music, but counted it no deprivation that his education in the subject was sparse. His mother, loving music, had despaired of her children ever learning a note, and rightly so; neither he nor Tobin could so much as hum on key. Pol, on the other hand, had a real affinity for singing, and after a time Rohan thought he heard his son's voice doubling Ostvel's. He glanced up, surprised. Ostvel's talent was rarely displayed, and never outside Skybowl or Stronghold, and then only after entreaties amounting almost to direct orders from his prince. How odd it was that he had been prevailed upon now.

Rohan was perusing trade agreements when a rider came in with reports from the Desert. Grateful to have his mind distracted from the problems of the *Rialla*, he attended first to Feylin's news about the dragons. She had spent the summer watching them and compiling population projections based on the number of hatchlings flown this year, and was pleased to inform the High Prince that the news was heartening. Barring any unforeseen circumstances, the dragons would hold steady in their numbers. There remained the problem of finding more caves so that the population could increase, but for now they were safe.

The news from Walvis and Eltanin in Tiglath was just as good. Desert troops were working well with those from Princemarch. Friendly competition in the arts of swordplay, archery, and horsemanship had seen many new tricks learned on both sides. Those of the Desert were better riders, but hunters from the Veresch did things with arrows that Walvis would have sworn were impossible had he not seen them with his own eyes. There was an amusing postscript to the effect that several men and women would be petitioning for a change in residence soon, for close proximity had accomplished the usual. Some twenty or so marriages were in the offing.

Thus it was that Rohan was smiling when Tallain approached him in the private section of the pavilion. "Ah, now, not more dispatches, I hope. Lady Feylin writes a clear hand, your father has the decency to employ a scribe—but Lord Walvis' scrawl has nearly blinded me!"

Tallain grinned. "No, my lord, no more parchments to read. You have a visitor. He calls himself High Lord Steward to Prince Miyon of Cunaxa."

Rohan's brows shot up. "How long have you kept him waiting?"

"The usual, my lord. Shall I admit him now?"

"Do that. When are their graces of Syr and Ossetia due to arrive?"

"Shortly, I believe. If your talk with this steward is overlong, I'll direct them to the antechamber, my lord."

"Excellent. Oh, by the way, Tallain, your father sent a note for you with his letter." He tossed the sealed parchment at the youth, who caught it eagerly. "All's going very well indeed at Tiglath. A rider will start back tomorrow morning, so you can include a letter to your father if you like."

"Thank you, my lord." Tallain tucked the note away in his tunic. "Shall I admit the steward now? And will you want fresh wine?"

Rohan winked. "I think the man is rather more hungry than he is thirsty. Give me a moment, then let him in."

The squire smoothed the grin from his face, bowed,

and left. Rohan relaxed back in his chair. He had a fair idea of the reason for Miyon's emissary, and was definitely looking forward to it.

Soon he was observing the barely polite bow of a short, chubby gentleman whose heavy beard and long hair all but concealed his face. Only the eyes—dark, shrewd, and watchful—were clearly visible. Many charming sentiments were expressed; wishes were given for the continued good health and happiness of the High Prince, High Princess, and their noble heir; Rohan received it all with a bland smile and did not ask the steward to sit down.

"If I may make so bold, High Prince—my exalted master is curious about the arrangements made for the youngest of Roelstra's daughters."

"The Princess Chiana?" Rohan asked, deliberately giving the girl the title to which she had no right. He decided to be obtuse for a while. "I understand she lives with various of her sisters, and at present resides with Lady Kiele here in Waes."

The steward bowed again, eyes signaling that he comprehended Rohan's ploy. "Perhaps I should amplify. My master is interested in whatever arrangements have been made for her future."

"She's free to go wherever she chooses and live as she likes."

"Your grace, I find it difficult to communicate with suitable delicacy the true nature of my master's curiosity."

"Then perhaps you ought to be indelicate about it," Rohan suggested affably, enjoying himself.

"Not to wrap it in too fine a silk, your grace—how is she dowered?"

"I am surprised to find Prince Miyon interested in the subject. My own curiosity is now engaged."

The steward's bejeweled hand combed nervously through his beard before he remembered himself. He shifted, shrugged, and said, "He is, to be blunt, concerned with what would come to the lady on her marriage."

"That would depend on her Chosen husband," Rohan replied smoothly.

"When Princess Naydra married Lord Narat, she received land around the holding of Port Adni, purchased by your grace from Prince Volog.''

"And a goodly bit it cost me, too," he admitted in a cheerful voice.

"Might one inquire if similar arrangements would be made for Princess Chiana?''

"One might inquire, certainly. But one might receive a more definite answer if one were Prince Miyon.''

The steward's plump figure bent in half at the waist. "May I have your gracious permission to withdraw, High Prince?''

Rohan waved him genially out, then called in Tallain and told him that under no circumstances was Prince Miyon to be admitted to his presence before Davvi and Chale had been spotted entering Rohan's camp. The youth chuckled his understanding, and when Rohan was alone again he filled his time with a letter to Feylin thanking her for her work. He wrote a separate note to Sionell, hinting at a lovely present from the *Rialla* Fair, and put it aside so Sioned could add a few lines if she liked. He was halfway through another letter, this one to Walvis asking for full details of various maneuvers, to be shared with Chay, when Tallain finally returned.

"My lord High Prince, his grace of Cunaxa desires speech with your royal highness.''

Rohan blinked at all this formality, then realized Tallain was speaking loud enough for Miyon to hear. He kept amusement from his voice and replied, "By all means, send him in. I hope you haven't kept him waiting.''

The squire bowed, straight-faced, and a few moments later Miyon was admitted. He nodded to Rohan, threw an irritated glance at Tallain, and sat where Rohan indicated.

"I have ministers enough to make pretty speeches for me," the prince said without preamble. "I shall be direct with you, cousin. What are you willing to give Chiana if she chooses me for her husband?''

"I had not know you were considering the match, cousin.''

Miyon condescended to smile, as one does when believing he holds the key to another's locked gates in his hands. "I could be persuaded to consider it, if there were profit to be had."

"My, my," Rohan murmured. "This younger generation. One would think the lady's charming person would be your primary motive."

"Romance in marriage is the luxury of a prince with safe anchorage," Miyon stated flatly. "What bargain can be struck between us, cousin?"

Rohan looked him right in the eyes. Miyon's were black, like the chips of glassy stone found at Skybowl. "What did you have in mind?"

"My support for your cause, in exchange for shipping rights at Tiglath."

"With Chiana as the—how did your man put it? Ah, yes: the fine silk wrapping."

"I would not ally myself with a commoner, naturally. My willingness to marry her would go far toward convincing others of her rights as opposed to Masul's."

"So much for romance. Is that all you want?"

"Free access to the harborage at Tiglath isn't unreasonable as a part of her dowry."

"A part," Rohan echoed softly. "What else?"

"Ten square measures of northern land to use as a staging area for my trade."

"And?"

"The two hundred gold pieces you gave her other sisters when they married."

"And?" Rohan asked again, patiently.

"Your armies the hell away from my border!"

Rohan flicked a glance at the water clock in the corner and smiled. "Don't tell me a simple little military exercise a full fifty measures from your border has made you nervous? You and your Merida armed with the best Cunaxan steel?"

"I came here to offer you—"

"You came here to be bribed." Rohan's smile did not fade, but his eyes and voice were frigid. "I know you, Miyon. You have three ambitions in life: a port, a rather large slice of my land to get the Merida off your neck, and recognition that you are a man worthy of sitting in conference with princes. The first two depend entirely on me. The third is your problem. I will not be the means through which you reassure yourself of your manhood.''

Miyon sprang to his feet, quivering with insult. ''How dare you!''

''Listen to me carefully, princeling. You want Chiana because you think she'll bring you all three of those things. Shipping rights at Tiglath, a chunk of my land, and accolades from the princes for your cleverness in outwitting me. Is that a fair summation?''

''It's the best offer you'll receive!''

''I think not. The day Chiana weds you is the day I cross your borders—*all* of them—with more troops than you could amass in twenty years. One of you greedy little royals on my northern flank is quite enough, and you and Chiana together would cause me no end of irritation. I know her, too, Miyon. I've allowed you to survive thus far—''

''Allowed me!'' Mayon shouted.

''Those advisers who kept you chained up during your early youth certainly didn't teach you any manners. Or perhaps you've spent too much time around the Merida. Do you know what they originally were? A brotherhood of trained assassins using razor-sharp glass knives. It's said they killed almost painlessly.'' Rohan leaned forward, palms flat on the desk. ''You may find yourself trying to breathe around a glass knife in your throat some night, cousin.''

''They have every right to the Desert! All those lands were theirs before your grandfather—''

''They have no right to it at all, which is why most of the other princes supported my grandfather. Miyon, you don't care a damn about their rights, except where they might provide an excuse for your own ambitions. And I'll tell you something else, princeling. I know you've been offered certain things by Kiele—but you don't trust her. And you don't entirely believe in this pretender, either.''

''How did you—'' Miyon stopped too late, his face crimson with rage.

''You're trying to build a bridge from the middle of the river, and whoever provides you with the most planks will have you on his side. I offer nothing, Miyon. I have no need of your support, especially not if purchased with my honor and my son's future. You can fall into the river and drown for all I care. You have my permission to withdraw.''

For an instant Miyon looked as if the killing fury in his eyes would find its outlet in a physical attack on Rohan. ''You and your Sunrunner bitch!'' he spat. ''Spying, manipulating—do you think the princes will sit still for it forever? We won't be ruled from Stronghold and Goddess Keep! We've endured the *faradh'im*, and we've endured a High Prince—but not both together!''

Rohan smiled. ''When you repeat this story, Miyon, be sure to tell it truthfully. I see by my timepiece over there that their graces of Ossetia and Syr ought to be in the antechamber right now, listening to every word. It would be terribly embarrassing to be corrected by them in public.''

Tallain, smart boy, chose that moment to step around the partition. ''Your royal highness, Prince Chale and Prince Davvi are waiting for your grace.''

''There, you see?'' Rohan beamed at Miyon. ''I was right. Give them wine, Tallain, and tell them I'll be with them shortly. Well, Miyon?''

Voice thin with rage, the younger man said, ''You have made an enemy today, High Prince.''

Rohan was no longer smiling. ''Your house and mine have been enemies since the day the first Merida found welcome at Castle Pine. I'm surprised it took you this long to figure it out.''

Miyon turned on his heel and strode from the pavilion. Chale and Davvi were instantly into the private area, and Rohan stood, greeting them with a comical grimace.

''I was afraid he was going to say something like 'You'll be sorry!' ''

''That was murderous,'' Davvi remarked. ''He's a vicious bastard, Rohan. Watch out for him.''

Chale, seating himself, fixed Rohan with curious gaze. ''I appreciated your point about a marriage between him and Chiana. What wouldn't the two of them come up with? But tell me, how do you know he talked to Kiele?''

''It has nothing to do with Sunrunners, cousin. Cabar of Gilad has a wife who adores her husband and loathes

Miyon. And my sister had opportunity to speak with her when our ladies spent the afternoon together the other day. . . ." He finished with a shrug.

Chale snorted. "Ah, yes, the redoubtable Princess Tobin. If I'd been twenty years younger, I would have given Chaynal a race for her, let me tell you!" He continued to eye Rohan, but now a faint smile played around his lips. "I was just remembering that innocent-faced young prince who beguiled us all at his first *Rialla*. Your father would be proud of you, Rohan."

"Thank you. I treasure that, especially from a man who didn't always agree with him." Rohan sank into a chair away from his desk. "Let's talk of more pleasant things, shall we? How do you like having Gemma with you?"

"Davvi's done a fine job of her education," Chale said gruffly. "She's got a good head on her shoulders, and a good heart to go along with it. She reminds me of her mother, my sister Chalia. But I assume you're asking how I like this idea of her and Davvi's boy, Tilal."

"His grace and I have been discussing it all morning," Davvi put in, adding with a rueful smile, "We agree that I've been an idiot not to have seen it sooner. And he's been kind enough to suggest that we hold the ceremonies privately, after the *Rialla*."

"In respect to my son and grandson, as well as to young Kostas," Chale nodded.

"Who can't be at all happy about losing such a prize. My lords, I can't tell you how pleased I am that at least *one* thing has turned out well this year!" Rohan gestured to Tallain, who brought fresh goblets of wine. They drank to the young people, perfectly in accord—a rare enough circumstance to put a wry smile on all three faces.

Chale said, "She's marrying a man who'll make her happy as well as make Ossetia a good prince when I'm gone." He paused, then shrugged. "You're right, I didn't have much in common with your father, Rohan, and you and I don't see things the same way, either. It irks me to agree with Miyon on anything, but your boy being a Sunrunner and a prince worries me, too. I like what I've seen of him, make no mistake. But he has many years of growing to do and power has ruined good men in the past."

"I understand your misgivings, cousin. I have them myself. But I also have faith in Pol's character and the training he's getting from Lleyn and Chadric and Audrite."

"And when he goes to Goddess Keep and finds out what he can do with sunlight and Fire? What then?" Chale cleared his throat and shrugged again. "Well, that's in the future, and I won't be around to concern myself with it. Tilal grew up at your court. He'll understand these things better than I ever could. In any case, I'm on your side in the matter of this pretender, for two reasons."

Rohan concealed his glee. "I'm grateful for your support, my lord."

"You ought to be grateful that Roelstra came before you," Chale pointed out sternly. "Only a fool would prefer another such as he to you. And from what I've seen of the boy—the thought of Roelstra's son at Castle Crag sickens me. That's my first reason. The second is Gemma. She and Tilal will have to deal with him if he's proclaimed, and she's made it quite clear that aside from her Chosen's feelings, she'll consider Masul an enemy all her days, after what Roelstra did to her brother." The old prince grunted. "Using the boy's pride to make him bear the worst of the battles! You know I often supported Roelstra—we all did—but that matter opened my eyes."

Rohan couldn't help saying, "And yet it was in battle against me that Jastri died."

"Do you think I'm such a fool as that? He may have been my nephew, my own dead sister's only son, but I know who put him in the way of his death. It doesn't make me fond of you that you led the troops that killed him, but I know who was truly responsible for his death."

Rohan nodded slowly. "Forgive me."

"Politics is an odd business," Chale mused. "Look at Saumer and Volog. At each other's throats for years, and now fussing over their mutual grandson and heir as if they'd never stolen a single sheep from each other. And if you're counting up real peculiarities, there's Roelstra's daughter as your regent in Princemarch." He sighed and shook his head. "You know, most of us are reasonable

people. Princes have to be in order to survive. Miyon
hasn't learned that yet, and that makes him dangerous.''

"As dangerous as my Sunrunner princess of a wife?"
Rohan said, smiling.

Chale looked startled, then burst into wheezing laughter. "Oh, your father would have loved that one!"

"Again, I'm complimented," Rohan said, grinning
now. "And may I say in return that my father would have
appreciated your reasoning and your support."

Chale wagged a finger at him. "I'm not saying I'll
agree to anything you say, mind."

"Cousin, I would be disappointed in you if you did."

"Then bring me some more of that wine and let's drink
to Gemma and Tilal again. And may your own boy find
it easier to win his Chosen lady!"

* * *

Sioned turned the full fury of her green eyes on her
husband. "How *could* you? It was going so well! Miyon
could have been ours! Chiana had him on the hook! All
you had to do was give her a little help reeling him in!"

With a patient sigh, Rohan said, "And if she had? It
would have been his perfect chance to humiliate me. All
he'd have to do is tell the other princes in council that I'd
agreed to his terms for taking Chiana, making it seem as
if I'd begged him to do so in order to win his support."

"It would have worked!" she fumed.

"It would never have worked. Listen, Sioned—he
wanted to outsmart me, prove himself more clever, have
something he could hold over me. Instead I've put him
in his place and let him know he can't out-think me.
Ever. Have you forgotten that he keeps Merida in his
princedom and at his court? That they've tried to kill Pol?
Do you think they could have done that without Miyon's
help, or at least his acquiescence?"

"You've made an open enemy. Is that preferable to the
veneer of tolerance?"

"I'd rather have him an enemy everyone knows about
rather than a pretended friend who might fool my *real*
allies. They'll beware of him now. And whenever he ap-
proaches any of the other princes, they'll remember that
he and I are opposed, and think twice about what he says.
And aside from all that, would you really want Chiana

on our border, scheming with Miyon against us? A woman whose very name means 'treason'? There was nothing else I could do. I regret that you disapprove, but it was my decision to make, not yours.''

She was silent for a time, then shook her head. ''I understand why you did it, Rohan. But I don't like it that you used me. And you did, you know—and Tobin as well, having us work Miyon and Chiana to where you wanted them.''

Setting Chiana on Miyon had been Sioned's idea. Rohan had neither encouraged it nor interfered; he had simply taken advantage of what she had done on her own. A pretty point of distinction, a sop to his conscience, that she would not appreciate. He was wise enough to keep his mouth shut about it. What he said was, ''You've learned almost everything a prince needs to know in order to govern. But you have yet to learn that sometimes people have to be used.''

''I suppose it's one of the things I didn't learn from Andrade,'' she said, quietly.

''She does it to perfection, with no regrets. It's not particularly nice, and it's certainly not noble or heroic. The difference between Andrade and me is that sometimes, like now, I hate things I've had to do. Oh, I admit I had a rollicking good time doing what I did to Roelstra my first *Rialla*. I enjoy gaming those too stupid to realize their own ambitions have led them along the path I want them to walk. I don't regret Miyon at all, because he had to learn to bow to me. As for the rest of them—''

Sioned smiled slightly. ''Let me guess. You wish they didn't bow quite so low.''

He nodded. ''It's why I value Chale and Lleyn and Davvi. They bow right along with the rest, but they know why it's necessary. The others just—do it.'' He glanced at the water clock and sighed. ''Over half the night gone. And tomorrow isn't going to be pleasant at all.''

''Rohan . . .'' She stood beside his chair and he circled her waist with gentle fingers. ''Let me help you sleep, love. You need it.'' When he smiled and shook his head, she went on, ''But you're exhausted. And so am I,'' she added frankly. ''I can't sleep if you don't.

Just this once, Rohan. Indulge your *faradhi* wife and let her work a little magic on you."

After a slight pause, he asked, "You will anyway, won't you?"

"Well. . . ."

"Oh, all right. I've had enough for today, I suppose. And the only thing I lack is an argument from my stubborn witch."

"You're welcome," she told him wryly, and he laughed.

A short while later they lay in each other's arms beneath a light silk sheet and a loosely woven wool blanket. Sioned curled close to her husband's side, her face bathed in thin moonlight drifting in through the screened window opening. She closed her eyes and threaded the delicate strands of silver into a soft net, placing it across Rohan. He sighed once, tense muscles relaxed, and in another moment was asleep.

She lay wakeful beside him until morning, listening to the steady, reassuring rhythm of breath and heartbeat that kept perfect time with her own.

* * *

Rohan looked at Andrade once, seeing her pen poised above the parchment, before he said, "His grace of Cunaxa."

Miyon stood, tall and lean and implacable. "I side with Prince Masul."

Lleyn's brows arched. The privileges of his great age and long years of rule allowed him to say, "The Lady Chiana will be disappointed."

Miyon's cheeks crimsoned. "I vote with my brains, cousin. Not my balls."

"Indeed," Lleyn murmured tolerantly.

Andrade made a mark on the parchment.

"His Grace of Ossetia."

Chale pushed himself to his feet. "I say this young man is mistaken," he growled, staring straight at Masul, who stood easy and relaxed near the water clock. "He's no more Roelstra's son than I am."

"Brother," Masul said, and gave Chale a small, mocking bow.

"Be silent," Andrade snapped as she wrote.

"His grace of Dorval."

Lleyn took some time about rising, and leaned heavily on his dragon-headed cane. "I have watched and listened most carefully, as befits this weighty matter before us. I have seen no proof that the Lady Andrade and Princess-Regent Pandsala were misled in their perceptions of the night in question. Moreover, I have seen no compelling evidence that this youth is justified in his claims. I regret any pain this might cause him, but I must in all conscience decline to believe him."

"His grace of Grib," Rohan said as Lleyn sat down and Andrade's pen scratched again.

Velden was instantly up, his pose aggressive. "I must disagree with our cousin of Dorval. There is no proof to contradict the claim. He must be given the benefit of any doubts any of us may have. I for one have no doubts. The evidence is certain. I accept him as Roelstra's son."

"His grace of Fessenden."

Long, lanky, lazy-eyed Pimantal unfolded himself from his chair. "Prince Masul," was all he said, with a slight bow in the young man's direction.

Rohan wondered what Kiele had offered him as he watched Pimantal resume his seat. "His grace of Syr."

Davvi got up, leaning slightly forward with his knuckles resting on the table. "I agree with our cousins of Ossetia and Dorval, and for their reasons. But I have another reason. Even if this man were Roelstra's son, and even if I were convinced of it, Princemarch was long ago won by all the rights of war, confirmed by law. I gained Syr in much the same way. It is true that I was the only male heir left of the Syrene house. But my claim rests on precisely the same rights of war as the claim to Princemarch. If this assembly chooses to violate its own agreement of the spring of 705, that acknowledged High Prince Rohan's rights of possession, then—" He swept the gathering with cool green eyes. "—then I assure you that the same principle, or *lack* of it, will hold true for me."

As astounded as the rest of them, shock betrayed Rohan into exclaiming, "Davvi!"

Sioned's brother met his gaze calmly. "I knew you wouldn't agree with this, Rohan. But believe me when I say that if a princedom won and lawfully confirmed can be so easily taken away and given to another, then I and mine will have no dealings with princes." He sat down.

It took Rohan a moment to recover. But his voice was firm as he said, "His grace of Kierst."

Volog levered himself up, cast a piercing glance at Masul, and said, "I'll take good governance and peace, demonstrated these many years, over this unknown farmhand who hasn't convinced me of anything but his colossal arrogance."

Miyon of Cunaxa stiffened with insult. "Have a care, cousin," he said tightly. "You will be seated at this table with him before the day ends."

Volog gave a bark of laughter. "Not damned likely, boy!"

"My lord," Rohan murmured in warning. "His grace of Gilad."

He wondered for an instant if Princess Kenza had managed to nag her husband into shaking off Miyon's influence. But Cabar stood, gulped, and mumbled words agreeing with their graces of Cunaxa, Grib, and Fessenden. As he sat and Andrade's pen rasped on parchment, Rohan turned his gaze momentarily to Saumer of Isel. His was the only vote still in doubt. Some perverse sense of the dramatic within him made him call on Clutha of Meadowland next, and the tension drew out a little finer, a little tauter.

The old man stood. "I say our cousin of Kierst has spoken most wisely of all. But, like our cousin of Syr, I have another reason, too. For longer than I care to recall, my land has been the battleground between the Desert and Princemarch. In the past fifteen years I've gotten used to peace. I don't intend to jeopardize it—because if any of you think that giving Princemarch to this boy will be as easy as all that, you're sadly mistaken. And who'd pay for it in burned fields and dead people? Me, that's who! I spent my childhood and youth and middle age watching armies lay waste to my meadows. I'll not have it in my dotage as well. No, thank you!" He plunked back down into his chair and turned his scowling attention to his hands.

Five against, four in favor. Rohan turned to Saumer. "His grace of Isel."

Volog's erstwhile enemy, grandfather with him of their mutual heir, rose reluctantly to his feet. "Cousins," he said, his voice heavy and strained, "I have considered this matter, as all of you have, with the whole of my mind and my heart. I do not agree with previous statements about evidence. I have seen no evidence one way or the other that convincingly refutes or proves either side. But I ask this. What right does a man have to his lands?

"The High Prince, while still in possession only of the Desert, quite rightly and wisely stated that in order to rule effectively, he had to know what he was prince of. We spent much time and effort uncovering precedent for holding our lands, and the treaties drawn up were of great satisfaction to all.

"And yet—if precedent and traditional right to what we hold is the highest law, where does that leave possession by right of war? If that is the paramount law, then we would all be at each other's throats—as in the past." He flicked a glance at Volog, who gave him stare for stare.

"If a man has the right to his lands, then he has the right to give them to his son. Usually the eldest, and one born of his wife's body—but there are several instances in the recent past of a younger son or an illegitimate one inheriting. If we take away that right, and if we decide that war is the more legitimate means of gaining a princedom or a holding, then we announce chaos and we might as well gird ourselves for battle here and now. For none of us will be secure in what we hold, from prince to most obscure *athri*."

He paused a long moment, then shook his head. "I do not disbelieve the Lady Andrade and the Princess-Regent. I do not disbelieve this young man before us now. But I do believe in the law, and in my own conscience. And both tell me that Princemarch by rights belongs to the son of the late High Prince Roelstra." He cast a quick glance around the table again, and sat down.

Rohan held in the long sigh that wanted to escape his chest, kept back the twist of bitter disappointment that threatened his lips. Saumer was not trying to spite Volog or anyone else; he was honest in his misgivings and in his beliefs. Actually, Rohan told himself with grim humor, he ought to be cheering the words that had come from Saumer's mouth: "I do believe in the law." He'd been working to instill those words and that belief in his fellow princes for over twenty years. And what a time to succeed!

Andrade broke the silence with a rustle of parchment. "The count is as follows. Ossetia, Dorval, Syr, Kierst, and Meadowlord against; Cunaxa, Gilad, Grib, Fessenden, and Isel for." She lifted her gaze from her notes. "My lords, it appears we have a deadlock."

Rohan did not meet her eyes, knowing what he would find in them. Masul was chewing his lip, the fingers of one hand drumming on the carved wooden support of the water clock.

At last Rohan got up, consciously drawing all eyes to him. "My lords, it is as the Lady has said. Both sides lack a majority. Firon being without a prince, and both myself and the Princess-Regent being obviously disqualified, I can see few ways of breaking this deadlock."

All of them sat up straighter at his implication, but it was Masul who voiced their question. "What do you mean?" When someone sucked in an outraged breath at his peremptory tone, he added, "My lord."

"I mean there are alternatives. Such proofs as are readily available have been presented, and have failed to convince one way or the other. But . . ."

He finally looked at his aunt. She nodded slowly, placing her long hands with their ten rings and gleaming bracelets on the table before her.

"What is it, my Lady?" Lleyn asked, his voice soft.

She answered, "The *faradh'im* have certain skills not generally known among the populace—or, indeed, among most *faradh'im* themselves. Some of us are able to catch quite detailed visions of the future, for instance."

Miyon leaned back in his chair with an angry gesture of one hand. "Your pardon, my Lady, but surely you don't propose to show us what the world would be like with Prince Masul at Castle Crag? I never heard of anything so—"

Andrade continued as if he had not spoken. "I have done such things myself, my lords. But what is relevant to us at present is something else. The past—and specifically that night twenty-one years ago—is in my memory. Using certain . . . techniques . . . I will be able to conjure that past for all of you to watch with your own eyes. It is a difficult thing, and possibly a dangerous one. But those of you who do not believe *me* will, I think, believe the evidence I will present before you.''

"And why should we believe this—or even allow it?" Velden exclaimed. "I've never heard of this supposed ability, either! Why should it be trusted?"

"You dare question the Lady's word?" Lleyn asked, his eyes like thunder.

"Peace, my friend," Andrade said. "He has every right to question. Would it satisfy you, Prince Velden, if I first conjured a scene from the past that you and I both witnessed?"

Cabar stared slack-jawed; Miyon was anxious and trying to hide it; Masul's lip curled scornfully. Pimantal looked intrigued, and Saumer, hopeful. He said, "If it will settle our doubts and if it is not too dangerous for you—"

"It probably is," she said with a shrug. "But I consider this person more so." She fixed Masul with a sardonic eye. "Well? Are you secure enough in your claim of truth to have the truth revealed to you through Sunrunner arts?"

"In which I have very little faith," he shot back. "But if their graces wish it, then why not?" He smiled.

"Very well." She rose and bowed to Rohan. "With your permission, my lord, I will retire to my pavilion and prepare."

"Will tomorrow serve, my Lady?" He was appalled by her sudden pallor.

"Tonight at sunset will do. I'd like to get this over with." Again she speared Masul with her gaze. "You've taken up quite enough time and energy as it is, and their graces have more important matters to discuss."

Without another word she walked from the tent, leaving an apprehensive silence behind her. Each prince looked at every other prince, and finally at Rohan. He cleared his throat.

But before he could say anything, Masul spoke—drawling, amused, yet with an undercurrent of hostility seething in his voice. "Well, cousin," he said to Rohan, "it seems your family witch is your last hope. But I'm not worried. Nothing scares me."

"Then you are a fool," Rohan replied tranquilly. "We meet here at sunset, my lords. I trust no one will object to the presences of the High Princess and my son, as well as the Princess-Regent."

There were no objections; there could be none. In renewed eerie quiet they left Rohan alone. He stood silent and unseeing for some time after they had gone. Then, sinking down into his chair, he put his face in his hands.

"Gentle Goddess," he whispered. "What have I done? What am I about to do?"

There was no one to answer.

Chapter Twenty-three

Of all the people in Waes that Sioned wished to see that noonday, the very last was Chiana. But the would-be princess was not far behind Tallain, who had run to the great blue pavilion at once with word of the princes' decision. Sioned had been there all morning, waiting in solitude and silence for her husband, wanting not even Pol to share the time with her. Tallain, respecting her obvious wishes, told his news and withdrew. But Chiana invaded close on his heels and paced the carpets with every intention of wearing them into the dirt.

"How could you allow this to happen?" she cried. "How *could* you?"

"Be silent," Sioned told her in a tone that ought to have warned her to do so immediately.

Chiana was beyond even rudimentary understanding of another's emotions—not her specialty to begin with. Sioned rose from her chair, a small frantic voice in her head demanding that Chiana be evicted at once, before Rohan could come back with his undoubted need for what little peace Sioned could give him. But Chiana continued to berate her, shrill and voluble in her furious panic.

"You had only to order it, and this pretender would be dead! My father would have executed him before he even opened his mouth! What use is the power of a High Prince if you don't use it? And now I must pay for this cowardice! I must suffer doubts of my birth! I must—"

Sioned bore it with phenomenal patience before her temper simply snapped.

"You, you, you! Is your precious self the only thing you can think about? Roelstra's daughter! If I'd ever had any doubts, they're gone now! Only the spawn of that vicious self-centered viper would behave so! Now let me be, Chiana, or I'll throw you out of here with my own hands!"

She had the odd sensation that it was someone else's voice shouting, someone else's hand that lifted threateningly. But sight of the emerald ring reminded her that the hand raised to strike was indeed her own. She swung away, nauseated. "Get out," she whispered. "Get out before I forget who I am."

"You seem to have forgotten who *I* am!"

Tallain's frantic voice rose in the outer chamber of the pavilion. "Your grace, please—"

"Is Rohan here? I must speak with him at once!"

Pandsala; all that Sioned needed at this point was another of Roelstra's daughters. She turned as the partition rustled and Chiana gave a blurt of laughter.

"Pandsala! Tell her! We demand the death of this pretender!"

Pandsala started at the sight of her half sister—and looked guilty. Sioned's fists clenched.

"Well?" Chiana snapped. "Go on! Tell her! If none of you has the courage, I'll order that bastard killed myself!"

"If he dies," Sioned heard that strange voice that was not her own say, "your death will follow, Chiana—and by my Sunrunner arts."

The younger woman gasped and turned white. "You wouldn't dare!"

A tiny smile hovered around Sioned's lips. "Would I not?"

At that precise moment Rohan stepped into the tent, and stopped instantly at the sight of the three women. He noted and dismissed Chiana's rage with one piercing glance. Then he regarded Pandsala for a moment, his eyes chips of colorless ice. At last he looked at his wife, a flicker of irritation spasming over his features. To her he said, ''I come here expecting respite, and find a battlefield.''

And with that, he was gone.

Chiana's mouth hung open. Pandsala looked as if she would either scream or attack her half sister, perhaps both. Sioned wanted to weep with the pain of seeing Rohan's eyes so cold and dead, his face carved in stone. Her own blood congealed into rivulets of ice, her own features drawing into a hard mask as she glared at the intruders into her husband's peace.

''Leave me,'' she snapped.

''I am not a servant!'' Chiana retorted, but without her earlier righteous fury. ''I am a princess!''

''Shut up, you fool!'' Pandsala hissed, and dragged her by one arm out of the pavilion.

When Sioned was alone, she spent a long time staring with blind eyes at the empty doorway. Then, with a brisk command, she called Tallain in and told him to fetch her son.

* * *

Having rid herself of Chiana through the simple expedient of pushing her into a nearby tent and shouting at the guards to keep her there, Pandsala set off after Rohan. She had a fair idea of where he would be headed. If quiet was his goal, then he would surely seek the river downstream from the encampment. She knew she would have, and her heart thrilled to recognize a similarity of impulse between them.

Sure enough, there he was—striding purposefully through the damp gravel at the water's edge, a slim figure in dark blue trousers, black boots, and a loose white shirt, crowned by blond hair. Pandsala snatched up her long skirts and hurried after him. When she was within hearing distance, well beyond the last of the tents up on the wooded slope, she called out.

''My lord! Wait!''

Rohan swung around with a furious movement, ready to snarl at anyone who dared intrude. And again Pandsala's heart quivered when his expression changed at sight of her. Though the ice and stone of him did not melt or soften, neither did he vent his temper on her. He would have done so with almost anyone else. But now he found in Pandsala, as he had not in Sioned, the respite he needed.

This was what she told herself as she neared him, and the catch in her breath was more at having him all to herself than at the exertion of her run.

"My lord—I'm sorry for Chiana's outburst. It was unforgivable."

"But then, so much of Chiana is unforgivable," he replied. "You didn't race after me to tell me this, my lady."

"No," she admitted quietly, her heart and respiration slowing. "I wanted to discuss some possibilities with you, my lord. Things that might save Lady Andrade the danger of a conjuring."

Blue eyes narrowed. "She's already told me that you have neither the skill nor the strength for something similar. Please don't suggest it, Pandsala."

"I would do it," she maintained, tearing her gaze from his to look at the river. "But it may be that neither of us will have to attempt it."

"Explain yourself."

She glanced up the wooded bank. "If you please, my lord, shall we walk a little farther? I can't see anyone, but—"

Rohan nodded, and they walked. After a time Pandsala spoke in a low, urgent voice.

"The princes are deadlocked without hope of persuading any of Masul's supporters to change their minds. You know as well as I that this means he will have to be recognized as ruler of Princemarch. Without votes enough to deny him, your own honor will demand that he be confirmed, no matter if there are five other princes who believe him false. Had there been six, or seven, then he could have been denied. But even then, even with only two or three princes to champion him, he could have mounted an army to fight for Princemarch, with those princes at his side. If he is denied now, there are five who will gird and supply him. I want war no more than you do, my lord. But war will surely come, and not just between you and Princemarch. All the others will be drawn in, and all our substance spent.''

"Succinct and accurate," Rohan said in clipped tones. "What do you propose as a solution?''

"If the results of the trouble cannot be removed, then we must go to its source. Masul himself.''

"And what would you do?''

She cast him a sidelong glance, drawing in a deep breath.

"What Chiana proposed just before you entered the pavilion. Kill him.''

Rohan stopped and turned on her. "Pandsala—''

"Hear me out, my lord! Please! I have killed using *faradhi* means before, we both know it.''

"So has Sioned," he snapped. "That doesn't mean either of you will do it again, and especially not now!''

"She has?" This was news to Pandsala, who reminded herself to rethink her opinion of the High Princess. "Then she will understand. I will do it, my lord, you can blame it all on me—and punish me as you see fit afterward. Masul is no son of my father—and even if he were, I couldn't endure seeing him in Pol's place at Castle Crag.''

"Stop this! No more!''

"My lord, it is the only way." She grasped his arm, feeling the strong muscles beneath the shirt. "All of this is my fault. Chiana was right about that. If I had not conspired with Ianthe and then with Palila, none of this would be happening. The responsibility is mine. I accept it freely. I will kill Masul by Sunrunner means in full sight of everyone. You and Andrade both will have the punishment of me—and if it's death, then so be it.''

For a wonderful instant she thought he was tempted. But then he snarled, "I won't hear any more of this!'' He pulled away from her, boot heels crunching angrily in the sand.

"Rohan, please!" She caught up again, seizing his hand in both her own this time, so hard that his topaz ring dug into her palm. The noon sunlight swept across his hair and brow, gilding his already golden fairness, sinking his eyes into shadow. "With Masul dead, and

with me punished however you like, there would be no
more danger to Pol!''

"With Masul dead, there would always be doubts! If
this were a viable alternative, I would have done it myself! Do you think I require others to do my killing for
me? I managed quite well enough killing your father!''
He wrested his hand from hers, closed both palms on her
shoulders. "What you're saying is madness. You know
it, I know it. Goddess witness that I'm close to a kind of
madness myself. Listen to me, Pandsala. Masul cannot
die until everyone believes not in him but in Pol! Once
that happens, his death is certain—but not because he
challenged me. I can't be the one to kill him, and neither
can you!''

"What difference would it make?" she cried. "I've
killed for Pol often enough before!''

For a moment Rohan did not fully comprehend. Then,
slowly, he searched her desperate, passionate dark eyes,
and the gold of his face paled to gray, like ashes. His
fingers dug painfully into her flesh. "What are you saying?" he breathed. "What have you done?''

Pandsala faced him, excitement like strong wine in her
blood, and told him the truth of the last fourteen years.

Rohan listened, unbelieving, to the frightful catalog of
her crimes. In growing horror he heard the words pour
forth, Pandsala's feverish voice and wild eyes giving
frantic reality to things out of nightmares. At last she
panted to a halt, hands clenched on his chest, Sunrunner's rings and his own gift of amethyst and topaz winking mockingly at him in the sunlight.

She had killed for Pol before. Not just that archer,
living torch on the battlements of Castle Crag. Oh, no.
And how efficiently, how logically she had chosen whom
to kill, and how.

Naydra's unborn son—her own sister's child—had been
the first, murdered in the womb a year after Pandsala had
become regent. Naydra had nearly died of the miscar-
riage. But with no heir, Port Adni would revert to Kierst
on Lord Narat's death. And Kierst was ruled by Pol's
kinsman.

Another sister, Cipris, had been murdered by slow
poison lanced through the parchment of her private let-

ters. Proposed wife of Clutha's heir, Cipris had died before she bore a male of Roelstra's line who might one day challenge Pol.

Then Obram of Isel. Saumer's only son had married Volog's daughter Birani; there had been no issue of the marriage before his drowning off the Iseli coast one spring. His sister Hevatia, wife of Volog's heir, had already borne the child who, with Obram's death, became heir to both princedoms. A united Kierst and Isel would one day be ruled by Pol's kinsman.

Lady Rusalka had died in a hunting accident shortly before her marriage. Lady Pavla had succumbed to a necklace with poison-tipped prongs barely a year after her marriage to Prince Ajit of Firon. Both women had been Pandsala's half sisters, and both had been killed for the same reason as Cipris.

There were more. Lord Tibayan of Lower Pyrme, resisting cooperation with Davvi on regulation of port fees and other matters along with the Syrene border with Ossetia, had paid for his intransigence with his life. So had Lady Rabia of Catha Heights, whose death in childbed delivering her third daughter had come just after her husband had blocked construction of a port at the mouth of the Faolain, a primary trade objective of both Syr and the Desert. Patwin had been much more pliable since his wife's death. Doubtless Pandsala had had this in mind when she'd killed another sister.

And yet another, two years ago—Lady Nayati, who had fallen to the knife of what had appeared to be a common street bandit in Waes while on a visit to Kiele. She, too, would produce no male heirs to challenge Pol.

This very New Year's Holiday, while Rohan and Sioned were planning the progress through a Princemarch conquered by Pol's smile, Pandsala had been busy conquering Firon through Ajit's death. She had grown impatient; she could not wait for the old man to die a natural death, and had hastened him to it with poisoned wine that had seized his heart and stopped it.

Finally, this spring, there had been Inoat and Jos of Ossetia. Dead in a boating accident on Lake Kadar, leaving Chale's niece Gemma the only choice as heir to the princedom. And with it rumored that Kostas would wed

Gemma, was it any wonder that Inoat and Jos had died? Small matter that Tilal and not Kostas would be Gemma's husband and prince; the effect was the same, another princedom ruled by another of Pol's kinsmen.

Pandsala had set her sights on Kiele this year. Unable to prevent the marriage to Lyell, which had occurred before Pandsala's regency, for some reason Pandsala had let Kiele live long enough to produce a son and daughter. But this year she had been singled out for death when she had championed Masul.

And other proposed murders? None other than Ianthe's sons. Their names were known, but not their location. Though nothing had been heard of them since Feruche had burned to the ground, Pandsala was convinced that they lived. She had sought Ianthe's sons for years, would search for them as long as she had breath—until or unless proof positive came that they were as dead as their mother. For these three, more than any other of Roelstra's grandchildren, would crave lands, castles, princedoms, power—and Pol's death.

Eleven deaths accomplished in less than fifteen years. And not a hint, not a breath of rumor, had ever been heard that they had been anything other than sad accidents or natural deaths. Nothing had ever connected them with the woman who looked up at him now, her fists pressed to his chest.

Rohan stared into Pandsala's fevered dark eyes. Sweat dappled her forehead. It was hot here in the sun, but the fire raging in her was even hotter.

Rohan tried to breathe around the horrible constriction in his chest. "Oh, sweet Goddess—*why?*" The question was a deathly whisper, harsh and hopeless. And with all the other truths revealed, he now heard the most terrible of all.

"For the son *she* gave you—the son that should have been *mine!*"

Panic leaped up and was beaten back with violent speed—for if she knew, he had to keep his wits, not give in to fear or rage or anything else that might destroy the sudden balance he sensed between them. It was a sick and twisted equilibrium, with Pol as its fulcrum: Rohan's love weighted against Pandsala's lies. But in understanding it, he found strength to preserve it.

For he must protect that balance at all costs. He had given her power and Princemarch and her pride, and she had responded with unswerving devotion to depleting the ranks of those who might oppose Pol. That this loyalty had taken so hideous a form was his payment for having used her so well, for having been so blind.

Blazing from Pandsala's dark eyes was hatred that had never been directed at Rohan. It was not directed at him now. By rights his rejection of her for Sioned ought to have earned her hatred. It had not. How could she hate the man who had given her a life, the man whose son she had worked for these many years? No, Rohan did not figure on the list of her hates.

Her father, yes, for exiling her to Goddess Keep. Sioned, who had Rohan's heart and body and mind. Ianthe, who had borne his son. These three she hated. But Rohan saw something more in Pandsala's eyes. She hated them because he had spent more of himself on them than he ever had on her. Jealousy was the core of her hate. Jealousy of Roelstra, whom Rohan had battled; of Sioned, whom he loved; of Ianthe, who had carried his child. They had claimed him and Pandsala could not.

So she had claimed his son's future. Murdered to show her love, twisted other lives to keep him safe. Created much of the world Pol would inherit, a legacy of blood and hate.

Roelstra's daughter.

Andrade had warned him, all those years ago. So had Tobin, and Chay, and Ostvel. But Rohan had been too sure of his own cleverness. Too arrogant in his own power to consider what use she might make of hers. Too willing to believe that she would work to the best of her abilities for Pol's cause in Princemarch.

Oh, yes, she had worked. To the best of her considerable abilities.

He could not speak, mortally afraid of saying anything to upset this terrible balance between them, which if overset might turn her against him and Pol. She held power over him that terrified and infuriated him. But he was as incapable of killing her now as he had been of killing Ianthe years ago at Feruche. *Coward!* he accused himself, and had to answer, *Yes.*

Pandsala's low, intense voice clawed at him. "His eyes—they might be mine, you know, in shape if not in color. There's something about him—things that don't speak of her but of me. I saw it in him from the first. He should have been ours, Rohan, not hers! She doesn't deserve him. I've seen how he looks at her with such love— love that should have been *mine*—"

"She—" He choked and like a swordstroke to his heart the knowledge was in him: *She doesn't know.* And abruptly the balance shifted to him. That one truth was more powerful than all her lies. She believed Pol to be Sioned's son. She did not know about Ianthe. And as the power surged in him, strong and deadly as Sioned sometimes described the flare of Sunrunner's power, he knew he would use that truth as ruthlessly as Ianthe herself would have done.

"I've thought of him as ours," Pandsala went on softly, almost dreamily. "When she's not nearby I can believe he's yours and mine. No mother in blood could love him more, want more for him. If you think what I've done is horrible, then think what his life would have been had I not acted. All those rivals that might have come from my sisters' marriages—I rid him of most of them and I'm glad! He'll be High Prince and *faradhi* and the most powerful man who ever lived! Think what I've done out of love for him, Rohan, things *she* would never have done!"

Her eyes glittered with enchantment at her work on Pol's behalf, actions that would haunt his manhood as High Prince and *faradhi*. The balance between that clean, proud boy on one side and this terrible blood-soaked woman on the other was suddenly intolerable.

"Sioned would never have done such things," Rohan said quietly. "But Ianthe would."

Pandsala stared at him without comprehension.

"Your sister! Pol's mother!" he shouted, shaking her until her head lolled on her neck, long hair tumbling about her face. "Did you think she lured me to Feruche and kept me there to indulge in common torture? Why do you think she let me go? She was pregnant with my son! The child you claim to love is the child of the sister you hate! Pol is Ianthe's son—and mine!''

Pandsala let out a keening moan and crumpled to her knees, huddled over, rocking back and forth with her arms clasped around her chest as if to hold her body together. Rohan stood over her and spoke words that splintered even the broken shards of her.

''The first time, I thought she was Sioned. The second time it was rape. I knew exactly who she was and what I was doing. She kept me there until she was sure, and then laughed and let me go. I went to battle, knowing that my son was in her belly. Sioned knew it, too—she waited, waited—and then went to Feruche to take the child, and razed the castle to the ground. How does it feel to know you've worked and schemed and murdered on behalf of Ianthe's son?''

Pandsala had killed children. Naydra's unborn son, Jos of Ossetia who had been only a little boy. She had left other children fatherless, motherless; she had taken children from old men, and women who could bear no more.

She had done it for hatred of Roelstra, rejoicing that a prince not of his blood would rule his lands, that heirs of his line would never sit at Castle Crag. She had done it for love of Rohan, rejoicing that the man her father and Ianthe had hated would rule Princemarch. And now she knew that the boy who had been her revenge was of Roelstra's blood and Ianthe's bearing. She gave a sob that sounded like her last breath and sank her fingers into her coiled hair, rocking from side to side.

''What you've done—Goddess—what you've done will burden him for the rest of his life,'' Rohan said. ''But *you* will burden him no longer.''

She looked up at that, face swollen with congealed horror and the tears that welled in her eyes but did not fall. ''If I have to die, let me die for a purpose,'' she choked.

''What purpose? Killing Masul?'' He wanted to demand why, if she was so loyal to Pol, she had not killed Masul long before this. But he knew that if she could have, she would have. ''Oh, no. He lives until he's proven a liar. I'll not spend the rest of my life hearing doubts of Pol's claim to Princemarch.'' He smiled thinly. ''And it's rather a good claim, don't you agree?''

She slumped, her hair straggling about her, and in the sunlight he saw the streaks of white through it. "Then kill me now," she said tonelessly.

"Pol can't afford it. If I put you on trial and you're condemned as you deserve, the burden on him will be the greater. So I won't kill you." *But, Goddess, how I'd like to, and with my bare hands. . . .* "Perhaps I'm the coward Chiana thinks I am. But after what you've done— I think the better death for you is the kind your father condemned you to years ago. I won't send you to Goddess Keep. You'll retire quietly to a manor somewhere— perhaps I'll rebuild Feruche for you," he suggested viciously. "Would you like to supervise its reconstruction, Pandsala? Would you?"

A shudder of loathing went through her. Still, she had courage enough to meet his gaze. "Whatever you wish, my lord. I am yours now, as I always have been."

"I don't accept such gifts as you offer. Do you even understand what you've done? Do you?"

"I know that I did it all for the best, for Pol. For you. I loved you both. Goddess help me, I still do. I regret nothing."

"You will. Believe me, in the years ahead, while you watch the Long Sand from Feruche, you will know what regret is."

He knew it now himself, for he could not kill her even though every fiber of him screamed for her death. It would be nothing more than justice for all the murders she had done, all the men and women and children she had destroyed in Pol's name. He was momentarily tempted. But the barbarian in him was the victor, pulling in harness for once with the civilized prince. Condemning her to a living death immured at Feruche was infinitely more cruel than if he had indeed thrust a knife through her heart. More vicious, and more practical.

No, he would not kill her, and he could not expose her crimes. He would have to live with this. And so would she.

"Get up," he ordered. When it seemed she had no strength to rise, he took her by the elbows and yanked her to her feet. She stumbled, scraped her hair back, and went down to the river to wash the stains of emotion from her face. Rohan watched impassively, wanting nothing so much as her death. He now understood the impulse as his own shame at having been so wrong, so fatally wrong. Was that truly what he couldn't stand? That he could make so hideous a mistake? He wished he could seek Sioned's counsel. But he forbade himself that comfort, that sure understanding. Forever.

When Pandsala had tidied her hair and smoothed her skirts, Rohan started back to the encampment. He heard her half-stumbling footsteps behind him. Wherever he was, whatever exile he condemned her to, he knew he would hear those footsteps behind him for the rest of his life—tripping over corpses.

* * *

Prince Lleyn required not only the support of his cane but that of his son's strong arm as he made his way into Rohan's pavilion. Chadric settled his father in a chair and stood beside him, his face carefully schooled to neutrality. Lleyn's expression was perfectly easy to read; he voiced both annoyance and curiosity at once.

"Very well, I'm here. Now tell me what it is that can't wait another instant."

Rohan stood before the old man. "Forgive me for summoning you here," he began quietly.

"You wouldn't have made it an order from the High Prince unless it was necessary. Tell me, damn it!"

"I need a great favor from you, my lord. From both you and Prince Chadric." He hesitated, then cast a glance at Sioned. Her head was bent, her fingers laced tightly together in her lap, her body utterly still. He had kept his promise to himself, had told her nothing. And how she resented it.

Returning his gaze to Lleyn, he went on, "Firon desires a prince descended from its own royalty. I ask you now if you would do me the favor of considering your grandson Prince Laric for that position."

Lleyn's parchment skin flushed slightly across the cheekbones and he fixed Rohan with a hard, questioning glare. But it was Chadric who spoke, his voice as bewildered as his expression.

"Laric? Why? Your son's claim is much stronger, coming through both you and Princess Sioned—"

"Be still," Lleyn whispered. His gaze now read into Rohan's soul. It was a very long time before he spoke in a voice like the rustling of dry leaves. "I thought Firon settled on Pol. Something has changed your mind. Something that occurred today. I do not believe it was the vote, but if that is the reason you wish to give, then I will accept it."

Rohan bent his head. "Thank you, my lord."

"With my grandson as Prince of Firon, you will have a sixth and deciding vote in Pol's favor. I understand this much. I will not ask you why this was not proposed earlier, when it could have saved us all a great deal of trouble."

Again Rohan nodded, almost a bow.

"But have you thought this through? You know I have no ambitions outside my own island. Chadric will take my place when I am gone, and after him his eldest son, Ludhil. For Laric there will be his mother's manor of Sandeia, or governorship of the ports, or whatever he likes and suits his talents. We do not meddle in the concerns of the continent, Rohan. We have no need to. It is one reason we thrive."

"I understand, my lord. But it is not possible for my son to inherit Firon or any portion of it."

He had just undergone a stormy passage with Sioned, Tobin, and Chay on precisely that subject. Understandably, they had all argued. And for the first time in their experience of him, he had shouted that it was his decision and his will and they would abide by the dictates of the High Prince or else. Stunned, hurt, and furious, Tobin had swept out of the pavilion in a rage. Chay had followed after a single eloquent glare. Speechless with betrayal, Sioned had refused to look at him at all. She remained only because Rohan had ordered her to be present during his talk with Lleyn and Chadric. He hated himself for not telling them the truth, but he simply could not bring himself to do so.

As for Firon, he had no choice. What Pandsala had done by murdering Prince Ajit had made taking the princedom impossible. He could not bring the dead back to life, but he could refuse to profit by the crime. Small comfort, when there were so many other crimes from which he had unknowingly gained so much.

"Pol cannot take Firon," he repeated.

"Why?" Lleyn asked. "Do you believe an excess of power would be dangerous? Or do you believe that Andrade will not produce sufficient evidence tonight?"

Sioned was the one who answered. Her low, quiet tones startled Rohan. "It is the perception others would have of an excess of power, my lord. You've had the care of my son, you and my lord Chadric. You know him. Do you think he would ever abuse any power he was given?"

"Of course not!" Chadric exclaimed. "Honor is as much a part of him as the blood in his veins. But that wasn't our doing, my lady."

"We will share the credit, if you please," she replied softly, and looked up with a faint smile. "But as well as we know and trust him, others would not. Or at least, they would choose not to. He will have the Desert and Princemarch. That is enough."

Lleyn still watched Rohan. "I've never known you to act out of imagined fears or threats."

"Yet we all have our secret terrors," Rohan responded. "Volog fears for his grandson that the eventual union of Kierst and Isel will be an uneasy one. Davvi fears that Tilal's marriage to Gemma, bringing him Ossetia's throne, will set him against his brother Kostas when the latter inherits Syr. You fear involvement on the continent. We are all afraid, my lord. Only some of us have the option of removing some of our fears.

"You could say that I am frightened for my son, and you would be correct. Enough burdens will be placed on him—the Desert, Princemarch, the title of High Prince, his Sunrunner gifts. Is it cowardice or prudence on my part to remove a probable cause for dissension, and threats not only to his power but to his life?"

"And you hope to do this by using my grandson."

"Yes," Rohan said quite frankly.

Lleyn tilted his head up and stared at Chadric, whose amazement had become worry. "Could Laric do it?" the old man asked.

"I don't know."

"Come, don't be modest about him! Could he rule Firon?"

Sioned leaned slightly forward in her chair. "My lords, would he be happy there? While I agree that it would be best for everyone else if Laric were to rule Firon, if it would not be best for Laric, then I am opposed to the plan."

Rohan shot her a dark glance that she ignored.

"Your beauty is equaled by your heart, my dear," Lleyn said. Then he sighed and shook his head. "I don't know. I've outlived myself, I think."

"I'm sorry to trouble you with this," Rohan said. "But I had to, my lord. Believe me."

"I do, I do." Lleyn squared his frail shoulders and said more briskly, "If I might have the use of a Sunrunner to speak with Eolie tonight at Graypearl, then we can let the boy choose. But it will be *his* choice, Rohan, not mine or even his father's. Modesty aside, I think he'd do very well. He'd be wasted on a manor or supervising the silk trade or the pearl beds. He's young, to be sure, and rather studious—but I seem to recall another young and bookish princeling who hasn't done too badly for himself." The old man cocked a brow at Rohan, who felt a smile touch his lips for the first time that day. "And the young are flexible, Goddess knows. They learn quickly how to be princes. I assume there will be treaties providing him with military support, should he require it?"

"Of course. I've drawn up a proposal for your inspection." He took the parchment from his desk and gave it to Chadric. "Should Cunaxa attempt anything, the Desert will invade from Tiglath. Volog will, I believe, provide naval support. And there is a stretch of the border between Firon and Princemarch that would serve for a garrison. If there's anything else you think Laric will need, please don't hesitate to add it."

"Generous of our cousin of Kierst," Lleyn remarked dryly. "But then, it's all in the family, isn't it? Tell me, Rohan, why not his younger boy?"

"Volnaya is only seventeen—not even knighted yet. Besides, Davvi's sons will one day rule Syr and Ossetia. Volog's grandson Arlis will unite Kierst and Isel when he inherits. Pol will have the Desert and Princemarch. They are all near kin to Pol. But Laric is not, Dorval is very far from Firon.''

''Ah, yes. The two will not merge as those others will. Although I wouldn't count on Kostas and Tilal working closely together, without someone keeping a very tight rein on both. But have *you* considered that with my grandson in Firon, Pol will eventually have four kinsmen controlling five princedoms among them? With Prince-march and the Desert combined, that makes six out of eleven. That's a rather threatening total—when you're not one of the six.''

''I've thought about it,'' Rohan admitted. ''And about Tilal and Kostas, as you've said. But though I know this kin-network is likely to fall apart in a generation or two, by then we'll all be dead and it'll be someone else's problem.''

''Someone else's secret fear.'' The old prince smiled grimly. ''Well, then, find me a Sunrunner who knows Eolie's colors, and we'll inform my unsuspecting grandson that he can become a prince.'' He eyed Sioned. ''No, my dear, you may *not* volunteer to be that Sunrunner. Andrade has sufficient *faradh'im* in her suite to spare me one this afternoon.''

Chadric helped his father up, supporting him as far as the doorway. The frail body abruptly straightened. ''I can walk,'' Lleyn snapped. ''Leave me be.''

''Of course, Father.''

When they were gone, Rohan turned to Sioned. She was staring at her hands again, unnaturally still. The fire-gold hair was in shadow, the brilliant eyes veiled by her lashes. It hurt to see her light dimmed, and to know that he had caused it.

''I know you don't understand,'' he began quietly.

''No. I don't.'' She lifted her face, her eyes dark. ''What did Pandsala say to you today? I don't believe your reasons for this any more than Lleyn does. What did she tell you, Rohan?''

He was tempted. Goddess, he wanted so much to let the truth flood out of him. Stubborn self-pity forbade it.

''You swore once never to lie to me,'' she whispered.

''I never have.''

Her eyes flared with sudden challenge. But after a time she looked away again. "Damn you."

Rohan sank into the chair Lleyn had used, feeling nearly as old as the man who had recently vacated it. And alone. Goddess, alone as he had not felt since his early youth, when he had dreamed and worked and slept and lived alone. Before Sioned.

He gazed at her proud head, bent now, and the ache in him was not so much for her pain as for his own, a selfish pain that was his punishment for what he had given Pandsala the power to do. But there was a cure for his pain, and for Sioned's. Neither of them had to be alone. Weak and cowardly he was—but he could not live outside the solace of his wife's mind and heart.

By the time he finished telling her, she had covered her face with her hands as if the words had brought pictures she could not bear to see. She said nothing for a long time. Then, at last, she whispered, "Her father watered a living green meadow with salt. She has done it with blood."

Rohan winced, remembering. That autumn and winter of his war against Roelstra, it had rained for more days than anyone wanted to count. With the first break in the storms, he and Chay and Davvi had ridden out to survey the plain where Roelstra's armies had camped. The troops were gone. In their place was a wide, shallow lake created by diverting a tributary of the Faolain. But before the water had been let in to drown the grasses and soak the soil to viscous mud, the entire meadow had been sown with salt.

Roelstra had had the power to order the befoulment of the Earth itself. Rohan had looked on it, the sharp fumes of rotting soil and salt thick in his nostrils, and nearly wept. He felt the same sick despair now.

"All that blood—" Sioned looked up, her eyes haunted. "It's on us, too, Rohan. We're trying to wash it clean, but it won't come off. She's just like Ianthe, just like her! Why didn't we *see?*"

"It was my blindness. Not yours. I won't let you blame yourself for my failure."

She shook her head stubbornly. Tears spilled down her cheeks. "We were warned, both of us. And we didn't listen. Oh, sweet Goddess—Rohan, what have we done? Roelstra's daughter!''

"None of this will touch Pol. Sioned, listen to me. I won't let it touch our son."

"He's not my son!"

He was up in an instant, taking her face between his hands. "Don't! He *is* your son!"

Tears streaked her skin like scars, and against her white cheek the whiteness of the crescent-shaped mark was livid. "Make me believe it. Make me believe I did the right thing when he was born—"

"If you doubt it, then tell him the truth. Now. Today."

Her eyes widened and he held his breath, fearing that the deliberate shock had been a mistake. But a moment later she shuddered and reached for him. He drew her up, folded her to his heart.

"I can't do that to him," she whispered. "Not so young." Another quiver coursed through her. "What a liar I am! It's myself I'm frightened for, Rohan. I don't want to lose him."

"You couldn't. Not ever. Sioned, he's your son. You're his mother."

After a time she nodded against his shoulder. "I have to believe that, don't I?" She pulled back from him, knuckling her eyes. "You haven't said what you're going to do with Pandsala."

"I can hardly reward nearly fifteen years of service with a public execution. Not without revealing everything."

"Another of our secret fears," Sioned added bitterly. "Let her live. She'll never talk. Let her rot somewhere."

"Who will we put in her place at Castle Crag?" He already had someone in mind, but wondered if her thoughts would harmonize with his.

"Ostvel," she said at once. "There's no one else we can trust as fully. Riyan can take over at Skybowl—he's young but he knows his home inside out, and he also knows about the gold. It has to be Ostvel, Rohan."

"Exactly," he agreed, relieved that the loneliness had vanished for them both. Then all other emotion was superceded by a vast weariness. "Sioned—I can't help thinking that if I'd done what I should have in the first place—''

''Kill Masul? Would it shock you to know that I agree with you?'' She gave him an unpleasant smile. ''But Inoat and Jos and Ajit and all the others would still be dead. Pandsala would have gone on murdering anyone she perceived as being in Pol's way. And who knows—when Pol had children, she might have killed Tilal's and Kostas' and Laric's sons, too, so all of it could be brought under Pol's rule. It's what Andrade's always wanted, you know,'' she added bitterly. ''Rohan, if you'd killed Masul, the only thing that would have been different—not better—is that we'd be murderers, just like her.''

Rohan held her to him again. ''We may wish we were barbarians. But we have the misfortune to want to be civilized. Goddess help us.''

''It's a stupid ambition,'' she answered. ''In such times as these, the height of folly.''

''I agree. But we still have to play out the little comedy. I'll have Tallain find Ostvel and we'll break the news to him.''

''Gently. Very gently.'' Tilting her face to his, she added, ''Rohan—could you have kept silent to me about Pandsala forever? Could you?''

He shook his head. ''No. I told myself that I could, that I must. But it seems I'm so made that I can't live apart from you in any way. I need you too much.''

Sioned smoothed the slowly silvering blond hair from his forehead. ''Beloved,'' she whispered. ''Beloved.''

Chapter Twenty-four

With the tension over Masul that morning and the nervous speculation about what Andrade would do that evening, nearly everyone had forgotten that the afternoon would bring ceremonies making knights of fifteen young squires. On a knoll overlooking the encampments there gathered the families and sponsors of the young men, but none of the usual gaiety attended on the scene.

"It's a poor celebration of knighthood for them," Maarken said to Andry, shaking his head. "I looked forward to this day my whole life."

Andry, who had not, nevertheless sympathized with Sorin, Riyan, and the others who had worked so hard and so long, only to have the supreme moment of their young lives blighted by the political troubles of their elders.

"It'll be special for them," he said, trying to sound confident, "no matter what else is going on. I remember you looked as if you and Lleyn were the only two people in the world at that moment. They'll feel that way, too—if only for that little bit of time. That's what's important."

"I suppose so."

Andry hesitated, took a quick look around at the others standing in little groups nearby, and decided he would not be overheard. "Maarken, have you talked to Hollis?"

Maarken stiffened. "No. Not today."

"I don't know why she's acting this way," Andry continued unwisely. "All during the time we were working on the scrolls, she talked about you and asked questions about Radzyn and the Desert, and now she won't even—"

"Do you know what you're talking about?" Maarken asked in a deadly soft voice.

Andry swallowed hard. "No," he whispered. "I guess not. But, Maarken, it's just that I—"

Frosty gray eyes the exact color of their father's glared down the finger's width that separated them in height. But after a moment Maarken sighed and gripped Andry's shoulder briefly. "Sorry. I just can't talk about it now, all right?"

Nodding, relieved that his beloved eldest brother had not seen fit to provide him with a broken jaw in payment for his prying, Andry turned his attention to the crest of the knoll, where the squires had assembled in strict order of precedence.

Fifteen of them stood in the afternoon sunshine, straight and proud in their sponsoring lords' colors, the hues of their fathers' holdings seen in the dyed leather of their belts. This made for sometimes garish results—Lord Sabriam's younger brother, Bosaia, for instance. The yellow and orange of their city of Einar competed to eye-popping effect with the already violent combination of pink and crimson in the tunic of Lower Pyrme, where he had been fostered. Riyan, in Clutha's light green with Skybowl's blue and brown in his belt, was luckier than most. And Sorin's tunic of Kierstian scarlet was brilliantly set off by Radzyn's red and white circling his waist.

There were no sons of princes being knighted today but, as a son of the most important lord in the Desert and grandson of a prince, Sorin naturally was first. Andry and Maarken stood with their parents, watching proudly as Volog slipped the golden buckle onto Sorin's belt and Alasen gave him one of the small loaves of bread baked especially for the occasion, together with a small silver vial of salt. Tradition also asserted that knights were given other tokens according to which court had fostered them. Kierst always presented the bread on a finely glazed plate, crafted by a master at New Raetia itself and rimmed in gold from the island's own mines.

Andry felt his heart twist suddenly. It might have been himself standing there, blushing a little as Alasen smiled on him. It *could* have been him—except that the ambition for knighthood had never burned inside him. All his fire was reserved for *faradhi* things. And it would be many long years before he had attained the status in his chosen realm that Sorin had achieved today in his. He cast a furtive look at his rings, and once more mentally added those that would bring the number to nine and then ten.

Alasen and Volog led Sorin over to his family. In the interval before the next young man was called, they had a few moments for hugs and congratulations. Andry embraced his twin fondly, proud to bursting—and yet when Alasen laughed and gave Sorin what she termed "Your first *real* kiss from a lady," he unaccountably turned away, unable to watch.

As the second squire was being made a knight, a quiet voice said at his shoulder, "It might have been you up there, you know."

Andry looked up at his father, startled and embarrassed that somehow his thoughts had been guessed. And for an instant he was afraid that he had indeed deeply disappointed this man he revered and loved, who had never truly understood his dreams. But Chay was neither dissatisfied with him nor angry. The gray eyes were loving, and the hand resting on his back was warm with affection.

Still, Andry could not help murmuring, "You're not sorry, are you?"

"I would be if *you* were. But if you're content, then so am I." He gave a soft chuckle. "Listen to how mellow I've become in my old age!" Then, seriously, he added, "Andry, I'm proud of *all* my sons."

He bit his lip and nodded blindly.

Younger sons and younger brothers came forward with their sponsors, and received gold buckles, bread, salt, and each *athri*'s special gift. From nearby, Rohan and Sioned and Pol presided over the whole, and the honor of being knighted in front of the High Prince, High Princess, and their heir was not lost on any of the young men so elevated. After making their bows to their lords, they turned, marched a few paces to the left, and bowed even lower to the royal trio. Smiles greeted each new-made knight: approving from Rohan, kind from Sioned, and a trifle envious from Pol.

Riyan made his appearance toward the end of the ceremonies, being the son of a relatively minor *athri* without important blood-bond to any royal house. He accepted the usual gifts from Prince Clutha and his eldest daughter, a statuesque lady of great dignity and a sudden mischievous smile as she gave the young man Meadowlord's traditional gift: a flask carved from the horn of a stag. The proportions of the animal who had contributed the horn must have been truly awesome, for the flask held enough wine to make a man blind drunk.

"I hope you won't mind if I share this first one with you in celebration," said Princess Gennadi. Riyan returned her grin as she undid the stopper, bright with silver and a circle of tiny sapphires, and expertly tilted the flask to spray a stream of crimson wine into her throat. Righting the horn, she gave it to Riyan. He offered it first to Clutha—who was shaking so hard with repressed laughter that he nearly missed his open jaws—and then took a large mouthful for himself.

"My lord, my lady," Riyan said to them as he re-corked the flask and hung it around his shoulder by its silver chain, "I wish for you what you've so graciously made sure of for me—may you never, ever thirst!"

Everyone was more than glad of the chance to laugh. Clay slapped Ostvel on the back and announced, "That boy's got style!" as Riyan made his bow to Clutha and Gennadi. Rohan, Sioned, and Pol were grinning broadly as the young knight approached and bent low before them.

Ostvel, rigid with nerves during Riyan's presentation, nearly wilted with relief as his son walked over to him. But he quickly recovered himself, turned to Chay, and said slyly, "Now, my old friend—are you seriously willing to see anyone with *less* style riding that beautiful dapple-gray mare?"

Chay might have been proof against Ostvel's blandishment, but when Princess Alasen turned the full force of her eyes on him and pleaded Riyan's case, he was lost. His wife saw it, and laughed.

"Give in, you old miser," she scolded, nudging him with an ungentle elbow. "You'd never be happy if anybody else rode Dalziel and you know it."

Chay groaned. But by the time Riyan joined them to collect congratulations and embraces, he was resigned. "Well, it looks as if you'll be riding off with my prize mare this year, thanks to your father—and a certain pair of big green eyes I should know by now how to resist," he added in Alasen's direction. "Sioned has a look just like that!"

Again Andry felt a delicate, exquisite twisting in his chest when Riyan bent over Alasen's wrist to thank her. When she smiled, the ache was worse. And when she glanced laughingly at him, those green eyes alight, he suddenly knew what was wrong with him.

To hide it, he looked away. It was the worst possible thing he could have done. Alasen was no fool. Only three winters his senior, she had lived at a great palace all her life and not in the relative isolation of Goddess Keep for the last six years, as he had. She had seen his like before, known the adoration of countless young men ever since she could remember. She knew exactly what he felt. And she would laugh, amused to have collected yet another heart, and pity him for giving that heart where it could find no home. Doubtless his feelings, so vital to him, would be to her just the worship of one more callow fool too young to know what love was. Bitterly humiliated, he compelled himself to have the courage to look her in the face.

What he saw stunned him.

Her eyes were clear and soft and gentle. She was not laughing at him. She did not pity him. She knew what he felt for her. But she did not smile in kind rejection.

Alasen might not love him, but she was shyly pleased that he loved her.

Andry's world turned to hazy colors, all unfocused around the green of her eyes, the ivory of her skin, the sweet rose of her mouth, the rich gold-lit brown of her hair. Sunlight spun through him seemingly of its own accord, and through it he felt her other colors: glowing moonstone, bright ruby, deep onyx. She gasped softly, feeling the woven light lace its brilliance around and through her. All the colors of late summer swirled around them, sweet and shining in a dance fitted to the music of birds and wind and the coursing of blood in their veins. Andry realized it was Alasen's first experience of her *faradhi* gifts, and in soaring joy knew it was something only he could show her.

Delight flushed her cheeks as she gazed up into his eyes, and they were the only people in the world for many shared heartbeats. But all at once there *was* a world again, its demand harsh and frightening as through their enchantment they both heard the name *Masul*.

He strode up to the place where all the other squires had been knighted. But his sponsor was not Kiele's husband Lord Lyell. At his side was Miyon of Cunaxa, whose bright orange tunic Masul wore. The outrageous presumption of the man, the sheer audacity of it, spread shocked silence over the knoll like a cloud. Andry's gentle glowing haze of color became so sharply focused that he winced. He saw with painful clarity the white fury of

Rohan's face, the crimson of Chay's as he fought down terrible rage.

The formula rang out mockingly as Masul knelt before Miyon and the latter said, "I have examined this candidate in all aspects, and found him worthy of my sponsorship for knighthood. Therefore I charge him to serve the Goddess and the truth, to live honorably and courageously in rich times and in bitter. In token of both I give him bread and salt, and in token of his new and honored state I give this golden buckle."

Loaf and vial were presented, and Masul's violet belt decorated with a large hollow circle of gold, pierced with gold. Then, grinning slyly, Miyon called one of his squires forward and a startled gasp went through the audience, for with the presentation of the final gift it was remembered that Cunaxa, home of the finest metalsmiths on the continent, traditionally gave as its special gift a sword.

Newly girded with a magnificent blade in a gorgeous scabbard set like the hilt with amethysts, Masul sauntered a few paces and made his brief, mocking bow to Rohan, Sioned, and Pol. The first nodded curtly, rigid with his effort at control. Sioned, equally furious, acknowledged Masul's salute with a grim stare. But the boy, for all his youth and inexperience, was the one who saved the disaster for them.

With absolute, proud calm, and in a clear voice that carried across the grassy knoll, he said, "Something mars your appearance."

Masul straightened up and stared. "What are you talking about?"

"Your belt." The corners of Pol's mouth lifted in a tiny, cold smile. "Violet with orange—what a painful mistake in color, especially to a Sunrunner's eyes. And I am certain it *was* a mistake."

"Violet is the color of Princemarch," Masul replied with scant courtesy to this stripling prince he could have broken in half.

"And Princemarch," Pol informed him pleasantly, "is mine. Be so good as to rectify the mistake, and remove the belt."

If he refused, there would be pandemonium. If he obeyed—

Miyon hastened forward and whispered something urgent in Masul's ear. The pretender's face turned several sequentially darker shades of red. Miyon said something else, and backed away. And Masul, salvaging what he could of a battle he had lost, undid the golden buckle so recently clasped around his waist.

"As you wish—my lord," he added insultingly. The sight of him juggling loaf, salt, and sword while trying to undo the buckle from the leather brought grins and even a few open titters of laughter. But Pol waited with perfect aplomb while Masul struggled to maintain his dignity and comply with a request he dared not refuse. Pol was in the right. Princemarch still belonged to him. Defiance now would be foolhardy.

The long strip of violet-dyed leather was freed. Masul held it in one fist, as if strangling a poisonous snake. Pol was wise enough not to extend his hands for it, and thus Masul did not have the satisfaction of dropping it into the dirt for Pol to retrieve. Tallain appeared silently at Masul's side, and before the pretender could even consider throwing it to the ground, took the belt and coiled it nearly as he returned to his post near the royal trio.

Pol nodded graciously. "Now you look much better, and your tunic is much easier on the eyes. You have our permission to withdraw."

Masul's green eyes bored into his. "Keep your precious color, princeling," he sneered.

"I intend to," Pol replied.

With Miyon in attendance, Masul stalked off down the hill. He was not even out of sight before someone, no one ever knew who, sent up a raucous cheer that was Pol's name.

Andry, who had watched the whole with his breath caught in his throat, laughed aloud and joined his family in its surge to Rohan, Sioned, and Pol. If there were disgruntled partisans of the pretender on that hillside, they vanished quickly in the wake of Pol's small, telling triumph.

A little while later, when everyone was heading down the knoll to their camps, Alasen caught up to Andry and asked, "I understand what Prince Pol did—and it was masterful—but why was that man knighted?"

"It wasn't just to irritate us," Andry agreed.

"Yes, our young prince did very well today, didn't he?" Ostvel said from behind them, where he walked with Riyan and Chay. "I thought the pretender would have a seizure! Pol's definitely his father's son, Chay."

"A fact Masul is currently cursing," Andry's father replied with a tight grin. "But if you'll excuse me, I'd like to hurry back to camp. I want to be the one to tell old Lleyn about this."

"Do it carefully!" Ostvel called after him. "He's likely to laugh himself into a fit!"

"My lord," Alasen said to Ostvel, "I still don't understand why—"

"Just for spite, my lady," Riyan said quickly. "Father, Tallain says we're to meet their graces immediately after this. We'd best hurry."

"Of course. Andry, will you see Princess Alasen safe to her father's care? We seem to have been separated from his grace in the crowd."

Andry would have kept her safe even if a thousand mounted knights suddenly thundered down on them. He suspected his face showed it as he said, "Of course, my lord."

"Good. I leave you in his capable hands, then, my lady." Ostvel smiled again at Alasen, and she smiled back.

"They didn't answer us," she said when they had gone.

"No." Andry couldn't bring himself to care. "My lady—Alasen—"

She blushed and his heart turned over. It was a very long time before either remembered that they were supposed to be going to her father's tents.

* * *

Andrade glanced up. Ostvel was holding her cloak over one arm, his face in shadow. No lamps had been lit, and the setting sun had turned the white tent to gray mist around them. She rose, smoothed her hair, and allowed him to drape the cloak around her shoulders.

"My Lady—"

"No." She heard her voice sharp with nervous tension, and clenched her fists beneath the concealing folds of material. "No," she said again, more softly. "All will be well."

"There's nothing I can say to dissuade you."

"Of course not. Hurry up. This must be done before moonrise. Is everyone assembled?"

"Yes."

"Then let's get this over with. I've had enough of this Masul person."

"As have we all," he muttered.

The late sun hovered in a sky washed pale yellow. Andrade mounted the knoll where knighting ceremonies had been held that afternoon. She smelled rain in the air, and fear not her own, as she stood outside the circle assembled on the hill. Twenty-five people stood around an empty firepit, a necklace of princely power threaded by *faradh'im*. When Andrade and Urival joined them, they would number twenty-seven—one of the multiples of three strictly prescribed for what she was about to do. Andrade found the mystical significance of three absurd, and suspected Lady Merisel had, too. But she did not dare flout traditions she knew nothing about.

Andrade had carefully planned the balance of powers, both political and *faradhi,* around the circle. There was nothing in the Star Scroll that demanded it, but her own sense of balance had focused the two conflicting sides directly opposite each other. Sioned acted as the Desert's Sunrunner, as usual; Rohan stood to her right, his eyes dark with guilt. Pol had insisted on his privilege as titular ruler of Princemarch—and Pandsala could not have joined the circle in any case, for the presence of persons who could appear in this kind of conjure was forbidden. Tobin, despite her mere three honorary rings and her lack of formal training at Goddess Keep, was acting as Pol's Sunrunner. On the other side of the circle were Miyon of Cunaxa and the four other princes who supported Masul's claim. *Faradh'im,* including Hollis, stood between them. Chale had selected Riyan as his Sunrunner. Andry had asked for and received permission to stand with Volog as his *faradhi* link in the circle. On his other side was Lleyn, with Maarken at his side. Lady Eneida represented Firon; Urival would stand with her. Young Sejast had volunteered to act as Davvi's *faradhi*. They completed the circle next to Sioned.

They were all looking at her with differing mixtures of wary apprehension, worry, and simple curiosity. Urival took her cloak at a gesture of her fingers, and she spared a glance for the swords and knives laid neatly out on a blanket on the grass. Ostvel would watch over them—and over Chiana and Masul, who also could not be part of the circle. Others stood outside, as well: Chay and Sorin with Alasen, Tilal and Kostas beside Gemma and Danladi. Pandsala stayed apart, seeming calm and confident until one saw her deep, shadow-bruised eyes.

Kiele had the temerity to approach Andrade, but one cold look kept her from speaking. She returned to Masul's side. The pretender arched a sardonic brow at the Lady of Goddess Keep, but if the expression reminded her of Roelstra, she did not allow herself to think it.

She nodded Urival to his place in the circle and entered it herself, standing before the firepit. Logs had been stacked in a heavy triangle, kindling piled beneath them, ready for Sunrunner's Fire. Andrade watched as the sun dipped lower, the sky gradually darkening. She had only a short wait before the moons would rise; this conjuring could take place only beneath stars. When the first of them winked into view in the east, she lifted one beringed hand. Urival stepped forward with a small flask. He opened it for her, took a small golden cup from his pocket, and poured out *dranath*-laced wine.

Andrade drank it quickly. Almost at once her head began to throb. She drank more; the ache faded to a glow of well-being, an almost sexual pleasure in the flow of blood through her veins and air through her lungs. Heat spread along her body, a slow uncurling of power that nothing in the Star Scroll had prepared her for. The sky went dark while she drank again. And it seemed to her that the stars exploded into being simultaneously, made of a million different colors that she could weave into the fabric of her memories.

She was startled when the logs burst into flame. She could not remember having consciously willed it, yet there the Fire was, flaring up toward the light-dazzled night sky. Someone gasped; perhaps it was herself. She did not know and certainly did not care. This was power beyond anything she had ever felt. It sang through her, promised delights of mind and flesh and spirit that enchanted her. Sweet, clean, omnipotent, acting on the already extraordinary strengths that had made her Lady of Goddess Keep, the *dranath* rushed through her and she nearly laughed aloud.

Andrade reached for the energies of the Sunrunners circled around her, wove their varying colors into a taut, shining fabric disciplined by her strong mind. It was a cloak she wore for only an instant before it melted into her flesh and became part of her augmented powers. So *this* was a sorcerer's way, she thought, *this* was what she had been so afraid of. How foolish! The ascent was dazzling. She had no thought for the fall.

Turning her face to the flames that leaped higher, higher with her every thought, she effortlessly caused the scenes of her memory to play out in smoky patterns superimposed on the red-gold heat. If there were gasps of fearful surprise, she did not hear them. She knew only the soaring glory of power.

The sailing barge swayed with the gentle motion of the Faolain River, the night sky bright overhead with stars. Palila lay in bed, straining in labor. Ianthe appeared, lips moving soundlessly, and as Andrade left the cabin she saw the princess sit beside Roelstra's mistress, stroking her hand. A staircase, steep and dark; a cramped, dim room, where two other women struggled to give birth, presided over by Pandsala. A third clutched her newborn fiercely to her breast. Andrade helped the other two as best she could, then left for the upstairs cabin once more. The night whirled dizzily, sickeningly around her as she stood on deck. The star-dappled water seemed to rise up, trying to claim a Sunrunner. When the world stopped spinning, she was given a swallow from a sailor's pocket flask.

Memories overlapped skittishly for a moment, the face of the kind sailor superimposed on that of a green-eyed corpse: Masul's real father.

Palila's door was locked. Women clustered in the passage, women who were supposed to assist at the birth. Andrade pounded on the carved wood, her rings shim-

mering in the light from a nearby lamp. Abruptly the door was flung open. Ianthe stood there smiling, a violet-wrapped bundle in her arms.

Palila lay spent against the white pillows now, a triumphant smile on her face. When Andrade turned, Ianthe was gone. She hurried into the passageway, where the princess stood with the child, and pushed the blanket from the tiny face. And suddenly Pandsala was there, holding another baby wrapped in gold-embroidered violet. Her face froze in horror at the sight of Andrade.

Roelstra's presence filled the narrow passage—tall, heavy through the shoulders, green eyes blazing. And while Andrade stared at him, Ianthe and Pandsala—and the children in their arms—were out of her view.

And then there were the five of them and the two violet-wrapped children alone in the cabin and Andrade took one of the babies and Palila screamed and Roelstra held a candleflame to his mistress' hair and she became a living torch and the child in Andrade's arms reached glittering claws for her eyes.

The power had hold of her now, dragon talons around her mind. No more did she control the visions that swirled and broke and coalesced again in the flames. She cried out at the agony ripping through her skull. It was the touch of an alien thing, a malignant fiery grasping *thing* tearing at her mind, clawing the *faradhi* colors away, that soft cloak of additional power gone now. There was only Andrade, her blood afire with *dranath*, her eyes blinded by a flash of starlight come to earth.

Clever Andrade, said a mocking voice in her mind. *So very clever! Daring to use* my *kind of power! Learn now that* this *is a sorcerer's way!*

She screamed, fell to her knees with her fire-filled head clutched in both hands, screamed until she had no voice left.

* * *

The circle shattered with Andrade's first cry. The Sunrunners lurched, some of them slumping to the grass, others held up by the terrified princes. Maarken stumbled over to Hollis, who lay senseless at Miyon's feet. Pol clung wild-eyed to Tobin as she moaned softly with pain. Barely catching Sioned when she began to crumple, Ro-

THE STAR SCROLL 457

han shouted for Chay and Ostvel. The fire and its hideous visions raged on, its roar punctuated by terrible screams.

Urival, with the knowledge and strength of his nine rings that had circled his fingers like fire since the first of Andrade's working, wrenched his own colors back from the tangled weave. Let Sioned sort the others out; let her worry about them. He flung himself to his knees beside Andrade, rocking her in his arms, his head nearly bursting and his stricken face contorted in the harsh red glow of the flames. He wrapped Andrade in his own colors, vainly attempting to shield her from encroaching darkness. The others were in danger, but he had no time for them. Not now, not when Andrade's cries were growing weaker. Hanging onto her, his rings burning his flesh, he sobbed and cursed into her silver-gilt hair.

Riyan, Andry—even Pandsala and Alasen outside the circle—all the *faradh'im* were nearly senseless with sudden agony no one not of their kind could understand. The unraveling of Andrade's power-filled weaving created a chaos of colors. Sioned struggled in Rohan's arms, her face sheened in sweat as she tried to sort through a blinding whirlwind of patterns that the ungifted could not see. Pol, giving Tobin over to Chay's strong arms, managed a few steps toward his mother and flung his arms around her waist. She cried out and held his bright head close, separating his glowing colors first. When he was whole again he slid to the ground, shocked and trembling still, but safe.

Sioned worked desperately as the shadows threatened, surged close to darken *faradhi* minds. She beat back the black mist in a frenzy, reformed the elegant shining patterns of Sunrunners nearly lost. At last she gave a great shudder and collapsed in Rohan's arms.

The fire died very suddenly, almost as if a gigantic fist had strangled it. No one saw Segev fall to the grass, seemingly in the same reaction as the other Sunrunners. Only he knew that his collapse came because Mireva had at last released him and the fire she had created through him. He lay in a forgotten heap, breathing heavily around a heartbeat so rapid that it slurred in his chest.

Prince Lleyn limped over to where Andrade was cradled in Urival's arms. He lowered himself to his knees, picked up one of her hands. His proud old face twisted with grief.

Chadric and Audrite approached Rohan where he bent over his wife and son. He shrugged off their compassionate hands, terrified by Sioned's spent face, Pol's uncontrolled shivering. Audrite murmured reassurance with a serenity not reflected in her eyes; Chadric gripped Rohan's shoulder and said, "They'll be all right. There's another who needs you now."

Rohan looked up, followed Chadric's gaze to where Andrade lay. He squeezed his eyes shut, shaking his head in negation of what he had seen. But when he looked again. . . . Tenderly he touched his son's hair, his wife's scarred cheek. Then he went to Andrade.

Alasen was sobbing in a strangled, helpless way in Ostvel's arms. Davvi was supporting Clutha, whose ashen face and glazed eyes betokened shock nearly as severe as the Sunrunners'. Some part of Rohan automatically took note of them all, a warrior keeping track of friend and enemy alike in battle. Sorin bent over his twin brother; Lyell and Kiele shrank back as Rohan passed; Chiana clung to Halian's arm, gasping with imminent hysteria. Pandsala huddled on the ground, hugging her knees. Tobin was gathered up into her husband's arms; Kostas and Chale had Riyan on his feet and coherent by now. Velden and Cabar and Pimantal stood in a little knot of fear.

Masul spoke suddenly, sounds that grated in the cold. "I don't think anything was proved," the pretender observed to Miyon, "except that they can prove nothing."

Tilal answered him, his voice low and harsh. "Close your mouth before I carve another hole in you to keep it company!"

Masul sounded vastly amused. "Is that a threat?"

Gemma straightened within the shelter of Tilal's arm. "Bastard," she hissed furiously. "Lying bastard! It's not only a threat, but I'll hand him his sword to do it!"

Rohan crouched beside Lleyn. His throat was too tight to ask what he feared to have answered. The old man met his gaze, tears running down withered parchment cheeks, and shook his head.

Impossible. Andrade could not die. Rohan gripped Urival's shoulder and the bent head lifted for a moment.

There was no accusation in the golden-brown eyes. There was only agony.

Andrade stirred slightly, her eyes opening, colorless and hazy. She saw Rohan and her lips curved in a tiny, rueful smile. "Pol," she breathed. "Safe?"

He nodded wordlessly.

"Sioned?"

Again he nodded, and the tension left her features. She said his name very softly, with love that was a knife in his heart. "No blame," she murmured, her voice thready now. "Forgive me—"

Forgive *her*? He choked and touched her face. The skin was so cold. "Please—Andrade, please. . . ."

"Sorry . . . I couldn't . . . prove . . ." All at once her gaze hardened. "Kill him," she said very distinctly.

Once more Rohan nodded. Andrade found Lleyn with her gaze and the old imperious command was in her face.

"He will die," Lleyn told her. "Fare you well, dear friend."

She relaxed back into Urival's embrace, looking up at him. Another small, gentle smile lifted the corners of her mouth. When the light left her eyes, she was still gazing at him.

* * *

He would not allow anyone else to touch her. He himself carried her back down the hill, half-blinded by tears that were rivulets of ice down his cheeks in the cold night air. They followed behind: princes and *faradh'im*, enemies, friends, blood of her blood, people of Roelstra's making and of hers. He held her closer, saw the breeze wisp strands of silvery hair about her forehead, saw the rising moons glitter off the ten rings and the chains and the bracelets. Soon enough he would remove them, all but the tenth on her marriage finger, and distribute them amongst her blood kin. And one of them would go to Sioned, as a reminder. But the tenth ring he would leave on her hand, where he would have put his own ring had not Goddess Keep claimed her long before he could, and the delicate chains he would keep for himself.

He heard the others disperse as they neared the torchlit encampment. A few were crying softly; some murmured of comfort or grief or political implication. He carried her into the white pavilion and placed her carefully on her bed.

The High Prince was the only one who dared follow him in. Rohan took a light blanket from the foot of the bed and drew it gently up around her waist.

"She and my mother were twins, but never much alike," he said quietly. "But right now their faces are the same."

Urival understood. Milar had always been the pretty one, the bright and lovely one. Yet Andrade's face in death was smooth, beautiful, its calm giving the lie to the restless impatient spirit that had been freed tonight. He folded her arms atop the blanket, fingertips touching each ring in turn.

"Forgive me," Rohan whispered.

Urival shook his head, glanced at the tormented eyes. "You of all people should know that she never did anything she didn't want to do."

"If I hadn't—"

He sighed impatiently, wishing Rohan would take his guilt somewhere else and leave him in peace with her. "And if there hadn't been the Star Scroll, and if Ianthe hadn't been a scheming bitch and Pandsala with her, and if Andrade hadn't brought Sioned to Goddess Keep—how long must I go on? There's nothing to forgive." He paused, then shrugged. "Perhaps someday you'll believe that."

"Perhaps."

They sat in silence for a long time. At last Urival said, "You have to know it now. Andry will follow her and wear the rings."

"Andry?"

Blue eyes almost the color of Andrade's narrowed in almost the same calculating way. Urival realized there would be echoes of her around him for the rest of his life. But never the same. Never.

"He's no more than a child," Rohan said.

"He's the age you were when you became a ruling prince. He was her choice. The only choice she could make. Not just for Pol's future, but for all *faradh'im*. You don't understand his power—and neither does he, yet." *And Goddess help us when he does*, he told himself.

"If Andrade willed it, then. . . ." Rohan cleared his throat. "I'm sorry for his sake, Urival."

Another silence followed, thick and heavy, like storm-clouds that would not break with rain.

"I heard no dragons," Urival said suddenly.

"Dragons before dawn, death before dawn," Rohan quoted, low-voiced. "Yes, I would have expected that, too."

A soft limping step sounded, and both men turned to find Prince Lleyn making his slow way into the pavilion.

"Your wife is asking for you," he said to Rohan, who rose at once. "Don't panic, boy, she's quite all right. Chadric and Audrite have been looking after her and Pol both." He took the chair Rohan had vacated and folded his hands atop his dragon-headed cane. "But you go to them now. We'll watch over her."

When Rohan was gone, Lleyn sighed and shook his head. "I always thought the wind would take my ashes to her at Goddess Keep—not that I'd watch her Sunrunners call up Fire for her."

Urival nodded. "You loved her as I did."

"No, not as you did. I spent all I possessed of that on my wife. Forty-six winters ago it was that she died. I see her in her son and her grandsons, but it's not the same."

"No, never the same."

"Masul will die for this, of course," Lleyn went on. "If I were younger, I'd do it with my own hands. But listen to me, Sunrunner. Don't you do it with yours."

He had never killed using the gifts; he wondered how Lleyn knew that this was precisely what was going through his mind now.

"She'd breathe down my neck the rest of my days if I allowed it—stubborn woman, your Andrade."

Yes, Urival thought, she was his alone, now that she was dead.

"I hope you don't mind if I wait with you. It's going to be a very long night."

"No, I don't mind at all. I think she'd want you here."

"Thank you, my lord." Lleyn bowed his head as if

Urival had been born royal. "I'll stay here, then. We'll wait together."

Chapter Twenty-five

Guards kept alert vigil against terrors bound to slither through the night now that the Lady of Goddess Keep was dead. They tensed at the sound of low murmurings, flinched at shadows cast on fabric walls by single candles. They tried not to see the sharp gestures, movements of impatience or pain or dread, arms that spread in helplessness or sometimes folded around a needing other. Long after the moons had nestled back into the embrace of the Veresch; long after the events of the day and night should have sent everyone to their beds; long after watchfires burned low and only the stars lit the encampment in pale silvery light, the whisperings went on and on within the many-colored tents.

Rohan thanked Chadric and Audrite for their care of his wife and son, saw them off into the night, and poured himself a large goblet of strong wine. Pol sat tense and wide-eyed in a chair near Sioned, who tried without success to hide her intermittent trembling. He poured wine for them, too, and paced off a slow triangle on the carpet: desk to window, window to chairs, chairs to desk.

"She asked about you," he said abruptly. "Both of you. To know that you were safe. Goddess help us. We mattered more to her than her own life."

Sioned set her goblet down untasted. Rohan spoke her name softly, aching for the terrible guilt in her eyes that matched his own. "No," she said, her voice raw with pain. "I can't bear it, Rohan. She made me everything I am, and the last time I spoke with her—oh, Goddess!" Her numb composure broke. "She died thinking I hated her!"

"Sioned, don't do this to yourself."

She looked up at him, her eyes bleak. "If I stop, will you?"

Pol shifted slightly, meeting Rohan's gaze with eyes much older than his years. "Father—Prince Lleyn told me what she said about Masul."

"And?"

"He won't have Princemarch. It's not just that it's mine by right. The people and the land accepted me. I won't give them over to him, not for any reason."

"They are yours, and you are theirs," Sioned murmured. She looked up at Rohan, her haunted eyes saying, *And he is Roelstra's grandson, with more right to Princemarch than he knows.*

"I'll fight for them if I have to," Pol finished.

"There will be no war." Rohan knew how empty that vow was. He gave his wife a weary, cynical smile. "Well, perhaps only a little one."

* * *

A larger war was being debated within Miyon's orange tent. He lounged on a padded couch, listening as Kiele and Masul discussed troop strengths as if they knew what they were talking about. Amusement played around his eyes and lips. Whoever fought this war, it would not be his own soldiers. He would get the others to do it. And when everyone was exhausted with battle, even the victors, his own fresh and ready army would seize great chunks of Firon and Princemarch and the Desert itself.

Lyell stood nervously by his wife's chair, ignored by all until he said to Masul, "Your pardon, my lord. It simply occurs to me that all this would bring a great deal of destruction which would be very bad for us all."

"Merchant," the pretender spat scornfully. "We speak of thrones, and you babble about trade."

Miyon hid a grin. Masul thought that being a prince was riding fine horses and wearing fine clothes, and enjoying the sight of heads and knees bent to him. He had never been strangled and starved by Desert armies, never seen the produce of his lands rot and rust for lack of transport to rich markets. Neither had he dealt with greedy, grim Merida, always clamoring for a war against the Desert that Miyon knew could only end one way. Perhaps he would send the Merida against the remains of Rohan's armies, once the latter had exhausted themselves in Princemarch. Yes, that was a good thought; they might just annihilate each other, and at the very least would so decimate themselves that it would be a generation before either had the strength to fight again.

"The princedoms function on trade," Miyon said softly. "But we are indeed speaking of thrones here, and not only that of Princemarch."

"How so, your grace?" Kiele asked suspiciously.

"Consider, dear lady." He snuggled back into the embrace of soft pillows. "Aligned with us are Gilad and Grib, Fessenden—and of course Isel." He chuckled. "What a merry time of it they'll have on their island, once they start the real war they've been flirting with for the hundred years since the last one! Grib and Gilad lie on either side of Ossetia, ready to pinch it between them like a dragon's jaws. Fessenden rides atop Princemarch—and will rein it into our hands. How many fronts do you think Rohan has armies enough to fight on? What use would Dorval be to him? Syr is a powerful ally—but once Clutha understands that his beloved Meadowlord will yet again become a battlefield, he'll save his troops for protecting his own, not for a fight he cares nothing about." Miyon sighed happily. "Rohan is mistaken if he looks for substantial help from any of his allies."

"I don't see that all this gets me into Castle Crag any the sooner," Masul said, glowering.

"Patience." Miyon smiled. "Watch them wear themselves out for a spring and summer. By then, not only will you walk into Castle Crag without opposition, but the others will be so exhausted by their wars that they'll have no strength to counter your more interesting proposals at the special gathering of princes you'll call to end the wars."

"And you, your grace?" Masul asked in silken tones. "I take it you won't be exhausted."

"Not in the slightest. I'll own the Desert from Tiglath to Feruche. You may have the rest. I'm not greedy."

"Of course not," Kiele murmured.

"Tomorrow should make a lovely little beginning for our wars," Miyon finished. "Remember that, and don't lose sight of the whole world for dreaming yourself at Castle Crag."

* * *

Pandsala slept, dreaming of just that place. She was a young girl again, strolling the gardens dug into the cliffs, and the sun was soft on her face and hair. Her sister Ianthe handed her a violet-wrapped bundle that squirmed in her arms. The child had golden hair and blue-green eyes.

"You're not the guardian I would have chosen for him, but you've done very well," Ianthe taunted. "You even love him! *My* son, and you love him! It's the best joke I ever played on anyone, the crowning scheme of my life!"

Pandsala stared in horror at Ianthe's child. Part of her wanted to thrust it away from her, hurl it over the walls to the deep gorge of the Faolain below.

Ianthe laughed. "But I'll take him back now. He's mine. More important, he belongs to our mother's people. I always thought it grossly unfair that she passed the gifts to you, not me. Think what I could have done with them!" She held out her hands. "Give him back to me now, Pandsala. Your work is done."

"No!"

"He doesn't belong to you," Ianthe explained as if to a dull-witted student. "Give him to us."

A shadow fell on the lawn beside her. She turned and saw her father, tall and green-eyed and adamant. He said, "Give him to us. It's time."

She clutched the infant to her breast. Calling on everything she had ever learned of power, she flung a bolt of Sunrunner's Fire at Ianthe, at Roelstra. Their flesh blackened and crisped before her eyes, but they were laughing as she killed them.

She began to run, tripped on the steps, fell, dropped her precious burden. She screamed again, terrified. But the blanket was empty.

Sioned appeared on the walkway above her, the emerald ring blazing as bright as her emerald eyes. She knelt and gathered the violet blanket, never taking her gaze from Pandsala's.

"What have you done?" she demanded, unfurling the cloth. "Look at the blood!"

Pandsala cringed away from the velvet that dripped fat spheres of thick red blood. They hit the sun-heated stones and burned to blackened circles. She touched one and her fingertip came away scorched, but there was no pain.

She looked up suddenly, relief sobbing through her as Pol came out of the castle to stand beside Sioned. But this was not the boy Pandsala knew; this was a man fully grown, tall and proud, the great topaz-and-amethyst ring on his finger. He looked down on her with remote curiosity and no recognition. Sioned took his hand. Claimed him.

Pandsala opened her mouth to reveal the truth. She could destroy Sioned by speaking of Ianthe.

Bud she did not. If she had killed Ianthe and Roelstra to keep Pol free of them, she could not reclaim him for them by telling him who his real mother had been. She could not do that to him.

Another shadow appeared, and for a panicked instant she thought Roelstra had escaped the flames. But it was Masul who strode forward, green eyes brimming with vicious glee as he swung his new Cunaxan sword at Pol's head.

"No!" she screamed again. Behind him were three more shadows, dark and menacing, more fatal even than Masul. Rohan must change his mind, he must allow her to remain regent of Princemarch—how else could she continue to protect Pol from the dangers that threatened him again and again and—

Masul laughed down at her and the sword continued on its slow, deadly, sunlit arc toward Pol's neck.

"NO!"

"My lady!"

She sat up in bed, shuddering, and stared without comprehension at the boy standing beside her. He held a candle. The flame danced light over his dark hair, into his eyes—green like Roelstra's, like the pretender's—like Sioned's. Their faces layered over his, joined by Ianthe's atop them all, and Pandsala shrank back from him. "Wh-who are you?" she breathed.

"My name is Sejast, my lady," he said, and the other faces vanished at the sound of his voice. Not more of the dream, then. Only a boy wearing a single *faradhi* ring on the middle finger of his right hand.

"Forgive me for violating your privacy, but—but I was

sent to find out if you were in any distress after what happened tonight.''

"I'm quite all right," she said, her voice infuriatingly thin and weak.

"I'm glad to hear it, my lady," he said with a shy little smile. "Some of the others aren't doing so well. But you're much stronger than they, I think."

"*You* don't seem much bothered." She swung her feet over to the floor, smoothed back her hair. "Are you so very strong?"

He blushed. "I'm not that gifted, my lady. If you're well, then I'll go and let you rest."

"Wait." She grasped his arm and he helped her to her feet, all respectful solicitude. "Get me something to drink."

He obeyed as she made her way to a nearby chair. She drank thirstily, needing the wine to wash away the last shadows of her dream.

"Do you want me to call a physician, my lady?"

"No." Feeling better, she straightened her shoulders and regarded him closely, searching for the elusive memory. She had seen him before, she was sure of it. All at once she had it. "Aren't you the boy who attends Lady Hollis?"

"I have that honor, my lady."

"I see." Having placed him now, she relaxed. This was no shadow, only a nice and helpful boy who had been kind—and who had better not say anything about what he might have heard. "I was dreaming," she said, "when you came in and woke me. I must have startled you."

"Not half as much as I did you, my lady." He smiled again. "I heard you call out and I thought it best to wake you if I could."

"My thanks. It was not a pleasant dream," she added wryly, relieved that she had said nothing to reveal herself. "And thank you for your attention, Sejast. You may go now. I'm recovered."

"Very good, my lady. But please try to rest. You look very tired."

"I will. Good night."

Segev grinned to himself as he left the tent. So much

for family instinct, he thought; Pandsala had not recognized a hint of her sister Ianthe in him. It had been a daring thing to do, but the night and Mireva's use of him and especially Andrade's death had intoxicated him. He had felt power rip through him like a blizzard of cold, stinging snow that burned with his own body heat and turned to fiery rivers of strength. His mind itched for the Star Scroll and the spells that would show him even more power. But he still had to wait.

Not for long.

He made his way to the High Prince's tents, careful to let his ring be seen by the guards. He paused outside Maarken's tent, listening to the voices, watching the shadows on the wall.

"Hollis—stay here for the night, you're not well enough to—"

"I want to go back and sleep in my own bed!"

"*This* is your bed! You're going to be my wife! Any bed I'm in is the one you should be in, too!"

"Maarken—leave me alone, I can't—"

Segev grinned again, barely containing laughter as the shadow that was Hollis broke away from the taller shadow's outstretched arms. He hugged himself with excitement.

Hollis snapped, "Stop acting as if I'm yours!"

She nearly stumbled over Segev in her flight from the tent. Suddenly it was as if Maarken's rasping cry of her name did not exist—or Maarken himself, for the matter.

"Oh!" she said, startled. "Sejast! Are you all right?"

He had grasped her elbow, and now slid his hand down to hers. Thin, chill fingers curled around his. "Are *you* all right, my lady?"

"I'm fine. But I'm glad you're here. Will you take me back to our tents?"

He cast one glance back over his shoulder as he escorted her. Maarken stood there in the entry of his tent, a lit candle flickering in his hand. By its light, Segev saw undisguised jealous hatred in the young lord's pale eyes. And grinned.

* * *

Ostvel had tried to give Volog's daughter back to him on the knoll, embarrassed by the girl's small, desperate sobs and the way she clung to him. But Alasen would not let go. Volog, after a gentle attempt to draw her into his own arms, shook his head and murmured, "Come with me. I doubt she's aware of much of anything right now."

It seemed true. It was accident that he had been near her in the first place, when Andrade's conjuring had gone all awry and the Fire had turned from vision to nightmare. Alasen's moan of agony, a tiny echo of Andrade's scream, brought Ostvel's hands out to steady her; the next thing he knew, she had buried her face against his chest and dug her fingers into his shirt. She trembled as if her slender body would shatter. Frantic for his son's safety, Ostvel tried to pry himself away. She only hung on tighter.

Davvi and Chale were helping Riyan; as Ostvel watched, Gemma and Tilal joined them. Riyan looked groggy but was fast recovering. Ostvel gave heartfelt thanks to the Goddess and to the tenderly protective spirit of his Camigwen that surely watched over their son, and turned his attention to the girl weeping hopelessly in his arms.

Volog seemed content to let Ostvel help Alasen back to the tents. He left them for a time, then returned to murmur, "Riyan's all right. Davvi's seeing to his comfort."

"Thank you for your care of my son, your grace," Ostvel said.

"And for your care of my daughter." Volog stroked Alasen's hair. "Poor child. . . . She's *faradhi*, of course."

Ostvel coaxed her to take a few steps. "Come along now, Alasen. It's all over. You're safe." He met Volog's eyes again. "What of Andrade?"

The prince shook his head.

Ostvel swallowed hard. Memories tumbled in him of his youth at Goddess Keep, growing up with Camigwen and Sioned and Meath and so many others who were Sunrunners. He had never felt the lack of what they had and he did not, had even hoped that one day he would earn the rank of chief steward there. Instead, he had accompanied Sioned to Stronghold, become Rohan's liegeman and friend and finally *athri* of his own keep. Andrade had ordered Sioned to the Desert, thus reordering all their destinies. Andrade had in many ways ruled his life for much of his life. It was impossible to think of her as dead.

Alasen was walking more securely now, but when Ostvel tried to unclench her fists from his shirt and hand her over to her father, she gave a despairing cry and huddled still closer.

"It's all right, my love," Volog murmured, one arm around her waist. "Only a little way now. My lord, you know more of the *faradh'im* than I. What happened here tonight?"

"I'm not sure, your grace," he temporized, although he had strong suspicions. "There are . . . certain things in which all Sunrunners present are joined, and tonight . . . tonight was dangerous." Even more so than the night Sioned had woven starlight, and not only Tobin and Pol, who had been nearby, but *faradh'im* hundreds of measures away had been caught up in it. Then, the tangle of colors had been sorted out by Andrade; Ostvel surmised that Sioned had done the work tonight. The other Sunrunners, no matter their level of training, had recovered, though they would all have raging headaches, if he knew anything about the breed. But Alasen had no training at all.

"Joined whether they like it or no," Volog interpreted, nodding at his daughter's bent head.

Ostvel nodded.

"Urival—or was it Sioned?—is very skilled."

He knew a leading remark when he heard one. "I don't think those of us without the gifts can ever really understand what happens to them, your grace."

"But you lived amongst them for most of your youth, yes?"

"I had that honor. When they talked of touching colors and seeing each other's patterns in light—" He supported Alasen as she stumbled. "Their powers are a mystery to me, your grace. But they are only people in the end, like the rest of us."

They reached Volog's scarlet tents. Ostvel began to wonder if he would have to sacrifice his shirt to the girl's fierce grip. Eventually, however, he and Volog persuaded her fingers to loosen. The prince placed his daughter on a low couch, covered her with a light blanket. Her green eyes were wide open and staring, blind to everything around her. Or so Ostvel thought until he turned to go, and she reached out both hands with a piteous cry of abandonment.

He knelt beside her, pressing her hands in both of his. "Hush now. It's all right, Alasen. You're safe. I promise you, my lady. Safe."

She searched his face and sense returned to her eyes. She almost smiled at him. Goddess, but the girl was beautiful, he thought with a catch in his heart that confused him. Her long lashes closed and he was glad that those eyes no longer gazed up at him with such trust, such gratitude.

Alasen whispered suddenly, "But she's dead. All the colors—and Lady Andrade is dead."

"Shh," he replied, aware of Volog hovering on the other side of the couch, watching. "Just sleep now, my dear."

Alasen's fingers moved convulsively in his own, then went limp. Ostvel waited until he was sure she slept, then rose tiredly to his feet. Joints at knee and shoulder hurt a little in the damp climate of Waes, so different from the hot, dry Desert around Skybowl. The dull aches reminded him of his age, fully twice that of the girl who lay on the couch, resting at last but not at peace. Another small hurt centered in his chest as he gazed down at her youth, her pale, strained face.

He turned to Volog. "She'll be all right once she's had a good long sleep, your grace."

"You must be getting bored by my expressions of thanks," the prince said wryly. "May I offer you some wine, my lord? We could both use it."

"At any other time I would accept gladly. But I really ought to go see about my son."

"Of course. Another time, then." He escorted Ostvel to the entryway. "I hate to ask it, but what do you think will happen tomorrow? Andrade is dead, the question of Masul is still unresolved, and I see no way out of this."

"The High Prince will find one. He always does." Ostvel thought of the Sunrunner Masul had undoubtedly killed; if it could be proven against him, he would die—pretender to Princemarch or not. "Good night, your grace."

He met Chay outside the perimeter of Rohan's tents. "I've been checking on our sons," the older man said. "All serene—though they'll not be fit to live with tomorrow, if I know *faradh'im*."

"My diagnosis exactly. I've just been with Volog. Alasen was stricken more than the others. She's had no training."

Chay looked grim. "Someone must have known her colors. Otherwise Sioned would never been able to find and separate her from the other Sunrunners, and we would have lost her to the shadows."

Ostvel wondered who it might have been who had touched and remembered Alasen's unique pattern of light. Then he shrugged; it was enough that someone had. "How does Tobin?"

"Well enough. She knew what was happening the entire time. She's stronger than she knows, and even stronger than she pretends to be," he added with a rueful shrug. Then he sobered. "I can't believe Andrade is gone."

"Nor I," Ostvel murmured.

"I can usually guess the workings of Rohan's mind—though I'm just that half-step behind him much of the time. But I'm damned if I know what he's going to do now." He shook his head. "I can't believe she's gone," he repeated.

Ostvel thought it best to change the subject. "Riyan is with Davvi right now?"

"What? Oh—no, he's with Andry at the Sunrunner tents. Sorin's going to stay the night with them. Maarken's holed up in his own tent pretending to be asleep." Chay grimaced. "I wish I knew what was going on with him. That girl of his is lovely, of course, and Andry tells us she's perfect for Maarken. But if she's in love with him, *I* haven't seen anything of it. Ah, well. They'll work it out themselves, I suppose." He squinted at the eastern sky. "Not much left of tonight."

"I wish there were. I'm not looking forward to tomorrow."

"Will the burning be here, do you think, or at Goddess Keep?"

"I don't know. Urival will have to decide, but I don't think he's in any state to make plans." He gripped Chay's arm lightly. "We won't be, either, unless we at least try to get some sleep."

"Ostvel, I can't even begin to think what plans to make—except ones for war."

* * *

Andry lay sleepless and afraid in the small white tent, not comforted even by his twin's presence nearby. He had been the one to delineate Alasen's colors—and Sioned had not been the one to separate her from the rest. Andry had done it himself. Through the shock and agony threatening to tear his mind apart, he had seen the luminous pattern that was Alasen begin to splinter. Panic had shoved aside all else. He had sensed the method used by Sioned to extract Pol from the chaos; instinct had taken over from there. The effort to calm Alasen's terror and keep her whole had wrung all the strength from him. The next thing he knew he was being helped down the knoll, led by Sorin's worried, soothing voice.

He could hear his twin's soft breathing nearby, the rhythm one of wakefulness, not sleep as Riyan's was in the other bed. Andry sat up slowly, holding his throbbing head between his hands.

"Lie back down, you idiot," Sorin whispered, instantly at his side. Andry groped for his brother's warm hand. "What is it, Andry? Are you all right?"

He could not seem to stop the sudden shivering that invaded his bones. "I–I just can't get warm," he stammered.

Sorin pulled another blanket from the foot of the bed. "Here, get this wrapped around you. Better?"

"Yes," he lied.

Sorin crouched beside him as he lay back. "I sent a squire to ask after the others. Everyone's all right, more or less. But the consensus is that you Sunrunners will be feeling tomorrow as if you'd had a four-day voyage on the open sea." He pressed Andry's fingers hard. "Goddess, you scared me!"

He let himself drink in his brother's solid, sane presence. Gradually the visions faded from his conscious mind, sinking into a locked place where only nightmares would have the key. "Are you going to stay here?" he asked, unashamed of his pleading tone.

"Of course. For one thing, Father ordered it. And for another, do you think I'd leave you when you're hurt like this?"

Andry remembered a time long ago when they'd both been very small, and the sunlight had suddenly assaulted his mind and gifts with brutal insistence. Frantic, Sorin had stuck to Andry's side for days thereafter. And there had been a winter when Sorin had sickened with a high fever, and Andry had defied his mother's prohibition and stayed with him, taking care of him until he was well again. It had been like that all their lives. He pitied those who had no twin, no second self to be there always—but even more, he pitied his brother Maarken for what he must have endured when his twin Jahni had died of Plague.

Sorin squeezed his hands again. "Do you think you can get some sleep now?"

"Yes—no. Andrade's dead, isn't she?"

Sorin nodded. "Urival's with her, and Lleyn, too, I think."

"Be thankful you can't see and feel what I do, brother," Andry whispered. "It was like a window of stained glass all in motion, pictures shifting and backlit by Fire—but then it shattered into a million pieces and I had to find the right ones, put the pictures back together again—Sioned did the work, but—I could feel all of them, all of us, the fear of the shadows—"

"It's all over," Sorin murmured. "Relax now, Andry. Just close your eyes. I'll be here."

He smiled faintly. "I've missed you, you know."

"Me, too. Listen, what if I ask Father if I can come visit you at Goddess Keep for the winter? He and Rohan have to figure out something for me now that I've been knighted, after all. That'll give them some time to think up what they want to do with me."

"What about what *you* want to do with you?"

"I never really thought about it," Sorin replied easily.

"They won't set me to the account books at Radzyn Port or anything boring like that, you know."

He chuckled. "A good thing, too. You never could add without counting on your fingers."

Sorin grinned, and Andry realized that sibling magic had worked again: his brother had made him laugh.

"It'd be interesting to help with the new port on the Faolain, thought," Sorin went on. "I like building things. Volog's got a little manor house that he's reworking just in case Alasen marries somebody who doesn't have a place suitable for a princess. I've had a great time there—" He broked off suddenly, whispering, "Andry?"

He cursed himself for letting it show on his face. "What?" he asked, trying to imitate Maarken's most forbidding tone. But evidently his older brother had been the only one to inherit that particular inflection from their father. Sorin simply stared.

"You—and Alasen?" he got out at last. "Oh, Goddess!"

"What's wrong with me and Alasen?" Andry challenged. "I may not be a prince and I don't have any lands, but I'm the grandson of a prince and son of the Lord of Radzyn and nephew of—"

"Oh, stop waving your credentials like a trade ambassador," Sorin chided. "It's just a surprise, that's all. I can't think of her as anything but a pest who grew up sort of pretty. But if you love her—"

"As if there's a chance," Andry muttered.

"Why shouldn't there be? Your lineage is just as good as hers. What's more, she's kin to Sioned and Pol. It'd be in the family. I think it's a great idea. Really."

"Do you?" He sighed. "Now I just have to convince her, and her father, and her mother, and—"

"You sound like Maarken. You Sunrunners—always finding shadows where there aren't any. Why shouldn't she accept you? You're fairly presentable, you don't eat with your fingers, you're smarter than the average plow-elk, and you wash regularly."

Andry couldn't help grinning again. "Thanks for building up my confidence!"

Sorin patted his shoulder. "Only too glad to help." But after a moment he grew serious. "But do you think you could give up being at Goddess Keep? It's all you've ever wanted, Andry. The manor on Kierst is beautiful, and it'd be more than enough for any man to run—and having Allie there would make it perfect for you. And you'd still be a Sunrunner, of course, probably attached to Volog's court. Actually, it'd be an excellent move politically. If you were their assigned Sunrunner, then when Arlis grows up and inherits the whole island—''

"I'd do it, for her," Andry said slowly. "But I won't have to leave Goddess Keep. Alasen will come there, and be trained as a *faradhi.*"

"Are you sure about that?"

"Sorin—I can't imagine anyone who has the gifts not wanting to use them, to learn everything they can about being a Sunrunner. It's the most wonderful thing in the world. It's—"

"I could set that speech to music by now, I've heard it so often," Sorin interrupted, grinning again. "All right, then—take her to Goddess Keep and make a Sunrunner of her." He wagged a monitory finger in Andry's face. "But I'll come along this winter to make sure your intentions toward her stay honorable!"

"Sorin!" Andry protested, outraged until he saw the teasing gleam in his twin's eyes. He took a playful swing at Sorin in retaliation, but sudden movement jostled the ache in his skull to new and inventive pain. He lay back and squeezed his eyes shut.

"Easy," Sorin advised, worried again. "You really should try to sleep."

"Not for the next little while, I'm afraid," said a quiet voice behind them. They turned, startled, and beheld Prince Lleyn silhouetted in the doorway. "It's nearly dawn—not enough time for a decent sleep. Lord Andry, if you feel up to it, Lord Urival asks that you attend him. I suggest," he added dryly, "that you feel up to it."

Andry hurried into his clothes and exchanged a single bewildered glance with his twin. Following Lleyn from the tent, he asked, "Your grace, do you know why Lord Urival wishes to see me?"

The old man cast him a sidelong look. "You don't know? Good."

The words did nothing for Andry's peace of mind. He

entered the huge white pavilion alone, almost trembling with unformed apprehensions. Urival stood before the tapestry partition that hid the sleeping area where Andrade lay. His hands were clasped behind his back, his face utterly still and expressionless but for the sorrow that dulled his golden-brown eyes.

"My lord?" Andry asked hesitantly.

Urival took the few steps that separated them, extending his hands. Andry looked uncomprehendingly at the two bracelets held out to him.

"My Lord," Urival said quietly.

And then he knew, and there was a roaring in his mind like a storm of Fire. Agony and exultation, grief and joy, terror and desire—Andry took the bracelets, clasped them about his wrists.

"My Lord," Urival said again, and bowed low to him.

Chapter Twenty-six

Far away in the mountains, Mireva paced and fretted. "Why do they do nothing?" she demanded for the fifth time of Ruval, who lounged near the open door of her dwelling, his chair tilted back and his feet propped against the wall. "This whole day long, nothing but baking in their damned tents like dragons in hatching caves, when they could be—"

Ruval laughed and she rounded on him furiously. He held up his hands in a gesture of peace. "Forgive me," he said, still smiling. "But what else can they do? You saw how they scuttled from tent to tent last night. Today they wait. By sunset they'll have made the pyre, and before the first star is out they'll gather to burn the old witch." He shrugged. "I still don't understand why you killed her, though."

"Could there ever be a better time? And when would I get another chance?" She poured wine from a bottle kept cool on the table. "She was vulnerable as she'd never been before. In any case, with her gone and her senile lover distraught, Segev will find it that much easier to steal the scrolls.''

She drank off the wine, set her goblet down, placed her palms together. ''I can almost feel them in my hands, Ruval. I must have them, I must. So much has been lost. It's incredible that Merisel wrote it all down. She was our most powerful and implacable enemy. And yet she seems to have known almost everything! Who told her? How did she gain such knowledge?''

He stretched his arms wide and eased his chair to the floor. Rising, he poured himself a share of the wine. Watching him, she felt her tension dissolve and something else uncurl in her body to take its place. He had experienced his final growth to manhood this spring and summer. His shoulders were broader with muscle, the lines of body and face hard and clean with the predatory beauty of a hunting cat. Even lazing back as he had been, or standing casually with a goblet in his hand, there was a feeling of contained power about him. For now it was purely physical; over the next years she would tutor him fully in other powers. Mireva's gaze roamed over him, and a slow smile stretched her lips.

Ruval recognized the look, and laughed. ''We really ought to celebrate Andrade's death,'' he suggested. Taking a long gulp of wine, he set down the cup. ''After all, they *won't* be doing much of anything for the rest of the day. No need to bore ourselves with watching them.''

''And have you a means of celebration in mind?'' she asked archly.

He only laughed again.

But a little while later, when they lay in a tangle of half-discarded clothes on her bed, she drew back and took his face between her hands. Fiercely blue eyes, hot with passion, glared at her for the interruption.

''Hear me,'' she said, breathing hard. ''Tonight we must watch most carefully, and every night until Segev is back with the scrolls.''

''Don't you trust my dear littlest brother?'' he mocked.

''If I didn't, he'd be dead.''

Ruval grinned down at her, turned his head to sink his teeth into her hand. ''And the same goes for me, doesn't it? But apart from that craven idiot Marron, I'm all you have, Mireva. Treat me sweetly, my lady, and I'll give you a princedom.''

"Treat *me* sweetly, my lord, and I'll give you everything from the Sunrise Water to the Far Islands.'' She tightened her grip on his face, dug her fingers into his hair. ''Remember that.''

"How could I forget?'' He grasped her wrists and spread her arms wide on the bed. "Will you do this with Pol one day?'' he asked, eyes burning even hotter now.

For answer, she called on the *dranath* that had been in the wine, using it and ancient sorcery to transform herself into the beautiful, willowy girl. She flung thick black hair over her shoulder, stretching widely, grinning in delight at the young, supple body she now wore.

Ruval laughed. "Fit for princes, indeed! May his Goddess pity him!''

* * *

It was a long walk to the cliffs where the ritual would be held. Rohan worried that the distance might be too much for Chale and Clutha, and especially for Lleyn. But Chale had Gemma and Tilal to support him; Clutha had Halian. Lleyn leaned on nothing but his dragon-headed cane, though Chadric and Audrite hovered close enough to irritate him into several sharp glances.

Andry had seen to the building of a suitable stone pyre. He and Urival had chosen a site where the rocky cliffs rose to their highest point, the sea immediately below. Stones had been piled up into a flat resting place, covered by a length of white silk velvet never unbolted since its weaving. A litter had also been constructed quickly from a single mighty tree felled that morning; every woodcarver at the Fair had been called on to smooth the struts and poles, a goldsmith had gilded the four handles, and a jeweler had set moonstones into them.

Rohan held two of those handles now, feeling the cool overlay of gold and the smoothly rounded gems in his palms. Chay had taken the other end of the litter, at Andrade's feet. Rohan watched the bowed dark head above the collar of gray mourning clothes, seeing suddenly how much silver had threaded through Chay's hair. Sioned and Pol walked to one side of them as they carried Andrade, Tobin and two of her sons on the other. It was

Andry who led the procession, the bracelets gleaming around his wrists. Urival followed behind with the Sunrunners. Highborns, their families and retainers, and finally the common folk trailed behind Rohan—whose back Tallain had insisted on guarding.

They set Andrade on the stones, bowed to her, and joined their wives and children. The ritual belonged to Andry tonight; he alone would preside. Not even Urival, who had known her and loved her so long, could participate as anything more than just another *faradhi*.

Andry came forward, lean and pale and moving with the strict grace of one whose control is too rigid to permit natural gestures. He paused while everyone assembled, and Rohan followed his gaze where he could among the crowd. Princes, *athr'im*, their wives and children and retainers; the Sunrunners to one side; great numbers of merchants and servants from the Fair across the river; all of them encircled by soldiers wearing the emblems and colors of the thirteen princedoms on their tunics, but carrying no weapons. Rohan wondered how many of them would soon be wearing colors and weapons in earnest.

Andry seemed to be looking for someone in particular, and a small muscle tightened in his cheek when that person went unfound. Rohan knew his nephew's face well enough to read it, even in its new aspect of Lord of Goddess Keep.

Water from a flask was scattered down the length of Andrade's white cloak as more people stood watching than had ever seen a Lady or Lord of Goddess Keep honored before. They kept a respectful distance from Andrade's family and the *faradh'im*. The ritual itself was long familiar to them all—but the one they held vigil for tonight had been the personification of the Goddess' power. There were many who looked askance at the young man who would replace her, and even more who considered him easy prey. Rohan felt a faint, grim smile move his lips as Andry, a slim gray shadow in the gathering gloom of dusk, let a fistful of Earth trail from his fingers down the white cloak. If anyone thought him weak, they were in for a surprise. They ought to know that a man born of Chay's family, Andrade's, and Zehava's was made of both power and strength.

It seemed Andry wished to go on record for those qualities, as well. He circled Andrade's pyre so everyone could get a good look at him. Then, facing west to the sea across her body, he held up both arms. His sleeves fell back to show bracelets that caught the last rays of the sun in silver and gold. His four rings tipped in tiny rubies shone as he suddenly stripped both bracelets from his arms and replaced them on Andrade's crossed wrists.

Rohan felt Sioned give a start of surprise beside him. He took her fingers and she met his gaze, bewildered. Rohan admitted to himself that if Andry had not explained it earlier, he would not have comprehended, either. The youth was putting everyone on notice that whatever Andrade had been, he would not be the same. When she had become Lady, she had used the bracelets of the man who had been Lord before her—a calculated act of humility, for she, too, had been very young when named Lady. But the gold and silver bracelets that had circled her wrists for most of her seventy winters would melt and vanish with the flames that consumed her empty flesh. Rohan did not know whether this was the action of an arrogant child or a man who knew precisely what he was doing. But he knew that sooner or later they would all find out.

Urival had been scandalized by Andry's plan, though he dared not object. Now he stood with bent head and slumped shoulders. He looked so old, Rohan thought, aching with pity. He held tighter to Sioned's hand, not wanting to think about a time when he might stand thus and watch his own beloved consigned to the Fire.

Andry gestured, and a soft breeze stirred the motionless Air, wafted across Andrade's body, fluttered the hem of her cloak and touched loose wisps of her silver-gilt hair. Tobin and Sioned had offered to help Urival make her ready, but he had jealously clung to the one service he *was* allowed to perform: washing her body, dressing it in a white gown, braiding her long hair.

The other Sunrunners moved to circle the pyre. Urival was the last to come forward, holding out a small silver flask of sweet oil to Andry. But the young man shook his head, returning the flask to the old man's suddenly shaking hands. Rohan nodded slowly in approval. Urival should have some part in honoring Andrade. It was only right.

He could smell herbs and spices heavy on the motionless air as thick oil was tenderly smoothed on Andrade's hands and brow and lips, and the four corners of the cloak were anointed. Urival stepped back, tears shining on his cheeks as Andry called Fire.

Sunrunners cloaked and hooded in gray bent their heads. The flames caught, rose, lit Andrade's strong, severe profile for a long moment. Rohan felt Sioned tremble—and then she was walking forward to join those of her kind in watching over the woman who had taken her in, taught her the nature of her gifts, summoned her to the Desert to become the wife of a prince. Tobin hesitated, then went to Sioned's side. Maarken was right behind her, and last of all Pol left Rohan to stand between his mother and his cousin. Rohan felt Chay and Sorin draw a little closer to him. Of all Andrade's family, they were the only ones ungifted with Sunrunner's Fire.

Andrade had hoped and planned what Rohan would be. Instead it was Pol who would be both *faradhi* and prince. There were soft gasps throughout the crowd as he joined the Sunrunners and gave them another reminder of what many would like to forget.

Rohan glanced around the cliffside. His eyes lit on Masul. Murderous, greedy, ruthless—everything Pol was not, Masul was. What if *faradhi* powers had been added to those vices? He acknowledged the reasons for the strictness of Andrade's training, her arrogant demand that all Sunrunners bend to her will. Sioned had not; but neither had Pandsala. She had given Rohan a bitter lesson in what could result when *faradhi* and princely powers combined in a single ruthless will.

Sooner or later there would be other princes who possessed the gifts. Pol, Maarken, and Riyan would not be alone for long. Andrade had trusted that her formidable will would instill discipline in such people to guard against abuses of power. But Andrade was gone, and Andry would take her place. He was too young, Rohan thought, frowning. Much too young.

"The same age you were when you became a ruling prince. . . ."

He looked sidelong at Chay. By the blazing light of the pyre, the proud, handsome face seemed carved in stone, generations of loyal *athr'im* and valiant warriors shining in his eyes. Rohan's gaze then sought his sister in the circle of Sunrunners, the ends of her black braids peeking out from beneath her gray veil. She was a most remarkable woman: princess and politician, warrior in her own right, born of a long line of princes. Coming from people such as these, Andry could not help but be strong. Perhaps in a way much different from Andrade, as his refusal to wear her bracelets had foretold, but strong just the same.

The first waiting period had passed, and the common folk began to come forward to make their bows to Andry and to the High Prince. Most moved quickly, wanting to be gone from this place where at dawn the *faradh'im* would call Air to scatter Andrade's ashes over the length and breadth of the continent. But some walked by slowly, staring at the great and the would-be great. Rohan received their salutes quietly, nodding to a few he noticed were frightened of him. And he felt Masul's eyes like pinpricks, knowing the pretender was seeing himself in Rohan's place as High Prince.

Most rituals began at midnight. For a Lady or Lord of Goddess Keep, things were different. At moonrise, the Sunrunners wove a delicate fabric flung out to all lands, touching all *faradh'im*, making them a part of this ritual as was not done for mere princes. This was the first many of the faraway Sunrunners would learn of the Lady's death; sustaining them in their grief and extending the weave to find every *faradhi* everywhere took time and much strength. Had this happened at Goddess Keep, where all Lords and Ladies had died in the past, there would have been hundreds of Sunrunners and students to perform this duty. But here there were barely enough to make this outpouring of power safe. A few were swaying a little on their feet, held up by their fellows as the work continued. Sioned sent Tobin and Pol back to stand with the family, both of them looking pale and drained. Rohan nodded approval to his son but did not put an arm around him for support, as Chay did for Tobin. Pol's eyes showed his gratitude before he turned to watch the Fire once more.

Rohan wanted desperately to touch his son, to break the silence decreed by the ritual, to speak to him of his pride and his promises for the future. Tomorrow, last day of summer and Lastday of the *Rialla*, would see Masul dead. Rohan did not yet know how he would manage it, but Masul would be executed. And if some still believed him Roelstra's son—well, they could not put a corpse on a throne. Rohan no longer could afford to care about discrediting the pretender. His death would be enough.

The princes and *athr'im* began to move, preparing to leave the cliff. Rohan was startled; surely it could not be past midnight already? But the position of the moons told him it was. And as Lleyn came limping forward, the means of Masul's death were determined by Masul himself.

He strode insolently past the Prince of Dorval, coming to a halt three steps from Rohan and Pol. His green eyes were wells of shadow as he turned his back on the pyre and broke the ritual silence that had reigned through the long night.

"There is only one way to resolve this, High Prince," he announced in a clear, ringing voice that brought gasps of shock from everyone but the oblivious Sunrunners. "I claim the right of challenge—just as you did when you battled my father in single combat. I will prove my claim on my body."

Old as he was, Lleyn could still bring thunder with his voice. "How dare you insult the solemnity of this night? Be silent in respect to the Lady we honor here!"

"She failed to prove your point," Masul returned flatly. "And in any case, I have no use for *faradh'im.*" He said this staring straight down at Pol, a faint, mocking smile on his lips.

Rohan felt the anger spasm through his son's body. "Your grace," he said quietly to Lleyn, "the Lady we honor would quite understand the arrogance of this young fool. And she would welcome, as I do, the chance to provide him with the death he deserves."

Lleyn bowed slightly. "I believe you are correct, High Prince. The Lady would undoubtedly laugh in his face."

Masul had stiffened in outrage, but quickly recovered his poise. "Then you agree to do battle with me."

"Did you think to fight my son?" Rohan smiled a very small smile, and even Masul recognized its deadliness. "I gather you think age is on your side in either case. Only a knight may issue such challenge. I've been expecting it since his grace of Cunaxa sponsored you yesterday. But it is also true that only a knight may respond."

"Father," Pol said in a low voice, tense with hatred, "Princemarch is *mine.*"

"That was never in any doubt, my son. But I do not intend that you soil your hands on this pestilence."

"I hear your sword has not left its scabbard in fifteen years," the pretender drawled. "Indeed, it has not left your Great Hall. I wonder whose you will have to borrow—and if you remember how to use one."

Rohan's smile widened a fraction. "As the challenged, I have the right to choose the weapon."

"And what will it be? Lawbooks thrown at fifty paces?"

"I trust you know how to use a knife for more than slicing onions."

The insulting reference to peasant's food went right past Masul. Someone had evidently warned him that Rohan was the best knife-fighter in three generations. He looked shaken for just an instant before he again recovered his aplomb. "Knives it is, your grace."

"No," Maarken said, suddenly appearing at Chay's side. "Swords. Yours and mine." He bowed to Rohan and Pol, his voice and phrasing strictly formal. "Your graces, I claim the right to act as champion against this pretender. His highness, my cousin, is too young, and you, my prince, long ago made a vow that I would not see you break. Not when my sword is here to serve you."

"Maarken—" Chay's voice was half-strangled.

"Father, I know what I'm doing. Not only has he caused endless trouble here among princes, but he murdered a *faradhi.*"

This revelation broke the last of any respectful silence that was left. The Sunrunners stayed in their ritual circle, but they all turned to the group of highborns. Those backlit by the flames were silvery-gray forms without faces; those looking across the Fire were made equally faceless by hoods and veils. But their rings—four here, eight there, and only one on Sioned's slender hands—swallowed the flames and spat them back in brilliant colors.

"Look at his hand," Maarken said. "He's wearing a Sunrunner's ring, taken from Kleve, whom he killed."

"It's true." Riyan, too, had left the circle of *faradh'im* now, coming forward with every evidence of relief that his information would be used at last. "He stayed at a manor house owned by Lady Kiele and her husband. I know because I followed her there one night."

Somewhere in the crowd, someone gave a sobbing gasp. Rohan would have bet his dragon gold that it was Kiele.

"Faradhi spy," Masul sneered.

"Murderer," Riyan shot back. "You left the evidence behind you—and there was one ring missing. The ring on your hand right now!"

Andry suddenly looked more like his hawk-faced grandsire than either of his parents. His eyes had gone nearly black with rage. He had known about Kleve's death and who had caused it, but that the pretender would dare to put a *faradhi* ring on his finger ignited something feral and deadly in the young man. He grasped Masul's wrist and held up the offending hand for all to see.

"A Sunrunner's gold ring," Andry said, "made from Sunrunner's gold. For this you will die."

Masul laughed harshly and snatched his hand from Andry's grip. "Mind your words and your manners, lordling. When I am High Prince, you Sunrunners will be watched at Goddess Keep by every court, not the other way around. Princes have a right to conduct their affairs as they choose, without the interference of *faradh'im* whose only power was the fear their late Lady inspired. I doubt you will be as formidable." He glanced around the assembly. "Yes, I killed Andrade's spy. All hold Sunrunners in such reverence—but they bleed and die just like anyone else. I wear one of their rings to prove it. Ask my sister, Lady Kiele. She watched while I did it."

Andry found her in the crowd, pressed against her husband's side, her stricken face proclaiming her guilt.

"My Lord—I swear I know nothing of—"

"Abandoning me, sweet sister?" Masul jeered. "What have you to fear? By tomorrow I'll hold Princemarch and nothing can touch either of us. I accept this one," he nodded at Maarken, "as my opponent for the challenge. He looks as if he could give me decent entertainment in a fight."

Rohan was privately astounded by the man's arrogance. All the bitterness of long years of believing himself Roelstra's lost son seemed to have risen up in the space of mere moments. He was paying back everyone who had ever thought him nothing more than a serving woman's bastard, everyone who had doubted what he had dreamed himself into believing was his true birth.

Maarken was still waiting for Rohan's answer. He gazed into the angry gray eyes, so like Chay's, and for just an instant remembered the little boy he and Sioned had saved from a dragon, the squire who had gone to war too young. Maarken still wore the garnet ring Rohan had given him as his first Sunrunner's token.

He looked then at Tobin, whose fingers were white-boned on Chay's arm. But her black eyes were adamant; neither Rohan nor Pol could engage in this battle. The honor of their house demanded that a member of that house be named in their stead. Chay nodded silently, his expression both furious and proud.

All at once he saw a graceful movement of gray silk skirt and veil. Sioned, who had stood apart with the other *faradh'im,* took a few steps forward. Her gaze never left his; in her was no anger, no stiff pride. Only sorrow for what had to be.

Rohan turned to Maarken. "It is for my son to say. Princemarch is his."

Pol held out one hand to his cousin, who took it and dropped to one knee before him. "We recognize your right, Lord Maarken—although we regret that you should sully your blade with this man's blood."

Masul gave a shout of laughter. "Oh, well said, little prince!"

Pol looked up at him with narrowed eyes. "Maarken,"

he said slowly, "win quickly—but make sure he dies slowly."

"As you command, my prince."

"Tomorrow, then, at noon?" Masul asked, as casually as if making an assignation with a woman.

"Noon," Maarken said after rising to his feet. "Now get out. You dishonor this ritual by your presence."

Masul gave him a mocking bow and departed. His allies followed, though they remembered to make their obeisances before Rohan and Andry. The rest stayed. The Sunrunners formed their circle again, gray shapes around the pyre. All was once more silence, the only sound that of the hungry flames.

* * *

Pol stood at his father's side, staring with blind eyes at the Fire. His mother had been in gentle contact with him while he stood with the circle, acting as buffer between him and the other *faradh'im* while light was laced across the continent. But now that tender, supporting presence was gone. He had never felt so alone in his life.

It wasn't the loss of her touch that disturbed him, nor his father's rigid silence beside him. Over the course of the summer and the *Rialla* he had experienced the power of the princely title his father had given him, and handled it to his own satisfaction. But twice now in two short days he had felt the incredible strength of his legacy from his mother. And that was a more difficult adjustment. Being a part of tonight's weaving had taught him the formidable ways of *faradh'im* intertwined, the breathtaking beauty of disciplined patterns of color. But last night, when Lady Andrade had died. . . .

His head still ached a little with the force of that battle his mother had waged against the shadows. He had learned the subtlety of her art, her fine, fierce command of her gifts. He had always thought of her only as his mother, but last night he realized how powerful a *faradhi* she was. His gaze sought and found her tall, slender figure, firegold hair shining even beneath the dull gray veil. She stood in the circle as a Sunrunner, though she wore only the emerald ring signifying her position as High Princess. He wondered suddenly which of her powers brought her the most satisfaction; he knew which she would give up if forced to.

Andry had made his choice long ago. As son of an important *athri* and close kinsman of princes, there would have been a castle or manor for him to rule, power and responsibility and honors. But he had chosen Goddess Keep and the rings that would soon number ten on his fingers. Pol felt none of the astonishment of the others at Andry's elevation. Especially not after his words to Masul. Absolute authority had rung in his cousin's voice, and Andry's face had matured almost overnight into that of a man twice his twenty winters. Andry was exactly where and what he wanted to be. He possessed everything he had always wanted—the *only* thing he had ever wanted.

Watching him with suddenly narrowing eyes, Pol wondered why. Maarken and Riyan had the same prospects as Andry: good lives as lords in their own keeps, as trusted and powerful councillors to the High Prince. Men to be reckoned with. But not as powerful as the position Andry now held.

Pol shifted his weight slightly, aware that Prince Lleyn was now accepting the support of Chadric's arm. Those two would teach him as they had taught Maarken. He would learn the ways of princes. He had no choice about what he would be. Neither had Maarken or Riyan. They were Sunrunners, too, just as he would be. Yet they would not have the tremendous power of being High Prince.

And that was where he and Andry were matched, he realized. A mere five years apart in age, they would be dealing with each other for the rest of their lives. Andry would be the one to whom Pol would go for *faradhi* training. And suddenly Pol's jaw set. He would one day be High Prince; he would not be ruled by his cousin of Goddess Keep.

It was not arrogance that made the decision, or jealous possessiveness of his power. It was simple self-preservation. He could not live in the kind of conflict he now understood had wracked his mother. She had been a Sunrunner before she had become a princess. But he was a prince first, last, and always. That he was also *faradhi* was a gift from the Goddess, and one he did not intend to squander. He would learn what Andry could teach him, and use it. But for his own ends, not those of Goddess Keep.

He wondered why he felt this sudden wariness of his cousin. There had always been much visiting back and forth between Stronghold and Radzyn, but the mere five years between them had seemed like many more to a small boy trailing after his older cousins. Pol had been only seven when Andry had gone to Prince Davvi as a squire and thence to Goddess Keep. To look at him now, cloaked in his new authority, was to look at a stranger.

Then he chided himself. He and Andry were blood kin. They shared grandparents, the Desert, Sunrunner gifts. Through those common bonds they could understand each other and work in harmony. There was no reason to doubt it. It would not be with them as it had been between Andrade and Roelstra, or the more subtle conflict between Andrade and Pol's parents.

And Pol knew that he, not Andry, was the culmination of Lady Andrade's ambition. She had wanted a Sunrunner prince, not a descendant of princes ruling all Sunrunners.

Still . . . Andry possessed something Andrade had not. The Star Scroll. Pol knew better than to discount the power that had ravaged Andrade's visionary Fire last night.

He frowned slightly, then shrugged. So long as Andry kept within the bounds of his own powers and did not challenge anyone else's, as Andrade had done—but was that in the nature of a Lady or Lord of Goddess Keep when dealing with a High Prince? Yet he could not imagine a situation in which he and Andry would come into conflict, and the frown melted from his features at the reassurance given by shared blood, shared background, and shared gifts.

Pol was surprised to see that it was nearly dawn. In the Desert, sunrise always seemed to creep across the sand, creating and then filling in shadows with light. On Dorval, dawn was a flood of sudden brilliance over the heights above Graypearl. But here in Waes he had found that daylight seeped across the sky in subtle tones that barely touched the land until the sun itself slid over the eastern hills. The stars were gone in half the sky now, replaced by a milky soft haze that dimmed in comparison to the flames still burning within the circle of *faradh'im*. He thought of what he had seen earlier that night, the land spread out before the flung weave of Sunrunner colors, the giddy sensation of flight such as a dragon must feel when first it discovers its wings. He looked up at his father; *azhrei*, Dragon Prince, they sometimes called him, which made Pol the Dragon's son. He felt a tired smile tug at his lips. Whatever else Andry might possess, he could never have that.

His *faradhi* senses stirred suddenly. The flames flared once, then sank into the blackened stones. Andrade was gone. Only a thin scatter of ashes remained of the powerful Lady of Goddess Keep. Pol felt his father's hand on his shoulder, the fingers tightening convulsively, and glanced up to find the blue eyes blurred with tears. He was surprised to feel his own eyes stinging. He had known Andrade only slightly. But her death was the passing of someone extraordinary who had worked for his birth and schemed to keep him safe.

The Sunrunners had broken their circle. They gathered now at the head of the pyre, exhausted by the night's vigil but with one more duty to perform. Andry began it, standing apart from them with raised arms and closed eyes as he called Air. A breath of it touched Pol's cheek, swirled lightly around the assembly, fluttered the Sunrunners' gray clothes. Pol felt himself responding, adding his own gifts without conscious volition. And he discovered how very easy it was to summon the wind, make it whirl with a force that lifted the ashes and indeed the very rocks that had built Andrade's pyre. There were gasps and flinches, but Pol paid them no heed, not even when Andry turned to face him and his father's hand gripped his shoulder even harder.

Pol could feel Andry's colors now. The other *faradh'im,* even his mother, drew back in the face of their combined strength. He sensed someone else for a moment, someone vaguely familiar and strictly disciplined, upon whose strength and training this power was built. But the joy of power itself soon made him forget that other presence. There was only himself and his cousin, and the sweet intoxication of their gifts.

The ashes moved. They became a stately vortex borne on Air, pulled higher and thinner until the spiral spread thrice a man's height over the awestruck crowd. Pol had tasted *faradhi* power before; this was the reality, the full feast of it, glutting his mind and body. And he understood Andry's single-hearted commitment, his need to be this above all things, a Sunrunner who called Air and summoned Fire, who could weave light and all the elements with the power of his thoughts.

The ashes, silver and gold fused with them in glittering pinpoints of light, were sent out over the land, wind drawing the mist ever more fragile. As far away as Dorval, as far as Firon and the Desert and Kierst, other breezes would pick up the fine dust until the invisible rain finally fell and joined with the soil. The last link between Andrade's spirit and body was severed, the substance that had once been flesh now spreading across the lands she had served so long.

"Pol."

He was dimly aware that someone was speaking his name.

"Pol. It's done. Pol, come back to us."

He looked up uncomprehendingly at his parents. His mother's green eyes were dim with weariness and, startlingly, fear. His father had a grip on both his shoulders now; he was the one who had spoken. Pol drew in a soft breath and tried to smile at them, suddenly aware of how much effort it took to make the muscles of his face respond. He was tired with a tiredness he had never experienced before, and it was remarkably difficult to stay on his feet.

His mother nodded slowly, her eyes no longer afraid. "It's all right now," she murmured to herself.

Of course it was all right, Pol wanted to say. He had only been doing what every Sunrunner could do.

But as people came to make their bows to him before returning to the encampment, he saw strange things in their expressions. Even Lleyn, even he and Chadric looked at him with new awareness in their eyes. Pol found it very odd.

But he understood only too well the expression in one pair of eyes. Andry never took his gaze from Pol's face.

And in that long, level look Pol found confirmation of his earlier wariness. Andry might be powerfully gifted in the *faradhi* arts—but Pol was just as gifted, and a prince.

Chapter Twenty-seven

"Instinct, of course," Sioned remarked with a casualness she was far from feeling. Rohan gave her a long, slow look that meant her tone hadn't fooled him a bit.

They had just seen Pol tucked up in bed, exhausted and swaying on his feet. He was asleep before his head hit the pillow, sunbleached hair bright in the dawn light filtering through the tent. Rohan had then taken Sioned in to their own section of the pavilion, made her lie down, and had then begun pacing the carpet.

"He didn't know what he was doing," she went on. "He just did it. I can't describe how it felt to have him suddenly *there,* all that raw young strength meeting and blending with Andry's, yet both of them separate. They simply threw the rest of us out of the conjuring, they were that intent on doing it all themselves. Young and very strong, both of them."

"I saw Andry's face afterward," Rohan said quietly.

Sioned sat up, hugging a pillow to her chest. "So did I," she was compelled to admit.

"I can see where he'd be angry, in a way. His first big moment as Lord of Goddess Keep, and his cousin who's going to be High Prince shares it with him, his cousin who's even younger than he is. But I didn't like what I saw in his face, Sioned. It reminded me of the Firedragon you conjured at Stronghold, the one that flew across the Great Hall and melted into the tapestry."

She shrugged. "Flashy, but effective."

"You know what I mean, damn it. Andrade was furious and suspicious. Andry looked at Pol the same way."

"They're both young, Rohan," she repeated.

"Young and very strong, you said," he corrected grimly.

She sunk her chin into the silk-covered softness, and was silent.

"He's my nephew, my own sister's son. This is insane."

Still she said nothing.

"Why should they come into conflict with each other? Their areas of power and influence will be totally different." He stopped his pacing and rubbed his hands over his face. "Goddess. If Andrade made a mistake in him—"

Sioned bit her lip, then said slowly, "Do you remember that *athri* from up near the Cunaxan border who asked you what to do about his sons?"

"He had a legitimate one and a bastard, and they both wanted to succeed him. As I recall, the Plague settled the question by taking both of them, and the holdings reverted to Tiglath."

"Yes. But when he told us about them, and their characteristics, it became clear that both were able enough to hold the manors very well. We talked about it all afternoon. Do you remember what I asked him at the last?"

Rohan nodded tiredly. "Which one, if he gave his lands to the other, would make war against the decision until he could take what he wanted?"

Again she was silent for a long time, and finally said, "Come to bed, my love. At least lie down for a little while, even if you can't sleep."

"It'll be noon before we know it."

"Yes."

"Sioned—"

"I know." She looked up at him. "I'm frightened, too."

* * *

Pol woke quite suddenly to a queer grayish light like dusk through the wire mesh window beside his bed. He leaped up, horrified lest he had slept past noon. But the haze was only clouds that had blown up since dawn. The sun made a hesitant appearance, then shied back behind a billow of slate-colored clouds. Pol tiptoed around the partition, saw that his parents sat with their backs to him, talking in low voices, and estimated his chances of sneaking out. Returning to his bed, he gathered up boots and a fresh shirt. He paused before leaving the pavilion; his parents were quiet now, and his mother's hand reached over the brief space between them to grip his father's hand, tightly. Pol could not distinguish the words she used, but the pain in her voice was achingly clear. He bit his lip and slid from the pavilion.

Tallain was nowhere in evidence, and Tallain was the only one who might have ordered him back into bed with impunity. The guards merely bowed as he paused to haul on boots and shirt. He ran his fingers back through his hair and hurried to the nearby tent where he suddenly knew Tallain would be.

His instincts proved correct. Not only Tallain but Sorin, Riyan, and Tilal were there, each with a section of Maarken's battle harness in his hands. They glanced up as Pol entered, and identical small, grim smiles came to all four faces.

"My brother is fortunate in his squires," Sorin remarked. "Here—your fingers are nimbler than mine, Pol." He gave his young cousin a vambrace. "Scour the inner part of that, will you? I can't get at the smaller bits."

Together they polished steel fastenings and silver decorations until one metal's shine was indistinguishable from the other. Leather was oiled to suppleness where needed, and inspected for stiffened strength where essential. None of them spoke unless to ask for a fresh cloth or to request an opinion about the readiness of a particular piece—opinions that always expressed satisfaction, but that were only spurs to more polishing, more oiling, more making sure that Maarken's equipment would be nothing less than perfect.

After a time, Tobin came in with her son's clothing. Her black eyes acknowledged Pol with a quick gleam. She laid out trousers, shirt, and tunic on a chair, smoothing them, her fingers tender on silk and velvet and buttersoft leather.

The colors dazzled. The shirt was Radzyn's white, with a red collar and yoke. Sky-blue for his Desert ancestors and pale blue for Lleyn who had knighted him were sub-

tly worked into the thin embroidered bands sewn down
the sides of the white leather trousers. But his own
Whitecliff's red and orange dominated the tunic, whisper-
light velvet that showed either color depending on which
way the nap was rubbed. In it, as his muscles moved
beneath the rich cloth, he would look like a living flame.

"If he dares get any holes in this, I'll take him over
my knee," she said suddenly. And only then did Pol
realize how afraid she was.

"I'll remember that, Mother."

Maarken entered the tent, his skin sun-bronzed and his
hair gold-lit after a summer spent in Princemarch, gray
eyes bright as quicksilver. He smiled easily at them all
before sliding an arm around his mother's waist.

"I mean it," she insisted, looking smaller than ever
next to her tall son. "This velvet cost me a fortune. If
you so much as loosen a single thread in a single seam,
I'll—"

"I know," he interrupted. "Stop worrying. And thank
you for the clothes. They're magnificent."

"Damned right, they are." She gazed up at him a moment, then reached up and took him gently by the ears
to pull his face down to hers. She kissed him quickly and
let him go. "I'll go find your father. Not that you need
any help in arming," she added with a fond glance at the
others.

"The only thing lacking is a sword, my lady," Tilal
said, rising. He went to a corner and pulled out a scabbard, presenting it to Maarken with a low bow. "I bought
this for my father, and he sends it to you with his love.
We'd both be honored if you'd use it today."

Maarken ran marveling fingers over the garnets embedded in the hilt, then tested the grip. "It's perfect. I—
Tilal, I don't know what to say."

"Just tell me you'll use it. I know you have your own,
but—my father also said that at his age, he's not likely to
use this for the purpose its crafter intended. And a sword
this fine shouldn't sit idle in an old man's feeble hand."
Tilal smiled. "*His* opinion of himself, not mine!"

"I've been to war with Prince Davvi," Maarken said
softly, meeting Tilal's green eyes. "I've seen what he and
a sword can accomplish. Thank you—and thank him for

me, as well. I'm just sorry it won't drink anything better than that bastard's blood.''

Tobin made a soft sound, but instantly recovered and said tartly, ''You'll wield that sword for your kinsman and your prince—and the Sunrunners, too, for that matter. I can't think of a more honorable first blooding for a sword than that.''

''You're right, Mother, as always.'' He glanced around the tent. ''And I can't think of more honor than to have princes and lords help me to arm. But it's getting late. We'd best get started.''

Tobin touched his cheek briefly, then hurried from the tent. Pol stepped back and watched as Maarken first got into his clothes, then stood still in the middle of the tent while Sorin, Tilal, and Riyan buckled him into his battle harness. Pol knew the theory, of course, and had assisted in arming Prince Chadric and his sons on ceremonial occasions. But he had never helped anyone don the accoutrements of war in earnest before, and hung back shyly, wide-eyed.

The red-orange tunic all but vanished beneath the chest- and spine-guards that were buckled securely at shoulders and ribs. The stiffened leather had been dyed the dark red of Radzyn and Whitecliff, and was studded with steel and silver across the breast. Maarken would be fighting afoot, not on horseback, so his clothes and armor were designed to permit as much freedom of movement as possible. When he was almost ready, he waved the three young men away and turned to Pol.

''My prince,'' he said quietly.

Pol looked up in awe at this cousin he idolized. Surely there was no finer young man in the world, no nobler young knight, no more admirable Sunrunner. And yet— Maarken smiled slightly, his eyes conveying understanding. Pol wanted to be the one to defend his own princedom, and cursed his youth and lack of experience in battle. He knew it must be wrong to want to prove himself in fighting, when his parents had worked so hard all their lives to spare him from living by the sword. But, coming up on his fifteenth year, and in the presence of the champion who would fight for him today, he realized that it would have been unnatural if he *hadn't* wanted to be in Maarken's place. He smiled wry assent to the look in his cousin's eyes, and shrugged one shoulder slightly.

Sorin came forward then with the belt, gave it to Pol. He fastened its white length around his cousin's waist, fingers nimble on the golden buckle given by Prince Lleyn. Then he accepted the sword from Tilal and presented it. As it was strapped on, he looked at Sorin and Riyan.

"Do you have what I gave you?" They understood at once, and handed Pol the knives he'd purchased for them at the Fair. He showed them to Maarken. "They're only eating-knives," he apologized, "not really suited for throwing. But Father always says that you should have at least one in reserve where your enemies won't think to look for it. Father keeps his in his boots."

"I know. I have a couple hidden—but these are quite welcome, believe me." Maarken slipped the knives into his belt.

Sorin asked, "Will you want the helm?"

"No. Nor leather coif, either. I plan to watch this bastard's face crumple, and hoods and helms only get in the way." He grinned suddenly. "Besides, it's damned hot out there."

Suddenly they were all silent, unwilling to acknowledge that it was nearly noon and Masul would be waiting. Pol gazed long and hard at his cousin, wishing he had words to explain his feelings—wishing he knew what those feelings were. They tumbled in him so quickly that he didn't know if fear or pride or love or hate or grim anticipation dominated. He touched Maarken's wrist briefly, saw the gray eyes smile down at him.

"Stay safe, Maarken," was all he could think of to mumble around a sudden lump in his throat.

"I will, my prince."

An unexpected visitor came in then—unexpected only by Pol, and respectfully welcomed by all but him. He felt guilty for the distance he wanted to put between himself and Andry, yet the wariness was stronger than ever.

Andry didn't seem to notice, however. He embraced his eldest brother and said, "Don't take this as an insult, please—but you must end this quickly. I don't want the stars shining on your battle. If these sorcerers could kill

Lady Andrade on the starlight, they'd have no scruple in doing the same to you. Guard yourself, Maarken.''

''You can't mean Masul has them on his side knowingly!'' Riyan exclaimed.

''I don't know what I mean,'' Andry snapped. ''I only know that this has to be done before nightfall. I don't know enough about the Star Scroll yet to be able to counter whatever they might attempt.''

Maarken nodded slowly. ''There are clouds enough to keep out the sunlight, Andry. And it's not even noon yet! I wouldn't be too concerned about the stars.''

''Well, I am,'' his brother said in curt tones.

''Maarken knows what he's doing,'' Pol heard himself say.

Andry glanced at him. ''He fights for my honor as well as yours.''

Pol nodded. ''I think we'd better get there first, by the way. If Maarken's late, Masul will only taunt him.'' He made an effort at Maarken's nonchalance, and shrugged. ''If for no other reason, he needs killing for the foulness of his mouth.''

Approval shone briefly in Maarken's eyes. He clapped Pol on one shoulder and said, ''Let's see an end to this, then. I'm stifling in here, and—''

Pol saw his face freeze, and turned. Hollis stood in the doorway, her long tawny hair wild around her shoulders, falling in tangled strands to her hips. Blue eyes, huge and dark in her pallid face, saw only Maarken. Pol's astonishment and devouring curiosity yielded to tact for the first time in his life; he collected the others with a gesture and led the way from the tent.

Whatever Pol had hoped they might say to each other to mend the breach that had been only too obvious since her arrival at Waes, Maarken's expression as he joined them plainly signaled that such things had not been said. Pol was suddenly furious with Hollis. Anyone with any sense knew that no man or woman should be sent into battle with the memory of fear-filled eyes. He'd watched and learned from the leavetakings at Stronghold this spring; even though no war was anticipated, a season spent on the Cunaxan border was always dangerous. Especially had he noticed the manner in which Lady Feylin had bid farewell to Lord Walvis. She had embraced and kissed him, then berated him for polishing his damned harness so bright that it pained her eyes to look at him. They had parted with teasing—much the same technique Tobin had employed a little while ago with her son. He'd seen men and women at Stronghold use the same cover for emotion as they said good-bye to warrior wives and husbands and lovers. Hollis would have to learn.

Andry was in the process of making things worse. "Maarken—she does love you, she's just been ill this summer and—"

Pol fixed Andry with what he hoped was an adequate approximation of his father's coldest look. Evidently it was more than adequate; the new Lord of Goddess Keep flushed like a schoolboy and looked away. But in the next instant the man who made Pol so uneasy had returned, and gave him a glance of equal iciness. They had met by *faradhi* means, they two, learned things about each other's strengths that had not yet been fully analyzed. And Pol had the sudden, sick feeling that whereas he would never come to open battle with Andry, neither would they ever be completely at peace with each other. There was too much power on both sides.

Gentle Goddess, why power? he thought suddenly as they started walking to the High Prince's pavilion where the rest of their family would be waiting. What did it gain? Roelstra had enjoyed setting princes against each other and reaping the spoils. Andrade had wanted to re-order the continent under Sunrunner rule. Pol's father wanted to form a fabric of law as wide-ranging as the fabric of light the *faradh'im* had spun last night. But what did Andry want?

More to the point, what did Pol himself want?

Troublesome questions flew entirely out of his head as he met his parents and the others outside the huge tent. Urival stood stiff and straight, as one who feared that relaxing any muscle would mean collapse of his elaborate defensive structure against grief. Chay was just as straight-backed, but without tension. He moved easily to embrace his son, confidence and pride in every line of him.

"Pol."

He started at the sound of his mother's voice, tight and clipped, totally lacking its usual music. He went forward automatically and she held out a plain, thin silver circlet. Only then did he notice that both his parents were wearing narrow bands across their foreheads, coronets carved so that the gold seemed faceted like a jewel. He smoothed his hair and set the circlet in place, feeling its chill quickly warm at contact with his skin. Rare were the times he had worn this symbol of his rank; the last time had been his farewell banquet at Radzyn, just before leaving for Graypearl to become Lleyn's squire. But today of all days he knew he had to remind everyone of his royal status—as if, standing beside his sternly regal parents, anyone would need reminding.

Rohan was inspecting Maarken's battle harness, tugging at a leather fastening here, checking a steel buckle there. Pol stiffened slightly, then realized that it wasn't that his father didn't trust the young men who had armed Maarken; he only needed something to do.

Finally Rohan nodded satisfaction and stepped back. In the interim they had been joined by Davvi and Kostas, Volog, Alasen, and Ostvel. The latter led Maarken's sleek and glossy stallion, caparisoned in Whitecliff colors. As if Ostvel were still chief steward of Stronghold and not an important lord in his own right, he bowed low to Rohan and said, "Your grace, all is in readiness."

Rohan inclined his head once. To Maarken he said, "As it is forbidden to engage in such things within the precincts of the *Rialla,* we've found a field across the river. It's perfectly flat, with no dips or hillocks to make things difficult. You'll wait on horseback until you're called, then ride up and make the usual salutes to me and Pol and Andry. Dismount then, and when Andry gives the signal, begin." He paused, then said, "Goddess blessing, Maarken."

As they started off, Andry tried to keep his gaze from Alasen, but could not. She wore a plain gown of pale gray, the color of a cloud come to earth. Her long hair spilled down her back in shining waves of gold-washed brown. The green eyes that were very like Sioned's refused to look at him; but she often glanced through the veil of her lashes at Maarken where he walked beside

Ostvel and the magnificent horse. Jealousy stirred in him, then vanished. What he had shared with her in the manner of *faradh'im* could not be rivaled by the sight of his warrior brother in all his brave finery. Andry had held the essence of her, shown her the joy of her gifts. He had restructured her bright glowing colors when she might have been shadow-lost. He had kept her safe. *Only let this be over soon,* he petitioned the Goddess, *and let me have the time to talk with her alone.* Alasen would understand and come with him to Goddess Keep, and he would teach her the wonders of being *faradhi.* They would be Lord and Lady together, with children to come after them, and—

He was brought up short by the sight of the crowds lining their way to the bridge. A strange rainbow fluttered below the gray sky as people waved ribbons of Desert blue and Radzyn red-and-white and Whitecliff red-and-orange—and Princemarch's violet. He wondered bitterly if they flung that color aloft for Pol or for Masul.

Pandsala joined them at last, empty-eyed. She bent her head to Andry and her knees to Pol, and took a place at the very end of their small procession. Andry frowned slightly. *There* was one he would have to bring back into the discipline of Goddess Keep. Princess-Regent or not, she was a Sunrunner; Andrade had loathed her and chosen to ignore her existence as much as possible, but Andry was not so sanguine about allowing her free use of the rings she wore. Andrade had been lax with Sioned, too—but whereas Andry trusted his aunt implicitly, he did not trust Pandsala at all. It would be an interesting knife-edge to walk, he told himself: keeping hold of the duty and loyalty all Sunrunners owed to Goddess Keep when some of those Sunruners were ruling princes. He glanced sideways at Pol. Andrade had thought to have the training of him; now it would be Andry who taught him *faradhi* arts. Along with them, he would instill in Pol a spirit of cooperation with Goddess Keep. He did not delude himself that it would be easy. But Andrade had broken the rule that *faradh'im* did not become princes; she had hatched the egg, and now it was up to Andry to teach the hatchling where and how he would fly.

But first they had to rid themselves of this pretender who had dared murder a Sunrunner.

The stallion's hooves rang loudly against the wooden bridge, echoing the thud of Maarken's heart in his chest. He was disgusted with himself for the apprehension. He had a fine sword; knives enough to back him up in the unlikely circumstance that he lost the greater blade; strength, youth, and the right on his side. For his princes and for his fellow Sunrunners he would kill Masul. He spared a tiny smile for the perfect harmony that mocked his fears of having the two parts of himself come into conflict. If being *athri* and *faradhi* both was always this easy, he had nothing to worry about.

But the future was precisely what was on his mind: the day's work before him and all the days that would follow. Would Hollis share them or not?

She had been frightened, distraught, wild-eyed when she'd come to him in his tent. Fever had swirled in her dark blue eyes, turning them nearly black with pinpoints of silver like lightning flashes through her soul. Folding her to his heart, elated that she was unresisting, he had felt the tremors shake her body that was almost frail in his arms.

"Beloved, beloved," he had whispered, "don't be afraid. I won't come to any hurt, I swear it."

"How can you know? How can either of us be sure?"

It was he who had drawn away from her, angry and desperately hurt. "If you have no faith in me—"

"I have every faith in you. It's *them* I don't trust."

"Who? What are you talking about, Hollis?"

"The ones who want all *faradh'im* dead. The sorcerers. I've read about their ways, Maarken, I've helped translate the scrolls. Even if Masul doesn't know about them or want their help, they'll give it to him. He's their challenge against us. Not only against the High Prince and his son, but all of us, all Sunrunners!"

Maarken told himself now that he should be reassured by her fear, for it meant she loved him still. Her pleas to be careful surely indicated a heart that was his alone. But just as suddenly her lips had turned cold under his comforting kisses, and she had extricated herself from his embrace with a terse reminder that the others were waiting for him.

As he had walked through the crowds to the bridge, he had seen her standing with the other Sunrunners. Hollis had been holding tight to Sejast's hand.

His family went on ahead of him when they reached the field. Ostvel stayed behind, holding the stallion's head while Maarken mounted. Gathering the reins, he looked down at his old friend's face.

"Remember he's larger than you are," Ostvel said. "Test him out. If he's slow with his size, use that against him. But if he's quick and strong—" Ostvel suddenly snorted. "Listen to me, advising you as if you hadn't been in your first battle at the age of eleven! And as if someone like me knew anything about the arts of war!"

Maarken smiled. "You know more than most, even if you never use it. I remember my lessons at your hands, before I went to Graypearl. You and Maeta used to drill me in swordplay until—" He broke off, wincing at her name.

"She'd be so proud of you right now," Ostvel told him. "She always was."

He nodded wordlessly.

"I'd better go take my place with the others."

"Don't worry, Ostvel. A quick victory for me, a slow death for him. I promised."

"To hell with your promise! Kill him however you can, as soon as you can." He hesitated. "I'll keep an eye on your lady for you."

"Thanks," Maarken replied awkwardly, not wanting to think about her. He must think of nothing but Masul's death.

The field was encircled with people now, half a measure away from where Maarken sat his horse. The highborns were strictly divided between the opposing parties. The common folk filled in between, everyone silent beneath the slate clouds. Maarken looked up, thinking that the sky seemed made of the gray ashes scattered at dawn, as if Andrade's spirit lingered to witness the pretender's defeat.

At the direction of Rohan's guards, an opening appeared on either side of the circle, one of them directly in front of Maarken. The crowd parted on the other side, giving him a clear view of Masul. He wore Princemarch's violet, damn him, and rode the horse he'd nearly killed in the race. It would be Maarken's pleasure to claim that horse for his own and treat it as so fine an animal deserved.

Despite the cloud cover it was still a warm day, muggy with a confusion of late summer and early autumn, as if neither season yet had dominion. Maarken felt sweat dampen his back underneath the leather and steel of his harness, and resisted the urge to twitch his shoulder blades against the trickle of moisture between them. At last he heard his brother's voice, indistinct at this distance in the open air, but he knew what Andry would be saying.

First, the identification of claims. Then the statement of Masul's crime. The pretender rode forward and halted before the High Prince, making no bow—not that anyone had expected him to. His head was at an arrogant angle as he made formal challenge. Andry heard him out, then turned slightly and spoke again. Maarken distinguished his own name and titles, touched his heels to his stallion's sides, and reined in neatly half a length from Masul. He bent his head to his uncle and his cousin.

"Be then our champion, Lord Maarken," Rohan was saying in long-established formula. "As this man seeks to prove his claim on his body, so you will prove ours on your own."

"I will, my prince," he replied.

Andry signaled both men to dismount. But Masul had one more thing to say.

"I demand assurance that he'll use no Sunrunner witcheries in this battle."

"Given," Maarken snapped before anyone could do more than stiffen with insult.

"Then remove your rings, *faradhi.*"

Maarken stared at him. Surely Masul didn't believe that old tale that a Sunrunner deprived of the rings was powerless. Sioned was proof enough of that; she had worn no ring but her husband's for fifteen years, and all here had seen ample demonstration of her continuing power. He glanced at Andry, who wore a scornful smile.

"Permission is given," said the Lord of Goddess Keep, "for we would not want the pretender distracted by his superstitions."

Maarken nearly laughed. Young as he was, Andry had a definite flair for this kind of thing. He bowed to his brother and stripped off his red leather gloves. One by one he removed the rings he had worked so hard to earn. As he did so, his urge to laugh died away. The six small circles in his palm, silver and gold with small rubies, and one more crowned with a garnet, were integral to his pride. They were part of what he was. He hesitated, then walked over and with a low bow gave them to Pol for safekeeping.

He saw a flicker on Andry's face, gone in an instant. "My prince," he said to his cousin, "I'll reclaim them soon."

"But they're still on your fingers, Maarken. Look."

There were thin bands of paler skin where the rings had been. If Andry had a flair, Pol had a positive genius. He smiled at the boy and Pol's eyes brightened in reply.

Chay came forward then, leading away Maarken's stallion. Miyon did the same for Masul's horse. Maarken put his gloves back on, flexing his fingers within thin, supple leather that would keep his grip on his sword firm and sure, and gestured for Masul to precede him out to the center of the field.

As he followed the pretender, he could sense Hollis' presence all along his skin. But he did not make the mistake of looking at her.

* * *

Segev shifted nervously at Hollis' side. He was on his own now, and he knew it. Mireva could do nothing, not in working her will through him nor in telling him what he ought to do. Starlight was her weapon; it was day. She was competent with sunlight, but the clouds blotted out the sun. He should have felt exhilarated by the freedom. He felt nothing but apprehension.

Swiftly he surveyed the crowd. Many for and many against Masul—but none of them with power to do what he could if he chose. If he had the courage. If he was willing to risk all for a man Mireva would eventually kill anyway.

No—not for Masul. For himself. Segev explored possibilities, projecting actions and their probable consequences. If he succeeded in killing Maarken with no one the wiser, then Mireva would have to favor him over Ruval when it came time to challenge Pol openly. But with the Star Scroll his, he would not need Mireva at all.

Who was likely to be trouble? he wondered, scanning the faces. No Sunrunner would dare any weavings—no usable sunlight shafted through the clouds, nothing to work with. He smiled in contempt at their weakness. But which of them might sense his own working? Pandsala was the obvious danger; her mother had been Ianthe's mother, gifted with the powers of the *diarmadh'im*. Sunrunner she might think herself, but Segev knew better. Urival was a strong possibility. Segev did not forget that he had sensed Mireva's starlit observations that night in spring.

But only Andry knew and understood enough of the Star Scroll to be a real threat. And that would only happen if Segev was careless.

He watched intently as Maarken and Masul faced off. The first clash of steel sent a spasm through Hollis. Segev had nearly forgotten her. She had escaped him for a time this morning, probably to go see Maarken. As if either of them would glean any comfort from the encounter. He glanced at her white, strained face with its huge eyes, and squeezed her hand reassuringly.

Maarken was perhaps a finger's width taller than Masul, but the latter was heavier through the shoulders. Still, they seemed evenly matched. Segev cast a quick glance at the water clock that had been brought here from Rohan's tent to measure the length of the battle. When the level in the lower sphere had risen one mark, Segev would act. Weariness would assail the combatants by then, and tension would draw nerves to the breaking point in everyone else. No one would pay any attention to the obscure "Sunrunner" youth who would decide the outcome of the challenge.

He hid a grin and pulled in a deep, satisfied lungful of the muggy air. He could wait.

Chapter Twenty-eight

Riyan watched with critical eyes as Maarken and Masul tested each other's fighting styles. There was no doubt that Maarken was the more polished warrior, elegant, graceful. But Masul fought with controlled heat, like a kiln fire stoked to searing strength. Maarken could take the chance of infuriating Masul in hopes that the resulting explosion of temper would make him careless. Or he could trust to his superior training and technique. For the present he played it conservatively, with feints and parries designed to show him Masul's weaknesses. But Riyan and every other swordsman watching soon saw what Maarken did: Masul's weaknesses were very few.

The pretender had had a masterful teacher. Riyan could well imagine that some knight in retirement at Dasan Manor had longed for amusement. Lacking sons of his own to train, discovery of so apt a pupil in so unlikely a place must have offered the perfect outlet for boredom. There must be many such young men throughout the princedoms, whose swords could earn them a way out of obscurity into a lord's or prince's permanent guard, and perhaps even to holdings of their own. Andry was proof that not every highborn's son was born to wield a sword; Masul showed that not all peasants were meant for the plow.

Still, there were certain moves of which he appeared ignorant. At first it seemed that Maarken might be overtrained, especially compared to Masul's brutal directness. But he picked up quickly on the differences in their styles, and when the fight began in earnest Riyan nodded slowly on seeing that Maarken had found the most important weakness. Masul excelled in one-handed thrusts and parries, but he had a bad habit of bringing his sword completely over his left shoulder to add extra force to an inelegant two-handed swing, as if he was hacking at a tree. Had he been able to trick Maarken into losing his balance, the blow would have been effective. But Maarken watched and sidestepped, and when the move had been tried twice, took advantage of its third use. He gave Masul time to bring his sword over his shoulder, fooling him with a purposely clumsy recovery, then swung his own blade in a deadly arc right at Masul's ribs.

The pretender saw it coming too late to evade entirely. His spine arched like an angry cat's, his right hand slipping from his sword as he struggled to maintain equilibrium. As Maarken's blade caught him in a wide swipe across his chest harness, his left arm and sword described a powerless half-circle in silver. The first whispers came from the hitherto silent crowd.

Riyan saw Maarken choose the emotional advantage rather than the physical one. Instead of following up on his opponent's distress, he took a step back and put one hand on his hip: the attitude of a master teacher waiting for an incompetent student to recover himself for the next lesson. Riyan could not hear what Maarken said, but the taunting curve of his lips was unmistakable. He evidently felt that Masul's unleashed fury would work against him far more effectively than a physical wound. As the pretender regained his balance and lunged forward to the attack, Riyan wondered if Maarken was right to risk it. The anger was still contained.

His attention was diverted from the next few moves by the sight of a young squire in Cunaxan orange and the silver knife badge who sidled around to this side of the crowd. Sorin stopped him, then grimaced and escorted him to where Rohan and Sioned stood. Riyan moved closer to hear what was being said.

"—your graces would care to make regarding the outcome," the squire finished.

"Your master has one hell of a nerve," Tobin hissed, her eyes on her son.

"Agreed," Sioned murmured, and Riyan's brows shot up at the wicked gleam that lit her emerald eyes. "But we'll accept the wager, nonetheless." She glanced at Rohan. "What do you think, my lord *azhrei* and husband? Free rights to Tiglath for the next ten years against. . . ?"

The High Prince smiled, and the squire took an involuntary step backward. "Against whatever you like, vein of my heart," Rohan drawled. "You're the gambler in the family."

"Thank you, dearest. You're so generous to me." She looked again at the squire. "My lord husband is a great believer in innovations. We have a project or two in mind that require large amounts of iron. Say, about 500 silk-weights."

The squire gulped at her casual mention of this colossal quantity. "I–I am ordered to accept whatever terms are offered, your grace. I shall inform my master at once."

"Do that," she purred.

Riyan looked a question at Sorin, received a bewildered shrug in reply, and sighed. Whatever Sioned had in mind, it was known only to her and Rohan.

Maarken was still toying with Masul, trying to loose the anger that could only help defeat the pretender. The crowd began to shout its preferences, cheering a well-aimed blow or an artful parry. As Riyan followed each attack and counter, he came to realize that whatever else he was, Masul was no fool. Too much depended on this for him to be tricked into losing his temper. Maarken seemed to sense this as well; his face set into grimmer lines and his sword swung with more ferocity, seeking not to taunt but to kill.

There was blood now on both men, gashes cut in arms and thighs, gouges taken out of leather harness and the skin beneath. Riyan tensed as Masul's blade sought to bury itself in Maarken's skull; the young lord swayed back just in time, but not quickly enough to avoid a glancing slice on his cheekbone. He riposted swiftly with a nasty cut to the pretender's already bruised ribs, where his earlier blow had laid open part of Masul's armor. The man gasped loudly and drew back, one hand clutching his bloodied side. This time Maarken followed through with a long step forward and a vicious swing of his sword designed to dissect the tendons behind the knees. Masul lurched out of his way at the last instant and fell to the grass.

Riyan's four rings dug into his flesh as his hands clenched in anticipation of the final blow. But it did not come. Maarken staggered slightly, shaking his head. And suddenly he raised his sword to strike at something that was not there.

Nervous laughter and derisive shouts surged through the crowd, quickly followed by exclamations as Maarken again thrust his blade at empty air. Riyan gave an incoherent cry as he felt trembling heat circle his fingers. He looked down at his hands, half-expecting the rings to glow, giddy with relief when he saw they did not. But they alerted him to a subtle and menacing prickle of the same heat in his mind. Maarken was struggling against some enemy seen only by himself—and his real enemy was recovering from shock and pain, heaving himself to his feet. Riyan closed his eyes, concentrating. An oddly familiar flare on the edge of his thoughts, intense fire just out of reach—his breath caught and he remembered when he had felt it before.

The assassin's death. The ancient power of his mother's family had responded to the use of sorcery then as now, answered through the burning of his *faradhi* rings. So he *was* of the Old Blood, he thought, fighting back panic as that blood allowed him to glimpse things that threatened Maarken's life as surely as Masul's sword.

* * *

Sioned clung to Rohan's arm, watching in horror as Masul rose up to renew the battle. But Maarken was flailing his sword at nothingness, whirling to attack things that were not there. "Sweet Goddess, what's wrong with him?" she gasped.

Tobin screamed her son's name. Masul, careful of the wildly swinging sword, approached and got in a telling blow with the flat of his blade on Maarken's spine. The young lord reeled, turned to slice a gash in Masul's arm. But it was as if he fought not one but two or more men, only one of them visible to the stunned crowd. Only his vast skills as a warrior trained to anticipate a dozen swords at once kept him alive.

"Sioned—it's them, someone's here who knows the old ways—"

She barely recognized Pandsala's voice, didn't even notice that for the first time the regent had addressed her by name. "What? What are you saying?"

Pandsala looked ill, her face as gray as her gown, her eyes nearly black. She was rubbing her hands, twisting the rings on her fingers as if they hurt her. "I don't know, I can't—oh, Goddess!"

Rohan and Sioned supported her as she swayed. "Sioned—if she's right, someone has to protect Maarken."

She knew at once what he was asking. She had shielded him from treachery years ago during his battle with Roelstra, weaving starlight at an impossible distance into an overarching dome through which arrows and knives could not penetrate. But this was different. He was asking her to pit her Sunrunner arts against something she knew nothing about. And there was no sunlight to work with, nothing to weave into a thick fabric of protection. Even if she could, would it be effective against sorcery?

Maarken twisted and fought, sometimes evading Masul's thrusts and sometimes staggering under their impact as he battled specters only he could see. The deep red of his battle harness and the orange-red of his tunic were darker now with another red, an ominous red. Like living flame he writhed and spun from visible and invisible warriors.

Living flame.

She let Rohan take Pandsala's weight. "Pol! Andry! Urival!" she cried out, and they were at her side even as the first blaze of conjured Sunrunner's Fire sprang up from the ground. She heard the screams, Miyon's furious shout that *faradhi* tricks were forbidden, and ignored all as she gathered in the colors of those around her. Sapphire and ruby and emerald and diamond and a dozen other gem tints dazzled and shone within the red-gold flames as they rose higher, higher, running up walls that were not there, meeting in a fiery arch that spread until it encapsuled the battlefield. People shrank back, faces crimsoned by the Fire, terrified by its intensity. Sioned grasped for every shred of *faradhi* power she could find around her, heedless of the soft despairing cries of Sunrunners already exhausted. But she kept Maarken out of it, cordoned off from the weave that must protect him.

The flames flickered, unsteady, as the sorcerer who had wrought Maarken's visions assaulted Sioned, battered at her with powers like yet unlike *faradhi* ways. It was as if their hands met on either side of a fine mesh screen, palms and fingers matched, the warmth of skin to skin tangible—yet never really touching. She fought back, drew even more from reeling Sunrunners until they had no more to give.

The Fire held, obscuring all view of the combatants within its dome. She could not know if her weaving had canceled the sorcerer's working. She wanted to believe that the frantic attack on her defenses meant she was succeeding. But she knew that the sorcerer must be found, must be. There was not enough left in the Sunrunners or in herself to sustain this for long.

Sioned felt a sudden loss, a retrieval of portions of power and color back to the *faradhi* who owned them. She could not stop to reclaim lost strength; she sought for and found more, moaning as she recognized the brilliant, nearly limitless force that was her son, offered up for her free use. As she had done once before when he was barely a day old, she drew on the raw power of him, and thanked the Goddess for his gifts even while begging her to keep him safe.

* * *

Pandsala struggled to rise from her knees, where Rohan had abandoned her when Sioned began her work. She was still a part of that work, could feel Sioned's imperious demand for her strength. Yet it was not like years ago, when she had been helpless in the Sunrunner's powerful grip. She could reclaim the larger portion of herself, and with it her conscious will.

She staggered a few steps, paused to catch her breath, and swept her gaze around firelit, frightened faces beneath the cloudy gloom. Who was it, where, how? Her rings burned her flesh. Her mind was ablaze. Yet for the first time there were two distinct sensations of power, overlapping in some places and remarkably similar, but different in subtle ways. One of them she could easily identify as the *faradhi* discipline, seized by Sioned. The other was strangely free of the High Princess, drawn instead toward another, matching power.

Suddenly she knew its source, knew him as instinctively as she knew how to breathe. Fierce eyes in a fire-stained, feral face—a face that had seemed eerily familiar to her before. The eyes were the wrong color, but the

face was suddenly an echo of one hated for half her lifetime, a face that laughed at her in nightmares that had
been true. Ianthe's face.

Pandsala almost screamed with the agony of knowledge. Ianthe's face, Ianthe's son, Ianthe's victory. She
tasted blood in her mouth, sorcerer's blood shared with
him, and knew her teeth had bitten her flesh. Her lower
lip was on fire, like the circles of gold and silver around
her fingers. Sunrunner's rings screaming in the presence
of sorcery. Physical pain snapped some thread of tension
in her, but instead of igniting fury she felt icy calm.

He was only a short distance from her. She pushed past
Chay, who held his nearly senseless wife in his arms,
shouldered aside Volog and Ostvel and the wide-eyed
Alasen. The boy didn't see her. He held onto the young
Sunrunner Maarken wanted to marry, his gaze intent on
the fiery dome. She moved closer, every muscle in her
body flowing smoothly and silently as water. Sioned's
demand for her strength in the Fire-weaving siphoned off
a little more of the *faradhi*-trained part of her, but she
kept the Old Blood for herself, felt its silken shimmer in
her veins like the trickles of sunlight seeping now through
the gray clouds.

Close enough to touch him now, to see the shadows
swirling in his eyes. Their shape and the thickness of
their lashes and the set of them in his face were all
Ianthe's. Their color, blazing green now with no hint of
gray, was Roelstra's. Pandsala's hands lifted to claw them
from his skull.

He saw her then, thrust the other woman away from
him. Pandsala lunged for him, an incoherent cry clot-
ting in her throat. This was one of those who wanted
Pol's life, his power, his destruction. Ianthe's youngest
son, Segev, who would want those things all the more,
even though and especially because Pol was his own
brother. The Old Blood screamed within her to let him
finish his work, promising powers undreamed of if she
would only side with her mother's people from whom she
had received her power.

Pandsala dug her nails into her nephew's shoulders. He
gave a small whimper of pain and tried to free himself.

She shifted her grip to his neck, pressed her thumbs to the hollow at its base.

Agony knifed through every nerve in her body. Her hands dropped from his throat to the blade's hilt embedded in her thigh. Her fingers groped through the slippery silk folds of her gown, already wet with blood.

It was not a thrust that should have killed her. It should not have hurt so much. Her mind knew that. But the knife was a thing alive, a steel snake slithering through her, severing all connection between brain and body, mind and power.

He shoved her down to the grass, smiling. "Dearest aunt," he whispered. But then his voice changed, deepened. Long ago she had seen Andrade demonstrate the arcane art of speaking through another person, using other eyes and ears. It was not Segev's voice she heard now. "It's the *faradh'im* who're feeling the pain—through you—and the *diarmadhi* in you that's keeping you alive. But not for much longer. Can you feel it in the knife? Iron doesn't kill us, only hurts. But anything cast with Merida poison kills."

She had no flesh, no voice, no will. Segev kept on smiling, kept on speaking in that other voice.

"They'll die through you. You're connected. All of them, all the weakling foolish Sunrunners. But not Pol. He's one of us. Did you know that? He belongs to us. Through Rohan, through Sioned, it doesn't matter. He'll survive this—and die a much more satisfying death. You won't be around to see it, but I thought you should know."

And Segev laughed quietly, gleefully.

Pandsala heard *faradhi* screams, felt their pain. Because of her. Smelled the blood pulsing from her veins. Felt the knife hilt warm and slick in her palm. Had no strength to pull it out, remove the iron poison that was killing Sunrunners or the Merida poison that was killing her. Saw the boy's face turn white as power flared in his eyes and shuddered through him. He smiled and this time it was Ianthe's smile as the red-gold flames died, and Pandsala with them.

* * *

The piercing shriek rose as if from a single throat. Sunrunners howled in agony as spell-caught colors flared to unbearable intensity, pulsed along already shredded nerves, threatened to explode their minds from the inside out. The fiery dome collapsed. The water clock, set on its stand nearby, burst in a shower of crystal shards. Sioned, writhing in her husband's arms, used her last strength in a frantic attempt to find order and pattern. But the cloudy sun-threaded sky above her was abruptly sharp-edged, the steel-gray of shadowed knives.

All of them—even Alasen in her ignorance of *faradhi* arts—all of the Sunrunners felt the slashing pain. But of them all, only one found enough strength to act.

Hollis lay still, glassy-eyed as she watched Sejast murder Pandsala. Her head was bursting, her lungs stabbing with each shallow breath, her body a mass of incandescent needles that bled flames. She did not understand Pandsala's scream, could not comprehend why her own agony coincided precisely with that scream. She saw Sejast kneel down with the other fallen Sunrunners around them, as if he, too, was dying.

Hollis looked at Pandsala's limp form just beyond him, at the knife protruding from her thigh. Everything had rough, snagged edges. She traced the angles of that shining knife, shining so brightly that it sank fresh pain into her eyes. She wondered why she was not dead, why she could still think—as the *faradh'im* around her could not. Part of her functioned quite normally, felt strong and in perfect control of her body and her colors, felt nearly as well as when Sejast came each night with his offering of hot, wonderful taze. But the rest of her knew this was illusory; for whatever reason, she knew she was close to death.

She saw the word written in elegant script hundreds years old. *Den*: death. But another word was superimposed upon it, a word heading a section of the Star Scroll. *Chian'den*: death by treachery and treason. The page wavered, became a sheet of Fironese crystal splashed with black ink. It shattered on the ground before her. She picked up a shard, read on it *chian'den*, and wondered which was illusory, her hands or the shaving of crystal.

Sejast knelt close to her, breathing hard, black hair framing his white face in jagged strands like strokes of ink on parchment. He was watching the combat avidly, fierce eyes laughing. *Chian'den,* Hollis thought. She had helped Andry translate those words, and Sejast had helped them both.

She heard a despairing cry, knew it had come from Maarken. He seemed very far away, struggling to rise as his enemy, whose name she could not quite recall, loomed over him and laughed. But the sword shining in that enemy hand was very close, immediate, ready to claim Maarken's life. Hollis breathed hard, part of her marveling at the magnitude of her fury that had seemed to fill her skull but had now narrowed to an incandescent needle sunk into her heart.

That calm, strong part of her rose up. Her rings were cold, brittle gold and silver circles around her fingers, filmed with dust as she crawled across the ground. They cut her flesh as she put both hands around the knife. She pulled it from the princess-regent's body, held it cradled for a moment between her breasts like a secret.

She was growing more comfortable with the renewal of power. Perhaps it was the cup of strengthening, sustaining wine Sejast had urged her to drink before coming here. She nodded, understanding at last and unsurprised. That, and all the other cups of wine and taze and fruit juice and even simple, innocent water he had brought during the spring and summer. All the sweet and potent drinks he had given her, laced with *dranath.*

She saw that her sister and brother *faradh'im* were no longer twisting in the grip of ferocious pain. She wondered briefly if Sejast had noticed it, too, had heard their weakening whimpers quiet as they caught their breath. She saw that to get to Pandsala, she had crawled around behind him, and that his back was to her as he crouched on his heels, arms extended toward Maarken.

Maarken. . . .

The tall, bloodied figure reeled as one dead drunk, sword wobbling in his uncertain grip. Masul stood back, grinning, as Maarken tried to gather himself for attack. The pretender took a step back, laughing outright as a half-blind thrust missed entirely. A contemptuous slap to one shoulder with the flat of his blade, a kick, and Maarken toppled again.

Hollis heard him cry out again—not in pain or fear but in utter desolation. He came to one knee and swung wildly at thin air, not even looking at Masul. And Sejast shook with silent laughter.

She put the blood-slicked blade between his ribs, forced it deeper and deeper until she fancied she could feel it pulse with the beat of his heart. Then she twisted. Thick redness spurted out onto her hands, her breast, her face. She turned the knife within his body until the heart-beat stopped.

* * *

The Sunrunners' abrupt collapse—and with them, the fiery shield—set even Rohan's rudimentary *faradhi* senses to jangling with pain. Sioned slumped to the ground, her breathing sketchy and her green eyes dark and wild. Pol, Tobin, Alasen—all the Sunrunners curled around their agony on the dry grass, frighteningly silent after the first terrible scream, as senseless as if a gigantic fist had crushed them.

Masul laughed and kicked Maarken down into the dirt. Rohan saw his nephew's sword come up again, aimlessly. The pretender seized the blade in one gloved hand, tossed it aside. Maarken cringed away from something unseen, fumbling for the knives in his belt. He lunged upward, sheer luck directing one of the blades into Masul's leg. The man grunted with pain, kicked Maarken over onto his back, and brought one boot down on Maarken's wrist. The second knife jerked as bones snapped. Masul straightened then, taking his time about positioning himself as if posing for the sketch of a commemorative tap-estry. Holding his sword in both fists, he raised it point down, ready to plunge it into Maarken's chest.

Rohan's boot knives balanced lightly in his fingers for a fraction of an instant before they slipped through the air, too swift to see except as a single long, glittering silver thread. Each embedded itself in Masul's throat, so close together that as they quivered with his startled movement, Rohan heard the click of the hilts against each other.

The sword dropped; Maarken rolled sluggishly to one side and it missed him by a hand's breadth. Masul's fin-gers and slowly crumpling body knew what his brain could not yet accept: he was a dead man. Wide with disbelief, his green eyes sought Rohan. It took him a very long time to fall to his knees. He looked down at the blood that poured his life out onto his chest, onto the ground, as if it ought to be someone else's blood. His lips moved, but the steel blades in his throat rendered him mute. Rohan watched unblinking as he pitched forward, total astonishment scrawled across his face, and died.

The giant's fist seemed to have closed around every throat, including Rohan's own. He tried to swallow, to find his voice. He could not. The silence was broken at length by the soft moans of dazed *faradh'im*.

Sioned clawed her way to her feet, stood swaying beside Rohan. He spared her a glance, then turned to his son. Pol was clinging to Sorin's arm, upright but just barely. Yet when Rohan started forward, Pol followed, determination substituting for physical strength.

Rohan pulled his knives from Masul's throat, cleaned them on the grass, and returned them to his boots. Pol cradled Maarken's head on his knees, wiping away blood-and sweat-caked dirt from his face, saying his cousin's name urgently. Maarken groaned, eyelids fluttering, then looked up.

His words nearly broke Rohan. "S-sorry, my prince," he whispered. "I—failed—"

"No!" Pol exclaimed. "You went out to fight a man, not a sorcerer!"

A harsh laugh claimed Rohan's attention. Miyon of Cunaxa glared at him and spat, "Is that the story you're going to use? Sorcery? A pretty excuse for breaking more laws than you ever wrote in your life, High Prince! The only sorcery here was what the *faradh'im* used—"

"To protect *both* men from treachery!" Pol cried hotly. "How dare you—"

"If you think I'm going to believe that, boy, you're an even bigger fool than your father!"

Rohan spoked very softly. "I did break the law by killing Masul myself. But I'll not argue circumstances with you or anyone else. I find myself tempted to break a few more laws by ordering my troops to cross your border. If you think you can get word north faster than I can, keep talking." He paused. "Otherwise, close your mouth and get out of my sight."

Chay was with them now, gathering his son into his arms as his grace of Cunaxa wisely, if furiously, followed Rohan's advice. Maarken made a feeble protest that not only was he quite all right, he wasn't a child. His father silenced him with a single look, then glanced up at Rohan.

"Now, before anyone else can make an uproar, may I get my son the hell out of here?"

Rohan flicked a finger; Tallain came running. "Tell the princes to attend me at dusk. And find a physician. Neither my wife nor my sister is up to it."

"I'll tend Lord Maarken, if your grace will permit." Gemma appeared, Tilal at her side. "Medicine is familiar to me."

"Thank you, my lady," Chay said, hiding most of his doubts.

But Tilal nodded confirmation and they carried Maarken from the field. Gemma, with Danladi assisting, made expert work of Maarken's wounds and bruises after giving him a sleeping draught that sent him mercifully beyond the reach of pain. Chay and Rohan watched it all, wincing as each wound was revealed and cleaned and bandaged, grateful for Gemma's skill and her assurance that there would be only a few scars. More worrisome was the crushed wrist; Danladi spent a long time over it, and even through his drug-hazed sleep Maarken groaned as it was bandaged. Time alone would reveal whether he would regain use of it.

Chay did not thank his prince for his son's life. Rohan would have been insulted by such words; if it was the duty of a vassal to fight for his prince, it was no less a prince's duty to protect his vassals. All that was understood.

Pol had been sent back to the pavilion with his mother and aunt, where all three tumbled into sleep as if they, too, had been drugged. Rohan assumed that Andry or Urival or someone had seen to the other Sunrunners in similar fashion. It was nearly dusk before Tallain came to Maarken's tent with shocking news.

"The princess-regent is dead, my lord."

Rohan was aware that he felt nothing, in the way that a stunning blow cripples emotion.

"How?" Chay rasped, unbelieving.

"There was only the one wound, a knife-puncture in her leg. She couldn't have bled to death from it. But she died just the same." Tallain looked as if he couldn't believe it, either. "Her sister, Princess Naydra took her from the field to her husband's tents, and asks what you wish done, my lord."

He was beginning to feel now, and his emotions shamed him. For he felt nothing except relief.

"My lord?"

"Yes," he responded automatically. "She'll be given honorable burning in state as befits a princess and a Sunrunner. At Castle Crag, I think—yes. Please tell Princess Naydra that if she'll do me the favor of arranging things, I'd be very grateful. And—and tell her that I share her grief."

The odd thing was that he did, in a way. He grieved for the intelligence twisted, the love based in hate, the gifts misused. But he was also shamefully glad that she was dead, that he would not have to immure her in some remote keep for the rest of her life. Her crimes were unforgivable, but in her own terrible way she had loved both him and Pol. Rohan cleared his throat.

"Are the other princes waiting yet?"

"No, my lord. When it looked as if you'd be longer here than dusk, I sent them word to come tomorrow morning." As Rohan frowned, Tallain turned defensive and a little formal. "Her grace the High Princess concurred that everybody needs to rest."

"Her grace the High Princess can be a graceless nag. Especially when she's right. Go reassure her for me, Tallain."

Looking vastly relieved, the young man bowed and left. Rohan then turned to Gemma. "My lady, have you finished?"

"Just now, your grace." She wiped her hands on a towel and returned it to Danladi's waiting hands. "There's no serious hurt done except to his wrist—although he'll be stiff and sore for quite some time, and one or two of the sword cuts will bear watching. As for his hand . . .'' She glanced at Maarken. ''I can't tell yet. But he shouldn't be moved for at least two or three days.''

Danladi smiled shyly. ''Considering the trouble we had to get the sleeping draught down him, you'll be lucky to keep him in bed for one, your grace.''

''He'll behave,'' Chay said gruffly. ''Or I'll skin what hide he has left.''

''I don't doubt it, my lord,'' Gemma said. But Rohan saw something in her expression that puzzled him. He arched a brow at her and she looked away, suddenly nervous.

''What is it, my lady?'' he coaxed. ''You've done me and mine a great service. Ask what you will.''

''Your grace, I want no payment for—''

''Oh, let me be generous,'' Rohan suggested with a slight smile. ''It's one of the few real pleasures a prince has, as you'll find out.''

''I don't ask for myself,'' she said quickly. ''But for Danladi.''

The other girl caught her breath. ''No, Gemma, please—''

''Hush,'' the princess commanded gently. ''She's been a sister to me for many years now. It's my wish that we become sisters in fact as well as in feeling.''

Rohan exchanged a puzzled look with Chay.

''I've been a princess all my life, though my title will change somewhat when I go to Ossetia after my lord Tilal and I are wed.'' She blushed becomingly at mentioning his name. ''But Danladi is just as much a princess by blood as I am. I would consider it a great favor if you'd ask Prince Davvi if it would be possible for Danladi to become Princess of Syr and my sister-by-marriage.''

''With Kostas?'' Chay blurted out, then apologized hastily as Danladi turned crimson to the roots of her hair.

''He thinks he wants me,'' Gemma said artlessly. ''But once I've left High Kirat, and if Danladi's dowered temptingly enough. . . .''

Gemma evidently had no illusions about Kostas' character. Neither did Danladi. She met Rohan's gaze squarely, blue eyes in a timid, fair face telling him silently that she wanted Kostas for her husband. He marveled that her love for Gemma had not suffered in the face of Kostas' preference; Danladi was surely unique among Roelstra's daughters in that she seemed to have not a jealous or possessive bone in her body.

But—Roelstra's grandson as future Prince of Syr?

Sweet Goddess, he was thinking like Pandsala. After all, another of Roelstra's grandsons would be High Prince one day.

"My lady," he said to Danladi, "I will be pleased to talk to Davvi as soon as it's opportune. If I may speak frankly, however—" He gave her a smile and she blushed again. "I think that once Kostas sees your pretty face around High Kirat after he's come to his senses, he's more than likely to lose them again."

"Th-thank you, your grace," she breathed.

He caught himself just in time from shaking his head in amazement. "I'll be subtle, I promise," he added, and at last she smiled.

As he walked beside Chay back to his pavilion, the older man gave a low whistle. "My, my, but you *were* gallant! Imagine, that pale little wisp of a girl being Roelstra's daughter! And wanting to wed Kostas, that colossal ass."

"Chay, I'm surprised at you. I thought you knew from personal experience that the right wife can be the making of a man."

"You always take refuge in jokes, don't you?" Chay asked sympathetically.

"You know me too well, damn you." They stopped outside the pavilion and Rohan looked around at the gathering dusk. "I can't take in what's happened the last three days. I keep thinking I'll wake up. Chay, how did all this happen?"

"The way things always do: while we weren't watching."

"I was watching," Rohan replied grimly. "I watched but I saw nothing, nothing at all."

"Go lie down and sleep. You're about to fall over."

He shrugged and entered the tent. Chay followed. "You don't have to hover around, making sure I obey you," he said a bit testily. "And what gives you the right to order me about, anyway?"

"The right of any elder brother. Now, be sensible and

go to bed. Believe me,'' he added ruefully, ''it'll all be
waiting for you tomorrow morning.''

Chapter Twenty-nine

She'll be all right now. She's sleeping.''
     Volog sat down heavily in a chair near his
daughter's bed. His hands came up to cover his face, and
for a moment Davvi thought he might weep in his relief
and weariness. But then Volog rubbed his cheeks briskly
and raked his fingers through his graying hair.

''It seems I'm forever thanking someone else for taking
better care of my daughter than I can. And the thing of
it is, she's always taken splendid care of herself. Until
now.''

''It's the shock of her *faradhi* gifts, cousin, no more
than that. Although I admit that's quite enough,'' Davvi
added.

''Yes. But the question is, should she go to Goddess
Keep and learn how to use such gifts, or try to forget
that she even has them? They've brought her nothing but
pain that I can see, ever since she set foot on board ship
to come here.''

Davvi did not answer. Volog gave him a speculative
glance, then pushed himself from the chair.

''I know,'' Volog said. ''It's not something I can decide for her.'' He led the way into the main part of the
tent, gestured Davvi to a chair, and beckoned a squire to
pour wine. ''I'm curious, cousin,'' he went on. ''How
did Sioned happen to leave River Run for Goddess
Keep?''

Davvi waited until the squire had bowed his way out
and they were alone, then said slowly, ''Sioned was only
a little girl when our parents died. I suddenly had a keep
to oversee. I was too busy to take much notice of her,
and she went pretty much her own way. But when I married Wisla, she was quick to see it—'a strange way with
the wind,' she called it. One winter night as we sat in

the solar, the fire went out and Sioned coaxed it back into being without touching it, without moving more than her fingers. Our grandmother and yours was *faradhi*. But it never occurred to me before that night that Sioned might be, too.''

"I've been just as blind with Alasen," Volog admitted. "You know, I often wondered what it might be like—I've even envied Sioned." He glanced at the partition behind which his daughter slept. "But not anymore."

"Sioned has found great joy and fulfillment in being a Sunrunner.''

"Alasen has not." Volog sipped at his wine. "Ah, well. As I said, it's her choice to make.'' He looked up as the squire came back in. "Yes? What is it?''

"A message from his grace of Isel, my lord." The boy handed over a folded and sealed square of parchment, and again bowed himself out.

Davvi snorted. "Let me guess. Saumer has experienced a revelation."

"No bet." Volog tore open the letter and scanned its contents. "Ha! It seems that not only Saumer but Pimantal of Fessenden has had a change of heart. Kiele is confessing to anyone who'll listen. She had word of Masul, brought him to Waes, believed his story, and taught him Roelstra's mannerisms to heighten the chance resemblance. She begged him not to kill the Sunrunner, and so forth and so on. I doubt any of it will weigh much with Lord Andry. But I find this very politic of Saumer and Pimantal, I must say."

"Especially in Pimantal's case, now that rumors about Lleyn's grandson and Firon are all over the camps. Volog, I need a favor. When Pimantal makes his conversion public, kick me when I laugh in his face.''

Volog grinned. "Agreed, if you'll do the same for me. Rohan has his majority now, at any rate.''

"Cold comfort."

"Indeed." He hesitated, then asked, "Davvi, what do you know of the Lord of Skybowl?"

If Davvi was surprised, he did not show it. "A good man, the best. He spent his early youth at Goddess Keep with Sioned—married a Sunrunner, in fact, though he's not one himself. You saw how fine a son he raised.''

"Mmm. Lord Ostvel was of great help to me with Alasen. I'd like to do something for him, if he'll allow it."

"I doubt he will. But if you approach Rohan and Sioned, they'll find a way around him."

"Advice I shall take, cousin."

* * *

By sheer force of will and a flat refusal to let the staggering pain in his head get the better of him, Urival got out of bed, dressed, left his tent, and started walking.

It was still early, the moons just visible between clouds. But it felt more like the deep black time before dawn. The last days had been an unrelieved horror and anyone with any sense was resting. But he had long ago acknowledged that sometimes he had very little sense indeed. So he crossed the bridge and skirted the silent Fair, heading for the field of battle.

He was more or less certain he knew what had happened. The two deaths besides Masul's, and the burning of his own rings, had told him much. He paused for a moment when the field stretched out before him, thinking about how he had found them: Pandsala, her dark eyes staring sightlessly up at the clouds; Sejast, prone with a knife stuck in his back. Hollis was sprawled nearby, propped on one hand with her head hanging, bright hair tangled around her face. Urival had looked swiftly around him. But no one watched; all eyes had fixed on the little knot of people around Maarken. Quickly he yanked the knife from Sejast's corpse. Hollis had lifted her head. There was blood all over her.

"He's dead, then, isn't he?" she said quite calmly.

"By your hand," he murmured.

She nodded. "Pandsala tried and failed." Suddenly tears rained down her cheeks. "Ah, Goddess, the Star Scroll—he knew, he knew, he was one of them, he wanted Maarken dead! Give me back the knife, he needs killing—"

"He's dead. And Maarken's alive. Hollis, listen to me!"

But she drew her knees to her chin, arms wrapped around them, and rocked back and forth, weeping, murmuring of *dranath* and the Star Scroll and sorcery.

Urival shouted Sorin's name. The young man glanced

around, left Andry to Lleyn's care, and hurried over. At Urival's direction, he gathered Hollis up to carry her. She buried her face in his neck for a moment. Then, looking at Urival again, she whispered, "Tell my lord I'm sorry. I beg his forgiveness."

"He'll understand."

"Do *you?*" Her eyes narrowed.

Urival nodded. "Take her back to the encampment, Sorin."

Hollis shivered, her gaze wild again, tears streaking through the blood on her face. "But there'll be no Sejast, and I'll die—you know that I'll die without him!"

Sorin stared at her. "My lady—"

"Hush," Urival whispered. "She's not responsible for what she says right now. Rest easy, Hollis. You won't die, I promise you."

Her hand reached out piteously. "Do you swear? I don't want to die. Maarken—I want Maarken, where is he?"

Urival placed his fingertips on her forehead and spun sleep around her. As long lashes descended to hide the anguish in her eyes, he told Sorin, "Don't worry. She'll be all right."

"If you say so, my lord," came the dubious reply.

Urival flinched in the darkness now as his boots crunched on glass. The remains of Rohan's water clock were underfoot, trampled and forgotten. He poked around, careful not to slice his fingers, and eventually found what he was looking for: the golden dragon that had decorated the upper sphere's lid. He turned it from side to side, rubbed his thumb over the proudly uplifted wings, then pocketed the emerald-eyed token and walked on.

He stopped when he saw the dark bloodstains soaked into the soil. Only a little of it was Pandsala's, spilled from a wound that should not have killed her. He had taken Sejast's body from the wash of blood on the ground and hidden it in the nearby trees. He went there now. Insects had not yet begun on the flesh, gorged as they were on the blood. For a moment Urival considered throwing the body in the river. There would be no cleansing Fire for this one. But he rejected the impulse; Rohan would want to look on the dead face, the other princes

would need proof that there had been a sorcerer present—
and Andry required a vivid demonstration of Sunrunner
fallibility.

He picked up the corpse and carried it from the trees.
Like Andrade, he had seen and frowned on the boy's
arrogant delight in his growing powers. But that was gone
now, leaving only this light, limp body, dark head tucked
to Urival's shoulder like a sleeping child. Who was this
boy who would never become a man?

With the compelling eyes hidden, Urival saw softness
that lingered around the lines of cheeks and brow, the
curl of the mouth. A boy arriving out of nowhere, speaking in the accents of the Veresch, fixing unerringly on
the two Sunrunners with the closest ties to the Desert,
knowing snatches of the old language. Knowing, too, the
uses of *dranath* and sorcery.

This "child" had lied his way into Goddess Keep, addicted Hollis to *dranath* that might yet kill her, cozened
her and Andry into letting him work on the scrolls. He
had spun sorceries hoping to kill Maarken. He had killed
Pandsala. Every Sunrunner present had felt his power.
He was an heir of the Old Blood, enemy of the *faradh'im*. And yet he seemed so young, so innocent.

Urival searched for reasons. Sejast's people had been
hidden for hundreds of years. Why now? Why him? What
was special about this boy? He had sought to aid Masul,
who claimed to be of Roelstra's blood. How could his
victory have benefited the sorcerers? What could possibly
connect sorcery and Castle Crag?

The first anyone had ever heard of *dranath* was when
Roelstra used it to enslave a Sunrunner. Alone of her
sisters, Pandsala had proven gifted—but no one had ever
tested the others. And she did not share the Sunrunner
aversion to water. *"My mother came from a place known
only as The Mountain."* The mountains of the Veresch—
whence Sejast had come to Goddess Keep.

Urival stifled a curse as the boy's head rolled back
against his arm. He'd forgotten in his haste earlier to slide
the lids closed—and the eyes were wide open to the starlight. Glazed. Staring. He'd seen eyes like that long ago,
dead green eyes lit by stars and framed by black hair.

Rohan's sword had gouged his throat, but still the face had smiled in death, as this face smiled now.

Nose, brow, mouth, jaw—not the mimickry of color and movement Kiele had heightened in Masul, but a *likeness*, the way a sapling is the young, half-formed version of the parent tree.

Ianthe had borne three sons before her death, sons everyone thought had died with her—and the mysterious fourth son—at Feruche. Urival had long known their names. And that all of them were alive.

One was dead now. Not "Sejast," but Segev. Segev, who had killed Andrade.

Urival carried Ianthe's son to the bridge. Aching with exhaustion, he paused in the center of the span. The Faolain was dark and deceptively quiet below him. Upriver the water thundered, but from here to the sea all was swift, powerful silence. Desirable silence.

The muscles of his shoulders and back tore as he hefted Segev's body over the rails and let it drop into the current. The gray-clad corpse surfaced once, then vanished forever.

* * *

"Urival came in just before midnight to tell us the boy, Sejast, was responsible. Sorcerer's get, living all this time at Goddess Keep. It doesn't bear thinking about, Meath."

"It can't become common knowledge, Sioned. Andry's going to have trouble enough convincing everyone he's as strong as Andrade was—if this was known, no one would have confidence in him at all. He let Sejast work with him on the scrolls." Meath downed his third cup of wine in two swallows. "Goddess! Andrade's death, and now this!"

Rohan pushed the flask across the table to him. "With no body to hand, we can say that the boy died the same way Pandsala did. The problem is, we don't really know why she died."

"I can tell you that." He glanced up suddenly, and set both cup and pitcher down hard on the table, spilling some of the wine. "Pol!"

"What are you doing up?" Sioned asked sharply. But Meath was already rising to give the boy a rough hug.

"Goddess, but I'm glad to see you! Sioned, don't make him go back to bed. He wouldn't sleep, anyway."

She shrugged. "Oh, very well. As long as you're up, you probably ought to listen so we don't have to repeat ourselves. Sit here by me, Pol."

He did so, settling into a place between her and Rohan. "You look tired to death," he told Meath.

The Sunrunner dropped back into his chair. "I've been on horseback ever since word came about Andrade. And you don't look so great, yourself."

"Why did Pandsala die?" Pol asked softly.

"Sioned was in charge of a powerful conjure, right? Every *faradhi* in the place dragged into it."

"And we were winning, too," Pol muttered.

"Of course," Meath said, surprised that he would even mention it. "You've got a lot to learn about your mother, y'know. From what's been described to me, all of a sudden you felt like the whole world was shattering around you. I'm not surprised—and I know exactly what it feels like. The same thing happened to me. I was in the middle of a conjuring and got a knife in me. And do you know why I didn't die?" He paused for another swallow. "I pulled it out."

If he'd had the energy left, Rohan would have been pacing the carpet. "You *faradh'im* are forbidden to use your arts to kill. Are you saying—"

"I've been reading Andry's translations," Meath interrupted. "The precise wording is that we're forbidden to use our skills in battle. And this is why. A working Sunrunner hit by arrow or sword or knife is dead."

"But why?" Sioned exclaimed. "There's no reason for it! Why should a minor wound taken during a conjure kill us?"

"I don't know. But think about this for a moment. There's a mention in the scrolls of the Merida and their glass knives. They worked for the sorcerers. Glass was said to be sacred. It became a matter of pride to use glass, almost a religion. It was their hallmark, their signature on a murder. But why glass?"

"Iron," Pol said abruptly and succinctly. Then he seemed to hear what he'd said, and his face changed. He reached across the table, poured wine for himself, gulped it down.

Meath nodded. "My reading exactly. The knife that

hit me and the one that stabbed Pandsala were steel. And I'm betting that Kleve's wounds weren't ones to kill him, either. He was trying to use the gifts, and the knife—''

''But the steel was removed,'' Rohan pointed out. ''It had to be, for Masul to sever more than one finger.'' He saw the Sunrunners look a little ill at that, their hands clenched instinctively into fists, and added, ''Forgive me. But I don't see how your theory works here, Meath.''

''I'm guessing that even though the knife wasn't in him all the time, each successive cut acted the same way, shocking his mind until he died of it. You told me Pandsala had only the one wound on her leg. And yet she's dead. You also said that just as suddenly as the pain began for the rest of you, it stopped. That must have been when Hollis removed the knife. The iron was no longer disrupting the linked conjuring. But Pandsala was already too far gone. Think of it like blood going to the brain through the big arteries in the neck. If they're severed, the brain dies. There must be something that happens inside us when we weave light or conjure Fire—something that iron breaks. Thank the Goddess that Sejast was not part of the Sunrunner conjuring when Hollis stabbed him.''

''And if the sorcerers formed the Merida,'' Rohan said, ''they'd make them use glass because they didn't trust them not to turn those knives on their masters. Meath, I'll even bet that the sorcerers forbade iron weapons in their presence. They knew why, but nobody else did. For someone ungifted, glass or steel wouldn't matter. Both kill.''

Sioned laced her fingers together. ''So here's another reason we must keep this quiet. If anyone knew how vulnerable we are to iron and to sorcerers pretending to be *faradh'im*—''

''We'd all be dead before next summer,'' Meath finished for her.

Rohan leaned back in his chair. He felt a million years old. ''Very well. Try this. Pandsala and Sejast died because they weren't strong enough for the power of Sioned's conjuring. This adds to her already substantial reputation as a *faradhi,* a nice bonus. Everyone around the two of them and Hollis was a Sunrunner and in no condition to see, let alone remember, exactly what went on. Sejast's body is gone—hmm, that's a problem. How about this: Urival, as chief steward of Goddess Keep, dealt with the corpse in private. That's only the truth, after all. We can tell Naydra the knife was poisoned. Urival has it right now, and he'll have to get rid of it. What have I forgotten?''

"Nothing that I can think of," Meath said. "You've a gift of your own, your grace.''

Rohan smiled faintly. "I thought you cured of that 'my grace' nonsense.''

"Certainly—your royal highness.'' Meath grinned at him.

Sioned rubbed the nape of her neck. "I think we can expect Chiana to be utterly loathsome tomorrow. Goddess give me the patience not to slap her.''

"Are the rumors true, that Halian's going to marry her?'' Meath asked.

"I wish him much joy of her," Rohan said. "And I pity Clutha more than I can say.''

"The one I feel sorry for is Alasen," Pol said. He got up and stood behind his mother's chair to massage her shoulders. "Better?''

"Thank you, hatchling.'' She smiled and leaned back into his careful, soothing hands. "Why Alasen?''

"Didn't you feel it? She was caught up in it, too. And it terrified her.''

"Alasen?'' Meath asked. "Volog's youngest girl?''

"Sunrunner," Rohan confirmed. "But once she learns to use her gifts—''

"I don't know that she wants to," Sioned mused. "She doesn't much like the idea of being *faradhi*, Rohan. We had a talk about it—Goddess, only six days ago? Is it really the last day of summer?''

"By dawn, the first of autumn.'' Meath pushed himself to his feet. "I've got to get some sleep. I'd suggest that all of you do the same, if I thought suggesting would do any good. And even I hesitate to give a direct order to the High Princess.''

"She doesn't obey *me*," Rohan said. "Why should she listen to you?''

"Stubborn as ever.'' Meath went to kiss Sioned's cheek. "I can hardly wait to get back to Graypearl, where I *do* have the authority to order Pol around.'' He gripped the boy's shoulder. "Eolie and I have a lot of work to do with you. And none of it has any bearing on being a squire."

"You mean you're going to teach me *faradhi* things?" He stared at Rohan. "But I thought Andry would be the one to—"

"Eventually," Sioned interposed. "But they'll teach you certain things you need to know."

"Good," Pol stated. "I'm not all that comfortable with the idea of going to Goddesss Keep not knowing any more than the usual new people there. I'm not usual; I'm a prince." He smiled as Rohan's brows shot up. "I don't mean it like that. I just mean that my position makes me unique. And I don't think Andry is going to relish having the ruler of Princemarch underfoot."

So Pol senses it, too. The unspoken words darted between Rohan and Sioned.

Meath stretched, bones cracking, and yawned. "I find you rather pesky, myself," he said amiably. "May I commandeer a bed in one of your tents, my lord prince?"

"Anything not already occupied by one of my female retainers," Rohan replied equably, and Meath grinned before bowing a good night.

"I think sleep is a very good idea," Sioned murmured after Meath was gone. "We've princes to face tomorrow and a very long ride back home to rest up for."

"Father, will we be going north to Castle Crag?"

"No." He elaborated on the harsh monosyllable with, "We couldn't be sure of getting back to the Desert before the rains begin. And you have to take ship for Graypearl. Lleyn's letting me borrow you for a little while longer, but has need of his squire—however clumsy and unlearned."

"Father!" Pol, who knew he was being teased and who also knew why, smiled. "I never get the chance to get arrogant about being a prince. Nobody lets me!"

"And a very good thing, too." Sioned rose, planted a kiss on her son's brow and said, "Back to bed. Rohan, leave orders with the guards not to disturb us, please? Urival and Meath were necessary, but—"

"Of course. Sleep well, Pol."

The boy paused at the partition. "Father . . . I know we won, but why doesn't it feel like winning?"

"I know what you mean," he said quietly, not attempting a glib answer that Pol wouldn't have believed anyway. "It didn't feel like it when I killed Roelstra, either. I don't know that it ever does, not when people have to die in order for us to win."

Pol nodded. "I understand. Try to sleep, Father."

"You, too."

Sioned was in bed when he finished instructing the guards and went into their quarters. Rohan stripped and lay beside her, flat on his back, staring at the blue ceiling.

"And what *have* we won?" he asked softly. "Pol's right to Princemarch. Freedom from Pandsala—though not from her crimes. Tilal as Prince of Ossetia one day. Lleyn's grandson in Firon. Look at what we've won, Sioned. And look at what all this winning cost."

She put her arms around him, shifting so his head could rest on her shoulder. She said nothing, and he was grateful.

"I love you," he told her. "You and Pol are the only victories that ever mattered to me."

* * *

Rohan had decided to summon all the highborns, not just the princes. The thirteen chairs and the huge table were taken outside into the weak morning sun. Each prince sat in his usual place, with wife, heir, and vassals, if present, standing behind him. The Sunrunners were grouped at a table nearby, where Andry sat to witness and seal any documents signed that day.

Lady Eneida of Firon had given over her seat at the princes' table to Chadric on his son's behalf, and looked relieved that somehow in all the chaos the problems of her people had not been forgotten. A private discussion with her before the general conclave had been most satisfactory; Laric would be welcomed with open arms by a thankful populace when he arrived in Firon sometime before winter began. And after the formal acceptance and acclamation of Laric's new position, a foregone conclusion, there would be one more vote against Masul. Cold comfort, indeed.

Chiana was, as Sioned had predicted, intolerable. She had taken possession of Halian's arm and was wearing her most elaborate gown and a brilliant smile, behaving as if she was already Princess of Meadowlord. Her sister Kiele looked on her with dull loathing; Maarken, still slightly groggy with the effects of battle wounds and the draught given him to ease the pain of his wrist, pushed her rudely aside when she attempted to embrace him in thanks for her deliverance. Rohan regretted the necessity for her presence, and again pitied poor old Clutha his declining years in her company.

Rohan took his time about the business of the extraordinary meeting. First there were several treaties to be signed—not many, as few had been willing to agree to proposals without knowing who would be ruling Princemarch. But now Rohan found them eager to accept the continuance of prior treaties for another three years. They could do little else when the High Prince made the suggestion—in polite tones but with ice in his blue eyes.

With the treaties out of the way, Rohan turned to Laric's confirmation as Prince of Firon. Lady Eneida detailed the twists and turns of ancestry that made him eligible, and affirmed that she and the Fironese people were more than willing to have him. To Prince Chadric she gave a diamond ring, gem of Firon, in trust and token for his son. Laric's acclamation was unanimous; again, it could scarcely have been anything else, not when the High Prince speared possible dissenters with his frigid gaze.

The vote was then taken that confirmed Pol's possession of Princemarch. A mere formality, of course, but one that Urival had been oddly adamant about the night before. It was his view that all princes should agree that he and he alone was the rightful ruler there. Not that anyone had dared say a word when Pol took the seat Pandsala had occupied during the last four *Riall'im*.

Ostvel was then presented to the assembly as Regent of Princemarch. A parchment was presented for his signature—Rohan's, Sioned's, and Pol's already being appended—that gave him Castle Crag outright. He was also given a new seal, the wreath of Princemarch circling a depiction of the keep itself. There was not a whisper of reaction as he signed and affixed his seal, gave over the ring betokening his lordship over Skybowl, and accepted the one Pandsala had worn. He stood behind Pol's chair, silent and solemn.

Rohan then called Riyan forward and gave him Skybowl, but in a different manner than his father had held it. A document similar to that making Castle Crag Ostvel's created Riyan Lord of Skybowl; no longer was either holding the property of the Desert or Princemarch. Riyan hesitated, looking at his father, asking silently if he should sign this instrument that would make him an *athri* in his own right and found their hitherto obscure family in the lands of two princedoms. Ostvel nodded once in assent. There had been a brief discussion with him, too, before the larger meeting, with Rohan and Sioned stating flatly that this was the way things had to be. Ostvel would hold Castle Crag and Riyan would have Skybowl, both keeps theirs by law. The elevation of a pair of landless nobodies—even though one of them was a Sunrunner—shocked more than a few people. But as Riyan signed the document and his father's ring was placed on his finger, no one breathed a syllable of protest.

It was Sioned's turn then, presenting a plan of her own that Rohan refused to have anything to do with. He listened stony-faced as she called Sorin forward and named him Lord of Feruche Castle.

Tobin straightened abruptly at her husband's side, startled. Chay took her hand and squeezed it hard, warning her to silence.

Sioned informed the assembly, "We are grateful to his grace of Cunaxa for offering to supply some of the materials needed to rebuild this important keep so that trade among northern princedoms may be protected in future as it was in the past." Miyon looked a little sour at this— all he dared show of his fury that Sioned had called him on their wager. Their bet had been on the battle's outcome, not the manner of its fighting. She sent a brief glance in his direction and went on, "Our beloved nephew will work assiduously, we are certain, for the safety of trade caravans as he supervises the building of his new castle. We confidently expect that by the time of the next *Rialla*, Feruche will be well on its way to completion."

Sorin bowed deeply, his eyes alight with excitement at this unexpected honor. Sioned gave him a fond smile along with a beautiful topaz ring in token of his new status. The look she gave her husband was one of veiled defiance; his objection was not to giving Sorin a castle, but that that castle was Feruche. To the end of his life he would have nothing more to do with the place.

He nodded to Prince Clutha then, who rose and cleared his throat noisily before ordering Kiele and Lyell brought forward to face him. "I've never held with this idea of the High Prince's, that *athr'im* should own their keeps. All mine hold their lands for *me*. Waes is mine to do with as I please. And it is my pleasure to reward this pair for their treachery, conspiracy, and lies by taking Waes from them."

Lyell turned sickly green; Kiele, white.

Clutha planted his gnarled fists on the table before him. "Years ago you were spared just punishment for your unlawful actions against Goddess Keep during the conflict with Roelstra. Penning in Lady Andrade and her Sunrunners with the excuse of 'protecting' them—bah! I didn't condemn you then because she and Rohan dissuaded me. But this time—this time no one has even tried to talk of mercy. I reclaim Waes. You are rejected, homeless, and landless. And I thank the Goddess that your father, the noble and loyal Lord Jervis, is dead and cannot learn of the shame you have brought on his house."

The old man paused for breath, fixing Kiele with a furious gaze. "You are truly your father's daughter. It seems I shall be accepting another such as my daughter-by-marriage. But I'll not have a second in my princedom, especially not in a place where I cannot watch her at all times."

Chiana lost her triumphant smile at that, looked daggers at Clutha. He ignored her, and Halian's outraged stare.

"But I don't believe in punishing innocent children for what their parents have done," Clutha continued gruffly. "Until such time as young Geir proves his loyalty and fitness to govern, my daughter Gennadi will hold Waes for me. As for Lyela, she'll be dowered well. No one will hold the children's ancestry against them, or, by the

Goddess, I'll have their heads.'' He glared around the table to reinforce his point. Then he addressed Lyell. ''That is all you may expect from me. Some would say it's too much.''

Rohan would not meet the old man's gaze. He wanted nothing to do with this, either, with Kiele's judicious and legal and necessary execution.

Andry rose from his seat at the small table. ''You have indeed been most generous, your grace. May I assume that Lord Lyell and Lady Kiele are no longer under the protection accorded *athr'im* by their princes?''

Clutha set his jaw, shaking his head. ''No. Do as you like.''

Lyell's eyes closed and his lips moved, presumably a plea to the Goddess for mercy. There was none in Andry's eyes. Kiele sank to her knees as the Lord of Goddess Keep approached, her tear-swollen face lifted in stark terror.

''My Lord! I beg you—it was all a mistake!''

Andry gave her an ironic little nod. ''Yes. And you'll pay for it, my lady.''

Lyell swallowed hard, then pulled his wife to her feet, holding her up when she would have fallen. ''I understand, my Lord,'' he whispered. ''May I be allowed to speak to his grace?''

Andry nodded again, and Lyell turned to Clutha. ''I am sorry for what has happened, your grace. And I thank you for your compassion for my children. I know that Princess Gennadi will treat them gently.''

The princess, visibly moved, opened her mouth to make reassurances. Her father silenced her with a look before she could draw breath.

Kiele stumbled, got her feet under her, and glanced wildly around the assembly for anyone who might help her. ''What about the rest of them?'' she demanded. ''What about Miyon, who believed in Masul as I did? Why aren't they to be punished, too? Why not take their lands, High Prince?''

Andry answered her. ''Your support of the pretender is not my concern. Your murder of a Sunrunner is.''

Scorn curled her lips. ''Liar! This is *all* because of Masul and you know it!''

He shrugged. "Believe what you like. It won't help you."

Kiele sucked in a breath, her hand lifting. Lyell grabbed it before she could strike Andry. She shook him off and whirled to face Rohan. But her eye was caught by Tallain, who stood behind Rohan's chair, and she blurted, "You! You're kin to my husband, you're his dead sister's son! Make them stop this!"

Tallain stiffened and took a step back.

"Sweet Goddess, you're cousin to my children! Would you see their mother destroyed? In the name of your mother Antalya, don't let them do this!" she shrieked.

Rohan didn't glance over his shoulder but he could feel Tallain's anguish, hear the tension in his voice as he replied, "I agree with his grace of Meadowlord. I'm glad my mother isn't alive to witness this. You are no kin of mine, but I will do my best for your children."

"How can that help *me?*" Kiele screamed. "Damn you, damn all of you—"

"Be silent!" Clutha roared.

Andry lifted one finger, and two *faradh'im* came forward—reluctantly, Rohan noted, no more convinced than Kiele that this was about to happen. One of them put a hand on her arm; she wrenched away from him, slapped his face.

"How dare you touch me!" she raged. "I'm a daughter of the High Prince! I'll have your rings severed from your hands—"

It was most unwise of her to remind Andry what had happened to Kléve. He nodded curtly at the Sunrunner, who took Kiele's elbows and held them behind her back. She thrashed and spat, screamed in her husband's face as he tried to calm her.

"Take her to where Masul's body awaits burning," Andry said quietly.

Kiele turned to stone. "Burning?" she echoed, as if she had not heard correctly.

"My brother, Lord Maarken, has asked that the late pretender be accorded battle honors," Andry explained—not to her, but to the others. "He is more generous than I."

She looked up at Lyell. "Burned?" she asked incredulously. "He's going to honor that lying bastard by Fire?"

Her husband gripped her shoulders, all his quiet fortitude gone in a gush of bitterness. "The lying bastard you swore to me was your brother! And it won't be just him, Kiele. It'll be us, too. Be grateful it's not Geir and Lyela along with us!"

Andry lost some of his composure. "Lord Lyell, you had nothing to do with the Sunrunner Kleve's death. You have been punished by your overlord. I do not seek—I have no reason—"

Lyell met him stare for stare. "She is my wife. I helped her, supported her in forwarding Masul's claim. I've shared her life and her bed. I intend to share her death."

He loves her—the idiot, Rohan thought. But he couldn't fault Lyell for his unexpected courage.

"I'd rather die with her, my Lord," he was saying to Andry, pleading a little now. "I was only concerned for my children. Now that I know they'll be unharmed. . . ." He shrugged. "I'm as guilty as she, in my own way. I knew what she was doing and I didn't stop her."

"But you—" Andry was truly flustered now.

Lyell almost smiled. His pallid face acquired a dignity as he faced death that it had never had in life. "I'll die one way or another. Let it be in the Fire, my Lord."

Andry looked to Rohan for help. Rohan returned his gaze expressionlessly, thinking, *I'm sorry, Andry. This decision is yours. This is Sunrunner's business, not prince's. And may you remember in years to come that there is a difference.*

The young man nodded slowly, whether in understanding of Rohan's silence or in assent to Lyell's request, Rohan had no way of knowing. But Lyell took it as acquiescence, and bowed.

After a moment Andry regained his self-possession and said, "I call on all princes and lords here present to witness the just punishment for murder of a *faradhi*: death by Sunrunner's Fire."

Kiele screamed then and did not stop. Lyell gestured the Sunrunners away. He caught his wife in his arms, one hand over her mouth to clamp her jaws shut, and half-carried her as he followed the Sunrunners toward the river.

Rohan saw something puzzling as the rest of the gathering moved to follow. Andry walked apart for a few paces, but all at once Alasen was at his side. She clung to his arm, speaking rapidly in a voice too low for Rohan to hear. Her green eyes blazed with intensity in her white face, but her attitude was more beseeching than commanding despite the fury of emotion in her eyes. Andry looked down at her in sudden anguish, the proud confidence of a Lord of Goddess Keep gone. All at once Rohan understood something that surprised him.

Sioned had seen it, too. She clutched Rohan's fingers and he felt in her body the urge to go to them, to stop this from tearing them apart. He put his arm around her waist.

"No," he whispered. "Let them be."

"But—"

"No," he repeated.

She pulled in a shaky breath and nodded unwillingly. Andry lifted a hand to brush Alasen's long, loose hair from her cheek; she flinched back from him. In those two gestures was finality, Rohan thought sadly. He wondered if either of them realized it.

Masul's body lay on the sand beside the Faolain. The wounds Maarken had given him and the gashes left by Rohan's knives were concealed by a black cloak that reached from neck to boots. Sunrunners formed a half-circle around him as Andry pointed to the place near the corpse where Lyell and Kiele would stand and die. Alasen had gone to her father now, openly pleading with him. They were close enough for Rohan to hear Volog's reply.

"No. It is the business of Goddess Keep, and none of ours. I understand your compassion and I love you for it, my dearest, but no one can interfere. Mercy is not shown to such as they—else where would the treachery end?"

Rohan saw the tears glistening in her eyes—so much like Sioned's in color and shape, but without Sioned's wisdom. Perhaps twenty years ago, Sioned would have begged as Alasen did now. But between that time and this had come long years of ruling and governing, making hard choices, fighting for the right to make those choices. He glanced at his wife and amended his analysis. Sioned would never have begged. There was a streak of cold practicality in her and she had always understood political reality. If she had not, she would never have been the right woman for him. If Alasen could not, then she was not the right woman for Andry.

The highborns grouped around the Sunrunners to witness the burnings. No ritual of Air, Earth, Water, and Fire would be followed here; no fragrant oil would disguise the stench of burning flesh. The flames called up by *faradhi* gifts would immolate one corpse and two living beings almost instantly. No one would wait in vigil while they burned, and no Sunrunner-called breeze would waft their ashes across the land. Few would have said they deserved even the honor of the Fire. But though Andry had protested, Maarken had insisted. And the new Lord of Goddess Keep had never gone against his eldest brother's wishes in his life.

Having failed with her father, Alasen now approached Rohan and Pol. She bowed deeply and without raising her eyes whispered, "Your grace, please don't let this happen."

Rohan said nothing, wanting to hear what Pol would reply. The boy did not disappoint him. He frowned and asked, "Don't you think they merit this, after what they've done?"

"They have to die, I know that. And I agree with it. But—" Her fingers twisted together. "Cousin, I beg you not to let their deaths be on Andry's hands."

"Ah!" Pol breathed, glancing briefly up at Rohan, who lifted a brow. "And what do you suggest, my lady?"

"Surely it wouldn't be too much to ask that they be— that death come before the Fire, so they're spared that. It would make no difference, would it? They'd still be dead. But mercifully. Without feeling the flames."

"Mercifully for Andry's sake, too?" he asked softly.

She nodded, still staring down at the sand. "For his sake more than theirs. Please, cousin."

Rohan found himself looking into blue-green eyes that asked him what he should do—if there *was* anything he could do. But it was too late. Andry was lifting his hands and any instant the Fire would blaze up. Rohan said nothing, hoping that events would take the decision from them. For if Pol challenged Andry's new power this soon, Andry would never forgive or forget. He explored the thought, saddened anew that he took it so much for granted that they would indeed challenge each other.

"My lady," Pol was saying, "I—"

Ostvel moved beside them, his wrist snapping forward to release a shining silver knife. It sank into the damp sand at Lyell's feet. He looked down, startled, then swiftly bent to pick it up. As the first flames billowed from Masul's corpse and reached out to engulf him and Kiele, he thrust the blade into his wife's heart. As she crumpled, he dragged the knife from her breast and plunged it into his own. They were dead before their clothing singed.

Andry swung around, glaring at Ostvel in blind fury. But Rohan, close enough to read his old friend's eyes, understood another surprising thing. Just as Ostvel had been Ianthe's death to spare her blood on Sioned's hands, so he had been the deaths of Lyell and Kiele to spare Andry—and Alasen.

Chapter Thirty

Hollis woke in unfamiliar surroundings. Instead of the white walls and bare necessities of the Sunrunner tents there was soothing soft blue silk, screened skylights left open to the sun, and elegant luxury. For a very long time she simply lay atop the cool sheets, too tired to do more than move her head and take in her surroundings. Eventually guilt stirred; she had no right to be here in the Desert enclave, as if she belonged with Maarken's family. She could not believe she had ever aspired to become one of them as his wife. Certainly that could never happen now. Even if he forgave her, she knew she would soon die.

A wide-shouldered shadow appeared in the doorway,

hesitated, stepped onto the deep carpet. Hollis recognized Meath and turned her face away.

Standing beside the bed, Meath chuckled quietly. "Well, you do look pretty awful," he told her. "But all you want is a few good meals and a bath. I'll see to the former at once—and you'll eat every bite, too! But though I'd purely love to assist with the latter, I think Maarken would run me through."

Unwilling to acknowledge it, she felt something akin to her old wry humor tug at the corners of her mouth. Goddess, how long had it been since she'd laughed?

"Oh, come on, Hollis." Meath knelt beside the bed and picked up one of her hands. "I didn't ride all this way from Goddess Keep to be met with the back of your head. Look at me. I can't do anything for you if you won't even look at me."

She wished he would go back to teasing her, or simply go away. His sympathy and kindness were impossible to hear without pain.

Meath signed. "I know my face isn't exactly to your taste, but it's still fairly presentable. It's even been called handsome on occasion—though I suspect the ladies who said so were a little drunk."

"Or it was *very* dark, and by your own design," she heard herself say.

"That's better! Now, can you sit up? Good." He propped pillows behind her back and she sank into them wearily, a smile flitting around her mouth. "I thought I saw some wine around here—"

"No!" She caught herself at the edge of panic and forced her body to relax. "I'm sorry. I *would* like something to drink, please."

Meath smoothed her hair back, his voice soft with compassion. "So he put it in the wine, did he?"

"And the taze, and anything else—oh, Meath—"

"Shh. We'll talk about that in a little while." He went to a table and poured out two goblets of a fine pale Syrene vintage. "One thing I'll say for life in the Desert— Prince Davvi supplies his sister with the best damned wines ever bottled. Now, this is a blend of mossberries and grapes from around Sioned's old home of River Run.

You'll have to visit it someday. It's a lovely place if you don't mind all that water!''

She smiled again, more easily this time, and sipped the wine. Meath talked about River Run and Syrene wines and the High Princess' knowledge of them, and gradually Hollis relaxed. He saw it in her face and interrupted himself in the middle of a sentence.

''I suppose you'd like to know what's been going on.''

She nodded. ''I don't remember anything after—after—''

''Understandable. Urival spun sleep around you good and tight.'' Meath leaned back in a carved chair that looked too fragile to hold his brawny frame. ''Well, let's see. First off, Firon now belongs to Lleyn's grandson Laric. He'll do a fine job with it, too. Smart boy. Sorin's going to rebuild Feruche for Sioned, and young Riyan's got Skybowl now that his father's going to be Pol's regent at Castle Crag.''

Hollis stared. ''All that, just this morning?''

''Rohan doesn't waste much time. You knew that Gemma Chose Tilal instead of Kostas, right? Well, there's a whisper or two that Kostas has already been Chosen himself—by Danladi. Maybe he'll be bright enough to accept her. She's a nice little thing. Doesn't have a word to say for herself, which is unusual for one of Roelstra's daughters. But Davvi's very fond of her and says she's a sweet girl, so I guess she'll be Princess of Syr one day. And speaking of Roelstra's daughters, that little bitch Chiana was hanging all over Halian today, all set to be wed to him and inherit when Clutha's gone. *That* should be interesting!''

''Thank the Goddess she's fairly stupid, for all her scheming,'' Hollis mused. ''And she's finally got her life's ambition, now that Halian's been fool enough to make her a real princess.''

''That about sums it up,'' Meath agreed.

''It's good news about Danladi.'' She pushed herself higher on the pillows. ''Being close to Gemma, the two of them should be able to smooth over any problems between the brothers.'' She smiled wryly. ''Politics!''

''And then some. Princess Gennadi has been named to take charge of Waes and of Lyell's children. I don't know much about her, but reputation has her a sly lady with an eye for a good-looking man." He paused and grinned. "Maybe I should ask for a transfer!"

For the first time in what seemed like forever, Hollis laughed aloud. "You're a miserable lusty wretch, and if you're not careful I'll tell Eolie on you!"

"Oh, she knows all about me," he replied breezily.

"But do you know all about her?" Hollis teased.

Meath looked startled. "What?"

She giggled. "Got you!"

"Maarken's got *you,"* he growled, "and welcome!"

Hollis hid a sudden wince by taking a long drink of her wine. After a moment she asked, "What about Kiele?"

"Dead." He rose to get the bottle from the table, poured more wine for them both. "She burned with Masul's corpse this morning. And Lyell with her."

"But he—"

"I know. Andry didn't want it done that way, either. But Lyell insisted. He loved her, you see. Besides, what kind of life would he have had, with Waes taken from him and nowhere to go? Gennadi will take good care of the children, and Clutha was adamant that they not be punished for what their mother did. But it really was the only thing Lyell could do, when you think about it."

Hollis bent her head. "She died badly," she murmured.

"She died before the Fire even touched her." Meath shook his head. "Damnedest thing I ever saw. Andry had just called up the flames and we were about to add to them and make it quick, when a knife appeared out of nowhere at Lyell's feet. He used it to kill her and then himself. They never felt a thing. I learned later it was Ostvel who'd thrown him the knife."

"Gentle Goddess." She met his gaze. "You know why he did it, don't you? So Andry wouldn't be a murderer, or any of the rest of the Sunrunners." A murderer like Hollis herself. She hid another wince.

Meath shrugged. "Andry's furious, of course."

"I'll explain it to him," she said firmly.

He smiled. "Big sister."

"Meath—please."

"Look, Hollis—I know what happened to you. So does Maarken."

She gave him a bleak smile. "And do you and he also know that I'm going to die? I have two choices, Meath. I can find a supply of *dranath* and be a slave to it the rest of my life, or I can free myself of it and die in the process."

"That's not true! You don't understand—"

"I know all about the Sunrunner corrupted by Roelstra. He died of taking too much—but it would have been the same if he'd stopped taking it altogether. I'm not going to be chained by a need for that drug, Meath. I'm going to ask Andry if I can return to Goddess Keep for the time I have left."

He looked at her in disgust. "You are depressing the hell out of me. Who ever taught you how to be so damned gloomy? I told you, you don't understand!"

They both looked up as someone else entered the tent. Tall, slim, dressed in a plain green gown, the High Princess flung her long firegold braid back over her shoulder in a gesture oddly reminiscent of Lady Andrade and gazed meditatively at Hollis. She wore a thin circlet across her brow, but it seemed an afterthought, or as if she had forgotten to remove it after some ceremony. The golden band certainly had nothing to do with her aura of regal authority; Hollis had trouble remembering that before her marriage this woman had been, like her, only an obscure Sunrunner.

But one descended from princes of Kierst and Syr, and chosen by Andrade to be Rohan's wife, mother of the first Sunrunner High Prince.

Still, for all her beauty and bearing and importance, her sudden smile was warm and empathetic. She might wear the circlet of royalty as if born to it, but she was still only a very human woman. Hollis felt her own lips curve shyly in an answering smile.

"Here you are at last," Meath said in relief. "What kept you? Sioned, talk some sense into this stubborn girl. I can't get her to listen to me."

"Going about it all wrong, as usual," Sioned answered lightly. "Get out of here, Meath. Go ride herd on my son, if you think you can keep up with him. We sent him to the paddocks to exercise Chay's horses while the final sales are going on.''

Meath rose and gave her an elaborate bow. "At once, your exalted royal highness.''

"Fool,'' she replied fondly.

She settled into the chair he had vacated, and when he was gone said, "I know precisely what you're enduring right now. You may think that I don't, but I do. Roelstra drugged me with *dranath*, you know, years ago. And I'm still here.''

"Forgive me, your grace, but I doubt very much you were addicted, as I am.''

"No,'' Sioned admitted. "But I nearly became so then, and later, during the Plague, when *dranath* was the only cure. And yet I'm still here,'' she repeated.

Hollis said nothing.

"You needn't die, my dear,'' Sioned told her gently. And reached into a pocket of her gown to produce a little velvet pouch. "We searched Sejast's things this morning and found this.''

"No! I don't want it!'' Hollis shrank into the pillows as if to get as far away from the *dranath* as she could. "Don't you understand? What if I agreed, and kept using it, and married Maarken—not only would I be living a life I'd hate, chained to the drug, but what if someone found out and attempted to control Maarken by threatening to keep the drug from me? I can't do that, your grace, I won't!''

"Did I say anything about continuing to use it? When Roelstra tricked me into taking *dranath*, I thought I was going to die, too. On the way back to Stronghold there were times—'' She broke off and shook her head. "I'm not saying this will be easy for you, Hollis. But by taking less every day, as little as you can stand, eventually you can be free of it. It's happened to me twice. It's living hell while it lasts, I won't lie to you. But Roelstra and the Plague nearly addicted me—and *I'm still here.*''

She wasn't aware of the tears rolling down her cheeks until she tasted salt on her lips. "Your grace—''

"You can do this, or you can indeed go back to Goddess Keep and die there,'' Sioned murmured. "Yes, I've been outside listening for quite some time. If you decide the latter, I don't think anyone would blame you. They all know what I went through. But all of us will be with you, Hollis. We'll take as long as you need to travel back to the Desert, and you won't have to go to Radzyn or Whitecliff or even Stronghold, if you wish it, until you're free.''

''Does Maarken know?'' she whispered.

Sioned nodded. ''I spoke with him earlier. He loves you very much, you know. And he has a great deal of love to give. Will you risk it, Hollis? Risk letting him love you enough?''

Hollis closed her eyes and leaned her head back.

''I hope you will,'' Sioned went on. ''You see, I have a wager going with him, and more than anything else, I hate to lose.''

Hollis knuckled her eyes free of tears and opened them—and saw Maarken standing beside Sioned's chair. He was exhausted. Bruises darkened his cheekbones and jaw, and one temple was swollen. He held himself stiffly, bandages bulky around his ribs and showing white at the open neck of his shirt, one sleeve rolled up to accommodate the splint applied to his arm. Those hurts and the healing swordcuts on his face were nothing compared to the open wound in his eyes.

''She really does hate losing, you know,'' he said in a thick unsteady voice.

''She won't get any practice at it now,'' Hollis told him.

Sioned smiled. ''I think I just became superfluous. I'll see to it you're not disturbed, my dears.'' She leaned up to kiss Maarken's cheek. ''Be happy.''

Hollis held out her arms to him. He sank onto the bed beside her, folding her wordlessly to his heart. It was a long time before she felt a slow, dull ache begin in her bones, a lethargy that brought a paradoxical restlessness. Fear sliced through her. *So it starts,* she thought, and her gaze went to the table where Sioned had placed the little pouch of *dranath.* She closed her eyes to it and held tighter to Maarken's strength.

* * *

''Your grace, I would speak with your daughter.''

Volog's brows shot up, and Andry wished he was ten

winters older, with all that time as Lord of Goddess Keep behind him.

"She's resting," Volog said. "Perhaps later."

I can't wait for later! he wanted to shout. He kept his mouth closed. Any such display would only emphasize his youth. So he waited, a thing at which he had never excelled.

"My Lord," Volog said at last. Andry heard vague unease with the new title. "The past days have been very difficult for her. As you must know. The revelation of her gifts—"

"Is precisely what I wish to speak to her about, your grace. Forgive me, but I really must insist."

"The decision must be her own," the prince warned. "If she wants to go to Goddess Keep, perhaps it's the best way of finding peace with herself and her powers. But if she chooses otherwise. . . ."

"I will respect whatever choice she makes, your grace." But surely she could make no choice but him.

"You understand it's a father's concern for his favorite child."

"My concern for her equals your own," Andry said incautiously.

The prince lifted one ironic brow that made Andry even more uncomfortable, but made no reply. He gestured to a squire and within a few moments Alasen came into the main section of the tent. Not a hair was out of place, not a crease marred her clothing. She was dressed for riding in a silk shirt of Kierstian scarlet, a black velvet vest, black trousers and boots. Obviously, she had not been resting.

"My lady," Andry said formally, "will you do me the favor of walking with me for a time?"

"Down to the river, perhaps?" she responded, perfectly controlled although her cheeks were very pale. But that might have been the effect of the vivid scarlet and deep black velvet. "Yes, I think it's time we talked, my Lord." She turned gracefully to her father. "May I?"

"Of course." Volog picked up an embroidered and fringed shawl, draped it over his daughter's shoulders, and kissed her cheek. "It'll be dark sooner than you think, and it's already chilly. Don't stay out too long."

Once beyond Volog's tents, Alasen spoke first. "I was at the paddocks earlier, watching the sales. Your father's horses brought excellent prices."

"They always do."

"The other day I was admiring a very fine mare. I was hoping my father would buy her for me, but Lord Ostvel had already purchased her. For Riyan, no doubt."

"No doubt."

They walked in silence past the white tents of Goddess Keep and the blue tents of the Desert, and then it was Andry's turn to make polite conversation.

"I've been in meetings all day with more people than I could count. But nobody I really wanted to see. I couldn't get away to come talk to you. Everything's been happening so fast. There wasn't any time before this for me to receive the princes formally as the new Lord of Goddess Keep."

"It's a very great honor to have been chosen by Lady Andrade."

"I know. It scares me some," he confessed. But more than anything else he was angry. The hostility in some eyes had confirmed his suspicions: if certain people did not like the idea of a Sunrunner as High Prince, they liked a prince's grandson as Lord of Goddess Keep even less. He would have to make them understand that he would not be ruled from Stronghold. Andrade had been too partisan. He could not be. His honor forbade it. His position as Lord of Goddess Keep came from his gift of *faradhi* powers, not his kinship with Pol.

"I know you'll do well, Andry," Alasen was saying.

With you beside me, I will, he thought hungrily. But he couldn't say that aloud. Not yet. "I finally got the chance to talk to my brother today as well." He smiled suddenly. "I thought he was going to hit me when I told him he had to ask my formal permission to marry Hollis. Until he realized I was joking, that is. You should have seen his face!"

She smiled sidelong at him, a hint of laughter in her green eyes. "Shame, my Lord! Your own brother! I'm surprised he *didn't* break something for you."

"But he would've been disappointed if I hadn't teased him!" Andry chuckled. "Besides, he was being so serious. It was fun to watch him turn red, with his mouth moving and no words coming out!''

''I still say it wasn't very nice. After all he's been through—''

Andry saw her sudden distress and said hastily, ''That's why he needed to laugh. My father says it's the sovereign remedy.'' He rubbed his shoulder ruefully. ''Maarken got in a good one anyway, once he figured it out and I let my guard down!''

Alasen chuckled. ''If you expect sympathy from me, forget it.''

They fell silent as they descended the gentle slope to the river, the crunch of their boots in the gravelly bank rhythmic counterpoint to late-afternoon birdsong. They took the direction opposite from the place where Masul and Kiele and Lyell had burned that morning, heading downriver past the bridge. A breeze off the nearby sea brought the tang of salt and the threat of early autumn rain from the clouds hovering offshore.

At last Andry could wait no longer. ''Alasen—''

''Please. Don't.'' She leaned her palms against a huge gray boulder. He stared at the scarlet and blue and white flowers woven across the black shawl, saw her shoulders shift nervously. ''I have to tell you this my own way, Andry,'' she said.

''All I want to hear is that you love me and you'll come with me and—''

''You want me to become a Sunrunner, like you.''

''You *are* like me. I've held your colors in my hands, Alasen, felt how strong your gifts are, how powerful you could become with training. Come with me, and I'll teach you everything.''

Alasen said nothing. Andry went forward, silent sand beneath his boots now, and his hand hovered for a moment near the hair coiled at her nape. But he did not touch her. Not yet.

''Only say you love me,'' he murmured.

''You already know. We've seen into each other, Andry. Something like that couldn't stay hidden.''

''I need to hear it.''

''You're very young,'' she said indulgently.

Pride stung, he took a step back. "Old enough to be Andrade's choice for Lord of Goddess Keep!"

"I didn't mean it like that." She would not turn and look at him. "I meant that I must be very young, too—because I want to hear the same words."

He put his hands on her shoulders, felt her slenderness and her strength. "I love you, Alasen."

"Those words are so easy for you," she whispered, her head bending. "What I have to say isn't."

Andry turned her to face him, bewildered until he saw her eyes. "You're not going to come with me. You're afraid of me."

"Please try to understand! I always suspected what I was. I think I always knew. There were reasons I didn't want it known, because of Pol, what he'll be when he's grown—I don't want to be wanted just because my children have a chance of being *faradh'im*. I have a right to a happy marriage and a life with a man who loves me, don't I?"

"That's what I'm offering you. And Sunrunner children as well."

"I know. And it's impossible."

He broke away from her. "But why? You love me—"

"Yes. I love you," she replied hopelessly. "Ah, Goddess, I don't want to hurt you, Andry."

"Then—"

"No. I can't." Her hands twisted together, slender and ringless. "I *am* afraid. What I've seen and felt of power terrifies me. I can't live with it. I won't."

"But it's not like that. What happened here—"

"No!" she repeated, pressing back against the stone like a hunted doe. "I won't go with you." She hesitated, then went on softly, "Andry, if you were only your father's son, with an inheritance like Sorin's or Riyan's, it would be different. But you're Lord of Goddess Keep. It's what you were meant to be—anyone who doesn't see that is a fool. Don't offer to give that up for me. I can see it in your eyes. I'd never ask that of you. It wouldn't be loving you to make you deny what you are. Just as I'd never be happy or at peace trying to be something that frightens me." Alasen touched his cheek briefly, regretfully. "I've thought about nothing else today. I try to see myself wearing the rings, doing what you can do—and I can't. You understand power. I'm afraid of it.''

''What are you afraid of?'' he whispered, and her face went ashen in the twilight at the deadly quiet of his voice. ''That I can do such things?'' A tiny gout of Fire flickered on the stone beside them, wafted over the river. It flared as he reacted to the fear in her eyes.

''Andry, please—this is hard enough for me. Don't make it ugly.''

''So we're to be civilized about it, are we?'' He nearly lost control of the hovering flame, furious emotion shaking in his chest and half-strangling him. She loved him. But she was not going to come with him.

''Stop it! Andry, why can't you understand? I don't want to be a Sunrunner! It frightens me!''

''This is what frightens you!''

Fire roared up from the river, Fire swirling in a whirlwind of Air and thick with brilliant diamonds of Water and dark clots of Earth caught in the influx of power. The column of flames leaped up to the dusky turquoise sky, glared into the depths of the Faolain. Narrow as a swordpoint at its base, it swelled river-wide and high as the trees.

''This is what you're afraid of!'' he called out above the rush of wind and flames. The wind whipped at her shawl and her hair, stung crimson into her white face. ''How can you say you love me when you hate what I am? *This* is what I am, Alasen—*this* is what power is about!''

He saw the horror in her eyes. Had he been anyone else, she would have loved him. Well, then, let her see exactly what he was, he thought bitterly, raging at a life that in giving him everything he wanted had taken her from him. He pulled her inside the maelstrom of spinning colors, forced her to create wild beauty with him. He lifted both arms and the fiery vortex burned higher, brighter, fed by their intertwined gifts. Windborne sparks plummeted into the water, shone and hissed before vanishing. Trees bent and shivered on either side of the river; birds startled to frantic shrieks fled their perches, some of them flying into the flames and their deaths. Water roiled, heaved, a shining red-gold wave crashing against the opposite bank.

Alasen stumbled away, clutching her shawl to her breast. Andry reached out with all his mind's force, showed her a fantastic spectrum of color, hues no eye had ever seen or named, made her feel the awesome strength of Sunrunner arts. But things that were glorious and beautiful to him horrified her. She screamed in terror as wind lashed at her body and power at her mind.

"Andry, please!" she sobbed. "It hurts! Let me go!"

The whirlwind guttered out. "Alasen—forgive me, I'm sorry! I didn't know it would hurt you! I only wanted—Alasen, please!"

But she was stumbling headlong up the slope, and vanished into the shadows of the wood as he called her name one last time, without hope.

* * *

There was little light to see by as she ran; the sun huddled behind the western hill, the trees ragged black silhouettes knifing into a sickly yellow-gray sky. And then there was no light at all while she stumbled through the wooded slope. She nearly sobbed aloud when she saw the watchfires, hurried toward them before realizing what her face must reveal to anyone with eyes to look. The flickering watchfires blurred and she wiped her eyes repeatedly, mortified as guards stared. At last she recognized her own scarlet tents, and the large one that was her father's. She burst into the pavilion, swaying.

Strong arms caught her and she slumped gratefully, hiding her face in a soft velvet tunic. But as her heart calmed from its frenetic racing and her mind gradually blotted out the flames, she realized it had been a mistake to come here before she had regained control of herself. She should never have let her father see her in this condition. He would blame Andry with the implacable anger of a parent protecting his dearest child. A new terror flayed her raw nerves as she thought of what might be said or done, what enmity might be created because of her.

She made an effort, pulled away from him. But it was not a Kierstian scarlet tunic that was damp with her tears. The velvet was dark blue with a black yoke, and covered shoulders broader and more muscular than her father's. Horrified, she found herself looking up into the deep gray eyes of Lord Ostvel.

"My lady," he said awkwardly, his face crimson in the bright lamplight. "Forgive me. Your father summoned me here, then was called away. He asked me to wait for his return. I didn't mean—but you were so—I only thought to help—forgive me," he finished.

He was stammering like a schoolboy, and she realized he was as embarrassed as she. Strangely enough, his discomfiture brought back a measure of her poise. "Thank you, my lord. I'm very glad you were here."

He looked down at his hands that still held her arms in a gentle grip, and swiftly released her. "I—your father said you were talking with Lord Andry," he said irrelevantly, taking a step back from her.

As he met her gaze again, the small grace of composure deserted her. He knew, or at least suspected. But he would never say anything. She saw that in his eyes . . . and something else. Through her stunned surprise she wondered why she had never seen it before—not in him, or in herself.

Alasen watched her hands touch his shoulders. She felt the warmth of him, the strength beneath the soft velvet. If Andry was Fire, quick and brilliant and dangerous, this man was Earth—enduring, patient, safe. Here was power that did not frighten her, eyes that demanded nothing. Only waited, aware now that she knew a thing only just admitted to himself.

With him there would never be the wild swirl of colors through her mind and heart. There would never be the shattering joy of first youth's passion. She would never know what it meant to be a Sunrunner and fly down ribbons of woven light. There would never be the glory of powers fully realized, gifts nurtured to fruition. Part of what she was would never find fulfillment.

But with him, there would be warmth, quiet strength, enduring tenderness, and peace.

Very gently, she slid her hands into his, a silent offering. His long figures closed around hers almost convulsively. Ostvel bent his head.

It was a long time before he spoke, and the words came

slowly. "My lady . . . Alasen . . . my life scattered on the wind with my Camigwen's ashes eighteen years ago. I became . . . my son's father, my prince's friend, Skybowl's lord. But I had no life. I did not know how . . . how empty I was, until you."

She moved closer, still holding his hands, seeking his warm strength, resting her weary head against the hard muscles of his chest. She could hear his heart like the beating of silken wings. She waited until the rhythm slowed, then stepped back and smiled serenely up into his wondering eyes.

"Come," she murmured. "We should tell my father."

* * *

Tobin, in the way of all ruthlessly practical people no matter what the circumstances, ordered dinner served in Rohan's tent—and ordered her family and friends to attend or else. The Lastday banquet would have been held that evening, the feast that was more spectacular with each successive *Rialla*. But not this year. Kiele's elaborate plans were forgotten, her servants and the splendid plates and crystal remained at the residence in Waes, and Princess Gennadi had the food distributed among the poor.

Only Chiana saw any reason for celebration. Cheated of her triumphant entry to the feasting on Halian's arm—and her chance to show off the grand banquet she had worked on with an eye to costing her sister a full quarter of Waes' yearly revenues—she settled for giving her own elegant dinner for those highborns who did not dare refuse her invitation.

Tobin surveyed her own arrangements, knowing full well that no one would appreciate them and that this food, too, might just as well have been given to the poor. Loaves of fresh bread, bowls of fruit, meat on silver trays, piles of vegetables—she expected almost all of it to stay right where it was on a long table to one side of the pavilion's main chamber. Watching her brother methodically peel, seed, section, and put a marsh apple aside untasted, she sighed with irritation. But she said nothing. He wouldn't have listened to her, anyway.

She had more success with her nephew and one of her sons. Though at first Pol seemed disinclined to eat, he succumbed to the demands of a healthy young appetite; Sorin had never willingly missed a meal in his life. Maarken, busy trying to tempt Hollis with food, was hopeless. So was Sioned, though she rallied enough to give Rohan a look of mock horror when he offered her a slice of the marsh apple; the fruit gave her hives. One never worried about Meath; he had been born hungry and ate enough for two. As for Chay—like Rohan and Urival he ignored the food in favor of vintage Syrene wine.

Tobin frowned her disapproval as Rohan gestured to Tallain and yet another bottle was opened. But she realized that the liquor was unlikely to make any of them drunk. They did not drink for any of the usual reasons: to forget, to celebrate, to dull the pain. They drank to get up the courage to talk.

It was the lack of any but the most desultory conversation that concerned Tobin most. There were things that needed saying, discussing, explaining. But not even she dared introduce any dangerous topics tonight. Not yet; not until everyone stopped looking so damned grim.

She was not insensible to the undercurrents of feeling; she shared their abiding grief for Andrade, their shock over the manner of the other deaths, and most especially the lingering weariness of the Sunrunners. But without talk there could be no understanding, and thus no dealing with the horrible events of this *Rialla*.

Yet there were people missing who should have been present. She beckoned Tallain over and asked him if he knew where Andry and Ostvel were. The youth shook his head and shrugged.

"I'm sorry, my lady. I left word at their tents, but. . . ."

Tobin gnawed her lower lip for a moment. "I see. Send someone to find them, please." She went over to Riyan, who was sitting beside Meath near the tapestry partition. They made as if to stand and she waved them back down. "Don't be silly," she admonished with a slight smile. "Riyan, what's happened to your father?"

"I haven't seen him since he went to see Prince Volog, my lady." He leaned forward and caught Sorin's attention. "Why did your lord want to talk with my father?"

"Oh, that." Sorin swallowed and shrugged. "He

wanted to thank him again for helping Allie the other day. She was pretty shaken, you know. Ostvel got her calmed down, more or less.''

"As you know so much, can you tell me where your brother is?'' Tobin asked.

"That I cannot, Mother,'' he replied easily. "But quite frankly, Riyan, if I were your father I'd stay out of his way for a while. Did anybody else see Andry's face when Ostvel threw that knife to Lyell?''

"It was mercy,'' Meath said slowly. "But I'm not sure it fit in with Andry's notion of justice.''

Tobin frowned. She agreed with the Sunrunner, but did not care to admit that she hadn't understood the reaction of her own son. It was a bad business, this not seeing one's sons while they were fostered. One remembered them as little boys, and the shock of meeting them again as young men was unsettling. It would be far too easy to wound their new adult pride by attempting to treat them as the children they had not been for years.

And now who was it, she asked herself wryly, who wanted to avoid something that needed talking about?

"Sorin,'' she said all at once, "get me a cup of wine.'' He rose to do her bidding, and she reflected that manners in the young were an excellent thing. She sat down near Meath and Riyan, saying quickly, "Tell me truthfully— what happened to Maarken while he fought?''

Meath blinked; Riyan, to whom the question had been directed, put down his fork and shook his head. "My lady, like the other Sunrunners I only caught glimpses.''

"I think you saw more than that,'' Tobin murmured. He flushed. "Forgive me, but—''

"I know,'' he whispered. "But it'll take some getting used to.''

Meath was looking baffled; neither enlightened him. Tobin said, "What did you see?''

Riyan looked down at his rings. "They burned. Perhaps that happened to Pandsala, too.'' He drew in a deep breath. "It wasn't so much actual *things* I saw as *feelings,* my lady. It was like—like fear had taken on shapes, half-misted, felt but not quite seen.'' His luminous eyes lost focus as he remembered. "Air alive with shadows. Things escaping from cages, all of them black and terri-

ble. Threats and dangers, some from childhood nightmares, others from—from all Hells. Feelings sneaking up
on you from behind, ready to tear your mind out and
devour it. Shadows you couldn't quite see, but you knew
they hid something hideous come to kill you and everything you loved—''

Pol had come over to them, drawn by the muted power
of Riyan's voice in the abrupt silence as all turned to
listen. His eyes were wide and dark, pupils swollen.

"I saw it, too," he breathed into the enthralled hush.
"It was just like that. You reached to drive it away and
it disappeared and something else just as deadly took its
place. But you couldn't really see it or touch it—''

The look in his eyes frightened Tobin. "Pol. It's all
right now. All over."

He gazed at her for a moment as if he didn't recognize
her. Then the muscles of his face drew into taut lines
much older than his years. "Is it? Sejast was only a little
older than me. Maybe he didn't know all that much. What
if there are more like him, older and more experienced,
waiting for the right chance?"

Urival was at his side, one hand on his shoulder. "Then
we shall deal with them. I wasn't going to propose this
yet, but I think perhaps I must. I'll return to Goddess
Keep and stay with Andry while he finds his footing there
as Lord. But I'm growing old. I've taught many hundreds
of Sunrunners in my life—and the last one I will teach is
you."

Pol stared up at him, brief incomprehension whisked
away by complete understanding—and gratitude.

Urival nodded. "When Meath says you're ready, send
for me. I'll come to you wherever you are and teach you
what you'll need to know. Andrade wished it."

They don't want him taught by Andry. The realization
horrified Tobin. The tall old Sunrunner turned his beautiful, implacable eyes on her, not without understanding
and even compassion. But she had no time to lash out in
her son's defense. Ostvel had come in, and Alasen with
him. The pair stopped just at the tapestry partition, the
tense quiet startling them both. Alasen's fingers sought
Ostvel's.

That single gesture was eloquent of all. Volog had

thought to reward him; he had been rewarded with the love and the hand of Volog's daughter.

Riyan was the first to get to his feet. He went to his father and clasped his shoulder, sharing a wordless moment as they looked into each other's eyes. Then he held out his other hand to Alasen. She placed her fingers within it; he raised her palm to his lips.

Sorin's jaw had dropped open in amazement. Tobin thought that very odd and resolved to ask him about it later. But all her questions soon became unnecessary. For as the others, led by Rohan and Sioned, came forward to embrace the couple and express their joy—more than welcome on this sad, strange night—Andry came in.

The silence was even more sudden than before, and just as terrible. Sorin set down the winecup and started toward his twin. Hollis took an involuntary step back, clutching Maarken's arm. Chay glanced around from making a remark to Sioned. She turned stricken eyes to Rohan; his expression changed and he drew breath to speak.

But Andry had already overheard too much. Tobin ached for his pain as he stared glassy-eyed at Alasen and Ostvel. The young woman's green eyes filled with tears. Andry's gaze went from her face to the pleading fingers she held out to him—and when he looked up again, at Ostvel this time, his eyes were incandescent with furious hurt.

"You should know better," he said very softly, "than to interfere in the affairs of Sunrunners, my lord."

Tobin understood then why Andrade and Urival did not want Pol taught by the new Lord of Goddess Keep. She raged silently at her kinswoman for showing Andry everything of how power was used and nothing of when not to use it. Andry lifted his hands, scant four rings glittering—and Fire gathered between his fingers to outblaze even that in his eyes.

Sickened, Riyan took a step toward Andry. "At least be honest about it," he rasped. "You don't give a damn about what he did for Lyell and Kiele."

Andry didn't seem to hear. Ostvel pushed Alasen toward Sioned and faced the young man, his eyes like winter.

The Lord of Goddess Keep held the sphere of Fire cupped between his hands, cold white-gold Fire like captured starshine, giving off light but no warmth. He looked briefly at Urival. "You should have read more in the scrolls," he murmured.

"And you should never have read them at all. I'm the only one who can give you the ten rings, Andry. Stop this or you'll never wear them. You may put them around your fingers, but they'll stay hollow."

The fury shone in his eyes, the Fire in his hands.

"Andry." Rohan spoke into the terrible silence. "Please."

The pale flames wavered as he heard the High Prince, his cherished uncle, say that word to him. He looked once more at Alasen's tear-streaked face, then down at the Fire. It died softly. The lines of his face crumpled into anguish for just an instant before he straightened his shoulders, his expression one of desperate pride.

"I regret. . . ." He bit his lip and tried again, and his mother moaned softly for the pain she could never comfort. "My Lord Urival, there's nothing to keep us here. Tomorrow morning we leave for Goddess Keep." *Alone,* his eyes said as one last time he looked at Alasen. He swept his gaze around the other faces, then bowed slightly to Rohan. He left the tent swiftly, not quite running.

Sorin was gone into the night after him before anyone could tell him not to. Chay slumped into a chair and covered his face with his hands.

"Gentle Goddess," he said in a muffled voice. "Why didn't I see? He's my son." His hands dropped to his knees and he met Urival's gaze. "Stay with him. Help him. He's so young, Urival. He's so young."

Tobin shook off Hollis' tender hand, stumbled into Pol's private chamber alone, and wept.

* * *

It was nearly dawn before Sioned gathered enough courage to ask.

"Beloved . . . how did you know what to say?"

Rohan turned his long-empty winecup between his hands. "His pride had been demolished. I had to restore it." He looked up with a bitter smile. "How many people have ever heard the High Prince plead?"

She nodded at his wisdom. "He might have killed Ostvel."

"I know. I understand it. I was about his age when I found you. If I'd lost you the way he lost Alasen—I might have been tempted to do the same thing."

Shocked, she protested, "You would never have—"

"Wouldn't I? Love is even more powerful than those *faradhi* gifts of yours, Sioned. Romantics would call us living proof of that."

"So you understood his pride, and humbled your own." She hesitated a moment. "Pol won't."

"No. But maybe he won't have to." Rohan set the cup aside and got to his feet, moving like an old man. "He'll have Urival's knowledge. And power much different than Andry's."

"You're not talking about being High Prince."

"Oh, no. Not that at all."

Chapter Thirty-one

Volog rode with them as far as the Faolain crossing, where in a sun-washed meadow he gave his most beloved daughter to Ostvel in marriage. On the same day Sioned fulfilled two promises: to stand with Hollis as she married Maarken, and to provide token of the union. She helped Maarken, whose injured hand was still useless, fasten around his new wife's throat a necklet of silver leaves clasping sapphire flowers. Then Sioned gave Hollis a simple chain made of gold to place around Maarken's neck. Three of its broad, flat links were studded with a ruby, a diamond, and a faceted chunk of translucent amber taken from one of Andrade's rings.

A prince's authority in recognizing marriages was equal to that of the Lord or Lady of Goddess Keep. Lleyn and Volog both stood with Rohan to lend extra honor to the couples joined that day. Meath pronounced the traditional words that should have been spoken by Andry; it would have been heartless cruelty for him to preside as the woman he loved wed another man. The new Lord was long gone in any case, riding with Urival and the contingent of Sunrunners back to Goddess Keep for his investiture. Sorin had accompanied his twin to represent the family during the ritual and because Andry was in need. Rohan, watching as Alasen placed a silver necklet set with luminous gray agates around Ostvel's neck, thought of his nephew with sorrow. Perhaps Sorin would be able to help him through this. Perhaps not. But as he saw Ostvel's careful tenderness while clasping moonstones and onyx at Alasen's nape, he knew that these two at least had found peace. He hoped that Andry would, too.

There was a feast that night, and Sioned at last wore the dress Pol had had made for her. Tobin, astounded by the red-and-silver gown presented by her nephew, was not persuaded to risk it in the dancing that followed until Pol himself led her out into the center of the meadow. Among Rohan's suite were several musicians—and the moment when Ostvel borrowed a lute and began to sing brought tears to Sioned's eyes.

"You didn't know, did you?" she asked Alasen, who listened wide-eyed to her new husband's music and shook her head. "He hasn't sung like that since—" She interrupted herself with, "I'm so happy he found you."

"Then smile," Rohan whispered, kissing his wife's bared shoulder.

They lingered for several days along the river, enjoying the late summer calm. The events of the *Rialla* had faded a little with every measure they put between them and Waes. Meadowlord was green and golden, as if summer lingered, holding its breath. There was no hurry to return to the Desert; the Sunrunners among them took turns scanning the Veresch, and no storms had yet gathered enough strength to spill from the mountains and shatter the delicate stillness.

After Volog and his retinue left them, returning to the coast to take ship for Kierst, they crossed the Faolain. The promise of continuing good weather allowed Rohan to act on whim, and he took most of the party north, leaving Meadowlord for Princemarch's lowlands. The rest would return to Stronghold and Radzyn by the usual routes, but there was a pass through the Vere Hills which, though not particularly steep or arduous, was not often used. The way was long and twisting, and it was shorter and faster to follow the river south. But they had time, and Hollis needed time to wean herself from the *dranath*. That alone clouded the soft, warm early autumn. Sometimes they lingered in one place for a day or two while she tested her strength against her addiction; with Maarken and Sioned and Tobin attending her, she refused the drug until she could stand no more. But the amount of it in Sejast's pouch diminished by a lesser amount each day.

Old Prince Lleyn stayed with them after telling Chadric and Audrite to head south to the sea and wait for him there. "Haven't seen this part of the country for years," he told Rohan. "Not since I was a boy and my father sent me on a grand tour. I'll tag along, if you don't mind. I'd like to see it again before I die."

Meath stayed, too, once again taking up his duty as Pol's guardian. By unspoken agreement between him and Sioned, he began to teach the boy some of the more basic *faradhi* arts. The results showed up sometimes when a tiny whirlwind would skitter across the road ahead, or dancing color touched the minds of the other Sunrunners. Sioned would arch her brows at Meath, watch her son give an apologetic shrug—and smile. Pol delighted in power just as she herself did, loved its beauty and joy. Let him learn the best of it now, she told herself. He had already found out the other.

The fourteenth day of autumn saw them in the foothills of the Veresch, to the west of and almost directly between Stronghold and Skybowl. It was stiflingly hot, even riding creekside through the woods. Sweat clogged Rohan's hair and his thin shirt clung soddenly to his back. He called a rest stop and turned in his saddle to survey the fifty or so riders, all of them drooping in the thick heat. As he settled again he made a wry face at Prince Lleyn and said, "You'd think a lifetime in the Desert would accustom us to this kind of thing. But I swear I'm about to melt!"

"Ah, but the heat you get there can suck water from stones. This is like high summer on the seacoast: air thick enough to swim in." Lleyn stretched, his old bones cracking, and smiled. "I find it quite comfortable, really."

Rohan laughed—then swore in startlement: there wasn't a cloud in the sky, but all at once a cool rain descended, drops indenting the road's dry dust. There were whickers from the astonished horses and exclamations from their riders. Rohan glanced around wildly. The invigorating shower extended the length of the column—and nowhere else. "What in the—?"

Sioned, shaking out her loosened hair in delight at the coolness, rode up to him and grinned. She gestured to the nearby creek, whence the water drifted up to sprinkle down, and said, "Don't look at *me!* If you want a culprit, talk to your son!"

Sure enough, Pol wore a mischievous smile and Meath was trying without success to appear disapproving. The boy urged his horse forward and said, "It's so hot, Father. I thought it'd be nice to cool off."

Rohan eyed him. "You did, did you? And what else have you been learning?"

He shook water from his face. "Nothing Meath will let me try—yet."

"Tallain," Rohan said to his squire, "ride back and let people know what's going on here."

"They already do, my lord. And who caused it." He looked consideringly at Pol. "Just don't soak the bedrolls, if you please."

Instantly contrite, Pol flicked a finger and the gentle rain stopped. "Sorry. I guess I wasn't thinking."

"Hmm," Rohan said.

Later, when they had made camp for the night beside a forking of the same creek, he asked his wife, "Should he be able to do that kind of thing?"

There was something in his eyes that kept her from a light answer. She hunched her shoulders briefly and stared into the little fire near their bedrolls. The night air was still very hot, but Sioned preferred having light to see by. She glanced around briefly. Ostvel and Alasen were not yet returned from their usual moonlit stroll; Maarken and Hollis were also absent, but not for romantic reasons. Though her dependence on *dranath* was waning, she was restless and wakeful for most of each night. Husband and wife paced together while he talked to her about Whitecliff, Stronghold, Radzyn, anything to distract her from *dranath*-hunger and reassure her about the life awaiting them. Sioned, remembering the way it had been with her, had comforted Maarken with the reminder that insomnia and its accompanying exhaustion were only temporary. But there were deep, pain-weary bruises under their eyes, and Sioned was saddened that their first days together should be shadowed thus, a longer and more painful version of what she and Rohan had endured.

Chay, Tobin, Riyan, Lleyn, and all the retainers except those on guard duty were already asleep, worn out by muggy heat. Pol was down at the creek with Meath and Tallain, trying to cool off with a more conventional wash than the one he'd given them all that afternoon. She heard muffled laughter and splashes that hinted at a water fight, and smiled.

At length she answered her husband's question. "I don't think anyone can say what's usual and what isn't for Pol. Or Riyan either, for that matter. I suspect Urival is the same as they. They saw most of what Maarken saw during the combat. I only caught glimpses, and so did the other trained Sunrunners."

"That's no indication—"

"Pandsala must have seen," Sioned murmured, not looking at him. "And she as much as stated that her mother was of the Old Blood."

"But she never got sick crossing water," Rohan pointed out. "Pol and Riyan do—and I remember Cami's hatred of water very distinctly."

"But Pandsala didn't have any Sunrunner blood, either. Pol does, through you. I think we can conclude that someone with only sorcerer's heritage doesn't, but something in *faradh'im* causes it whether the Old Blood is there or not."

"You're reaching," he said flatly.

"Am I?" Sioned picked up a twig and poked at the fire. A spark danced up nearly to the trees overhead. "Pandsala could cross water without difficulty—and that alone made her different from the rest of us, suspiciously so. She could sense when sorcery was being used. I felt her drag herself out of the weave I tried to protect Maarken with. And there was something strange about her colors, Rohan. I'd never noticed it before, because the only other time I was ever in close contact with her was the night her father died. I grabbed onto anyone I could then—even Pol, day-old though he was. I've been thinking about that lately.''

"You sensed the same in him?''

"No. But I wasn't looking for it. But consider, my love.'' She met his gaze across the fire. "When Pandsala withdrew most of herself from my conjuring, what she left behind was *faradhi*—or the parts of her that were *faradhi*-trained. I only had a glimpse of what she took with her. It was very like what we are, yet subtly different.'' She paused, frowning as she tried to find words. "Like almost identical mirrors reflecting back and forth. But not angled quite right. Strange depths in each that didn't match the other.''

Rohan mulled that over. "When Pandsala's gifts were first discovered, Andrade went back in the genealogies as far as she could, and nothing on Roelstra's side even hints at the gifts. So Pandsala's heritage was only of the Old Blood, through her mother. Not Sunrunner at all. Yet she learned the arts. Because Riyan could sense what Pandsala could, Cami probably had the same heritage along with her *faradhi* gifts.''

"Either that, or it's in Ostvel the same way it's in you. But we're not discussing Riyan,'' Sioned told him softly.

"No.''

"Pol can't cross water—that makes him Sunrunner,'' she said. "But he also sensed the visions Sejast used to assault Maarken. That makes him part of the Old Blood.''

"It makes him a sorcerer,'' Rohan said grimly. "And sooner or later he's going to figure it out.''

"What of it? We've always said that Maarken will be his example of a Sunrunner who's an important political power as well. In this other, he'll have Riyan to look to. No one could accuse that boy of being a sorcerer! Pol will understand.''

"And will he understand where that second heritage came from?''

Sioned gasped. "Rohan—''

"I'm sorry, love. But he's bound to realize it someday.

He's grown so much this spring and summer, Sioned. Perhaps it's time he knew. He's old enough to understand.''

"No! Not yet. Rohan, please. Not yet!" She held out one pleading hand.

After a moment he took her fingers. "You know, of course, that the longer we wait. . . ."

"But he's still so young. He wouldn't really understand why—"

"Why his father raped his mother?" He gave a small, bitter laugh. "I suppose so. Lleyn's teaching him to be too civilized, Sioned. Only barbarians comprehend rape."

"Stop it. Don't do this to yourself, Rohan."

"It's true, though, isn't it?" He shrugged and let go her hand. "Once again, for all my pretensions to civilization, I did the good barbarian thing. I killed Masul. You know, Sioned, it doesn't count for much that I resisted so long. Better to be an honest savage and just *do* it."

"If you say next that if you'd killed him when we first knew of him, Andrade might still be alive, I'll—"

He smiled ruefully. "No threats. You're all too likely to carry through on them. Very well, no second-guessing. But there will always be those who believe Masul was indeed Roelstra's son. Somehow, I can't bring myself to care very much, as long as Pol's safe. But we'd better have a damned good explanation ready for him when he asks where his gifts really come from."

She stirred the fire again with the twig, staring moodily into the glowing red coals. "There's never been a word spoken anywhere, Rohan, in fifteen years. As far as anyone knows, you and I were imprisoned by Ianthe at Feruche and then let go. Even if someone knew that the child she bore was yours, they assume he died along with her when the castle burned." She met his gaze briefly. "I don't want him to know the truth. Ever. I don't want to hurt him."

"*I* don't want to lose him," he whispered. Sioned flinched, and he gestured aimlessly with one hand. "A lapse. Ignore it. I'm just tired."

She was wise enough to let the matter drop. Banking

the fire, she stretched out on the blanket. Lying close together, they stared up at the silent, dangerous stars for which Pol had been named.

* * *

"Oh, excellent, Sioned!" Meath rubbed his hands together gleefully. "Fresh stew tonight for dinner, thanks to that hawk of yours!"

The bird had settled daintily back on her wrist and was preening as if she understood every word of the praise. The hawk had indeed performed beautifully. Sioned had flown her once or twice during the journey, but never yet at prey. Today, however, she had brought back a rabbit twice her own size, deposited the kill gracefully at Sioned's feet, then leaped back up to her mistress' hand.

"And she only tore a little off for herself," Pol observed, adding the rabbit to the two small birds taken down by his and Tobin's hawks. Rohan and Alasen had yet to fly theirs; he gestured gallantly and she rode forward, loosening the bird's hood but not yet revealing the fierce black eyes in an amber face. She glanced back over her shoulder at Ostvel and smiled.

"If she makes a good catch, my lord, will you sing for us tonight?"

His brows arched. "It's a wife's duty to provide for her husband's needs. Why should I reward you for doing your duty?"

"Ostvel!" Chay reprimanded, grinning. "That's no way to talk to a bride of less than twenty days! Especially one who hasn't seen your keep yet. Until she does and approves it, she can still *un*-Choose you. So take care!"

Alasen was laughing as she waited for Ostvel's answer. "Well? Will you sing if I provide your supper?"

"No lullabyes," Lleyn told him sternly, eyes snapping with mirth. "I don't think singing her to sleep was exactly what she had in mind."

"Providing for *my* needs was more what I meant," Alasen teased.

"You know," Sioned remarked, "I thought I'd seen his last blush years ago. Seems there are a few left. Congratulations, Alasen!"

"Enough!" Ostvel roared, causing the hawks to shake their feathers irritably. "A song for a decent meal, eh?

Very well, my lady. But it had better be a sizable catch.
I find I've a hearty appetite these days.''

"Legitimately come by," Tobin drawled, winking at
Alasen.

Sioned handed her own hawk to a servant after hooding
the proud head and smoothing the iridescent blue feathers rippling down the bird's back. A memory of Camigwen tugged with painful suddenness at her heart. Ostvel's
lute had been her wedding gift to him, mostly silent since
her death. But Alasen had brought back his music.

The hood was removed and the amber-faced hawk flew.
Gorgeous bronze and green and gold pinions flickering
in the sunlight, she called out her joy in free flight. But
instead of ranging through the low hills for grounded
prey, she gave voice to a triumphant cry and wheeled
northward.

"Damn!" Riyan exclaimed. "We'll never catch her if
she keeps on like that!"

Sioned gave in to temptation and wove a few threads
of sunlight together. She followed the hawk, eyes closed
and spirit soaring. *This* was what it meant to be *faradhi:*
skimming as free and wild as if she, too, had wings,
borne along on wind and sunlight and her own strength.
After all the pain and trauma her gifts had brought her
during the *Rialla*, this, the most beloved of her powers,
was sheer delight. She flew with Alasen's hawk above
rich hillsides and meadows tucked between them, saw the
bird circle above a valley and then dive too swiftly to
follow even at sunlit speed.

"Come on!" Sioned cried, "I know where she is!"

It was a wild ride she led them, galloping through rolling foothills and jumping their horses across branches of
a stream that within a measure became a summer-thin
river. Thundering along its banks, Sioned called out a
warning as the watercourse narrowed through a rocky,
tree-lined defile that compelled them to ride slower and
only two abreast. Pol splashed his horse through the shallows to catch up with her and Rohan. She could hear
Meath cursing behind her, and Tobin laughing like a
madwoman, and Chay yelling at them all to slow down.
Sioned did no such thing, and when the path widened

again, she coaxed her mare to prodigious speed through the forest.

All at once they burst out into the valley she'd glimpsed on sunlight. Sioned pulled her horse up short, gasping at the sight. A broad, lush flatland spread before them, fully ten measures long and half that across at its widest point. Trees heavy with fruit grew up the slopes, and lofty pines towered at the higher elevations where ragged gray stone thrust to the sky. The river wound its way on the eastern side, surrounded by meadow thick with blue and crimson flowers that together turned the land purple. In the distance, as the valley narrowed, was the sunlit shimmer of a small lake, tall grasses bending gracefully in the breeze, alternating gold and silver-green. Sioned caught her breath and flung an excited smile at Rohan, whose blue eyes had gone slightly glassy as he gazed at the beauty around him.

"Like the hollow of the Goddess' hand," Tobin breathed. "Sioned—are those *roses* climbing up that hill?"

"And wild grapevines, too," Chay affirmed. He turned to one of the grooms who had managed to keep up with them. "Go back and get the others. We camp here tonight." With a glance at Rohan's transfixed face, he added wryly, "And maybe for the winter!"

Rohan didn't hear him. He spoke his wife's name in a voice vibrating with suppressed excitement. "Tell me what the soil's like."

She blinked. "Rohan, it's been years since I—"

"Do it."

She jumped down off her horse and threw the reins to Pol. Walking—wading—into the ocean of wildflowers, she pulled off her riding gloves, knelt, and dug her hands into the rich dark earth. She squeezed it in her fists, inhaled its fragrance, sifted it through her fingers. The daughter of a farming lord remembered her lessons of a lifetime ago; she tested the soil with knowledge that had no use in the beautiful, dead Desert. Rising, she gave her husband a brilliant smile.

"This will grow anything you care to plant in it. Not that anybody should even have to test it by touching it— look around us! I've never seen anything so perfect!"

He nodded slowly, light dawning in his eyes. He dismounted and walked forward alone, the sun finding bright reflection on his blond hair, and the others watched in bewildered silence. All but Sioned; she knew exactly what he was thinking, and could barely restrain herself from telling everyone else.

At last he returned, and surprised even Sioned by seizing her around the waist and swinging her up into the air, laughing in triumph.

"You're right, you're right, it *is* perfect!" he cried. "Sioned, it's the most beautiful place in the world! And it's ours!" He kissed her and set her down, then turned to the others. "Pol! Where do you think we should build your palace?"

"My—" The boy nearly fell out of his saddle. "Father!"

Tobin gaped at them. "Palace? What are you babbling about?"

"Oh, you know—walls, floors, painted ceilings and tapestries and carpets and—"

"And huge windows and stained glass and gardens and fountains and—and *everything!*" Pol finished exuberantly. "I can see it all right now!"

"So can I!" Tobin started herself with the words, and laughed. "You're mad, every one of you! Where are you going to get the stone?"

"That's the nice thing about being rich!" Rohan grinned at her.

"Father—we won't have to spend a thing. Rezeld Manor!"

"Where?" Chay asked.

"It's a holding we visited this summer—remember, Maarken? They owe us," he added to his mother. "And they've got a quarry."

Rohan nodded happily. "I'd almost forgotten!"

"Hold it right there," Chay ordered. "I assume you're going to explain that later, but what I want to know right now is what in all Hells you're talking about."

"I gave Castle Crag to Ostvel for a reason, you know. I want a new palace that embraces both the Desert and Princemarch. This valley isn't too far from the pass leading to Stronghold. And this is where the *Rialla* will be held in the future, not in Waes." He pulled Sioned to him and kissed her again. "So my Sunrunners won't have the bother of crossing the Faolain anymore!"

A little while later Lleyn arrived with the rest of the party. His approval was instantaneous for the valley, a new palace, and a new site for the *Rialla*.

"Clutha won't mind, and Gennadi will be grateful not to have it hanging over her head every three years. Besides, I've always felt the High Prince ought to have an accessible residence. Castle Crag is an impossible place. This. . . ." He gazed into the valley and nodded. "This is indeed perfect." The old man grinned suddenly. "By the way, did you find Alasen's hawk?"

"Oh, Goddess!" Sioned exclaimed. "I completely forgot!"

She wove sunlight while the servants and guards began organizing their camp for the night. But her efforts met with no success and she apologized to Alasen, who shook her head and smiled.

"She'll show up again, once she's fed full on whatever she caught."

"I gave her to you, and I don't intend to lose her through my own stupidity," Sioned replied. "Let's go find her. Pol, Rohan, Ostvel, come with us."

Maarken joined them after seeing Hollis comfortably settled in the shade with Lleyn to keep her company. She shook her head when he asked a silent question with his eyes.

"I'm feeling quite well, love. And I haven't had any wine since yesterday morning. I think it's over, Maarken—or nearly so."

He kissed both her hands and smiled.

Lleyn poked his leg with the end of his dragon-headed cane. "You've had her all to yourself for days now," he scolded. "Allow an old man to flirt with your pretty wife out of your hearing. I promise I'll make only the most scandalous suggestions, guaranteed to put a blush back in her cheeks."

"Old lecher," Maarken accused fondly.

They rode away from the trees, following the course of the river toward the lake. Rohan was full of plans that

Pol amplified, the pair exchanging ideas as if they'd rehearsed this for years.

"And over there we'll plant an orchard, and a grove of nut trees."

"More grapevines up that hill—"

"If we hold the *Rialla* here, we'll have to have a racing circle—but at the end of the valley so there won't be so much dust."

"Could we set up a horse farm with it?"

"Now, wait just a—" Maarken began, but neither heard him.

"Excellent! Nothing elaborate, just stables and a paddock—we'll breed for color! What would you say to a pasture full of golden horses? We can coax Chay into giving us a few good mares and a stud—"

"*Giving* you?" Maarken said, more loudly.

"Selling, then," Pol laughed. "You wouldn't begrudge us a few horses, would you?"

"Dangerous question," Sioned put in. "What about this palace?"

"A foundation of Rezeld stone, but a facade of that wonderful grayish marble from that quarry north of here—you remember we saw it this summer, Pol. It'll shine silvery in the sun and rose-gold at dawn and dusk."

"With a blue tile roof," the boy affirmed. "Kierstian ceramic. Father! I have an idea! Why not have something from every princedom, the way it is in the Great Hall at home?"

"I like it," Rohan announced. "We'll have a whole palace to work with, after all."

Alasen had been listening to all of this with wide eyes; Ostvel, with an indulgent grin. He touched her arm and said, "Tobin's right, you know. They're utterly mad."

"Ha!" Sioned scoffed. "This from the man who redid Skybowl from cellar to tower, and before that changed Stronghold from one end to the other, and before *that* ruled Goddess Keep for all that Urival held the title of chief steward! I know exactly how you're going to spend your first year of marriage, Alasen: wondering which room at Castle Crag you're not going to recognize next!"

"A vile slander, unworthy of a High Princess," Ostvel told her. "Aren't you supposed to be finding a hawk?"

"A graceless change of subject, unworthy of a regent!" she shot back, laughing. "But you're right. Let's see if our wayward friend is airborne again."

They stopped half a measure from the lake. As she wove light once more, Maarken asked his uncle, "Why hasn't anybody lived in this valley before? It's beautiful, according to Sioned it'll grow anything, and it's not badly situated, though a little far from the main roads. Why do you think—"

He broke off abruptly. Rohan was not listening. He had reined in, his body rigid, his face turning to the north where the small lake spread its shimmer before the embrace of the hills narrowed. Sioned drew back from the sunlight and stared at him. He was tense with expectation, eyes shining. Sioned exchanged a wry smile and a nod with Maarken.

"That's why," she said.

Dragons.

Upwards of thirty adolescents and hatchlings, watched over by five adult females and a sire, flew down from the high hills into the valley. They wheeled in dizzying patterns before landing to drink at the lake. The hatchlings were nicely grown, almost half the size of their elders, sleek with good summer feeding in the Veresch. Some plunged into the lake for a wash, earning annoyed snarls from the others as they stirred up sediment.

The horses sidled nervously. The dragons condescended to give the humans a single disinterested glance before proceeding to ignore them.

"I wish Feylin could see them," Rohan murmured. "Look at those beauties!"

"Mother . . . how does he *do* that?" Pol whispered.

She shrugged. "He's dragon-bred, too, you know." Suddenly she straightened in her saddle. A reddish-brown female dragon sprang up from the lakeshore and soared lazily above them, calling out softly. Sioned calmed her restive horse and rode forward a few paces. The dragon spiraled down, wings spread wide to show their golden undersides and head extended to peer at Sioned. A raucous howl of greeting presaged a masterful display of flying skills, ending in a happy plunge into the middle of the lake that splashed water nearly to the shoreline.

"It's Elisel!" Sioned waved. The dragon rolled over and over in the water before sculling to the shallows and standing erect. Another cry of joyous greeting sounded, and wings were shaken in a shower of sparkling drops.

"Elisel?" Rohan asked.

She glanced at him, embarrassed. "My dragon. I've been calling her that in my mind. It means 'little wing.' "

He smiled. "And people accuse *me* of being foolish about dragons! At least I never put a name to one!" He paused, then added thoughtfully, "But then, I never had my own dragon, either."

"You think I do?" she laughed.

"Well, just look at her—showing off for you, calling out as if she'd been looking for you! I'd say you do indeed have your very own dragon, Sioned."

She stood in her stirrups and lifted one hand, her emerald aglow in the sun. The dragon spread her wings in answer. Sioned wove light, careful to keep from touching the dragon—but Elisel strode out of the water directly into Sioned's sunlight. She caught her breath as the contact showed her a dazzling array of colors. They whirled and danced in a living rainbow that intensified in speed and light until she grew dizzy and her mind cried out.

The maelstrom of color softened, slowed. And through it she sensed apology, curiosity. Stunned, Sioned reorganized her thoughts and spoke to the dragon.

My name is Sioned. Have you a name?

The dragon came closer, her head tilting in a strangely human gesture of inquiry. Sioned began to dismount. She felt Rohan's cautioning hand and glanced at him with a reassuring smile. But the weaving tugged at her, and through it she sensed a petulance that astonished her.

He's my—my mate. His name is Rohan. He's the sire of the boy over there—the hatchling man with hair like sunshine. The hatchling's name is Pol. Elisel, are you understanding any of this, or am I just talking to myself?

Her frustration was almost palpable, even to herself; the dragon whined and shook water from her wings, shifting as if the emotion made her uncomfortable.

"Sioned—" Rohan came to stand beside her.

"That's it," she breathed. "A language of emotions."

"You mean you're communicating with her?"

"I'm not sure." She hesitated, then put an arm around his waist, leaning against him, and let her love for him flow through the sunlight. Elisel looked uncannily surprised for a moment, her eyes widening. Then she shuffled a few steps closer and hummed low in her throat, eyes half-closing in an expression of pleasure, her head swinging from side to side on her graceful neck.

"I'll be damned," Sioned murmured. "I'm telling her I love you—and she understands me!"

"I thought it might be something like that. Keep it decent, Sunrunner." He grinned at her. "She's only a three-year-old. I won't have you corrupting an innocent dragon."

"Oh, hush!" Moving closer to the dragon, she tried once more in speech. *Elisel! My name is Sioned, and my mate's name is Rohan. Do you have a name?*

The dragon looked bewildered. Sioned bit her lip, groping for some means of communicating with her. Then she had it. Imagination painted a picture of dragon sires on the sand and females choosing them; whimsy put Rohan standing among them and herself walking forward to take his hands. She concentrated, conjuring the scene within the skeins of sunlight—not too difficult, only a variation of what she did with Fire. Elisel warmed to the picture, humming again, and this time her pleasure surged through the weave.

This was the way to do it, then. Sioned made a further picture of Skybowl, the way she herself saw it when Sunrunning, the way a dragon would see it in flight. She showed the dragon the keep crouching beside the lake. Elisel called out happily and swayed back and forth. Colors ricocheted through the air, all the bright blues of water and sky. Sioned let them wash over her without trying to assimilate them all. She formed a vision of Stronghold, again from a Sunrunner's—or dragon's—point of view, then focused down on herself and Rohan and Pol standing in the courtyard. This time images came back, and so powerfully that Sioned winced a little. A mountain aerie, richly green with summer foliage, elk and deer easy pickings; the gentler heights of the Catha Hills in winter, storms flashing across a dark sky viewed from the snug safety of caverns. Within each picture was a myriad of colors and subsidiary images: rivers, fish, wild deer and elk, other dragons, trees, birds, flowers, flight patterns to and from each location, surrounding countryside with human settlements hazed over in dark warning colors—too much information for Sioned to take in.

Elisel! Please! Slower—you're hurting me!

The images abruptly terminated. The dragon fluttered her wings, whimpering concern. Sioned concentrated again, trying to project reassurance. She formed her own distinct pattern of color, the shades of emerald and sapphire, onyx and amber embedded in her consciousness, more a part of her than her own name. *This is me. Sioned. These are my colors.*

And at last it seemed the dragon understood, for the pattern appeared to hover duplicated in the air between them, oddly elegant when filtered through a dragon's perceptions, an image of Sioned's face superimposed. An instant later another structure appeared, complicated with colors Sioned had never seen before. Interwoven with this was a picture of the little red-brown dragon with her gold underwings.

Elisel! Sioned told her in triumph. And the dragon hummed and swayed. She spoke the word aloud—and could have sworn Elisel winked at her. "She knows her name!"

"Good Goddess," Rohan breathed. "She understands you. All my life I've wanted—Sioned," he interrupted himself with sudden urgency, "ask her if it's all right that we're here."

"Do you think I need to? She likes us!" She laughed and kissed him. The dragon's humming took on the same low note as when Sioned had communicated her love for her husband. Rohan pulled away, blushing a little. "Oh, she likes you, too," Sioned assured him playfully. "But I think you're right about asking her if it's all right to build here."

"But we couldn't! Not now. If this valley belongs to them—"

"Let me ask, love."

Stepping away from him, she wondered how to convey so complex an idea. She showed Elisel Stronghold again, then changed the picture in her mind. The keep now rested down the valley, rising tall and proud, people going about their business within and without. Curiosity again from Elisel; the great eyes peered southward as if a castle had indeed appeared there. She looked at Sioned, bewildered, head tilting in that oddly human gesture. Imagination's picture expanded to include a large paddock where golden horses grazed in the sunshine. Elisel perked up and Sioned nearly giggled; the dragon was seeing easy prey.

But the picture Sioned created was suddenly given back to her in changed form: instead of long-legged mares and stallions, Elisel rather wistfully pictured plump white sheep. The Sunrunner altered the vision accordingly and showed her a pen near the lake, stocked with ewes and lambs. The dragon rumbled with delight and gave Sioned a view of the whole valley from flying altitude—complete with castle, paddock, horses, people, sheep—and dragons stopping off for a drink, a swim, and a free meal.

Sioned did laugh then, and her approval of the plan met and merged with the dragon's. *So you like sheep, do you? You can have all you want in exchange for letting us build our palace here!*

Elisel shook her wings and projected Sioned's pattern of color once more into the space between them. Woven through it was a view of winterswept hills that must be this group's southern home in the Catha Hills. The invitation to join them was very clear, not only across the plaited sunlight but also in the huge soft eyes. Sioned had no trouble conveying her regret; she showed Elisel Stronghold again, and the dragon actually sighed.

All this time the other dragons had been refreshing themselves at the lake, completely oblivious to the revolutionary contact taking place nearby. But now the dragon sire bellowed stern warning and took to the sky. He circled the lake, snapping his great jaws at hatchlings who seemed inclined to linger and play in the water. One by one the other dragons soared windward, mature females keeping adolescents and hatchlings in line.

The horses trembled as the sire swept over them and roared at Elisel. The little dragon gave a start and jumped to attention like a reprimanded soldier. Sioned smiled and gently unthreaded the sunlight. Elisel whimpered again with the loss; Sioned felt like echoing her at giving up the splendor of her colors and the warmth of their communication. The dragon took flight, circled once over the lake, then joined her kind as they flew south.

Sioned watched until they disappeared. Only then did she feel Rohan's touch on her shoulders. She turned, met his gaze.

"It was wonderful," she said softly. "Indescribable."

"For the first time in my life, I truly regret not being *faradhi*."

Her heart swelled with pity that he would never know what it was to touch one of his dragons. "Rohan—"

He shook his head, smiling. "Later. When you've had time to think it all through. When you can find words to describe the indescribable—because I want to know *everything!*"

Pol approached them, still on horseback. "What did she tell you, Mother? What did she say?"

Sioned looked up at him. "We can stay here, and we can build our palace—as long as we provide the dragons a free meal when they stop over! This valley is on one of their flight paths between the Veresch and the Catha Hills. Oh, Pol—I can hardly wait until you learn to use your gifts!"

"So I can talk to a dragon of my own?" He laughed in excitement. "I think you're the only one who can teach me that, Mother."

"Well, if you're giving lessons. . . ." Maarken put in.

"Once I figure out how it happened," she promised.

A sharp, frightened cry startled them. High overhead a small, swift shape darted across the sky: Alasen's hawk. Ostvel kicked his horse to a gallop, following the bird to the top of the valley. The others hurried after, and finally came upon him in a wooded slope, where a thin waterfall drifted down a cliff. With autumn rains it would swell to a roaring torrent, and perhaps with winter it would turn to a column of ice. But now it was like frail white gauze, nearly silent.

Ostvel was on foot, his horse tethered nearby, and gestured them to silence as they rode up. His gaze was fixed on a stripling pine. In an upper branch was a flash of amber and green and bronze.

"So your big cousins scared you, eh?" he crooned to the hawk. "It's all right now, little one. They're gone. Why don't you come down now? Alasen, call to her."

She slipped from her saddle and glided toward him, whistling the low, three-note call to which the hawk had been trained to respond. Feathers rustled. She whistled again, holding out her arm invitingly. A few moments later the bird leaped down with a cry both forlorn and relieved and settled on her wrist. It took Alasen some while to smooth feathers and coax wings to fold; when she had, Ostvel slid the hood over the bird's head.

"Well," he said. "at least we know what to name this place."

"Lost Hawk Valley?" Maarken asked whimsically.

"Ah, no," Rohan said, and there was that in his voice which drew all eyes. He smiled. "What else could we call it and our new palace but Dragon's Rest?"

Index of Characters

* Sunrunner

ABIDIAS (658–701). Lord of Tuath Castle. Died of Plague.

ABINOR. Lady of Rezeld Manor.

AFINA. Kiele's childhood nurse.

AILECH. Afina's sister; deceased.

AJIT (657–). Prince of Firon. Six wives, including Pavla (713).

ALADRA (676–694). Roelstra's mistress.

ALASEN of Kierst (696–). Volog's younger daughter.

ALLUN (685–). Lord of Lower Pyrme.

*ANDRADE of Catha Freehold (649). Milar's twin. Lady of Goddess Keep 677–.

*ANDRY of Radzyn Keep (699–). Son of Chay and Tobin; Sorin's twin. Fostered at High Kirat 711–713; Goddess Keep 713–.

ANTALYA of Waes (679–701). Sister of Lyell. m698 Eltanin. Mother of Tallain. Died of Plague.

ARLIS of Kierst-Isel (710–). Son of Latham and Hevatia, grandson of Volog and Saumer; heir to both princedoms.

ATHIL (680–703). Father of Ianthe's son Segev.

AUDRITE of Sandeia (670–). m692 Chadric. Mother of Ludhil, Laric.

AVALY of Rezeld Manor (703–). Daughter of Morlen and Abinor.

BAISAL (650–). Lord of Faolain Lowland.

BIRANI of Kierst (688–). Daughter of Volog. m708 Obram.

BOSAIA of Einar (698–). Brother of Sabriam. Fostered at Lower Pyrme 710–.

CABAR (687–). Prince of Gilad. m705 Kenza.

*CAMIGWEN (676–701). m698 Ostvel. Mother of Riyan. Died of Plague.

CHADRIC of Dorval (664–). Son of Lleyn. m692 Audrite. Father of Ludhil, Laric. Fostered at Stronghold 677; knighted 683.

CHALE (645–). Prince of Ossetia.

CHALIA of Ossetia (650–695). Chale's sister. m680 Haldor. Mother of Jastri, Gemma.

CHAYNAL (668–). Lord of Radzyn Keep. m690 Tobin. Father of Maarken, Jahni, Andry, Sorin. Battle Commander of the Desert 695–.

CHELAN (670–). Father of Ianthe's son Ruval.

CHIANA (698–). Roelstra's daughter by Palila.

CIPRIS (687–708). Roelstra's daughter by Surya.

CLADON (681–). Lord of River Ussh.

CLUTHA (644–). Prince of Meadowlord. Father of Gennadi, Halian. Grandfather of Isaura.

*CRIGO (665–698). Addicted to *dranath* by Roelstra.

DANLADI (694–). Roelstra's daughter by Aladra.

DAVVI (665–). Prince of Syr. Sioned's brother. m686 Wisla. Father of Kostas, Riaza, Tilal.

DRESLAV (646–). Lord of Grand Veresch.

ELTANIN (678–). Lord of Tiglath. m698 Antalya. Father of Tallain.

EMLYS. Lord of Dasan Manor. *Athri* at whose home Masul grew up.

ENEIDA. Fironese ambassador.

*EOLIE. At Graypearl.

*ERIDIN. At Goddess Keep.

EVAIS (674–). Father of Ianthe's son Marron.

FARID (638–704). Lord of Skybowl. Killed by Merida.

*FENICE. At Goddess Keep.

FEYLIN (684–). m706 Walvis. Mother of Sionell, Jahnavi.

GARIC (642–). Lord of Elktrap Manor.

GEIR of Waes (707–). Son of Kiele and Lyell.

GEMMA of Syr (694–). Daughter of Haldor and Chalia.

GENNADI of Meadowlord (667–). Daughter of Clutha.

*GERIK. Ancient Sunrunner.

GEVINA (679–701). Roelstra's daughter by Vamana. Died of Plague.

GIAMO. Innkeeper on Dorval.

HADAAN (634–714). Lord of Remagev. Rohan's distant cousin.

HALDOR (656–701). Prince of Syr. m680 Chalia. Father of Jastri, Gemma. Died of Plague.

HALIAN of Meadowlord (680–). Son of Clutha.

HEVATIA of Isel (682–). Daughter of Saumer. m707 Latham. Mother of Arlis.

*HOLLIS (691–). At Goddess Keep.

IANTHE of Princemarch (676–704). Roelstra's daughter by Lallante. Mother of Ruval, Marron, Segev, Pol. Killed by Ostvel.

INOAT of Ossetia (664–). Son of Chale. Father of Jos.

ISAURA of Meadowlord (700–). Granddaughter of Clutha.

JAHNAVI of Remagev (711–). Son of Walvis and Feylin.

JAHNI of Radzyn Keep (693–701). Son of Chay and Tobin; Maarken's twin. Died of Plague.

JAL. Guard in Chay's service.

JASTRI (688–704). Prince of Syr. Son of Haldor and Chalia. Killed in battle.

JAYACHIN. Waesian merchant's daughter.

JELENA (689–701). Roelstra's daughter by Palila. Died of Plague.

JERVIS (655–701). Lord of Waes. Father of Antalya, Lyell. Died of Plague.

*JOBYNA. At Goddess Keep.

JOS of Ossetia (709–). Son of Inoat.

KARAYAN (660–689). Roelstra's mistress.

*KASSIA. At Goddess Keep.

KENZA (683–). m705 Cabar of Gilad.

KIELE (681–). Roelstra's daughter by Karayan. m704 Lyell. Mother of Geir, Lyela.

KIERA of Einar (698–). Sister of Sabriam and Bosaia.

*KLEVE (681–). Itinerant Sunrunner.

KOLYA (696–). Lord of Kadar Water.

KOSTAS of River Run (687–). Son of Davvi and Wisla. Fostered at Swalekeep 700; knighted 708.

LALLANTE of The Mountain (655–679). m673 Roelstra.

LAMIA (683–701). Roelstra's daughter by Karayan. Died of Plague.

LARIC of Dorval (698–). Son of Chadric and Audrite. Fostered at High Kirat 710; knighted 718.

LATHAM of Kierst (683–). Son of Volog. m707 Hevatia. Father of Arlis.

LENALA of Princemarch (674–701). Roelstra's daughter by Lallante. Died of Plague.

LLEYN (637–). Prince of Dorval. Father of Chadric.

LUDHIL of Dorval (694–). Son of Chadric and Audrite. Fostered at Fessada 705; knighted 714.

LYELA of Waes (709–). Daughter of Kiele and Lyell.

LYELL (683–). Lord of Waes. m704 Kiele. Father of Geir, Lyela.

*MAARKEN of Radzyn Keep (693–). Son of Chay and Tobin; Jahni's twin. Fostered at Graypearl 702; knighted 712; Goddess Keep 712–719.

MAETA (670–). Commander of Stronghold guard. Myrdal's daughter.

MARRON of Feruche (701–). Ianthe's son by Evais.

MASUL (698–). Pretender to the throne of Princemarch.

*MEATH (673–). At Graypearl.

*MERISEL. Ancient Sunrunner.

MILAR of Catha Freehold (649–701). Andrade's twin. m670 Zehava. Mother of Tobin, Rohan. Died of Plague.

MILOSH of Fessenden (699–). Pimantal's youngest son.

MIREVA (659–). Sorceress who raised Ruval, Marron, and Segev.

MIYON (689–). Prince of Cunaxa.

MORIA (684–). Roelstra's daughter by Surya.

MORLEN (674–). Lord of Rezeld Manor.

*MORWENNA (684–). At Goddess Keep.

MOSWEN (692–). Roelstra's daughter by Palila.

MYRDAL (645–). Retired commander of Stronghold guard. Maeta's mother.

NARAT (667–). Lord of Port Adni. m705 Naydra.

NAYATI (684–717). Roelstra's daughter by Vamana.

NAYDRA of Princemarch (673–). Roelstra's daughter by Lallante. m705 Narat.

OBRAM of Isel (680–711). Son of Saumer. m708 Birani.

OSTVEL (673–). Lord of Skybowl. m698 Camigwen. Father of Riyan.

PALILA (669–698). Roelstra's mistress.

*PANDSALA of Princemarch (675–). Roelstra's daughter by Lallante. At Goddess Keep 698–704. Regent of Princemarch 705–.

PATWIN (691–). Lord of Catha Heights. m709 Rabia. Father of Izaea, Sangna, Aurar.

PAVLA (687–713). Roelstra's daughter by Palila. m713 Ajit.

PELLIRA. Guard in Pandsala's service.

PIMANTAL (657–). Prince of Fessenden.

POL of Princemarch (704–). Rohan's son by Ianthe. Fostered at Graypearl 716–.

RABIA (693–715). Roelstra's daughter by Palila. m709 Patwin. Mother of Izaea, Sangna, Aurar.

RASOUN. Overseer at Skybowl mines.

REVIA. Guard in Chay's service.

RIALT. Merchant's son at Graypearl.

RIAZA of River Run (694–701). Daughter of Davvi and Wisla. Died of Plague.

*RIYAN of Skybowl (699–). Son of Ostvel and Camigwen. Fostered at Swalekeep 711–713; at Goddess Keep 713–718; at Swalekeep 718–.

ROELSTRA (653–704). Ruler of Princemarch, High Prince 665–704. m673 Lallante. Father of Naydra, Lenala, Pandsala, Ianthe; Gevina, Rusalka, Alieta, Nayati;

Kiele, Lamia; Moria, Cipris; Pavla, Jelena, Moswen, Rabia, Chiana; Danladi. Killed by Rohan.

ROHAN (677–). Prince of the Desert 698–; High Prince 705–. Fostered at Remagev 690; knighted 695. m698 Sioned. Father of Pol.

*ROSSEYN. Ancient Sunrunner.

RUSALKA (680–712). Roelstra's daughter by Vamana.

RUVAL of Feruche (700–). Ianthe's son by Chelan.

SABRIAM (695–). Lord of Einar. Brother of Bosaia, Kiera.

SAUMER (659–). Prince of Isel. Father of Obram, Hevatia.

SEGEV of Feruche (703–). Ianthe's son by Athil.

SINAR (610–678). Prince of Kierst. m635 Siona. Grandfather of Sioned, Davvi, Volog.

*SIONA (614–679). m635 Sinar. Grandmother of Sioned, Davvi, Volog.

*SIONED of River Run (677–). Sister of Davvi. m698 Rohan. Princess of the Desert 698–; High Princess 705–.

SIONELL of Remagev (708–). Daughter of Walvis and Feylin.

SORIN of Radzyn Keep (699–). Son of Chay and Tobin; Andry's twin. Fostered at New Raetia 711–.

SURYA (665–690). Roelstra's mistress.

TALLAIN of Tiglath (700–). Son of Eltanin and Antalya. Fostered at Stronghold 713–.

TIBAYAN (642–714). Lord of Lower Pyrme.

*TIEL. At Swalekeep.

TILAL of River Run (692–). Lord of River Run. Son of Davvi and Wisla. Fostered at Stronghold 702; knighted 712.

TOBIN of the Desert (671–). Rohan's sister. m690 Chaynal. Mother of Maarken, Jahni, Sorin, Andry.

ULRICCA. Goldsmith in Waes.

*URIVAL (653–). Chief Steward of Goddess Keep 681–.

VAMANA (658–686). Roelstra's mistress.

VELDEN (683–). Prince of Grib.

*VESSIE. At Goddess Keep.

VOLNAYA of Kierst (702–). Volog's younger son.

VOLOG (659–). Prince of Kierst. Father of Latham, Birani, Alasen, Volnaya.

WALVIS (685–). Lord of Remagev. m706 Feylin. Fostered at Stronghold 697; knighted 703. Father of Sionell, Jahnavi.

WILLA. Giamo's wife.

WISLA of River View (663–717). Princess of Syr 705–717. m686 Davvi. Mother of Kostas, Tilal, Riaza.

YARIN (690–). Lord of Snowcoves.

ZEHAVA (638–698). Prince of the Desert. m670 Milar. Father of Tobin, Rohan. Killed by a dragon.

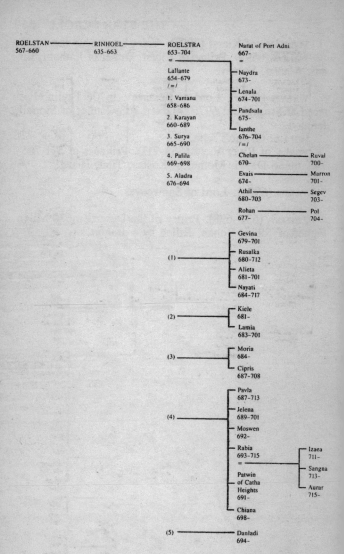

ROELSTAN ———— RINHOEL ———— ROELSTRA   Narat of Port Adni
567–660   635–663   653–704   667–
                                      =
                                      Lallante   — Naydra
                                      654–679   673–
                                      / = /   — Lenala
                                      1. Vamana   674–701
                                         658–686   — Pandsala
                                      2. Karayan   675–
                                         660–689   — Ianthe
                                      3. Surya   676–704
                                         665–690   / = /
                                      4. Palila   Chelan ———————— Ruval
                                         669–698   670–   700–
                                      5. Aladra   Evais ————————— Marron
                                         676–694   674–   701–
                                                         Athil ————————— Segev
                                                          680–703   703–
                                                         Rohan ————————— Pol
                                                          677–   704–

                                      (1) ———————— Gevina
                                                          679–701
                                                   — Rusalka
                                                          680–712
                                                   — Alieta
                                                          681–701
                                                   — Nayati
                                                          684–717

                                      (2) ———————— Kiele
                                                          681–
                                                   — Lamia
                                                          683–701

                                      (3) ———————— Moria
                                                          684–
                                                   — Cipris
                                                          687–708

                                      (4) ———————— Pavla
                                                          687–713
                                                   — Jelena
                                                          689–701
                                                   — Moswen
                                                          692–
                                                   — Rabia ——————— Izaea
                                                          693–715   711–
                                                          =   — Sangna
                                                       Patwin   713–
                                                       of Catha   — Aurar
                                                       Heights   715–
                                                          691–
                                                   — Chiana
                                                          698–

                                      (5) ———————— Danladi
                                                          694–

Genealogy
(as of 719)

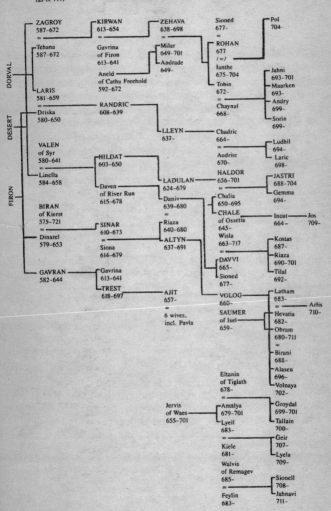

DAW

New Worlds of Fantasy

STEPHANIE A. SMITH

☐ SNOW EYES   (UE2286—$3.50)

When the mysterious mother who abandoned her returns to claim Snow-Eyes for the goddess known as Lake-Mother, Snow-Eyes is compelled to go with her to the goddess' citadel—there to face betrayal and a confrontation with her own true nature.

☐ THE BOY WHO WAS THROWN AWAY   (UE2320—$3.50)

The spell-binding sequel to SNOW-EYES! Gifted with a musical magic and a shape-changing talent he can scarcely control, Amant struggles to rescue his cousin caught in a terrifying spell halfway between life and the realm of Lord Death.

MELANIE RAWN

☐ DRAGON PRINCE   (UE2312—$4.50)
☐ THE STAR SCROLL   (UE2349—$4.95)

In a land on the verge of war, Rohan and his Sunrunner bride would face the challenge of the desert, the dragons—and the High Prince's treachery! *"Marvelous . . . impressive . . . fascinating . . . I completely and thoroughly enjoyed DRAGON PRINCE."* —Ann McCaffrey

TANYA HUFF

☐ CHILD OF THE GROVE   (UE2272—$3.50)
☐ THE LAST WIZARD   (UE2331—$3.95)

Magic's spell was fading, but one wizard had survived to wreak madness and destruction. And though the Elder Races had long withdrawn from mortals, they now bequeathed them one last gift—Crystal, the Child of the Grove!